THE

DEAD

MEN

J. C. Harvey is the fiction pen-name for Jacky Colliss Harvey. After studying English at Cambridge, and History of Art at the Courtauld Institute of Art, Jacky worked in museum publishing for twenty years, first at the National Portrait Gallery and then at the Royal Collection Trust, where she set up the Trust's first commercial publishing programme. The extraordinary history of the Thirty Years War (1618–48) and of seventeenth-century Europe has been an obsession of hers for as long as she can remember, and was the inspiration behind the story of Jack Fiskardo's adventures, which begins with *The Silver Wolf*, and continues here with *The Dead Men*.

THE
DEAD
MEN

J. C. Harvey

ALLEN&UNWIN

First published in Great Britain in 2023 by Allen & Unwin,
an imprint of Atlantic Books Ltd.

10 9 8 7 6 5 4 3 2 1

A CIP catalogue record for this book is available from the British Library.

Hardback ISBN: 978 1 83895 344 7
E-book ISBN: 978 1 83895 346 1

Printed in Great Britain by TJ Books Limited

Allen & Unwin
An imprint of Atlantic Books Ltd
Ormond House
26–27 Boswell Street
London
WC1N 3JZ

www.atlantic-books.co.uk

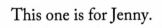

This one is for Jenny.

Contents

Author's Note

Greetings, gentle reader.

Those of you coming to *The Dead Men* from the beginning of Jack Fiskardo's adventures in *The Silver Wolf* will already know something of the appalling destruction wrought across Europe by the Thirty Years War. For those of you new to this period, very briefly therefore, the war began in 1618 as a religious conflict, between the Catholic Holy Roman Empire, full of the zeal of the Counter-Reformation, and the new 'reformed' religions of Calvinism, Lutheranism and Anglicanism. Like all religious wars, it soon came to be about anything but. By the time, in 1630, that the Lutheran King of Sweden, Gustavus Adolphus, brought his army into the war (on the pretext that the Holy Roman Emperor threatened Sweden, but really because he wanted the Empire's Baltic ports), the quarter of a million soldiers fighting in the war hailed from every country in Europe; and there was not a single nation, from Scotland to Spain, that did not have a stake in its outcome.

When it finally ended, after the armies had fought themselves to a standstill in 1648, twenty per cent of the then-population of Europe had perished as a result. By comparison, European mortality in the First and Second World Wars has been estimated as between five and six per cent. It was a terrible, terrible war, so terrible that even those going through it at the time understood that what they were suffering was unprecedented. To survive in it as a soldier would have taken immense courage, resourcefulness and *luck*; to thrive in it, as Jack Fiskardo (for the most part) does, would have taken qualities even rarer and more particular. That was part of my interest in exploring this period as his background – what would you have had to become to get through it? What would you have had to give up? What acts committed? What, within yourself, would you have had to live with? And what would the cost of all this be to you? Jack is older now, and with age and rank come responsibilities, even for a loner such as him. The lives of the men about him will be developing and changing, there will be partners, children – how will our hero, our eyes into the war, negotiate all that?

The other aspect of the war that fascinated me as a writer is the fact that it produced so much in the way of words. The appetite for information, for the latest news from the war, was ceaseless. To paraphrase Orson Welles in *The Third Man* here, in Germany for thirty years under the Habsburgs they had warfare, terror, murder and bloodshed, but they produced memoirs, journals, chronicles, letters and diaries by the score, and in the corantos, so began the first popular, international, press. Which, if you will allow me, leads me into the discussion, necessary for any writer of historical fiction, of what in *The Dead Men* is based on actual historical fact, and what is simply me, the author, leading you as reader through a landscape of my own devising.

So: the corantos, French, Dutch and German, are real, and one of the best was the English *Swedish Intelligencer*, which was indeed published in London by the booksellers Nathaniel Butter and Nicholas Bourne, and was compiled from many sources with quite extraordinary skill by the Reverend William Watts, of St Alban's Church in Wood Street in the City of London. And Nicholas Bourne was an infinitely more cut-throat and better businessman than the unfortunate Nathaniel Butter ever turned out to be.

The Swedish army did indeed sweep down into Germany in a seemingly unstoppable advance between 1630 and 1632, much to everyone's amazement, or horror, at the time, and there was indeed an anti-Habsburg pact between Sweden and France that financed this invasion, and was the reason for its initial unprecedented success. (And how intriguing it would be, thought I, if Cardinal Richelieu had overreached himself in setting it up. History loves irony.)

The war did indeed promulgate any number of myths and superstitions, as such dreadful times so often do, including magical mists; and the *spiritus familiaris*, or unwitting bargain with the Devil; and the hard men, who were proof against any weapon made of iron or steel. Carlo Fantom, Jack's sworn enemy, is a documented example; you can find just about all that is known of him in John Aubrey's late-seventeenth-century *Brief Lives*. And Quinto del Ponte, or Quinti Alighieri, crops up in Walter Harte's 1791 history of Gustavus Adolphus, but in other sources too, as an example of a Habsburg double-agent who did, yes, pass on information leading to an attack.

Pasewalk ('Passewalk') was one of the many towns almost wiped from the map over the course of the war, but the fate of Magdeburg was a watershed. On 20 May 1631 a city of 25,000 people was annihilated over the course of a single morning, with some 40,000 soldiers running amok through her streets. There are appalling reports of gang rape and torture, even of children, while the fire-storm that should never have started left maybe 200 of Magdeburg's almost 2,000 buildings standing, and suffocated or burned many of the casualties to death. A census in 1632 listed just 449 inhabitants, and much of the city was still rubble even into the eighteenth century.

Poland's winged hussars flourished from the 1570s to the early 1700s; in copying their appearance Jack will, I hope, be seen only as doing honour to the legendary status of this elite cavalry force. And with soldiers of so many nationalities fighting in the war, they did indeed evolve a sort of military Esperanto between them, much like the slang of the grunts in the jungles of Vietnam. One tiny part of it was the use of the term 'Maria' for gold. And (again, according to Walter Harte), Gustavus Adolphus did indeed discover six tons of gold while campaigning in Poland in 1628, hidden away in the castle of Strasberg (now Brodnica) and, like Jack Fiskardo, helped himself to the lot. And from such tiny seedlets, whole plots and books do grow.

THE
DEAD MEN

N

NORTH SEA

THE DUTCH
REPUBLIC

ENGLAND

Haarlem ● ●Amsterdam

London ●

THE SPANISH NETHERLANDS

HESSE

R. Rhin

St Etienne-des-Champs ●

Paris ●   FRANCE

—— Border of the Holy Roman Empire

0   50   100 miles

0   50   100 km

Cast of Characters

PART I

On the island of Usedom, off the coast of north Germany

The invading Swedish army, including:
    Jack Fiskardo, captain of a troop of military scouts, or
    'discoverers'
    Zoltan, his lieutenant
    Ilya, 'The Executioner', his sergeant
    Sigismund, 'Ziggy', his horse-master
    The Gemini
    Karl-Christian von Lindeborg, 'Kai', his ensign
The scouts themselves, including:
    Ulf, Elias, Sten, Thor, Luka, Ansfrid and Ulrik; then Per,
    Jens, Alaric and Magnus
Milano, Jack Fiskardo's horse

In the great camp, or 'Camp Royal' at Stettin

Gustavus Adolphus, King of Sweden
Quinto del Ponte, a messenger and double-agent

Somewhere among the ruined farms and villages along the Oder

Carlo Fantom, 'Charles the Ghost', a Croat one-time hired
    assassin, now a mercenary in the army of General Torquato
    Conti
Salvatore, his sergeant

In Paris, at the Palais du Louvre

Armand du Plessis, Cardinal Richelieu
Tino Ravello, intelligencer, messenger, fixer in the service of
    Cardinal Richelieu

In London

Nathaniel Butter, bookseller and entrepreneur
Nicholas Bourne, his business partner
Mrs Butter, his wife
Belinda, 'Belle', his daughter
Rafe Endicott, his assistant
Mr William Watts, a clergyman, writer and editor
Cornelius Vanderhoof, a Dutchman
Clayton Proctor, landlord of the Mitre Tavern
Miguel Domingo, a Thames waterman, native of Capo Verde
Mungo Sant, a Scottish mariner, captain of the *Guid Marie*

Encamped with General Åke Tott, on the Swedish front line

General (later Field Marshal) Åke Tott, 'The Snowplough'
Achille de la Tour, a Frenchman. One of General Tott's
    aides-de-camp
Colonel Ancrum, a Scot
Edvin, his ensign
Rosa, a washerwoman
Roxandra, Pernilla and Kizzy, three old women

In the town of Forbach, on the border between France and Germany

Rufus, a headsman of the Roma
Yuna, his wife
Emilian, his son
Benedicte, his brother, a seer

*In the town of Schwerin, in the Duchy of Mecklenburg,
north Germany*

Emmanuel Vincent, a writer and researcher

Henricus Anderman, of Antwerp, and Theodore Brunner, of
    Brussels: proto-foreign correspondents

Hauptmann Erlach and his men, soldiers in the pay of the
    Prince-Bishop of Prague

Viktor Lopov, their prisoner, the Prince-Bishop's archivist

At the Dunqerqer, an ancient tavern east of London on the River Lea

Aaron Holland, youngest member of the Holland crime family
    of London

Josh Arden, one-time mariner and pirate, now retired

PART II

Also in the Camp Royal at Stettin

Felix Stromberg, Physician Royal

In the town of Wolgast, on the coast

Herr Gruber, an innkeeper

Frau Klara, his neighbour, madam of a modest brothel

Sophie and Katya, her whores

August von Hoch, a horse-dealer

M'sieu, a stallion, reputedly worth one thousand thalers

With Rafe Endicott

Dart, his dog

PART III

In Hoffstein, on the Elbe, ancestral seat of the Prince-Bishop of Prague, now deserted. A place of dark secrets

Leo Franka, the Prince-Bishop's disgraced gunsmith, sent into
    exile here
Ava, his daughter
Otto, his son

At the sack of the city of Magdeburg

Dr Silvestris, Kai's old tutor, and Frau Silvestris, his wife
The households of the Brandts and the Hannemanns, their
    neighbours
The Imperial armies of General Tilly and of General Pappenheim

In the village of St-Etienne-des-Champs, Picardy

Robert, landlord of the Écu de France
Mirelle, his sister
'Cou-Cou' Marin, Robert's intended

PART IV

In Amsterdam

Yosha Silbergeld, a wealthy merchant, part owner of the *Guid Marie*
Zoot Vanderhoof, his housekeeper

On the road to Prague

The Pilgrim Players, a group of travelling players from the Red
    Bull Theatre, London, including:

Henry Kempwick, leader of the players
Andrew Frye, their dramatist
Alembert, their leading man
Martin, a child actor
Lucy, a musician
Blanche, their wardrobe mistress
Saul, a handyman of sorts

In Prague itself

Stefan Safran, a printer, brother to Ziggy
Danushka, his young daughter
Matz, an old soldier and trickster
Frau Viki, his partner, a seller of trinkets at the Charles Bridge
The Prince-Bishop of Prague
Magister Ieronymus, Steward to the Prince-Bishop
Vainglory, an immense bronze cannon

In the Giant Mountains, on the border between Bohemia and Poland

Pyotri, a pigboy
Egan, his brother
Lenka, his brother's wife
Christina, 'Tink', an orphan
Josuf, Marcus and Hendrick, children of the village
Boris, Pyotri's prize boar

And finally… in Crossbones graveyard, in London

Bess Holland, matriarch of the Holland crime family
Abigail Skinner, her maid

PROLOGUE

Osnabrück, 1644

C HILLY OUT HERE, *nicht wahr?*

Through that door there, you'd find it rather different. Through that door there is light, and warmth, and a continual bustle back and forth, despite the lateness of the hour. Round-shouldered secretaries scurrying along, satchels of documents clutched to their hearts. Messengers, heads bobbing and one hand held perpetually aloft as they search for the swiftest way through. Lawyers and jurists, deep in their secrets, stalking in pairs as if tied at the foot. Mapmakers too – board gripped in one hand, compasses and rule in the other. And in those warm and well-lit rooms beyond, ambassadors and delegates from every court in Europe, from Utrecht to Madrid. Oh, full of strangers, this city, and full of strange new words as well: *Peace*, there's one not been heard from in a long, long while. *Negotiations*, there's another. It's an exciting place to be, through that door there.

Not this one, though. The secretaries and messengers, they pass this door without a glance. Nothing behind this one but a guardroom – thick pamment tiles on the floor, bare plaster walls (much rubbed at what is shoulder-height, if one were sitting down), and no better furniture than a pair of joint-stools and a lopsided table, on which sit two squirrel-size, curly handled, lidded steins of soft dark beer, a draughts board, and the heavy elbows of a pair of thick-set veterans: Münster and Munich.

Munich can tell where Münster comes from because Münster's accent is as solid as a cabbage, and the ubiquitous

buff-coat, as worn by Münster, appears to be of the type of good
Russian leather that won't let in the wet, supplies of which have
not been seen in further parts of Germany in years. Münster
can place Munich because Munich's accent is fierce as popping
fat, and he wears show-off breeches with ribbons of Bavarian
white and blue laced down the sides. Time, playing with both,
has pocked Munich's nose and broken the veins in Münster's
cheeks. No better company than these, and every bit as chilly in
the room as out. No, nothing of interest here.

Münster leans forward; the leather of his buff-coat creaks.
He cups the bowl of a clay pipe in one hand as delicately as if
it were a bird's egg. A puff of the pipe, an eye across the board.
There are any number of counters Munich's side of the table,
rather fewer his, and on Munich's side, a scatter of coins as well.
Münster lets his eye glide across the coins, drains the last of
his beer, then, reversing the pipe, uses its stem to indicate the
square of dark beyond the door. 'A night like this, it was,' he
remarks. 'Puts me in mind. Just like to this, in fact. Stars in the
sky, and frost in the air, and clear up to heaven.'

'What night?' Munich replies, still studying the board.

'The night I saw the Dead Men.'

Munich takes two of the four legs of his stool off the floor,
leaning back to survey his opponent at arm's length. 'You're
telling me you saw the Dead Men?'

Oh. A *story*.

'It was spring of thirty-two,' Münster says. He takes a long pull
of his pipe.

Munich, arms folded, has all four legs of his stool back on the
floor. 'Was it indeed?'

'Spring of thirty-two, and my company, we'd set our camp,
and we were hoping as we're not so far from Gottingen, though
where we were on the map, God knows. It felt a damned long
way from any other living soul, I tell you that. And bitter cold.

Clear cold. Stars bright as diamonds,' Münster continues, using his pipe-stem to point out the stars, as if they are there on the guardroom ceiling.

Slowly, the arms unfold, like a knot coming undone. 'I been to that part of the world. I've marched them roads in Saxony. Go on.'

'And a small world it is, my friend. Maybe you might have marched along the very road of which I speak. For that road is where I find myself, taking my watch. Twenty paces one way, twenty paces back, counting 'em off, as you do. I make my turn – I see a mist is rising up behind me.'

'You saw that?' Munich exclaims. 'Then it's true?' He nudges his stool up close to the table, drops his voice. 'How they would raise a mist, and travel through it?' The voice drops lower; there's a nervy glance over one shoulder before he speaks again. 'The Dead Men?'

'All I can tell you, friend, is what I saw,' says Münster. 'But this same mist – it had a strange odd way to it, that's sure. It starts to gather round me. It rises to my waist, and then my face, then it closes right over my head. I look down and I've disappeared, and the stars above, they're fading too. And I do think, I ought to get me out of this, I ought to call out to my company – when through the mist I hear a sound.'

'What sound?' Munich asks, in a whisper.

'A little sound. *Klingel-klingel*, we would say, where I come from. Tinkling, like frost in the twigs on a tree. A little dainty sound. But not from one tree shivering on its own. This is like a forest. And under the tinkling, I hear this.' And Münster hooks his mug from off the table and starts knocking out a rhythm on the tabletop: *one-two, one-two*.

'Horses,' comes the response. 'God above.'

'Horses,' says Münster. 'And every minute getting louder. I can't tell if they're behind me, or in front. If I'll see 'em now, or next. I'm stretching my eyes and my ears to make out anything at all, and the mist is coiling all around me, when of a sudden it gives this mighty swirl in front of me, like water – and there they are. Coming down the road in double file.'

'And it was…?' says Munich, in the tones of one who hardly dares to breathe, let alone speak.

'The Dead Men? I am sure of it, my friend. Sure as I'm sitting here,' says Münster, sitting back. 'I knew it at once. One, there's the mist. And two, it's the silence. Sure, there's the tinkling of the harness, and every so often one of the horses, it 'ud blow a snort, but the men? Not a sound from 'em. Not a word. I'm stood there in the road, goggling, like this, d'you see –' (and Münster rounds mouth and eyes and drops his arms to his sides, slack) '– I'm turned to stone I am, that terrified, and all the while they're going round me like I wasn't even there. And the horses – they have wings. Oh yes,' Münster continues, in response to his audience's gasp, 'that's true and all. Wings. May God strike off this hand if it's a lie. Tall as angels. Cleaved the mist. When they went past I saw the stars again. And right in their midst, I see this one horse, with its ears curved up like the horns of the Devil, and the way it was weaving its head about, I knew that one weren't making place for me nor any man, so I give way. And it passes by me, close as I am to you, and snaps its teeth. And the rider glances down at me, and that is when I know,' Münster ends, triumphantly, 'that's when I know for sure. That's him, the Dead Man. I could have reached out, touched his stirrup. There.'

'Saints and angels!' Munich exclaims. 'You look in his face?'

'I did. I couldn't stop myself.'

'God in his heaven!' says Munich, with his stool once more reared up off the floor. 'So what did he do?'

Münster is tapping out his pipe against his boot. 'What d'you mean, what did he do?'

'To you,' Munich replies. He sounds baffled. 'The Dead Man. What did he do to you?'

'To me? Why, nothing. What should he have done? He passed by, him and his, back into their world, and the mist cleared, and I found my legs, and staggered back to camp and into mine. And lived to tell the tale,' says Münster, digging his tobacco pouch out from his pocket. 'Someone has to. Else where would all the stories come from, eh?'

There's a silence. Then: 'Let me be sure I have this right,' Munich begins, slowly and heavily. 'This here's the spring of thirty-two.'

Münster inclines his head.

'So this was after Prague, and all that they did in Prague...'

'That would be so,' Münster agrees.

'You've got your green lads and your drummer boys, they're seeing his shadow in the crack of every door – by God, if but half a word gets out as he's nearby, half your company hightail it for the hills, and you expect me to believe as they rode past you—'

'Round me,' Münster corrects him, mildly, as he repacks his pipe.

'—round you, on the road, the Dead Man, the Dead Men, all of them, and they do NOTHING to you? NOTHING? And you expect me to believe you? God help us,' says Munich, striking the table, so the counters jump across the board, 'nearly thirty years of war, and that's as much as any of us has to show for it, tall tales and tobacco smoke and that's it. Hogwash, my friend. Hogwash!'

'He did do something, point of fact,' Münster replies. 'Now you do put me in mind.'

'WHAT?' Munich bellows, rising from his seat. 'WHAT? WHAT DID HE DO?'

Münster flicks a few shreds of tobacco from his coat. 'He *winked.*'

PART I

July 1630

CHAPTER ONE

Ghostland

'It seems we have another little enemy to fight.'

Ferdinand II, Holy Roman Emperor

NOW – WHERE WERE WE?

On an island, it turns out, though one so lightly separated from the rest of Germany and by tides so low and amiable, there are places a man might ride from island to mainland with his horse hardly wetting its belly. Amongst the new recruits tumbled out here, out the great galleons and the flat-bottomed transports, the sackful tumbled into his tender care reveal themselves as the sons of fisher-folk from the Stockholm archipelago, who seem delighted to find the country they have just invaded so very similar to home.

Two hundred transports, all told. Thirty-six galleons; thirteen thousand men. The island of Usedom has been overrun. It takes two days for all thirteen thousand to come ashore, by which time the supplies unloaded with the first have already been consumed, but what would an army be without the odd little oversight such as that?

Forage, he tells them. Use what you know. If you lads are fishermen, you go fish. He feels himself inhabiting this new role as he says it: Jack Fiskardo, *Kapten*, who says, now, listen, lesson number one: God help you, from here on in you are discoverers, army scouts (or you will be before I'm through with you), which means you'll spend your life up country, miles ahead of the rest of the army, with no-one to count on but the man wearing your boots.

A moment while they work that out. A moment while those who work it out the fastest explain it to the rest.

We look after ourselves, he says. Start getting used to that here. To add to the unreality of it all, they've made this landing in July, so it's past midnight, yet everything – his hands, the lads chasing fish through the shallows, the water itself, the sky above – is all the same fluttering, pulsing cornflower blue.

On the far side of the channel separating Usedom from the mainland, dark and spiky as a crown of thorns, the town of Wolgast, in silhouette.

He holds his hands out before him, into the indigo light. The whole story of his life is there, inked into his skin: the criss-cross for each battlefield; the trio of waving lines for each crossing of the seas; around the thumb the narrow black band for his old commander, Torsten the Bear, tied with its inky bow. *I am this war made flesh*, he thinks. And then turning his left hand over, there, burned into the pads of the palm:

GFRN

GFRN. *Gefroren*. Frozen. Hard. Don't waste your bullets. Many, many years ago he had his fortune told, his entire life, supposedly, laid out for him by a man who was blind as a stone and almost mute, but the only soul, he thinks, of all those he has known who might be entirely unsurprised to find him sat here now.

A little cough, for politeness' sake, and the boy, Kai, sits down beside him (it being an ensign's duty to be as constantly about his captain as a shadow), in that splendid suit of blue and gold, now so sadly watermarked from its adventures on arrival here (and shrunk too, he notes, about the boy's limbs), and starts some tale of childhood days and long white nights at some summer house in the archipelago, and how his nurse would bring him treats from the table of those banqueting out on the terrace below. The sons of the fishermen gawp at him as if he had just fallen from the moon, and snigger behind their hands. Kai, gamely attempting to emulate the other officers amongst Fiskardo's scouts, had gone plunging straight over the rail of the galleon, just as they had done, and the weight of gold thread on his clothes had nigh-on drowned him. The episode has already become one of the favourite tales of this company and its landing, embroidered and embellished at each handing-on. Now one of the fisher-lads, deftly throwing a fish onto the sand, calls out mockingly, 'Has 'e brung 'is little golden spoon?' and, in some presumption of agreement, slides his own gaze up to that of his captain, sat there on the bank with Kai beside him.

He thinks, Not *this* company, *mine*. He takes a narrow prospect of the josher. Yes, that little bit of varnish to this one: cock of the walk outside the house, the favoured child at home; best fed, best loved, no doubt, as well. Some mother's hand put that embroidery on the lad's shirt, at neck and wrists. How it must have hurt her heart to see him sail away.

He's sentimental where mothers are concerned.

But because this is his company, because he is its captain, and because years back, there had been another boy – younger, bullied, also loyal – now he gets to his feet and calls out, 'You – name?'

The answer comes back, 'Ulf. Ulf of Torsby!'

He crooks a finger. The lad approaches, splashing up the bank.

He lowers his head, and as he does so, Ulf of Torsby shrinks into himself a little. Kai is not the only one about whom tales are told. 'You use that tone to any of your fellows in this company again,' he says, 'you will regret it. Is that clear?'

Ulf of Torsby hangs his head. 'Yes, Kapten. Sir.'

Little bastard. All the same, it's Ulf of Torsby had the balls to crack the joke, to catch his eye, and on returning to those others in the stream, it's Ulf of Torsby is being given the commiserating pats on the back.

Meantime, Kai – Karl-Christian von Lindeborg, of Castle Lindeborg in the county of Uppsala, no less – gets stiffly to his feet, as one does when one is young as this and one's pride is tender. 'I too can forage,' he announces, and off he goes, those shrunken breeches rising up above his kneecaps at each step.

A shout of laughter from behind him. His officers – Zoltan, Ziggy, the Gemini, the Executioner – are hunkered in the dip there, and Zoltan, it transpires, has been composing his will. Now Ziggy has taken it over. 'Item,' he hears Ziggy declaim, at full pitch, 'item, my boots. Which I leave to the cheese-makers. Item, my fine moustache, which is to be put upon a string and made into a diversion for the cat. Item, my cock and balls, which are to be stuffed and varnished, and given to the artists, to use when next they must depict a god!'

They are all of them still half-deaf from the thump of those Baltic rollers on the island's eastern side. His hair feels thick with salt, the skin on his face made tight with it. Here though, facing the lagoon, the thump and boom is distant. There are cottages; there are little farms, although all deserted now, of course. The population of Usedom, such as it was, has taken to its boats and fled. In its place, scattered across this open landscape, there are regimental flags and battle standards, snapping in the wind. Messengers, galloping back and forth. The peep of bugles. Encampments, gatherings. Thirteen thousand men. And this one small band amongst so many others, his.

He folds himself back down again, there on the bank amongst the salt-grass. Over there, the future awaits, cunningly masquerading in the shape of Wolgast and, more to the point, raised up on its sconce, its fort. Either it has one more day to live, or they do. His hand goes to the pendant at his breastbone, the silver wolf, scratched and niello'ed now with age, but still the only compass he has ever had, or ever needed, come to that. Grace alone, faith alone. *Gott mitt uns.* We'll see.

This war, this German war, is twelve years old. It has already swallowed the armies of Duke Christian of Brunswick, and of the Danes. It has drained Bohemia of blood and blackened it with smoke; down on the Rhine it has turned the Palatine and all about it to a wasteland. It has given birth to tales of horrors and marvels, of prodigies and portents not heard since the time of the Norse. It has chewed its way through the troops sent by the Dutch and English. It has sucked in regiment after regiment of Emperor Ferdinand's soldiers, and those of his cousin the King of Spain, picked its teeth with their bones; and every one of those armies, Catholic, Calvinist, Lutheran, claimed God was with them too. *And now us*, he thinks. This army: this army of the Lion of the North, His Majesty Gustavus Adolphus of Sweden.

He keeps it to himself, but it seems to him God is an unreliable ally.

Kai returns. He returns with a round flat basket over one arm, and with a little old man and a little old woman, like the figures on a weathervane, bringing up the rear. There being a lady now present, Zoltan and Ziggy get to their feet. The Gemini and the Executioner also being present, the little old woman tucks herself in behind her husband at once. He hears Kai telling them, in flawless German, *'Don't be afraid. Here is my company, those are its officers. This is our captain.'*

He goes forward. 'Kai, who are these?'

'Herr Tessmann, Domini,' the boy replies. 'And his wife Frau Tessmann. Bette.'

He sees Frau Tessmann give the boy a fond quiet glance.

'They have a little house and farm,' the boy continues, pointing through the trees. And then, swopping back to Swedish, They wished to see us. He lowers his voice, glances at the Gemini, adding, They had heard all the Swedish had white hair. They wished to see if it was true.

And indeed Frau Tessmann, from behind her husband's shoulder, is now peering at the Gemini, with their candle-flame white hair, and tittering softly to herself.

And tails and horns, Kai continues, abashed.

'Tails and horns?' He laughs, swopping to Deutsch now himself, holds out his hand. 'That would be me. Fiskardo, Herr Tessmann. Jack Fiskardo.'

Herr Tessmann takes the hand in both his own, which are soft and dry with age, and pumps it, as farmers do. Frau Tessmann removes the cloth from the top of the basket. Inside, there are duck eggs, layer upon layer, nested on straw. Astonishing bounty. 'Kai!' he says, amazed, and the boy's face flushes up with pleasure.

I said that we would pay, he admits.

'Indeed we will pay. Herr Tessmann, how much for these fine eggs of yours?'

Herr Tessmann removes his cap, scratches his head, squints upward from this daring angle, and announces that these eggs will be four pfennig the dozen.

Pay him five, he tells Kai. Five a dozen, and we'll take them all, and we want sweet butter to cook them in too.

He raises an arm. This may be the one and only time anyone went foraging equipped only with good manners, and returned with such a result. This army, even with its thirteen thousand, might be ludicrously short of men, they may be almost out of cash (so rumour has it), they may, in fact, be marching on nothing but faith and earnest promises, but this morning, his company at least has—

'Breakfast!'

Clams, flounder, shrimp, the odd dozy perch, all chopped and fried together; a certain amount, it must be said, of seaweed and sand; the eggs piled on top, yellow as the butter and as soft. 'I must admit,' says Zoltan, 'this is by no means as revolting as I feared.' He raises his spoon in acknowledgement to the Tessmanns – still watching, still apparently fascinated that these men from the frozen north should do anything as commonplace as eat. 'But it is a strange thing,' Zoltan continues, lowering his voice, 'all their neighbours are fled. Why are they not gone too?'

'Herr Tessmann says they are too old,' Kai answers, seriously. 'He says they fled before, but not again. And Frau Tessmann fears to leave their animals.'

'You speak good German, Kai,' his *Kapten* hears himself say, and the boy flushes up again.

'My tutor was from Heidelberg.'

'Your *tutor*!' Zoltan exclaims, with a bellow of laughter. 'Of course!' Anywhere else in the world, the status of Kai's birth would have doors being opened, bows being swept; here, however, it is everyone's favourite jest.

But Kai continues. 'It is the greatest shame we must make war against his people.'

Puzzlement on Zoltan's part. 'Your tutor, he was a Catholic?'

'No indeed!' The boy sounds shocked to his core. 'No, he was of God's true faith, of course.'

'Then we make war *for* him, not against him,' Zoltan points out.

'I think we make war *on* him,' Kai says, quietly. 'On all these people. They will be lost beneath our boots.'

Now Kai's captain hears himself ask, 'Where is your tutor now?'

'Magdeburg. He and his family, they are in Magdeburg.'

Magdeburg is one of the few cities to have made those earnest promises of support. It is surrounded, unluckily, by many that have not.

He looks at the Tessmanns, how they hold onto each other in the wind, the little old woman with her hand in her husband's, like a bride. Ask the men who write the rules, and there is no pillaging nor plunder in the Swedish army. *Yes*, he thinks, *and I'm the Queen of Spain*. He stands up. 'Ulf!'

'Yes, Kapten!'

'Take five of your friends, put a guard upon the Tessmanns' farm, and if any other company comes sniffing round, you tell 'em Fiskardo got there first.'

A mighty grin. 'Yes, Kapten. Yes, Domini!'

Domini. These names keep attaching themselves to him. Domini, master, is one; *Fransman*, the Frenchie, is another, *'shtiana*, a third. Why do they call you that? Kai had asked. He'd sounded as if he were contemplating taking offence, that perhaps being part of an ensign's duties too. (Don't ask me, he'd told the boy. I was older than you before I knew such a thing as an ensign even existed, and I never in my life imagined I'd end up with one.)

'Tr-cz-iana,' he'd explained, spelling the word out, saying it slow. 'In Poland. A battle, a year ago. It's where I was made captain. By your king.'

And the boy's eyes grew wide.

'Your king has a habit of hazarding himself,' he'd continued, explaining. 'Getting too close to the fire. He had four Cossacks after him, but I had Milano.' And he points to where the horses wait in their usual patient line, heads down, doing whatever a horse does to get some sleep under the midnight sun; Milano, with his ringleted mane, standing out amongst them even from here. 'And I was first, and he was fastest.'

They say Gustavus Adolphus lost his footing as he came ashore. Stood up, clutching handfuls of Germany in each fist, gave thanks to God for putting it so easily within his grasp. It's a good job Lutherans do not believe in omens.

Wolgast. Jack Fiskardo and his discoverers, they take its measure, report back: There's the fort, up on its sconce, another little channel of water, then a castle on a tiny island of its own, then the town. Upon sight of the Swedish cavalry, the men defending Wolgast pour down the sides of the sconce and out through the earthwork like ants when you kick their nest, but it's not excess of fighting spirit, this, no, it's utter terror, it's *Let's get it over with.* You can feel the entire army take in its breath before it falls upon them, and then the men defending Wolgast, God help them, then they die – they die upon the field, they drown within the river, they are shot within the boats in which they try to flee. When the world is calm again, *'shtiana's* new recruits edge down to the water and look upon the bodies swilling about in the shallows; venture out to inspect those left on the field. One or two of them throw up, but only one or two. The rest crouch down, peer and marvel, just as he once did himself. It's no soft nor easy life, that of a fisherman, and just as well.

This is how fast it comes upon you, he tells them. Life to death. Do they have a little more the measure of it now?

Next up is Wollin, and a march of forty miles along the Baltic coast, and if they take Wollin they will have strongholds either side the lagoon of the Oder. Jack finds himself and Zoltan picking their way around a field of tangled grain, sprung from last year's unharvested crop, through a forest of green bracken as high as their heads. On the far side of the field, the Gemini do the same. The sun pours down its heat; insects criss-cross lazy lines in and out the green shade above them. Jack takes a pause, points to the two white-blond heads on the far side of the field, bobbing in and out of sight, unmissable as signal flares. 'D'you think we should have them stop bleaching their hair?'

Zoltan is elbowing aside stems of bracken sturdy as an officer's baton. 'I think we should have left them where we found them, that pair of freaks,' Jack hears him mutter in reply.

'What, in a pit, in Poland?' In a pit in Poland, villagers gathered round it, stones in their hands. Neither of the Gemini has ever offered an explanation as to why, but it don't take much to work one out. 'The dew falls on us all,' Jack says, piously, and gets as expected a snort in reply, and then Zoltan comes to a dead stop, pointing down.

There is a corpse laid at their feet. What was once a man: the skin now no more than human parchment, the bones at wrists and legs protruding, white as chalk.

'Germany,' says Zoltan, under his breath, as if no more need be said.

Jack crouches down. The front of this one's skull is blackened, the face consumed. Whoever this was, he was killed by having his head put into a fire. He tries to remember the last time a corpse – any corpse – made him do more than speculate who might have killed it, but small chance of an answer to that here. This part of Germany has had armies marching through it ever since the war began. This same war in which he did his growing. Now here he is again; a veteran at twenty-four.

He holds his left hand over the skull, where the nose would have been, over the cracked and yellowed teeth, the cheekbones burned away, the mournful void of the sockets from which a man once viewed the world. He thinks of silent Benedicte, with his blindly rolling pebble-white eyes, and he feels in his hand, with its message of scars, something... some urgent thing. He looks at the skull again, its blackened emptiness. *Why are you shouting at me?*

'You think we know what breed of man it was did this?' Zoltan asks.

'I would be very surprised if we did not.'

Zoltan straightens up. 'Germany,' he says again.

And then a shout in earnest from the far side of the field. He stands. The Gemini are pointing toward Wollin, from which smoke is now rising, and there is Wollin's garrison, racing away, taking flight like game.

Well. That was easy.

NOW SOUTH TO Stettin, at the mouth of the Oder proper, another thirty miles, and once again it's Fiskardo and his discoverers are ordered to go ahead, check out the lie of the land. Where do these orders come from? Kai wants to know. 'Ultimately, Åke Tott,' Jack replies, as Åke Tott's messenger turns his horse about, departs. 'General Åke Tott. In the wars in Poland he knew my old commander, Torsten the Bear.' Below Tott, there is General Baner; and between them and Baner, Colonel Ancrum, a Scot, one of many in this salmagundi of an army; below Ancrum his lieutenant colonels, majors, other captains; the regiment's quartermaster, its provost, clerk; its standard-bearer, chaplain, blacksmith, trumpeters and the not entirely reassuringly named barber-surgeon. An entire farmyard full of both cockerels and pecks. The first regiment he ever found a place in, back in Germany, all those years ago, could muster a scant five hundred at its strongest; now, Ancrum's alone is double that. Everything in this war grows bigger, or grows worse, and if it can, does both.

'They put us at the front because they know how good we are,' Ulf of Torsby declares. According to Ziggy, Ulf rides like a sack of cabbages; according to the Executioner (after Zoltan, third-in-command) the lad is too full of himself by half, but the life of an army scout seems to be suiting him. Face by face the new recruits have begun acquiring names. There's a front row coming into being: along with Ulf, there's an Elias (one of those quick-to-it lads); a Sten (the joker of the company); and a Per (lanky as Jack is himself). There's Jens (freckled, top to toe); there's an Alaric (earnestly intense); there's a Magnus (a great blonde bullock of a lad); there's an Ansfrid. Ansfrid? ''Cos 'is mum's a Norge.' There's even a Thor, who (his Kapten notes) keeps himself to himself, perhaps in consequence of the fact that God sent him out into the world with one eye so much smaller than the other; and then there's Luka, who looks just the same as the rest – too fresh of face and soft of cheek, you would think, for any of the deeds that will be asked of him – except that he must have been hatched from an egg half the size of all the rest. Last of all, there's Ulrik; last because he's the lumberer, walrus-size, and always at the back.

Ulf has developed the habit of starting the day by leading his comrades in an enthusiastic drill: whirling his sword above his head as if he were casting a net; not a few times, his comrades have started the day diving to the ground to save their necks. Jack knows he is unusual in bothering to drill his recruits at all; most of the army takes the attitude that natural wastage is what hones a fighting force, but he was trained, taught and tended as a scout, and by one of the best, and would not be here now (ungrateful little sod that he was) without. So yes, he makes them drill. They set fire to their hair with lengths of smoking match-cord; try to free sword from scabbard too fast and at the wrong angle and get the blade stuck; get their thumbnails caught between flint and frizzen on their muskets and hold their powder flasks upside down and trail black powder all over their feet; but he makes them drill. I will have you loading and reloading in the dark, he tells them, before I'm through with you. Because as *Kapten* he suspects the likelier reason to make such active use of them is that, with the possible exception of Kai (and even he is a younger son), their loss would be a nothing: if you can believe the rumours, there are another forty thousand conscripts waiting back in Stockholm, while Zoltan is Hungarian, the Executioner by birth a Muscovite; Ziggy's family are Bohemian refugees and, as for the Gemini, God knows where they call home. And Colonel Ancrum, he suspects, knows, likes, trusts none of them. Torsten the Bear had a reputation, a wild man of the woods; and then—

Then if you were Ancrum, and found yourself with this oddity amongst your captains, this man who by repute is *gefroren*, frozen, proof against any weapon made of iron or lead or steel, who wears the token of a hard man about his neck, wouldn't you put him at the front too, just to see what happens?

Stettin is in sight. He sends Luka, who is agile as a weasel, up a tree with their spyglass. 'I see the castle,' comes the report, shouted back down, and then, 'By Christ, they're off again! That's the garrison! On the run! The people are on the walls!'

He thinks of some of those little places he fought through in Poland. He asks, before he can stop himself, 'Are they alive?'

They are indeed. There is a pretty little meeting outside the walls between Gustavus Adolphus of Sweden and the Duke of Pomerania. Duke Bogislaw looks sick and tired, King Gustavus buoyant as ever. Meantime, Fiskardo and his discoverers are sent in through the city's gates to flush out any mad-for-glory snipers that might by some chance have been left behind.

They come into the city from the east, Stettin's castle rearing up before them like a land-berg. The walls behind them may be full of folk and noise, but the streets before them are as empty as if the world had come to its end. Over the rooftops an Imperial flag, the Habsburg eagle, trapped on its broken pole, flaps and beats above them, as if bewailing how it has been forsook. Faces bright with excitement, and with the Executioner hissing orders and imprecations behind them, the sons of the fisher-folk make a more than creditable stab at it, the chequerboard game of feints and darts down the streets, and now there's a gatehouse, so they ease the gate open, wary, and there beyond is a courtyard, and there within it an entire commissary-worth of supplies: half-laden wagons packed with barrels of beef, crates full of bottles, chickens hanging from a rack, sacks of bread, wheels of cheese, hams, garlands of dried herring, all of it abandoned in confusion. Ulf and his fellows stand at its centre, turning round and round, somewhere between delight and disbelief: Food! Forage! Rations! 'Take every crumb,' their *Kapten* tells them, 'fill your packs and fill your pockets, do it now,' then out the corner of his eye sees Kai approach something the size and shape of a catafalque, shrouded in canvas; sees the boy lift the canvas back, spring away, and go straight down on his arse, skittering back across the ground on heels and elbows, with a cry of 'Holy *GOD!*'

Two animals: huge, spotted, snarling; prowling left to right. A pair of leopards in a cage. His men surround them, all amazed. The Executioner hunkers down, peering in, those warts and whiskers pressed to the bars of the cage, and one of the animals backs up, squats down, pisses itself. It's the male. The female, hackles in a crest, swipes at the bars of the cage with a paw that makes the metal ring. *There's a moral there*, thinks Jack.

And then behind the cage, there's movement; there's a man, crouching down, seeking to hide himself behind the barrels and crates, then scurrying for the gate. The Gemini catch him with ease; lift him up under the arms and pin him against the wall. The man wears a buff-coat like theirs, but the strangest pair of breeches in harlequins of yellow, green and red. 'Quinto del Ponte!' the man shrieks, pointing at his breast. 'Quinto del Ponte, Quinto del Ponte!' He seems to think he will need dumb-show before they understand this is his name.

'*E chi o che cazzo è Quinto del Ponte?*' he asks, and the man does a splendid job of apparently going limp with relief, and replies, '*Sono il servitore del generale Wallenstein.*' I am the servant of General Wallenstein. These beasts were a gift from him, to the Emperor.

He finds he still remembers enough Italian to ask, You are their keeper?

Del Ponte nods.

He looks across to the animals' cage. There is a bowl in it, broken, dry; a single bone, licked down as smooth as the sea licks a stone. *Their keeper my arse.* He turns back to Del Ponte and says, So now you can join us, and make them a gift to a king.

Del Ponte demurs. No, no, I am nothing. No soldier. I am – I am a trader, only. Please, you may keep the creatures, but please, you will let me go.

He leans forward. Del Ponte quails. The rare occasions Jack Fiskardo finds himself before a looking-glass, he is amazed at the man who glowers back. That cold pale gaze, blank as a wall, as if whatever lives behind it isn't him at all, but is instead this Myrmidon, this thing that, if it ceased to fight, would surely sink and die, the way it's said a shark will do, should it cease to swim. Not so many years ago he was pretty enough to seduce his colonel's whore – now look at him. Yes, and look at his conscience too – the aches, the tender spots, the bruises that never fade. He can remember, when he was younger, when it wasn't this face stared back at him but something so much softer and more hopeful, joking that he'd end up a big ugly bastard; it's still a shock to see how true, in every way, that has turned out to be. Then again, every veteran in every company knows the value of making themselves look as alarming as possible: they stud their buff-coats, wax their hair into whipcords, plait it into strings; the Executioner grows out his side-whiskers and nourishes warts the size of gooseberries; the Gemini make themselves this crazy mirror-image of each other; Ziggy, as horse-master, dyes his horse's tail with carmine and his own topknot the same. If nothing else, it has encouraged Death, so far, to find easier prey, and judging by the terror on Del Ponte's face, the effect certainly works on him. But does Del Ponte speak German? Soon find out.

'You know what His Majesty Gustavus Adolphus of Sweden would say to that?'

Del Ponte, glancing from him to the Gemini and back, shakes his head again.

'He'd say, you're with us, or against us, friend. So which is it to be?'

Night falls, only of course it don't. The leopards, sated on chicken, with a bucket of water let gingerly into their cage through its cunning little door, lie on their sides, bellies heaving with content. And Jack Fiskardo and his ensign Kai lean over the cage and chat.

'Why do they keep running away?' the boy asks. 'The Emperor's army – why do they not stand and fight?'

'They're stretching our lines,' Jack replies. 'The only place we have where we can reinforce or resupply is the beachhead back on Usedom. The further we get from it, the faster, the better for them. Their commander, General Wallenstein, is no fool. His field marshal, Torquato Conti, even less. He will harrow the earth ahead of us. He'd sooner have his own troops starve than leave us as much as a peapod.'

The leopardess, beneath them, extends all four of those mighty paws, toe by taloned toe, and opens her eyes as if their conversation is of interest.

Kai, looking down at her, asks, 'What will become of them?'

'They will go to Stockholm,' he says. 'To the Djurgården, I would think. A whole island for them to range about on.'

Kai looks mournful. 'Poor beasts,' he says. 'They are so far from home.'

As are we all.

'Signor del Ponte says they are worth five hundred thaler,' the boy continues, in a marvelling tone. And lo, at the boy's words, there is the man himself, still in that outlandish costume, sidling into view. Something prompts him: extend the conversation. Let Signor del Ponte come up if he will.

'When I was much the same age as you,' he begins, 'I helped disembark a horse worth all of that.'

The boy's eyes widen once again. Everything is new to Kai, the boy spends his days agog. 'A horse worth so much?'

'So I was told. The Buckingham mare. She was being shipped to Stockholm too.'

And here is Signor del Ponte himself, ducking his head in greeting, steepling his hands. *'Buona sera, buona sera.'* And then in German, 'My friends.' He comes closer. 'I am intrigued,' he begins. 'You speak Italian, Captain. Excellently, if I may say so.' An ingratiating smile. 'A man who speaks Italian is as rare in these climes as – well, these.' A hand waved over the cage.

It comes to him that Quinto del Ponte's costume is exactly what a man would wear if he wished not to be taken seriously. 'Yet you are here,' Jack replies.

'Ah, yes. My business takes me everywhere. *Il mondo è il mio mercato*, as they say.'

'Sadly you are at the limits of my Italian, Signor del Ponte,' he says, 'as you are at the limits of your own range.'

'Ah, so.' Hands in the pockets of those harlequin breeches. 'But yet I am intrigued. How is it that you speak Italian at all?'

'An old acquaintance. When I was first a-soldiering.' And then just to see, he adds, 'Another trader, like yourself. One Tino Ravello.'

Quinto del Ponte's face congeals instantly, a response so swift even a dissembler as practised as this one can't hide it. The boy,

Kai, eyes darting from one man to the other, aware something has happened here, but nothing like fast enough to work out what.

'Well then!' Del Ponte declares. 'I believe I know the man. Or I have heard the name, at least.'

'Indeed? How small this great world can be.'

Del Ponte waits a moment, rocking on his toes. 'Then my curiosity is sated. Captain, I bid you *buona notte*.'

The leopardess watches him go.

'He is a little strange,' says Kai, uncertainly.

'He is a *lot* strange. I think we keep a careful eye upon him.'

'But he knew your friend,' Kai points out, as if this must be proof of good character.

'He knew the name, sure enough. But the Tino Ravello I knew was an intelligencer, a spy. I wonder quite what our Signor del Ponte may prove to be.'

The leopardess is on her feet. She lifts her head – her head that is both chamfered and square, and as if pulled from the mass of her body between the finger and thumb of her creator. Jack lays his hand to the top of the cage, feels the heat of her breath, her whiskers stiff as salt-grass. The blood and ivory of the inside of her mouth. Then she yawns, and the yawn extends into a yodel of complaint, of feline huff; with just enough of a growl to it so you know to pay it due heed. *You remind me of someone*, he thinks.

All these shades, all these echoes, all these ghosts, a whole land full of them. And only one that matters.

His hand lifts to the silver wolf. *Where are you, you son of a bitch? Where do you wait for me? What stone are you hiding under now?*

CHAPTER TWO

This House Where Nothing Moves

'… a country unpeopled, and rendered waste…'

Count Galeazzo Gualdo Priorato, *An History of the Late Warres*

IT'S A COMMONPLACE with all those who meet him, all (rather fewer) who live to tell the tale; how insignificant his appearance is. Nothing about him stands out, nothing whatsoever – middling height, middling build; stronger than he looks, but you could say that of any cavalryman. In the old days, before the war, there were plenty who forgot meeting him altogether, in the panic of some inexplicable fever, or the tiny wound that suppurates, turns black. All that has ever made him memorable is his lard-white pallor, yes, as if he is himself recovering from illness, and the scarf knotted Croat-fashion at his throat, and when he shows them, which is but rarely, his tiny, wide-spaced teeth, like a lizard's, like pips, within the pinkness of his gums.

And of course the silver wolf, the token affixed to the front of his coat. Here he sits: Carlo Fantom, Charles the Ghost, here in this house where nothing, any longer, moves – not the dog in its kennel, the man at the door, the boy on the stairs, the woman in her bed, the infant in its cot, the maid in the attic. Not even the bird at the window in its cage. In the houses on either side he can hear his men, working through them, room by room – the stoving-in of doors, the clatter up those wooden cottage stairs, the shriek or scream of capture, or more rarely the shots and shouts of resistance. But here in this humble room, all is peace. Because this is what he does, this is how he thinks of it: he brings peace.

He moves his boot across the floor a little, left to right. The liquid on the floor is sufficient for the movement to create a ripple, as across a pond. Tumult to left and right, but in here only silence, order, calm. It comes to him, on this small rise of feeling, almost of nostalgia, that this is how it used to be when he earned his bread the other way. When he had served the great, the mighty thing all on his own, when he watched its passage through so many, when its power had been such that sometimes he had almost felt it pass through him, as well. His men will never understand that, the respect that it deserves, but he does, he, Carlo Fantom, and he never took a life, not as soldier or assassin, without acknowledging it, that moment when he—

Call it what it is. That moment when he is God.

He moves his boot again. The formless waters.

No, it is gone. It has passed.

He gets to his feet. To be honest, they depress him when they're dead. All that struggle, all that desperation, that vitality, to simply disappear? The eyes no more than marbles, the body slack. Something gone from it; the hand pulled from the glove. Puppets, cut from their strings. It seems a sort of cheating.

He goes to the window. How mean this place is. All these little dorps hidden away at the end of their rutted lanes. Could you even call this one a village? No, it is a nothing, and now it will be a less than nothing, just like all the rest. *Lay it to waste.* The fire and the sword. Those were Conti's orders. Leave the Swedish nothing but ruins to hide themselves in. It had reminded him of his own promise as an assassin, his watchword: *no loose ends* – no suspicions, no retribution, nothing, not for his employers, not for him – nothing but silence, fulfilment and peace. Nor had there been loose ends, ever; it was his guarantee, his reputation, it was a promise he had kept—

All save one. One escapee, one single instance—

He rolls his shoulders, like a horse throwing off flies. So far away, so long ago – pah.

All the same, it rankles. He might have snuffed the boy out as a child; but no. Then when their paths crossed, in Hertzberg, when Hertzberg was such a place where every path crossed, then he might have done it – again, no. But (he tells himself) has anything more been heard of his one loose end, from that moment all those years ago to this? It has not. So what does that suggest? Yes, that the war has done his work for him, and the boy is long dead.

Only – oh, what is this? What is it? Even as that thought is disappearing, pulling its tail behind it, out of sight, there's that snap of light again, across the inside of his head. It's new, this, it has not yet disclosed its meaning, but every time it happens, it bids him raise his hand and place it on some surface – window, wall – and prepare to feel that surface shake.

He rests his hand, his left hand, against the leading of the window, the bumps of solder, fragile glass, cracked here, there, everywhere. His men have caught something out there. He sees a stockinged foot, he sees it kick, kick again, judder, then flop. *Ach*, what is this? Is it a warning? Is he being fanciful? It feels the way cannon-fire feels, heard way, way off, almost too far to hear, but you register it, nonetheless. You feel it, deep inside you, in your gut.

He turns away. It's a low business, this. Low and mean –
purgatory for a man like him. These peasants – he cannot help
but think how he is nothing but the man who sets his terriers
on rats, while that civet cat Quinto disports himself within the
Swedish camp; Quinto, that idiot, that two-legged louse... the
thought that, as Quinto insists upon putting it, he and Quinto
should share a stable, *Aiee, jebati!* Fuck.

He goes outside, raises his arm, circles it above his head, sees
his men look up, the whole gang of them, from whatever it is
they have there on the ground. Time to be gone.

And then he feels it once more. Something out there, was
not there before. He cannot name it, he cannot shape it, but he
can feel its mighty hunger, he can feel the weight, the mass of
its intent—

Again, he rolls his shoulders. How fanciful! How sick this
dead land makes us. Oh, for a fight worth the name!

He calls to his sergeant: 'Salvatore!' and the man turns about,
detaches himself from the group gathered round whatever it is
they have there – the clothes so wet and muddied, the face now
so misshapen that it's impossible to tell if it was male or female.
But they've left it lying on its front, so female, probably. The way
they will keep on crawling, as if they could get away. It was one
of the first lessons he learned, how if you destroy their women,
you break the men as well. There is no actual lust involved in this
for him, unless the one being despoiled is proud enough and fair
enough for the despoiling to truly make a difference (and yes, he
admits, he does have some little reputation there); it is simple
efficiency, that is all. So he chooses those men like Salvatore,
who do have specific appetites to sate, and then those men like
Salvatore, they in turn choose those others who are simply weak
enough to follow. Because otherwise (another glance at the thing
there on the ground), who could possibly desire *that*?

Salvatore – Salvatore of the broken nose – comes forward.
Salvatore has had that broken nose for years now – another

souvenir from Hertzberg. Someone flattened it across his face with such vehemence that his nose looks like a frog: the body squashed, the fat thighs his gaping nose-holes. All these years it's been getting worse and worse, such that Salvatore snorts now, when he breathes; has to do so with an open mouth. It'll be a relief to be rid of him, for a while.

But Salvatore is eyeing him with suspicion. Does Salvatore too see something that wasn't there before? Does he see distraction? Does he sense unease?

'*Kapetan?*'

'We're done here. You go east. Be sure you clear out everything that way.'

'And you?' Snort. 'Where do you go?'

'I go back to camp. I am to wait,' (an inner snarl) 'to hear from Del Ponte.'

CHAPTER THREE

The Letter-Lock

'Written intelligence is very dangerous…'

Sir James Turner, *Pallas Armata*

S TRANGE HOW IT works, this sense that there is something out there, was not there before. The way it seems
to wait, until some wholly disconnected notion trips
over it, and then the way your thoughts come back to that
loose stone over and over again. Kick at it, poke at it, will not
let it be. As a phenomenon, it is one with which Tino Ravello
is all too familiar.

Tino Ravello – eh, not quite the man he was. Time has set
about Ravello the way a cook might set about a carrot, paring
off a little here, a little there: narrowing his flanks, thinning the
upright chick-fluff of his hair, poking in the flesh of his cheeks

and putting brackets around that smiling mouth – a warning, perhaps, for those with sense enough to see it, that what comes out of there will have clauses, subtext.

In compensation, however, it has made him a man of sufficient importance to be standing here. Here in this tiny room, examining his own reflection in the room's one narrow window, while the great and good – the great and good, Ravello thinks, the not-so-good, and those not to be trusted as far as one could throw a *boule* – of this great city finish their business, oblivious, in the chambers beyond the room's surprisingly thick and solid little door.

Ah, Paris. Those bastardly Londoners would have you believe their city is the greater, its population the more numerous, but in truth at this point the two are neck and neck, and Paris is far, far the more beautiful. She has her Notre Dame, her Pont Neuf, her Tuileries; marking her eastern edge, she has her terrible Bastille (and if you walk there, from the Tuileries, you have walked across pretty much her entire width – think of that!). She has her Place Dauphine, her Place Royale, edged with buildings so straight and true and fine, you would think they had been lowered from Olympus. She has her streets where live the lower folk, and that give proof of their commercial enterprise by being thick with muck, through which coaches and fiacres dart back and forth, splattering rich and poor alike. She has her little dogs that run at you, for no better reason than to show off their paces, and her exquisite mam'selles, who dress themselves with such finesse, no man can tell if he is following a comtesse or a whore. She has no fewer than two hundred courts in which the energetic can play *jeu de paume*. She has her Sorbonne – the man for whom Ravello waits is its dean. And atop the sloping vineyards of Montmartre, she has recently acquired a brace of sturdy windmills, which visitors to Paris are already using as a handy landmark. You would be hard-put to find a Protestant church in Paris at this date, but if you wished you might go say a prayer in its solitary Lutheran chapel, in

the Swedish embassy. Some might think it odd that Sweden
has been extended such religious courtesy, but few would be
foolish enough to say so. And certainly not here, here within
the Palais du Louvre – that maze of stone, a Minotaur around
its every corner, glowering down upon the great khaki rush of
the Seine; the only thing within the city to pay what goes on in
here no heed at all.

And here at the back of the Louvre, above this almost
forgotten courtyard, Ravello waits. He's good at waiting. It's
one of his greatest talents.

But the man for whom he waits is even better at that game
than he.

The smaller the room, the greater the secret, is Ravello's experience, and this one is so small he could stretch out his arms and
press his fingertips upon its walls. They call them closets, such
rooms as these, but truly, knock a few pegs into the walls, it
would be a cupboard.

He gives himself a stretch – up on his toes, hands clasped
above his head. He is unused to dressing as he is today, and his
clothes irk him.

And the greater the man, the more numerous the retinue.
Seeping through that surprisingly solid little door, Ravello can
hear their voices still. The door will not admit their actual words,
but Ravello recognizes the tone, the earnest, serious murmur in
which one delivers those necessary promises of service, loyalty.

He turns away, back to that narrow window. A man, he
thinks, might stand just here and view all the doings in the
courtyard beneath, and – unless one of those below looked up,
at just the right moment and at just the right angle – expect to
be completely unobserved. Here at this back-end of the Louvre
nothing happens nowadays – pigeons strut, cats sashay along the
balustrade then flop themselves down to sleep on the leads in the
sun. A workman, somewhere out of sight, sings out a melody,

while walloping something with a mallet – one cannot turn a corner in Paris these days without finding some edifice being torn down, and another put up. But thirteen years ago, down in that unregarded courtyard, a man named Concino Concini found Death a-waiting for him, and the whole fortune of France was changed. Concino Concini, *soi-disant* chief minister of France, forced to his knees and his brains blown out across those very cobblestones. In response, they say the Queen Mother had all the windows from her apartments facing the courtyard filled in. Could not bear to look upon the place where the man who (by repute) was in her bed even more frequently than was its warming-pan met his end. Petitioned her son to move her to the new wing he was constructing. And was refused. Moved to a new palace, the Luxembourg, instead, and filled the entirety of its ground floor with a painted biography, vast canvasses from the brush of Master Rubens of all her hardships and her triumphs, from her birth as a grand-daughter of the Habsburgs onwards; including one showing mother and son reconciled as they have never been in life, he as Apollo, she both blonde and blameless, innocent as Christ. As she never has been, either.

Ravello's reflection gazes back at him, as does whatever lurks behind the friendly invitation in his eyes. A friend – dead these many years – once told him he had the perfect face for an intelligencer, a keeper of secrets, precisely because he did not. He is not sure this is true any longer. He thinks he is acquiring the face of a man who has seen too much, knows too much and has lost too many.

The windows opposite stare back at him; blank and blind as ever. And King Louis XIII is still chilly-hearted; and Marie de' Medici still sits in her new palace, fattening upon her own venom like a scorpion. Sometimes, Ravello wonders how anyone can take these royals seriously.

A little cloud runs between Ravello and the sun, like a reminder. *Balthasar, hello*, he thinks. Balthasar, the Shadow

Man, so fine a scout the joke was that he never cast one. Balthasar who has been in his grave, a shadow now himself, these – what? Seven years? Yet who still, whenever he arrives in Ravello's head, glares at him and gives that same loose stone a hefty kick. You lost that boy, is what Balthasar says. I found him, you lost him.

Oh, but surely. The boy had a right. He was grown. I only told him what he asked. And by God, if ever there was a lad could take care of himself...

No, let's take this in order, because these things always have a beginning, even if as yet this one has no end; and the beginning of this one was down in that dusty courtyard. There was a man, Jean Fiskardo, Balthasar's brother-in-arms, who held Concini down as Concini's skull was blown clean as an egg, and who then disappeared, seemingly from the entire face of the earth. There was the running mad, in consequence, of Jean's poor English wife. There was her seeming self-murder; which turned out to have been actual murder, plain and unadorned; there was Jean's own reappearance, in a grave, in Picardy; and worst of all, the fifth act in this tragedy, there was the fate of their son. The fate, Ravello knows (as he stands here, waiting, waiting, waiting), that Balthasar would hold him responsible for without a doubt. For a moment he eyes his reflection again, asquint, as if seeking to sneak up on himself. No, it's not loss he sees there, it's guilt.

The voices beyond the door have ceased. He turns. The door opens.

'Eminence,' murmurs Ravello, bowing low. Because the man now entering, sharing this tiny space – for all that he has the look of a provincial tax inspector, for all the delicacy of build, the mournful eye – this man one should take as seriously as death.

'Oh, up, up, up,' says the Cardinal, summoning Ravello back to his feet. 'No more of that, God spare us.' A hand flapped at the world beyond the door. 'Those – those *dissemblers*, Ravello. I know exactly what they are, they know I know, yet still they smile and bow and smile and bow... Come, come with me. Through here. Into my office.'

There are those, Ravello knows, who wait all their careers to be admitted into the Cardinal's private office. To look at it, you would wonder why. A window, curtained; a fireplace, its firedogs dozing, this summer's day, un-needed, side-by-side; one old-fashioned, high-backed plumply cushioned chair into which a man might sink when the day's business is done; and several others, pushed back against the panelled walls, that look as if they had been chosen to be as comfortless, as encouraging of swift decision-making as possible. Books and rolled documents form an untidy stash against the long wall of the room, where they have been summarily pushed from the table; and on the table itself there reposes the *carton* and rag-paper model of yet another addition to Paris's new builds. Double height; ashlar masonry sketched in with delicate watercolour; pedimented attic storey; all set around a single central courtyard in which bushes of green silk threads, combed and rolled into cones and spheres, wait in their thimble-sized planters to be rearranged at whim. 'Very elegant,' Ravello comments. 'Very – restrained.'

A thin smile. 'Le Nôtre is already at work on designs for the garden,' the Cardinal tells him. 'Assuming, of course, that I am here long enough to see it.'

The parlous state of the Cardinal's health is well known. At times he shudders with an alternating fever; at times the pain of urination makes him weep. He is beset by megrim headaches, when he must view the world through shapes that shimmer like the feathers of the phoenix. But this time it does not seem to Ravello that the Cardinal references only his health. 'Eminence?' he says, as a means of encouraging more.

A sigh. 'You see before you,' the Cardinal says, 'a man attempting to keep his balance on a *bascule*. I am trapped between His Majesty and his mother. If one does not tip me, the other will.' Another sigh. He puts out his hands, and presses down upon the air. *Calmez, calmez...* 'To business,' he says. Yes, business, always. 'You have it? My letter?'

'Yes, Eminence,' Ravello replies. His own hand goes to his ruff. He rarely wears such an item (that persistent annoying rustle under your ear every time you turn your head, and then the fact that, compared to the flat, falling collar, ruffs these days are far from *à la mode*), but this occasion is as formal as his life gets. Also—

Also those many robust pleats and runnels, they do still make excellent hiding places, for anything made of paper in particular. Using index and middle finger, he extracts the letter and places it in the Cardinal's open palm.

Cardinal Richelieu tilts his head to examine it. 'This is how you received it?'

'Exactly as it was.'

'From the man himself?'

'From Del Ponte, yes,' says Ravello. He adds, 'To all appearances, it is untouched,' because to all appearances it is, the scarlet seal in place, the squared-off folds as neat and sharp as when they left the desk of His Eminence all those weeks ago.

His Eminence gives a thin, sad smile. 'Yet what is it we are told about appearances?' He waves the letter back and forth, as if the better to assess it. 'Well then,' he says, and slips a thumbnail under the seal – his own seal: the shield with its three chevrons topped by the wide-brimmed *galero*, the extravagant ribbons. He opens the flap, tips the letter on its side and shakes it, and out into his palm falls a tiny pleated ribbon of paper, like the tail of a miniature kite. A letter-lock. A letter-lock, *picked*.

The Cardinal frees another sigh. 'I cannot tell you,' he says, 'how depressing it is to be so often correct.'

He drops the letter back into Ravello's hands. Ravello takes it, smooths it out – first the side with his address, written across the letter's own verso (*Sig. Tino Ravello, By Hand to the Carpenter's Hat, Annecy*), and then the other. It is clearer to see, then, the place where the creases meet and where there is now a tiny strip missing, hidden in the fold; originally cut loose on three sides, then pleated, bent back upon itself, threaded through; the lock that anyone opening the letter would inevitably tear away. Anyone not meant to be opening the letter in the first place.

So now, the obvious question. 'Might I ask,' Ravello begins, 'what service – what role was it – Signor del Ponte performed for you?'

The other gives him a quick, sharp glance. 'Oh, he was not as you. He was merely a go-between.'

Yes, but between you and who? Ravello wonders. 'A messenger, in other words.'

'Indeed, or so I thought.' A pause. 'He came to me through the Prince-Bishop of Prague. And the Prince-Bishop's recommendations have served me well before, very well. And he was of use to me – good use – in our business in Italy.' Our business in Italy being the pestilential complications of who succeeds to the throne of Mantua and who controls the kingdom of Savoy – an ally of France, or (God forbid!) a puppet of the Habsburgs. 'Which will,' His Eminence continues, 'I fear, one way or the other, be the death of me.'

And Ravello, looking into the face of the man he has served so long, finds himself thinking, *I am not the only one to be ageing here.* It's an unsettling thought. 'What would you have me do?' he asks.

The Cardinal rocks back and forth a little, as if regaining equilibrium. 'Find him,' he says. 'Del Ponte. Find him.'

'Eminence?' Ravello is amazed.

'Find him, speak with him, turn him. Promise him whatever he asks. Whatever he is being paid by the Emperor, better it. Double it. No price is too great. And bring him here, to me.'

'Eminence,' Ravello begins, even more amazed than he was before, 'it would be my honour, but where? Where would I start to look?'

'Oh, I know where our friend will be,' the Cardinal replies. 'He will be in the Swedish camp. He will be exactly where I sent him, when I was fool enough to still believe he worked for me.' He peers at Ravello, fixes him with sad, unsentimental eye. The face of a mournful hedgehog; it is perhaps the Cardinal's greatest asset. 'Since we must assume he is most thoroughly the Habsburg now.' For the first time he sounds bitter. He turns away, and when he turns back, he is the man of business once again. 'So that is where you must go, too.'

'Eminence,' Ravello begins. 'Your wish and my will are one and the same, as ever, but to reach the Swedish – it might take me weeks.' *If it can even be done.* What would it entail, passing through one front line? Passing through another? And in between the wasteland, as everyone knows, that the war has made of northern Germany – the ruined villages, the towns a-tremble behind their gates, and God knows what horrors rampaging across it—

He stops himself. This is what his employer does: as everyone else speeds into panic, the Cardinal slows down. With an effort, Ravello forces himself to do the same.

'Eminence, what is it that Del Ponte has? What messages did he carry?'

The Cardinal turns; he moves to the curtained window. 'There was another letter,' he says. 'Previous to this. This is what Del Ponte has. And I must have it back. Do you understand me?'

Ravello takes a breath. 'Yes, Eminence, but—'

'This is your speciality, is it not? To travel about, unseen? To dance between the lines? No –' The Cardinal raises his hand. 'I need not know the how. I only need to know the if. *If* you can retrieve it for me. Because if not –' and the hand now indicates the dusty courtyard, '– that will be my fate too. So. Can you?'

What a question, thinks Ravello. What a question, of course he can. Will he? Yes. Does he want to?

No.

Here he sits at the edge of the Seine – hidden, as much as one can be, from the Palais du Louvre and its Argus eyes – occasionally raising his own to the exuberant statue of France's Henry IV (now there was a king!) up there on the Pont Neuf above him, and turning the immediate future about in his head. And examining, like the master-tailor that he is, its re-cutting. New coat, old cloth. *Dannazione.* Damn.

What Ravello had intended for himself this year was retirement. The travel he had planned was not up into the cannon-blasted badlands of north Germany, but south; south to that familiar rambunctious border country between Italy and France, specifically a tavern long known to its regulars as the Carpenter's Hat, and the only place these days Ravello ever thinks of if he thinks of *home.* His imagination saw him there (not here, spoiling his boots with the mud of the Seine!), but sat there on its terrace, bottle of Rousette to hand, waiting for the right moment to enquire of its landlady as to whether the quick-moving *piccola ragazza* now waiting tables at her mother's side is not, in fact, also Ravello's own. He can hear Balthasar: 'And that, my friend, is why you should have lived your life as an honest scout, rather than a cunning intelligencer. *We* get to retire.'

Leave me alone, Ravello tells him. *Don't I have enough to concern me already?* And with an effort, twists his thoughts away. To business.

So, there was another letter. Containing what? Mentally he fans out ahead of him all the various options the Cardinal might have currently in play – truces, treaties, hands in marriage… Refusals, rebuttals, outright threats… He plays a sort of inner spotlight over them. Nothing stands out.

On the far side of the river they are cutting down a tree. It has already been shorn of its branches, which lie in a pile at its feet; now workmen are dismembering its trunk, taking it down, length by length. The whack of axes, the ricochet of sound under the bridge; echo upon echo.

Very well then, that fifth act. Balthasar died. He died, and Ravello, prompted by some skew-whiff sense of rightness of his own, told Jean Fiskardo's son everything he knew about the circumstances of his parents' deaths, and off the lad went, white-hot for vengeance, into the chaos of the war in Germany, whence he has not been heard of from that day to this.

He lifts his eyes from bank to bridge – still limestone-white, still seeming to bounce across the waters. It had been a favourite vantage point of Balthasar's, he remembers, who had been particularly taken by the many grotesque carved stone *mascarons* there beneath the cornice – the horned devils, leering gnomes, moustachioed kings. 'D'you see?' Balthasar used to say. 'There will always be someone watching you. Or some*thing*.'

Ravello gets to his feet. He will not be heading south. No, he will collect his horse, he will head toward the Bastille, he will leave the city by the Port Saint-Antoine; he will head east. He will make for Hertzberg, on the border with Germany, as he has done so many times before, and there he will wait for the Roma. The great secret to Ravello's travels, the means by which he manages to move about almost invisibly, carrying his secrets from one place to the next, is that he makes his journeys in company with those the world wishes to pretend do not exist – and what the world wishes to pretend does not exist, it doesn't see. And let's not forget, if you are looking for something, even more for *someone*, how useful the Roma can be. Wasn't it they, after all, who located Jean Fiskardo's grave in that tiny village in Picardy, all those years ago? And with the Roma, he will travel into Germany – *and if this is the death of me*, he declares to Balthasar, in his head, *I hope you will be satisfied*.

But first, a posting inn. Because ahead of him, Ravello is going to send a letter. Because an agent always has agents of his own. Because if, after this last piece of business (and he swears to himself, this *is* going to be the last), if Ravello is indeed to bid adieu to the spider-web of information he has spent his life a-building, it will need to be left in safe hands. And because it is time, therefore, for his protégé to graduate. *Mon cher Achille*, the letter will begin. Our patron, our esteemed patron, has a little problem. Its name, you will be unsurprised to hear, is Quinto del Ponte.

And we might go with him. For Ravello, this journey will mean dusty roads and buggy beds in down-at-heel country inns without number; it will mean arriving in Hertzberg travel-stained and short of temper and feeling every one of his years. Whereas we might do it as easily as by turning the page.

It may seem perverse therefore, but as so many tales like to do, we are going to head off in the opposite direction altogether. For all that its buildings and its solitary bridge are stained such an infamous brown with the smoke of its addiction to sea-coal; for all that its palaces look like they were put up by goblins, not by gods; and for all its drizzling weather and comical cuisine, its whispered disquiets and ridiculous, untidy politics, we are going to head across La Manche, to Paris's great rival. We are going to London.

The Correspondent

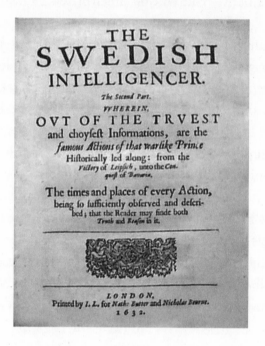

'Our method is this: to handle every Story by it selfe, and then to bring all together…'

William Watts, *The Swedish Intelligencer*

THERE ARE AS many ways to tell a tale as there are tales to tell.

Nathaniel Butter sells books, as do so many, from St Paul's Churchyard – south-east corner, by St Augustine's Church, under the sign of the Pied Bull. Nathaniel's bookshop, fragrant with the smells of virgin paper and new-cut leather, is one of the larger of those many round St Paul's, with a meeting room above, which Nathaniel encourages the Stationers' Company to make use of, as a subtle reminder of his status amongst them. As a somewhat less subtle reminder, in pride of place upon the display set out before the shop, there is always to be found Butter's edition of Master Shakespeare's *King Lear*, in which Nathaniel aggressively maintains copyright. Lear is bolstered, like a monarch surrounded by his bodyguard, by the plays of Thomas Dekker, of Beaumont and Fletcher, by editions of the *Iliad* and *Odyssey*, by commentaries on the law and books of verse; and then surrounding these in turn, fanned out like the common soldiers that they are, books of ballads, books of jokes, books of self-help (*The English Gentleman's Way to Wealth* sells particularly well), tracts, polemics, and those headline digests, those gazettes, of all the doings of the world known as corantos. For the English gentlewoman, there are pamphlets on the restoration of the complexion and on washes for the hair. In fine weather, Nathaniel's oldest child, Belinda, in summer gown, can often be found at the corner of the display, tidying the stock, shaking from it the dust of the London streets or even raising a book (oh, the lucky, lucky book!) to her mouth, to puff upon it; an artless frown of feminine vexation on her pretty face. After Belle has stood outside it a little while, the bookshop tends to fill.

In wet weather, Rafe Endicott, Nathaniel's assistant, is set to stand outside with a tarpaulin. The rain runs down his arms, and down his neck, but it is enough for Rafe simply to stand where Belle has stood, and to know that when he is finally allowed back into the shop, and Mrs Butter hustles him through it and down the steps into the kitchen before he can drip on any of the stock, Belle will be waiting for him with a cloth to rub his hair, and that rueful little smile of hers to warm his heart. Rafe can never think of that kitchen, with the feet of those walking along Watling Street level with its window, without also seeing the hazelnut sheen of Belinda's hair, and hearing the gentle movement of her lips as, head bent, she reads to herself. Belle's younger brothers – two of the most dull-witted clod-polls imaginable – are pupils at St Paul's School ('Ten pound a quarter!' their father declares, whenever either boy appears at home, in a tone pitched somewhere between pride and outrage), but neither of her parents had bothered themselves with Belle's education at all. Yet as Rafe endured his poverty-stricken years of studenthood in Cambridge, Belle, as if to keep him company, had taught herself to read; a feat Rafe finds as impressive as it is heartbreaking. Belle and Rafe have known each other ever since, as a schoolboy himself, Rafe first began running errands for Endicott's Rare Books and Fine Prints. Belle and Rafe are in love. Belle and Rafe are secretly betrothed. This is by far the greatest secret that the old Pied Bull has ever kept.

This morning, however, Rafe stands not in the shop nor in the kitchen but in that room upstairs, and it is not the grandees of the Stationers' Company to be found there, but his employer, and Nathaniel Butter's business partner, Nicholas Bourne; them sat one side of the table while Rafe stands at the other. The circumstances remind him of the interrogation, a matter of a year ago, before he began his employment here, when Butter had brandished a copy of *King Lear* at old Endicott's only child and demanded, 'What's this then, hey?'

'I – I suppose it to be the most purely tragical play in all the English language,' Rafe had begun. He had been at something of a loss. Freshly graduated, finally in possession of his degree, was he being asked here to demonstrate the breadth of his studies? At the time he had never even seen the play performed. In this last year, however, he has seen three performances of *Lear* alone, including one, at the Red Bull Theatre up in Clerkenwell (which likes its drama emphatic, and its revenges comprehensive) where Regan had gone up in silken flames on stage, Goneril been eaten by an ancient British bear; Lear had breathed his last in Cordelia's arms, rather than the other way about; and the play had ended with dancing as Cordelia and Edgar wed. Then, however, standing before Mr Butter, he had been nonplussed. 'The most Greek of all Master Shakespeare's tragedies—' he had continued.

'WRONG!' Nathaniel Butter had been pink with delight. 'Wrong, wrong, wrong! It is a crown quarto! And stitched and in wrappers but unbound – unbound, mark you! – like this, it is one shilling and fourpence!'

Also this morning at the table, albeit sat back a little, there is a third man, who wears the long plain gown and short white collar of a clergyman, and who has just been introduced to Rafe as the Reverend William Watts.

'I believe Mr Endicott and I are acquainted,' Mr Watts comments, sounding kindly. Having shaken hands, he has withdrawn his own into the long sleeves of his gown. The room has not had a fire in it since March, and London's summer, thus far, has been a bit of a niggard as to heat. Mr Watts continues, 'I believe I have seen you at my church, Mr Endicott. St Alban's, in Wood Street.'

'Why yes, you will have done,' says Rafe. 'My friend, Cornelius Vanderhoof, he introduced me to your services.' He blushes. He is unused to being noticed. 'And I have seen you here, sir. In the shop. You purchased a copy of *L'Académie Française*, I believe. And a German wordbook.'

Mr Watts smiles, a small, private smile. 'I was contemplating a journey,' he admits. 'I travelled much, when I was young as you. You are a German-speaker yourself, I am told, Mr Endicott.'

'At Cambridge. As a sizar.' Rafe blushes. A sizar acts as the servant to others in order for his college to fund his keep. It is not a thing to be proud of. But Endicott's Rare Books and Fine Prints had finally breathed its bankrupt last during Rafe's first year away, his father likewise. 'Translation. It was a part of my duties.' He keeps his gaze well away from Nicholas Bourne as he says it. Cambridge being Cambridge, some few (but enough) of those treatises Rafe had translated were of the most radical, sectarian stamp conceivable. Nicholas Bourne's politics, Rafe suspects, are such that he would have such writings publicly burned.

Mr Bourne shifts his weight; his chair creaks. Something about Nicholas Bourne puts Rafe in mind of those places he has read of at the bottom of the world: the Lands of Fire, where great fields of mud seethe perpetually, like milk in a pan. Nicholas Bourne is that: a field of mud, which occasionally swells up into some vast carbuncle, bursts and subsides. In the past when Rafe is about, the mud has oftentimes swelled up into Mr Bourne's favourite joke, a persistent mishearing of the word 'sizar' for 'lazar' or leper. This morning, however, it seems there is something else has him a-seethe. 'To the matter, Nate,' says Nicholas Bourne.

'The matter, yes.' Nathaniel Butter leans forward. His eyes bulge with eagerness. He is a small man, standing; Mrs Butter tells him often that he cuts a more imposing figure seated, once he pulls himself up straight ('Nathaniel! Be a better Butter!'). And he is a small man in a hurry where this present matter is concerned; any day now one of his rival booksellers must surely come up with the same idea as he. On the table before him there lies a copy of one of the corantos, his and Bourne's own, the *Weekly News*. Or, to give it its full and proper title, *The Weekly News from Italy, Germany, Hungaria, Bohemia, the Palatinate, France and the Low Countries*. Nathaniel Butter believes long titles lure the reader in. He begins.

'Do you know what this is, Rafe?'

'I believe it is thruppence, Mr Butter,' Rafe answers, promptly.

'WRONG!' comes the answer. Nathaniel Butter sits back, mighty pleased. 'It is bread on the table, that's what this is. It is wood for the fire. It is slippers for Belle. It is *your wages*, young Endicott. Fifty issues a year, ten shilling a twelvemonth subscription, and it outsells anything in the shop.' He leans forward again, brandishing the *Weekly News*, rolled now, at Rafe, as if it were the baton in a race. 'And it is our intention, Mr Bourne's and mine, to start another. All anyone reads these for at this present moment is the news from Germany, so that is what we shall give 'em. With the help of our well-travelled friend the Reverend Watts here.'

Mr Watts bows his head. Rafe looks at him in astonishment. 'You plan a journey into Germany, sir?' It seems the wildest of enterprises for such a sober soul as this. All the news from Germany is terrible, especially now the Swedish King has brought his army into the war; the only reason the corantos are read is for accounts of atrocity after atrocity. To go into Germany sounds akin to a descent into hell.

'Not Mr Watts,' says Nathaniel Butter. 'Not Mr Watts, young Endicott, but *you!*'

When he comes to reconstruct the scene in his memory, as he will do that evening in the Mitre Tavern in Wood Street, for example, sitting with Cornelius and still dazed by the day's events, at this point Rafe will remember himself as being so entirely astonished that he had taken a step back. '*Me?*'

'Yeesss, youooo!' Nathaniel Butter had replied, mimicking his assistant's amazement. 'Why – you speak the lingo, don't you? You told me you learned it for them German book fairs.' (Another thing old Endicott got wrong, in Nathaniel's opinion, wasting his time and his money on any market other'n that here.)

'I speak it, yes, sir,' Rafe had begun. 'But you are talking of my *going into* Germany—'

'An opportunity for you, young Endicott. A *fine* opportunity.' Nathaniel Butter has repeated this so often to himself that he has quite come to believe it. And there are other reasons to wish Rafe Endicott far away, that tiny sway to the young man's body at mention of Belle and her slippers being high amongst them. Latterly, Nathaniel has begun to suspect he sees something of the same reaction in his daughter, too, at mention of Rafe's name, albeit cunningly suppressed. But topmost reason of all, this business of a new coranto. It is astonishing what appetite there is amongst Nathaniel's countrymen for news from abroad, and this is what will give his new enterprise its edge – it will not be mere digest, mere repetition, like all those others, based on whatever gazettes arrive at the Thames-side wharves. No, it will be based on exact and singular observation, intelligence gleaned on the ground, at the point. It will not be speculation, it will be hard and fast and first-hand fact, and it will sell accordingly. He even has a name for it – *The Swedish Intelligencer*, that's what it will be called. By God, with a name like that, it will fly from the shelves. London will have never seen the like. Because that's what counts in this trade, as Nathaniel will tell you – it ain't the words, it's the numbers. Get that right, you're singing. Which is why Nathaniel Butter at the sign of the Pied Bull lives and flourishes, and old Endicott's, which was also once here, facing the cathedral, is but a memory, an empty shop-front, a dusty trestle, then nothing at all.

The Reverend Watts is clearing his throat. 'It is not our intention to expose you to any jeopardy,' he says, at the look of horror on the young man's face. 'You must not place yourself in harm's way in the least. Our thinking is that you may travel about in Germany, but safely, and simply in speaking to those you meet, collect for us true and proper information on the progress of the war. True and proper, not the mere repetition of nonsense, such as the other gazettes offer. It is the only way to do it, to be there upon the ground. Sound out the truth of all the tales. It was how I engaged myself in my younger days. And I would do it again, did I have my youth still.'

'But if I am *there*, and you are *here*—' Rafe begins.

'A correspondence,' says Mr Watts. 'You will return to me, regularly, by letter whatever you hear of, or see, and I will construct from it a narrative, and Mr Bourne and Mr Butter here will have it printed up and sold.'

'A correspondence?' Rafe begins. His mind seems capable of no more than snatching at odd words as they float past.

'Exactly so. The Thurn und Taxis post is a miracle of organization, even in these unhappy times. In every town of any consequence in Germany there will be an inn displaying their yellow-and-black – a posting inn, don't you know?' Mr Watts's smile is so encouraging Rafe cannot help smiling back, exactly as if he understood every word the other said, rather than them blowing past him like thistledown. 'They have a relay system from one place to the next. It all debouches into Brussels, from where there are regular carriers back and forth to London. I have known letters to make the journey in a week, or even less.'

Mr Bourne is coming up once again to the boil. A word pops from his mouth. It sounds like 'stipend'. Then he once more slackens in his seat.

'There you go, yes,' says Nathaniel Butter. 'Thirty pound. Thirty pound for one year's work.' He sits back, remembers Mrs Butter, sits up and forward again. 'What do you say to that, young man?'

'And it will be a service of true importance,' Mr Watts is saying. 'To bring to the widest notice an account of the exploits of a Christian army against that of the Emperor – to do this will be a matter of note.'

Note. Importance. Rafe's brain appears to wish to bring these words to his particular attention. Suddenly he finds he is thinking of Belle. Of note, of importance. And with money in his pocket. That will be him. He is none of those things now. He looks at Mr Butter and Mr Bourne, and understands without any doubt that if he refuses, he will be out on the street. And of a sudden he understands something else too, that he has been handed something here, he has been gifted the means to release Belle from that kitchen. To be able, in one year's time, to take her by the hand and lead her forth, to stand with her and announce, *Nathaniel Butter, I love Belinda and I will be wed to her, what's more.*

Thirty pounds is scarce more than his annual salary. 'Sixty pounds,' Rafe hears himself announce. 'Sixty pounds for this service for you, Mr Butter. And I will needs be released from my contract with you to do it, so you must have me declared a Freeman of the Stationers' Company, sir, and provide me with a proper statement of this new employment.'

'*Sixty?*' Nathaniel's splutter reaches quite across the table. '*Sixty?* You must think I'm made of money. You must think my brains are *cheese—*'

'One hundred and twenty of those annual subscriptions for this new coranto, Mr Butter, and you have my costs covered, that is what I am thinking. I think also that you would have the greatest difficulty in finding anyone else to undertake this for you, although, please, if you wish to try, I will bear no ill-will.' He lifts his voice a little. He can hardly believe this *is* his own voice. 'But my price for this is to be declared a Freeman of the Company, and to have a statement written up that I will be paid sixty pounds. And I will take twenty of them up front. The journey will be arduous, I have no doubt, and I will have expenses on the way.'

THE MITRE TAVERN in Wood Street is a place for bookmen, with many a small and comfortable room (octavo-sized, one might describe them) in which a man can retire to do business, or simply sit down with some reading matter and a good glass of wine. It is in fact as noted for its cellar as it is for its twenty-something fireplaces. Sat in a first-floor room, looking out over the Mitre's noisy courtyard this summer evening, are Rafe and his friend Cornelius Vanderhoof; on the table between them a wine from the top end of the Mitre's list, a white Bordeaux. Cornelius, as usual, will be picking up the bill.

Cornelius's background, and his access to the funds for such evenings as these, is something of a mystery. The man lives modestly enough – two rooms above a self-effacing little office in Green Dragon Court, hid behind the rows of print sellers and bookshops, with 'Vanderhoof' over the door. Yet when he comes into Butter's bookshop (which is how he and Rafe met, over the purchase of, yes, a *King Lear*), he buys in folio size, and he has his purchases bound in full leather, and gilt upon the spines. Visiting, to deliver this new customer's first purchases, Rafe had come away with the information that 'Vanderhoof' was this new customer's mother's name. He had been astonished by this. What small currency Rafe has in the world of bookselling comes entirely from his father's name. Why would Cornelius do business under his mother's?

At this point in an ideal world, Cornelius would have leaned forward and said because this is England, and England expelled its Jews three centuries ago, and my father's name is Silbergeld. But then of course in an ideal world he'd not have had to say anything anyway. Instead Cornelius had given a small wry smile and answered only, 'It is simpler so.'

I see, Rafe had replied, although he didn't, not at all. And the business is...?

Another mystery. Cornelius buys some things, and sells others, but nothing he buys or sells ever seems to touch the ground. His business exists, like swifts or swallows, or gaudy birds of paradise, perpetually aloft. Transporting further purchases to Cornelius's office, Rafe has walked in on traders from Muscovy, merchants from Norway, and once, magnificently turbaned and robed, a gentlemen introduced to Rafe as a native of Persia. But never once has he seen the unloading or loading of goods – none at all. It is a far cry from Nathaniel Butter's crammed cellars, and the bundles of books and loose-leaf to be found on every step of his stairs.

When not in his office, Cornelius is to be found at the theatre: the Salisbury Court, the Fortune, the New Globe, the

Red Bull; stood there upon the nutshells with the groundlings, and shouting and groaning and huzzahing his way through a performance as loudly as any of them. On the one afternoon a week that Rafe has free and can accompany him, the two of them usually follow up the play by retiring to the Mitre, to discuss what they have seen in depth – the text, the actors, even the quality of the scenery. Very often, especially if they have been to the Red Bull, Cornelius is still wiping the tears of laughter from his eyes, so much do the on-stage drolleries of the actors there delight him, such that Rafe has in the past found it incumbent to point out that in the Shakespearean original of *Julius Caesar*, for example, there was in fact no amusing trio of clowns following Mark Antony about, nor in any production other than at the Red Bull was Calpurnia a wanton, with the boy who played her sporting papier-mâché breasts. The productions of the Holland family, who own the Red Bull, are not known for artistic subtlety. 'Oh, I am sure, I am sure,' Cornelius had replied, wiping his eyes anew. 'It is your English foolery. Your English wit.' Rafe has never known a man so entirely stage-struck. 'No other nation is like you. In Amsterdam we respect everything, and here you respect nothing! Not even your own Mr Shakespeare!'

Not this evening, however. This evening Cornelius is of a very different humour. 'Germany,' he says. The fine-grained skin of his forehead is pleated with distress.

'The players from the Red Bull are going into Germany,' Rafe informs him. 'Or some of them at least. Henry Kempwick is taking them. I think there has been a falling-out between him and the Hollands; now Henry has formed a new company, the Pilgrim Players, he and Andrew Frye. Henry believes they will make their fortune over there.'

'Yes,' says Cornelius, no happier than before. 'And if Mr Kempwick had asked me first, I would have told him no, too.'

'But *you* went into Germany,' Rafe points out. He is a little peeved. It has come into his thoughts that the next time he sits here, maybe a year from now, everything will be changed. He will be changed, beyond measuring. It seems to him the Mitre ought to show some consciousness of this, and if it cannot, then certainly his companion should. He has a peculiar awareness of the nearness of the mighty Thames (just there, at the bottom of Bread Street, that's all) as if it were waiting for him. He would like to be toasted, cheered, tonight, not cautioned.

His friend's face – neat-featured, smoothly and expensively barbered – becomes even more serious-looking than it was. Only once before has Rafe seen Cornelius so grave, so lost in his own thoughts as this, after they had sat through *The Jew of Malta* at the New Globe. This business of Cornelius's being in Germany is yet another mystery. 'It was my vow,' he had said. 'I told my family, I would come to London, I would open up a bureau for us here, but I must be allowed to go into Germany and look for my friend first.'

Cornelius had shared his boyhood with a foundling, so the story went, some child taken from the streets and provided with a home. A kind of infant St Michael the Archangel, is how Rafe imagines him, from Cornelius's description of the lad's doings, fierce and valiant beyond his years. Rafe, to be honest, rather resented the prime position the memory seemed to hold in Cornelius's affections, and had cheered, silently, when at the conclusion to the tale, it turned out this paragon had done something bad enough to have run off rather than face his punishment. At great expense the family had managed to follow the boy's path down the Rhine as far as Heidelberg, but even with Cornelius's final effort, had been unable to find any further trace of him.

'Yes,' Cornelius says now. 'Yes, I went into Germany. And if I had known of it then what I know of it now, I would never have done so. You have no idea.' He shakes his head.

'But I will not be in those same parts as you,' Rafe begins, but Cornelius stops him.

'There is no part of Germany now that is without the war. That unhappy country, it is nothing but one army after the last.'

'Germany for me,' Rafe begins, with a little heat, 'is a lease on my own shop. Germany for me is to have my own business, like yours. It is to be free, it is to be a man. And beyond that, it is –' and he takes the case with Belle's picture inside it from his pocket, opens it and places it on the table. The Butters had Belle's likeness taken recently; half Cornelius's savings secured this copy of it, in secret, from the artist. It is in grisaille only, being cheaper, and the grisaille emphasizes the rueful nature of her smile, but also, to Rafe's mind, brings out that tiny, rare top-note of defiance in her expression.

'Yes,' says Cornelius, thoughtful, grave. 'I understand. She is all.' He fills Rafe's glass, and then his own.

'And I am no hero,' Rafe assures him. 'Trust me. I will expose myself to no danger at all. I will gather information, feed it back to Mr Watts. That is all.'

But Cornelius shakes his head. 'Rafe, I am sure, every man who goes into Germany thinks that, and every man, when he is there, finds himself brought to some place where he is presented with things he would never have believed possible, and if he is wise, understands, he should not go beyond it. Because beyond that place –' and Cornelius lifts his shoulders, opens his hands. 'Beyond, there is only death.' He lifts his glass and drains it. 'So promise me, my friend. When you find yourself at *your* place, you will do as I did. You will turn about, and come home.'

So far from being cheered, Rafe finds it is now he who must do the cheering. 'Well. I have to get myself there first,' he says, because this is his first hurdle, and it is a wholly unexpected one. 'I need to get myself to Hamburg, and it seems there is a dearth of sailings that would be of any use to me.'

'Yes, I am sure,' Cornelius replies. 'There is nothing like the trade with Germany that there was.' Then he brightens. 'But perhaps I can assist. My family has an interest in a ship. It is one of those few still make that voyage. Her captain is a Scotsman. She is called the *Guid Marie.*'

AND THEN OF COURSE there must be the farewell with Belle – one week later, his passage all arranged, and a mere five minutes snatched at dusk outside the kitchen in the Butters' miserable yard. 'You will wait for me,' Rafe says. He has Belle's hands in his, but to hell, at this juncture, with them being overlooked. Her fingers are warm and curled within his own and there is something so definite in the feel of them, in this linkage between them, that Rafe finds it hard to believe the moment can ever end. 'One year, Belle, that is all. I will come back with enough for a lease on a bookshop of our own, I will come back a Freeman of the Stationers' Company. You will wait for me?'

'I am yours, Rafe,' she answers. 'I am yours and you are mine, and that is all that need be said.' But in the dark little courtyard, Rafe sees her eyes are shining, their surface even more liquid than usual.

'Belle,' he begins, 'don't cry, dear one, please—'

She frees one hand, holds it up, forestalling him. Closes her eyes, bows her head. From that hidden mouth emerge the words, 'My parents wish for me to marry Mr Bourne. They have given him my picture.'

Something like a mill-wheel grinds into agonizing life within Rafe's chest, crushing all beneath it. It feels as if it is pressing the air out of him. 'But you will wait, Belle, you will wait for me. You will tell them no—'

'I cannot,' she says. 'I cannot defy them.' Rafe hears himself give a gasp. But then she glances up at him and there it is, that tiny sparkle of defiance, small as a mustard seed. 'But I cannot think Mr Bourne will wish to wed a wife who is sickly.' Then she covers her mouth and coughs – once, twice, three times: *ehu, ehu, ehu.*

'Belle!' he exclaims.

'We must be clever,' she says. Someone is calling for her from inside the house. Belle glances back over her shoulder. 'One year, Rafe. I will hold them off for one year. After that, you must be there for me.' Over her shoulder she calls out, 'Coming, Mother! I will be there directly.'

The kitchen door comes open. Nicholas Bourne is there. He holds the door for Belle, then as he closes it, looks directly out at Rafe, left there alone in the yard. There in the gap between door and frame is the light and warmth of the kitchen, and Mrs Butter, rising to her feet, bustling toward her daughter, and Belle's white shoulders, the lovely curve of her neck, the back of her head, and the door is closing, it is closing, she is gone. Burned onto the image in Rafe's mind, the face of Nicholas Bourne (that schemer! That London Machiavelli! That bubbling field of mud!), grinning like a fox.

He turns his own face up toward the evening sky. *I will get that door open again*, he tells himself. *I will get that door open, I will get Belle out of that kitchen if it is the last thing I do.*

The image stays with him. It is there when he rises next morning, so early there are still a few last stars in the sky, in his lodgings (one room) in Fish Street. It is there as he washes in cold water at the pump, lifts his pack onto his shoulder, and makes his way downhill to Queenhythe Wharf. It is there as he disturbs, in the misty blue of early morning, a waterman, crouched over his pipe, and negotiates with the man to take him downriver, to the Blackwall Basin. And the name of the ship they are heading for?

'The *Guid Marie*,' says Rafe.

The waterman flaps a hand, turns his back and walks away.

A second waterman is found. The negotiation founders once again. 'Mungo Sant's ship?' the man says, and laughs. 'That bloody robber? Not I.' Rafe tries a third. The same. Rafe is flummoxed. Is he to be thwarted this early in his quest? He pursues the man, beseeching – is he to walk to Blackwall? Is he to swim?

And then a shout. Another waterman advances up the stony slope of Queenhythe Wharf. Rafe, watching him, finds himself thinking at once, *Othello*. 'I know Sant,' the man says. He surveys his fellow watermen with what looks very like contempt; Rafe with a kind of curious pity. 'I will take you.'

Rafe's shilling is handed over. The man settles Rafe at the stern and shoves off. The gravel of Queenhythe Wharf scrapes beneath Rafe's backside, with but so few narrow planks between him and it, and then is gone. The rowboat settles into the Thames instead, and down the river they go. The new tide is with them, running them as only water can, under the bridge with but a modest bump and splash and past the Tower, where a chill damp breeze, the first breath of the new day, plays across the river's face. The roofscapes of the city slide past, one rising behind the last as the waterman pulls away, slide past in layers, like scenery on stage. Rafe relaxes his grip upon the gunwale. He has never seen the city quiet as this. By contrast the river seems to have been awake for hours – there are halloos, there is movement on every deck, there are buckets being drawn up, fishing lines thrown out. Now they are at Limehouse, and all the buildings cease at once, and there are fields, and a man watering cattle at the river's edge. Rafe sees the sails of a windmill, and thinks at once of Cambridgeshire, of all the years of his life that have gone before and the complete unknown of what will follow. He thinks, *We might turn back*, but then it is with him again, that memory of the kitchen door closing, with his Belle the other side of it. And Nicholas Bourne's smirk, as he thinks of it now, his smirk of triumph.

He clears his throat. He feels in need of conversation, something to stoke the fires of his courage. Wouldn't it be fitting if this came from a fellow whose business is the transport of the intrepid traveller?

'A fine morning,' he comments.

The waterman, broad of shoulder as a bull, mighty of thigh, wholly impassive of feature, says nothing. Rafe can hardly shake the man's hand as he pulls at the oars, so he points at himself and says, 'Rafe Endicott.'

The man eyes him for the space of one more pull. 'Miguel Domingo,' he replies.

'I am to travel into Germany. Hamburg,' Rafe tells him. But again, no reply, only the creak of the oars, the swirl of the water. 'That is a very great way away,' he adds, in case the man should not be aware.

Miguel Domingo, watching his oars as they pass a buoy, replies, 'It is not so far.'

Rafe is taken aback. Startled, he replies, 'It is, to me.' Creak. Swirl. He tries again. 'And where do you hail from, Master Domingo?' A word of understanding, from one traveller to another, it would be most welcome – *yes, your journey is a great one, sir, but no doubt you will accomplish it, I am certain.*

'San' Saviour,' comes the reply. 'San' Saviour, in Southwark.'

'I mean,' says Rafe, after a hunt for the words, as the fellow surely was not born here, under London skies, 'where did your life's journey begin?'

Miguel Domingo looks Rafe full in the face and answers, 'You call it Capo Verde.'

Here is Deptford. Here is Greenwich. And here, at Blackwall, is a ship stood out midstream, to which Miguel Domingo turns his boat. This, then, is the *Guid Marie*. Her cracked, worm-eaten figurehead, grimacing like a gargoyle, looks down on them as they approach; her side rears so high above that looking up at it is like gazing up at the curtain wall of a castle. Rafe cannot think how he is meant to get up there. Miguel thumps the flat of his hand against that oaken wall and bellows upward, 'Ho the *Guid Marie*! Ho within!' and a human voice responds with something unintelligible, in an accent that seems to Rafe briny as Neptune's and spiky as a thistle. A face appears, way above at what would be the battlements. Miguel shouts up at it, 'Sant! I have your passenger!' and the face yells down, 'Domingo? You lay your hand upon my boot again, ye bastid, I'll turn my cannon on ye!'

'That is Mungo Sant,' Miguel says, turning to Rafe, then shakes his head and adds, 'You poor devil.' He has shipped his oars. Rafe is still trying to work out how one gains entrance to this – this – ark, when there is more noise from above and a ladder is let down, slapping against the ship's side, a ladder of rope so thick it might have been intended for giants, the lower part of it slick with weed.

'You go up,' Miguel tells – no, *instructs* – him. He pulls the ladder forward. The boat they are in tilts horribly. Rafe, donning his pack, is off-balance, and reaching out, makes a grab, and feels for one terrifying moment the whole edifice of the *Guid Marie* nudge toward him. Gulls wheel and squeal above her, as if the movement has awoken them. Nothing is static here; nothing can be trusted. He puts a foot upon one of the ladder's slick green rungs, and the entire thing contracts quite horribly beneath his weight. He reaches up, grabs at another rung, while his foot gropes, blind, for – well, a footing – and then he senses Miguel begin to pull his boat away, so there is now nothing beneath him, nothing but the Thames, and this mountain to climb above. He hangs for a moment petrified above the watery abyss and then the same voice as before shouts down, '*Mr* Endicott, shift ye bluidy arse, mon, the tide is with us. Or I'll sail with you hanging there!'

He dare not look up. He dare not look down. In his mind's eye, he puts Belle's face at the top of that oaken wall, and climbs toward her.

CHAPTER FIVE

A Baptism

'... neither the army nor the Cavalry alone, no not a company, must march without discoverers: which must be sent out, not only by the direct way where the enemie is like to come, or you are to march, but to scoure all the by-wayes on either side...'

John Cruso, *Militarie Instructions for the Cavallrie*

THE LAGOON OF the Oder is some thirty miles west to east, and maybe half that north to south. It frets and fritters away its entrance into the Baltic in winding channels, in causeway and marsh, in brackish water-courses that hardly seem to move at all. If you are on the lagoon's western side, the landing site on Usedom and the town of

Wolgast are safe behind you; but to the east there is Wollin, and out beyond that—

Well. That's what they are here to find out.

'Think of this,' Jack tells his now not-quite-so-raw recruits, who can each of 'em get off a round in a minute and a half, and some of 'em even less; who are beginning to measure the days in the yellow horn the reins have rubbed into the palms of their hands, in meals munched from those same hands (Food! Forage! Rations!), in body-stink, 'as the first roll of the dice in a game of *bräde*, yes?'

Kai is the only one to have an Ah! of comprehension on his face. Plainly, backgammon has yet to reach the fishing villages of the Stockholm archipelago.

'Think of it as the first pokes and prods in a fistfight. Before you go to it in earnest.' He draws it out for them, in the dirt – there, top left, Wolgast, there, top right, Wollin, and there at the bottom, Stettin, the tip of this upside-down triangle, pointing down into the rest of Germany, and in between these three, the entirety of the delta of the Oder, and it's theirs.

Ah!

Oh, that's clever. They'd had no idea that's what they'd been about.

Where next, Domini?

Altdamm. Altdamm sits opposite to Stettin, close enough that the two might almost be the same place, except that Altdamm, like Wolgast, like Wollin, also has a fort, a garrison, packed tight with the enemy's troops; and between them and it, a shallow stretch of water, and somewhere under the water, a causeway. Which it is their job as scouts to find, because there's no waiting on the tides in this business, nor, come to that, for the light of a new day, and if you have to ask why, you're in the wrong job.

They can't risk losing a horse by some mis-step over the causeway's edge, so they have to find the causeway with their feet, edging along under that pulsing midnight not-quite-sun that runs water and sky one into the other. At one point a rocket is fired at them from the fort, illuminating everything as clear as if you were holding up a lantern. The recruits watch the last flaming fragments hiss down into the water all about them and in their new polyglot yell back, '*Tack! Tack, freunde!*' Thank you, friends! There are no more rockets after that. Instead the garrison at Altdamm makes a break for it to Stargard, twenty miles to the east. So the army of the Lion of the North makes a midnight march across the causeway, falls upon Stargard as it sleeps, and you can guess the rest.

Think of it as the sun at your back, in your face, spangling the next water-course, marbling tidemarks across your horse's belly, its legs; drying your shirt to your skin. Think of it as the fords you locate and the bridges you stand guard over; as the roads and trackways you do scour, indeed – the broken gun carriages, shorn of their cannon, that you haul out the field gates where they fouled; the abandoned carts you pull to the edge of the road; the dead horses you drag out of ponds to keep the water sweet for the troops coming after. It shocks them all, how damn untidy a thing is a war, the mess it makes – they who grew up wasting nothing, who made use of every bit of flotsam the ocean blessed them with. Now they find discarded hats, lost gloves, broken sword belts; boots with the sole a-flap. 'Keep 'em,' says their captain, says Fiskardo. 'Bring 'em back to camp; if you can fix 'em, you can sell 'em.'

Fiskardo. God's love, but he's a strange one. Even shipboard, on the journey over, as they huddled below deck, them and three hundred others just like 'em, and a pair of veteran master-sergeants to see order kept; all of 'em swopping what they knew of what they'd be a-doing in this new life and who their officers would be, when Fiskardo's name came up, there'd been this reaction to it – the one master-sergeant sucking his breath in, then whistling it out, the other rounding his eyes. 'And good luck to you, my boys,' the first had said. Then he'd seemed to relent. 'Mind, he'll not lose many of you, you can count on that.'

Won't he? Why not? They'd already been preening themselves, there below decks, as the ship rose and fell and the farm-boys spewed and moaned; now it seemed having this Fiskardo as their *Kapten* would be another reason to brag.

'A'cause as he's a hard man, ain't he?' the other had replied. 'Can't be killed. Nor any of those ride with him. Damned, yes. Killed – no.'

Did they believe it?

Of course not. But—

But, look, there's times he's right there with you, right when you need it – showing how to pad a breastplate (which take some getting used to, them), explaining the difference in the way a drum sounds if the drummer's standing still or if he's on the march, or spotting when they've a laggard like he's eyes in the back of his head; but then there's times you can see as he's gone off in that head of his to some place of his own and no-one bothers him, not the Gemini, not even Zoltan.

'I reckon that's why he's a discoverer,' Luka had offered one evening as they sat about their fire. 'It's a'cause he likes being away from all the rest. Don't you reckon? That's how he wants it. Out on his own.'

Where next, Domini?

'Kammien.'

Kammien. Which is another fifty miles back up toward Wollin, on top of the God knows how many they have travelled already, and where there is need for them to find a road for Ancrum's wagon-master to use to bring supplies up from the great camp now at Stettin. The road is found, the Gemini go back with news of it; next morning here comes the wagon-master, rolling by; then the infantry and then Ancrum himself, with his smooth pink face and his smooth white hair and his nose up, as ever, and not a glance to them what found the road for him – and God above, riding at Ancrum's right shoulder that's Quinto del Ponte, ain't it? Quinto del Ponte, harlequin breeches a thing of the past, all of a-wiggle with silver braid. What's he doing here?

Turns out Del Ponte has found himself a place in Ancrum's general staff.

Doing *what*? they want to know.

'God knows,' Zoltan tells them. 'There are such men. Work their way in like worms into cheese.'

Meanwhile, Kammien falls.

Where next?

Back to Wollin. Back to Wollin, back and forth, because that, apparently, is how you stitch your invasion into place; only when they get there, Wollin is a mess; all the people sour-faced and complaining at the men they now have billeted upon them, and if it's not the billeting upsets them so, it's the earthworks and defences that have been dug through their gardens and their fields. Their captain takes one look at the place, the state it's in, draws off into a consultation with Lieutenant Zoltan (while his company – saddle-sore and rank as goats – slide off their mounts to sit upon the blessed earth and wait), then leads them out of town to the lagoon. 'We make camp here,' he says.

They can fish. They can wash themselves. Those of them with the squirts can find a private little bush behind which to loosen their knotted bowels rather than having to do it at the side of the road with their fellows looking on and jeering. The Executioner goes back into Wollin, taking Ulrik with him – Ulrik who's built, they joke, with all the height and heft and meat got left off Luka – and the two of them return with sacks of rye bread and a whole cheese, the size of a pumpkin. And a little way away there's a sluice-gate to the lagoon, and the sluice-gate keeper's house beside it, and as they eat, and as the noise of their talk and their laughter and even the odd burst of song goes up into the darkening sky, the sluice-gate keeper and his son move cautiously down toward them, carrying a couple of jugs.

Their captain goes to greet them, and you have to say this of him, for all he looks like your worst fucken nightmare (after the Executioner), for all those eyes of his make you feel you're being worked at with a bodkin, he does have the knack, with folk, of talking it away. That rare big smile of his, and the way he holds himself, so he don't tower over folk, or not so much. After a little while more the keeper's old mum comes out, carrying a bowl of pork dripping to put on their bread, and then his missus, with another jug of that fruit wine, which is more than decent stuff, to put a bit of heat in your belly for bedtime, and then another boy who quite plainly is a daughter, for all they've put her in doublet and breeches and chopped off her hair, and Christ, don't that say something of the times these folk have seen.

And now the sluice-gate keeper and their captain are in conversation, and it seems there is a service they can do the man. The enemy, General Conti's troops, when they came through here, just for spite they sunk his little sailboat, and he and his boy, who is no older'n Golden Spoon, they haven't the muscle to raise it. It lies there, the man says, by the jetty.

There is nothing with a boat as part of it that Fiskardo's company can't tackle. The strongest swimmers jump into the water with ropes, work them under the boat's hull, tie them fast; the brawniest take the ends of the ropes on shore and start to haul, with the swimmers directing the boat, as she begins to stir, round toward the bank. There's weed, there's eels, there's blooms of mud, but she moves. Sten, who has the habit of putting a voice to anything, gives the boat a dainty female squeal as she comes nearer, as her bow breaks the waters – 'Oooh, one more, boys, one more! Make it a good'un!' – and then the short-arses, Luka and Golden Spoon, they get the task of bailing the water out, once she's nearer shore. So when the body floats to the surface, on its own great bloom of muck, it's Golden Spoon it bumps against first.

Golden Spoon gives a shriek, falls backwards, submerges, in what can't be no more than a coupl'a feet of water; comes up, streaked with mud and streaming weed, and scrambles for the bank. Those on the bank drop their ropes, they're laughing so hard. The body rotates in its cloud of mud. Ansfrid, who feels the need to prove he's good as the rest of 'em, despite his mum being from Norway, goes down into the water, drags it to shore.

Oh, the poor sod. He's been took to pieces. The eyes have gone, and while it might have been the eels did that, somehow they doubt it, because the man's hands have been taken too, hacked off at the wrist, and that's inhuman, that is, to throw a soul into the water when he can't see to swim to safety; and with no hands can't swim in any case.

'Who is it?' their captain asks.

'Our neighbour,' the keeper says softly. His wife and daughter are in tears. 'Gregor. We took off when the soldiers came –' he gestures to where his wife and daughter stand weeping, faces hidden against each other's necks. *I have women. You understand.* 'We called for him to come, we waited as long as we could, but Gregor he liked a drink. He must have been in his cups. When we returned, his house was empty, and our boat was down there.'

Gregor lies upon the ground. Other than the black pits of his eyes, he is all the same wet waxy grey. Even his butchered wrists are now washed pale as pork. Their captain hunkers down, tilts his head, like he's following a thought. 'Did you see the men who did this?' he asks. 'Did you spy anything of them at all?'

And the keeper answers, at once, 'My boy did.' He puts his hand on his son's head. 'The one in charge, he had this red scarf at his throat.'

And the captain straightens up, and there's a glance goes between him and Zoltan, and it holds everything of how many years they have done this, all they've seen and God alone knows how much more besides.

'Come,' Zoltan says. 'We'll help you dig his grave.'

Åke Tott's messenger finds them the next day. 'Lost ourselves,' the captain tells him, unblushingly. And now, it seems, they are to work their way back toward Wolgast, which feels like going back to an old friend, so fine – but why not push south?

It's a better question than they can ever know. Because those earnest promises of support are still promises only. Because Sweden has not the funds to raise the men to move an army southwards. Because they need allies that as yet have not materialized. Because time is their enemy, and the Emperor's friend, and as King Gustavus Adolphus and Åke Tott and General Baner and every other high-up in the general staff know full well, and as more than a few of the veterans have worked out too, without that situation changing, within a very few months Germany will be doing to them exactly what she has already done to the armies of Ernst von Mansfeld, Christian of Brunswick, Christian of Denmark and everybody else: starved, and exhausted, and broken them. And it won't matter one damn bit how fast you can load and fire your musket then.

THEY'RE OUT BEYOND Anklam, where Anklam's river makes its turn, and the country round them is a devastation, worse than anything they've seen. The fields burned up or trampled through, no livestock, none, no people either; threads of smoke on the horizon every way you look, and birds – birds everywhere. Flittering about in the hedges, or taking off into the skies, and the endless racket of their chirping and twittering – God have mercy, it's like even the birds have run mad. Anklam itself is under siege – part of Torquato Conti's force has taken refuge in Anklam's castle, and when the wind brings it to them, they can hear their Swedish cannon, knocking on the castle door, as they say – so they already know to keep their wits about them; and then they turn to make their way down this little lane, and all the chirping and twittering stops at once, like someone slammed a door.

They dismount and fan out. It's a little like working their way through the streets of Stettin, except (so the thudding of their hearts informs them) now it's different. You have your sword in your hand. You have your pistol cocked. You stare at what's ahead so hard it makes your eyes go dry.

What's ahead is a farmhouse and a good big barn – or what was a good big barn – and both of 'em burned out. There's six, seven little houses too, no more than cotts, with nothing but blackness at their windows, like poor old Gregor and his eyes. There's an orchard, apples rotting on the ground. There's a cow, burned up where she stood, poor thing, in her byre, likewise a pen of pigs. Who did this, Domini?

'I have no doubt we'll find out.'

But why kill the animals?

'Luka,' says the captain, 'it's so we can't eat 'em.'

They come into the farmyard. Their thudding hearts are stopped, momentarily, by the sight of a man hanging out of a window (the farmer, by his clothes), but he's long dead, his blood dried right down the wall. There's another man, younger, lying dead by the farmhouse door. A third, just inside. And then another door. 'Brace yourselves,' says Ulf, because there's that smell, the one makes you want to not get it in your mouth. They force the door open, pushing and shoving it against all the burned stuff on the floor – charred wood, and twisted clothing, and then within the room—

The room is shuttered, so they think first of all it's sleepers, lying in the gloom. Then Kai comes up behind them. 'What is it?' he asks, and by immediate consent they all shuffle up, shoulder to shoulder, so that Kai can't see.

Ulf turns Kai about and leads him outside. 'It's women, Kai. It's girls.'

And now here's the captain. They wait while he takes in what lies about the floor, and after a minute he herds them all outside, and he shuts the door. And they stand in the sunshine, mute.

Elias says, 'They was trying to defend 'em, weren't they?' Back home he has sisters too. He swallows hard. 'The farmer and his boys. They was trying to keep the women safe.'

The day after, working their way along by the river, they start to snuff that other stink, of human shit, and find a ditch that's been used as a latrine. Maybe a mile further on, another body awaits them, only this one is no farmer. His boots have been taken, so in fact it's his stark white legs they spot first of all, but otherwise he's a trooper, just like them, however much his human juice has stuck his shirt to his rotting chest. Kai goes forward, like he'll close the man's eyes, but the captain hauls him back. 'Woah, woah, woah,' the captain says. 'You see those blotches on his neck? That's not rot, it's typhus. Trust me, I would know.'

And then from the trees between them and the river, the Gemini emerge, and they have that look to them, like hounds who've just spotted a bird tumbling to earth. There's men in the woods; men encamped, drunk and making merry; and what Fiskardo's discoverers should do now, they know, is go back to Anklam and make their report, but fuck that.

What they are going to do instead, their captain says, is make a net. He, Zoltan, the Gemini, they will be one end of it, and they will chase the men down to where the rest will be the trap. 'Fight so they remember you,' he tells them, 'and you won't have to fight them again. And don't forget – every man who fights under me, what is he?' And he holds up his left hand.

Gefroren!

*

It's a sort of limbo, waiting in ambush. Ulf has to keep reminding himself not to hold his breath. Beside him, flat to the earth,
Elias whispers, 'Do you think it was some of these did that to
those girls?'

Ulf thinks for a moment, then replies, 'I don't care.' None
of them has spoken of it – not what they found, nor how they
moved the bodies from that room in the farmhouse to the
orchard. They'd needed blankets to carry them, like rubble,
those soft ruined shapes. When he thinks of them, Ulf finds he
is thinking of the clothing on the floor – discarded, blackened,
trodden underfoot. 'That's their problem, if it weren't.'

One man has got to his feet, gone to the fire, gone to the
cauldron bubbling upon it, lifted the lid—

Ulf finds he knows exactly what's coming, the second before
it does. The crack of shot, and the man falls, knocking the
cauldron into the fire.

Those watching seem unable to work out what has happened,
or how. Then the Gemini, on horseback, streak across the
clearing, one of 'em one way, one the other, firing as they go.
Something else is happening behind them, where the captain
went – too far to make it out, with all these damn trees in the
way, but there's a speed to it is putting Ulf in mind of being
on the deck of his father's boat, out past the Skagerrak, and
watching as a pod of orcas destroyed a group of seals.

Now they get it, those men about the fire. Now they're
running for their horses – no, stupid, that's where the Gemini
are now – now they are grabbing up their weapons; now they
are looking all about them, now—

Another crack of shot; another pitches over. Now they're
backing up. Now they're turning. Now they run. There goes
one, straight for the riverbank—

And three more, running straight to where Ulf and Elias lie
hidden. Elias, on his elbow, awkward, raises his pistol, fires – and
misses. One man throws himself behind a tree, and a shot goes

into the trunk above Ulf's head, spattering one eye and filling his mouth with bits. The other two are still coming. Ulf lifts himself onto one knee, and fires, and now there's only one. He and Elias, they charge the man together. Ulf, who has yet to draw his blade, who in fact has wholly forgotten he has a blade there to be drawn, reaches the man first, and on furious reflex, swings his fist. Then Elias leaps on the man's back, and the two of them are rolling on the ground. Elias is yelling something. It comes to Ulf that the first man is still somewhere there behind him, that Elias is trying to warn him of this. He spins about. The first man is indeed still there, reloading, making a mess of it, fumbling. Ulf finds he has his sword in his hand. But now the man fighting with Elias has his hands at Elias's throat. Ulf leaps on top of the rolling bodies, sword held before him, and part shoves, part watches, as it goes into the man's buff-coat and whatever is beneath. The leather resists; so does whatever is under the coat. The man gives a yell. The three of them separate. Ulf, staggering back, collides with a tree. Elias is on his knees, bawling. Now more men running through the trees, the whoop and holler of the Gemini, in pursuit. The one Elias had been fighting, he's on his feet, is blowing hard, swinging left to right, and behind him Ulf sees the first man, pistol reloaded, get to his feet, sight them along his barrel, and out of nowhere, Ulrik, great lumpen Ulrik, ploughs the man down flat, yelling over one shoulder, 'You're welcome!' and is gone.

Elias's opponent puts a hand to his waist and it comes out bloodied. He's cursing at them. In fits and spurts Ulf comes to realize the amount of noise there is about him: the huffs of breath, the shouts, the shots, the streaks of movement through the trees. Elias has got to his feet. A tiny moment of nothing, and then they hurl themselves upon the man, like dogs bringing down a bull, he to one side, Elias the other; the man staggering and whirling, trying to shake them off, and *No you fucken don't*, says a voice in Ulf's head, *not again*. He has his sword held like a spear, like he was spearing fish, like he was spearing that old sack, stuffed with

straw, the way the captain has them do it in their drill, and he
thinks of the farmhouse, that darkened room, the orchard where
they had buried the bodies, the apples rotting on the ground,
and he holds the man by the back of his collar with one hand
while with the other he puts the sword in, under the man's coat,
running him through. And that's all it takes. Fishermen no more.

Down where the river curves through the woods, that's been
left to Luka and to Kai. Luka seems perfectly happy with this,
but to Kai it feels like banishment. At home he is disregarded,
his mother's late-in-life surprise; and here it seems he is the
baby too; all his comrades are older, bigger, stronger, even Luka
has more status than him. He had never dreamed he could miss
home so much; the father to whom he always feels he ought
to introduce himself ('My duty to you, sir, I am your youngest, Karl-Christian'); his smiling mother, always looking over
Kai's shoulder to someone more significant; his nurse, who
he misses most of all. He aches with homesickness, and hates
himself for it; he hates his ridiculous stained and shrunken
clothing too. *I'm no better than the mascot*, he's thinking, and
then most hatefully of all, *I'm the joke*. He's standing in this fog
of private misery when a man appears in front of him, wraps an
arm about Kai's throat and begins pulling him toward the river.
Kai gives a yell. He starts to fight the arm, because what else do
you do to the thing that's throttling you, and the man curves
his other arm over Kai's head and stabs him in the shoulder.

It seems to Kai he hears his own flesh scream in outrage. He
thinks he feels the knife's edge scrape a bone. He shrieks. He sees
Luka running toward them, but the man is already backing into
the river, holding Kai clamped before him like a shield. With
terrible speed they are afloat. The water is swift and cold and
deafeningly noisy; at Kai's mouth and round his face in rippling
muscular rills. The man, tugging Kai with him, is swimming
one-handed for the river's far side. Water rushes over Kai's face;

when his head comes clear again he sees others have joined Luka, come running down to the riverbank. Now the river is at its swiftest, and deepest. If his captor lets go of Kai here, he is going to drown. Now they are where the water rushes round and over rocks, and a tree has got caught amongst the rocks, and the terror of drowning, of being discarded here, has Kai grab at its branches, grab at them one after the other in a frenzy until somehow he gets a solid grip on one, solid enough that the man holding him feels it, curses, and brings his fist down on Kai's head. Kai is once more underwater; as he surfaces, gasping, this time he spies Ulf, waist-deep, pointing, then with hands cupped round his mouth yelling, but the river is far too loud to hear. He clings to his bit of tree with even greater desperation than before, then for no apparent reason finds he has been freed from his captor's grasp. He twists his head about to see how, and there behind him the man is being propelled straight out of the water; horror on his face, chest and belly all exposed. There is a shot. The Gemini are there, pistols raised, but it is Thor who stands at the centre of the echo, and Thor's musket which shows that tell-tale twirl of smoke. Then the branch tears away altogether and Kai is in the torrent once again. Then he is not. He is being grappled with, pulled at; coughing and spluttering he feels himself being lifted from the water, sagging front and back, carried like an old wineskin, carried against his captain's hip as his captain strides from the water, Kai under one arm, the other dragging Kai's abductor in his wake, and all his brothers-in-arms at the water's edge are cheering.

Zoltan is wading down to meet them. 'Kai,' his captain is saying, as Zoltan splashes past, 'you are going to have to sodding learn to bloody swim!'

Zoltan is bending over the body. 'Jacques, you're right!' Zoltan shouts. He lifts the scarf, trailing at the man's throat. 'It's a Croat!' He peers closer. There is purple froth bubbling from the man's chest. 'And he's with us still!'

Kai finds himself deposited on the bank. His captain has gone splashing back into the water, to where the man lies, gasping, staining the water all about him. His captain lifts the man's head up by that red scarf. 'Good day to you,' his captain says, bending over. That little silver pendant slips from his shirt. 'One of your countrymen. Carlo Fantom. Charles the Ghost. I'd like a word with him. Any idea where I might find him?'

The man's face seems to stiffen; the last of the bubbles die in the froth. 'Now that,' says Zoltan, with satisfaction, 'is the face of a man who died watching hell open up before him.'

'Or that is the face of a man who knew Carlo Fantom's name,' says the captain. 'Knew it damn well. He's here, Zoltan. I feel it. I know it. He's here.'

They build a fire and sit Kai down beside it, on someone's saddle, and the Executioner appears, with his pouch of needles and his bobbin of silk, and a flask of aqua vitae too, which he pours into the new mouth there all a-grin in the meat of Kai's shoulder, and which hurts so much Kai falls off the saddle altogether, and must be helped back onto it, wiping tears of anguish from his cheeks. Then he must be stitched, which would also be agony, were it not that Sten is there and takes it on himself to provide a sort of commentary: a mouse-size squeal as the needle goes in, as if the wound itself were speaking, a tiny high-pitched *Ahhhh!* of relief as each stitch is tied. The Executioner bends to his task; Kai's brothers-in-arms crowd in to watch. Who's this Carlo Fantom? they want to know.

'He is a man your captain is hunting for,' the Executioner tells them, in that rumble of his. He offers the flask once more to Kai. Sten does his mouse-sized wail and the needle goes in again. 'Your captain has been hunting for him almost all his life.'

The heat in Kai's belly has given the fire raging in his shoulder something else to think about. Why so? he hears Luka ask.

The Executioner gives a sigh. 'Because when your captain was a very little child – even younger than you, little lord,' he says, nodding down at Kai, 'this man first took from him his father, then his mother, and he would have killed your captain too, if he had found him.' Another sigh, a shake of the head at the wickedness of the world. 'But that, thank God, was not to be.'

Kai's audience is a-gawp. This is more than they have ever heard before.

'The Croats are good soldiers,' the Executioner continues. 'This one, though, he is monstrous.' (Says he, who looks so like a monster himself, yet is now balancing Kai's arm tenderly within a sling.) 'And there is such enmity between our captain and this man, Lieutenant Zoltan swears the two must hunt each other even in their sleep.'

Silence, as they digest this. 'Carlo Fantom,' says Per. 'That's a devil of a name.'

'He is a devil of a man. And he too wears a silver wolf.'

Kai feels the glances of his audience meet above his head. Another hard man.

'But why'd he do it, this here ghost?' Luka asks. 'Why'd he kill our captain's folk?'

'Black work. The man is an assassin. He was paid so to do.'

'Who paid him?'

'That,' says the Executioner, 'I am sure, will be the first question our captain has for him.' He gives Kai's arm in its sling a gentle pat. 'There, you are whole again.'

Now Kai is lifted to his feet, guided forward. He finds he must concentrate to walk in a straight line. Now he sees they have set up his tent for him, and the kindness of this might almost make him weep. 'Not the –' he begins, as they lay him down. 'Not the –'

'What's that?'

He tries to lift himself up on his good arm. Oh, his head is so heavy! 'Not the – not the baby any more,' he manages at last.

A cackle of laughter. 'No. No, now you been *baptized*. Sleep tight, Golden Spoon!'

'Goldie!' A chorus of shouts. Kai surfaces, as from the river, which is indeed where his dreams had taken him all night, and from which he struggles free, one-winged.

'Goldie! Come on out, there's orders! We're breaking camp!'

He gets himself up onto his knees, rubbing his eyes. There's Ulf, Luka, Sten; Ulf carrying a bundle under his arm. Behind them, the unmistakable activity of horses being readied, tents taken down. But his companions are all somehow altered. Ulf's doublet now appears to be of green velvet; Sten sports a ridiculously fancy hat with a mighty feather in it; and Luka is wearing boots that come so high up his legs he has to walk without bending his knees. 'What's happened?' he asks. 'Where are we going?'

'Back to old Åke Tott. Anklam's ours,' Ulf tells him. 'We went in with Ziggy. Had a look about. Ziggy got another dozen horses; we got this for you.' He proffers the bundle.

Kai, still off-balance, staggers to his feet, with his good arm shields his eyes. His head feels like it's being thumped, over and over. He squints. 'What's that?'

''Ave a boggle.' The bundle parts into two, and shows itself to be a pair of breeches and a soldier's coat, buff-leather, tabbed at the shoulders, scalloped along the sleeves. He holds it up, one-handed. He hears himself gasp.

'It's loot, not plunder,' Ulf tells him, meaning stolen honestly, not taken by force. 'Captain says we can't have our ensign running round looking like he oughter be an acrobat on stage. Now shift yourself, Goldie. Captain ain't waiting, not even for you.'

So back to old Åke Tott it is.

And then, for a little while, nothing happens. And then, everything does.

⸻ ❧❦ ⸻

Esteemed Revd Mr William Watts, Rafe writes.

I write to you from Hamburg, where I disembarked but yesterday, staggering across dry land in much the same way as I have been staggering across decks and pitching myself down stairways and tumbling across my cabin within the Guid Marie *these two weeks past, but it seems my 'sea-legs', as it is the sailors call them, took it upon themselves most unreasonably to manifest the very night before I was set ashore, and now must be exchanged for my old land-legs and I am told to expect that this will take a day or two.*

Indeed, if he flexes his legs he seems to feel within them still the awful pitch and yaw of the ocean, the terrifying glassy-green dips and slopes, streaming with foam.

Of the journey here, sir, I will say only that the sea is a mighty and powerful thing; that those men who make their living upon her must be of a different breed to you and I; that for the first week I had more conversations with the bucket placed beside my cot than with any of them; and that should our captain Mungo Sant *ever sustain a scratch or graze or knock such as those I carry with me from his ship, you would find the word* PIRATE *glaring at you from under a single layer of his skin. I begin to understand why the watermen were so averse. I am astonished that Mr Vanderhoof should be acquainted with such a rogue, truly.*

An uprush of noise from the room beneath. Two families are bedded down there, two families at least, and the women of each have been in conflict since dawn. Now a man's voice, impatient, beset; the wail of children.

Nonetheless, my passage here has indeed been accomplished, and I write you from a good clean house close by the docks, the Green Boar.

He smooths the paper out again. His desk is his knee. He sits here, under the tile and rafters of the roof, sunlight spotted across the floor wherever a tile has slipped, innocent of every possession but what he stands up in (not that there is even any space to do that), cross-legged upon the mattress that he had to drag and bully up the stairs himself. He cannot remember when he ever felt so happy. How wonderful it is to be in this new place, and to be this new Rafe Endicott – so buoyant, so much master of his destiny, so *free*. No, more than free – invincible. Unstoppable. He is an adventurer. He is a knight upon a quest. He is Perceval, he is Gawain, he is Siegfried – damn it all, he is a *hero*.

But Mr Watts, in honest truth, beyond my safe arrival I know not what to tell you, sir. The speed of the Swedish advance has swiped the breath from everyone. They are here; no, they are there. The Hamburg corantos, sir, have them riding upon reindeer as they sweep across the land; and speak of them as knowing neither hunger nor cold; soldiers who are more machine than men. No-one has the truth of what is happening in this country; even those to whom it happens. All is on its head—

Beneath him, the sound of what might be fire-irons being hurled across the room. In answer, the crash of what can only be a chamber-pot. A shriek of outrage. The argument has reached its pitch.

– and Hamburg has become a gathering place for all the unhappy people who once again find themselves fleeing before the conflict as little birds upon the shore flee the onrushing wave.

He pauses, examining that last sentence from both sides. Yes. It is good, let it stand.

Nonetheless, I have endeavoured to gather all the information that I can, and what I have for you thus far is this.

He pauses for a moment, tapping his pencil on his knee, bringing his thoughts into order. On the floor below, a door slams.

After His Swedish Majesty made landing, upon an island so small as to be beyond the notice of anyone but the forces of King Neptune, he has dedicated himself to securing the lands on either side the Oder river with such success that there is now a great fan of territory that is, in effect, Sweden-in-Germany. The Emperor's commander in the north, one Torquato Conti, has drawn his forces back to his stronghold of Gartz, while the Swedish lion flies above the towns of Wollin, Stettin, Wolgast, Stargard, and any number more. All have fallen to him, one after another, as one tree brings down the next. I enclose below a map, sir, of my making, which I hope will make all clear.

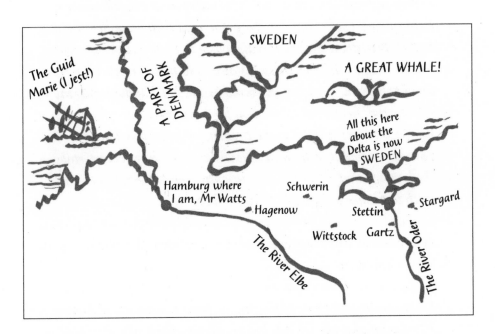

Beyond that, however, there is naught but panic and confusion. I am told the Swedish raise mists and miasmas and travel within them, invisible; I am told their victories come from the fact their army is composed of men who have compacted with the Devil and sold their souls in exchange for invulnerability. I am told that every night, armies of the dead march across the land. You never heard such desperate story-making. Thus do our fears make idiots of us all.

He takes a breath.

Mr Watts, I thank you with all my heart that you have made me part of this your enterprise, but you see my dilemma, sir. Everyone I speak with has a tale to tell, but I am unable to ascertain the truth of any of them. If I am to gain better information for you, sir, there is no doubt but I must work a way eastward, to the Oder. The landlord here assures me there are good roads forward of this place, part of the old route by which salt was brought across the country, and if I follow them to Hagenow I will find a posting inn, and then on to Schwerin and to Wittstock. So I will make haste to Hagenow as speedily as I can. You might write to me at any of these, if you wish. It would oblige me greatly if you could assure Mr Vanderhoof of my safe arrival here, and thank him for his kindness in arranging my passage, for as full as the town is of folk, so is Hamburg's harbour empty of ships, and so few vessels willing to undertake the journey that everyone I speak with wonders how in future, with the times so out of joint, they are to live.

Ah, Master Shakespeare, as ever, you have the words for it. A happy thought.

I wonder too if there is any news from Germany of Henry Kempwick and our friends in the Pilgrim Players?

How pleasant it would be to encounter them, to describe to them his quest. It is the kind of thing, he knows, that Mr Kempwick in particular would glory in. Perhaps there might even be a drama in it, of some sort. There was for Perceval, and for Gawain too.

And so I close my first report to you, sir, assuring you of my good spirits, and my duty to you and to Mr Butter in all.

Raphael Endicott, by his hand.

And then

PS – And if you are able, sir, to give to Miss Belinda Butter my willing service too.

His quill hovers. Should he cross that out? No, let it stand. A knight should write his lady. Besides, what cares a gallant knight for paternal mutterings against him? Exactly nothing, is what. All the old folktales – many of them German, now he thinks of it – they all tell us that.

Eastward to the Oder. What a splendid title for a memoir that would be!

CHAPTER SIX

The Men Who Write the Rules

'Man's life's a game at tables, and he may
Mend his bad fortune, by his wiser play.'

George Herbert, *Wit's Recreations*

A SK THE MEN who write the rules, they'll tell you the Swedish army allows itself no women. No officers' ladies, sighing their way in silky boredom through their days in their billets in Stettin (no queen on her way with another ten thousand conscripts, come to that); in the camps, no soldiers' wives digging out their fire-pits, boxing their children's ears; no women sutlers setting out their stalls with their supplies of baccy and playing cards and new beer and grog; no farmers' daughters, tearfully searching for Trooper Olaf or Sergeant Erik (because he promised to wed her and what if her belly should swell?). No, none of them. All those flashes of colour you see out the corner of your eye, those bright bursts of soprano chatter and the bawdy cackles late at night or (just as often) the yelp of a man taking a knee to the cods, they are mere figments of your imagination. So say the men who write the rules.

But the men who write the rules, they've never tried to wash out a shirt. And consequently have no idea what being ridden on all day can do to a shirt-tail, nor how depressing it is to see the same old spray of droplets across your sleeve, day in, day out, fading from red to brown; nor how a hole in a stocking means by the end of the day a blister on your toe, and you limping along at half the pace you might have made, and your fellows waiting for you whether they like it or not, and I rest my case. An army may march on its stomach, but it gets up in the morning because it has clean linen.

Rosa knows this. Ten years ago, when this war itself was but a babe, Rosa washed the shirts of the men who came over with Ernst von Mansfeld, who were supposed to have Friedrich of Heidelberg (the cause of all this) back in his castle by Christmas, him and his English princess-wife. Then, after Mansfeld's bubble burst, she washed those of the troops of Christian of Brunswick. Then those of Old Father Tilly (still campaigning somewhere down there to the south), and thus can tell you, there is no difference whatsoever between the pong of a Papist and that of a Protestant. Then it was the turn of the army of Christian of Denmark, until he took to his ships and fled back home. She has washed Saxon shirts, Westphalian shirts, Bavarian shirts and those of the men of Hesse. Now, it is the turn of the Swedish shirt, to be scrubbed and twisted in her strong, rough, reddened hands. Rosa collects sheep's wool from the hedges, and rubs her hands with it before she sleeps. You're a washerwoman: your hands are how you earn your living, just like a soldier with his sword. It serves you to keep 'em in good order. Rosa knows the tricks.

So here in the camp of Åke Tott, first thing she does is find
the water (every camp there's always water, lake or river, has
to be), then she spies out this place down by the water where
there's big old rocks, set like steps, all smoothed for her by Time
itself and perfect as a surface where the dirt can be beaten out
of the shirts once they've been soaked; and a little bosky, bushy
place where laundry can hang and dry. So she pitches her tent,
laying her claim, unpacks her tub and fills it with water and lye,
and sets up shop. And the camp grows and the weather behaves
itself and business is good.

She's less than amused therefore when this company of
discoverers, maybe the last to come into camp, pitch their
tents all round those handy bushes, and right in front of her
as she kneels there (paddle in hand and a shirt stretched over
the rock between her knees), their horse-master leads their
horses into the river to wash the sweat off their hides and
lets 'em dung there. True, there's not a horse-master made
who don't rank their beasts higher than any human soul (and
this one, with his pulled-up, red-dyed sprout of hair, has even
made himself look like one of his charges), but who wants
their shirts rinsed in water smelling of that? So she waits a
day, to let these men get their bearings and a decent night's
rest, because they're all unshaven and bristly as boars, they've
all the starey-eyed look of those who've been out on the roads
for weeks on end; and no-one but a fool tries to reason with a
man when he's short of sleep. Also, she asks about a bit, and
what she hears suggests that *Vorsichtig! Approach with caution!*
might be the smart thing to do. She watches them. She listens
to them talk – 'Rotwelsch', it's called, that cant this army uses:
Swedish, German, English, Scots, mixed and mingled as the
moment demands, seasoned further, as it were, with whatever
is to hand. Them what see monsters under the bed, they say
it's what the devils snarl at each other in hell, but Rosa is made
of stronger stuff than that.

So after a day she plaits her mass of brown-black hair and coils it atop her head; pinches a bit of pink into her cheeks (cheeks that years of working out of doors have freckled like her very own dotted veil), eases her washerwoman's shoulders (sturdy as a milkmaid's yoke), into her good bodice of Lyons velvet, and with caution, true enough, makes her approach.

'Ho! Kapitän!'

He'd been crouched down, speaking with two of his men; now he turns and stands. Rosa resists the urge to retreat. Oh, the height. Oh, the face. Oh, those eyes. Forbidding ain't the word.

'We share a ground,' she begins. She scrapes her foot across it, just to be clear. 'This ground.'

The eyes narrow. 'Is that so?'

'I'm in need of a clean place to work,' she points out. 'And you're in need of a laundry-woman.'

She sees him look down at his shirt-front – grimed and grey and the linen as limp as something dead. 'Suppose I say we take care of our own laundry?' he says next.

'That's what you've been trying, is it? Did you wash that shirt with you in it?' And when she sees from his face that yes, in effect that must have been exactly what he'd done, she follows up with, 'That's why you need me.' Now she has her hands on her hips. 'But your horses, they dirty up the water.'

One of the men standing with him, the glossy handsome bugger – yes, he looks like a man would relish getting his laundry done – he says, 'The fräulein makes a case, Domini.' The warm smile of a man assuring her he's on her side. Then he smooths his wide moustaches with his hand, like a dog licking its chops, and she gets his measure, right enough.

The other has turned aside, so all she can see of him are his side-whiskers and his prodigious great ears. It's oddly beguiling – who would have thought that one of these could be such a simple thing as shy?

Back to the captain. She looks square up at him. 'You let me stay here, and you water your horses some place else, I'll do your shirts for free.'

Again, the eyes narrow. 'What's your name?' he asks.

'Rosa.'

'Whose camp have you come from?'

A lie under that gaze is only going to drop to the ground between them and squirm itself to death. 'Torquato Conti. His.'

'And how was that?'

Again, that straight look up. Rosa has no time for those don't say it as it is. 'Conti is the Devil. His men are locusts, they are the plague. They are burning everything. They all think they are going to die, either of fever in camp, or at your hands out of it. It's nothing to them, how foul they are.'

That *zzzzip* of understanding in his face. 'Rosa,' he repeats. He holds out his hand. 'Jack Fiskardo.'

'Oh, I know who you are,' she answers. 'Everybody does.'

THREE THINGS ABOUT Åke Tott. One, he likes a place for a headquarters that stands out good and high, so all his troops can feel his presence. Here it's a tithe barn: a chequerboard of beam and brick four storeys high and honeycombed with windows, as in this part of the world such buildings are, before which Åke Tott's death's head standard ('Tott' and 'tod' being so close as makes no difference) flies at the height of a maypole. And two: Tott's nickname. Bestowed upon him by Gustavus Adolphus himself, Tott's nickname is 'the Snowplough' because he clears a path for all the rest. Tott's camps are always way to the fore of the rest of the army, and in this case, rumour has it they are already so far forward they are off their maps.

Tott has a squat little face, like a gnome, all the features gathered together in the bottom half beneath a bulbous, balding forehead. His expression sits perpetually somewhere between amusement and perturbation, like a man risen halfway out of a chair. Third and last: he has a settled aversion to Scotsmen (an historic slight from one Alexander Leslie – it need not detain us here). Also, despite a high-born Swedish mother, Tott is in fact a Finn, and who knows how they tick? The Finns foretell your fortune in a sneeze; have gods of beer and turnips, speak of ogres in their woods with beards of moss, and believe in steeds of iron, forged by trolls. How is the notion of a man made impenetrable any stranger than these? So when Ancrum, in his usual windy way, is favouring Tott's general staff with his view of Conti's numbers (vast) and intentions (to come to battle as soon as he can) and Tott feels his own thoughts wandering off to gaze out the window, then spies the scorn on the face of that captain amongst Ancrum's discoverers, he raises a hand, silencing Ancrum, and asks, 'Fiskardo? You disagree?'

Fiskardo. No-one knows anything about Fiskardo, other than that one thing, which everybody knows, and really, once you know that, what more do you need?

'No more than an observation, Fältherre,' Fiskardo begins. 'But when we've encountered Conti's men, we've never seen more than their backsides, running away. Also, they have fever in their ranks. Bad enough that they leave their dead where they fall.'

A murmur round the room.

'And now there are women coming into camp here—'

'There are no women in the Swedish camp,' Tott says at once.

'In that case, Fältherre, there are mysterious entities within this camp who look like women—'

Laughter. Soldiers like a laugh, and look most favourably on any man can bring a joke to earth, no matter what else may be said of him.

'—and the women are always the first, sir. They always know.'

'What do the women know?' comes the question, from the lower reaches of the table.

'Everything, in my experience,' Tott puts in. More laughter. Tott sits back, gnome-like features brimming with pleasure. The usual tedious making of reports, this morning it's going rather well.

Says Fiskardo, 'They know when the tide has turned.'

In they come, in they crawl, homeless and leaderless: left-overs from the army of Christian of Denmark; starvelings, God help us, from that of Christian of Brunswick; wide-eyed lads straight off the farm; squads of horsemen coming into camp under the home-made banner of some local grandee; freebooting wanderers, growling and snarling in Polish and Czech. And then the first out-and-out deserters from the army of the Emperor, the first of the turncoats. Yes, they are unpaid. Yes, they are unfed. Yes, many of those left behind are sick. The Emperor's army is all confusion. He would play any trick to stop you, these men say, but right now all the great commanders in his army do is throw blame, one at the other. No-one even knows who is truly in charge. 'The tide runs with us,' Tott writes to his wife, another Swedish gentlewoman. 'The gods are smiling.'

SOMETIMES THE GODS make it so easy.

They hobble into the camp with the sunrise, each leading the next. One is bent double, tapping her way along with her sticks; one freakishly tall and with a strip of leather tied over her eyes, and then there's the third, who you'd think might be in charge of the other two, save that she has the moony smile of a half-wit, a madwoman's froth of hair, and instead of walking, trips along making dance-steps. One or two of the sutlers give them food, just to be rid of them, and sometimes one of the whores will guide them through the jumble of tents, because it can do no harm to store up credit with the angels by a kindly act. Otherwise these three are all but invisible; not only women, but elderly to boot. It takes them hours to get through the camp to the water, then when they do, at the last moment their way looks to be barred by a string of horses being led off to the blacksmith to be reshod. The horse-master, up aloft, carmine topknot turning this way and that as he overwatches the horses, he doesn't see them; the troopers urging the horses along, nor do they; the lieutenant, urging the troopers along, nor does he; but his captain (whose mount has the wildest mane of curls), he has his men stop in their tracks, to let the women teeter and totter across the path, and only then does he let the horse-master continue on his way.

'That them?' Roxandra asks, from behind her blindfold.

'That's them,' Pernilla answers. She rotates her head, beneath the hump of her shoulders, to keep horses and riders in view.

'And that's him?'

'Oh, that's him all right. Kizzy, I hope those boys of yours know to thank us for this. You could brand leather with my feet.'

'He's pretty,' Kizzy puts in. She does a turnabout, there where she stands, bare feet *la* and *la* and so. Something with Kizzy is always in movement – her hands, her wide mouth, her tapping foot, the sit of her head, her jittery look.

'You think they're *all* pretty,' Pernilla tells her.

'Oh, not *him*. No, I mean his friend.'

'Yes, he was pretty.' Pernilla is still staring after the horses. 'Well now, Jack Fiskardo. You have took your time, sir.'

'Which one was pretty?' Roxandra wants to know.

Milano kicks out at the horses from Anklam, tries to bite the blacksmith. Unheard-of bad behaviour. 'Domini, he's an old boy now,' Ziggy says, gently, as one breaking bad news. 'These marches tire him. Put him out of sorts.' He points over to the new mounts. 'Take one of those. Take two.'

He refuses. Milano, he had explained, would never forgive him. Besides, fine as they are, none of those looted from Anklam have ringlets in their mane, nor that trick of putting their nose in his pocket, as a greeting.

'What's got into you?' he asks, rubbing round Milano's ears. 'It's not so long ago you beat four Polish Cossacks to their prize.' But there is grey at his horse's muzzle, and threading through that outlandish mane of curls, and just recently a new hollow has opened up in front of Milano's hip. Ah me.

He's here, he tells his horse, standing with him, forehead to forehead, and no, of course he doesn't think Milano can read his thoughts. He knows Milano can.

Carlo Fantom. I feel him here. He thinks of the soldier in the river, the man's body, face up, breast shattered. The trail of blood, the trailing ends of the scarf, tied in that Croat fashion at the man's throat.

But how do I get my name in front of him? How do we lure him out?

Meantime, thanks to Rosa, their shirts are washed and Kai's new breeches have been taken in to fit him rather less piratically than before. Ah yes, Kai. Kai has also acquired a nickname. Jack has heard the yell – "'Ere! Goldie, sir!' – twice now, and as everyone knows, nothing says your fellows have accepted you clearer than that, and unless his captain's eyes deceive him, as he and his officers sit about their fire of an evening, there's now a couple of tiny plaits keeping those golden curls from obstructing Kai's ingenuous view of the world. Nor is Kai the only one to be so dressing his hair. 'Have a look at that,' Zoltan had said, summoning him. 'Just look at that boy,' as Ulf strolled past with a whole head of rattling quills, like a porcupine.

The recruits, a little way off, sat about a fire of their own, are trying their hand at a song – something about crowns of flowers and I love you the best. Zoltan begins, 'D'you think Fräulein Rosa would favour me, if I made her a crown?'

'Charm not working as it should?' Jack enquires solicitously.

'She shows no interest in me at all,' says Zoltan. 'It is the greatest mystery.'

'Oh,' says Kai – Kai who now sits with them of an evening as a brother officer should, and doesn't always blush and shake his head when the bottle comes his way, either. 'She tells me it is because you are too handsome.'

'*Too* handsome?' Zoltan straightens his back.

'Much too handsome,' says Kai. 'She says a man like you will have had hundreds of women.'

Zoltan strokes his moustache. 'Not *hundreds*,' he says, modestly.

'So she says you must be poxed,' Kai concludes.

Amid the eruption of laughter, a snort from the Executioner, of such force that the man must wipe his coat.

GIVEN LONG ENOUGH, all those pedlars and sutlers and whores, they create a sort of high street. It's where you go to sell your plunder, or to buy: thicker woollen stockings for the winter, a better pair of gloves. There's a leatherworker, if you're in funds and have your heart set on one of those soldier's coats of elk-hide; there's a butcher, the front of whose counter is tasselled with rabbits and game-birds and any such little thing as couldn't find its way around snare or net; there's a baker's stall, with his mighty oven heating the air all around, and the aroma of fresh baking luring its usual throng. There's a seller of swords as well, if that doled out to you when you enlisted no longer fits the bill. The man displays his wares with a padlocked chain run through their hilts, and the rattle and clank as his customers handle and weigh and appraise makes this the noisiest place in the street. 'Is it Solingen steel, this blade?' his customers ask, eyeball-ing the blades down their length, and the sword-seller always answers, 'Oh, better. Better!' There is hardly any better steel than Solingen, but a sword made with it might cost a month's salary, which is why one of the few to wear one is Fiskardo, and yes, his was as plundered as plunder can be; the hand he took it from still twitching. And now here's the man himself, the usual path opening casually before him, because this trestle-and-canvas high street is also where you find aniseed candies for your snappish steed and, unless Jack misremembers, is where, at the leatherworker's, he had spotted a backgammon board. You can use anything for counters – pebbles, leaves, bits of bread – but you need a board.

He likes the game of *bräde*. It was his old commander, Torsten the Bear, first taught him how to play, in an attempt to give this unexpected new recruit something to do other than pick fights and talk to his horse. When you begin a game, it's nothing but raw luck, but the further you advance, the more moves you make, the more you realize, it's he who makes the most skilful use of that luck will be the winner, always.

Much. Like. Life. The crowd has parted, once again, but not for another officer – no, it has parted for that washerwoman, running through it at such speed her petticoats are all a-froth about her ankles, windmilling her arms, crying out, 'Captain! Captain!'

Jack has to put his own arms out to stop her. 'The devil is it?'

Her strong-featured face with its high colour and its freckles, it is all disordered. 'Captain, they are fighting! The boys!'

Here is Ulf, on his knees, head tipped back, blood on the front of his shirt, and Kai pinching Ulf's nostrils closed in an attempt to stem the flow. And the rest of the recruits gathered about them, fretful as angry bees. Now what?

''E gussed your nabe, Kapding,' Ulf informs him.

Who did?

'Edvin.'

Edvin as in Ancrum's *ensign* Edvin?

'Yeh, hib,' Ulf replies, squinting up at his captain over the purpling bridge of his nose. 'Gussed your nabe and when I told hib to go fug himself, he took a swig ad me.'

I see, says his captain. And this happened because?

Horses get hungry, that's why, and now Fiskardo's troop has a dozen more than before, the ranging-abroad for green fodder had taken his recruits into pastures Ancrum's crew regarded as theirs. So there was a clash, in which Ancrum's ensign takes their captain's name in vain ('He *gussed* you, Kapding!'), and when Ulf retaliates, knocks him flat. So then Ulf did what?

'Bulled me lebber on 'im, the gunt,' Ulf replies. "E soon fugged off theb.'

Pulled his leather. Drew his sword. On a soldier of superior rank.

'Bud I din't use it,' Ulf replies, as Kai breaks in with, 'It was in *reply*, Domini. It was in reply *only*.'

'Yeh, it wod in rebly.' Holding his own nose closed now, Ulf turns his head and spits. 'That's wod it wod. *'N* 'e darted it.'

Well. Let us hope Colonel Ancrum sees it likewise.

Predictably, Ancrum does not.

Trials in the Swedish army take place in the open air; a practice designed to create a sense of impartiality, plain dealing. It is another bright blue day; a sportive little breeze lifting the proudly waxed quills of Ulf's hair, where he stands, hands tied, between two of the provost's men. The court, if you can call it such, is drawn up in battle lines: there sits Ancrum at a table outside his mighty tent, provost on his left and one of Åke Tott's lieutenants on his right, and opposite, standing, Jack Fiskardo with all of his discoverers behind him, as if every single one of them is on trial too – as indeed perhaps they are. The presence of the lieutenant is a surprise – a neat young fellow with an enthusiastic look, and the strangest, lopsided haircut, one side up by his ear, the other at his shoulder, and tied with a bow. It takes Jack a moment to realize the lopsidedness must be intentional. Also a surprise: the appearance, behind Ancrum's chair, of Quinto del fucking Ponte.

Edvin, Ancrum's ensign, is one of those unlucky low-waisted youths with long torso and short legs, as if the top half of his body is a graft. Edvin testifies unblushingly that Ulf attacked him, unprovoked.

Outrage amongst the supporters of the defendant, with Kai's treble – 'But it is *not so!*' – soaring above the rest; Kai, of them all, the only one innocent enough to believe that an injustice need only be pointed out to be universally recognized and instantly righted.

He steps forward: Jack Fiskardo, with his polar glare, his tattooed hands; with (by repute) that silver wolf hanging over his black heart. At Zoltan's insistence, he has at least donned his officer's sash and changed his shirt. He walks past Edvin (the boy shrinks away), to a spot a yard in front of Ulf. 'Gentlemen, in any army, these fallings out will happen,' he begins. He lifts himself up a little, making the most of his height. 'Wise men treat them as they deserve.' He lets his gaze fall on Ancrum as he says it. 'We train these lads to fight. They settled their differences as they are trained to do. With honour,' he adds, 'honour' being one of those words never fails to back an idiot like Ancrum into a corner. 'And he was no more unprovoked than I am Cicero.'

A pleasing ripple of surprise through his audience. (Give me the name of an orator, he'd told Kai. And make it a good one.)

'After all, I understand my own name was maligned as well.' ('He said as you was a damned and godless rogue, Kapten,' Ulf had declared. 'A damned and godless rogue, and everyone knew it, and that you tricked yourself out like a heathen, and now you was having all of us do the same.') He fixes Ancrum with his most frigid glare. 'Should I be demanding satisfaction for that?'

'His blade was bared,' the provost points out, unhelpfully.

'*After* he was struck. This was a nothing. Fisticuffs between two boys with red stuff in their veins, that's all.'

'No, no,' the provost persists. 'These are issues of the utmost seriousness.' It being his blasted job to present them as such. 'His blade was bared, and unprovoked, against a superior. This is of the gravest consequence.'

Ancrum nods his head in sage agreement. How the man loves a rule-book. 'Indeed, for let us not forget,' Ancrum begins, like a preacher – Ancrum who lives in a world where really the only thing audible is the sound of his own voice – 'the ultimate penalty for such an act is death.'

A gasp from Ulf, drowned in Jack's own bellow of laughter. 'Anyone who wants my lad's head over this will have to come through me.' *And you know what they say about me.*

But now Quinto del Ponte is leaning forward. Quinto del Ponte has Ancrum's ear. A glance toward Ulf, more murmuring. He steps away; a man who's said his bit. Ancrum and the provost consult. Now Tott's lieutenant leans in to join their conversation. Ancrum busies himself for a moment with the papers under his hand. Finally, he says, 'This court acknowledges that there was provocation on both sides.' A glance at Del Ponte. 'It seems we have a witness.'

We do? To the best of Jack's knowledge Quinto del Ponte had been nowhere near the fight. And then as he feels Jack's eyes on him, the man flicks his own gaze upward, meets Jack's for just an instant, and taps at his chest with a small, conspiratorial smile.

'Nonetheless,' Ancrum continues, 'insult was offered to the superior rank. Both the accused will be fined their next month's pay, and for he who showed his blade, five lashes, in addition.'

'I'll take it!' Ulf exclaims.

Out comes the frame, dragged by the provost's two guards-men, bumping over the ground. Ulf is skinned out of his shirt and his wrists are tied above his head. It amazes Jack how

vividly he remembers that stretch, and the sudden coolness of
the air under your arms. And the fury there had been in his
heart at such usage too. Here, one of those idiotic re-routings
of the human brain has Ulf shivering with what looks like
laughter, at least until the first blow lands. The guard deliv-
ering the punishment, Jack sees, has an eye on Jack himself
– *Yes, you do know what they say about me* – and is trying to find
some slightly more merciful manner than usual of wielding
the whip.

All the same, it's a bloody business. The first stroke and the
blood flees the skin all along its track, then rushes back; where
the second stroke meets it the skin breaks at once. Ulf stands
the first three strokes as if speechless, then a sort of ululation
breaks from his mouth that seems to contain the shock and hurt
of all three lashes all at once. He remembers that as well, the
way the agony mounts up, in waves. 'Stand straight, Kai, open
your eyes,' he says to Kai, who is wobbling beside him. 'If Ulf
can take it, so can you.'

Ulf, cut loose, manages a step or two on his own before falling
forward into the arms of his comrades. 'It is not the pain, it is
the shame of it,' says Kai, gulping down his distress.

'Oh, Kai, there is no shame in a flogging,' Zoltan assures him
in a fatherly tone. 'In Poland I saw a lad take a dozen lashes like
that, take them without a sound. And these days he outranks
the pair of us.'

'That's a lie,' says Jack. 'I cursed away with every oath I knew.'

He glances down. Kai's amazement is so naked you can't help
yourself.

'You were flogged, Domini?'

'I was. I was, and I deserved it.' There, now the story must
be told. 'When I was first in Torsten's regiment there was a
man, a sergeant like Ziggy, took a fancy to Milano. He made
me an offer. My horse means a lot to me, Kai. When I had
nothing – not meat for my belly and hardly a shirt for my back

– I had him. So I refused. The man thought to help himself. We fought. I got a dozen lashes for it, but I kept Milano. Kai, was Signor del Ponte anywhere in sight when Ulf was fighting with Ancrum's boy?'

'No,' Kai answers, 'no, truly, Domini, I am sure of it, he was not there at all.' Another gulp, a sniff; the boy wipes his nose upon his sleeve. *Oh, Kai,* Jack thinks, *if your nurse could only see you now.*

'What happened to the man?' Kai asks. 'The one who tried to take Milano?'

'Oh, he went his ways,' Zoltan answers, 'he went his ways.'

Went his ways into the grave, a mile from Torsten's camp, with his skull knocked apart. There are those you meet with in battle, then there are those others who are something else. Thus far, there have been four of those, the first, back in Amsterdam, when he was just thirteen. But Jack Fiskardo is no longer thirteen and he is trying very hard not to have that total increase.

This, he thinks, *was a sod of a day.* He finds he has wandered almost to the lakeside, down near to Rosa's tent, down to where the grass is still green, as opposed to yellowed under the passage of many feet, or worn away so entirely that the soft grey earth is bared. But here there is green, so one can sit upon the ground, which is the proper place for contemplating all the frailties of mankind. It's rare, these days, for him to find himself alone like this; as captain there is always some question waiting for an answer; some problem or other begging for him to find it a solution. Ah me indeed.

He looks out across the lake. He wonders what it has in the way of fish. He wonders if there might be time to find out. He remembers being taken fishing as a boy, he remembers catching a pike, the intoxication as this monster was pulled from the depths – outrageous beginner's luck, but not entirely so. There had been baiting of the water, there had been a big fat oily mackerel on the hook.

Bait, he finds himself thinking. *Baits and lures.* There is something trying to bring itself together in his thoughts, with that familiar simmer of anger to thicken the mix. Ulf is his trooper. This is his tribe, his family, God-damn, cross one, cross all – *Trick ourselves out like heathens, do we?*

And now, behind him, someone clears their throat. He turns about. It's Åke Tott's lieutenant. 'Now how is it,' the man begins, in the tone of one who has rehearsed this opening with care, 'that a whippersnapper such as that can stand there, tell a bare-faced lie, yet it is the other lad gets the flogging?'

'A mystery,' Jack agrees. 'But then if a full-blown fuckwit can be a colonel...'

A moment's pause, and then an escape of laughter so high-pitched it seems to take the lieutenant by complete surprise as well. Recovering, Åke Tott's lieutenant extends his hand and announces, 'Achille de la Tour.'

'Jack Fiskardo,' says Jack. (In Rosa's tent, the man tenderly anointing her face, her mouth, her neck, her naked breasts with a twist of lamb's wool freezes, and in that woodwind Muscovite accent of his, whispers, *'Yoperesete!* The captain!')

De la Tour continues. 'How is the prisoner?'

'Smarting,' Jack replies. 'But he'll live.'

De la Tour edges closer, a man with something more to say. 'I must admit, Captain, I have been curious to speak with you. I knew your father.'

At the look of disbelief on Jack's face, he corrects himself. 'Perhaps *knew* is to put it too strongly. I saw him, once. In Paris. He was far too – how to put it? Far too *unofficial* a presence to be bothered with chitchat. Too unofficial and, frankly, too intimidating for a mere cadet. We were all of us in awe.' A shake of the head. 'And you have his look, you do indeed.'

'So I am told,' Jack replies.

He puts that edge to his voice. De la Tour shoots him a wary glance. 'You are not disposed to speak of him?'

'Let's say that where my father is concerned, I have learned to be circumspect. Tell me – how does a Frenchman become one of Tott's general staff?'

'Oh, that,' De la Tour replies. 'A relative. A diplomat.'

'Do you have influence with Tott?'

'Me? Not one iota. But my uncle? Certainly.' Another wary check before he speaks again. 'You ask because…?'

'Have Tott send us back out there,' Jack says. 'We're off our maps, yes? My troopers have the makings of good scouts, but they'll learn nothing here. The more time they spend in the field, the better. If Tott wants intelligence of what's ahead, send us to get it for him.'

'You are volunteering, Captain?' De la Tour asks.

'I am.'

De la Tour tilts his head back. 'You understand, in honest truth, we have no idea what's out there. None at all.'

'In honest truth, I never have had,' Jack replies.

De la Tour rocks a little on his toes. 'And I suppose,' he says with a smile, 'some distance just at present between you and Ancrum – no bad thing?' More rocking back and forth. 'If I may say one thing – I have never forgotten the impression your father made upon me. It was a great shock, when I heard he had been – well, *lost*, as he was.'

'And to me,' says Jack.

De la Tour holds out his hand again. 'I will speak with *le général* Tott,' he says.

Jack walks down to the water's edge. Stones crunch under his boots – little flat stones, good for skimming. He picks one up, sends it out over the water. Three skips. Picks up another. Tries with that. This time, five.

My father.

Another. Six.

My father the man who never came home.

Who rode away without a backwards glance. You might say

he did so as a man of honour; you might say he did so in pursuit of glory. You would be just as right or wrong, in either case.

And here stands his son, here at a lake in Mecklenburg, skimming stones as an alternative to the endless conflict with his father in his thoughts. Stoops to select another stone, purplish in colour, perfectly rounded, and sends it out across the water, kiss, skip, kiss, skip, out, out, out... five, six, seven, eight, *nine*. Not going to better that.

'Most impressive,' Zoltan says, coming up behind him.

The sort of fool grin only Zoltan ever gets to see.

Zoltan continues. 'I passed Tott's lieutenant as I came down here. Anything I should know?'

'I think we will do better back out in the field than here,' Jack tells him.

Zoltan produces a heavy sigh, places his hand over his heart. 'Ah, bella Rosa,' he murmurs, 'it was not to be.'

'And I think we would do best to make a little space for ourselves out there. Do you remember,' Jack asks, 'at Trzciana, the winged hussars?'

Zoltan draws his head back. 'Trust me, I am unlikely to forget.'

'I was thinking,' says Jack. 'Why should it be the Polish have all the fun with that?'

SUNRISE OVER ÅKE Tott's camp. A sliver of pink rising over the water; birds stalking the shallows. Rosa, waking, moving her lover's arm from round her waist, stretches her legs and cocks an ear. She hears noise outside – cackles of laughter, twiggy snaps and rustlings. The sound of soft items being thrown about. Her laundry!

She pulls herself up and outside, and there are those three crazy old women: the one on sticks pulling the linens of yesterday's wash from the bushes; the blind one, standing as tall as if she is on stilts, running each shirt through her fingers; the zany with her mass of hair, catching and folding them as they fall. Each shirt leaves the blind one's hands with some croaked comment: 'This one's had it. This one will be gone by Christmas.' 'This has some life left in it still.' 'Ah, this one is good for years and years!'

'My ladies, what are you doing?' Rosa asks, amazed.

The one on sticks squints up at her. 'An inventory,' she says. 'We're almost done.'

The zany has taken up one shirt and is dancing with it, eyes closed, an arm about its waist, the other holding its cuff to her cheek. 'Give me that,' Rosa says, going to her, snatching it away. The zany old woman smiles at her, still humming her mad little tune. There are flowers bobbing in her froth of hair, leaves, bits of vine, so fresh there is a ladybird crawling amongst them. A butterfly dips up and down over the old woman's brow. It is a shock, Rosa realizes, looking at this old soul's face – the arc of her eyes, the fullness of her lips – to see what beauty this one must once have had, long, long ago.

From the fancy-work at its collar, the shirt looks to be one of Lieutenant Zoltan's. 'Ah,' says the one on sticks, hobbling up, head angled Rosa's way, 'she's right. He's pretty. But he's not the one for you, my Lady Soap-Bubble, is he now? He's not the one a-lying in your tent.' And before Rosa can respond to this with more than a gasp, she says, 'Now, listen, you. We've a message.' She straightens up, as far as she can. 'We've a message for the captain, for Fiskardo. Give me your word as you'll pass it along, and we'll be on our way.'

'Ilya!' Stooping, Rosa re-enters her tent, kneels to shake the Executioner by his shoulder. 'Ilya!'

He comes awake like something surfacing, a sea-monster perhaps, with his great fleshy ears and the ridges of his brow. A kindly gargoyle, is how Rosa thinks of him, blinking, rumbling, the way men do before they have their wits in place. Oh, she will miss him. Oh, she will.

'Those three old women,' she tells him. 'They said they had a message for your captain. They said to tell him they will see him again when he has the horse.' She spreads her hands in bafflement. '*What* horse?'

This early in the morning, that high street of trestle-and-canvas is quiet, but it's one of Quinto del Ponte's favourite hunting grounds, all the same. Men half awake, unguarded, are even more susceptible to flattery than they would be otherwise, and how many times has the witty compliment, the skilful teasing-out of some unguarded comment provided him with exactly the information he was after? It's certainly worked with Ancrum. A couple of instances, no more, of good-natured shock at how little General Tott seems to appreciate that skilled warrior Colonel Ancrum, and Ancrum is already sharing with him how and when the regiment will shift to the Camp Royal at Stettin, and when Her Majesty is to be expected with all those reinforcements, and the plans for the reception, for her arrival. Ripeness is all... dancing through his thoughts go notions of reward, regard, a commission; and even if all that should come to naught, then still, he has his letter.

His letter – imagine, as he presents it to the Prince-Bishop, imagine, as he whispers, 'No, no, no-one knows of this, your Grace, no-one but you, I, and the man who wrote it, and here I deliver him into your hands.' Such golden dreams. Such a future! And how pleasing it would be, to have him, Quinto del Ponte, the Prince-Bishop's favourite for once; him and not that – that lurking nightmare, Carlo Fantom. Whatever the rumours might be of Fantom's paternity, *hah*.

So here he goes, strolling from one group to the next, sharing an early morning greeting here, some wry comradely comment there, a whispered word of manly approval to the one with that sleepy-eyed doxy on his arm, who stands there yawning, fluffing her curls. A rueful admission he could never get a mistress like that himself. The girl blinks at him, unfooled, turns her attention back to the *Brötchen* she holds in both her hands (thinks Del Ponte), like a rat. He ponders wandering away, but then—

'*Ach! Le streghe!*' says Quinto del Ponte, as the three old women pass. He shudders in comic mock-horror. 'Haste away, old witches, haste away!'

Two of them, the crookback and the blind one, continue on as if not hearing him. But the other turns, comes dancing toward him; skip-step, skip-step, bare feet here, there, here, there. She points at him, her finger bumpy as a twig. 'We see you,' she says.

The bleary girl, watching, wipes her mouth.

Quinto del Ponte makes the horned hand at the old witch: *get away!* She takes no notice. Her mass of hair nods at him, scattered with withered stems, brown and dry. He sees with revulsion that it is beaded with lice as well. 'Oh, we see you,' she says. She leans toward him. Her eyes are bloodshot, her breath is foul. Del Ponte is horribly discomfited. He feels the old hag has turned the tables on him. To be so assailed, and in front of witnesses!

Now she is speaking again. 'We see your evil heart. We see your filthy soul.' Another step forward. 'But the Dead Man will cleanse you. He will cleanse you from the earth, just as my boy said he would. Just as he will your master.'

She has taken up a fold of his shirt. She rubs it between finger and thumb. 'A year or so in that at the most,' she announces, with an evil grin. 'Not long now!'

CHAPTER SEVEN

The Knight Errant

'Travel, in the younger sort, is a part of education; in the elder, a part of experience.'

Francis Bacon, *Essays and Counsels Civil and Moral*

Dear Mr Watts

You find me, sir, if I have my present location aright, between the towns of Lauenberg and Hagenow. It being the rule hereabouts to journey in company if you can, and not at all, it would seem, if you cannot, my landlord at the Green Boar arranged for me to travel on to Lauenberg with a carter, a transporter of hides.

Which had made for an aromatic start to his adventures, to say the least.

*Indeed, Mr Watts, my own linen still at moments reacquaints
me with that particular aroma, of new leather and old meat.*

No, thinks Rafe. He scratches this through. Not at all the
style in which a knight errant should present himself, as stinking
of the tannery.

*After much delay in Lauenberg I was at last directed toward a
wagoner, who (for an amount more in keeping with the charge
for a seat in the Lord Mayor's carriage) was willing to add me
to the travellers he was taking as far as Hagenow. You find me
therefore one of seven, not including our wagoner—*

All of whom again have a particular aroma of their own.
Before him are two thick-set youths, who remind him of
Belle's clod-hopping brothers and who are heavily scented
with manure; beside them a thin, unhappy-looking fellow,
with shadowed cheeks, who partakes almost constantly of
camphorous snuff from a thumbnail grown into his personal
scoop; then there is a young mother with her tiny child, who
in her gentleness and care reminds Rafe poignantly at every
glance of Belle; and beside Rafe there is a man who has
introduced himself twice now as Matthias Frink, of Bremen, a
corn-factor. Herr Frink sits with his wife, Frau Frink, who is
pungent with musk. Both have expressed, and more than once,
their distress that the state of the world requires them to travel
with manure, with camphor, and the gentle, whey-like odour
of the nursing mother.

*And it is a very curious thing, Mr Watts, how no-one can see
a man with notebook and pencil, deep in his own thoughts,
without interrupting those same thoughts to enquire what it is
he is writing.*

'London,' says Herr Frink, looking round his fellow travellers to be sure he has their attention before returning his own to Rafe. 'You know Herr Jessop, I am sure?'

'I regret not,' Rafe replies. 'London –' (he finds himself sketching his city's dimensions in the air) '– London is a place of many souls, and I know only the smallest number.'

Herr Frink's eyebrows rise. 'Herr Jessop is a great corn merchant,' he explains. 'A great corn merchant. Of Norwich.'

'There you have it,' Rafe explains. 'You see, Norwich is one place, and London another. And I have never been to Norwich, although I hear it is a fine city.' The eyebrows rise yet higher. 'Cambridge,' Rafe offers. 'Cambridge I know.'

'He does not know Herr Jessop,' Herr Frink confides to his wife.

'*Ach,*' she replies, shaking her head.

The camphor-scented gentleman leans forward. 'You must write of the terrible army,' he informs Rafe.

'Yes,' Rafe agrees. 'I do. The Emperor and the Swedish, both. I will.'

The man shakes his head. 'Not of the Swedish. Nor of the Emperor.' He leans yet further forward, bringing the smell of camphor with him. 'Our army of the dead!'

'Ah, yes,' says Rafe. 'The armies of the dead, I was told of them in Hamburg.' Disappointment clouds his neighbour's visage.

'And of the raising of the mysterious mists,' Rafe adds.

The camphorous one opens his mouth, raises a finger. '*And* of the hard men,' Rafe puts in.

The finger droops. The mouth closes.

'Has 'e heard of what the Devil do?' one youth asks the other. His companion turns to Rafe. ''Ave you 'eard what the Devil do?'

'Very probably,' says Rafe. *He sends unwanted companions to plague the hard-working writer with their interruptions, Mr Watts.*

''E waits, you see,' the youth continues. ('So he does,' says the other.)

''E waits until 'e finds a traveller on 'is own.' ('Minding his business, like,' the other puts in.)

'An' then 'e offers 'im a bargain. A great pig, say, or some other fine thing. And 'e sells it 'im –' ('This traveller,' the other youth puts in, helpfully.)

'For nothing, do you see? Or almost nothing. And then 'e 'as 'im.'

'How does he have him?' Rafe enquires.

'Why, 'e 'as 'is soul!' The youth sits back. Tut-tuts of horror and exclamations surround him. 'D'you see, that man is *curse*-ed now.'

'But why is he?' Rafe asks.

'A'cause – a'cause of this accursed thing as 'e 'as bought. And the only way to lift the curse is 'e must sell whatever fine thing 'e 'as bought for even less.' A nodding of the head. 'Sprite-us – sprite-us famlus, is what it's called.'

'*Spiritus familiaris?*' Rafe suggests.

'That's it! Sprite-us famlus. You write that in yer book.'

Truly, Mr Watts, whatever else this war may generate, its greatest product must without doubt be its stories.

The young mother, in her world of two, looks up, gives him the sweetest, blankest smile, adjusts her shawl over the head of her infant and the curve of her breast, and goes on with her nursing.

The wagoner gives a cheery shout. 'Here we are, good souls, safe and sound and the Lord keep you so. Hagenow.'

Hagenow, Mr Watts. The war has not left much of Hagenow.

Shops, there are but three. Inns, but one, and Rafe its only guest, as far as he can judge. He asks, is there a posting inn?

and the landlord takes him outside, turns him about, and points down the street, where is—

What must, from its great burned gable, and its diamond-paned windows (all now peeled from their frames and leaning out over the street), have been another inn, one time.

'But what happened to it?' he asks, and the landlord answers, 'Well now, young gentleman, we has this thing, I don't know what you'd call it, but we has this thing we call a *war*.'

So much for Hagenow. Walking the town (there being nothing else to do) Rafe encounters an immense, black-painted carriage, like a strong-room on wheels; its timbers studded, its windows covered and grilled, with two great horned oxen being backed into its traces, bellowing and tilting their heads. There is also a considerable number of armoured horsemen, with a sort of braggarty loudness to them, all curvetting about it in the road. An enormous flag is being wielded at their head; as Rafe crosses the street it unfurls: one half black Habsburg eagle, one half a dripping scarlet heart, on a field the colour of mustard. He wanders closer, and one of the guards sees him watching. 'Hey, you!' comes the shout. 'You fuck the fuck off the way you come, or it'll be the worse for you!'

Rafe returns to his solitary room. It occurs to him that he has had enough, for the time being, of his fellow man. It occurs to him that no matter what the traveller's tales, it might be a very pleasant thing to journey on tomorrow on his own.

THE OLD SALT ROADS, thinks Rafe. The Old Salt Roads. He likes the words, their feel in the mouth, the sense of human permanence they evoke. He likes the roads as well, which are excellent indeed, great square cobblestones runnelled with the passage of wheels innumerable over the passage of years immeasurable. They remind him of the ancient pavement unearthed beneath

London's Guildhall; from the times of the Caesars, so the antiquaries said, when Joseph of Arimathea brought the Holy Thorn to England. Might these roads be as ancient as they? He finds he has a sharper interest in such matters since coming into Germany, a greater sense of the history of all folk, in fact. It is surprising how comforting this is. *The way we do go on*, Rafe thinks – leaving our works behind us, no matter what almighty conflicts slice their way through our lives, on and on and on. Like to this road, in fact: the clear straight path behind and that in front, showing the way as sure as a line ruled across the page of an atlas. Up this slope, down that. There is a breeze. There are just enough clouds to keep the sun from becoming oppressive.

Dear Mr Watts, he begins, in his head. This is something else that delights him, how well the business of walking and that of writing consort together. A step, a word; a mile, a page.

Dear Mr Watts
    You must forgive the trivial nature of today's notes, but beyond the great pleasure a man may take in his own company, I have little to offer you.

All the same, when he set off from Hagenow, being the solitary traveller for quite so many hours is not how he had envisioned the day. Would the road to Schwerin truly be as empty as this? Has he mistaken his way? He is also disconcerted to see how low the sun has fallen in the sky. He will not reach Schwerin today.

Very well, Rafe tells himself. He has food in his pack – bread, sausage, even (carefully rationed in his flask) a little remaining of the Green Boar's schnapps. The weather is fine, it is dry, the breeze not cold at all. He is a true knight errant, he is lord of himself, he is the hero of his tale. All he need do now is find some sensible and sheltered place in which a knight errant might spend the night.

And there it is! Just such a place, what in England he would call a shepherd's bothy. He walks up to its door, peers inside. Espies a mossy floor of verdant green.

Rafe settles himself in a corner, his pack for a pillow, draws up his knees and drapes his jacket over them. *Why, this is not so bad,* he tells himself, *this is endurable.* He makes his modest supper, and allows himself to finish the schnapps. He is sure Perceval would approve. And tomorrow Schwerin will await him, and so too, back in London, will Mr Watts; and there, he reminds himself, there is Belle, the prize at the end of his quest and every step he takes is one that slowly completes the circle back to her. What, compared to that, is one night spent out of doors?

He takes out Belle's picture, as he always does, presses it to his lips. 'Good night, my love,' he whispers, and feels the familiar frisson and rise in his loins as he does so, in anticipation of the night when he may turn to her for real. But no. Perceval, he is quite sure, did not do *that.* Instead he arranges himself, curled on his side, jacket over his shoulders, head on his hands. He sleeps.

He wakes. He wakes disordered. He is unable to place himself. Why is he wet-through on his uppermost side... why is everything around him wet, in fact? And why is everything grass and weeds?

Ah – he begins to come back to himself. This light is dawn. This wet is dew. He is in Germany, and something has jumbled through his dreams all night, some great unhappiness, that is why he feels so muddled now. It had been something to do with the road...

Yes, something to do with the road. There had been a press of people on it, pale-limbed, blank of face, and as he stood watching them, some trick of the landscape had the wind sough all about him in such a manner as to almost replicate the sound of weeping. And there at the top of the field had been another building, a sort of chapel, perhaps, with a narrow pathway leading through the grass and weeds to its door, and he had understood that the people, who had all suddenly vanished from the road, were instead to be found inside it. And what had seemed to be the wind was now the up and down of song!

In his dream he had climbed the path; the music – yes, it was surely music – growing more distinct with every step. He had been confident that the moment he opened the door, everything would be resolved. And he had opened it—

And the music had stopped at once. Not a sound. And nothing inside, nothing – not pew, not pulpit, only this empty, bare-walled space, with a pool of black water on the floor where the rain had got in.

Now Rafe shakes his head. He wants these images gone from it. He makes to get to his feet—

'*Oh!*' he groans. 'By the *bowels* of *Christ!*'

He is entirely unprepared for how entirely unsuited the human body is to sleeping on the ground. His whole left side feels as if it has been tenderized, like beefsteak. His fingers are stiff with cold, and his right hand must have fallen into contact with a nettle, and itches like the very devil. His jacket has left his shoulders overnight, and the dew has soaked him as it has every other thing within this – this – what is this? He had thought it was a shepherd's hut, but now he sees it is a ruin, an absolute ruin, the walls all tumbled and booby-trapped with nettles and bramble, what is more. He staggers to his feet, stumbles through what was its doorway, eases himself upright as painfully as if he were rusted.

He is mortally ashamed of himself for doing so, but the first thing he does is look up to the top of the field, to see if, as in his dream, there is a building there.

Of course there is not.

He puts a hand to the back of his neck. Yes, he remembers now. In his dream he had closed the door, and as he did so, it had felt as if some agency was helping to close it from the inside. And that pool of black water on the floor – even to think of it sets off a shudder.

Oh, come now, he tells himself, sternly. A man who lets his fancies get the better of him on such a quest as this is lost indeed. *Good Lord*, he thinks, *look at me. My hands are all a-shake. Sort yourself out, man.* Next, it will be a stranger offering him a pig for sale, at bargain price!

He is brushing what he fervently hopes is no more than mud from the sleeve of his jacket when he hears the clop of hooves.

Rafe is again the only upright thing that he can see. There are no other travellers upon the road, no livestock in any of the fields, yet the clop-clop grows steadily louder. He turns about and there, breasting the road, come the ears, the blinkered head, of a horse, pulling an open-sided wagon behind it, of the sort that at home might be piled high at harvest-time. Only this one is empty.

It comes closer. The horse – stolid, hairy, a proper Dobbin – seems to have no interest in anything other than the ground beneath its muzzle. Clop-clop, on it goes, solid plod by solid plod, one to the left, one to the right, oblivious of its passage through this empty landscape. Should he make it stop, Rafe wonders, take a hold of its bridle, wait for some owner to appear? Or is it a local horse, knows full well its way, the business that it is about?

He comes up to the wagon, close enough to look in.

There is straw across the bottom of the wagon. It is—

Stained. It is—

Pinkish.

Rafe's mind begins rotating images of the carts he has seen in Smithfield market, back in London, those left outside St Bartholomew's after the butchery of the day is done. He thinks of that he travelled in only yesterday. But this is not the same wagon, nor the same horse, no, this is not the same at all. He is looking; he is trying not to look. His mind is fleeing from such a thing; his mind is attempting to make sense of it. He seems to hear again that soughing of the wind. *But this need not be human blood*, he tells himself; *no, why should this be human, it might be any number of other things else.* The horse is simply plodding home, the owner of the cart might any minute come puffing over the hill in pursuit of it; might be somewhere out there sleeping, just as Rafe was himself, only moments ago. He looks back to where the cart has come from – no, the fields there are as untouched as that in which he stands: sadly tangled and weed-strewn but no sign of disorder, damage, indeed there is no sign of anything. The horse plods on. The wind soughs, that strange broken sob. Rafe is left standing there.

Something small drops from the back of the wagon, to the road. Rafe bends toward it – he cannot help himself.

It is the tiny shoe of a child.

CHAPTER EIGHT

A Little Bird

'... to play the roguing Gypsy, to wander up and down the country, roguing and cheating with telling Fortunes, as Gypsies do.'

Giovanni Florio, *Queen Anna's New World of Words*

AH, HERTZBERG. SHE may not have quite the beauties of Paris, but she is just as beloved by some. The road in along the river, thinks Ravello, dreamily, where the air is so thick with the malty, lemony aromas from the Rauchmann Brewery that it has you licking your lips. Her market square, her famous Mermaid Clock, the bosomy mermaid herself, whose noontime appearance the crowd beneath, in the marketplace, never fails to greet with lusty cheer. His room at the Golden Oak, his faithful room (as Ravello thinks of it): the bed made up afresh for him with a sprig of rosemary left on the pillow, and the shadows of the leaves of the Golden Oak itself, dancing their dance of the seven hundred tiny veils across the matting on the floor. And best of all, after such a journey as he has endured, and is enduring – hands slick with rain, his horse steaming with it, and some kind of defect, just revealed, in the crown of his hat – best of all, supper at Fat Magda's. Knuckle of pork that falls off the bone if you but stare at it; crackling as explosive as shrapnel; Magda's famous salt-raised bread, the crumb so chewy and resilient you have to pull it apart with your thumbs; and a jug of Rauchmann's famous doppelbock to wash it all down with, dark as a moorland stream, strong enough to take your legs away. And time to reminisce. Dissect the doings of the war with Mesdames Magda and Paola, perhaps; catch up with those two youthful oddities Jo-Jo and his sister Ilse, see how life has been treating them. Ah, Hertzberg.

But, this is not she. No, this is Forbach. Which has but two points of interest for the weary traveller: one, its hospital (and how prescient were those Franciscans, thinks Ravello, to site their hospital here, where so many must at one time or another have contemplated the journey before them, felt that falling of the spirits and decided No, not another step); and two, its border crossing into Germany. Forbach. One of those places where the gods release their spleen (not to mention this pestilentially inconstant weather): there are always delays, there is always annoyance, one always arrives here later than hoped, and with your inner reserves reduced to naught. And just to make being here even more dispiriting, there is the line of folk Ravello sees trudging toward him, out of Germany, like a slow leak. How is he meant to do this? The closer he has got to the border, the more impossible the task has seemed.

Serve you right, says Balthasar, in his thoughts – Balthasar who spent weeks in that same hospital, nearly died in it. *And if you've caught your death, I'll be waiting for you there, as well.*

The storm, having soaked all those beneath it, departs, behind the many towers of Forbach's castle. Ravello's horse gives itself a shake; his stomach gives a growl; somewhere in the marketplace behind him, someone begins dinging a handbell. A cry reaches his ears: 'The famous Pilgrim Players! The Pilgrim Players of London! Here for one night only!' And then the same in French, or a sort of French at any rate, and then for good measure, in German too. Dong, ding, dong. Of a sudden, Ravello's gloom reverses itself. No, enough. One night more on such a quest will make no difference whatsoever. Supper for him, a stable for his poor soaked steed, and the diversion of a play.

An hour later, belly somewhat appeased (not Fat Magda's roast pork, more's the pity, but a decent meal of herb soup and fried fish), he lets his feet guide him back to the marketplace. The players have gathered quite a crowd, although to Ravello this looks likely to owe as much to bafflement as to appreciation. The stage displays a young lad, in a woman's nightdress and a string wig painted yellow, lying down upon a cloth painted with rough stripes of varying blues. His clasped hands hold flowers at his breast. Is the boy meant to be dead? Is he, in fact, meant to be a beauteous maiden? Ravello's attention is also taken by the actual maiden stood to the side of the stage, strumming the saddest of laments on her guitar; a wonderfully plump and pretty fair-haired English rose. Then another figure arrives on stage, clad all in black, strides back and forth and left to right, declaiming. It produces a skull from behind its back, and begins to address the skull. The audience hoots with laughter at such antic behaviour. *Ah*, thinks Ravello, *Hamlet!* And at that moment, feels a hand slip into his pocket.

Some years before, when still under the sunny skies of Italy, Ravello's duties had included acting as escort to an English *milord* – a milord his eminent employer believed would be helpful in frustrating the ridiculous scheme, then much noised about, of marrying the heir to the throne of England to a daughter of the King of Spain. The English prince (now the English King) had finally been decently married to a sister of King Louis himself, so all had ended well enough; meantime back in Italy Ravello had found himself assisting the milord in acquisitions for his art collection: coins, gems, paintings, sculpture, and a curious book of drawings, the work of one Leonardo of Vinci, retrieved from the palace of the unhappy Duke of Sforza. One of these drawings in particular had stayed with Ravello – a soldier, very old, indeed antique, surrounded by four figures, all grotesque, one of whom reads his fortune in his palm while another, behind him, steals his purse. It had been a shock to him to realize that these four hideosities were intended as Roma; perhaps why the drawing has remained so clear in his memory. But it is exactly that stealthy movement he now feels taking place behind his back. He spins about. At the same moment he thrusts his hand into his pocket to see what has gone from it, only to find not a lack, but an addition. He draws the small object out, and finds himself staring at—

– the tiny model of a bird.

To anyone else, it would seem they had been the butt of some child's prank, but to Ravello this means something very different indeed. This, to Ravello (the walnut-shell body, acorn head, the single sparrow feathers as wings), means that far from him finding his Roma, his Roma have found *him*.

He looks into the crowd. On stage behind him, Hamlet informs his audience, who have maybe a dozen words of English between them, that there's a divinity that shapes their ends, whether they like it or not. *How right you are*, Ravello thinks. Before him, at the edge of the crowd, he sees a woman who meets his stare with her own bold gaze, raises the brocade collar of her jacket between her fingers, and thus, bids him follow. Easing his way through the audience (now cheering Hamlet along in a swordfight), he follows in her wake.

She leads him across the square. The *Ooooh!* of the crowd grows faint. She leads him down a narrow twitchel, behind the houses, down toward the river. Then down a set of stairs, and along the bank of the river itself. So garlanded is she with silver that even above the sound of the water he can hear her necklaces and bangles move across each other. The two sounds meld. He calls out, 'Yuna – where are we going? Where are you leading me?' and even as the words leave his mouth she turns, and he sees down there by the water the camp, the tents, the fires. A man, standing – red hair, tasselled cap hiding his missing ear. Rufus. And beside Rufus his brother, Benedicte, getting to his feet with the gentle caution of the blind.

Yuna waits for him to come up to her. 'We were ever ahead of all of you,' she says. She sounds amused. 'Come. We will take you to the one you seek.'

CHAPTER NINE

Between the Lion and the Eagle

'Behold here as in a Glass the mournful face of a sister Nation, now drunk with misery...'

Philip Vincent, *The Lamentations of Germany*

Dear Mr Watts—

The line of folk shuffles forward. Rafe feels himself nudged onward, as he has felt himself nudged before, by the lumpish youth behind him. Or rather, by the goat attached by a length of twine to the lumpish youth behind him. He tries again—

Dear Mr Watts
You find me here at last in Schwerin—

'*Guter Herr*,' he exclaims, turning round, 'I cannot move forward any further than I have. I cannot move forward any faster than I am. I can do nothing to improve your, or my, position here.' *Other than wring your wretched goat's blasted neck.*

The youth stares back at him. It seems to Rafe his words have made about as much impression as water does, moving round a rock. The goat, having sampled the edge of Rafe's coat, now nibbles at his satchel. Rafe's feet continue aching. The line of folk continues sweating in the sun. Schwerin has closed its gates, reinforcing this decision with a line of halberd-wielding sergeants-at-arms, and is admitting travellers one by one through a tiny door in the gate-tower to the left. Rafe can remember being taken to see such guards linking arms and blocking off the streets to the Tower (and more to the point, its armoury), when old King James died – 'No good will come of it, treating those who live here in such fashion,' his father had said, loudly, bravely, but even so, then the guards had still been part of London, part of home. Here, they strike Rafe as something very different.

The goat nudges him again. Behind it and its lumpish keeper, a fellow of vast proportions driving before him a sow of equal hugeness, piglets squealing under her enormous teats. Then a milkmaid follows, with her cow. More snorting, squealing swine and then another of those enormous oxen, which every so often lifts its head and deafens them all with its bellow, while the yokel at its head, unaffected, leans back against its massive shoulder, rolling a straw back and forth in his mouth. This, Rafe imagines, must be how Japheth felt, waiting to lead Noah's menagerie into the ark; Japheth, who the scholars say was the progenitor of all the peoples of Europe, so far back it was before the years were even counted, and now here we are again, abandoning our homesteads, herding ourselves and any animal we can save into our little towns, terrified of anything beyond their walls. He wonders dully if the enlargement of this thought might prove wordily fruitful.

Dear Mr Watts—

Another nudge. 'Sir!' Rafe begins in protest, turning about, at which the boy points at the door and announces, 'It's you next.'

Why so it is.

The room beyond the door (and Schwerin visible beyond that – Schwerin with all its promise of a bed for the night, of hot food, of a bowl in which to soak his burning feet) holds a table bearing taper, wax, seal, and ink in three different bottles, carefully demarcated: red, green, black; and a pile of paper cut into narrow strips. Sat behind all these a gentleman who bears on his chest an almighty bronze medallion of the town itself. A town clerk. A gatekeeper. A man who in this little world is God. 'Your name, sir?'

'*Ich heisse* Rafe Endicott,' Rafe begins. He is preparing to spell it out, as he had done in Hamburg, Lauenberg, Hagenow… 'Eeeya, enna, deeya…'

The man stares back at him. 'You are from where?' he asks, tilting his head to fix Rafe with his eye and revealing the fact that he has the most oddly off-centre front teeth.

'London. England.' Rafe begins searching in his doublet. 'I have here papers, for my business in Germany—'

'Your business?' the man repeats. 'You are Englander?' The eye is goggling. 'What is your business here?'

An excellent question. What should he call his business here in Germany? He looks up, and out, into Schwerin itself, and at the eager crowd gathered there, heads bobbing this way and that; waiting, presumably, for the latest news, or to greet friends and family – and he has neither.

'I am a writer,' Rafe begins. He finds himself attempting a vague mime – see, here, my one hand is my paper, this other, a pen. 'I write, I report, I record, this war. Your war. I send news of it back to England…' His voice dies away.

'You record this war? You send news of it? Reports? To whom? For why?'

Of a sudden, Rafe sees where this might go. A shriek of *SPY!* and one of those sergeants from outside will be in here; there will be the blade of a halberd at his throat. 'No, no,' he begins, 'I was unclear in my explanation. My apologies—'

The gatekeeper leans back from the table. Rafe can see the screech building in the man's throat. Those folk at the townward door have sensed something too, are peering in – and then there is a man elbowing his way through them, a man in a steep-crowned hat, tall as a sugar-loaf (very different to Rafe's own sat-upon pancake), who exclaims in German, 'Ah! Most finally you are here! My beloved!' and seizes Rafe by the hand. The stranger turns to the man behind the desk. 'My beloved,' he begins. 'No, my apologies – I mean of London, my friend.' Rafe, amazed, begins. 'No, no, I fear you are mistook—' and the stranger kicks him in the ankle.

'My friend,' the man repeats. He gives Rafe a look that is both hotly eager and full of warning. He turns to the gatekeeper. 'My friend of London,' he repeats, in the same appalling German as before.

The gatekeeper peers from Rafe to this stranger, who is now pumping Rafe's arm. 'You will vouch for this man, Herr Fincent?' the gatekeeper asks.

'Yes, yes, of course! My friend of London! My most important friend!'

The gatekeeper gives Rafe one more narrow look, then, moving ink and seal before him, signs across a paper in black ink, stamps across the signature in red, puts one mark in green in the margin, folds and seals the whole with wax, holds it out to Rafe and says, 'One night. Then you must present your papers here again to me.'

'Of course, of course!' the stranger replies. He claps an arm about Rafe's shoulders. 'Well now, my friend! To have you here it is so good!'

Rafe makes to take the paper. The man draws it back. 'And for one night,' the man says, holding out his other hand, 'we will take from you one schilling.'

The Black Bull at Schwerin – at last. A prosperous-looking house, with pillared doorway and that yellow-and-black of the posting inn set up above the gate to its yard. Certainly prosperous enough to be able to produce a basin of hot water, in which its newest guest might soak his feet, but it seems this same guest must dine first, with his rescuer. 'Emmanuel Vincent,' the man had said, in English, his arm lodged round Rafe's shoulders as he hurried Rafe onward through the streets. 'Emmanuel Vincent. Delighted to make your acquaintance, sirrah. Well, well, you never know who will arrive here next!'

Emmanuel Vincent now sits opposite Rafe at a table at a window, facing out toward the street. Rafe is momentarily reminded of his last evening with Cornelius, at the Mitre Tavern – or would be, were it not that also sharing the table are Henricus Anderman, of Antwerp, and Theodore Brunner, of Brussels.

On the other side of the window sit a family of Schwerin's beggars; the father staring at his feet, the children in their mother's lap, cupped hands extended, pleading for alms. It occurs to Rafe that if these had been livestock brought in from the fields, rather than people come from some ruined village, they would have been fed and watered, stabled, bedded down by now. For all the radical nature of some of those tracts he translated as a sizar, Rafe's own politics remain of the very gentlest sort, but it seems to him that for a town so clearly making a very good thing out of this war, Schwerin might be more charitable to those the war has left strewn along its streets.

Cambridge, good God, he thinks. It seems extraordinary that it was he, the same person, who was there as sits here now.

Emmanuel Vincent has ordered supper: a roast capon, a dish of peas and fatty, smoky bacon, chopped up small and cooked, somewhat strangely but not unpleasantly, with pear; also a jug of beer, which Rafe has half-emptied already. Until the food appeared, he'd had no idea how ravenous he had become, as if his body had temporarily given up on all idea of sustenance as a bad lot. Mindful again of those poor souls starving outside, he hopes he is not making a glutton of himself. Also, he is very much aware of his own dusty, unshaven, unwashed state, compared to the crispness of his companions.

'So,' says Emmanuel Vincent, dabbing a finger, cowled in his napkin, to his mouth. 'Another chronicler of our sad times. Another Englander, to boot!' His fine hat, complete with flashy hatband, sits on his knee, rather as if it were some expensively collared pet. 'I must look out for you, Friend Endicott,' he continues. 'Perhaps you will prove to be a rival.' The tone is jocular, but Rafe has the sharp and instant intuition that this probe into him and his doings is being poked in earnest. Is this why he was rescued at the gate, so that he might be interrogated?

'Yes,' he says, carefully, 'I suppose that is what I am. A chronicler, indeed.'

Emmanuel Vincent's hot dark eye grows hotter yet. He exchanges glances with Anderman and Brunner. He makes a little beckoning gesture. More!

'I am employed by Nathaniel Butter,' Rafe informs them. 'Nathaniel Butter and Mr William Watts. They have sent me to report upon the war. They plan a coranto—'

'Ah, a coranto! An English coranto!' Anderman leans forward. 'I am so employed also by my father, Herr Endicott,' Anderman says, in courteous if imperfect English. A glance to his left, where Brunner is busily emptying the dish of peas. 'Theodore is so by his godfather, Abraham Verhoeven. We all are chroniclers. The same so you.'

Rafe can just imagine the fury this information would engender back in London. Rival corantos... and from Antwerp and Brussels, as well, both of which are Catholic, and can only mean these are corantos supporting the Imperialists. The troops of Torquato Conti, in other words. And where does Mr Emmanuel Vincent sit, in such matters?

'My uncle and I,' Vincent is saying, 'we plan a book.' His tone is such that there can be no doubt, compared to this, a coranto is very small beer indeed.

'A book?' Rafe repeats.

'A book.' Vincent sits back, eyes a-shine with anticipation. 'I am to travel all across Germany, collecting all the stories from the war that I can. My uncle would be here himself, and plans to join me, but my aunt is ailing and detains him.' A sigh, and Vincent raises his eyes to heaven. 'Women!' he concludes, in jocular tone, although Rafe would bet the price of that fine hat that Emmanuel Vincent's experience of women extends no further than having his aunt scrub his face with handkerchief and spit.

Theodore Brunner, having chased down the last of the peas and wiped out the bowl with bread, now addresses Rafe, asking, 'There is news from Hamburg? There are stories you have heard, perhaps?'

'I am afraid I have discovered very little,' Rafe begins. 'All I have at present are the usual tall tales...'

Three pairs of eyes focus themselves upon him at once. 'The usual tall tales,' Rafe repeats, at something of a loss. 'Armies that transport themselves by means of magical mists. Or armies of the dead,' he continues, seeking to make light of it. 'The old legend of the *spiritus familiaris*. And of the men who cannot be harmed by any weapon made of metal—'

'Those who wear the silver wolf,' Anderman comments, sagely. 'Yes, we have heard much talk of them.'

Says Brunner, 'There are men, now, out there, east of us, whose horses they have wings.'

'Indeed?' comments Anderman. 'That I had not heard.'

'Yes, indeed,' says Brunner, gravely, nodding his head. 'I was told this only yesterday. No force will go near them.'

'Dear me!' Rafe exclaims, merrily. 'And there was I, imagining the worst I would face out there were the men who were bullet-proof!'

His companions turn to him. They seem to be entirely at a loss. 'But surely you cannot believe such stories!' Rafe begins. 'It must be obvious to any man of sense that such are simply part of the disorder of the times—'

'You will go out beyond Schwerin?' Anderman asks, wonderingly. 'Why? How?'

'*Why*,' Rafe replies, with a little heat, 'because I am here to gather actual fact, not foolish rumours, and as to *how*, by finding some other travellers to travel with.'

'Mr Endicott,' Vincent begins, 'those foolish rumours as you call them are the very tales your readers crave. This is what they read us for, to feel their hearts shudder in their breasts. The towns aflame. The peasants, butchered in their hovels. The maidens, violated. With our book, I intend a chapter for each.' He sits back.

'But surely,' Rafe tries, 'it is our duty to sift through such tales, to bring to light the truth in what we hear—'

'Oh, Mr Endicott,' says Vincent, with a sad shake of his head. 'This is Germany. What is truth? Out there –' (he waves an arm) '– anything is possible, even horses with wings. While I have been here, I have been told of talking well-heads, of walls that drip blood, of statues that weep! But the trick, sir, is to let the stories come to you. Wait by the gate, sir, as I do – do not go out there in search of them yourself! What, place yourself between the lion and the eagle? No-one does that. No-one goes further east than here. Utter madness. Nothing has travelled east of here in weeks.'

A boy has appeared at their table. '*Eine Groschen*,' he announces, holding out his hand. No-one else moves. Anderman looks at his plate; Brunner looks at Rafe. Vincent is suddenly occupied with brushing his fine hat.

'Well,' says Rafe, digging in his pocket, 'I thank you for your good advice, gentlemen, but I feel I must at least make the attempt.' He drops a groschen into the boy's grubby palm. A small high voice a-yelping in his head tells him that he has just paid out the equivalent of a day's London wages on a single meal. 'Wittstock,' he concludes. 'That is my next destination. And if I discover anything of account *out there*, I will of course endeavour to let you know.'

The boys bites the coin, inspects the result, deposits it in the pocket of his apron, holds the hand out anew. 'Each,' he says.

The Black Bull lodges Rafe in a room above its yard. It greets his question as to whether there might be any letters waiting for an Englishman with blank-faced bafflement, but it provides a basin of hot water, in which Rafe soaks his feet until he can separate sock from blister, and a bed with a mattress; albeit sheets and pillow, he is informed, will be extra. Rafe tips himself back upon the mattress as it is. His spirit seethes within him. No, he will not be deterred. He will not lurk and fatten here. (*Three groschen? For one meal?*) He will get himself out there, he will uncover such things as will have Anderman and Brunner and Vincent reporting *him*.

He hears Vincent's voice down in the yard, exclaiming, 'Pulled from their graves? How many?'

But what if Vincent is correct? What if, truly, there is nothing travelling east from here? Can he journey on alone? Perhaps he should buy a horse. Does he know *how* one buys a horse? And how much should one pay? Those twenty pounds – what riches he had thought them, what security, and now it seems the entire universe is bent on separating him from them, bit by bit; the wagon to Hagenow, a bed there, a bed here, his suppers... Is this – can he do this? Does his heart quail simply because – well, because, or should he heed its warnings?

Something is digging into his back. He grubs around in his pocket. It is the tiny shoe. He holds it up before his eyes. Yes, now he understands why he had picked it up off the road, why he had brought it with him – not from any hope of uniting it with its wearer, but because the tiny shoe, in its way, is truth.

Dear Mr Watts
　　Schwerin, I find, is not a place to tarry. I will push on to
Wittstock with all the speed I can—

From outside in the yard, where he has already been dimly aware of the neighing of horses and the crunch of wheels, a shout: 'Get out of it! You shit-spat beggars out the Devil's arse, here ain't no place for you!'

Rafe sighs, gets to his feet, goes limping to the window. *I am*, he thinks, *so very tired of noise*. To his amazement, he sees it is dawn. He must have slept. And there at the gate to the Black Bull's yard, an altercation of that ugly type he feels might well be Schwerin's speciality: a man – a soldier, unmistakably, in helmet, back- and breastplate – manhandling a child half his size. The boy appears to have been trying to evade the man's grasp by shinning up a drainpipe; or perhaps the man had caught him in the act, and is now pulling him back toward the ground. The boy raises his arms, hands curved in threat: Rafe sees the boy's long fingernails are filed to points, like claws. A defiant hiss of fury, then he twists in the man's grip and escapes. '*Fucken* gyppos,' the man is saying, as he comes back into the yard. 'Worse than the fucken *kikes*.'

But that same great black closed carriage from Hagenow, that is down there too.

Rafe pulls on his stockings, squeezes his feet into his shoes, throws everything he has into his pack, clatters downstairs and out into the yard. 'Hi!' he calls.

The soldiers, gathered round the carriage, stare back at him. 'Whose arms are those?' he calls, indicating the dripping heart, the mustard-yellow flag.

He who had been manhandling the boy, who might be the captain, Rafe supposes, from the extra cord upon his sleeves, replies, "Is Grace the Prince-Bishop of Prague!' For good measure he then adds, 'Fuck off!'

'Do you have room for another passenger?'

'No fucken passengers 'ere,' comes the reply.

Rafe digs into his pack. He thinks he knows what counts in Schwerin. He holds out a golden guinea, flashing in the light. 'Where are you headed?' He cannot let this chance go by. 'I will travel a-top, if I must!' He tilts the coin again, and marvelling at his own ingenuity adds, 'One now, and another from my – from those awaiting me.' Of a sudden it had felt like no bad thing to imply that he has friends expecting him. Who is this new Rafe Endicott whose mind finds routes so speedily, along such unaccustomed roads? 'Gentlemen, please – your destination. Where do you go?'

There is a snarling consultation. There is much pointing toward the carriage, as if it were worthy of some particular consideration. Then, 'Hoffstein,' comes the reply.

Hoffstein? The name means nothing. 'Will you pass by Wittstock?'

An exchange of glances between the soldiers. 'Nearer'n you are here,' one offers.

'Then, gentlemen,' Rafe announces, 'I believe we have a deal!'

DEAR MR WATTS, Rafe begins, in his head. Plod, plod go the oxen, left to right the carriage lurches. Where Rafe sits, on its roof, the motion is horrendous. He finds he must fix his eyes on the horizon, as he did on the *Guid Marie*. Also there is some

persistent knocking, some sort of percussion from within the carriage, a steady tap-tap-a-tap coming from beneath him, through
its roof. Would a little conversation serve as a welcome distraction
from it and his nausea, both? He fixes the soldier riding alongside
to his right with what he hopes is a pleasing smile.

'Do you know Hoffstein yourself? I had not heard of it.'

The man stares at him a moment. 'Ho yes,' he says. A snigger.
'See Hoffstein and die, mates, ain't that what they say?'

Laughter, all about him. Rafe has no idea what it is he has
said. He fixes his eyes once more on the horizon.

*Dear Mr Watts, here I be, where precisely I know not, but
headed for Wittstock.*

I see a body of water up ahead. I see a field.

I see a dead horse in the field.

The horse lies facing downhill, front legs curled beneath it,
like a cat's. Its eye sockets regard the landscape before it with
calm sagacity, even as a crow stalks along its backbone and
nettles grow through its ribs. *This is where it lived*, thinks Rafe
(lurch to the left, lurch to the right), *this is perhaps the field in
which it was born and here it died.* He finds a sort of solace, both
peculiar and melancholy, in the thought. And there at the top
of the field, the house of its owner, also an empty ruin, its own
bones on display.

And there in the ditch at the side of the road, a bundle of
rags, which some instinct Rafe never knew he possessed before
registers as what it is, then has him look away.

*Dear Mr Watts, here I be, crossed over into this strange country
called The War. Where the dead watch over the living.*

The road dips. The horses turn sideways, the oxen plod
on; Rafe finds that he must grab the sides of the roof, brace

himself not to go spilling off it altogether. Now he sees a milestone, a marker. He scrambles to the side of the roof, peers down and reads—

WITTSTOCK
80

Very strange, but there is what appears to be a small black dog curled up beside the milestone, lying in the long grass, tail over nose. It is quite the most contented-looking creature Rafe has seen in days.

He gives a groan, closes his eyes. Another eighty leagues or miles or whatever it is, but another eighty of them, lurching from side to side up here. Tap-tap-a-tap comes that annoying percussion once again. On they go.

The day comes to its end, as it will, as it must. The land on either side of the road begins to change in that way the countryside does at evening. Space contracts; shadows well up from each dip and hollow. Rafe's escort, as he tries to think of them, turn off the road, dismount, plant their flag, tether their horses; leave them to get what sustenance they can from the grass at their feet, make up a fire and sit around it, passing a bottle back and forth. Their conversation is lewd, their presence raucous. Rafe has no desire to join them, so makes a solo camp under a nearby tree. He finds a chunk of dry bread in his pack to chew on. He drains the last of the water from his flask, then this new Rafe Endicott tells him he should refill it for the morrow. He remembers passing over a bridge before they turned off the road, and with care, in the gathering darkness, makes his way back toward the sound of water. There is the bridge; rushes growing at its foot. There, water lilies, cups closed now, held up above the water as they sleep, in the brave moonlight (he hears himself describing it so to Belle) like so many ivory chalices.

And there – good Lord! – as he stoops by the bridge to fill his flask, with water seeping into his shoes, a rustle, and a small black dog comes nosing toward him.

Rafe straightens up. He has no idea what kind of animal one might find out here, but in London, his instinct would be to take care. The dog might be rabid, it might be ferocious, a dog that once earned an honest living and now, with that living taken from it (he thinks of the ruined house), now it has taken to the highway and turned bandit.

The dog sits, scratches, stands up, wags its tail. There are places where its fur has been rubbed away, as on a worn suede glove, and really, it is very small. And very, very thin; its ribs distinct as separate fingers, as if it stands there being offered up by a pair of invisible hands.

Rafe breaks off a small piece of dry bread, holds it out. The dog at once snaps it from his fingers. Rafe breaks off another piece. It disappears as fast.

Rafe, with a sigh, crumbles the last of the bread, scatters it upon the bank, stoppers his flask and goes back to his tree. His escort are silent, or snoring. One man, presumably meant to be on guard, is sat propped by the roadside, but even he has his head lowered, his shoulders rounded in sleep. Rafe tells himself that he is young and hale and that another night spent out of doors amongst such company will make a splendid tale one day. He begins rehearsing it – the tone of voice (that of one now amused by the daredevil follies of his past); the opening phrase – 'Ah, Belle, on such a night as this' (thank you, Master Will). *Think on that*, he tells himself, *think on taking Belle to the theatre as your wife; think on how Henry Kempwick and his players are out there somewhere and by God, if they can survive Germany, so can you.*

Good Lord, there is the dog again. Sniffing at the rear of the great black carriage, out there on the road. Giving an excited little *whuff* or two.

Somehow Rafe does not think his escort will turn out to be kind-hearted men where small creatures are concerned. He goes to the dog, which wags its tail again at his approach. He picks it up (it is light enough to hold in one hand), bids it an urgent *shush!* It turns in his grasp to lick his face. At that moment, from within the carriage, Rafe hears a voice in as urgent a whisper as his own, asking, 'Who is there? For the love of Jesus, who is there?'

In the moonlight one of the oxen gives a snort, stamps a hoof. Rafe looks over at once to where the soldiers lie, to where the guard slumps, but there is nothing, no movement, no answering noise. At the back of the carriage he sees there is a step, as for a footman. It creaks horribly when Rafe climbs onto it, but again, none of the soldiers stir. Above it there is the tiny slit of a window – ungrilled, this one, and when he tries it, its slide slips back.

Standing on the step, he peers down into the carriage. At first in the darkness he can make out nothing at all, then there is movement. For a moment, peering in, Rafe cannot work out what it is he's seeing, then with horror he sees the carriage's occupant is wearing a sort of miniature of the carriage itself upon his shoulders, studded and grilled and locked about his head, from which a pair of eyes stare out, mournful as a whale's.

'Great God!' Rafe exclaims. He starts backwards, almost loses his balance.

A mouth moves within the cage. 'My name is Viktor Lopov,' the mouth continues, urgently. 'I am a prisoner of the Prince-Bishop of Prague. Who are you? Do you have water? Who are you?'

'I am a traveller, an Englishman,' Rafe hisses in reply. A gasp from within. He places the little dog upon the carriage's roof, where it watches Rafe pass his flask through the window.

'Oh, thank you! Thank you! God have mercy!' says the man in the cage, and he drinks; at least he seems to manage to tip something through the contraption around his head. The flask is handed back. The cage is at the window again. 'You must help me,' comes the voice from within. 'You *must* help me. Once we arrive in Hoffstein, I am *dead*.'

'But what can I do?' Rafe asks. The dog is now hanging over the side of the roof and has begun a low growling. It comes to Rafe that the dog is trying to warn him – yes, the guard there, as he casts an anxious glance over his shoulder, he sees a change in outline. The man is stirring.

'You must help me!' comes the voice again, even more desperate than before.

'Yes, yes,' says Rafe. 'I will, I will, but not now. I cannot now!'

He slides the window shut. He hops down, the dog held to him. He jumps back from the carriage, just as the seated soldier rights himself, rubs his face, gazes witlessly over. Rafe, scarce daring to breathe, freezes to the spot. The man subsides back into sleep. Rafe, still holding the dog, tiptoes back to his place by the tree. *Good God, good God*, he thinks. *What to do? What am I to do?*

CHAPTER TEN

Here We Are

'... lay your embuscadoe before the dawning of the day, and place Sentinels in places convenient, where they may be unseen: some on trees, others couched on the ground...'

John Cruso, *Militarie Instructions for the Cavallrie*

THE NEXT DAY dawns, to the unlovely music of his escort readying itself – snarls and curses as they greet each other, snarls and curses as they take their horses down to water them at the stream. He who has the task of watering the oxen, lugging two pails up from the riverbank, stands before them, unbuttons his breeches, takes out his member and pisses over the animal's muzzles as they drink. 'What?' he demands,

as he sees Rafe looking on in horror. 'They love it, don't they?'
Returning his attention to the animals, he tells them, 'We get to
Hoffstein, I'm gonna have *you* roasted, an' I'm gonna have *you*
made into knackwurst. Hah!'

Here is the captain, bellowing something about a rendezvous,
and by God, any man not ready in five minutes will regret it.
Rafe takes a gulp of the morning air, for courage. 'Good day
to you!' he begins. 'I did not introduce myself before. Remiss
of me.' He holds out his hand. 'Rafe Endicott. I am a – a –
traveller abroad, in this your lovely country.'

The captain eyes him for a moment, then says, 'Erlach.
Hauptmann Erlach.' If he has a Christian name, plainly he is not
about to share it. Then, full of suspicions: 'What you got there?'

Rafe had placed the little dog inside his shirt. Something had
warned him, if it was on the ground, either man or horse or ox –
most likely man – would give it a kick. 'Ah, a new companion,'
he says, as the dog sticks its nose up, licks his chin. 'It, er – it
found me. Last night. Down by the water.'

Even greater suspicion in Hauptmann Erlach's eye. 'You
been wandering about?'

'To fill my flask,' Rafe says, hurriedly. He lifts the flask from
his pocket, as evidence. 'But I did notice, from the carriage,
there seemed to be some sound or other. I wondered, is there
someone – are you transporting...' Erlach is glowering at him.
Rafe's voice crumbles in his throat.

Erlach lowers his eyelids, regards Rafe as might a bird of
prey, assessing the panic of some tiny creature beneath. He
leans forward. There is a gust of musty breath so odorous Rafe
almost expects to see mushrooms growing in there, not teeth.
'Listen, you,' Erlach says. 'We don't know you from a fuck'ole
in a fence. There's a lot can happen to travellers out here. A *lot*.
Them friends of yours, it 'ud be a shame if they were all to be
left waiting for nothing, eh? Think on *that*, next time you feel
like wandering about.'

*

It is brutally hot. They pass through woods, and are tormented by flies, along roads so little used for so long that branches rattle along the carriage's sides. They come out of the woods, into a landscape so devastated that the few buildings left within it are mere scattered runs of walls a few bricks high, or corners of nothing, left as if bracing themselves. They pass a church, its tower thrown down and stretched across the ground like the neck of some great dead dragon. They pass by water, a succession of lakes and ponds, and the flies become bloodsuckers. The soldiers curse. Rafe, now walking alongside the carriage, beats at the air about him with his hat. He cannot imagine what the temperature must be like inside the carriage itself. Beside him, one of the guards – he who had so personally watered the oxen – dismounts as well. The two of them are almost in step. *Now*, thinks Rafe, *now say something*, but how to start a conversation, what stratagem to use? He has to find out more about the prisoner, but how?

His heart is beating as fast as if it were angry with him. There is the whirr of a fly past his nose.

This new Rafe instantly reaches up to the shoulder of the man beside him, making a violent brushing motion with his hand. The man jumps, makes as if to draw his sword. 'An insect, sir,' this new Rafe says, explaining. A sunny smile. 'A stinger. I believe it had you in its sights.'

No thanks, but no retaliation, either. 'Your prisoner,' Rafe begins, after another step or two.

'What of 'im?' comes the response.

'Does he have water? Does he not need food?'

A hoot of laughter. 'Missing breakfast is the least of his fucken troubles, believe you me.'

Rafe tries again. 'Who is he? How did he offend?'

'He's a thief, innit,' says the guard, scratching at the back of his neck. 'A lying, cheating thief.'

'Indeed?' says Rafe. 'How dreadful!' He lowers his voice. 'Are you allowed to tell me more?'

The man eyes Rafe sideways, then drops his own voice in turn. 'The Prince-Bishop,' he begins. 'He's about making this mighty cannon, ain't he. Vainglory, its name will be. A work of wonder.' He nods his head for emphasis.

'How splendid!' says Rafe.

'Yea to that. But that – that little runt in there, he's a secretary-man, a paper-pusher, and what he tries to do is fiddle the costs of it.'

'Disgraceful!' says Rafe.

'Yeah, innit,' says the guard. 'And when he was found out, he run, like the guilty sod he is. So then we had to go all aways up country to find 'im, and bring 'im back.'

'Indeed?' says Rafe. 'What perfidy!' *When*, he asks himself, *when did I learn such posturing? Why, I could be on stage myself!*

But the guard is staring at him. 'You what?'

'Perfidy,' Rafe repeats. 'Treachery, deceit. What will become of him now?'

The man leers. 'Hoffstein,' he says, with grisly satisfaction. 'So if I was him,' and now he raises his voice, 'the hours when all I'd to worry about was an empty belly an' a bit of sweat, I'd make the most of them!'

Bringing up the rear, the little dog comes to a sudden halt. Tongue out, it checks to the left and then to the right, gives a sudden *whuff!* and runs up the length of the column, until it gets to Rafe. You'd almost think it had seen something. You'd almost think it thought they were being tracked.

No-one takes any notice of it at all.

On they go. Rafe once again has the dog as his passenger, the small head hanging at his breast. He opens his shirt to give the dog some air, pours water into his palm, smooths it over the dog's muzzle, then over his own face. *Surely*, he thinks, *surely, when we make the rendezvous, we will stop, we will rest!* Now the road is climbing. The trees fall away. They emerge onto a high, wide plain – yellow grassland, with a line of woods on either side and the great bowl of the sky above, harshly blue. The dog gives a final, exhausted *whuff* and settles down, resigned. Above them a skylark dips and soars, dips and soars. Rafe's eyes are watering, a haze of heat gyrating before them; when first he sees it, he thinks it is a scarecrow. But a scarecrow dressed in that same mustard yellow as his escort.

It is staked upright. Flies buzz around it in a frenzy. And hanging from a string about its neck, below the bloodied mouth, a piece of board. And scrawled upon the board, the words—

GEH ZURÜCK

Or as Rafe reads them—

TURN BACK

Carriage and escort sway to an astonished halt. Rafe feels his stomach turn, bile gather in his mouth. His escort cluster round the scarecrow, peering at it, as if it were about to come alive and tell them how this fate had befallen it. It is, apparently, one of those very men with whom they were meant to rendezvous. Erlach, still on horseback, rides round and round, in a fury. 'Who did this?' he demands, as if thinking one of them might know. 'Who did it? Whoever did it, by Christ they'll pay!'

Yes, but who did do this? And where are they? Erlach's men have fallen to a murmuring amongst themselves.

'Peasants!' Erlach declares. 'It'll be fucken peasants, or outlaws, or deserters. Safest thing to do, press on. Press on!'

The decision is made. On they go.

Less than a mile ahead, another signpost waits for them. This one has no head at all. But someone has propped up its

outspread arms with musket-rests, and stretched on a banner
between them—

TURN BACK NOW I DID NOT

The escort hold another conference. It is plain they are of
a mind to take this signpost's advice. Erlach is furious. 'You
spineless rags,' he roars, 'are you men-at-arms or –' (pointing at
Rafe) '– green milk and jelly, such as he? We go on!' He flourishes
his pistol. 'Or any man as won't, he can meet his maker here!'

They go on. Rafe (green milk and jelly) has climbed up onto
the step at the back of the carriage once more, which feels
marginally less perilous than being on the ground. There is
again a banging on that little window. '*Shhhh!*' he tells it. 'Not
now!' A muffled plea from within. 'Not now!' Over the roof of
the carriage he sees there is now something waiting for them in
the middle of the road. A mound of earth, and sticking out of
it, a pair of naked feet, and in between the feet another notice—

TOO LATE

Everything stops. The lark, the wheels upon the road; the
haze of dust, it settles too. The escort look from one man to
another, either dumbfounded or (thinks Rafe) as if they sense
all too clearly they have come to the end of something here.
And as they sit there, out of the sunlit silence comes a voice. A
male voice, young and clear and strong:

> Ein Feste burg ist unser Gott
> Ein gute Wehr und Wa-a-a-ffen

Erlach, at the front, turns his horse, comes galloping back.
'Which of you's singing?' he howls. 'Which of you bastards is
singing?' The banging upon the panel is thunderous. Rafe slides

it back. There is the mouth again. 'Luther's hymn!' it tells him, hoarse with terror. 'That's Luther's hymn!'

'I know!' Rafe hisses down.

'It's the Swedish!' the prisoner all but screams at him. 'They use it! It's their battle song!'

And now it is not one voice singing, but two:

> Er hilft uns frei aus a-al-ler Nott
> Die uns jetzt hat betro-o-offen.

Desperate, Rafe tries to see where the voices are coming from, but there is nothing – nothing but the breeze stroking the grass, the strength of the sun, the brilliant deep green of the trees beyond. His escort – idiotically, it seems to Rafe – are moving forward along the road as if lured by sirens, encouraging each other, calling out 'What do you see?', 'What is it, is it there?' But now the voices are four:

> Der alt böse Feind

And now they are eight:

> mit Ernst er's jetzt meint

And now more, louder and louder, ringing from the trees, the sky:

> GROß MACHT UND VIEL LIST

And more still:

> *SEIN GRAUSAM RÜSTUNG IST*

And more again, a cathedral of voices all about them, and still not a singer to be seen:

> *AUF ERD IST NICHT SEINS GLEICHEN!*

The song ends in a shout that seems to echo back at them from the dome of heaven itself. Then – silence. The breeze across the grasses, the far-off shivering of the leaves upon the trees.

And then, the sound of hooves. At the apex of the road, where iron-hard track meets sky, there appears a single horseman. Rafe hears himself give a gasp. A shout from his escort. They see it too.

The solitary horseman turns his horse about. Up it rears.

The horse has wings.

It charges at them, full-pelt, straight down the road, raising behind it a dust as thick as smoke, and as it charges it seems to pull the other horsemen with it, out of the woods on either side, streaming out from the trees, the horses with their tails flying and their riders shrieking like banshees—

– and now there are men rising from the plain of grass on either side of them as well. Erlach is screaming out orders and his men are pelting back toward the carriage as fast as their horses will carry them, but Rafe's own first impulse is not of fear, it is astonishment. It is almost elation. He has never seen anything to compare to this, the speed of it, the precision – one minute nothing, the next, all this. Then one sorry laggard in the escort, at the back, his horse catches its foot, two of the horsemen streak out from the pack, one to the left, one to the right, their hair as bright and white as candle-flame, spurring their horses on, and they catch him.

It's as if they'd somehow thrown a pot of red paint over him. The man disappears from his saddle as completely as if he had never been.

The world, at this point, explodes.

The pair arrow in on another, catch him, lift him from his horse, over its neck, carry him between them for a yard or two, then he is gone as well. There is a noise like a china plate being snapped, somewhere by Rafe's ear. There is an unearthly, deafening thrumming in the air, a noise that assaults the heart and senses all at once. There is that snapping sound again, and from one of the oxen a great bellow of despair, and all at once the carriage cants to the right. The ox is on its knees. The wheel nearest to it gives a crack, the carriage tilts yet further, then more than tilts. The carriage is going over. A shout of terror from within. Rafe, jumping clear, lands on hands and knees, the dog leaping round him, barking furiously. The ground is like a drumskin, thudding with the hooves of horses, the air is pierced with screams and cries, and still that sound, that deafening, disorienting *THRUM, THRUM, THRUM*. The carriage is on its side on the road; one of the oxen yoked to it is dead, while the other is roaring and tugging at its yoke in frantic attempts to free itself. That snapping noise again – *Ah! A bullet*, thinks Rafe. He has no idea what has happened to the dog. He rolls over, and a horse (ungainly as a cow from underneath) passes right over him, a horse painted blue one side, yellow the other, legs in stripes like a barber's pole, hooves kicking for purchase on the air, rider whooping with triumph. Another shriek from within the carriage, where the door is being assaulted from inside; the prisoner frantically trying to batter his way free. Bent double, Rafe reaches the carriage, clambers on top of it like a shipwrecked mariner climbing up a rock, wrenches at the door. Nothing. Wrenches again. Still the door will not open. Fingers claw at the grille over its window. Rafe shouts, 'Get away! Get away!' and jumps with all his weight on the door, almost falling in as it gives way. A pair of arms reaches out toward him. He grabs them, exhorts, '*Push! Push!*' and the carriage gives birth, tumbling Rafe from on top of it and Lopov from within. Another horseman thunders past. The tail of the horse is scarlet, like a banner, streams like silk; the rider has a great scarlet plait issuing from the top of his head, bouncing along behind him, and his face – his face – his face, good God, it is a *skull*. The two of them, Rafe and Lopov, cling to each other, Lopov still with that outrageous contraption locked about his

head. Riderless horses canter back and forth about them. Rafe
sees one of their escort – the trooper he had spoken to – surface
from the long grass, holding his side, and come staggering
toward them. That pair of horsemen with the bright white
hair are riding back and forth across the road, and shooting
down at anything that moves. Rafe understands their escort is
no more. He understands that where he sees a knee or an arm
raised amongst the grasses, there will be a man, dead or dying,
beneath it. He raises a hand (his left – he will never cease to be
grateful it was his left), yelling at the trooper to come to them,
and as he does there is a terrific concussion all down his arm and
he is flat on his back on the ground. Something is spattering all
about him, like rain. He lifts the arm, and spattering is over his
face. It is warm. 'You've been shot!' Lopov cries. On his knees,
he tries to catch Rafe's waving arm, to fold it against Rafe's
chest. Rafe hears Lopov's voice, the shriek of 'You've been shot!'
but it is as if it is both in his ear and being shouted at him down
a well. He gapes at the hand and sees at once that something
terrible has befallen it, great wrongness: the hand is swelling
like dough, and the middle finger is pouring forth blood like a
hose. A sheet of pain falls over him; the world grows dark. In
desperation he tries to hold onto the one tiny point of light left
at the top of the well, above his head, and suddenly *BANG*, the
cover is lifted off the well and the world roars back in on him.
The trooper is kneeling in front of him, held by the scruff, held
the way a hunter might hold a rabbit, by this enormous youth, a
sort of infant giant, half of whose face is again painted blue, and
half of it gilded yellow. The infant giant throws back its head
and yells something wholly unintelligible to one of its fellows.
It gives the trooper a shake, as if to bring its prisoner to proper
notice. It yells again. There is a sort of buoyancy to its speech,
the phrases lap at each other, like waves. A shouted answer,
in the same extraordinary imbricated tongue. The infant giant
snarls what can only be an oath, whatever language it is in, and

spins the trooper away from him. The man goes sprawling. Now the infant giant peers at Rafe and Lopov – and yells again. Rafe closes his eyes.

He opens them in sun so bright it makes his eyes water, and sees there is now a horse standing over him, a horse with a mane of dark and shining ringlets, like a woman's hair. The dog is barking at it. The horse shrills a whinny at the dog, and the dog, with a squeal, is gone. The horse shakes its head. Bells tinkle in its mane. The front of its skull, the mighty timbering of its breast and legs, have had the bones painted in, in thick white chalk. It is a skeleton horse. It is a creature from a nightmare.

And there is a man leaning over the neck of the horse. The sun is behind him. Something in his grip, shining, metallic, like the head of a snake. 'Oh, Christ!' says Rafe. 'Oh, Christ! God save me!' and registers that he is speaking English, that he will go to meet his maker like the Englishman he is.

The man dismounts, with liquid ease, a-shiver with weaponry as his feet hit the ground. He comes closer, peering down. He too has that white stuff on his face, and great dark circles blotted round the eyes, dark lines drawn in over his lips. The teeth, the face of an ogre.

He crouches down. His eyes are bright as suns. The white on his face cracks round the mouth. A beaming smile. Also in English, and with immense good humour, this apparition says, 'Well now. What have we here?'

The well-cover drops over the well. Rafe is in darkness. He thinks, with perfect clarity, *I am dead.*

THE AFTERLIFE.

The afterlife has trees, and a soft breeze which, as Rafe watches, turns the leaves of the trees this way and that above him. It has birdsong, and some other sound, softly regular and suggestive of a sort of rhythmic adhesion and release. It has a sky of summer blue, across which spoonfuls of cloud move at a speed just swift enough to be pleasing. It has a golden-haired angel, who kneels at his head, and wishes him good day.

Oh. He is perhaps not dead.

'Can you sit, please, Herr Endicott?'

Yes, he can. Sitting, he sees that he is out of doors. Trees on either side of him, their heads caught in the breeze; shafts of green sunlight. And tents – here, there; triangular tents, like so many houses of cards. And some sort of bedroll beneath him. And his left hand in a sling across his chest.

'Can you stand?' the angel wants to know.

Yes, to his surprise, he can do that too.

'This is excellent,' the angel says. 'Then I am to take you to our captain.'

With the angel as a human crutch, Rafe makes it to his feet. He feels pleasantly light-headed, as if he had drunk wine on an empty stomach. 'Please to take care, Herr Endicott,' the angel says, then adds with equal gravity, 'you spilled much sauce.'

Again that softly regular pull and release, pull and release. Amongst the trees, any number of horses, pulling at the turf, moving together like gleaners in a field. Tethered close by, a placid ox, chewing its cud. Rafe looks at the ox. He remembers. 'Where am I?' he asks.

'Oh, this is our camp,' the angel explains.

'You know my name.'

'Yes, Herr Endicott.'

'But I know not yours.'

'My name is Lindeborg, Herr Endicott. Karl-Christian von Lindeborg.' And the angel bows to him, from the waist. 'I am honoured. Now, please – you will follow me to our captain?'

Yes, he will. Past those many horses, through the trees, in and out the shafts of sunbeams. Now he smells smoke, and the most ravishing aroma of roasting meat. Now he hears voices, now he sees, hanging from a tree, a banner. Blue at one end, yellow at the other, and written across it the legend—

HÄR ÄR VI

Rafe sounds it out, in his head: *här är vi*. Here are we? Of course! Here we are! Why yes, indeed!

Lindeborg leads him forward. ('Take care, Herr Endicott. The ground has holes.') A youth – not the infant giant, but the same make and breed, clearly – strolls past, wearing a jacket of mustard yellow, with the cuffs at his elbows. For a moment Rafe thinks with faint hope this might be that one surviving trooper, before the wearer turns and he sees his mistake. 'Eh,' the youth says, peering at Rafe, then with great good humour, '*Gooder morgen!*'

Rafe reaches out a hand to Lindeborg. 'There was a trooper,' he begins. He dreads the answer. 'One of my escort. Is he – did he...'

'Yes, he is gone,' Lindeborg replies.

'Gone? You mean...'

'Our captain says to always let one go.' Lindeborg smiles, as if this is the most natural thing in the world. 'One to tell everyone else, so that they know to keep away.'

Now they pass – what is this thing? A wooden frame, two curved poles as tall as Rafe, lined up and down its height with painted feathers, cut from leather, which move a little in the breeze. Rafe lifts his good hand to them, wonderingly, lets it pass over them – ah, the thrumming sound! Of course! And there is another, in fact they are passing a veritable aviary of such, set up in lines, each one with a void at its base to fit behind a saddle. How cunning! And now a group of men sat round a fire, whose unconsumed fuel appears to be the Prince-Bishop's carriage, and upon which roasts part, Rafe suspects, of the dead ox. His mouth is watering.

'Domini!' his guide calls out. 'The English, he is here, he is awake.'

'Herr Endicott!' One of the men by the fire gets to his feet. He comes forward. A loping walk, long legs; the swing of a buff-coat, studded at the seams. There is still white paint in the roots of the man's hair, and some of that dark stuff lingers round the eyes, which have a particular pale glitter, perhaps in consequence. A small black dog runs forward with him, yipping a greeting. 'How does the hand?' the man asks.

For the first time, Rafe dares to looks down. There in the sling across his chest, against the hardened bloodstain on his shirt, is his left hand, three fingers as they should be, and one, the middle, which at the knuckle now bears a row of strong-looking stitches holding a seam of skin, crimped like pastry. It is neat as the nub end of a candle, but there is nothing beyond it. No rest of finger, no fingernail, this. *Hah*, thinks Rafe. *My finger, it is gone.* Here is this, this unfinger, instead. For a moment, all strength seems to leave him. He grips his guide by the shoulder.

'Vastly improved,' he answers, bravely.

'Excellent!' comes the response. 'I'm delighted to hear it.' The man extends his own hand, which is oddly marked across the back. 'Jack Fiskardo, Herr Endicott. I am the captain here. You are our guest.'

Rafe looks from the hand to the man and thinks, *Yes. Unmistakably. This is the one in charge.* And then this other, new, Rafe Endicott suggests, *Make an ally.* He indicates the dog, pirouetting round them. 'He has taken a liking, I see.'

'She,' the man replies.

She?

'Take a look.'

He does. Ah, *she.* 'And you know my name,' says Rafe. 'But other than my helpmeet here –' (Lindeborg turns up his face, beaming) '– I know no-one.'

'You know *this* one,' the captain says, and points back toward the fire where sits a wisp of a man, high of forehead, thin of cheek, wide of nostril.

'Mr Lopov?' says Rafe. 'Good Lord, sir, you are freed!'

Lopov lifts an arm. He seems to attempt to make politer greeting, something with words in it perhaps, but he is chewing like a horse.

'Are you hungry, Herr Endicott?' the captain asks.

'Oh,' says Rafe, 'oh, good God, *yes!*'

The angel helps him sit, carves at the joint above the fire, fills a wooden plate, passes it with great solemnity to Rafe, and for some minutes there is nothing but the glorious experience of sating hunger with juicy beefsteak, and for Rafe, the novelty of balancing his plate with thumb and three fingers only.

'Now, Mr Lopov has been telling me of his business,' the captain says, once Rafe has ceased eating long enough to look up. ('Oh, no, no, I am nothing,' Lopov murmurs indistinctly.) 'But what,' Fiskardo continues, 'is yours?'

Now there's a question. Sat here, soldiers walking all around him, what Rafe is here to do seems even more outlandish than it did before. 'My business,' Rafe begins. 'My business is this: I am employed to uncover all the information that I can of this war, to make it into a regular report and send that to England.'

'And who so employs you?'

'Mr Nathaniel Butter. I send him all that I find, and it is edited, and printed up, and published.'

'Into one of these,' Fiskardo says next, and brings from his pocket a tattered coranto.

'Yes, so exactly,' says Rafe. How delightfully unexpected, that a coranto might be found even out here! And yet – 'No, not like that. This is one of those from Antwerp, yes? In praise of the Emperor? That is not what we intend at all,' he continues, bolder by the minute. 'No, ours will be in support of you. Your army, sir. Your Swedish king. He is our hero.'

'Is that so?' comes the reply. Those pale eyes glitter. 'We're your subject, are we?'

'Exactly, yes! Your victories, your armies, your campaign. And everyone will read of it.'

'Everyone?'

'Yes, indeed. The appetite for news, in London and abroad – it is vast, sir. Vast. Circulation has increased by leaps and bounds, even since the Swedish landing.' It amazes him that he should have these easy phrases at his command. 'The corantos are read all up and down. But ours – we are determined, sir, ours will be the standard by which the others are judged. It will include nothing but what I have verified myself. Ours will be the one read before all the rest.' But strangely, even as he says it, he feels an intimation of dismay. Why is that? Has he left something out in his account? No, he has not. But if not, why this horrid sense of having taken some mis-step?

'And you would write of us?' Fiskardo is saying. His head is at a tilt, as if this idea is of the greatest interest. 'Of me, and my discoverers, here?'

'Most certainly, sir! I will include this –' Rafe waves a hand (how strange it feels! That current of air in the space where his middle finger was, and that strange ache, like the echo of actual pain! He hopes Belle will not be frightened by it), '– all of this – in my next report, believe you me!' And then he stops. 'Oh no,' he says. The horror in his tone is such that Lopov looks up too.

Fiskardo peers at him. 'Herr Endicott, are you well?'

'Wittstock,' Rafe says. 'I must make haste to Wittstock, Captain, all haste, I cannot stay here. I must to the posting inn.' The scenario unrolls within his head: where he is, and *where he is supposed to be*. No Wittstock, no report. No report, no employment. No employment, no Belle. No future at all. 'May I implore you, Captain, may I ask for your aid – forgive me, but I must, I have a duty, sir, a contract. I cannot break it. Everything depends upon it.' He reaches into his pocket for the miniature of Belle, opens it up – surely Belle would melt the hardest heart? 'You see, sir, I am – I have an understanding. I am affianced, Captain. And if I do not meet my contract, if I do not make my report, my contract will be ended and all my hopes, also.'

Fiskardo has drawn his head back, narrowed his eyes. 'I suppose you might continue on to Wittstock,' he says, considering. 'You might indeed. We might even provide a horse to get you there. But anything you meet going that-a-ways –' he jerks his chin, '– will kill you. Then again, anything you meet going the other way will most definitely kill you. Added to which, you will starve.'

Rafe gapes at him. With awful imminence he feels the wrack of all his plans washing about his feet. He sees that kitchen door, he sees that damned kitchen door closing again, and he here, and all his hopes the other side of it. 'But I have no other choice!' he says. 'What else am I to do?'

CHAPTER ELEVEN

The Dunqerqer

'... forthwith the Ley, gathering itself again into one
channel, mildly dischargeth itself into the Thames...'

William Camden, *A Chronological Description of England*

EAST FROM THE City, far enough east so that the great
square stump of the tower of St Paul's is no more than
a smudge against the sky; beyond even the Isle of Dogs,
where it hangs down into the river like the lolling tongue of
a hound; out so far east in fact that there is nothing about
you but reed-bed and marsh, and your only companions are
curlews and wagtails and the odd ruminating cow, out where

the landscape is reversed, so that it is the fields that are worn
low and the paths that stand out high between them, out where
the Thames finishes its great swinging curve, the River Lea
comes down to meet it, throwing itself into contortions to do
so like a wounded serpent. It is the strangest landscape. So few
trees you might count them on your fingers, and no houses to
speak of, none at all, until you reach the tiny hamlet of Poplar;
yet here, set apart, where the Lea makes its last turn back
upon itself, there is an alehouse. The Dunqerqer is its name.
It has a peculiarity – well, it has two. One is only visible if you
are down at water-level on the Lea itself and happen to know
where to look, in which case at high tide you will discover that
there is a channel cut beneath the building, so that a boat may
drift right underneath, in through the bulrushes like Moses,
and come to rest with the floorboards of the Dunqerqer above.
A quick rat-tat-tat with the end of an oar, and a trapdoor
opens, and any little thing you might have in the boat with
you – flasks of Genever, say, thick French satins, Italian cut
velvets; nutmegs, peppercorns, oranges – can be whisked up
out of sight before you can say 'And what might the customs
duty be on that?'

The Dunqerqer is little enough, as an enterprise. There
are no other dwellings here on this low marsh, and even if
there were, the Dunqerqer doesn't have at all the look of a
place you might choose to sit down in of an evening with
your neighbours. The yellowed plaster of its walls swells out
between its timbers in a manner suggestive of a dirty sponge;
in more than a few places the plaster has given up its battle
with gravity and fallen off altogether, revealing bare sticks of
wattle; and the whole of the leeward wall is held in place by
three enormous timbers, big enough once to have been part of a
galleon, which lean their mighty weight against the Dunqerqer
in desperate manner, like three tall men attempting to hold
shut a door. Even its name is a deterrent: Dunkirk is where a

seaman ends up if he has offended against the gods sufficiently to fall through the ranks of privateer and pirate both. The Dunkirkers are notorious for their attacks on merchantmen, supply ships, private yachts, even inoffensive fishing smacks – all alike, all prey. Would you, retired, boast of having been one of their number? You would not.

But even the least-loved must have someone who looks upon them fondly. In the case of the Dunqerqer it is he who is now approaching it on horseback, on one of those raised-up pathways, he who now swings himself down from his horse and with something of a swagger approaches the Dunqerqer's door: a fresh-faced, curly-headed lad of fifteen years or so, with clear grey eyes and an open-hearted expression – Aaron Holland.

'Old Josh!' he calls. 'You in there, are yer, Old Josh?' A private grin, for where else would the man be? He waits a moment, looking about. It is still early enough in the day for water and sky out there to be the same pale pearly blue, the sun showing only as if in that place on the horizon the sky has been rubbed thin. 'You up yet?' he calls again. 'You a-risen?'

A dull percussion from inside. It comes closer to the door. A surly growl that might be '*Waddyawant? Ooozit?*' This is the Dunqerqer's other peculiarity, its solitary year-round occupant. Aaron's grin grows wider. ''Tis yer landlord!' he calls out; under his breath he adds, 'You old bear.' He taps upon the door again. 'Now open up!'

The door comes open. A man stands there in his nightshirt. His face glitters with grey bristle; he has an untidy iron-grey plait reaching down between his shoulder-blades. There is more grey fur at the placket to the nightshirt, and on the sinewy arm holding the door ajar. An old bear indeed.

The man turns his head. One eye, or rather one socket, is sunken, empty, a little cave, overhung with the vegetation of a seventy-year-old eyebrow. Even now, Aaron finds it as terrifying to look into as he did as a child. To hide this, he continues cheerily, 'You well, are yer, Old Josh? You been keeping good, 'ave yer?'

'You can go fuck yourself, you wee shite,' the old man replies, turning away.

'Now don't be like that,' Aaron persists, following him in. A quick glance around the room, for as a Holland, the watchword is always and ever *you can never be too careful*, but it's all as you'd expect – discoloured plaster, disfigured by the damage of many a drunken collision, beams still black with tar, that suspiciously creaky floor, and not another soul than he set foot inside for months – years, probably. 'What'ud my grandma have to say to that, eh?' he asks, almost flirtatiously. 'Old Bess? What'ud she say to you being so curmudgeonly?' Inwardly he's sniggering at his own daring – Old Josh Arden, once the scourge of the Dutch coast, a man whose mere name cleared the seas, now washed all a-ways up here. A man who without them, the Hollands, might as well be standing as a scarecrow in a field. 'You oughter remember—'

Aaron finds he is suddenly prone, laid out along the floor, the *wallop* yet resounding through his skull being the only clue as to how he got there. But now his head is being lifted, head and shoulders both, by Old Josh, who has a fistful of Aaron's shirt in his grasp. 'You was saying?' the old man asks, standing over him, bringing his face down close to Aaron's, turning it so that the hideous socket is all Aaron can see. 'I can *hear* fine this side of me face, even if I cain't see. Something you had to tell me, was there? Something I has to remember?'

'Nothing, Old Josh, nothing,' Aaron says, hurriedly. He fights the urge to look away. The smell of unwashed ancient skin is so strong he can taste it. He scrambles to his feet. 'You're all right, Old Josh, you are. We ain't got a quarrel, you an' me.'

'And you just remember that, *boy*,' Old Josh tells him. He turns away again, pads off. Aaron takes the chance to pull his shirt straight. Rubs at the back of his head. *Hooked me legs out,*

the old bastard. Hooked 'em right out from under me. He wonders
if he will tell his grandmother, but if he does, he thinks, she'd
only laugh. You cheek Old Josh, she'd say, you push that man
too far, you're lucky you get up again at all.

Old Josh returns. He's carrying a lidded basket in his hands.
'In there. This is hers,' he says. 'Old Bess. Brussels lace, five
yards of it.'

'That's the stuff!' says Aaron, gratefully. He takes the basket,
holding it as carefully as if it were the sacramental host, lifts the
lid. Inside the lace is billowy as fresh-whipped meringue. 'Me
little sis,' he confides. 'New petticoats.'

'An' there's this,' Old Josh continues, producing a package
from under his arm, 'come with it.'

'What's that, Old Josh?'

'Mails,' Old Josh tells him. 'Mails for London. Come through
the German post to Brussels.'

Aaron is leafing through the package, from one letter to
the next. 'There's enough of 'em, ain't there? God a'mercy,' he
continues, holding one up. 'These've been in the wars!' He peers
more closely at the spray of stains. 'Fuck me, is that blood?'

'Whether it is or whether it isn't, they're all to go to a Mr
Watts, care of the Mitre,' the old man announces. 'The Mitre
in Wood Street. You know that one, don't'cha? An' I paid an
extra five shilling for 'em. Me good deed for the day. I figure
someone must'a been waiting a good long time for those. So
you drop 'em off at the Mitre an' whatever you get, we'll split it.'

'You don't fancy the jaunt into London yerself then?' Aaron
asks, all innocence. 'A day away from all this – that don't appeal?
All what you have here?'

In answer, Old Josh curls a fist at him. That tattoo across his
knuckles, of a mouth of hell, is still just visible. No, of course
Old Josh ain't about to go into London himself; the reason
being that as far as the rest of the world is concerned, the man
is meant to have been dead these twenty years and more.

'I figured I'd leave all o'that to you,' the old man says. 'Give you the chance to *prove* as we ain't got no quarrel. Fair enough?'

SO HERE IS Aaron Holland, making his way along Cheapside, under a sky no longer pearly blue but heavy with the promise of a late summer downpour. He has that bundle of letters from Germany snug in his shirt, and is pondering what, to the mysterious recipient, they may be worth, because in Aaron's experience, folks who patronize the Mitre have deep pockets. Eschewing its front door, Aaron turns into Wood Street, then turns again into Mitre Court, then waits a precautionary moment, an eye on the street behind him. The Holland family have rivals, the Skinners, and this side of the river, you never know when there might be one of them about. Satisfied that this time there is not, Aaron eases his way via its back door into the Mitre itself. Lets his eyes adjust from the brightness outside to the dark within, and looks about. Clayton Proctor, that's who he's looking for, and there's the man himself, making his way up from his reputedly splendid cellar. Aaron waits until Clayton Proctor has the bottles in his hands safely stowed on his shelves, then, stepping up smartly, greets him with a 'Good day, Mr Proctor – how's business with you?'

Clayton Proctor is three times Aaron's age, easily so, a husband and father, prosperous, well known, but all the same, such is the reputation of the Holland family, to be greeted by even one of its youngest is enough to have a man consider his answer carefully. 'Well enough, Master Holland,' Proctor replies, slowly. 'Well enough.'

Aaron gives him an easy smile. He's no stranger to this sort of reception. The Holland family run a controlling interest in taverns by the dozen; taverns, theatres, stews – for years Old Bess Holland herself has run Holland's Leaguer down in Southwark, the finest, most luxurious brothel London has ever seen, famed in song and story. Old King James (so unlike his milk-and-water, kill-joy son, who seems to have no understanding of the jaunty nature of the people of his capital at all), he was a patron; it's Bess's proudest claim. Old King James, the old Duke of Buckingham – 'all the nobs, and all their knobs', is what Bess says. Those were the days. But Old King James has been in the ground for five years now, and it's no secret, how the Hollands are casting about for business ventures more respectable. The Mitre is just such a place as they might cast their eye upon, and Clayton Proctor knows it.

But not today. 'Now would you,' Aaron begins, disclosing the corner of the packet of letters at his breast, 'would you know of a Mr William Watts, Mr Proctor? I've a little something here I think as he's been waiting for.'

'There's a Reverend Watts,' Clayton Proctor begins, uncertainly. 'Rector of St Alban's, up the street. Would it be him?'

A clergyman? Possibly, but that would be less exciting than Aaron had hoped. Less lucrative too. Your bishops and archdeacons, sure, their livings make 'em fat, but your humble City rector? Poor as the church-mice, them. Oh, how Aaron longs to be wealthy himself, to be in charge of some proper bit of business of his own! Sometimes he thinks his dealings with the Dunqerqer have been given him only because no-one else would put up with Old Josh; sometimes he thinks it is because both he and the Dunqerqer are the smallest, least significant of all the Hollands' enterprises, and he and it have been thrown together for no better reason than that. Had his father or his uncle walked in here, by now they would be seated at the best table in the house with a bottle of the Mitre's finest there before them, and Mr Clayton Proctor bowing down as before the throne of God.

'Because if it's him, he's sat just over there,' Clayton Proctor is saying, pointing a finger. 'Him and Mr Vanderhoof, d'you see?'

*

'Nathaniel Butter believes he has absconded,' Cornelius is saying. He is outraged.

'I am sure he does not,' Mr Watts tells him. 'I am sure it is only his concern for Rafe would have him speak so intemperately—'

'He has no concern for Rafe at all,' Cornelius tells him, bluntly. He empties his glass – his second, such is his ire. 'None whatsoever. All his speech was of his twenty pounds, and how Rafe had made away with it. And it has been almost three months now, Mr Watts, and nothing. Not a word since Hamburg. What are we to do?'

William Watts hangs his head, over his own, untouched, glass of Muscadine. 'I fear, Cornelius, that I have acted in a most foolhardy manner. I fear my agreement to Mr Butter's plan has exposed your friend to dangers we could not compass. But we must not lose hope. Rafe is – he is – he is determined, he is resourceful –' But is he? Is he? William Watts feels at this moment he is describing some other man entirely, not young Endicott – helpful, biddable, well meaning, the very definition of an innocent abroad.

'He rages,' Cornelius is saying. 'Mr Butter. When I was in the shop, he even raged at poor Belle for coughing, shouting that she was discouraging the clients, and how else was he to make good his loss? Then he raged at Mrs Butter too, for defending her daughter. Mrs Butter says she will take Belle away to Epsom, until she is recovered. She says Mr Butter's temper is not to be lived with. These were her very words.'

'Good day to you, gentlemen,' says Aaron, coming up to them. 'Now which of you two good souls would be Mr Watts?'

Mr Watts, much surprised, gets to his feet. 'Why, that would be me,' he admits.

Of course it would. That threadbare gown, all shiny at its wearer's corners, the unstarched collar; that little cap fitted over his head… beyond these letters, William Watts is of no interest to Aaron Holland whatsoever. Also, to Aaron's youthful eye, Mr Watts appears almost as ancient as Old Josh. Mr Watts's friend, though, the Dutchman, he looks worth knowing, he and his good jacket and good boots and would that be a glazed silk, the gentleman's shirt? Aaron wonders. 'Aaron Holland,' he announces, sticking out his hand, and is even more intrigued when Cornelius, likewise rising to his feet, says, 'Mr Holland, forgive me, but I think I have seen you before this. At the Red Bull, sir, in Clerkenwell. Could that have been you?'

'Why,' says Aaron, 'it could have been, it could have been indeed. The Red Bull theatre, yes –' (modestly he drops his gaze) '– that is an enterprise in which I have an interest, sure.'

'And you have I think essayed upon the stage yourself? I saw a very fine Ariel there, only this last month.'

Aaron flushes up, pink as a sunrise. 'Why yes,' he says, eagerly, 'why yes, that was I. O'course,' he adds (the long-suffering man of business once again), 'we've all had to turn to, ain't we, all of us in the company, since Mr Kempwick went off on his adventures.'

'There!' Cornelius exclaims. 'I knew it! I said to myself, even as I saw you with Mr Proctor, why, that is Ariel, that is his look, his very eye – and there was a child with you, Mr Holland, came up and took your hand, a little maid – quite wondrous lovely, Mr Watts,' says Cornelius, as if in explanation, as Mr Watts looks from one to the other, all amazed.

'My sis,' Aaron tells them. 'My sort-of sis.' Aaron's sis and her unforgettable good looks are a source of immense pride to the Holland family, who appreciate the value of such things. But even so, she ain't the business here.

To it. 'Mr Watts,' Aaron begins. With a flourish, he brings the packet of letters from his breast. 'My interests run as far as Brussels, sir, and in the course of 'em, I do occasionally pick up mails, for London.'

A strangled gasp from Mr Watts.

'An' it so happened as this last did bring me these,' says Aaron, fanning the letters out to display them to best advantage. 'O' course, the carrying of 'em, it was not without expense,' he begins.

But the old fellow, Mr Watts, is already reaching for the packet. 'I know that hand!' he says, pulling it from Aaron's grasp with a force that takes Aaron aback. 'Cornelius, it is his hand!' Now the fan of letters is spread out across the table. 'Oh, thank God, thank God!' Mr Watts exclaims. Now he is opening them, one after another. 'Cornelius, look at this!' Displayed, disclosed, line after line of scribble, interspersed with little maps, with diagrams, with lists – *Now that's got to be worth something, sure*, thinks Aaron, *just from its reception alone*. 'Oh, the dear boy!' says Mr Watts. He seizes his glass; he drains it at a swallow. 'This is everything we could have asked for, everything! Why he has even numbered them – one, two, three, four – look at this, Cornelius, look at this!' Mr Watts finishes triumphantly, brandishing the final missive, numbered '9', and headed 'FROM SCHWERIN PLUS TEN DAYS'. 'Our friend is safe! Our enterprise is saved! Sir –' he turns back to Aaron, '– you have done us a greater service here than you can know.'

Try me, thinks Aaron. 'I am very glad to know it, sir,' he begins. 'The expense of doing so was not small, but to be of service to two such gentlemen as yourselfs—'

At this point Cornelius places upon the table a coin whose delightful *donk* informs Aaron it is solid gold even before Cornelius has moved his hand away. A laurel, from the reign of old King James; twenty shillings at least. 'This will cover it, I am sure,' Cornelius says. There is a firmness to his tone that Aaron understands instantly: not such a gull as he might look, this one, not by no means. *Business*, thinks Aaron. *Business!*

'Ah, bless the dear boy, bless him!' Mr Watts is saying, scanning the letter in his hand. 'He writes here that he left

Schwerin in the company of gentlemen from the household of the Prince-Bishop of Prague – Catholic without a doubt, but no matter, no matter.' He continues reading.

'That will cover it most handsomely,' Aaron says to Cornelius. 'And it may be that if there are more letters coming by the same route—'

'Oh my word, Cornelius, he writes they were surprised! There was an ambush!'

'Indeed, Mr Holland, there may well be more,' Cornelius answers, then to Mr Watts, 'Read on, Mr Watts, please – what more does Rafe say?'

'And he sustained a hurt, a wound upon his hand –' Mr Watts looks up with a face of agony, turns the letter over, turns it about (Rafe has used every last inch of the paper: part is written one way, part the other, the last section upside-down to all the rest), '– oh, now he writes it has healed. Thank God, thank God!'

'Well then,' says Aaron, 'I will make it my particular business to have 'em looked about for, sir, and brought here safe to you. Rely on me.'

'Oh my dear good God!' Mr Watts exclaims, so suddenly and at such volume the nearest of the Mitre's other patrons turn to stare. 'My dear good *God!*' He is waving Letter No. 9 wildly before him. 'He writes here – our friend, Cornelius – he writes here that he has *enlisted! He writes that he is with the Swedish army!*

PART II

October 1630

CHAPTER ONE

Dear Mr Watts

'A letter: een breef.

A letter missive or an epistle: Een sendt-brief.'

Henry Hexham, *A Copious English and Netherduytch Dictinarie*

NOCK, KNOCK, KNOCK.
'Mr Watts, sir! 'Tis Aaron Holland, with yer mails!'

From our campsite, sir, and the sun just peeking.

Dear Mr Watts

I do hope my last did not alarm you. In fact I have great hopes my new situation will find future communication between us runs as if on threads of silk. I have been given my own messenger, Mr Watts, the captain's ensign, who has undertaken

*to carry my letters whenever we are nearby a posting inn. And
will also, need I say, collect any there may be from London.*

*And I am most advantageously placed to pass to you, sir,
all the latest of the war itself. Thus I can tell you that the
countryfolk, who are beset by raids from Torquato Conti's camp
at Gartz, petition the King to turn his armies thither—*

'Scribbler! Time to go! Captain says put the pen and ink away
and shift yer arse!'

'I CONFESS, MR Vanderhoof, I am amazed. It is as if we are
there beside him. The night attacks, the coming up by water
upon these little towns about the Oder – I have followed these
marches almost minute by minute. And the information he has
– I am amazed. Anklam, do you know, the town of Anklam –
our friend tells us it rose up against its occupiers and opened its
gates to the Swedish itself!'

'I am delighted, Mr Watts,' says Cornelius, smiling, 'that you
are so well served. I hope Mr Butter is now satisfied also?'

*On the road, Mr Watts, in fact on horseback. Please to forgive
the pencil.*

*We now in great haste are to sound out the country into
Mecklenberg, west of us; our captain (whatever else may be said
of him) having a golden reputation as a Discoverer, as they call
it, or scout—*

'Still scribbling, Mr Endicott?'
'Still scribbling, sir.'
'Will you make us all famous, I wonder?'

'Should you ever do anything of account, Captain, I will record it with your name most prominent, for sure.'

When the captain is amused, something happens in those pale eyes of his. It puts Rafe in mind of the play of light on water, of ripples catching the sun. Kai watches them, gaze twitching from one man to the other, like a duster in the hand of an over-anxious maid.

'You are become a man of spirit, Mr Endicott, I find,' the captain says.

'Yes, sir,' Rafe replies. 'I put it down to the company I keep.'

I would describe my messenger to you, Mr Watts, so you may know something of the composition of this army.

'Captain, if you have a moment – if I might enquire…'

'What is it, Mr Endicott?'

'I had heard, sir, that every Swedish family with two sons or more has given one up.'

'Entirely true, Mr Endicott.'

'But from the lowest to the highest, sir? The same for all?'

'The same for all. Kai!'

'Yes, Domini?'

'Come here and explain to Mr Endicott what a well-born little bastard you truly are.'

This child, Mr Watts, comes over and says how it is his honour to serve me, and how very much he admires London, that great city, as he calls it. I ask him how does he know it, and he replies he was there for King Charles's coronation, all his family, the Lindeborgs were there, within the Abbey, with the King! He said he thought the Abbey so enormous a building he expected birds to be flying about the tops of its columns, but that of course he was very little then, and full of foolish imaginings, as such little children are. I ask him how old he is now; he answers proudly, 'Why, now I am twelve.'

'MR WATTS! ARE you within, Mr Watts?'

'Ah, Master Holland! Do you bring more letters for me?'

'I do, Mr Watts, I do indeed,' Aaron replies, disburthening himself of the letters within his shirt, his pockets, and the one tucked into the band of his hat. 'Blimey, 'e's well named, your scribbler, i'nn'e?'

This from near to Rostock, Mr Watts, after we found fine, clear passage into Mecklenburg. The town of Bartz the King took first. Then both town and fort at Damgarten. Three days after this, Ribnitz. I have drawn here another map for you:

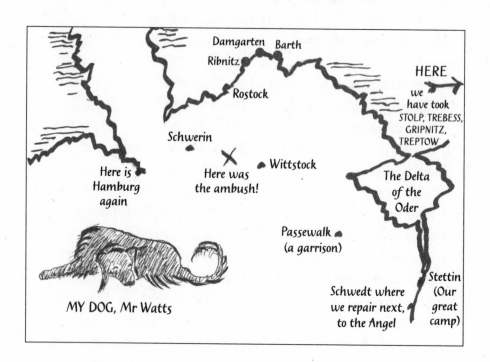

At Damgarten our soldiers, it was said, made a game of flinging the enemy out at the windows, to save, so the story went, their shot. I said I hoped this was not so; no, no, I am assured – it was. So now to open a window for another man is to put an end to him, and is one more term to add to their soldier's lexicon, along with 'sauce', for blood, if you should take a hurt, as I had; and then for gold, which (and my brothers-in-arms make no secret of this) is desired every bit as much as victory or glory, that they term 'Maria', and speak of her as a man might his mistress, vying with one another to detail all the beauties of her form, the glow in her eye, her feel in the hand, and above all how she doth raise the spirits of all who possess her, et cetera et cetera.

One learns not to startle too much at such language, but I must confess, the naughty sacrilege of this was such that even I was took aback.

Meantime, behind us we hear Stolp and Trebbess (forgive me, I have no notion of the spelling) and Gripnitz and Treptow are all now held in Sweden's fist.

Rafe sits back on his elbows, pushes back his hat. He sits against a small rise, perhaps thrown up in case of flooding, while before him at the bank of the Oder, his company water their horses. Darting in and out between the horses' legs goes the dog, stopping to lap at the water here, and then there, as if she is their court-appointed taster.

Dart…

She pauses by Milano, lifts her nose, wagging her tail. Milano lifts his dripping muzzle and waters her, like a plant.

He calls. Let's try this, why not? 'Dart!'

In and out the horses' legs, up the bank, straight to him.

The captain, watching. 'So she has a name now, does she, Herr Endicott?'

'Yes, sir,' Rafe calls back, as Dart nuzzles his face. 'So it would seem!'

Mr Watts, I feel I must tell to you something of our captain. He is a riddle of a man. He speaks (and I have heard him do it) seven languages – French and English, which he says he was born with, then Dutch, Deutsch, Swedish, and can pull from the air turns of phrase in Polish and Italian too. 'I too am a stray dog, Mr Endicott,' said he, 'and we learn to bark each new master's language, or we starve.' I think perhaps I may have looked a little out of countenance at such proficiency in quite so many tongues, for he laughed, and bade me not to fret. 'It is as much as I could do, Scribbler,' said he, 'to scratch out my name in any of 'em.' (He did show me, however, that he can hold a pen and scratch it out as easy with one hand as the other. Am I right, that Alexander could do the same? You will know better than I.)

Also (and here I must confess I blush), these tales of the hard men – not to beat about the bushes, Mr Watts, but it seems our captain is one such. At least, he wears beneath his shirt the medal of a silver wolf, by which all such men are meant to know each other. Which is a most puzzling thing, as he also most certainly bears his share of scars, including a curious thicket of them within the meat of his left hand. I asked how it was he came by his silver wolf, and he leered toward me, and said he would tell me, but feared it would cause me to have bad dreams.

'Mr Endicott!'

'Yes, Captain!'

'Mr Endicott, you are walking as if you still had a horse between your legs.'

'I feel as if indeed I do, Captain.'

'Mr Endicott, you give us all much amusement here.'

'Then I am glad to be of service, sir.'

Truly, Mr Watts, the blistering of the feet is as nothing compared to the chafing of the saddle. To be well-leathered, or a true-grown leather-arse, a veteran of much campaigning, here is accounted the greatest compliment. I cannot even guess how many miles we cover in a day. Every roadway, every track, every tiny trickle of a path, all must be investigated.

My messenger awaits. I close in haste with two further items, although I declare I have not assayed as yet the truth of either: one, that the Emperor is so enraged at the conduct of his campaign, he has removed his own great general Wallenstein from office; and two, Mr Watts, the strangest rumours, all around, that in France the great Cardinal Richelieu is just as like to be cast aside. It must be the season for great men to fall. Like leaves.

Sir, your servant always.

PS. How does Miss Belinda and the family, I wonder?

WILLIAM WATTS PUSHES back the mass of papers on his table, pinches and rubs at the bridge of his nose. 'Cornelius,' he says, 'I have corantos here from Amsterdam, from Paris, from Antwerp, from Frankfurt, even – none of them has such grasp. None of them has the same accuracy of information as we.' He rubs his hands, reaches for his inkwell with his quill. 'We will set a benchmark, Cornelius, truly!'

'Do we know where our friend is now?' Cornelius asks. 'I am disposed to see if I can get a letter back to him.'

'Write to him at the town of Schwedt,' says Mr Watts, lowering spectacles from forehead to nose to be sure. 'With his last, he said he was headed to Schwedt.'

From Cornelius Vanderhoof to Rafe Endicott, by hand to the Angel, Schwedt

My intrepid friend

Although our lives here in London would (I have no doubt) seem dull to you beyond describing, describe them I will, as you so figure in them. To begin, I must tell you that the first instalment of 'The Swedish Intelligencer' moves toward publication, and at a dinner this week at the Stationers' Company, I hear Mr Butter was so moved as to propose your name for a toast, as a Freeman of the Company and, as he termed you, 'our resolute correspondent'.

But, before you become swell-headed, you are not the only traveller to send news home. I learn from Aaron Holland that there is at long last word from Mr Kempwick and his Pilgrims. They crossed over into Germany at Forbach, and are on their way to Munich, and Henry Kempwick writes (and so we must believe it!) that they are all in the finest of health and spirits, that they have met with the greatest approbation and success, and that Master Shakespeare plays as well in Germany as ever he did at the Red Bull or even the old Globe.

Meanwhile, Belle and her mother remain in Epsom, while Mr Bourne is here in the city, plotting and planning some new venture. Apparently even the thought of returning to London's dust brings on a relapse of Belle's condition. I have heard Mr Butter mention it; while I believe that Mr Bourne's lack of concern for her daughter's health endears him to Mrs Butter not at all, and that Mr Bourne is aware his suit is fading, and turns his hand to his new business ventures in what the French would call a pique. I have of course passed on to Mrs Butter and to Belle all your humble service and good wishes, and I end here, my friend, with my own to you.

Cornelius, at our old table, at the Mitre.

Rafe Endicott, one-time bookseller's assistant, half-rises from his table in the Angel Tavern, Schwedt, lifts the letter to his lips, and kisses it. 'She is mine!' he calls out, to anyone who might be passing. 'She is mine, still!'

But what is this? No indulgent smiles, no teasing ripostes. He looks about the room. His brothers-in-arms have gathered into corners, faces dark with anger, talking low.

Dear Mr Watts

I write you here in Schwedt, sir, which to my amazement I am told is halfway between Stettin and Berlin, so I leave you to draw your own conclusion, where it may be this army intends to go next. But here in Schwedt, Mr Watts, we make an unaccustomed pause, because of this — to the north of us, we hear the Imperialists have taken Passewalk. Three thousand of them come out of Gartz, utterly rout and destroy our 140 men, which was all the defence the town then had, and fall upon the townsfolk, crying GIVE US MONEY OR GIVE US BLOOD, using torture upon the men and such violence upon the women as you may at worst imagine. Where they found children hiding in the cellars, they thrust whole stooks of straw down in amongst them and set it on fire. They burn the churches, massacre the ministers, then masque up and down in the churchmen's robes, laughing and saying 'How finely does Passewalk burn!' Of two thousand folk, they say not above two hundred survived.

It has made us all and the King His Majesty most sensible of the situation of Magdeburg, for all that she is twenty thousand souls to Passewalk's two. It would be impossible for a city the size of Magdeburg, and so well defended, to fall as Passewalk has done, but even so, the rage amongst the men here, it is of such settled force, you might squeeze it from the air.

I am told the army will make response by shifting ourselves closer to Gartz, to winter quarters in the great standing camp, or leaguer,* at Stettin.

* My messenger informs me such a standing camp is known as a 'Camp Royal'.

'Captain? Forgive me — I disturb you, sir.'

'You do, Mr Endicott, but that has never stopped you yet.' His captain stoops down; Dart gets up on her hind legs for him to stroke her head.

'You are much affected by this news from Passewalk, sir,' Rafe begins. He hears a sigh.

'It is a bitter thing,' his captain says, 'to fail.'

'To fail, sir? How is it you have failed?'

'Where there are those you should protect. And you cannot, or you do not, but it is they who suffer. They are dead, yet you are still alive. It is a bitter, bitter thing.' He lifts his head. 'You had a question, Mr Endicott.'

Rafe looks into his captain's face. 'No, sir,' he says. 'Now I think is not the time.'

THE SWEDISH INTELLIGENCER

The first part. Wherein, out of the truest and choicest informations, are the famous actions of that warlike prince historically led along:

'Good day to you, Mr Butter!' Cornelius announces, as he enters once again the premises of Nathaniel Butter. It is coming up to nine of the clock on a bright October morning. Clouds chase each other behind the tower of St Paul's, the trees in the churchyard toss their heads; all is motion, flurry and excitement. 'Mr Butter, it is a splendid day, sir, I hope I find you well.'

'You do indeed, Mr Vanderhoof, you do indeed!' exclaims Mr Butter, as he turns about and straightens his back. Although the summer's heat has left the City, Mr Butter, Cornelius sees, is sweating, no doubt from his labours unpacking the many crates there before him. And although he is here in his shop, Mr Butter is also in his shirtsleeves, with them rolled up most informally above his elbows.

'Mr Butter,' Cornelius says, 'I am here, as you no doubt guess, sir, to buy issue number one of our *Intelligencer*.'

'And I would most willing sell you one, Mr Vanderhoof, my friend, most willing.' But,' says Mr Butter, indicating the empty crates and showing Cornelius a face all a-shine with delight, 'as you see, sir, as you see, our first printing, it is gone – we are sold clean out!'

CHAPTER TWO

Ripeness Is All

'... the Imperialists being led by one Quint, who had before run away from the King, fall upon the outer Guards of the King's Camp, and cuts them off; putting the whole Army into danger.'

William Watts, *The Swedish Intelligencer*

AN ENORMOUS GEOMETRIC earthwork is coming into being around the Camp Royal at Stettin, complex and many-cornered as a star. Gates and sentry-posts have been slotted into its towering, hard-packed sides, field paths wide as roads have been rolled across it, and at every zig or zag there is a built-up sconce, buttressed with timber, and a gun platform, with cannon pointing out three ways at once.

The only part of the camp not yet completely enclosed is its southern edge, where there is a wood, rustling with the winds of autumn, and where those with an interest in such things may find the ruins of an ancient abbey, now home to Fiskardo's company of scouts. Beyond the wood the skin of the earth collapses into an area of blocky granite defiles, sliced through and through with narrow cuts and many almost-silent streams of water, snaking their way down those rocky sides. Tree roots and ivy grapple across the rocks; a path steep enough to have any horse descend it sideways leads down and round and through.

Rafe sits with Viktor Lopov at the edge of the wood, looking down upon the nearest gun platform; then a little further off the ancient angled shape of the abbey; and considerably further off than that, like an endpiece to the view, Stettin itself. Rafe would far sooner be in the abbey than here. Firstly, although the greater part of their quarters has been in ruins for centuries, the rooms around the cloister are still in good enough order for Rafe to be able to look up and see ceiling, as opposed to sky, which seems the greatest luxury; secondly, he finds the architecture of the abbey most intriguing. Its ruined nave is now their stables, with the columns becoming ready-made dividers for the horses' stalls, and right beside Milano's stall there is a column whose carved capital is twin, exactly, to one in the crypt of St Paul's – a favourite of Rafe's since boyhood. One side shows an industrious vigneron pruning his vines, but he is bending over, and if you go round to the column's other side, the man's naked buttocks are on display. So did he who sculpted the one come here and sculpt the other? Rafe would like, at this moment, to be making a sketch of the vigneron, to enclose with a few reflections on the nature of antiquity in his next letter to Mr Watts. It would do something to distract him from the teeth-on-edge sensation that the wind creates on the end of the unfinger.

At his feet, Dart sits with her nose to that same wind, taking the measure of the day.

Dart is one of the few creatures to bring a smile to Viktor Lopov's face. Sudden noise (and there is no other sort, within a leaguer the size of this) makes Lopov jump, horses make him sneeze; his one and only talent seems to be for getting in the way. Indeed, Rafe has learned that the surest method of locating Lopov is to listen for the shout of warning as the man wanders into one peril after the other: straying too close to an equine backside, failing to see the wagon about to roll down on top of him.

'You would not know,' says Lopov now, 'that this was the same dog.'

Indeed, you would not. From being the threadbare, rib-thin scrap Rafe could put in his shirt, Dart is now as silky as a thoroughbred. Her once rat-like tail is a flag; her paws have become elegant high-heeled tippy-toes. 'All her coat is grown back,' Lopov says, approvingly.

'The one they call the Executioner,' says Rafe. 'He made me a salve for her skin. It has worked wonders. Truly,' he begins, turning to his companion, because it seems to have become one of Rafe's duties to jolly Lopov along, 'when I first heard his name, or I should say the name they have for him, I feared this was his very occupation. Yet he is the most kind-hearted of men. It was he tended my hand. His fellows call him as they do only because he is so ill-favoured they say that, like an executioner, he should wear a mask.' He shakes his head. 'Soldiers are the strangest breed. The cruel, the courageous, the compassionate, so mingled together. Their nature is – it is baffling.'

Before it collapses into those granite defiles, the land rises a little for the wood, as if in preparation for the plunge. Where they sit, this gives Rafe and Lopov a perspective on the nearest sconce, the island kingdom of one Corporal Arvinius. Arvinius has proved an accommodating neighbour, and like all gunners is endlessly willing to talk about his guns, with the result that down on the sconce this morning, the scouts are being given an artillery lesson – that magical combination of angle of elevation, size of charge, projected wind-speed and basic cross-your-fingers that determines how high and how far a cannonball will travel, and where its death-dealing blow will land. They can see Arvinius now, moving back and forth amongst his cannon, hands unconsciously caressing trunions, barrel as he speaks; and the scouts obediently lowering their heads to inspect touch-hole and bore. A little way off, their captain stands, arms folded, waiting.

'Fiskardo,' comments Lopov.

'Exactly.'

'To be in this world, yet to fear none of it,' says Lopov, with a sigh. 'How that must be.'

They contemplate together how that must be. Then, 'He was much intrigued by your first coranto,' Lopov remarks, and Rafe's writer's heart grows warm as a hot coal, puffed upon. 'He had young Lindeborg sound it out for him, every word.' Another sigh. 'And here I am, a woodlouse.'

'Oh, hardly that, Mr Lopov!' Rafe assures him. He gives out so many of these assurances a day, he finds that all he does now is wait for Lopov's voice to drop into that familiar gloomy register, then utter the usual platitude in response.

A silvery trumpet call. Dart lifts her ears; they see Fiskardo turn his head.

'No, I am nothing here,' Lopov insists. His nostrils twitch. 'Not that I have ever been of much significance. My filing systems, my tabulations – they were never of interest to anyone but me. But I had my office in such good order, Herr Endicott! Now look at me.'

Below them, they see Fiskardo lope away toward the cloister, in the direction of that trumpet call.

'It was Vainglory was my downfall,' Lopov continues. 'That wretched gun. Fifteen tons, Herr Endicott! Fifteen tons! Who could use such a thing? Who could even move it? I could make no sense of the business at all. I found promissory notes, for example – the same note, but for two different debts. I consulted with the foundry-master, with Leo Franka – a man of note, Herr Endicott, a man who had been trusted even by the gunsmiths of the Doge in Venice! But no, he was as baffled as I. We were buying copper from the Swedish, from the mines at Falun, and there are very few the Swedish will do business with, but there is a merchant in Amsterdam who they use as agent – the amount of the debt to him was recorded against another name entirely! Herr Franka wrote to him, to ask, was this a new partner, but no – Yosha Silbergeld was as much at a loss as we! We compiled a list of these errors, I sent a memorandum – how should I organize these documents, I asked, the same project cannot be in so many places at once – and in a single day, my world was taken from me. Accused, pursued, vilely imprisoned. As you saw.'

Another trumpet call. Kai can now be seen running along the path from the abbey in their direction.

'And Leo Franka, my supposed accomplice? He simply disappeared. Gone, *pouf*, into thin air, in shame, I was told, at being a part of our conspiracy. *What* conspiracy?' Another sigh. 'It was when I heard that, I knew I had to run. Vainglory. Never was a gun better named. It is ruin to all who have to do with it – why, whatever does that child want with us?'

'Gentlemen!' shouts Kai, running toward them, panting. '*Snabbt!* No, I mean *schnell!* As much *schnell* as you can find! The captain requires your presence instantly!'

Mr Watts, this is a most perplexing aspect of military life – one minute all is calm, the next, everything about you is in hubbub and riot.

All around the abbey is a-boil. Every last one of the scouts has run out to the road, where men on horseback are sweeping in amongst them. There is that trumpet again. And there at the roadside is their captain, on one knee, head bowed – there are his officers behind him, heads likewise bowed and uncovered, and now, on a splendid chestnut steed, quite the finest horse Rafe has ever beheld, swinging himself down from its back, here is a portly gentleman with red-gold hair cut short, *en brosse*, and red-gold beard as sharply pointed as a spindle, and as he advances on their captain he is saying *"shtiana!* How many Cossacks have you dealt with today?' And their captain is replying, 'None as yet, Majesty, but the day is still young.' Rafe is a-gawp. The following rolls through his head as on a banner: *I am the greatest idiot in the history of creation. It is called a Camp Royal because it contains a king.*

There is more conversation, enough for Zoltan and the rest to stand upright once again; there is a particularly affectionate greeting for Kai ('Ah, Lindeborg! Do they treat you well?'). In his head Rafe has already begun upon a description of Gustavus Adolphus for Mr Watts (*he does have goggling eyes, exactly as they show him. He has a sort of brisk, informal way of speech. He dresses like a common soldier!*) when he sees the King turn to Fiskardo and in that brisk, informal manner hears him ask: 'And where is this English? Where is this one who writes?'

'Oh, our scribbler? He's about, Majesty.' And then a yell. 'Mr Endicott! Your presence, if you please. Get yourself down here.'

There is a peculiar singing in Rafe's head. All he can think is that he must get himself through the ranks of Fiskardo's company without tripping over anyone's feet. He himself seems to have double the usual number of limbs to organize, yet somehow he is walking forward, and Fiskardo is coming closer, and then beside Fiskardo, at his captain's shoulder, there is that face, topped and tipped with red-gold bristle. He hears himself say 'Majesty'. To his fury, at this moment of all moments, someone is pulling at his coat, then he realizes this is Zoltan, and that he is meant to kneel. He does. He is staring at the King of Sweden's boots, which are creased at the ankle and have a green stain from His Majesty's stirrup. Now there is a hand, in a glove, in front of his nose.

Boots may be boots, but the glove is a work of art. It is beaded. It is tasselled like a rug, and all around the wrist are twists and knots of gold thread, so deeply and luxuriously worked it is as if the hand emerges from a sunburst.

The glove jiggles, as if for attention.

Rafe raises his own hand to it, hardly daring to touch. Is he meant to kiss it, he wonders, as a Catholic would the hand of the Pope? Then he remembers seeing Fiskardo bow his forehead to that hand, mere minutes ago, minutes in which Rafe seems to have lived a lifetime. He does the same. A scent – sandalwood – fills his nose. He also manages to expel the word 'Majesty' a second time; it emerges in a tone as deep as if there were an organ in his chest.

He hears Fiskardo say, 'Rafe Endicott, Majesty, of London. A celebrated writer in that city. A great seeker after truth.' A pause. 'And a man of spirit, also.' Now someone – Zoltan again? – has their toe in Rafe's arse. Ah – he is meant to stand.

'Herr Endicott!' The eyes goggle. The point to the beard lifts up – perhaps that is a smile? 'Herr Endicott, you write of us?'

'I do,' Rafe agrees. 'I do! It is my greatest honour—'

'Herr Endicott, why does your king not send me money? Why does he not send me men? His father sent both to Mansfeld, when the war was young. Why does he now not send more to me?'

Rafe is speechless.

'Is it not his own sister whose lands we fight to restore? Are we not of the same faith, the same beliefs? Should we not each support the other?'

Some furious engine in Rafe's head has taken over all the usual processes of thought. *Yes, but,* he wants to say, *when the war was young, the King had a Parliament that listened to him. Now he does not.* He opens his mouth.

'Perhaps, Your Majesty, when he reads of your exploits, it will prompt him.'

In the silence that follows, a second furious engine in Rafe's head tries to tell him he has just committed treason. The two engines are about to pull Rafe's brain asunder, down its mid-seam, he is sure, when the King gives a bark of laughter. His Majesty strikes his own knee. 'Very good, English, very good!' His Majesty turns. His groom holds His Majesty's horse. His Majesty remounts. The moment is finished. 'The King,' Rafe murmurs, faintly.

'Yes indeed,' he hears Fiskardo reply.

'Did you see his horse?' Rafe asks.

'I did.'

'Did you see his gloves?' Rafe asks next. His throat feels blocked; his eyes feel oddly full. Fiskardo is smiling broadly; his eyes have that sunlit flicker to them. And then there comes the shouted greeting from the horsemen gathering behind the King, and as Rafe watches, everything in his captain's face is changed, as abrupt as pulling down the visor of a helmet.

'Ah! Fiskardo! My friend! We meet again!'

Quinto del Ponte. Quinto del Ponte, accoutred like an officer, with silken sash of Swedish blue.

'Signor del Ponte,' says Jack, as evenly as he can. 'Every time I see you, you have managed to float that little bit higher.'

Del Ponte modestly acknowledges this to be true. And here too is Ancrum, with his epicene features and that snow-white hair. A prickle of irritation runs through Jack like the leading edge on a wildfire.

But no time for that now. 'It is a fine day for riding,' His Swedish Majesty declares. 'Let us go up to those woods.' That mighty chestnut steed, its head is already being pulled around. 'Fiskardo, you and Lindeborg will ride with us today. And bring the English,' comes the shout, over His Majesty's shoulder. 'Let him write of this – there is no substitute for seeing for oneself!'

*

Here they go, along the road to the woods. As they pass,
Arvinius and his men at the gun platform set up a cheer. His
Majesty acknowledges it with a wave of the hand. He turns
about. 'English!' he declares. 'Write this – our bones are iron,
our blood is cannonballs!'

'I will indeed, Majesty,' Rafe calls back. *Here is me*, he thinks,
*in conversation with a king – wait till Mr Butter hears of this! Wait
till I can tell Belle!* He feels that he should pinch himself. He
cannot stop grinning.

Now they are amongst the trees. Rafe is distracted by
everything – the rump of that chestnut steed up ahead, the reins
of his own mount, the autumn light falling through the trees
and the way it splashes to the ground; the fall of the earth at
that granite edge, the shine of the Oder. *Somewhere amongst all
this*, he thinks, *somewhere here there is the reason*; why one enlists,
becomes a soldier, risks one's life...

Beyond the reach of human sight, but out there lurking all
the same, there is, he knows, Torquato Conti's camp at Gartz,
the twin to this, also edged by the Oder and no doubt just as
fiercely fortified. There are rumours of skirmishes, raiding
parties. What heroics! What glory!

'Ah! Meester Endicott! Eeenglish!'

From the warmth of the greeting, you would think the whole
of Quinto del Ponte's life had been leading to this moment. No
less surprising is the fact that the greeting is in English itself.

'Eeeenglish, I hear of you! We must speak together, yes? I
practise your language, she is very strange. We speak soon.' A
doffing of the hat, and Quinto del Ponte moves past, on his
way. In his wake, as if on the man's trail, Fiskardo rides past
in silence, his face that solid mask of animosity. 'Kai!' Rafe
whispers. He lifts his hand to hide his mouth as Kai rides up
beside him. 'What's up?'

Kai lowers his head. 'We do not like Signor del Ponte,' he replies, quietly. 'We do not trust him.'

No, we do *not*.

The path through those rocky defiles curls to the right and leaves a stark edge, a fall of twenty feet, to the left. A bird, perhaps a kite, hovers overhead, its wings a-ruffle. In front of him Del Ponte leans toward Ancrum, murmurs something, then with much bowing and doffing moves off to the side, out of sight.

What are you up to, you human horse-fly? Taking a piss?

His Majesty, perhaps inspired by the view, begins to propound upon the justness of their cause, the beauties of this country, its current unworthy exploiters. Think how Germany has suffered! Think how she suffers still! He reminds them of the imminent arrival of the Queen, of the troops she brings with her, of the glories ahead. Then His Majesty moves on, surrounded by his bodyguard, and Jack nudges Milano off to the left with his heel. Del Ponte, still mounted up, comes back into view.

Reins knotted at the pommel of his saddle, Del Ponte is now wholly absorbed by something he holds in his hand, something small, and with a glint to it. A compass?

No, a notebook. Del Ponte looks, he writes. He looks, he writes again, flipping back and forth from one page to the next. Look up, flip back, scribble, scribble. Then he tears one page from the notebook and tucks it in his pocket. And so absorbed is Del Ponte in his task that the fact he is being moved up on here is lost to him.

The hovering bird wheels away with a scream. The heel of Jack's boot nudges Milano a second time. Milano, in horse terms, is an officer himself, and never yet would tolerate having another horse in his way, so just as Jack had known he would, Milano stretches his neck and nips Del Ponte's horse on the arse.

Del Ponte's horse, at the edge of that twenty-foot fall, staggers back, and away; Del Ponte makes a grab for the reins, and the notebook falls from his hand, bounces straight over the edge and is gone. Nicely done!

'Signor, forgive me,' says Jack. 'My fault entirely. I misjudged my beast. What was it that you lost? Can it be retrieved?' He dismounts, peers down. Del Ponte, for all his protestations of *No, no, it was nothing*, is glaring as if he would dearly love to have his own horse nudge Fiskardo right over that granite edge to join whatever else now is down there.

'Tell me what it was,' says Jack. 'I will make it good, I promise you.'

Another glare. The King and his bodyguard have turned their horses about, are going back down into the camp; Del Ponte does the same.

As everyone knows, the best way to deal with a disgruntled horse, like an out-of-sorts trooper, is to tire him out. And now Milano knows the way to the woods, let's take him there again. Enjoy that splendid view in solitary peace and quiet.

At the edge Jack dismounts, lies down, chin on his hands. This is where it went over, so, Del Ponte's notebook – where did it come to rest?

There. There's that same glint as before. Some tiny thing at the foot of the drop, held there by brush and scrub.

He measures the drop, eases himself belly-down over the edge. There are finger-holds, and roots, and ivy, there are granite ledges just wide enough to take the edge of your boot.

There are places sharp enough to scrape you through your shirt, and closer to, the scrub is thorn. Not going to be easy.

Hanging from one hand, keeping his weight as close to the rock-face as he can, slowly and carefully he crouches down. There is the glint again, and so long as he doesn't disturb it, it's within reach—

It's like the thing can see his hand approach. There it goes, sliding another six inches down the shaley slope, even deeper under those thorny twigs than it was before. And the arm he's hanging from is screaming at him to pull up, pull up, and one boot keeps slipping. And the light is fading.

Take a breath. Hold it in; hold it—

At the widest possible stretch he comes in round and under it, makes a grab, feels something more within his hand than grit, then his boot slips fully and finally from the ledge, the root and stem clutched in his grip come away and he's flat on his back at the bottom of the slope, with the edge of the drop there above him and thornbush all around, impenetrable.

He stands up, rubbing the back of his head. Something tells him, *down* was the easy part.

Oh, to be lithe as Luka. Oh, to be *short* as Luka, who could no doubt scamper up this rock-face in a breath. Instead Jack must heave and balance and slip and grab, and heave again, until he is below the lip, looking up at its fringe of grass-roots, at the point where he let himself down and there are no more handholds or ledges left *and this is not going to work.*

He calls, 'Milano!'

Nothing. 'Milano!' He can hear his horse up there, tearing at the turf.

'Milano!'

Milano's head appears at the cliff edge, reins dangling.

'Drop your head, you idiot!'

The reins fall within reach. He gets them wrapped about one wrist. 'Now back up! Back up!'

Milano backs up. Grabbing with his free hand, scrabbling with his feet, Jack gets an elbow over the lip, then a knee, then is lying on the edge with his horse peering down into his face. 'You,' he tells Milano, 'need to remember who to thank for them aniseed candies, you do.'

In answer, a snort.

He digs a hand into his pocket. Let's see what we have here.

It's cunningly made. A leather cover, silver corners, narrow enough to slip into your boot, let alone hide in a pocket. He flips the pages against his thumb.

Gibberish. Over the years various attempts have been made to teach Jack Fiskardo his ABCs, and none have worked – every time he looks at a letter, all he can see is the thing it reminds him of – tripods, a gibbet, an eye, a chair. He can just about recognize his own name, but that's it. So he's not expecting to be able to read anything in the notebook; but he's not expecting this, either – page after page covered in dots and hooks and swirls, the odd bit of numbering, and any number of abandoned sketches of what might be a bare tree, or maybe some kind of implement. Beside one, an extra line of jiggled scrawl, then the ragged edge of the page Del Ponte took away with him. 'Does this mean anything to you?' he asks Milano, who has come ambling over, no doubt to check whether what his owner has in hand is not an aniseed candy of some sort.

Behind him, down in camp, he hears the trumpet call as a guard post rotates its guard. One very easy way to find out what this is: ask the man who wrote it.

Let's take this slow.

He walks Milano through the camp, which is emptying before them: groups of men one after another making their way into Stettin – its taverns, its bakehouses, its girls; but when did a discoverer follow the herd? He walks on until he reaches the lanes where the tents get bigger and grander with each successive one. There is Ancrum's, with his standard flying before it, and there, set back a little, is another, like Ancrum's had pupped.

He peers inside. One of those familiar little canvas rooms with table, lantern, a rope-framed bed; and Edvin stood before him, looking as lost as if he'd just been dropped there from the moon.

'Knock, knock,' says Jack, pleasantly.

Edvin turns about. He holds a little wooden casket in his hands. Its lid gapes open; so do Edvin's chops.

'What might you be doing here?' Jack asks next.

Edvin puts the box down. It is completely empty. He answers, huffily, 'Might ask you the same thing.'

'And so you might,' says Jack. 'But since I'm the captain, and you're hair on the army's backside, how about I get my answer first?'

Edvin mutters, 'Looking for Signor del Ponte.'

'There's a thing. So am I. Any idea when he might be coming back?'

'Nah,' says Edvin, and for the first time the boy isn't sounding huffy, he sounds simply at a loss. 'He's took off. His cloak is gone, and his boots as well. All his clothes.'

All his clothes? 'And what was in there?' Jack asks, pointing to the box.

'Money. And a letter. All gone.' The boy shakes his head. 'When 'e comes back, I'll tell 'im you was here.'

'Edvin,' Jack begins. 'You truly do have holes in your net, don't you?' It's low of him, he knows, but he can't resist. 'As my trooper Ulf would say.' He points to the casket Edvin still holds in his hands. 'The man's took his clothes, he's took his kit, he's took his gold and you're still expecting him back?'

Centuries before, the monks of the abbey of Stettin built themselves a refectory. They built it with a vaulted ceiling which, although it has lost most of its plaster, has otherwise resisted the worst that four centuries of wind and weather could do to it; and they built it with a splendid fireplace, with a block of local granite for a mantel. Time has taken the top third of the chimney, so when the wind is in the south, the fireplace smokes like the Devil, but when the wind is a nor-easter, as tonight, the fire still draws perfectly, and the room

is made as cosy as one could wish. The scouts have equipped
it with a table, made of wormy panelling pulled from the walls
(scouts are nothing if not handy), they have bodged together
a set of stools, and the room now has as much the fraternal
feel of a guardroom as one could ask for. And sat here this
evening either side of the fire are Lopov and Rafe; and at that
knocked-together table are Kai and Ulf, with Luka, Ulrik,
Elias, Magnus and Thor as audience. Kai has their backgammon board before him, and is teaching Ulf how to play. There
is the smell of tobacco smoke, and the pleasing, fruity aroma
of schnapps. There is the air of men (and gently snoring dog)
at ease.

'That's a five, and a four,' Kai is saying. 'So you can move
four pips with one counter, and five with another. Or, you could
move one counter nine pips, d'you see?'

Ulf, heavy with concentration, gives a grunt. This game had
looked so simple when he sat down – now it's making him feel
like his brains have sprung a leak.

'If you move nine pips, you can block me,' Kai says, helpfully.

'I KNOW,' Ulf replies. Magnus bends forward as if to offer
his advice, in turn; Ulf glowers at him. Magnus straightens up.
And then, from outside, there is the sound of a horse. Ulf, with
a prayer of silent gratitude, lifts his head. Who's this?

Now the sound of its rider, striding through the cloister
toward them. And they know that stride. Dart lifts her head,
gives a *yip!* of welcome, gets to her paws.

Jack enters, slaps the notebook on the table. 'There will be a
prize,' he announces, 'for anyone can tell me what the devil this
is. Endicott –' (as Dart pirouettes about him) '– call off your
hellhound.' He looks about. 'Also, where *is* everybody?'

'They are all gone into Stettin, Domini,' says Kai. 'The
reception for the Queen Her Majesty. There will be much merry-
making tonight. And many sore heads tomorrow, I think.' He
peers at the notebook. 'Kapten, whose is that?'

'It *was* Quinto del Ponte's, only he lost it. And now he has disappeared. And not into Stettin, I think.'

The notebook is picked up, and examined, and shrugged over. It is passed to Thor, who holds it to the little eye and shakes his head; it is passed to Kai, who says, 'I cannot read it at all. Herr Endicott – can you assist?'

'I fear not,' says Rafe, turning the notebook this way and that. 'Although I think that it may be a secretarial shorthand.'

'May it?' says Jack. 'In that case, Mr Lopov, you are my last hope.'

Lopov comes forward. He takes the notebook, and at once turns it about, so the front cover becomes the back. 'Yes, it is a secretary hand. I think it is in cypher, from right to left, but these marks here, these would indicate speech. It is perhaps a record of comments, overheard.'

'Mr Lopov, you amaze me,' Jack tells him.

Lopov's cheeks acquire a girlish blush. 'But these,' he continues, more confidently, turning through the notebook to the page of sketches, 'these are something different.'

'Can you make that out?' Jack asks. He points to the line of jiggled scrawl.

'Oh yes,' says Lopov, happily. He turns the book about again. 'This reads *fiume*. Which means—'

'River,' says Jack. *River*. Only one river hereabouts, the Oder. Which means perhaps one reads the page with 'River' at the bottom, as if you had it at your back. Now look forward. What would you see?

There, those rocky defiles. There, the path through, that brings you into camp. The camp that for this one night is almost emptied out.

All the machinery between his ears, all of it in motion at once. He asks, 'Do we have a moon tonight?'

'No, Domini,' Magnus replies. 'We are in the dark of the moon tonight.'

No moon. And the camp emptied out. And now he's thinking of another night, and another walled town, not even so very far from where they are now. A walled town and an attack. Torsten the Bear. A walled town and an attack, and a moonless night just like to this. And leading a gang of boys through the streets of the town as those streets went up in flames: Hans, who was the only one who ever got it; Gunter, that little glutton; Matz, a con-man in the making; and Stuzzi, who he understands now loved him, and would have died for him, and did. And who is even now the most innocent, the least demanding of all the many scars upon his conscience.

'Domini?' he hears Kai ask, uncertain.

Not a tree, not some kind of implement, but a map. The way through the towers of granite, all there, sketched out to perfection. And then you creep down through the wood, and take the gun platform, and its cannon, and you turn them upon the rest of the camp—

And so we are caught, with all our counters on the wrong side of the board.

'Mr Lopov,' Jack begins, 'I need you to carry a message. I need you to go up to the sconce and have Arvinius prepare his guns such that very shortly he will be able to fire over the wood and down into the rocks. And tell him to please God get his calculations right, because the wood will have us in it. Do you understand?'

'Yes, Kapten,' Lopov replies. 'Yes of course, I understand, but why—'

'He may take some convincing, Mr Lopov, seeing as this comes from you. Convince him. Do not take no for an answer. Do not be gainsaid.'

'No, sir, I will not, but surely he will ask the reason—'

'The reason, Mr Lopov, is going to be all too damn apparent all too soon. The rest of you, you are going to collect every firearm, every grain of powder, every bullet you can find, and come with me. And bring those bottles of schnapps, as well.'

Endicott is on his feet. 'Captain, do you mean me too?'

'No. You, Mr Endicott, are going to take Milano, and you are going to ride like shit-fire into Stettin and bring back every man you can.'

'I, sir?' Endicott looks horrified. 'But sir! But why—'

'Because if you can see the thing to do, Mr Endicott, you have to do it. Don't you agree?'

'But Kapten – Domini –' (this from Kai) '– what is it? What do you see?'

He puts the notebook down on the table. He takes a breath. 'Gentlemen, I think we are about to come under attack.'

Pandemonium. But pandemonium of two very different sorts. His discoverers on their feet and running for their weapons at once; while Lopov and the Scribbler are running into each other like hens with a fox in their hen-house. He grabs one by the back of the collar, then the other, pulls them both along with him. No more thinking, no more talk; the time for that is done. Instead, this: Move. Act. Do.

It is full dark now, outside. 'Mr Lopov,' he says, 'do you see the sconce?'

Lopov nods.

'Do you remember what you tell 'em?'

A squeak.

'Do you take no for an answer?'

A vigorous shaking of the head.

'Very good, Mr Lopov. Get yourself up there. Go!'

Off the man goes, disappearing into the darkness like a rabbit. Now for the Scribbler.

Who is protesting, pulling back: 'Sir – *sir!* I beg you, a moment – sir, I have never ridden a horse of such mettle as Milano. Surely, one of the others—'

'Then you will be amazed,' says Jack, 'how easy he makes it.'

He is already making a cradle of his hands. 'I ain't debating this with you, Endicott. I need every other man with me. This is an order. Up.'

He pitches Rafe into the saddle. He pushes the reins into Rafe's grasp. 'Oh, God,' he hears Rafe say. Milano turns his head, as if examining who he has up there, and gives a twitch, as if to settle this unaccustomed rider into position.

He goes to his horse's head. 'Listen, sweetheart,' he tells Milano, 'you are the best horse in the world. And you are going to have to run as you have never run before, you understand? That's my good boy.' Then, looking up at Milano's rider, he says, 'Keep your knees in and the reins loose. He'll do the rest.' Then he swipes Milano over the haunches with his hat.

A leap, a blur. Rafe's wail. Milano has taken him at his word. Dart goes bounding after them.

And here are his discoverers, bristling with pistol and musket.

Now for the woods.

A wood at night is a different place, a different thing. Full of sound: the stirring of leaves, so like a woman's silken skirts, trailing across a floor; the mast-like creaking of the trees. A wood at night is a place waiting for something to happen.

He has them lying in an arc along that granite edge. The first of the stars appear. There's the scream of a vixen, somewhere out there in the night. He can almost feel all those hearts skip a beat. He whispers, 'You know why you need to be able to reload in the dark now, not so?'

There is just enough light to make out Ulf's teeth, in his grin, as he answers, 'An' we do, Captain, an' we do.'

Then Thor – Thor with his sharpshooter's eyesight – inches forward on his elbows.

'Do you see something?'

'Reckon I do,' comes the reply.

Jack peers out into the darkness. He makes out nothing. 'Thor, you and that little eye of yours. How many?'

'More'n us,' says Thor, who would no more waste words than he would a bullet. A wriggle, as if the boy is lining himself up. 'Yeah, I see 'em.'

'On your mark, then. You fire, we'll be ready.' As he speaks, he curls his fingers about the neck of the first of the bottles of schnapps, the neck now wedged with dry grass and with a length of match as a fuse. Another trick of Torsten's. Jack shields the small red eye of the match with his other hand. 'Remember, once you fire, they will know where you are. If they can see you, they can aim at you. So you shoot and you move. Understood?'

Back comes the whispered chorus: 'Yes, Domini.'

Beside him, Thor has steadied the barrel of his musket against his outstretched arm, let out a long slow breath. 'Here they come,' he says.

The *fzzzt* of ignition. Thor fires, and at once rolls to the left. An unmistakable human yelp, out there in the darkness. *By God, the boy could see something. Him and his little eye!* Jack lifts the bottle, blows upon the end of the match to make it bright, and hurls it in the direction of the yelp.

Let there be light.

The bottle hits the ground and explodes, the schnapps igniting in an arc. It illuminates the upturned faces of maybe a dozen men, down in the drop, making for the path – a forlorn hope, sent forward first; nothing like enough to be the main force. Thor fires again, and this time a man falls. The thornbush is now burning as well. He feels Kai push another bottle into his hand. This one he aims at the path itself. A wall of flame, and of course it's liquid, it runs, and it illuminates everything – the side of the cliff alight, the path alight, the thorn crackling in the heat, and more men pushing forward. Now a third of Torsten's bombs, from Ulrik – thrown too long, too hard. 'Make 'em count!' Jack roars. He sees Magnus at the cliff's edge, scrabbling at something lodged there – a grappling hook. Elias rolls into place beside Magnus, points his pistol straight down over the edge, fires, and the rope on the hook goes slack. Magnus kicks the hook back over the edge. 'Move!' Jack tells them. For God's sake, surely Arvinius can see this? What is taking the man so long? Even the branches over the drop are in flames. Ulrik throws again, right on target, and illuminating not faces but backs, men scrambling to get away.

'They're running!' Ulrik bellows.

'Wait, wait, wait,' Jack tells them. 'Reload. There'll be a second wave, there'll be more.'

The thorn burns out. Smoke fills the drop. The stars still wink and sparkle in the sky.

Here they come. More, more, many more. *Oh, Scheisse*, thinks Jack. *It's all up to the Scribbler now.*

And here is the Scribbler; here is Rafe, head empty of everything but this extraordinary sensation of speed, of having a horse of Milano's calibre carrying him along. It is as if they are in flight! It is like being liquid, like being air, as if he is riding music! The road curves and he finds himself leaning into it, and Milano answers, easing with him – by God, faster yet! He ducks himself down along Milano's neck, repeating 'Stettin! Stettin!' as if the horse will recognize the word, as if it can understand, as the outline of the city grows sharper, darker, separates from the sky. 'Stettin, Stettin!' Rafe cries again, and Milano seems to elongate, nose bouncing against the air, nostrils agape, snorting it in; sweat scalloped along his flanks, thud, heart, thud, hoof, thud, thud, thud—

Only now there are men ranged out along the road, spreading out to bring him to a stop, and Milano knows them, he recognizes their shapes, their voices, the *woah, woah, woah*, and yes, he starts to slow, to pull up, because he is a good horse, an obedient horse, a *smart* horse, as he has been told so many times – only this time, this time, on this good hard road there is some part of him that is going to go on galloping into that starlit night forever.

'Gather the men!' Rafe shouts. He sees Ziggy, he sees the Executioner (who could mistake those ears?). He sees the Gemini. 'Gather the men!' he shouts, as Milano rears and dances beneath him. He cannot believe he has used such a phrase – just as if he were a soldier himself! He tightens the reins around his hands, he keeps his seat! 'Gather the men, we are under attack! Alarm, alarm, alarm!'

And now the second wave is on the path, and these mean business; these have sharpshooters of their own hidden within the rocks, and are using them to creep up closer under cover of each volley. 'There! Block them!' Jack yells. The rattle of another round of shot – *yes*, he thinks, *but how much do we have left?* Magnus's bandolier is empty, Luka's also, and there are only two of those bombs of Torsten's left. Ulrik takes one, he takes the other – *Ready, aim* – a shot shatters the bottle in his hand. Ulrik reels away, hand across his face. Jack throws himself flat to the cliff edge, pistol in his hand, sees a man on the path, a perfect target, sets it up, shoots – and the sleeve of his buff-coat, soaked in schnapps, instantly goes up in flame. 'Domini!' he hears Kai shout, behind him. 'Domini, you are on fire!' He pulls his arm from the jacket, throws it to the ground, and as he stands there a double meteor shatters the branches above them and plunges down into the rock and earth below. The air is full of twig and leaf and whistling particles of granite. Arvinius has the range. Shouts from below, shouts, screams: *RÜCKZUG! RÜCKZUG! GO BACK! GO BACK!* And now he thinks he also hears the barking of a dog. He turns – there are lights, there are torches coming through the trees, there are men, there are horses, he hears Kai's shout again: 'That's Dart!'

He gets to his feet. 'Quinto!' he roars, into the darkness, into the chaos below. Not one chance in hell the man himself will be there to hear it, but it is something, to stand there, to roar. 'Quinto, wherever you are, I will have you! I will have your fucken hide!' Two more from Arvinius's cannon boom through the air and down into the defile. The earth shakes. A trio of flashes from amongst the rocks. Just for an instant he has an image of himself, white-shirted, up against the darkness of the trees, just long enough to think *this was stupid of me* and then—

   If they can see it, they can aim at it.

He knows he must have taken a bullet. Nothing else could throw a man over with that force. It's he who took the bullet, sure, but it's Luka who is screaming. He lifts a hand to reassure the boy (*I have been shot, I know, I know*), and as he does a belt of agony pounds through him, from breast to spine. There is a smell of burning. Is he still on fire? Luka is shrieking, 'The Kapten! The Kapten!' Someone has an arm about him – Ulf, who looks down at him, then exclaims, 'Kapten! Oh no, oh God!' He cannot get his breath. He cannot speak. There is a hollow opening up between his lungs. All he can do is lie there, gasping, at quite how much it hurts to gasp. Ulf is trying to sit him up, and he feels himself, or feels his body, bellowing with pain, but all that comes out is this long, dry *Haaaaaah* of feeble disbelief. He looks down at himself. There is a hole in his shirt, still smoking, right over his heart. The light of the stars is failing, failing... There is no breath, anywhere. He has been cored. He lies back. Enough.

CHAPTER THREE

A Hero Lies Here

'If the wound do not penetrate into the Cavity of the Breast, but is only in the musculous Flesh, it must be cured as Wounds in the Fleshy parts…'

Richard Wiseman, *Severall Chirugicall Treatises*

Dear Mr Watts

Forgive the unsteadiness of my pen, Mr Watts, but there has been a plot, a plan, laid most vilely by a traitor in our midst, one Quint—

Clamour outside. Rafe's pen stutters across the paper. He hears Zoltan's voice, taking command.

—a plot to raid into our Camp Royal and wreak God knows what havoc upon it, on this one night when all those that would otherwise be about the camp had gone into Stettin to welcome Her Majesty, and this concatenation of circumstance – it damn near spelled the end of us. BUT, WE CONFOUNDED THEM, Mr Watts, my company and our captain, we drove them off, only I fear we have paid most tragically for our victory—

More noise out there, and now with purpose: cries of 'Lights, lights' and 'Let the man through!'

Mr Watts, I must leave off, the surgeon is arrived.

Felix Stromberg has made something of a study of bullets and their caprices, as they wander through the human body. Most particularly, he has made a study of that which since the battle of Dirschau in '27 has been lodged under His Majesty's shoulder-blade, which gripes most painfully if His Majesty attempts to wear the usual heavy steel cuirass, and which has taken all feeling from two of the royal Swedish fingers. As both man of science and Physician Royal, therefore, he is used to being called upon when those in need of his attendance are significantly higher up the pecking order than this, this troop of discoverers, way out in their ruined billet here on the edge of the camp, a long, dark and unexpected ride from his comfortable rooms in Stettin, not to mention the pleasures of this evening's reception for Her Majesty.

But such is life; such were his orders. He bends to his patient anew. 'If I might have a little more light – *tack*, my friend, thankee,' as the fearsome-looking fellow who has apparently appointed himself as surgeon's assistant drops his lantern lower. 'Yes, splendid, *perfekt*.' Lord, what creatures these discoverers be. He with the lantern – the fleshy features of a veritable troll. And look at these two, one at each of his patient's shoulders, holding his man steady. Hair like the seed-heads of the dandelion!

On the table before him, his patient continues his staccato gasp for breath. 'Slow and shallow,' Stromberg instructs him, giving his patient's shoulder an encouraging pat. 'Try to breathe slow, yet shallow. That is best.' He looks up, to be sure he has the full attention of his audience, and indicates his patient's breast, rather in the manner of a chef displaying some unusual delicacy. 'You see here,' he begins, 'the rupture of impact, the open wound –'

And so you do. Although that open wound does have the most curious imprint round it, which the fanciful might almost see as legs, a head, a tail…

'– the essential structures of the chest, not only breached in themselves, but with the invader embedded within. This, on first examination, was my fear. All else – the debrading of torn matter, the suppression of bleeding – proceeds from the need to follow the projectile in its track.' He folds his hands over his low-slung paunch, as if to keep them out of mischief. 'But in this case –' (a merry grin) '– in this extraordinary circumstance, upon further examining the wound, what do I see? Some great contusion, sure –' (and indeed the bruise upon his patient's chest is vast, the length of the breastbone and already twice its width) '– but nothing of that greater damage I would expect. No bursting flux of blood. No sign of the deep penetration that at such a site must prove fatal. You will readily perceive the same if I open the wound so – if you would hold him steady, gentlemen, my thanks again – and you will no doubt understand my puzzlement.'

The audience presses closer. 'Christ, Jeeesus!' the patient exhales.

'Ah, and the faculty of speech has returned!' Stromberg exclaims. He looks around, beaming. 'Excellent!'

At the back of the crowd are Lopov and Rafe. Lopov has his hands pressed to his cheeks. 'Our poor captain!' he repeats, over and over again. 'Our poor captain! Did you see him, when he was brought in?'

'I did,' says Rafe, who has no wish to relive the memory (the dragging arms, the head loose on the neck).

'Insensible!' Lopov continues. 'And that terrible wound!'

'Mr Lopov, we must have hope,' Rafe tells him.

'Yes, yes,' says Lopov, 'I know, yes, yes – my friend, is that the little dog? Is she hurt too?'

It is Dart, indeed. But the noise she's making is not the howl of something hurt, it's more a sort of gudding, like a heartbroken infant. 'Dart?' Rafe calls. He moves a step or two away, into the cloister. 'Dart, where are you?'

Is that the skitter of her claws? 'Dart! Where are you, little girl?' There she is, at the entrance to the nave. 'Come here, lass!' Rafe calls, crouching down, but already she is gone, back into the darkness of the nave itself. 'Dart!' he calls again, and she reappears, then once more doubles back, pausing only to make sure that this time he is following her.

Dammit! thinks Rafe. Behind him he hears Stromberg's voice, holding forth anew. 'Dart, this is not the time for games!' Yet he follows her into the nave, feeling the cold of the stone all about him, the stir and movement of the horses. There is but one lantern in the place, up where Milano is stabled. 'Dart!' he calls, and there she is, sat up against Milano, muzzle raised, a look of piteous supplication in her eye, and there can be no doubt what so distresses her: Milano himself.

Who lies on his belly, front legs doubled beneath him, neck curved, nose resting in the straw. Just like that horse in the field, that same calm resignation in his pose, that same great, heavy stillness. There, says the writerly part of Rafe's brain, wagging a finger, there is a lesson, how swiftly we learn to recognize death, on the scantiest experience. The rest of Rafe's consciousness ignores it. He drops to his knees. There is the horse's eye, half closed, and all the depth gone from it, all connection to the world. 'Oh, Milano,' he hears himself saying. 'Oh, Milano, why?'

Footsteps behind him. Here is Ziggy, bringing in the usual armful of fodder, because horses must be fed no matter what. He sees Rafe, kneeling. He stops. He sheds the armful. He too comes forward. Now he too is on his knees, pressing a palm to Milano's chest, where that mighty heart has stopped, clean as a clock. 'Milano!' Ziggy says, sitting back upon his heels. He turns a face of tragedy to Rafe. 'Ah, God in heaven,' he says. 'How are we going to tell him?'

'So in this case,' Stromberg is saying, 'in this *unique* case, I conclude that nothing has been carried into the body whatsoever.' He lowers his head to his patient's mouth. The man yet gasps like a fish. 'Yes, that will ease,' Stromberg assures him. He straightens up. 'Therefore, gentlemen, my decision is to treat this as a contused wound, albeit one with the *strangest* nativity.' He smiles and folds his hands once more. 'So, a soft dressing, and a simple sarcotic, to assist in the drying and the restoration of the flesh. Terebinth in gum Arabica, olium chamomile, olium hypericum. A little honey. I will have it made up and brought to you. As an anodyne, I will use olium papaver. I would advise, however,' he continues, looking round at his audience, and mindful of how well such a jest has gone over in the past, 'I would advise your captain bearing in mind that whereas cats may have nine lives, we men are given only one.' He lifts the silver wolf high enough for all to see, the silver wolf that now carries embedded in its breast a round lead musket ball. 'He is, I think, unlikely to be quite so lucky again!'

He waits for the laugh, but laughter there is none. Did they not hear him? 'I was saying, he is unlikely—'

Another of these rascals has come to the doorway, this one with a topknot red as blood itself, who knocks upon the wall where the door might once have been. The crowd makes space for him. 'Domini,' the man begins. He is turning his hat in his hands. Where a woman might wring her hands, a soldier does this – turns his hat round and round, by the brim.

The patient lifts his head. He can still manage no more than three words at a time, but he does his best. 'Ziggy,' he begins. 'What's up with.' Another breath. 'You?'

⁂

Dear Mr Watts
  Today, we buried our captain's horse. We buried him with every honour, and we all helped dig his grave.

No, it is no use. Rafe is too heartsick even for his usual charm to work, of turning the world into words. Outside, where shines the slimmest crescent of new moon, like God put down his wine glass when its foot was wet, in the square of open ground within the cloister, his brothers-in-arms celebrate Milano with strong drink and battle songs and a mighty bonfire, made above the ground where Milano now lies – Milano, his bridle, his saddle, his blanket and a scattering of aniseed candies. And above the archway through to that open ground, there is now a new, pale, sharp inscription, cut by young Kai as he sat upon Ulrik's shoulders:

En hjälte ligger här
A hero lies here

If nothing else, thinks Rafe, from the depths of misery, it will give any future passing antiquary food for thought.

Rafe is not one of those stood about the bonfire. Rafe is here, on his own, in what had been Milano's stall; the stone of the nave numbing his nates, feet stuck out into the straw, bottle in his fist and as drunk, he thinks, as he has ever been in his life. He killed his captain's horse. Some ignorant bit of horsemanship, his over-eager urging, carried him away and now Milano is dead. It is a terrible thing to think. This can never be forgiven. It can never be put right. He will carry this with him to his grave.

Two pairs of boots resound down the nave, and enter his unsteady field of vision. He looks up, wipes his cheeks.

The Gemini.

Rafe has never been in such close proximity to the Gemini before. Frankly, it perturbs him; and when they sit down on either side of him, it perturbs him even more. He has never exchanged a word with them, either; indeed, he has never been able to make out a single thing they say. They seem to have a unique language all their own. He has heard of this phenomenon amongst those who have shared a womb, but still it baffles him, how these two make their way in the world. Where have they come from? Where might they call home? Even when he has heard them speak to others in the company, it has been the briefest of exchanges only; the only souls you might say they hold actual conversations with are each other.

'Ingleeeesh,' says one.

It seems to Rafe some formal introduction is required. He makes to shake hands with them, but cannot decide which should take precedence, so placing the bottle carefully between his knees, with great concentration, he crosses his arms and thus manages to shake hands with both of them at once. 'Rafe Enckidot,' he says.

'Konstantin,' says one. 'Kazimir,' says the other. They nod their heads. Up close they are rather less alike, one's eyes are deeper-set; their noses are differently shaped. Also, does he imagine it, or do those heads of bright blond hair not show dark roots?

'I am from Lonun. London,' Rafe says next.

Kazimir indicates himself, his – well, twin. 'Riga,' he says.

Ah, *Livonia*. Is that the language they speak? Rafe nods his own head, with drunken, sage-like understanding. Kazimir – or is it Konstantin? he has forgotten already – speaks again. 'Vin shear badix,' he says. At least, that to Rafe is how the sounds resolve themselves.

To Rafe's astonishment, Konstantin – or is it Kazimir? – responds in perfect Latin. '*Est tristis*,' Konstantin says.

Now Rafe understands. The Latin is a translation, for his benefit. 'Yes,' he says, tearfully. 'Yes, I am sad. I am very sad. The captain's horse – I fear I murdered him.'

Konstantin nods his head. Is that in understanding, or agreement? Rafe feels his eyes fill anew.

Konstantin lays his own hand on Rafe's, patting it. '*Hoc manducare*,' he says, eat this; and Rafe sees Kazimir is holding something toward him – a rusk of some sort, field rations, generously smeared with something dark as pitch. It smells, not unpleasantly, of earth. 'What is that?' Rafe asks.

'Carne-piu,' Kazimir replies. 'Carne-piu par-valtz.'

Again, Rafe has no idea what the actual words might be. 'Carne-piu?' He takes the rusk and brings it to his nose. The smell of earth is overlaid with something else, a sort of oily promise.

'Eat,' says Konstantin. '*Laetificat cor*.'

It cheers the heart. 'Well,' says Rafe, 'my heart is most definitely in need of cheering. Thank you, gentlemen. *Gratias tibi*.'

They nod. They get to their feet. Rafe takes a bite of the rusk. Carne-piu. Ah – it has seeds in it, little nutty seeds, that pop between his teeth. It is perhaps a darkly northern version of bread dipped in oil; certainly that oily, musky savour is its only taste. He watches the Gemini depart – what quaint fellows they are, they hold hands, as they go! – and is chasing the seeds around his mouth when he realizes his lips and his tongue are tingling. Is this the first symptom of a syncope? he wonders. The precursor to an apoplexy, as his heart collapses under its load of guilt? He waits for his vision to narrow, for the cold sweats to begin. Certainly he has deserved no less. Even Dart has deserted him. Normally of an evening she would be beside him, the warm curve of her skull under his hand, smooth as the back of a spoon, and it would be a fine and comforting thing, to have it there. He thinks of her, how she had sat with her head pressed back against Milano's cooling shoulder, her eye fixed on Rafe's own until she saw that he understood, finally, what had occurred. She came to let us know! he tells himself. She *did* let us know. And what idiots she must have thought us, as she howled her message of bereavement down the nave. How little of the world we know, how little do we understand!

Ah, here she comes! He hears her tiptoe, just as if she had heard his thoughts – and why should dogs not hear our thoughts, thinks Rafe (amazed at how speedily his disordered mind puts forth this explanation), when they hear so much that we are deaf to? Yes, here is Dart, and with her—

His captain. Fiskardo.

Fiskardo, one hand spread across his breast, easing himself down to sit beside Rafe. In the other he too holds a bottle. Dart, pushing a way in between them, sits leaning up against Fiskardo's side, her head back, her eyes on Rafe, just as she had sat against poor dead Milano. *There*, she seems to be saying, *I will not lose this one, too*. Rafe cannot look at the man without seeing him as he was when he had himself walked to Milano's stall, supported on either side, how he lowered himself down, even though it must have been agony to do so, how he had tried to gather his horse's head into his lap, had lowered his face into Milano's mane...

'The Gemini said I would. Find you here,' his captain says.

He still cannot take a proper breath, thinks Rafe. The thought pierces like an arrow. No, he must cleanse his conscience, no matter what. 'Captain, I have to tell you – I think it was me. I think I killed Milano. I let him run too fast. I should have held him back. I am – I am on the rack with this, sir. I think it was me.'

'You think that? Is that why. You are here?' His captain shakes his head. 'It was his time, Rafe, that's all it was.' A deep sigh. 'I think he tried. To tell me so. I think he tried to tell me so. For weeks.' He lifts his bottle, but charily, not over-raising the arm. 'To Milano,' he says.

'To Milano,' Rafe echoes, unsteadily. 'He was the noblest of steeds,' he begins.

'Yes,' says Fiskardo. 'Yes, he was.'

'When he carried me, the solid earth disappeared. I felt as if I was riding through the stars,' Rafe hears himself say next. It is as if his mind is running about in ten different rooms at once.

'Yes,' comes the reply. 'I know that feeling. Knew it. Knew it well.' A moment's silence, then, 'Everything I love, I lose.'

'Oh sir, don't say so!' Rafe exclaims.

'Thus far,' his captain says, 'thus far, at least, my record. Is unbroken.'

That scarred left hand is at his forehead, his eyes have closed. Rafe has never seen a man look so entirely comfortless. For one terrible moment, he thinks he is about to see his captain weep, a thing which would be almost as bad as watching his own father do so as the bailiffs of the Stationers' Company had removed the last of their stock, all those many years ago. *Dammit*, thinks Rafe, *dammit, this time I will find something to say. I will not sit here with my tongue tied.* There is a peculiar resolution in his thoughts, a sort of rushing forward.

'Do you ever think, sir, how there must be some design to the course of all our lives?' There, now everything in his thoughts is falling into place at once. 'Some great design, only we see it not?' Yes, that is it! He nods his head – ah, look, the toes of his boots nod back! Delightful! 'Some great design, for all of us—'

He stops. He sees his captain is looking quizzical. 'No, go on, Mr Endicott, please.'

'But do you see – if there is a great design, and our lives are but the following of it – and after such a miracle as your own survival, sir, can we doubt it? Should we, should we not take comfort from that?' He waves his bottle to and fro for emphasis. 'And if only we could see the whole, and where it led, and how each happening was mother to the next – what comfort, what wisdom—'

'Mr Endicott,' his captain says, 'take breath.'

He does. His head feels hot.

His captain eyes him, head to one side. 'Rafe, have the Gemini. Been feeding you that black butter. Of theirs?'

'Yes!' says Rafe. Suddenly he is euphoric. 'Yes, sir. It had the strangest savour.'

'It's known to be. Somewhat strange in its effects, as well,' his captain tells him.

'But don't you think, sir? Don't you think?' Strangely Rafe now finds he can't recall what it is that he should think, exactly, but no matter. His head is full of stars.

'I had my fortune told me once,' his captain is saying. 'The whole design, as you would say. All laid out for me, by a blind man. A Roma.'

Rafe is amazed. 'You did?'

'And I regret to say. It made no sense whatsoever.'

'Oh,' says Rafe, crestfallen. But still, how tantalizing! 'But what was it? What did the Roma tell you?'

'Well,' says his captain. He is smiling. Yes, he is smiling! 'It was a very long while ago, so it is all somewhat. Jumbled now, but there was a deal of snow, I remember that. And many. Little birds. And a hall of mirrors. And a man there who seemed to be waiting for me. The Roma. Called him the Dead Man. Perhaps I am meant to. Fight him. And there was a room. Full of gold.'

'A *room* full of gold?' Rafe marvels.

One of his captain's rare great smiles. 'To the ceiling, Mr Endicott.'

'Why, that is extraordinary!' Rafe exclaims. 'That is extraordinary, Captain!'

'Is it?' comes the reply. 'It did seem so, once. Now, though, I think this world has not. Much design to it at all.'

Rafe looks up at the capital above them, that so unaccountably matches the one from his childhood. 'It is because we cannot step back far enough,' he says with decision. There, the vigneron agrees with him. Has parted the foliage and is nodding in agreement! That's it, that's it! 'If we could but see what these stones have seen, if they could but speak – do you ever think, sir, how that might be?'

His captain has his hands pressed to his breastbone, where all his air has been consumed in a cough – no, his captain has his hands pressed to his breastbone because he is wheezing with laughter! Excellent! *Laetificat cor!*

'And what makes you think,' Fiskardo asks, when he can speak again, 'that the stones would have any more sense. Than the men who put them there?'

He is trying to rise. Rafe has to help him to his feet. They stand together, swaying. 'I am on leave,' Fiskardo says, hand to chest, as if holding himself together. 'For the first time in my life. As a soldier. I am on leave. Zoltan has made himself. My nursemaid, so we leave you in the care of. Ilya. Try to be with us still, when I return.'

'I will, sir, I will!' says Rafe. 'Where is it you will go?'

'Stromberg is sending me. Back to the coast. Out of.' Another wheeze. 'Harm's way. The end is off. My breastbone. It must stick itself. Back.'

'Perhaps,' Rafe says, brightly, 'you will find your room full of gold.'

'Hah. I would settle for finding. Another horse.' But his captain smiles down on him still. 'You are a good fellow, Scribbler.'

'Yes, sir. Thank you.'

'But no more of that. Black butter while I'm gone.'

'No, sir. You have my word.' He watches his captain limping away. Oh, he has something more to say, something most important! 'But I will write this, sir. I will make a brave account of all. I will make you famous, I promise you!'

CHAPTER FOUR

My Lady Soap-Bubble

'Conception is nothing else but an action of the Womb, by which the prolific seeds of the Man and the Woman are there received and retained, that an Infant may be engendered and formed out of it.'

The Accomplisht Midwife

IT'S HAPPENED TO her before. There'll be a month when she doesn't bleed, then maybe there will be a second, but soon thereafter, one morning she'll wake hot with blood. Or she'll straighten her back as she lifts herself up from the tub, and feel the child silently, meekly, slip away. But the not-bleeding has never persisted as long as this. It's never caused her to pause, all of a sudden, bend double, vomit her breakfast up onto the grass. It's never caused her to have to move the button on the placket of her skirt. July had become August, had become September, and this one – it stayed hooked into her, this one.

She imagines her womb like her tub, she imagines the child stood with its feet spread wide, legs braced either side of that treacherous drain.

And September had cooled into October... And she has started to imagine it having a face, a name, a sex (the other washerwomen tell her it must be a boy, because it's sticking so far out of her already). She imagines cradling it in her arms, and it makes her breasts ache. She imagines a birth-day, she counts forward: it's going to be a springtime child.

She imagines a father.

They're not so very far away, she tells herself. *The Camp Royal at Stettin, he'll be there. I could let him know. I should let him know. Perhaps.*

Still she hesitates. This jelly-child, it has to have time to set.

She imagines other things. She imagines there being a wife, somewhere in far-off Muscovy; she imagines asking for him at the Camp Royal and being laughed at; or worse, the mournful shaking of a head – oh, how much worse would that be! She imagines him denying her – no, in fact she can't imagine that, she cannot think he ever would, but there are so many other things out there that could go wrong, and only one thread, one line, one course where everything goes right. So much safer to stay put.

Autumn sits itself down to stay. The bushes behind her tent, where that mad old woman Kizzy had danced with Lieutenant Zoltan's shirt, they lose their leaves. There's a morning when she wakes and finds she's looking up at a fur of frost on the outside of her tent, and inside, her breath steams. She imagines dying, in childbed, she imagines the child dying in childbed. She sees how the camp is clearing – companies sent out here, there, everywhere, to stiffen the defences through the winter of all the towns now flying the Swedish flag. She thinks of how a woman heavy with child cannot run.

October. November...

She feels how she can no longer bend over her tub, but has to come up to it sideways, on her knees, and how there are fewer and fewer men, so less and less linen, and how cold the water is now, and how far she must walk to gather fuel, and then one morning, kneeling, scrubbing, her belly swaying beneath her, she feels the child give her a kick. Not the little flutterings there had been before, which she maybe thought she felt and maybe thought she did not, but a proper hefty kick. 'Oh,' she says. Strokes her hand across her belly, and there it is again, as if tracking her palm from inside, *wallop*, another kick, unequivocal. I'm ready. Get us out of here.

FORTY-THREE MILES NORTH. Forty-three miles straight into the oncoming winter, that's where Stettin lies.

She tells herself, *That's nothing*. She's done fifteen miles a day before, and carrying her tub on her back, what's more, like a tortoise carries its shell. She tells herself, *You can walk that*. She makes her plans. She sells her tub, and her tent, and buys a pair of boots of Russian leather, to keep her feet dry, and a soldier's old buff-coat, with tatters of blue and yellow braid on the sleeves. Her own winter clothes are too tight for her now anyway. She buys hard rusks, dried deer-meat, the sort of wide, flat honey-cake you can snap into pieces. She buys gauntlets, fur inside. She asks about, she finds who's moving on, and buys herself a day's ride with one of the woman-sutlers, and a night in the woman's wagon, sitting up, propped against a wall of those little barrels of baccy, but the woman will only take her so far; the woman has her own living to make, she's even talking of heading for the Imperialist camp at Gartz. 'Why?' Rosa asks, and the woman shrugs. 'This lot,' the woman says, pointing with her pipe-stem at the camp behind them, 'they can conquer all the towns they like, but that won't pay their bills. Nor mine.'

Maybe thirty miles left, maybe a few more. The road goes up, it goes down. The ups are harder than she had expected, the downs are icy, but at least the ride in the wagon had got her beyond the empty country left around the camp, where it had sucked the world around it dry; every so often now there are other folk in sight. She walks with the old, who can only shuffle; with those with handcarts, who still have something to save, they're slow too. So are those with children, children who waddle along, holding a fold of skirt or the corner of a cloak, so swaddled and lagged they are hardly able to bend their limbs. The second night she follows those ahead of her off the road and into a barn, easing open the door to see heads by the dozen lifting out the hay – women, one or two big-bellied like her, old folk, children, and a few with that haunted, speechless look to them like they can't even remember what their names might be no more. No men, unless they be toothless ancients, mumbling and staring. When the familiar dark music reaches them of men in armour on the road, the rattle of arms, the tramp of marching feet, everyone ducks down their heads, Rosa too; they keep the littlest children silent with their hands across their mouths. 'Where are you from?' she asks the women nearest to her, once the road is quiet again, and the women name places she has never heard of, little villages, wiped from the map. *Where are you going to?* would be the better question. They must have tramped for miles; their feet are bound up till they are the size of loaves, and when they unwrap them, wincing, she sees some of them have toes that are black, and some of the children have the same tight, shiny-looking places on their fingers too. She strokes her belly, she tells the child in there, *That will never happen to you.* She pulls her feet, in her own good boots, out of sight, under her skirt. She shares the honey-cake. She asks them, do they know which is the road to

Stettin, and one of the women tells her, yes, find the road by the river. Follow it.

No, no, says another. Keep to the lanes, the byways. *Soldateska, soldateska.* The big roads are what the armies use.

Yes, but which army?

Soldateska, the woman says. Her expression is that of someone finding themselves talking to an idiot. *Soldiers, all the same,* and the others nod their heads.

Rosa spends the night pulling and picking the braid off the sleeves of her buff-coat.

Next morning there is snow dusted under the hedges and the air is cold enough to make your teeth ache. She's been out in the winter weather before, of course she has, but then she was with hundreds more, following an army, and then too she did not have the child inside her to keep warm. It makes much more difference than she had thought – her belly is like the outer curve on an old tiled stove, releasing its heat into the air.

Wait till tomorrow, some of the women say. Too cold today, too cold, stay here, but 'here' is no good to her, and who says tomorrow will be any better? She and a dozen others make their way back to the road, slipping and sliding, but Rosa is the only one with child, she's slow, and it's understood, it's every woman for herself, and soon she is on her own. She puts her head down, nose in her scarf, times her steps by her breathing, tries to keep steady. She starts humming under her breath a lullaby she remembers from her own childhood: Sleep child, sleep, your father tends the sheep... When her hands begin aching, her fingers in particular, tingling and burning along the cracks left in them from scrubbing at her tub, she folds them under her arms. She tries not to let her mind wander back to that moment, as she and those others left the barn, the looks that had been exchanged between those staying and those departing, the looks that had asked, *Is mine the right decision, or is yours? Will you end up dying because you stay – or will I, because I go?*

The small of her back starts to complain, then the muscles in her legs. She grows breathless, pauses, looks up, and there, thank God, is the river, the great silver ribbon of it, the land about it flat as if it had been ironed. Quills of sunlight move across the countryside, as if searching for something. The sky ahead, unbroken, right down to the horizon, is as vast and grey as the side of a mountain. And three bodies of pike moving along the road, looking from this distance like combs for carding wool, and just the glint on the pike-heads tells you how mortal they are. And at the head of the column a great flag, and on it a great eagle.

Keep to the lanes, the byways… the roads are for the armies, the little places for the little folk. *Zehr gut.*

There is no frost in the lanes, so they are thick with mud. You have to pull your boots up from it, every step. She tries to pick a way along the verges, following the tracks of all those who have done the same before her; wonders where are those folk now? At every rise she stops, and looks about until she spies the river, gets her bearings, then she goes on. Her body has opened the maw of its new appetites, ravenous for food and greedy for rest. She chews on a rusk to quiet herself down, and tries to stop her thoughts from racing ahead, into the cold there will be tonight, and the darkness, and the perils of the dark.

Another rise. It comes out at a crossroads. She is so weary. It's as if her bones have gone to sleep, and she has to wake them, all of them, one after another, every time she wants to move, just to put one foot ahead of the other. She has to rest. She's miscalculated this, she knows she has. This land is too big, the weather too heartless, the miles too long and too many.

Don't think of that. Find rest, that's all you have to do. She scans the landscape ahead – a barn, a cott, a ruin, anything with shelter, anywhere she can sit down.

She has sunk down upon the bank. Is she asleep now? There's a clop, clop, clop, the creak of wheels. And a cracked old voice,

singing – another song from her childhood. They used to call it
the Grandpa Dance:

> *Oh, the grandpa*
> *Took the grandma*
> *And the grandpa*
> *Was the groom*

She makes herself open her eyes and raise her head. What
is this?

A pony-cart is approaching the crossroads, basic as such a
thing can be: a piebald pony with a belly on it as round as her
own, and the cart no more than boards and a pair of wheels.
One old soul up atop, singing, banging out the beat with her
fist, another driving, and a third skipping along behind. And
the one driving has a strip of leather over her eyes.

Rosa clambers out onto the road, halloo-ing and waving her
arms. The cart comes to a stop.

'Well now, my Lady Soap-Bubble!' comes the cackled
greeting. And then the pipe-stem pointed at her belly. 'What
have *you* been up to, eh?'

They help her on board, and off they set again. 'Where are
we going, my ladies?' Rosa asks.

'Ah,' says Pernilla, 'we've a rendezvous.'

'Who with?'

'His kin,' comes the answer. The pipe-stem points at the pony.

'But where?' You can see the snow-clouds massing up on
the horizon, like the breasts of so many dark grey pigeons, all
jostling together.

'Arnulf knows where,' Kizzy calls back. She's skipping along
now at the pony's head.

Arnulf?

The pony, of course. Another cackle from Pernilla. 'Why,
you didn't think it was Roxandra finding our way, did you?'

*

Breadcrumbs of snow start to fall, then there are flakes, then great fat feathers from those pigeons' breasts – gently, slowly, spinning down. She brushes them off her belly, wraps the buff-coat more tightly round her. Now she is nervous again. 'We will need shelter,' she says.

'Trust us, little mother, trust us. All will be well.'

You have to peer through the flakes to make out what's ahead, and even then it withholds itself. A stand of trees, leafless and fragile, but something dark within it. Now the dark thing has shape. A tent. Big enough for there to be separate facets to its roof, with many different props holding it up, and a carpet laid on the ground at its door. And two more ponies, spotted like dominoes, like Arnulf, with a windbreak set up behind them, and a wagon behind that; and both ponies pulling at the turf as if the snow were happening some other place entirely.

Arnulf gives a whicker and breaks into a bouncy trot. A woman appears at the doorway to the tent, stooping to emerge, then standing upright – a woman in a wide red skirt and a wide-brimmed hat. Her shape stands out; then a boy joins her, and as soon as she sees them, Rosa's thinking, *Roma*. She turns to Pernilla, alarmed, and finds the same word is in her head a second time. *Oh*. Roma, of course, all of them. How did this never occur to her before? What should she do about it, in any case – get down? Run away?

Kizzy has gone skipping forward. *Oh*, there are men coming out of the tent as well – one in a long pale robe, one with a head of hair so fiery-red even the falling snow can't dull its colour. And then another, in boots and buff-coat, like a soldier, who hangs back. The one in the long pale robe moves with his hands held out – *Oh*, he's blind. The red-headed man is leading him forward. They come up to Kizzy, and the man with red hair kneels to her, and she strokes his head, then goes to the man in the long pale robe and lifts his hands to her face.

'Who are they?' Rosa asks, in a whisper.

'Her boys, of course,' Pernilla answers. She sounds surprised that this should not be obvious. 'Our nephews. That's Rufus, that's Benedicte. Kizzy's sons.'

Kizzy's sons. And the woman in the great wide skirt, with silver garlanded about her neck, from collar to belt, is Yuna, Rufus's wife; and the boy is their son, Emilian. And the other man, who hangs back so?

'Signor Ravello,' Pernilla tells her. 'A friend.'

They sit in the back of the wagon and watch the snow come down. Rosa has a sense that she is not permitted in the tent, and that the three old women are out here with her to keep her company. The wagon has cushions and pillows across its floor; it's a deal more comfortable than jars of baccy, and the steadiness of the falling snow is making her eyelids heavy. Does she doze? Does she sleep? She knows that at one point Roxandra leans across, places a hand on her belly. 'They say a boy,' Rosa tells her, embarrassed. 'That's what I'm told.'

Roxandra's hand is heavy. Rosa feels the baby move, as if to push it off.

'Nonsense,' Roxandra replies, behind her blindfold. 'That's a daughter. Any fool can see that.'

Signor Ravello walks past, carrying a blanket to put over his horse. He gives the wagon a sort of trimmed-off salutation as he passes. His face is harrowed with lines, his clothes as deeply wrinkled as if the wrinkles have been sewn into them, his boots dark with riding and with wear. His horse is as good and big as anything she saw ridden by the scouts, but shaggy as a dog. The pair of them, horse and rider, bear evidence of weeks and weeks of unaccustomed and relentless wear. Where would they have come from, to be here?

The woman, Yuna, and the blind man, Benedicte, come out of the tent, and there is a three-way consultation between them and this Ravello. At one point Ravello points to the sky, where the snow is lessening, but when he does so, Yuna shakes her head.

'What is it he wants?' Rosa whispers.

'*Ach.* He wants to get on to Stettin tonight. Some *gadjo* fuss.'

'Stettin?' She struggles upright. 'But I want to get to Stettin too!'

'We know, little mother, we know.'

Now Kizzy comes out of the tent, the boy with her, holding a blanket over Kizzy's head like a palanquin. The man makes his case to her, every so often glancing back at the wagon. Rosa has the strangest notion, that she is herself the subject of discussion here. Kizzy listens, speaks, the man bows his head, acquiescent. Something astonishing occurs to Rosa. 'Is it Kizzy who is in charge?'

'Of course it is,' Pernilla replies. 'It's Kizzy is in charge of *everything.*'

Kizzy, under her canopy, walks away. Yuna comes up to the wagon. 'It is too late to travel on today,' she says. 'Dame Kezia says there are too many gadjo on the road. Too many folk we don't know, and don't know us. We go no further.' She looks across to Rosa. 'So, tomorrow, Signor Ravello will take the little mother on to Stettin with him. Yes?'

AND JUST HOW will Signor Ravello take the little mother on to Stettin?

Riding pillion, that's how. A folded blanket behind his saddle for her to sit on, and for a mounting block, the hub of the wagon wheel, plus a hefty push from Roxandra. Rosa hasn't ridden pillion since she was a child, and her first thought as she tries to balance herself is, *This was never intended for a women with a baby in her*. And the man, Ravello, shifts about himself as she gets into position, in a manner that makes her feel he wishes she were not there, either. But then he shows her how she can hold onto the solid high back of his saddle, and the sky up above begins to clear and reveal some blue, and all she has to do is endure this, and she will be in Stettin. Which means Ilya. Ilya! A tiny uprush inside her at the thought. Oh, but what if – what if all those things that might go wrong, now in fact do? What if any one of them does?

To take her mind off all the possible *what ifs*, she tries to make conversation with the man, with this Ravello.

'Thank you,' she says.

It takes a moment for him to respond. Then, '*Prego*,' he says. 'You are welcome.' Then, 'The Roma like you. Dame Kezia says you were mannerly to them.'

'It never hurts to be mannerly,' she replies.

He seems to think about this. 'Why are you travelling to Stettin?' he asks next.

'My man is there.' It is like a little sip of something sweet, something strengthening, to speak of him. And now he might be so near! (*Oh, but what if—*) 'He is a discoverer. A scout.'

'Ah.' Another pause. 'I rode with a company of scouts when I was first in Germany,' he says, and she thinks, *Well, if I liked you any better, I might see if you know mine*, as she has a sense Fiskardo's name in particular will have travelled; but then she feels him sigh, and he adds, 'But I think they must all be long dead now.' And it is a strange thing to have the solidness of a man's body up against her own, like this, and for it not to be that of the father of her child. It makes her self-conscious, it makes her feel too much conversation should be avoided, so after that they go on in silence. The baby swings back and forth inside her to the rhythm of the horse as if this was no more than a hammock.

The man twists about. 'There,' he says, pointing, and as she follows his pointing finger she hears herself pull in her breath. 'The castle. Stettin. Do you see?'

Yes, she does, she does! And a great dark earthwork, like a giant slow-worm, zigging and zagging its way about the town.

The last few miles, they seem to take ten times as long as any that came before. Added to which, she's readying herself for how it can be when you try to get into a camp, how the guards amuse themselves in quibbling and cross-questioning you, and if you are a woman on your own, telling you that you must come into the guardroom and wait and all the rest of it, but this Ravello, he leans down as they come up to the gate, gives his name like it's an order, and the guard drops his halberd at once and waves them through – through the raw-looking gates that still smell of pine, and in – in past banks of earth big enough to make mannikins of both those on top of them and those walking about beneath.

'Will I take you to your scouts?' he asks. But she is wary of arriving in front of Ilya riding behind another man; she is truly nervous now, so she says no. So he dismounts; he hands her down. 'Good day to you then, Madame Rosa,' he says. 'And good luck.'

She steps aside from the road, taking a moment to stamp some strength back into her legs, to waken their pith; and to comb her hair with her fingers. She pulls her clothes straight, beats the worst of the journey from her skirt. There are pathways leading all across the camp, and she has no idea which might be the right one, but she spies one of the leaguer women, at her stall selling hot grog, so she goes up and asks politely as she can, 'Do you know where are Ancrum's discoverers? Fiskardo's company?'

The woman nods her down the road, then calls her back and presents her with a ladleful of hot grog of her own.

On she goes. Mind the wagons, moving everywhere, mind the horses, and mind the men, all turning to stare. But everywhere the pathways meet, she asks; and every time she asks she is pointed on again, and if there are nudges and sniggers behind her back, she ignores them.

At last there is almost no further to go. The opposing wall of the earthwork is there before her, and trees – countryside – beyond that. There is a gun emplacement, and just before it some ancient ruined place, with horses outside, and a young man, throwing a stick for a pretty black dog. He looks most unsoldierly. Hardly any beard, and ink-stains on his fingers, and (she notes as she comes nearer) on his cuffs too.

Oh, her back aches. Oh, her legs too.

'I'm in search of Jack Fiskardo,' she says.

'Are you?' the young man replies. He sounds astonished. He is trying not to look at her belly. The pretty dog has sat at his feet, cocked an ear.

'Or his discoverers,' she tries.

'Why then,' the young man says, this time pointing at the ruin, 'we are all in there. But our captain, he is on leave.'

'Is your sergeant—' she begins, and he looks so relieved, at the thought of there being someone he can hand her on to.

'Yes, yes,' he says, and then redeems himself: 'Please, good lady, take my arm.'

He leads her in. The dog runs ahead, like a herald. There is stone underfoot, and stone overhead – and voices, male voices echoing toward her, and suddenly one exclaims, 'Fräulein Rosa!' And it is Kai, little Kai, although not so little now, she sees, and there, Thor, she remembers him, and then the one who got himself whipped, and then there is Ilya, her Ilya, pushing his way through. He stops. 'Rosa!' he exclaims, in that particular accent of astonishment, as if you must name the person in front of you before you can believe they are there. And then he sees her belly. *Well*, she thinks, *he will either come forward, or go back, it will be one or the other; one way or the other, I will know.*

He does neither. 'Rosa,' he repeats. He drops to one knee. '*ROSA!*

ACHILLE DE LA TOUR has taken up residence in a triplet of rooms in Stettin, and has also acquired some sort of share in servants who can not only provide hot water on the instant, enough for Ravello to wash these weeks and weeks of travel from his body, but who also offer new linen to then clothe that body in; replacing the vinegar stink of Ravello's own sweat and the apple-scented perspiration of his weary steed with something much more befitting civilized company, something with lemon balm to it, thinks Ravello, taking an appreciative sniff of his sleeve. And a fire, breathing warmth across the room. One might almost forget the wastelands outside exist, sitting here; here with beeswax candles adding their own faint scent of honey to the air, with wine on the table, a napkin for his fingers and what would that be in the tureen, steaming away?

'I am speechless,' Achille is saying. 'Forbach to Stettin. I had no idea you would make such a journey yourself. And Paris to Forbach, before that. Good God.'

'I tell you, Achille,' Ravello answers, shifting discreetly from one tender bum-bone to the other, 'it has almost done for me. For no-one but His Eminence, and even then, never again. I thought I was younger than this.' He points to the table. His stomach is growling so fiercely it is as if it would lead him to it, on hunger's leash. 'What awaits us there?'

'Buttermilk soup,' Achille informs him. 'Most nourishing for the traveller, I am told. They make it with bacon. And to follow, pressed duck. And wine, of some sort, although –' (he lifts the stopper of the decanter, sniffs) '– I think they do not understand wine in Pomerania. But eat, please, before I ruin your appetite with all the latest news. His Eminence,' he continues, filling Ravello's glass, 'our poor beset Cardinal. The court is in schism, don't you know. The gloves have come off

and the gauntlet been thrown down, with the Queen Mother
and her wretched Habsburgs to one side and the Cardinal to
the other. Apparently the King's health threatens to collapse
entirely, he is so torn between them. I am sure you can imagine
the state of the Cardinal's own. Yet still he holds out. His voice
in the King's ear, it is all that we have. Reine Marie, by all
accounts, is thriving. Tell me, how does Germany, since you
have travelled clean across it?'

'It trembles,' Ravello tells him. 'The Emperor has spread his
armies all across it, and it trembles still. Both the Frankfurts,
Cologne, Leipzig, Berlin – all expect to have His Swedish
Majesty arrive at their gates next.'

'Whereas, did they but know,' says Achille, darkly, 'the
situation here – neither men nor money. We may very like be
sitting here next winter too. Or whatever of us is left by then.'

'You are becoming a strategist, I see,' says Ravello.

'Dear Lord, no. I am but an infant in such matters. The
duck is splendid, don't you think?' says Achille, taking another
forkful. 'Before they bone it, they stew it with juniper berries.'

'And Quinto del Ponte?' Ravello asks.

'Ah, what a tale hangs there!' Achille sits back, as if to give it
space. 'Whether the man was in the pay of the Queen Mother,
whether he was in that of her Habsburg uncle, whether he was
in business on his own account – a mystery. Likewise, where the
treacherous little monkey might be now.'

'*Where* he might be?' Ravello echoes. 'He is not here?'

'No longer, no. I was on his trail soon as I could get to Stettin,
but he was long gone. Apologies, I know that this was not what
you wished to hear.'

No, not by any means. *And so much*, thinks Ravello, *for we
will take you to the one you seek*. It's a shock. It's more than a
shock. He feels years older, on the instant; he feels every blasted
mile of that journey here. His Roma have never failed him so
before. Now where to look? Where to even begin?

He realizes Achille is still speaking.

'It seems he provided Generalissimo Conti, at Gartz, with details of our camp and its defences. A raid was attempted; need I say it was foiled. Quinto vanished ahead of it.'

'If the man has gone,' Ravello begins, 'I believe he was in possession of a letter—'

'Also gone, and yes, he was. He was noted for the care he took of it. What was in it?'

'It was a message he had carried for His Eminence,' Ravello begins. He licks his lips, his mouth has dried. 'Not a recent message, but of great importance all the same. Certainly of great importance to the Cardinal himself. I was sent to retrieve it. It, and Quinto himself. I think –' He puts his hand to his brow. The image of that dusty courtyard is before him, the Cardinal standing at the window, pointing down. 'Achille, Quinto del Ponte must be found. Him, or it.'

'But where?' Achille asks, staring at him. 'But how? He could be anywhere—'

'No, he will be *somewhere*,' Ravello snaps. 'Men like Quinto do not disappear; they have livings to make. He will have left a track, he will be – he will be *computable*. He will have an aim in mind, it can be followed, he can be hunted out.'

'Ah,' says Achille. 'I see, yes. Possibly.'

'Who knew him, when he was here?' With practised hand (ball of the thumb, knuckle of the first finger) Ravello brushes up the tips of his freshly trimmed moustache; an aid, he always finds, to the ordering of his thoughts. 'Who did he speak to? Who did he spend time with?'

'Ancrum,' says Achille. 'A Colonel Ancrum. But Ancrum has so smeared his reputation in this matter that the King has sent him back from whence he came, tasked with raising a regiment. If the man succeeds in raising another two, then it might be worth him trying to return. But I wouldn't hold your breath.' He ponders a moment, holds up a finger. 'There is one other. A captain amongst the discoverers. He kept his eye on Quinto. It was he, in fact, gave the alarm and foiled the raid. His reputation is a little *skiddy*, let us say, but he is a great favourite with His Swedish Majesty.' And Achille gives a little shrug, as if to say, who can account for such things?'

'Is he here?' Ravello asks. 'If he is in camp—'

'Sadly, he is not. He took a hurt and is on leave. The most curious thing,' says Achille, leaning forward, 'but I knew his name. Knew it at once. You might do so too. Fiskardo. Jacques Fiskardo. His father played a part in ridding us of Concini, all those years ago—'

He looks up, at the sort of sound more commonly associated with choking than eating, and jumps to his feet. His guest is the colour of the soup. 'My friend! Do your travels tell upon you? Are you well? Are you quite well?'

CHAPTER FIVE

M'sieu

'An HORSE is... a creature sensible, and therefore so far as he is moved to do anything, he is thereunto moved by sense and feeling.'

John Astley, *The Art of Riding*

IT WAS DUKE Wartislaw I who made the town of Wolgast, and ever since the people of Wolgast have had reason to appreciate what a good turn he did them, siting it so with the castle protecting its harbour, and the island of Usedom blocking the Baltic's winter storms. Further north, the sea is already sluggish with ice, and soon it will cease to move entirely, become this petrified mass, still holding the corrugations of the last watery thought to move across it; but here at Wolgast the sea will be open until February at least; some winters it hardly freezes at all; and thank St Elmo, patron saint of mariners, with

his church down there on the quay, for that. And just as well
– there is an army out there to reprovision, resupply. You can
imagine how busy the harbour here must be, how crowded with
masts and rigging; how bulgingly full Wolgast's warehouses –
warehouses that stretch up into the town, so that the crates, the
sacks stuffed so full a man can hardly lift them, the barrels of
goods from the ships moored at the quayside finish this part of
their journey sliding over the long-buried skeletons of Slavic
tribesmen; over the foundations of their temple to Gerowit, god
of war; they pass houses first put up by the Danish invaders who
slew those tribesmen; and then they find themselves locked away
in storerooms and strongrooms all guarded by these new invaders, the Swedish. One whole quarter, near enough, of Sweden's
wealth, of everything she has, is being funnelled down into the
north of Germany – seriously, thinks Zoltan, standing on the
quayside, how can anyone imagine, on our own, that this can
be sustained?

But (he tells himself) let's not fret over that today. Of much
more concern to us right now is the finding of a stables, both for
our own horse, Reena, and for that from Anklam being ridden
by our unsmiling companion, and after that, let the day bring
what it will. His gaze wanders down the quay. The harbour
here in Wolgast is a gathering place for all those in the town
whose business is horseflesh – the buying of it, the selling of
it, and the slaughtering of it, in the case of any animal that
staggers ashore in too bad a state to save; the war in Germany
wasting horses at even more barbaric rate than it wastes – well,
everything else. The alehouses where this business is done line
the quayside, many now with auction arenas thrown up behind
them, and all with stables – not there, Zoltan thinks (doing the
usual triage across such places in his head), that one looks like it
was set up only yesterday; not there, too small and old and mean
– ah. There. Perfect. He dismounts, gestures encouragingly to
his companion to do the same.

Where Zoltan has come to a stop is outside the alehouse of Herr Gruber, and the emporium run by his neighbour, Frau Klara. Herr Gruber calls his alehouse the Fat Herring, while Frau Klara's has an empty scabbard hung above its door, which ought to make the nature of its business clear to anyone. It's only a little after sunrise, with one of those wintry dawns paling the sky, and Zoltan has to rat-a-tat on Herr Gruber's door once and twice and once again before its yawning proprietor appears. Yes, there's a room. Yes, there's stabling. No, he will not lower the price for either. The two of them (Herr Gruber casts a suspicious eye at the second horseman, still aloft, and every bit as unfriendly-looking as before) can share the attic, and think themselves lucky.

So Zoltan and Jack lead their horses round behind the Fat Herring, to where its stables are to be found.

Meantime, the door to Frau Klara's bangs open, and there stands Sophie, the oldest of Frau Klara's girls. Sophie is cushiony of shoulder and of hip, and, as of this moment, stands cocooned in the blanket from her bed, pale and plump as a silkworm. She raises a hand to her mouth and yawns, produces a chamber-pot from under the blanket and is about to swill its contents at the drain when she hears the tread of boots returning from the stables. She turns her head. 'Frau Klara!' she yells. 'There's gentlemen!'

Sounds from within the house. In the meantime, Zoltan reappears. Sophie looks him up and down. She lets the blanket slip from one shoulder. ''Allo,' she says.

Jack also reappears. Sophie gives him the up and down too, but says nothing.

Here is Frau Klara. Frau Klara has cheeks rouged as red as the bull's-eye on a target and brows of an unlikely sooty black, and once upon a time it would have been she standing here at the door with her chamber-pot. But she worked hard, she nurtured neighbourly relations with Herr Gruber, and now it is

not. Two girls work for her, instead: Sophie and Katya. A few
months ago Katya was hoeing beans and playing handy-dandy
with the ploughboy; the changes in her life since then have left
her stunned. Sophie and Frau Klara regard her as something of
a simpleton, and any man Frau Klara doesn't care for the look
of gets handed on to her.

Frau Klara notes with satisfaction the entanglement of
eye-beams going on between Sophie and Zoltan. Holding the
door invitingly wide, she speaks. 'Will you step in a moment,
sir? Refreshment, a chance to rest your bones – we are a humble
house, but such comforts as we can offer are yours. Nice clean
girls – and all most reasonable,' she adds, as Zoltan does indeed
step in, dipping his head and grinning broadly. Then she sees
Jack, and a calculation takes place across her hectic features. She
puts her head back. 'Katya!' she yells.

The yard returns to its previous quiet.

The door to Frau Klara's comes open once again. Jack goes to
the bench by the door, sits, sticks out his booted legs, puts his
hands behind his head and tilts his face to the sky.

Some half hour later, by the sun moving round the helm-
shaped tower of St Elmo's, Zoltan re-emerges, tucking in his
shirt. Crosses to Jack, sits down beside him. 'That was a very
pretty girl,' he says, with satisfaction.

'Glad to hear it,' says Jack. 'Now, can we get looking for a horse?'

It seems to Zoltan that the mood here is not quite what he
would expect. 'Don't tell me,' he says. 'You take the one with
the dark hair, yes?'

'As it happens, no,' comes the reply.

'The devil why not? What was wrong with her?'

'She was scared,' says Jack.

Zoltan heaves a sigh. 'Listen, Jacques,' he says, 'these are not
like the punks in camp. You got to gentle them along. Hunch
up a little. Smile – no, not like that, Christ, that would scare
even me—'

'Zoltan,' says Jack, 'I hate to be the one to break it to you, but handsome as you are, when it comes down to it, these girls don't like you any better than they do me. You want to know the best thing we could do, for any of them? Disappear. So why bother?' He turns away. 'And I did pay her,' he adds.

There is a moment's affronted silence.

'Brother,' says Zoltan, finally, 'I love you. But ever since you lost Milano, you are like an emerod. A God-damned *pain* in the *arse.*'

Noon, and the quayside is as full as a fishing-ground holds gulls. Outside the Fat Herring, Sophie and Katya are running back and forth with trays of pretzels and jugs of beer and the air is threaded through and through with horse-noise, whinnies and whickers and good full-throated neighs. Deals are being done at the speed of a spit into a palm, sealed with a slosh of tankards, and there is talk, too, in particular of a ship coming in from Köslin on the morrow. There's a new face amongst the dealers, a fellow calling himself August von Hoch, and while he's a bit of a blowhard, without a doubt, he's boasting that he has something very special coming in aboard that ship, a stallion with a pedigree to make your mouth water, and what's more, the beast was the bargain of the year, to boot.

Sunset sees Katya, at her attic window, idly plaiting her hair. She sees those same two young men as before return along the quay, apparently empty-handed. Incurious, she follows their progress to Herr Gruber's door. 'We must have seen near fifty horses today,' the one with the moustaches is saying, as they wait for Herr Gruber to answer. 'And you're telling me, not one of them was worthy of you?'

'No,' comes the reply, floating upward. 'I'm telling you, not one of them was worthy of Milano.'

The Fat Herring and Frau Klara's share a wall. Sound carries. Katya hears boots going up the Fat Herring's stairs. One flight, two, three – they are in the attic. This means, in effect, that Katya and the two men will be sleeping next door to each other tonight, separated only by two skins of plaster and the ribs of wattle in between.

Katya says her prayers. She gets into bed. After a little while she hears snoring from the room next door, loud as a length of chain being dragged across the floor. The ropes under the mattress squeak; footsteps pad across its floor; she hears its window open. Someone next door is wakeful. Pulling her bedclothes round her, Katya goes to her window, in turn. Sophie has suggested Katya might find being squashed flat rather less unpleasant if she tried making a little conversation with the gentlemen first, and Katya thinks now that the one who is wakeful will be the one who paid her for nothing, and that perhaps she might feel less stupid talking with him than she would with those others, the ones who squash her. She eases her window open, peers out and round. She can just make out the man's hands upon the windowsill. "*Tag*,' she says, nervously.

A moment's surprise, then the response comes back. His voice, she remembers it. "*Tag*, little one.'

Taking courage, Katya wraps the bedclothes more tightly round her, leans out a little further. Now she can see his profile, tilted up to the night sky, and his bare throat. 'Ain't you cold?' she asks.

'I'm used to it.' Although his voice, to Katya, sounds warm.

'What are you doing?' she asks next.

'Looking for my old horse,' he says. 'He's up there somewhere.'

Katya too tilts her face up. There's no sign of a horse up there that she can see. 'You here looking for a new one?'

'That we are,' the man says.

'Couldn't you find one?'

'Not yet. We'll look again tomorrow.'

'There's lots of horses get unloaded here,' Katya offers. 'Every day.'

'True.' She thinks now that he has turned toward her. 'But a horse has to choose you, as well as you choosing it. You have to find each other.'

'Jacques!' A grumpy-sounding protest from the snorer in bed. 'The hell – close the window!'

The man leans out far enough for her to be able to see that he has his finger to his lips. 'Shhh,' he says, then she hears the window close and he is gone.

Katya goes back to her bed. The moon rises. Wolgast sleeps.

IT'S WOLGAST'S SEAGULLS wake him, yawping away out there in outrage at some disturbance of their dock. He lies there, idly rubbing at the place on his breastbone where it still aches, and where the heart beneath it still complains as well. *What do you want?* Zoltan keeps asking him, *What is it we are looking for?* and the only answer he can come up with he can't make, because it is too witless: *I want a horse that talks to me. I want Milano.*

Floating up the stairs comes the voice of the man himself, Zoltan, and then the delighted giggle of a woman taking a compliment – Frau Klara, by the sound of it. Zoltan could charm the pearl out from an oyster. *How does the man do it?* Jack wonders. *How? Whereas they look at me and only pray as I'll leave 'em alone.*

He pulls on his boots and his jacket – he has healed plenty well enough to be able to do that for himself once more, to raise an arm above his head. Or to hold a set of reins, if only there were any worth the holding. Ah me. He goes to the window. That plantation of masts, the geometries of rigging, the billowing white of half-furled sail, and there, rammed in the midst of them, and no doubt the cause of the seagulls' indignation, a big Baltic trader, with a pennant in Köslin's blue and white streaming from her stern.

And then, also from outside, a commotion. Shouts of warning, a sudden rush of folk along the quay, toward the church, and then a falling back, and then a noise, if you can imagine this, such as a man might create if he were sawing through a trunk of iron-hard wood, with a new and unoiled blade, and the wood by some mischance had a length of pipe embedded in it. Zoltan appears on the quayside, just as the scream, the screech, the God knows what you'd call it, as it reaches its *fffff*fortissimo. 'God bless us and save us!' comes Frau Klara's squeal. 'What in the name of heaven is that?'

That's a horse, Jack thinks. *No, that's a stallion*. Nothing else in Nature can produce a noise like that. The rush of folk has come to a stop outside the church, there are people pointing to its door. Even the sailors on the ships in harbour have straightened their backs to stare. That scream again. It has an echo to it, as if it's coming from within an interior.

The two girls are running back along the quay. He sees Zoltan's girl, the little pudding, stagger to a halt, hears her call out, 'Oh, Frau Klara! Frau Klara! 'Tis terrible! The mad thing, it's done gone run right inside our church!'

'Well now, Captain!' Herr Gruber announces, as Jack comes up. 'Here's a right to-do!' Zoltan, standing to Herr Gruber's other side, nods toward the church and says with a grin, 'You won't believe this. There's a horse in there.'

The door to the church is part-ways open. Darkness inside but also, yes, something in there barging about; and a divot of crumbled stone gone from the edge of the step where no doubt an iron horseshoe hit it; and a boy being lowered to the ground by the step, a boy grinding his teeth in pain and holding himself with the tilt of one nursing a broken arm. 'Fucken stomped me!' the boy is saying. 'Run fucken mad, it has!'

The crowd has divided itself, Jack sees, as crowds so often do – he, Zoltan, Herr Gruber at what you might call its neutral middle, then to one side a group of men in the baggy breeches, the wood-soled shoes of mariners; and to the other a man in a fur-trimmed coat so splendidly flocked and figured it wouldn't look out of place on a Lord Chancellor. 'That fellow there,' Herr Gruber continues, 'August von Hoch. His horse broke loose as they was leading it along the quay. Christ, it's a size! And the boy there, he's sweeping out our church, and the beast sees the door is open and what's it do but run inside!'

'Tis a desecration!' shouts a voice from the crowd. From within the church, another of those fearsome screams, loud enough to make you wince. 'Tis a devil-horse!' shouts another.

The owner of the devil-horse spins about, the fur-trimmed edge of his coat a-flying. 'You provoked it!' he bellows at the mariners, and then to the crowd, 'And that is as fine an animal as any of you people is ever like to see!'

'Provoked it?' The sailors are incensed. 'You any idea the trouble it's give us? Took four of us just to get it off the boat!'

'We had to hood it before it 'ud even move!'

'An' even then it kicked at everything we passed!'

'The bastard thing's possessed!'

Another man comes running up, breathless with self-importance. 'Harbour-master's on 'is way,' he says, 'with 'is blunderbuss. That'll sort it.'

August von Hoch gives a groan. Within his coat he seems to crumple. 'Good people, please! That is a thousand-thaler horse in there!'

Which is – *which is as ridiculous a claim as you would expect from a fellow with that coat in his wardrobe*, thinks Jack. Reena is as tidy a beast as you could ask for, and she cost eighty; while Milano (best horse in the world) came to Jack for – well, to be honest, for nothing at all. 'You paid a thousand thaler for a *horse?*' he hears Zoltan exclaim, incredulous. 'Jesus! You must be as crazy as it is!'

'Of course I didn't pay a thousand thaler for him,' Herr von Hoch snaps in reply. 'He was the bargain of the year. But that's what he's worth, make no mistake. His grand-dam was the Buckingham mare.'

The Buckingham mare? By God, there's a name from his past. There's a memory. The docks in Amsterdam, and the Buckingham mare, that pretty bay, stood on a gangplank, her Arab head lowered, glaring at the men who had been unloading her, refusing to go either up or down. But she had moved for him, this vagabond, as he was then; she had let him lead her, docile as a lamb. It's one of the very first times he can ever remember having been proud of himself. At least, in that part of his life, that part when he was on his own.

The noise of something heavy toppling over in the church. 'We don't care if it dropped out the cunny of the Winter Queen herself!' declares the same voice from within the crowd. 'Gerrit out our church! Gerrit shot!'

'*Meine Herren*, please,' Von Hoch beseeches them. 'Be reasonable. I'll pay fifty thaler, fifty thaler here and now for anyone will get him out of there.' He waves a heavy-looking purse above his head. 'Fifty thaler. Who's up for it? Who'll give it a try?'

Jeers in response. 'Do it yourself!' 'Make it five hundred!' 'Gerrit shot!'

'One hundred,' Jack hears himself say. The memory floats away; back in the here and the now he is facing Zoltan, who puts a hand on his arm, saying, 'Jacques!' and who clearly approves of this notion not at all; and Herr von Hoch, who seems now to see Jack for the first time, and to be making up his mind whether he approves of him or not.

'You reckon you could do it?' Von Hoch asks.

'For one hundred, I'll try.' He casts a glance at the crowd. 'And I don't see no other volunteers.'

'Ah, damnation!' says Herr von Hoch. 'Damn it to hell! That blasted horse! Nothing but trouble from the moment I clapped eyes on it!' He glares at Jack. 'And if he knocks you down and stomps on you? I don't want no suit of damages from you.'

'You won't get one. Now what's it to be?'

'Ah, damn it! Damn it to hell!' Herr von Hoch declares. 'Done, then. You get him out, a hundred thaler.'

Zoltan still has that hand upon his arm. 'Jacques, this is crazy. Look what it's done to the boy.' (Still down, now floppily insensible, and the colour of whelk-meat, to boot.)

'You have your weaknesses,' Jack replies. 'I have mine.'

'Mine don't kill you,' Zoltan points out.

'*That's* a matter of opinion. Besides, that horse ain't going to hurt me. I knew his grandmother. I'm almost family. Oh, come on, Zoltan, you old woman,' says Jack. 'That's a thousand-thaler horse in there! I have to do this, you know that.' He moves toward the door. 'You just keep the bloody harbour-master out the way. I'd be a damn sight more scared of him and a blunderbuss in there than I am of some runaway horse.'

Woah. Will you but look at that.

Spots of sunlight before his eyes. That same cold smell there always seems to be inside a church, but in this one, horse piss too, lakes of it, by the stink, and (as his eyes start to work) all along the floor, balls of dung. And a row of pews, knocked sideways, a lectern on its back on the floor, and off to the side there, where the church is at its darkest—

Yes indeed. A horse. He can make out the curve of its neck. And the stamp of a hoof, and the constant old-soul chuntering noise of a horse at the end of its patience with everything.

'Christ Almighty,' Jack hears himself say. 'Jesus, you are big.'

Its head comes up. There's something over its head, pulled crooked. Looks like a sack. *Yes, they hooded you,* Jack thinks. *They hooded you and that only made everything worse.* No bloody wonder it fled in here.

It's paddling its feet, uncertain. He thinks perhaps it is not so very old, he thinks (God help us) that it might grow bigger yet. The height of its head. The length of those legs!

Now he spies the trailing end of its halter. He takes one more step forward, talking to it all the time, not words, just sounds: *Woah, woah, woah.* This might be easy.

He takes another step. He sees how it must have been pawing at the hood, here in the dark; he sees where it has scraped along its muzzle, trying to free itself of this thing, he sees the white of one rolling eye, he sees the glister hanging from its jaws and he sees how it is furious, and terrified, and furious by turns, and he takes one step more. He says, 'Let's have a proper look at you. Let's get you out that thing,' and he does it without even thinking; his hand simply goes to the knot of the hood, skewed all awry under its jaw—

It's like a detonation. Up it goes, rearing up, front legs swinging like clubs, that rolling eye, and the scream again, that great open-mouthed scream, only this time he is close enough to see right down its gullet. He is back against the wall, pasted to it, those front legs swinging round his head. The black fists of its knees, the charcoal shading of its belly, its stones, then the wet pink loll of its tongue, a sudden close-up of the portcullis of its teeth, and then its head bangs against his. He hears it happen – *clonk.* He thinks he feels his brains slap from one side of his skull to the other. He's seeing stars. He slides down the wall. He thinks how the last thing he'll know will be the horse standing over him, making ready to bring those hooves down on him. He opens his eyes.

The horse is maybe ten feet away; weaving, back and forth. Its neck is arched, head held back in order to see him, the hood still slanted piratically over its face. It sounds as if it is talking to itself.

A shout from outside. 'JACQUES!' The horse jerks its head. 'JACQUES! Do you need us? Are you alive in there?'

'We're good, we're fine!' he shouts back. 'You stay out there!'
An eye to the horse. It hasn't moved. Colour from the stained
glass behind the altar, sliding over it; its ribcage pulsing in and
out like bellows. He looks down at his shirt. Dung, blood, horse
piss, all over him.

He gets to his knees, to his feet, puts a hand to his eyebrow.
Fuck. Damn, that hurts. Blood on his fingers. The sting of it in
his right eye. That head-butt broke the skin. 'Oh, you truly are
a devil,' he says. 'What would your grand-dam think of such
behaviour?'

One ear has been freed of the hood. He keeps talking. He
sees the ear relax, little by little. He sees the eye stop rolling.
The flow of equine grumbling ceases.

'All right, M'sieu,' he says. 'We'll try that again.' Crouched
down, small as he can make himself, he reaches out his hand –
slowly, slowly, slowly. At last the horse extends its neck, as if to
meet him halfway. He hears it make a little grinding noise, deep
in its throat, the sound of a horse intent on inspection.

Its whiskers tickle across his palm. *Snuff, snuff, snuff.* He feels
the round of its nose, the velvet of its muzzle in his palm, sees
the connection happen in the horse's eye: *this creature, this smell.*

'That's better,' he tells it. 'That's the way.'

Still at arm's stretch, still crouching down, he goes for his
pocket. You go shopping for a horse, you go prepared. He brings
out a candy. Holds it out. It too is inspected, in his outstretched
palm, and is mumbled into the horse's mouth and rolled about,
to try it, but then with a sort of dowager-ish pudeur, let fall to
the floor.

Not a fan of aniseed. Very well; we have other inducements
to try.

He takes the little screw of fenugreek from his pocket, scatters
the seeds across his palm, crouches down again, and waits.
The horse lowers its nose and sniffs. Out comes its tongue.
Works over his palm until not a seed is left, pushes his hand

up, mumbles at the back of it, has him spread his fingers to investigate between them, then coats them with drool as well – you can almost see it thinking, *What ambrosia is this?* And then, turning its head sideways to do it, eyeing Jack himself, *And who is this god, who produces this for me?*

And now he's close enough. *Woah, woah, woah.* As it pushes at his left hand, Jack lifts the back of the hood from behind its ears with his right, pulls it over the horse's lowered head and it's free.

It's so astonished that it takes a step or two backwards. Shakes its head, as if to be sure the hood is truly gone. The soft trill of a neigh – is that relief? Pleasure? Then it lowers its head and looks at him, dead on. The way they do, to fix you.

'There,' he says. 'There, you see me now, eh? What do you think?'

Now he stands up himself. 'So let's have a proper look at you.'

The horse comes forward, as if to help. Oh—

Oh, everything. The turning of the neck, the sculpting of its face, the meat of its breast, the jump from flank to hip, the landscape of withers and shoulder, *those legs*, everything, even the bitten-in curve from fetlock to hoof; and the colour of it – this deep dark grey, dappled and dotted, like it had been rained on while its paint was wet, like faery rings; and a mane and tail black like ebony, shining like satin.

He lets out his breath. Is it fanciful to think he can see the lineaments, the delicacy of the Buckingham mare in the grooving of that face, in its carriage? All he knows is that he would give a thousand thaler for this horse this minute. He would give *two*. 'And ain't you something,' he whispers. 'Ain't you a marvel, hey?'

It reaches its nose forward. It snuffs his face – his nose, his mouth. It mumbles the wallop on his forehead. 'I know,' says Jack, looking at where it has scraped itself. 'We match.'

A snort.

'Oh, you can talk as well, can you?'

'Jacques!' comes the shout again. 'The hell is going on in there?'

'We're good! Make a road, we're coming out!'

He has the end of the halter in his hand. 'Come on,' he says, and the horse tucks itself in behind him and follows him out, penitent as a scolded child.

The *Ooooh!* of the crowd makes it startle again, paddling its legs; the sun makes it shake its head. 'God almighty!' says Zoltan, coming up. 'Have you seen yourself?'

'Zoltan, I was never better. Look at him. Ain't he something? Ain't he just the most beauteous thing you ever saw?' Another *Oooooh!* from the crowd, this time of agreement. There's even a little applause. The horse paddles its legs once more, but this time as if adjusting its pose. *Oh, you damn show-off, M'sieu!*

And here comes Herr von Hoch. 'That's my thousand thaler!' Von Hoch crows. 'That's my boy!' Then, 'Here – what happened to the hood?'

The horse snaps its teeth at him, with a sound like castanets. Herr von Hoch retreats.

'One hundred thaler,' says Zoltan, taking charge.

'Why certainly, certainly,' says Von Hoch, from a rather safer distance than before. He takes out his purse. 'Here's ten, here's another ten – Brunswick silver thalers, they are, you can't get them no more...'

'And take my advice,' says Zoltan, as the last coin is counted into his palm. 'Keep him hobbled, and pay for him to have a stable on his own.'

'Oh, I'll do better than that,' Herr von Hoch declares confidently, putting the purse away. 'I'll put out his eyes. No more trouble with him then, eh?'

There is – if a crowd can give a gasp, all at once, there's that. 'Put out his eyes?' Herr Gruber repeats, faintly.

Herr von Hoch sees how the crowd has fallen silent. 'What?' he says, into the hush. 'Ain't you people ever heard of that?

Blind him, keep him crib-tied – he can still cover a mare. Get me just a couple of foals from him, I'm laughing.' And his hand reaches out to the halter.

He will think, afterward, will Jack, how at this point there was nothing in his head whatsoever beyond the one firm resolution that Von Hoch was not getting his hand on that halter, not as long as the world still turned. 'So how much did you pay for him?' he asks. It's playing for time, that's all, no more than playing for time, while he digs, mentally, *double*-digs through every possible alternative. Throw Von Hoch in the harbour. Break his fucken neck. Vault onto the horse's back and flee.

'Me?' says Herr von Hoch, proudly. 'Three hundred. Three hundred thaler. Like I said, he was the bargain of the year.'

The bargain of the year. 'And you didn't think that odd?' Jack enquires. 'A thousand-thaler horse, and you get him for under half of that?'

'Fellow didn't know his business,' comes the reply. 'But I know mine.' And Herr von Hoch's hand reaches out again.

'What did he look like, this fellow who made so bad a deal with you?'

'Think you might know him, do you?' says Herr von Hoch, nastily.

'I might,' replies Jack. 'Little fellow, was he? Dressed in black?'

On Zoltan's face those ridiculous moustaches have acquired a curl, the way they do when under them there hides a grin.

'He keep his gloves on, while he spoke with you?' Jack continues. 'Hide his hands?'

'His gloves? Of course he kept his gloves on, it was bitter cold.'

'So you could see his breath?' Zoltan enquires, joining the conversation.

'His breath?' Von Hoch stares from one man to the other. 'What is this?'

'*Could* you see his breath?'

Von Hoch gapes at them. 'What *is* this?' he says again.

'You tell him,' says Jack.

Zoltan puts a heavy arm round Herr von Hoch, who eyes it nervously. 'My friend,' Zoltan begins. 'You're new to these parts, ain't you?'

'You might say that,' says Herr von Hoch, still eyeing the hand upon his shoulder. 'What's that to you?'

'So you wouldn't know what bitter fortune can befall a man round here. A stranger, such as yourself. Who meets another stranger. Who offers him a bargain. The best deal of his life. My friend,' Zoltan continues, turning Herr von Hoch to face him, 'you stand in mortal peril here.'

Herr von Hoch gawps back at him. 'I do?'

'You do indeed. The fellow who sold that horse to you – it is the most devilish of all his devilish devices.'

'Most devilish?' Herr von Hoch repeats, in bewilderment.

'Oh, good sir, yes indeed. That horse,' says Zoltan, pointing (the horse peers at his finger, as if it thought it might be good to eat), 'is his. And as long as you possess it, so are you. That horse –' (declaiming now with the zeal of a preacher) '– will be your ruin. You will watch your business fail. Your dear ones will sicken and die. You will be struck down like Job. And when that horse is all that you have left, the man who sold it to you will reappear, to claim what is his own.'

'His horse?' whispers Herr von Hoch.

'His horse,' Zoltan replies, 'and *your soul.*'

The crowd lets forth a wail. ''Tis the Devil's bargain!'

''Tis the Devil's horse! Just like I said!'

''Tis the spiritus! 'Tis damnation!'

Herr Gruber is crossing himself in the frenzied manner of one hunting fleas. Herr von Hoch clutches at his heart. 'I knew it!' he exclaims. 'I knew it! No normal animal behaves as that one does. Yet I saw only the money I could make from him. The Devil tempted me – he closed my eyes – shut up my reason – God forgive me – what am I to do?'

'There is only one thing you can do,' says Zoltan. 'There is only one way to break such a devil's bargain. You must sell on what was sold to you. Otherwise, the curse will stay with you, and you are doomed.'

'But who would take it?' says Von Hoch, turning to the crowd as if for succour. The crowd, predictably, draws back, as if he'd just revealed a leper's bell. 'Who'd have him now? I'd take a thousand thaler, right away—'

'No, no, no,' says Zoltan, wagging his finger. 'It must be for *less* than you paid. But as to who, my friend, there you have me. I am at a loss—'

'I'll take him,' says Jack, off-handedly. 'I'm in the market for a horse. This one would do.'

'You?' says Herr von Hoch. 'You'd take him?'

'Sure I would. I'll give you a hundred thaler for him, here and now.'

'But you—' Herr von Hoch begins, then checks himself. 'But he – you said – now just a minute here—'

'*Sell it to him!*' Herr Gruber roars. 'Before we're all cursed, same as you!'

Zoltan holds out the hundred thaler. 'Here,' he says, smiling.

But Herr von Hoch has narrowed his eyes. 'A hundred thaler,' he echoes. 'You think I'm going to sell this horse to you for a hundred thaler? You think I don't know what this is? D'you take me for a fool?' He turns to Zoltan. 'If this horse is cursed, if any man buying it is cursed as well, how come your friend here's so keen to have it, eh? Answer me that, if you can.'

Zoltan flashes his excellent white teeth. 'Oh, he don't have to worry,' he replies. 'He and the little fellow in black? They have an understanding.'

'An understanding?' Von Hoch repeats. 'What kind of foolery is this?'

Zoltan spreads his hands, as if to indicate that what comes next is no fault of his. 'Show him,' he says to Jack.

From the neck of his shirt, Jack pulls the silver wolf. Lets it swing back and forth on its cord. 'Oh, by God,' they hear Herr Gruber say.

The blood leaves Herr von Hoch's face. His voice has dried to a tweeting falsetto. 'Give me my money,' he says.

'You're sure?' says Jack. 'I'd not want you thinking ill of us—'

'My money!'

'And it is a very splendid horse. You could sell it to another for far more than we can pay.'

'No! My money! Now! I'll take it now!' And Von Hoch snatches it from Zoltan's hand. 'Here,' he says, turning to Herr Gruber. 'Take this! This is for my bill! I'll not stay here another minute – you people – this land – this war – the Devil walking abroad – tricks and knavery!'

'Yeah, an' what about our church?' comes the shout. ''Oo makes good that mess?'

'An' the boy!'

'And us! Our time unloading the beast, as well!'

Herr von Hoch is surrounded.

'And I think this is the point where we might take our leave as well,' says Zoltan, under his breath, to Jack. 'Don't you?'

Back they go along the quay. The horse has its head up now. It walks with a bit of a swagger. And here comes a man with braid on his sleeves, hurrying along with a blunderbuss over his shoulder. 'Where's the hubbub?' he asks, as he passes.

'Down there,' Zoltan says, directing him. 'Fellow tried to skip out on his debts!'

YOU GET THE horses, says Zoltan, I'll get our kit.

So there he is, stood at the trough in Herr Gruber's yard, with Reena and the Anklam horse one end of it, and this, this *prodigy* the other. The horse looks even bigger in the daylight

than it did in the church. Its coat is wondrous. Here in the light
it looks like it's been marbled, and it keeps up this background
chorus of little self-congratulatory grunts as it drinks. Reena
and the Anklam horse are exchanging glances. *You'll get used
to each other*, he thinks. Also: he'll need a bridle, he'll need a
saddle; how will he ride; what will Ziggy make of him; I cannot
wait to see Ziggy's face.

'You, M'sieu,' he tells the horse, 'have some very big
horseshoes to fill.' And then a glance at the horse's feet, the size
of them; like plinths. 'Well, no, you don't,' he says. 'Compared
to yours. But size isn't everything.'

He hears Zoltan, coming down those creaking stairs. He
hears Frau Klara's voice, then Zoltan's again, and then a pause,
which Jack is damn sure marks the snatching of a kiss; and then
he sees there are those two girls at the kitchen door, the one
(Zoltan's) pushing the other girl forward. Who rolls her eyes,
then comes toward him. *Ah*, he thinks, *so you do have a bit of steel
in you.*

The girl calls out, 'You found a horse!'

'Yes,' he answers. The horse gives him a nudge in the
shoulder. 'I guess I did.'

She comes a step closer. 'Does he have a name?'

Now that's a good question. He looks back at the horse. 'Yes,'
he says. 'He does. I think his name's M'sieu.'

M'sieu lifts his head, gives a snort.

Here comes Zoltan, with their kit. And he's brandishing a
news-sheet, a coranto.

'Have you seen this?' Zoltan calls. 'You're famous!'

CHAPTER SIX

The Salamander

'The salamander kills not only such as it bites, by making a venomous impression, but it also infects the fruits and herbs over which it creeps.'

The Works of Ambrose Paré

O H, THIS PLACE is foul. Fleas assault his ankles; when he moves his feet to be rid of them, the straw upon the floor releases not only the stink of old beer, but of human piss, and (he thinks) of vomit too. Quinto del

Ponte would like to remove his feet from the floor entirely; he would like to curl up on this joint-stool with his arms about his knees and touch nothing, anywhere, about him (other than that yet another drunken sot would be bound to stumble into him, even so); he would like to be gone. Everything here might kill. The tankard before him is so tarnished he can taste it, then the ale in it is sour; the candle upon the table is of such unrefined, cheap tallow that every so often it gives a sizzle as it reaches yet another fragment of animal held within the wax, and adds to the surrounding miasma (itself contaminating his lungs with every breath!) the stink of burning cow-hide. Crazy shadows disport themselves upon the wall in front of him as the other patrons variously fall over themselves, take drunken swings at each other with their fists, grope the serving girls and are smacked around the head; all of it lit by the colours of the fire. It is as if he has his back turned to one of the circles of hell. 'This place –' he begins, and shakes his head.

This place – far enough into Germany for Conti's troops to have been replaced by those of General Tilly. Getting here has worn a lesion in the sole of Quinto's boot and, worst of all, emptied his pockets. 'I walked about the town,' he tries, hopefully. 'There is a bakers here, if you tell them your flag, they will make it for you. We might shift there.' He is aware his hands are making optimistic motions of kneading dough. 'With cheese,' he says. One hand now sprinkles something appetizing but invisible. 'Or cinnamon. Poppyseeds...'

His companion – no, it is so blank, so wholly without connection to the world, you cannot even call it a stare. The lard-white chops, like an invalid, the russet-brown eyes of a stoat. You can see the likeness to his father the more, the older he grows. And the sheeny gloss of his jacket, and the whiteness of his shirt. Carlo Fantom's pockets aren't empty, you may be sure of that.

'This place,' Carlo tells him, leaning forward into the candlelight, 'is all you deserve.'

This, Quinto feels, is grossly unfair. 'I provided those men with everything, all the information they could need. I drew up a map!'

One, two, three, four go the cards upon the sticky tabletop. Carlo plays against himself; there has been no invitation to Quinto to join in. 'I showed them exactly which path to take,' Quinto says, his mind searching, even as he says it, for any path of his own that might get him out of here.

'And what did they find, when they took it? Men lying in readiness, men lying in wait, cannon with their range. Cannon. I tell you, Del Ponte, I am not the only one to wonder if what you guided them into with such care was not simply a trap. One laid with your connivance, what is more.' Down go more cards – five, six, seven, eight.

Quinto del Ponte's face is a mask of horror. 'Why would I do that? You know I would not do that. Why would I do that, and then come here, to meet with you?'

'Because you are a doubler, Signor del Ponte. You are the card with two faces,' his companion says, picking up a card in those odd, small, pointed-looking fingers of his and turning it this way and that in the candlelight to make the point. 'You are a Janus, are you not? You are the strumpet who takes one man's money and sleeps in another man's bed.' A sigh, as if at the falseness of the world, when all along this one, as Quinto knows full well, this one is as duplicitous, as treacherous as – as – as if there were a deadly salamander on the table between them, not a hand of cards. Very much as if. Carlo Fantom uses poisons, amongst his other resources for removing souls from this world, and uses them so skilfully that by reputation he has dealt death in a handshake, from the briefest touch of his very own skin. He *is* a salamander. Quinto del Ponte's gaze drops to the cards upon the table, now being picked up and shuffled anew. Nervously, he folds his own hands in his lap. Thank God for the letter, nestled against his heart! His manumission out of here, out of places like this; his pass into those where no-one has empty pockets nor must live with holes in their boots.

'I have but one master,' he says. 'His Grace the Prince-Bishop. He knows it. So do you. If His Grace sends me to be amongst our enemies, what am I to do? And it was you who gave me my orders, you who told me, *go amongst them, gather information, bring it back to us in Gartz.* All this I did. Am I to be punished for it?'

'No, Signor del Ponte,' comes the reply. 'You are to be punished because you failed. You are to be punished because your masters are displeased, and most of all, you are to be punished because all this reflects so poorly upon me.' A second hand of cards fanned out upon the table. 'You are to be punished because you are an idiot.'

A sudden upsurge in the noise behind. Glancing round, Quinto sees that one of the serving girls has been offended so grossly that she has walloped the offender over the head with her hefty wooden tray. The man is on the floor, his companions leaping to his aid; the girl's defenders, meanwhile, are shielding her in turn. The girl can be heard declaring, 'An' you try that again, you fucker, I'll pull your cock off at the root!' She sounds very young – young enough, he sees, to have lifted his companion's gaze for an instant, before judging her as the harridan she no doubt is. *Christ save us*, thinks Quinto, *these harpies* – and then he wonders who here would rush to his aid? No-one at all, is the answer. He has fewer defences even than her, that ghastly shrieking thing.

'You know this game?' Carlo Fantom continues, examining the cards as calmly as if nothing had happened behind them at all. 'There is so much time to kill out of the field, I learn all the games I can. The Swedish favour boardgames, so I hear, but I prefer cards. This one, the French call it *Cul-bas*. Arse-down. You must match cards. He who cannot, loses. He who can no longer play, he loses everything.' He looks up. As close as that expressionless face ever comes to a smile. 'And you – you can no longer play. You are out of the game.'

Quinto is aware that there is liquid in his throat. When he swallows it, it burns. 'If the raid miscarried it was not because of me,' he begins. He sees Carlo Fantom is reaching for something in his jacket. What is it to be, a stiletto? Pocket pistol? Poison dart? He sees himself down there on the filthy floor, fleas playing hopscotch over his lifeless body. 'I did everything I could – I thought only to act as I had been ordered.'

Carlo has laid a printed paper on the table. 'Read this,' he says. 'You have English, yes? I see your name in there. Read what the world says now of you.'

Why, it is only a coranto. A London coranto. Quinto del Ponte draws the candle nearer, lowers his head. He reads.

'*Quint?*' he exclaims. 'They are calling me *Quint?*' Not even his proper name? He is incensed. 'Oh, and look here! All this from the report of an English, a witness in the Swedish camp – yes, I am sure! I know the man they mean. Those damned scouts, he was – he was nothing but their *scribe*, their mouthpiece – he says that I *ran away* from the King? *Mine* was the loss and shame? They lost men, sir, they lost men, you mark my words, and as for the shame, to leave themselves so open to attack – and now they traduce me! They blacken my name!'

He turns the paper over. Of a sudden, a different name leaps out at him. 'There!' he exclaims. 'You want to know who was responsible, there!' His finger stabs. 'Jacques Fiskardo – you see this? "One Jacques Fiskardo, a gentleman-at-arms in the service of the King, at the outer guard, took the alarm" – there, you see?' he ends, triumphant. 'If the raid failed, it was his doing. By God, he obstructed me from the first. Him and his *damned* discoverers.' Quinto sits back. 'And to think, I did him service.

Fool that I am, I thought he was as you.' He smiles with relief. Surely now he has absolved himself?

For the very first time in the conversation, engagement between his words and his listener. Awful engagement, like a silent thunderclap. 'Describe him,' Carlo orders at last. 'This Fiskardo.'

To have Carlo's attention is even more alarming than to have his contempt. 'A captain,' Quinto del Ponte begins. His words fall over each other. 'The – the coldest-eyed man I ever saw. He leads a company of discoverers, of scouts. A ruffian – like his men. One of them drew his sword on the colonel's ensign. I intervened – I said the villain drew in his own defence. I thought that might carry me some favour with the man, with – with Fiskardo, but no. He was contrary to me from first to last.' He dares to peek across the table. He is astonished by what he sees there. Is it disbelief? No, is it rage? Is that why the strange working of the man's left hand – flexing and flattening, flexing and flattening, as if it feels a cramp – is the man about to make a fist?

'And in what way,' Carlo asks, his voice oily with menace, 'did you think this Fiskardo was as me?'

'Because he wears a –' Quinto del Ponte's hand goes up to his own shoulder. 'A –' he taps nervously at his jacket. 'A – one of those,' he says, eyes fixed on the badge on the shoulder opposite. The upreared stance, the curling tail, the savagery of teeth and claws. 'A silver wolf.' He swallows again. 'Do you know him?' he asks.

No answer. The most violent struggle is taking place on his companion's face. Quinto watches it, horrified, enthralled. Something there, something of even more moment than his own doings, vastly more. Finally, Carlo Fantom begins gathering up the cards from the table, shuffling them into a pack. 'You will return to Prague,' he says. 'Your name is out there, your failure is out there, you are no further use to anyone here. You will go back to Prague, you will make yourself of service to the

Prince-Bishop in any and every way you can. You will redeem yourself with him. Perhaps with me.'

Good God above, thinks Quinto, his companion's hands are shaking! But now he is already imagining himself back in Prague; he is thinking of how he will present his letter (there in the lining of his jacket; there above his heart!) to the Prince-Bishop, he is thinking of what he will say as he presents it. 'Your Grace, at great danger to myself, I have preserved this for you.' Or perhaps, 'Your Grace! I deliver the Cardinal of France into your hands!' He looks up. The hatred in Carlo's expression, even for Carlo, is extreme. 'Will we travel together?' he asks, all his terrors upon him once again.

'No,' comes the reply. 'I will stay in Germany. Tell His Grace the Prince-Bishop I will take service under General Pappenheim. I have – I find I have unexpected business here.'

CHAPTER SEVEN

Two Days in November

''Tis said the Cardinal employed all manner of industry
and all sorts of submission to the Queen Mother to
reconcile himself to her favour, but all in vain... the
order was at last signed for the Cardinal's removal.'

Guillaume Girard, *A History of the Life of the Duke of Esperon*

HOW DID IT come to this? How could he have been
set against his monarch in this way? *Oh, ever-patient
Christ*, the Cardinal prays, as he is thrown left to right
in his seat, *give me your strength to endure this.*

He had sensed the Queen Mother's influence a-growing. He
had felt it in the air outside his rooms, the corridors where fewer
and fewer waited for him. He had heard it in the whispers.
He had heard it, above all, in the silences. He had felt it in

the glances at his back, those looks as sharp as knives. The Habsburg faction at the court: it waxed, he waned.

But this has happened before, he had told himself. This has happened before, so do as you did then. Flatter, amend, atone. Go to her, go to her in her palace, the Luxembourg, make your apologies in person, beg forgiveness on your knees—

A clod of mud hits the side of the carriage. He hears his driver curse, lash out his whip, he hears the horses' panicked whinnying in response. Thirteen years before, when the mob had learned of Concino Concini's assassination, then too, they had given chase to his carriage like this. They had almost thrown it from King Henry's bridge. And he had fled – but that time, thirteen years ago, the King had been but a youth, a callow boy. There had been exile – painful, wracked with fears – but it had ended, as he always knew it would, with him being recalled to his monarch's side, his counsel sought, his words revered. Now though – now—

He had gone to the Luxembourg. Was this but yesterday? The 10th of November, that evil, evil day; he had gone to the Luxembourg and she had closed its doors against him. She had barred him from his king. He had forced his way into the chamber where they sat together, mother and son – oh, her fury! She had called him 'valet' – valet, he!

He hears his driver curse once more, he feels the carriage swerve, its fragile wheels rock up onto the pavement, down again.

It is her agents have whipped up this mob. He had left the Luxembourg with the laughter of her people in his ears; he had left the palace with the Queen Mother herself waving him on her way, her victoricus farewell: You are fallen, Monsieur le Cardinal, you are done!

He had meant to flee. Instead, in desperation, this – this last throw of the dice, this pell-mell journey from Paris to Versailles, to where he hears his king is now, this one last desperate attempt to save himself.

And if this fails? What will await him then? Exile once more, to Poitou? Imprisonment? The headsman's block?

His bowels ache. His heart not so much beats as seems to spasm in his chest. The carriage rocks again, he must brace himself against its sides, and finds his arms have barely strength enough to do it.

Peccavi, peccavi, I have sinned—

Yes, but for France! Always, all for France! Are all his plans, his stratagems to come to this? Concini died for France, though the man never knew it. No-one has ever known. When the mob pursued the Cardinal's carriage through the streets thirteen years ago, they were pursuing the very man who had rid them of Concini's menace – Concini, who would have chained France to the Habsburgs for good, made her their lackey. True, there had been other deaths, but they were part of the whole, they were needed, yes, they had to be! If he had been able to avoid them, surely he would have done – but it was France who required them, demanded them, France who had to have his secret kept, France for whom anyone who might have betrayed it, had to be—

Removed.

Has he been betrayed? His letter, has that been his undoing? Has King Louis learned of it? Or does it sit, even now, on the soft, fat lap of the Queen Mother? It is twelve miles from Paris to Versailles – will the hand of some soldier of the guard fall upon his shoulder, as it had fallen upon Concini's? When he steps from the carriage, is that how this journey will end, with him forced to his knees, as that mindless ruffian Jean Fiskardo had forced Concini to his?

And then the man, Jean Fiskardo, had looked up. Looked up, and straight into Richelieu's face, as he stood at the narrow window in his closet, watching it all. Looked up, and instantly and unmistakably, had guessed, had understood everything.

I have sinned—

The surface of the road changes under the carriage's wheels. He feels his bowels register the change. He is a sick man, yes, he is sick, but he will not plead for mercy, he will not beg. If it be the King's will—

But France, France! Who will defend her, if not he? Who will steer her course? There is no other hand but the Cardinal's own can pilot his country over the rocks, there were no other eyes but his who saw the use to be made of this Swedish king, this enemy of France's enemies, this perfect ally, this Lion of the North.

And so he had written his letter. And not one moment's peace has he known since.

He hears the fountains. He sees the lights. They have reached Versailles. The carriage comes to a stop. He takes a breath, and waits. Its door is opened. He heaves himself up, steps out and down. He hides the trembling of his hands within the sleeves of his robe. *Concini died for France. And I, if I must, will do the same.*

Triumph! Triumph! Victory! The most glorious, glorious day! The King it was, placed an arm about his shoulders, the King it was, sat him by the fireside in his private chamber, the King it was, looked him in the face and said, 'If I must choose between you and my mother, I cannot choose the Habsburg side.' The King who said, 'Come. Tell me of your plans. Tell me how we keep France safe and whole. Tell me. Tell me how.' And they had talked, all night long, talked as they once talked when the King was but a youth, and he had unfolded all his plans – a treaty with the Swedish, money for this army to ride on down into Germany, to chase the Habsburgs to the very gates of Vienna itself. Yes, victory! Exile, disgrace, yes, yes, but not for him! The Cardinal sinks back into his seat. He is a man transported, he is a man transformed – vigorous, dynamic, full of force. His coachman plies his whip, the horses, the fresh horses, from the King's own stable, they will have him back in Paris before dawn. Victory, victory! Complete and total—

But that letter! That damned letter! Out there – somewhere – still!

CHAPTER EIGHT

A King of Snow

'The day before Colberg was taken, was there a League
concluded betwixt the Kings of France and Sweden...'

William Watts, *The Swedish Intelligencer*

S O THERE YOU have it. Two men sit down together in a
private chamber in Versailles, talk all night, and almost
before you can catch your breath, Reine Marie is back in
exile; His Eminence the Cardinal is back in his suite of rooms
in the Louvre; and Sweden – that northern nothing! – starts
this new year, 1631, with an alliance with King Louis that
gives her a million livres a year for doing exactly what she was
doing already. The Day of the Dupes, is what they are calling
it in Paris, this 11th of November past, that momentous day,

and it is extraordinary the difficulty one would have in Paris
now of finding anyone, *anyone*, from page-boy to prince of
the blood, who has not, did not, does not, always give the
Cardinal their most enthusiastic and unquestioning support.
And right at the end of this chain of consequences, almost
eight hundred muddy miles away from Notre Dame, or the
Tuileries, or the graces of the Place Royale, Jack Fiskardo
finds himself sitting in his guardroom with a man who for the
last God knows how many years had thought him dead, and
who is now—

'Signor Ravello, you are goggling,' says Jack.

'I dare say I am,' Ravello answers. 'I dare say I will. I dare say
you will get used to it.'

Also sat here in the guardroom are Zoltan and Achille de la
Tour. In honour of France's glorious alliance with these Viking
conquerors, and the three days of revelry and fireworks with
which it has been marked, Achille wears his very best today:
he is as padded as a counterpane, as beribboned as a hobby
horse, and his every movement is accompanied by a silken
rustle. 'Gentlemen,' he begins, getting to his feet (a gentle
tsshhh tsshhh tsshhh). 'Our business here today can be summed
up in three words. Quinto del Ponte. Quinto del Ponte and
everything we know of the man. Or rather, don't. Such as, his
present whereabouts, and in particular, that of this notorious
letter. In fact, as I understand it, Signor Ravello, we would
leave the man in peace if we were only in a position to restore
the letter to its author.' He sits down again (*tsshhh*). 'Do I have
that right?'

'If a choice must be made,' Ravello agrees, 'then yes.'

'I have a question,' says Jack. 'I have several hundred in fact,
but this is the first. Do we know who wrote this letter?'

A glance between Ravello and Achille, light as the tap of a
finger. 'We do,' Ravello says, with the subtlest underlining of
that *we*.

'But you are not about to share that with us.'

'No,' says Ravello, 'we are not.'

'You may take it that the writer is a friend to Sweden,' Achille puts in. 'A significant friend. Which is why we have the blessing of Fältherre Tott, to, ah, involve you in this matter. Of Fältherre Åke Tott, and – well, let us say, even higher than he.' He sits back. He looks from Jack to Zoltan, and Zoltan to Jack. 'Gentlemen,' he begins, buoyant as ever, 'you may confirm this with the Fältherre himself, if you need—'

'Oh, trust us,' says Zoltan, 'we have.'

Achille deflates. *Tsshhh.*

'Second question,' says Jack. 'What is in this letter?'

'That,' says Ravello, 'no-one knows but the man who wrote it. He and Del Ponte. And, God help us, whoever Del Ponte may think to pass it to. So where might he have taken it?'

'Friendly territory,' Zoltan suggests. 'Which would hardly be Gartz, for him. Not any more. Some other camp? Some other force?'

'I hope that is unlikely. Del Ponte is an intriguer, not a soldier. His oldest connection seems to have been to the Prince-Bishop of Prague. He was in the Prince-Bishop's household for a number of years.'

'Is that so?' says Jack. 'Well, well. This may just have become rather easier.' He leans back. 'Kai?' he calls.

'Yes, Domini?' says Kai, coming to the doorway. Very prompt. Suspiciously so, in fact.

'Would you find Herr Lopov? Ask him if he would be so good as to join us here.'

Victor Lopov. *What an oddity of a man*, Ravello thinks. So wide of nostril, so hollow of cheek, as light of build as a girl, and looking as if he would bolt out the room entirely, given half the chance.

'Herr Lopov,' Jack begins, 'would you introduce yourself to these gentlemen?'

The mouth opens, the mouth works about what must be words; nothing emerges.

'Don't be afraid, Herr Lopov. Remind us who it was employed you, before you found yourself here.'

'The Prince-Bishop of Prague,' comes the reply. A nervous cough. 'I was his archivist.' Lopov dares to dart a glance at Ravello. The tips of his ears seem to glow. 'You must not judge me, sir. I know that here he is amongst your enemies.'

'Signor Lopov,' says Ravello, 'be at peace. You are not the matter here. You will think this ridiculous, but we are endeavouring to track, as we sit here, a document. A letter. It was in the possession of Quinto del Ponte. It left Stettin with him. And there is – there is a connection between this man, Del Ponte, and the Prince-Bishop of Prague.'

Viktor Lopov's eyebrows lift, as if caught by a breeze. 'He was in the Prince-Bishop's service?'

'So we think. Now is it possible, do you imagine, that this letter might have made its way to Prague? To the Prince-Bishop?'

'It is possible,' says Lopov, 'yes, of course, it is possible…'

'But?'

'Might I ask its nature, this letter?'

'Good question, Herr Lopov,' says Jack, quietly.

'It was – it was private, and it was confidential. And the author wishes for it back. As a matter of – of importance, shall we say.'

'And is it – would its return be worth money, to its writer?' Lopov enquires.

No price is too great, thinks Ravello. 'Yes. I believe so. To the writer, yes.'

'Because they wish its contents to remain – private?'

'I think we may take that as a given, Herr Lopov,' says Jack.

'And might I ask,' says Lopov with a wriggle, as if screwing himself down into his seat, 'what language the letter would have been written in?'

'I believe, in French,' says Ravello, after a moment's hesitation.

'And how we might recognize it, if it can be found?'

'It will bear a seal. Three chevrons, a crown, and some, ah
– ribbons.'

Viktor Lopov takes in his breath. His nostrils round like
blowholes. 'The Prince-Bishop of Prague received a great deal
of correspondence. An immense amount, in fact, in every tongue
you could name. The paperwork associated with his position
and his court, it was extraordinary. The business of keeping
track of it – it was endless. It necessitated systems. Categories.
Many of them.'

'We understand, Signor,' says Ravello, with a heavy sigh. 'To
trace one letter – which may never have come into the Prince-
Bishop's possession in the first place. We understand.'

'But if it did,' says Lopov, 'it will not be in Prague. The
Prince-Bishop keeps nothing of such worth about him in that
city. He used to say Prague was far too great a target to keep any
document of value there.'

'Is there somewhere you think it would be instead, Herr
Lopov?' Jack asks.

'Oh, certainly,' says Viktor Lopov. 'If it is with the Prince-
Bishop, I can tell you exactly where it will be. To the cabinet.
To the very folder.' He squares his narrow shoulders. 'It will be
in Hoffstein.'

'Mr Endicott!'

'Captain, yes!'

'Paper, Mr Endicott! Pencil too.'

The paper is brought.

'Now, Herr Lopov,' says Jack, 'Hoffstein. Draw it out. Show
us where this place is.'

'Why, here,' says Lopov. Rafe, pressing himself to the wall
and hoping thus to go unnoticed, sees Viktor draw a long
irregular line – 'Let us take this for the coast,' he says. He draws

another line, slanting off the first. 'The Elbe.' He adds a dot at
either end: Hamburg; Prague. Then two more. 'It is here, do
you see? It is below Magdeburg, but before Dresden. There is
a great forest on the other bank, as you come near, then many
of those fisherman's jetties, and then a sort of promontory, and
there it is.'

'Which side, Herr Lopov?'

'Which side? Oh – this,' says Lopov, tapping what would be
the Elbe's eastern bank. 'It is in the territory of Saxony.'

'Saxony is neutral,' says Achille, peering over. (*Tsshhh, tsshhh.*)

'No such bloody thing,' says Jack. 'So. Miles below us. *Miles*
below us, even as our front line is now.' He glances up. 'I think
even Fältherre Åke Tott would not venture so far.' He walks
around the table, examining the map. 'Herr Lopov – shift
yourself, Scribbler, you are in the way – Herr Lopov, describe
Hoffstein to us, if you will.'

'It is a very little place,' Lopov begins. 'A village – one of
those that winds its way uphill – and upon the hilltop, a castello.
There is a square – very small – with linden trees. It was the
first seat of the Prince-Bishop's family. It is almost a ruin now,
but he had a laboratory set up there, a workshop. Like the old
Emperor, the Prince-Bishop had a great interest in alchemy
and such-like arcane science. He used Hoffstein as a – as a
retreat.' There is a little sweat on his forehead. 'And for – for
incarceration,' Lopov finishes, with a gulp.

'And who is there now?'

'I think there is no-one.'

'You *think*?'

'It is his *way*,' says Lopov, sounding beset. 'If Hoffstein is
abandoned and forgotten, everything there is kept secret, do
you see? This is how he thinks of it. That is why he keeps his
archive there.'

'I wonder what he's hiding,' says Jack. Another circuit about
the table.

Achille clears his throat. 'Captain, I should say – you were put forward for this task exactly because of your skill at surviving up country.'

'And for my susceptibility to flattery, eh, Achille?'

'By no means!' Achille protests, in the offended tone of one who had meant that, exactly, and thought he had got away with it, what's more. 'But if it would make a difference, if you require more men, we are empowered to offer them—' He breaks off. 'Signor Ravello, is that not so?'

'It is,' says Ravello. 'Although you never heard that from me.'

Jack lifts his head. 'That's a handsome offer, but I'm going to refuse it.'

'Refuse?' repeats Achille. 'But why?'

'Because, Achille, if you take something by force, that is the only way you can keep it. And if we attempt this, we will be almost three hundred miles south, and on our own. If we make an attack on Hoffstein, the Prince-Bishop cannot but hear of it, and retaliate. How then are we to be resupplied? How reinforced? We will be besieged. And all we are there to do is see if we can find this letter. Whereas if we take it by stealth – then the Prince-Bishop need never know that we were there at all.'

'But how could that be done?'

'Oh, I can think of a way.' He puts back his head again. 'Ulf!'

'Yes, Domini!' An even speedier appearance at the door than Kai.

'Ulf, are you *all* waiting out there?'

'Yes, Domini!' comes the cheery reply.

'Then you can all go get the loot from our ambush, can't you? Where we freed Herr Lopov, and acquired the Scribbler? All the uniforms and that damned ugly flag.'

The map has been removed. In its place on the table in the guardroom there now reposes a pile of sad-looking jumble, misshapen from its months of storage, and in many cases, ravaged of its braid and buttons too. And across the table like a cloth, a mighty standard – one half black Habsburg eagle, one half a dripping scarlet heart, on a field the colour of mustard.

'There,' says Jack. 'That's how. We go in under the Prince-Bishop's own colours. We kit ourselves out like we were his, and we walk straight in. And then, God willing, fast as we can, we walk straight out again. With this infernal letter, if it be there.'

For a moment, there is silence. Then Achille says, 'Well. I for one am inclined to applaud.'

'Then is our business done here? Because unless there was food upon it, I never yet spent time sat at a table that I didn't think could be better spent doing anything else.'

Achille has raised a finger. 'One thing, Captain.'

'And what is that, Achille?'

'I believe there is a horse?'

THE ABBEY AT Stettin now boasts a paddock, in which it is M'sieu's daily pleasure to parade – neck arched, tail stiff, one eye to his audience.

'Oh, but he is prodigious,' says Achille. 'I had heard he was a wonder, but he truly is.' He lays one hand on the paddock's rough top rail. 'Although I am amazed that he don't jump that, the size he is.'

'He does,' Jack answers. 'Then he thinks he is lost and starts yelling for me, and I have to turn out to find him. I fear he is none too bright. And he is a mighty great show-off, what's more.'

M'sieu has picked up his water bucket and is shaking it as a cat might shake a mouse. Then he throws it at the fence. Having made sure of his audience's full attention, he does another trot past, trilling all the way.

'A mighty great show-off, and as noisy a horse as I have ever known. But he is also as you see him. And you have to forgive such beauty anything.'

M'sieu high-steps past a third time. Achille watches him, eyes wide. 'I wonder how he will do on a march?'

'I have no idea. But I think three hundred miles will be an excellent way to find out.' He turns toward Ravello. 'We can't tempt you to join us?'

'*Madonna*,' says Ravello. 'Twenty years ago, maybe. No, I will wait for Achille to let me know of your success, and then, my friend, I plan to slip into a graceful retirement.'

M'sieu breaks off to the right, where Rosa stands with the Executioner. Pokes his nose between the rails, turning his head to sniff at her belly. Rosa extends a hand and rubs at the rosette between his eyes. M'sieu closes his eyes and turns his nose the other way. 'And like all those blessed with good looks,' says Jack, resignedly, 'he is a shameless flirt.'

'You will be without your sergeant, for this venture down to Hoffstein, I think,' says Achille.

'I think you're right. We only need a dozen or so for this in any case, and I seem to have no shortage of volunteers. Even the Scribbler is petitioning me to let him come along. But Ilya will stay here. He and Rosa are to wed.'

'Ah!' says Achille. 'Delightful! Congratulations!'

A moment's silence. Then Jack says, 'You are goggling again, Ravello.'

'Forgive me,' Ravello answers. 'You cannot know what it is, to lay eyes on you. I keep thinking, what would our friend Balthasar say, if he could see you now?'

'You know what he'd say. He'd tell you to stop goggling too.'

'I think he'd say how proud he was of you,' says Ravello. '*Dio*, I have at least a hundred questions of my own.'

'Fire away, then, Signor. Fire away.'

'Did you find your man?' Ravello asks at once.

'Not yet. But I will. Or rather, the plan is, he'll find me. That's where the Scribbler comes in.' And at Ravello's look of puzzlement: 'I'm bait.'

'You're bait?'

'My name is bait. My father's name. I don't think he'll have forgotten it. It means I'm a loose end. Maybe his only one. Nothing drives him wilder than that. Only –' (a rueful smile) '– there's not much sign he's taken it, as yet.'

'*Dio*,' says Ravello again. Then, 'Tell me – did you ever go to Picardy? To your father's grave?' It feels odd to speak of the man like this. Ravello was rightly wary of Jean Fiskardo in the flesh – everyone was wary of Jean Fiskardo in the flesh – but, old soldiers. You know how it is.

'And why would I do that?' comes the even-toned reply. Even-toned in a manner that warns you off as effectively as ever Jean Fiskardo raising his fist.

To honour the man, perhaps? Whatever else one might think of Jean Fiskardo, there was no faulting the man's courage. 'Jacques, you should not judge him too harshly. He did what had to be done. He didn't think of the cost.'

'But the cost wasn't his alone, was it?' comes the reply. 'My mother paid a fairly hefty price as well.' And then, 'I don't judge him, Ravello. I just keep him where he was. Which was, mostly, far away.'

'Ah,' says Ravello. A change of subject. He looks over to where the Executioner is shepherding Rosa back into the warm. He asks, 'And you never wed? No family of your own?'

'I can't think that will ever be for me.' Jack nods to where Ulf stands at the paddock rail with Sten, Magnus and Per, all of them no doubt dreaming, just as Jack did once himself, of the day when a horse such as M'sieu might be theirs. 'This is my family. Such as I am ever like to have. And you?'

'Ho,' comes Sten's voice, in what Sten must imagine to be an approximation of horse aristocracy. 'Ho yes, look at me. Look at me hold me tail up. Look at the size of me noble bollocks!'

'Ah,' Ravello replies. 'That is under investigation. A project for my retirement.' A long moment of consideration, and then, 'Have you been happy, Jacques?'

And an equally long moment of consideration before there is a reply. 'Yes. Happier than for a long time I ever thought I would be, at least.'

WINTER ON THE ODER. Snow piles up on Stettin's high-pitched roofs, descends in curtain-falls on the unwary. The trees by the river wear tinkling coats of ice; the clinker in the sentries' braziers freezes solid. *That's* when you know it's cold. Torquato Conti, indisposed, coughs and groans his way toward Christmas. A canker or imposthume or some such is eating him from the inside out. The Emperor removes him from command, and sends him home to Italy, and one Count Schaumberg succeeds him, anticipating, no doubt, a month or two at least in quarters, in peace and quiet, as no-one makes war in wintertime, it's understood, but no-one seems to have told the Swedish that. On Christmas Eve they drive Schaumberg out of Grieffenhagen, then by God out of Gartz as well. Then they take Kustrin. Then they take Klempenow. Then they take Landsberg. Rafe's pen can hardly keep up. *We have, in total,* he writes, *between July last and now, took eighty cities, castles and sconces. Eighty, Mr Watts!*

Rosa, thimble on her finger, on the same hand that now bears a wedding ring, lays the uniforms taken in the ambush on her belly, as on a worktable, and humming to herself, one by one, makes them presentable as she can.

Upstream the snows begin to melt. The fields on either side
the Oder flood, starting each day with roundels of ice floating
upon them, flat as pansies. The trees watch their reflections
in the flood, but their mirror shrinks a little every day; the sun
has that first tint of returning warmth; the colour of the sky
changes, rising from almost no blue at all on the horizon to
something deep and vivid as the Swedish flag.

Jack sits down with Lopov's map, calculating, calculating.
Go with the army moving down the Oder, down to Frankfurt.
Work a way around above Berlin. Head west, to the Elbe. Three
hundred miles. At least three hundred miles. He lies awake
at night, planning, calculating. Who goes? Zoltan, of course,
Ziggy (their one and only speaker of Czech). Ulf, Ulrik, Elias,
Ansfrid. Kai. Sten. The Gemini. Luka. Thor. That's twelve.
Lopov. The Scribbler. *And me*, he thinks. Plenty.

Dear Mr Watts

   *You have, I am sure, heard of the great alliance now
brought into play between the King of Sweden and the
French. There were bonfires burning in the camp here at
Stettin for three whole days in celebration, and cannon
firing day and night, so that a man might hardly hear his
own voice toasting our brave fortune. The King, it is said,
will lead his armies down into Germany in his own royal
person; meantime we, Mr Watts, have an expedition of
our own. I cannot say more of this, on pain (so the captain's
orders) of him leaving me here, so if this should be the last
you hear from me for some little while, do not be anxious on
my behalf. I will return with tales to tell!*

THE DAY BEFORE they are to depart, Jack puts a saddle on M'sieu and takes him out for one last gallop, Stettin to Gartz, twenty miles, straight down the Oder, fast as he can. And by God, M'sieu can run. You give him the message and he is gone – half horse, half cannon. On this frozen ground he even sounds like artillery, hoofbeats echoing like thunder through the air, and his stretch, the reach of those great legs – it's as if the horse himself wants to see how fast he can go. Past the flooded fields, under the naked trees, and into that strange territory of little lakes that stop and start and bend away to nothing, and that's where she's waiting for him, this tiny figure, cloaked, behatted, sat there by the path, cooking catfish over her fire.

M'sieu (rearing, snorting) crashes to a stop. 'Well now, Captain,' she says, getting to her feet, as his horse comes down to earth with such a wallop that he sends the birds from the trees. 'Fancy meeting you!'

He thinks he remembers her. Although her face seems fuller than when he last saw her, in camp, after Anklam, and her eyes seem brighter too. 'Fine horse,' she comments.

Her name comes back to him. 'Kizzy,' he says.

'That's me. Are you hungry, Captain? Sit down here with me. Eat.'

She puts the pan on the bank between them. As they eat, he feels her eye him. 'You have the look of one about to make a journey,' she says.

'That I am.'

Behind them, pulling up the yellow grass in sheaves, M'sieu keeps up his usual commentary of snorts and warbles. 'It's good that he's so noisy,' she says next. She brushes off her lap. 'And how does our Lady Soap-Bubble? Is she wed?'

It makes him laugh. 'Good soul, how could you know that?'

'Oh, I know many things,' she says. 'I know what a long and wanton road you have to travel, Jack Fiskardo. I know you will be tested. I know who you are, and I know who you will be.'

The birds have started their cawing again, circling the trees. She raises her hands, claps them together. 'Shush!' she says – and every single bird is mute. M'sieu falls silent. Even the noise of the wind has ceased. A fish jumps from the water in front of them, and falls back into its circle on the stream without a sound. Here he sits on the riverbank, and it is as if every sound has been deadened, as far as ear can hear or eye can see. He can hear nothing but the beating of his heart. There is a tingling in his forehead, and he knows that, he has felt that before. He looks at her in wonder. He almost expects to find himself struck mute. 'Who are you?' he asks.

'You know who I am,' she says. 'I am like my son. I am one of those who sees the road.' A little sigh. 'You'd not think it so hard a thing to do, but it seems there are few enough of us can do it.' She turns to him. 'Stand up,' she says. And when he does, she puts herself on tiptoe and pulls his face down close to hers and says, 'Listen to me, Jack Fiskardo. The one you are searching for, he knows you are here. And he will find you. In the dark places, in the fire and flame, where you cross over, he will find you. Be ready.'

And then he feels her lips against his cheek. It's like the wind has fingertips. Sound returns to the world with the touch of it on his skin.

'Your son,' he says.

'Yes. Benedicte.'

He has his hand over the place where she kissed him. He says, 'Will I see you again?'

'You will. After the crystal forest. You will see everyone again. All the circles will complete.'

He takes her hand. 'Kizzy, tell me how you do this. You and Benedicte. Tell me what you are.'

'Oh,' she says. Now she is laughing. She reaches up to his cheek and gives it a little pinch, like you would a child. 'There is greater by far than me out there, Jack Fiskardo. You might even get to meet her, one fine day.'

PART III

March 1631

CHAPTER ONE

Hoffstein

'The Elbe takes its head from the Mountains of
Resingbrig, or Gyant Mountains, between the confines
of Bohemia and Silecia, and usefully watering diverse
Provinces and Principalities, after a very long course
wherein she takes into herself divers other rivers,
becoming navigable for great barkes, she disgorges
herself into the North Sea.'

Count Galeazzo Gualdo Priorato, *An History of the Late Warres*

S HE'S A HANDSOME river, the Elbe. The Oder might seem
to arrive in her course almost by accident, simply welling
up to fill the dips and wrinkles in Pomerania's farmland;
but the Elbe has design. She has mountain chasms, she has
waterfalls, rapids, ravines. She has forests that might have

lain undisturbed since the first folk ever to be German hunted through them, wrapped in bearskins, armed with axes made of stone. She has three mighty cities – Hamburg, Magdeburg, Dresden – dividing her conveniently into parts, and ferries criss-crossing her, here, there, everywhere. She has barges and rowboats and unsteady home-made rafts; she has channels deep enough for merchantmen. She has, supposedly, water nymphs, Undines, long hair trailing behind them through the reed-beds, muscular tails twisting over in the water with that big-fish swirl and splash. She has, along her banks, fields that were harvested last autumn, and are now being ploughed over for the spring, and sown anew, just as they should be. She has farmhouses with roofs, and with smoke coming from their chimneys, not staining the blackened holes of their windows; she has churches whose bells still ring. She has strongholds, castles, high above the wide curves in her course; and vertical cliffs of marbled sandstone, eroded into an edging of stacks, with green above and green below, as if the forest had slipped, like icing on a broken cake, and all these things are going to matter and not just here, and not just because war is nothing if not geography, but because wending their way through all this are Jack Fiskardo and his scouts.

'We are travelling,' says Rafe, bouncing along on his mount from Anklam, fat with her winter oats, 'with the spring. Do you see, Captain? Every wood we pass through, more leaves than the last. Every field, greener!'

'We are travelling south, Mr Endicott,' says Jack. 'I think you'll find it has a thing or two to do with that.'

They pass by Gartz, or what remains of Gartz. They pass companies of foot, men who jeer at the scouts, aloft on horseback, and promise to save a beer for them in Munich. They move away from the wide plains of the Oder, and into wooded country, travelling with four up front – two to stay there, two to come back and confirm the rest can move. They cover fifty miles, they cover sixty, seventy, eighty, more. They must be beyond even Berlin by now, not so?

'Way beyond, Mr Endicott.'

They change course. The sun rises behind them, and as it sets, sends streaming banners of pink and flame into their watering eyes. They keep to the herders' trackways where they can; in single file they follow paths untrodden by anything but deer and wild pigs and woodsmen. Their captain had every fourth horse shod backwards before they left (another old trick of Torsten the Bear), so the trail they leave is not some single caravan moving south, but looks like any day's traffic – some one way, some the other. When the country opens up again, he has them travelling between first light and sunrise or after moonrise only; at the zenith of the day they are hidden away, flat on their backs, looking up at the sky. The land begins to lift, the roads descend; and from a wooded hillside they watch as a whole company of Imperial artillery grumbles its way along the road at the hillside's foot, the guards so dilatory that not one realizes the scouts are there, a mere fifty feet above them. Rafe cannot remember when he ever had such a whirl of glee in his stomach, not since he was a child in London, lying awake in his bed, awaiting on the stroke of midnight the bells of New Year's Day. Hoffstein. In his mind's eye he has given it marble pavements, cedar shutters, pillars, waving cypresses – unlikely, he admits, in Saxony, but his mind's eye seems peculiarly confident of the fact. Something like their abbey, but grander by far. The romance of it! The daring! 'This brave adventure, Viktor, eh? This brave adventure!'

Viktor says, 'You do not know Hoffstein.'

'True. But I will. We all will.'

'You will not. You do not know its reputation. Even when I was in the Prince-Bishop's household – none of us was ever at ease when we were there. And those who entered the castle as prisoners, *none* of them were ever seen again.' And Viktor pulls Dart to him, and refuses to say another word.

They find the Elbe, and once they have her, they let her be their compass. Where she winds and curves, they wind and curve; where she has left part of herself behind, in ox-bows and standing water, they work a way around. They track her from hilltop and heathland. They see her villages, her hard-trod roads, her farmsteads. Says Elias, 'What's happened to the war?'

Says their captain, 'Trust me, it won't have gone far.'

They set snares for rabbits when they make camp, go out a-hunting deer. They chew down on hard rusk, and fantasize about the feel of bread in the mouth. They sniff themselves and mourn the loss of Rosa; they wonder if she has had her baby yet. ''Tis a terrible dangerous place, childbed. 'Tis like a battlefield for them,' says Ansfrid, mournfully. 'My brother, he lost two good wives that way.' They show Rafe how to make a Swedish torch – take a dry log with a flat end, cut a star into it, light a fire on the star and it burns down into the log and keeps on burning for hours. 'How ingenious!' says Rafe. 'Viktor, look at this! Feel the warmth from it!' They pass by Magdeburg, on the opposite bank – 'Why,' says Rafe, 'she has as many spires as London! And so well fortified!' he adds, seeing her city walls, the fort guarding the approach from their side of the river. A shoal of islands – some great, some small – split the Elbe before her into two, and from the largest, a bridge spans the deep current, with windlasses to lift its central section up. Just as with London Bridge, in fact. 'A noble city!' says Rafe, swept all of a sudden with homesickness. The spires, the cathedral, the bridge, the hills behind, so like the heights of Hampstead, where he had dreamed of picnicking with Belle. His fingers find her miniature in his pocket, give it a squeeze.

It is just as well the fortifications are there. Magdeburg also has a small Imperial camp on her doorstep, and from behind the city, there comes the desultory boom of cannon. 'My old tutor,' says Kai, sounding unhappy. 'Dr Silvestris. He and his wife, they are there. They have a house by the marketplace.'

'I am quite certain,' Rafe assures him, 'His Majesty, the Lion of the North, we will find him here on our return. He will sweep all before him, never fear.'

On they go, picking their way along the edge of fields, looping through wood and forest. They have been travelling like this long enough to have forgotten there were days when they did anything else, that's all Rafe could tell you, when they come across a clearing full of tents, or rather the Gemini do, and send Luka back with word, and when the rest of them come up, the Gemini have been waiting there so motionless that no-one in the clearing has even noticed they are there yet. Fiskardo steers M'sieu out of the undergrowth and the first man to see him falls over in simple shock.

'*Guten tag, gute leute*,' Fiskardo says, as the man scrambles up, as the women scatter, dragging their children with them, fleeing into the trees. Good day, good people. He dismounts. M'sieu, disburdened, shakes himself. Fiskardo holds out his hand. The man who had fallen over regards the hand with horror, as if he were being offered a smoking grenade. There are babies wailing. There is a dog on a rope, barking furiously at M'sieu. At Rafe's breast, Dart struggles and whines.

Fiskardo crouches down, quiets the dog, stands, offers the hand again. This time, the man shakes it.

'*Hallå*,' the man says, uncertain, but daring. As he talks, his eyes dart over Fiskardo as if they can't stop themselves. He has the look of one who might already be crafting this encounter into a tale for his grandchildren: *The day I met the Swedish.*

'Why are you here?' Fiskardo asks.

Because the other bank, where their village is, is full of soldiers. More and more each day. We came up here to wait it out, until they're gone.

Whose soldiers?

One or two more of the man's neighbours have come to join him. They hold knives and axes; one has a musket, but keeps it shouldered.

We don't know whose, the man says. The Emperor's, we know that. But all heading north'ards, downriver. Opposite way to you.

They swop some of their venison for sacks of dried peas, bargain for a barrel of beer. On they go.

'Why'ud there be so many soldiers going north'ards?' Sten asks, as they sit around in their own camp that evening, under the stars.

'Maybe we took Frankfurt-on-the-Oder,' Ulf suggests. 'Maybe we took Berlin.'

Next morning Thor, sent up ahead, comes hurtling back saying he sees an army marching in the opposite direction to them, along the Elbe's other bank.

An army?

'Thousands,' Thor says. 'I ain't mistaken, Domini.'

'Show me,' says Jack.

They've made camp on a bluff, one of those walls of rock with green above and green below, but even before he and Thor have picked their way to the edge of it, he knows the boy is right. There's that unmistakable murmurous noise – when you first hear it, like a wood with a wind working through it, and then as they make their way nearer, like a river, only one tumbling over rocks, and then like it's a torrent, in flood. The silvery sound of thousands of horses, the tramp of regiments of men. A bugle call, clear enough to make you jump. Then you see them – from this distance like a river of smoke, of dust, flowing along beside the water. He takes the spyglass, and directs it at them. He sees the ragged black shape on a banner held above the dust, the shape that even from this distance can only be a Habsburg eagle, then he sees another. And not a single craft upon the river – all disappeared like magic. He gives the spyglass to Thor.

'Look up there,' he says. 'As far up to the front as you can. What are those flags?'

'Blue and white,' comes the answer. 'Chequers, blue and white.'

'That's Bavaria's colours,' Jack tells him. 'And that, methinks, is Pappenheim. One of the Emperor's generals in the south.'

'Where's he headed?'

'God knows. But that's one hell of a lot of men.'

On they go. The land is smoother here, as if it has been patted down. There are water meadows. There are fishing boats. There is some great dark forest, stretching almost unbroken to their right, with paths coming down through the trees, each one ending at the river in a jetty.

'Are we getting close, Herr Lopov?'

Lopov draws in his breath. 'I think we are near.'

'Get out those uniforms,' Jack says. 'Ulrik, you are now our flag-bearer.' Up goes Ulrik to the front, while the rest of the scouts strip off and don their mustard-and-blood. 'And from now on, you speak Deutsch,' Jack tells them. 'You want to tell Ulf to fuck off, it's *Verpiss dich*. We got that?'

And then where the Elbe eases round into another great swinging curve, there is a long fat divided highland, like a lobster claw, and spooling a way up the divide to its tip, the pale thread of a road, and a scatter of little dwellings along it, and what might be three tall trees, coming into leaf, at the top, and beyond them, a tower.

Close to, the road is so steep the lesser riders must dismount. Close to, the middle of the road is a gravelled chasm. Water must have run down here all winter, it seems to Rafe as he struggles up it, mindful of M'sieu's great backside there above him; and the horse's mighty hooves, and skittish unpredictability. At one point he thinks he hears the *bok-bok-bok* of hens, but tells himself he must have imagined it. The houses either side of them are shuttered, all closed up; the silence going up the road

is that of absolute desertion. He concentrates on not turning an
ankle, a mishap that on London's cobbles has befallen him all
too often.

There are the linden trees. The ground around them is
bare earth (no marble pavement), bare gritty earth broken by
tree roots like old arthritic fingers, clambering free. There is
an ancient-looking pump, and an empty basin beneath it. An
odd-looking little building behind the trees, circular, a sort
of tempietto, with columned doorway and portico above, but
its roof appears ruinous. He looks up. There is a round stone
tower, built on a basement skirt of dark rock. Iron bars across
its windows. They walk or ride through an archway, and they
are standing within a dusty, weed-strewn courtyard, denuded
in many places of its paving stones. There is another tower,
opposite – square, this one, also of stone, and painted across
its lower storey and very much faded, again that monstrous
chimera, part eagle, part bleeding heart. A wall, marking the
edge of the courtyard, the drop to the river, and the Elbe visible
beyond. A pair of antique lopsided cannon, poked through the
wall, as if to pull faces at the countryside beneath. There are
no cypresses. There is no pillared walkway. He turns to Viktor
Lopov. 'This is it?' he asks. 'This is the Prince-Bishop's castle?
His place of retreat?'

'This is it,' Lopov replies. There is sweat on his forehead, his
nostrils flare, his face is grey. 'Hoffstein.'

FRIDAYS, IN THE Franka household, they eat fish. They may
no longer have neighbours to monitor whether they do, but
nonetheless, every Friday before sunrise, Otto Franka clambers
over the wall out of the garden, trying not to wake his sister's
hens nor plant an accidental foot in her potager, picks his way
downhill to the riverbank, and stands there in the chill and the

quiet, watching the mist unravel itself over the water, listening to the rustle of the reeds, waiting for the plop and turn of
warming, wakening fish (or is it an Undine? Now that would
be a catch!), and periodically jiggling his line in a manner
designed to mimic the exact motion of some good big juicy
fly, all disoriented with his springtime waking and sat there
stropping his feelers while he, like Otto, comes to terms with
the world in which he finds himself, and makes what peace
with it he can.

This is why (thinks Otto) he hasn't put a gate in that garden
wall. Made the path, sure enough, cut back the undergrowth of
ivy and bramble, even dug in a few steps for the steepest parts,
but those are temporary, they will be gone one day (just as he
will be, just as they all will be, one day), but knocking down a
yard of wall, putting in a gate, however much easier it might
make his life, make all their lives, that would be permanent.
That would mean they are staying here: he, Ava, Tata; that
would mean there is nothing after this, nothing beyond this,
that this is all there is for them, and all there will ever be. Thus
the thoughts of Otto Franka, standing here on the bank of the
Elbe, in the same spot where he has found himself thinking
those exact same thoughts so many times before.

Two hours later, with the sun fully risen in the sky, Otto
stumps his way back uphill, the bag Ava made him for his catch
soaking his shoulders. Otto gauges where he is in his trudge
uphill not by looking up, and thus being faced with the reality
of the castle, but by counting steps, by keeping his eyes on his
feet. He can always feel the castle there, of course he can, even
when he's fishing, but it's a personal battle between him and
the cursed place – how far can he get up the hill before he has
to turn his gaze toward it? Before he has to admit to himself,
it is still there (and he is still here). But he does well today,
he thinks, he is almost up the hill, up through the first spring
green, before he lifts his eyes, and then when he does the first

thing he spies is his sister, in their garden, over its crumbling wall; his sister, waving an arm above her head. A warning.

There are irises, pushing their new leaves up through the winter-rot of the old. A constellation of wood anemones dancing beside the path. A bird is singing. His shirt, at his shoulders, is wet through. He opens one palm – *What?* – and his sister points up toward the castle, and hisses, 'Otto, there are soldiers here! The Prince-Bishop's men!'

His stomach folds in on itself, like it was being kneaded, like dough. Some hard knot at its centre.

He comes up to the wall, which is no more than rubble, clambers over. He should have made that gate when they first arrived. 'Where is Tata?'

'Inside. Asleep in his chair.'

Their father has the recent habit of wandering away. Ava says it is because his thoughts wander too, and he follows them; in Otto's opinion, it is all of a piece with his father's love of contrary behaviour whatever has been his age. Tata's whereabouts are the first important question in this unwelcome circumstance; the second is—

'Is the Prince-Bishop with them?'

She shakes her head.

Be thankful for small mercies. Otto goes into the house, puts the sack on the table, sighing as he straightens up. Recently, it has begun to feel as if his body is in a constant state of annoyance with him. *This place*, he thinks, *it is getting to us all.* Ava has pinch marks at the corners of her eyes; her arms, which in Prague were white and soft and bore glittering bracelets at the wrists, have grown sinewy with her gardening and show a tan. Unthinkable, before. As unthinkable as a Catholic not eating fish on a Friday. If he and Ava end up old as Tata, will they still be here then? Will they die here, facing each other over their single table? Sit there, mummify, slowly turn to dust?

Oh, Tata has awakened. His father has tottered up to the table with those newly hobbled steps of his, and with the one arm that still obeys him, waves aside his son's greeting to inspect the contents of the sack. This, for a man who was once consulted all across Europe, grandee to grandee, court to court.

His father pulls from the sack the body of a bream. 'Ech,' his father says, in disgust.

'Listen, Tata. We cannot be choosy, we will starve.' Otto is lifting down his good coat from its hook as he speaks, thinking, *Should I shave? Change my shirt? Dare I keep them waiting while I do?* He turns back to Ava and asks, hopefully, 'Is the same man with them as before?' The previous visitor to Hoffstein had been extraordinarily affable. Asked to be shown around, admired the views, disappeared into the archive for a mere five minutes and with apologies for his rudeness in doing so. Not what they had been anticipating at all.

'No. Otto, I think they have prisoners. Two prisoners.'

Now his gut is a cushion, being turned over, punched. This is bad, oh, this is very bad.

It gets worse. 'I think one of them is Victor Lopov.'

Lopov? He goes to the window, peeks uphill. He sees two guards at the archway, two men with crazily bright, pale hair; he sees horses in the courtyard behind them. Ava is saying, 'Do you think he is here because of Tata? Because of us?'

'No,' Otto says at once. 'No, it can't be.' But he has at once that terrible suspicion that it is. He peeks again, steeling himself. 'I must show them we are here,' he says, quietly.

'Otto!'

'I have to, Ava. We have no choice.' Then, lifting his voice he says, 'Tata, don't go outside. Stay here, with Ava.'

'Eh?'

'Don't go outside. Not on your own. Not with the soldiers here. Wait till I'm back.'

IN THE END, it is so ridiculously easy. Ulrik puts his shoulder to the door in the square tower, and the lock gives way at once. They go in, into an echoing, stone-flagged corridor. Up a short square flight of stairs. A passageway, with curved ceiling, low enough that anyone tall as Fiskardo, as Zoltan, as Ulrik, has to hunch. Even for Rafe the space is claustrophobic. There is a window at the end of the passageway, many little roundels of glass, and on the floor before the window, a dead bird. Must have got itself trapped in here; no more than dust and feathers now, poor thing. Rafe picks it up. Under the dust, the feathers are Indian yellow. Why – a canary! He has seen canaries for sale in Piccadilly, at Gresham's Royal Exchange; the tiny bird offered for as much as a hogshead barrel of wine. Yet this one was – what, let out of a cage, to flap its way to despair? Who would own such an expensive little novelty, only to abandon it, to let it perish here? Beating its wings out against a window and a world it could never reach again?

He puts the dead bird down upon the windowsill. There is – there is something about the level of dilapidation and spoiling in this place that feels almost spiteful. Dart, at his heels, puts up her nose. For a moment he is not sure which one of them is reassuring the other.

There is an arch off to the left. It leads to a wide square chamber, looking out over the river one side, the courtyard the other, and just as bare. There is a painted decoration of some sort upon the floor, so worn away as to be less there than not, and five mismatched chairs, two with their cane seats broken through. If a room could grow weeds, this one would. Fiskardo, at the front, has come to a halt. 'Viktor, this place is derelict.'

Says Lopov, 'You do not understand. Follow me, then you will.'

In the corner of the room another door, and beyond it a spiral stone stair, leading up, leading down. 'What's above?' the captain asks.

'Bedchambers. Our way is down.'

Down they go. Door number three. Ulrik kicks the lock; it too gives way at once. The room beyond is low enough in the tower for there to be greenery touching its windows, and it is lined, from floor to ceiling, with shelves and drawers and cubbyholes. Some are narrowly horizontal, stacked with papers, some narrowly vertical, holding portfolios, some, with rolls of paper protruding from them, are in rows of squares. It's like being in a beehive, facing the walls of cells. There are three tall thin windows, foliage dancing beyond them and giving down upon a vertiginous view of yet another skirt of rock; but otherwise every inch of wall is covered in this intricate furniture of ordering and categorization, all joined and fitted to perfection; the edges sharp, the mouldings flawless. The wood is – no, thinks Rafe, the woods *are* walnut, mahogany, ebony, olive. He smells cedar. He looks up. Along the cornicing are roman numerals, let in, one to each section, in mother-of-pearl. There are ivory labels to every shelf; if it is then subdivided, the subdivisions are labelled too, lettered in scarlet or gold. The stringing of the shelves has been water-gilt. The pulls for the drawers – are they amber? And out of every cell, every opening, there poke those documents in ribboned rolls, or leather folders, or papers layered one upon the other like the layers in a pastry. Rafe is open-mouthed. Not since his college library in Cambridge has he seen anything like this, and what a contrast to the neglect that came before! 'Mr Lopov,' he begins, 'is this yours? This is your archive, sir?'

Lopov inclines his head. 'It was.' He lets his fingers trail the edge of one shelf, the way another man might caress a strand of his lover's hair. 'I designed it, to be fitted out so. It took much thought, much care.' He looks around, sighing. 'And all for what, I ask myself now.'

'In order that you might find Ravello's letter for us, Mr Lopov, remember?' comes Fiskardo's voice. 'And we might quit this place, as unnoticed as we came in?'

'Oh, yes. Those steps, if you please.'

The steps are brought. They are as elegantly worked as the shelving. Viktor Lopov mounts to the top, reaches up, pulls on a gilded knop at the corner of a shelf, and as they watch, with the muffled sound of chains running and weights descending, as in a clock, an entire section of shelving first shudders slightly, then swings toward them. Dart, startled, barks at it, furiously. Within there is yet another room – octagonal, and with no windows at all, but the same wooden floor, in continuation, and just as carefully lined with shelves and drawers, and just as full of papers. 'Do you see?' asks Lopov, quietly. 'This is what the Prince-Bishop hides away here. The secrets of other men.'

He crosses the room, pulls out a drawer, lifts out the ribbon attached to its front edge – the base lifts, again the smell of cedarwood – and as they come forward, peering, there, in the velvet-lined interior on a scatter of other papers, is a letter. One thick sheet of paper, folded three times over, tied with a cord and with a dangling seal. 'I said it would be here,' says Viktor, modestly. 'If it was anywhere.' He holds the letter out to them. 'Three chevrons. A crown. Ribbons.'

'Good God,' their captain says. 'Mr Lopov, if I had not seen that with my own eyes, I would not have believed it possible. I take my hat off to you. We come three hundred miles and you know the very drawer. Astounding.' He takes the letter, folds it about its heavy seal, puts it in his pocket and asks, 'And what's through that door there?'

What door?

'There.' Dart is scratching at the skirting board. 'There, she sees it. Follow the line.'

There is a minutely wider, darker, vertical line at the edge of one section of shelving, which Dart now has her nose to. You can follow it: up, then along, beneath the edge of a shelf at a little more than head height, then down the other side. 'Lopov, how does this one open?'

But Lopov is retreating from the door, across to the other side of the room. 'I have never seen it open. I do not know.'

'You don't know?'

Lopov shakes his head.

'Very well then, we will open it ourselves.'

But how? A knop? There is none. A hidden handle? They run their fingers round inside the shelves, under the papers, stand on tiptoe to stretch into the cubby-holes. 'I can feel the draught from it,' Fiskardo tells them. 'This opens somehow.' Ulrik puts up both arms and shoves at it. Ulf lies along the floor and pushes at the skirting. 'Gerroff,' he tells Dart, who is licking at his face, delighted at this new game, but no movement, not even a creak.

'What's beneath us?' Fiskardo asks.

'Nothing,' Lopov answers at once. His nostrils flare.

'That was a very speedy answer, Mr Lopov. You're sure of that?'

Lopov licks his lips. 'There is supposed to be a well.'

A well?

'An old well. Very deep. It is one of the stories told about this place. But I have never seen it.' He licks his lips again, a snake-flick of the tongue.

'Mr Lopov,' says Fiskardo, 'you are lying. Now why would you do that?'

Lopov says nothing.

'Is there a well down there, Mr Lopov?'

'Yes,' says Lopov, in a whisper. 'But it is old, the water is bad. It is not used.'

'Does this door go down to it?'

'It might.' Another whisper.

'Mr Lopov, do you know how this door opens?'

'No. I promise you. I never knew it was here. Captain, please—'

'Domini?' Ansfrid has appeared at the door, breathless. 'Domini, the Gemini – they say there's someone coming up the hill.'

'We will continue this, Mr Lopov,' says Fiskardo. 'This place is plenty strange enough without mysterious locked doors. Thank you, Ansfrid. You will stay here, if you please. The rest of you, follow me.'

Ansfrid takes up position at the door. Rafe looks over at Viktor Lopov; Viktor Lopov does not meet his eye. Rafe clears his throat. 'I do not think,' he begins, 'that it is a good idea to lie to him.'

'I am not lying,' says Viktor, sullenly. 'I did not know this door was here.'

'But you knew there was a well down there.'

'*Everyone* knows there is a well down there. It is – it is what Hoffstein has. But I have never seen it. And I have no idea where that door may lead.'

'Then we had better get it open and find out.'

Impossible not to feel intimidated, stood here between these two – these two oddities, with their white-blond hair, waiting, waiting. Also, toiling up to the courtyard has left him breathless anyway; Otto Franka runs to plumpness, if not fat. He is shaped like an eight, like his name. He tries to make conversation: 'A fine day, gentlemen.' He feels them exchange glances over his head. 'Was your journey easy?'

'*Hoc est stultus*,' says one. This is an idiot.

'*Hoc est stultus timidus*,' says the other. A frightened idiot. It seems not to have occurred to either man that Otto might speak Latin too – or perhaps it has, and neither cares.

The door to the square tower comes open. A man advances toward him, hand outstretched, a man with a sprout of dyed red hair coming off the top of his head. Did he spy the same colour on one of the horses, on the creature's tail?

'*Dobrý den! Ahoj!*' the man says.

'*Ahoj!*' Otto answers. He is wholly taken aback by the friendliness of the greeting, likewise that it is in Czech.

'I am Sigismund,' the man continues, in Deutsch this time.

'Otto Franka,' says Otto. 'I am – I am the caretaker here.'

'Ah, so!' The man, Sigismund, looks round. 'Beautiful,' he says, seeming to mean the overgrown courtyard, the two towers.

Otto is even more confused than he was before. He casts a glance at the other men, ranged about the open doorway. At some level (he will realize later) he registers their peculiar motley, that all of them wear the Prince-Bishop's colours, true enough, but that not one has an entire uniform. He registers too that this Sigismund looks round again before he speaks, that he checks back to the men standing at the door, that he seems to look back to one of them in particular, the tall one, stood with his arms folded. He cannot see Lopov anywhere. Nerving himself, Otto asks, 'May I enquire – do you have others with you?'

'Others?' Sigismund wears an expression of polite interest. Another quick glance back over his shoulder; another bright smile. 'No. No others.'

Otto is wholly, utterly confused. 'Oh. Oh. Then, do I, er…'

'Yes, do,' says this Sigismund, encouragingly. 'Good day!'

TWO DAYS AFTER he had been plucked off the street in Prague, Leo Franka awoke in his cell (it was a room, its door was locked, there was a guard outside, what would you call that?) and found he could see nothing out of his left eye. He lifted a hand to investigate, and although he told the hand, the arm, to move, it did not. It is still disobedient, even now.

Over the course of the following day, Leo's stout left leg also seemed to leave him. At least, it was there, but it wanted nothing to do with him. That was when he composed himself to die. An apoplexy. There was a history of such in his family. He comforted himself with the thought that at least that misbegotten ingrate the Prince-Bishop would get nothing more from him, he beseeched the good Lord to guard Otto and Ava, closed his eyes, and waited for the next hammer-blow to fall upon his poor tormented brain. When he opened them again, however, he was still alive, still in that room, and there was a man sat watching him; a man with peculiarly hot, feral eyes in an oddly pale face.

'My thinking,' the man began, 'was that we should put you from your misery here and now. But His Grace the Prince-Bishop is more merciful.'

The Prince-Bishop, Leo was assured, still valued his old servant, whatever had been his crimes and even with him reduced to such a half-man as he was now. In Leo's head there yet remained all his knowledge, his skill, his understanding of the complex character of metals in the casting of a cannon as great as Vainglory. He would therefore continue to live, in order for such knowledge to remain available to the Prince-Bishop, but from such a place where his contact with all others might be controlled. Where he would be able to make no further enquiries into the financing of that great work, and the thalers that have already vanished into her, as into a vat of molten ore.

'It was,' said his visitor, 'so very foolish of you, so to do.'

If he acceded to this, his visitor informed him, then his son and daughter would survive the father's foolishness. If not, then—

They would pay the price. For the son, the quarries, or the galleys, perhaps. For the daughter, a brothel, obviously. 'She is old for such,' his visitor had said, as if he had given this the most detailed consideration, 'so she would not last long; but one can see how proud she is. Perhaps I will break her to it myself.'

And his visitor leaned forward, knitted his small fingers together under his pallid chops, and asked Leo which it was to be.

Over the months of their exile, cautious use of his left leg has returned to Leo Franka, as has a bitter understanding of his family's plight. If the Prince-Bishop has sent men here, they will be here for him. The sooner they speak with him, pick what they can from his brains, the sooner this will be over, and the sooner they – damn them – will depart. Leo Franka's arm may be a jellyfish, his leg as pliant as a withy, and the vision in his left eye no more than a series of colourful smudges, but he is still stubborn, he is still determined, and it is still he who is head of this family, by God.

He waits in his chair, good eye half open. He sees Ava make her way back out to the garden, shaking her head. He pushes himself up, hobbles to the door. He has to be careful with the handle, make sure he keeps a hold of his stick, as drop that and *feh*, he can be there for the next half hour, trying to pick it up. His hands, which were once so cunning – now look at them. Shake like leaves. Twitch, like they are giving up the ghost.

The door, finally, is open. With careful deliberation he moves out, down the path, and then he puts his left foot down on that damned uneven road, and is at once almost down on his *prdel*. Almost.

'Now then, oldster! Can't have you out here, falling about!'

The hand – the strong, young hand (he registers both in the voice as well) – catches him, steadies him, holds him till he has his breath. He peers up and round – yes, there is his rescuer, a youth like a young ox, and another, who is pretty as a girl. And a mighty great horse with them.

'In you get, oldster.' The pretty lad has already gone around him, is holding the front door open, is inviting Leo to go back inside. 'We'll be bringing our 'orses up an' down here,' the young ox tells him. 'You stay safe in there.'

He hobbles back into the house, sits down. He hears his daughter still out in the garden, talking to her hens. He wipes one fluttering hand over his forehead, presses it to his mouth. *These are never the Prince-Bishop's men*, he thinks. *Never!*

In the archive it is Ansfrid's opinion that they should take an axe to that door and chop a way through. He and Rafe have cleared the shelves of papers, to Lopov's silent distress; they have tugged and shoved at the shelves themselves, opened drawers, felt around inside them – all to naught. The door (it is more and more obvious it is a door, every time you look at it) defies them. They sit on the floor, the three of them, and stare at it. 'It just don't make sense,' Ansfrid is saying. 'We can see it. Why can't we open it?' He picks up a paper from the drifts of them now on the floor, balls it up, throws it at the door. Dart goes running after it. She skids against the door and gives a yelp. A panel of the floor has sunk beneath her paw. And the door is no longer flush with the rest of the shelves and cubby-holes; it is at an angle. It has moved.

Rafe gets to his feet. He crosses the room – his sense is he should do this on tiptoe – pushes at the door, and the whole section swings back, smooth and easy as you like. And revealed, another spiral stair.

They creep down it. Ansfrid is in the lead. At the bottom of the spiral, maybe twenty steps down, just where the light from above gives out, another door. 'Fuck this,' says Ansfrid and, shoving his way past Rafe and Viktor Lopov, stomps back up the stairs. They hear him cross the room above their heads.

'Viktor,' says Rafe, 'this is extraordinary! Don't you think it is? Aren't you excited by this?'

Viktor puts his head against the wall and closes his eyes.

Ansfrid returns. He returns with Elias, and a loaded pistol. Elias shoots out the lock. The stink of black powder in the tight space of the stairs is enough to have them all coughing, but this door now swings open too. Another stairway lies ahead of them, running straight down against the wall. It is very dark, but it is not wholly so – moving one behind the other, they can make out the edge of each step, enough to follow them down, or to follow Dart, who goes pattering ahead, then at the bottom—

At the bottom, a sort of tunnel, or a tunnel-shaped cavern, running off in either direction, left and right. The air moves through it. It is cold. It smells wet; it smells of stone. Tiny, irregular shafts of light, thin as canes, silvery-grey, play in the top level of the darkness. Rafe looks at the floor, where the stair ends. It is dark, and irregular, but flattish. *That's bedrock*, he thinks.

Says Elias, 'Are we under the courtyard? Are we between the towers? Is that where we are?' He sets off to the left. Dart does not follow. Dart whines and growls.

Elias comes back. 'Not that way?' A glance at Lopov. 'What's up with him?'

Lopov is sat upon the stairs. He has his head in his hands. 'I am faint,' he says. 'I am unwell. The air – I will not go further.'

'You stay with 'im, Scribbler,' Elias says. He looks off to the left again, shrugs – it is dark that way, very dark, it must be under the round tower – and sets off to the right. Ansfrid follows. There is just enough light to make out their faces as they work their way round the edges of the cavern. Their conversation floats back, ringed with echoes. 'What's this here?'

Here, here, here… It's eerie, as echoes always are. Rafe finds himself looking off into the darkness to the left. The air feels colder that way too. Presumably, that way is the well.

'Nah, nothing. Empty.'

Empty, empty…

'Oh ho ho! Lookit in there! There's the wine! Thank you very much!'

Off the footsteps set again, the pale dot of one face, then another. Then an angry expletive. 'Shit! Not another fucken lock!' A pause, in which Rafe imagines Elias recharging and reloading his pistol. Sure enough, the flash of firing, the *bang* of the report. Lopov, behind Rafe on the stairs, gives a shudder and holds his head. Dart gives a whimper, pushes her nose against his face.

The sound of a door being eased open and protesting about it. Then, for a moment, nothing. Then a shout. 'Jesus! Jesus *Christ*!' It's loud enough to bring Rafe to his feet. Above their heads, the final cane of light has changed its colour. Not silvery-grey, not any more. It is as strongly yellow as the plumage on the dead bird.

UP-A-TOP, IN THE courtyard, the scouts are watching Otto make an uncertain departure. 'Excellently well done, Ziggy,' says Jack. 'I should think we had him fooled there for all of ten seconds at least.'

Ziggy turns about, raises his hands. 'Apologies, Domini.'

'No matter. We have what we came for. Let's get out of here.'

And then the door from the tower bursts open, and there is the Scribbler. He runs straight to them. 'Captain, please, sir – you must come with me! Herr Lieutenant, you too, sir. Please!'

They follow him. Up the stairs, through the arch, into the chamber. Down the stairs, to the archive. Through to the octagon. 'Ah, the door!' Zoltan says. 'You have it open!'

'All the doors!' comes the mysterious reply.

Down a stair. Down another stair. Negotiate a way round Lopov, at the bottom, sat there with arms about his knees. Jack pauses. 'What is this place?'

'It's a cavern, sir. A natural cave, beneath the courtyard. Do you see, the light comes in through peeps in the rock. And there are rooms dug off it. You will see!'

And then Ansfrid's voice. 'Kapten! Kapten! This way!' Jack sees Ansfrid at the cavern's end, jigging from one foot to the

other with excitement. Zoltan has gone ahead. 'Are you ready?'
Endicott is asking. 'Are you ready, sir?'

Ansfrid and Elias are standing together at the far end of the
cavern. No, they are standing at another door, so dark you can
barely make the thing out, but it's heavy-looking, that's for sure.
It's taking the two of them to open it, to pull it back. 'Do you
see, sir?'

'Do you see what we found?'

'Do you see? It's real, Kapten, it's real!'

The door is open. The entire front of Zoltan's body changes
colour, goes as yellow as if he were stood in front of a church
window. Jack hears the gasp, although it is almost a shout.
Zoltan has dropped to his knees. Jack goes forward. He sees.
He spreads wide his arms, as if in welcome. He hears himself
say, as if none of this was any surprise at all, 'Oh, yes.'

'We found it, sir!' Endicott cackles behind him. 'We found it!
Your room full of gold!'

CHAPTER TWO

Maria

'Gold will be slave or master.'

Horace, *Epistle 10*

Gold.

No, that's not enough. To say only that is nothing like enough.

Gold in little bags of coin – escudos, crusados, florins. Chests of gold, too heavy to lift. Gold in wrinkled ingots, the size of your thumb, piled in ziggurats upon the floor. Bangles, necklets, chains of gold, that spill and pool like water. Plattens, church plate, ewers, goblets, chalices. Gold-handled knives. Golden forks. Nested bowls, all cupped together. Golden earbobs, shaped as quatrefoils, like hooplets, like bells. The statue of a stag, whose fur shimmers, whose antlers are solid gold twigs. A curious flat gold mask, white shell and greenish stone let in around the eyes. A tiny golden mannikin, wearing the head of some kind of beast. Another, winged like an eagle. The gold head of a griffin, or some such – hooked beak, golden ears raised like a dog. A ring, set with a pale blue stone, the exact blue, pale but warm, of a bluebell. His hand reaches out for that; nor does he pull the hand back.

'We found it, sir! Your room full of gold!'

There is the golden cover for a book, pulled from its binding – the Lord enthroned on high above, nailed to the cross below. There are crucifixes of every type and size imaginable, some strung together, as if they were no more than keys, some waiting on their own; crucifixes granulated, pierced, bound round with yet more gold, with or without a tiny golden Christ. One by one the scouts come down that narrow stair and through the cavern, and stand in the room full of gold and stand, and stand, and stand – speechless. Breathless. At one point Elias has to sit upon the floor and put his head between his knees. Endicott goes round and round them, staggering from one man to the next, laughing and gesticulating like he's been at the Gemini's black butter once again.

There are gold thimbles, gold shoe buckles, weskit buttons, thin gold pins for pushing through the hair. There are enamelled dolphins, there are golden mermen, there is a golden frog. There is a golden galleon, sails spread, perfectly rigged, with golden timbers crossing her deck and a lidded hold, in which lie a scatter of crystals of – what is it?

Ulf puts one to his tongue. 'It's salt!' he exclaims. 'Good God a'mighty, all that for nothing more'n salt!'

There are golden boxes for snuff, for baccy; there are grilled vinaigrettes; there are gold tampers for your pipe. There's a bag of golden aigrettes, to dress up the ribbons on your jacket. There are empty gold frames for cameos, for jewels. There's a golden inkwell, with a lid that closes with a snap, could sit in the palm of your hand; there's an ivory pen with a golden nib. And a roll of what might be cloth, were it not so heavy, and if it could not be pleated and folded, and then the pleats and folds *stay*.

They empty the wine cellar. They have no idea what they might be drinking, but what does that matter? They are armoured with gold. There is not one man amongst them does not now think himself invincible. They sit in the courtyard as the stars come out, toasting one another, asking, 'Have you seen Maria?'

Oh, I have.

She's a big lass.

She's a *fine* big lass.

Big enough for all!

Where did she come from?

'Pillage, ain't it,' says Ulf. 'The sort of pillage you can get away with when you're the fuckety Prince-Bishop of Prague. And now we're going to fuck *him*.' He sits back. 'I'm buying me a fleet of fishing boats.'

'I'm buying me a harbour.'

'I'm buying me a horse like the Kapten's. No, I'm buying ten!'

Viktor Lopov finds the smallest bedchamber, as high and as far away from the room full of gold as he can; rolls himself into the smallest corner, facing the wall. He tells them he is sick. He looks as if he might be trying to burrow out of Hoffstein altogether.

Says Zoltan, 'In Strasberg, in Poland, they say the King found six tons of Polish gold hidden in the castle.'

Jack, stood in the centre of the room, soaked in light yellow as buttercups, says quietly, 'I think this might be more.'

'I take it we will not be leaving here as swiftly as we thought?'

'You would be right in that.' He has the ring with the pale blue stone on his thumb, is rolling it back and forth across his fingers.

'And that when we do leave, this is coming with us?'

'You would be right there, too.'

'Our boys,' says Zoltan, 'our boys will go home rich.'

'We're all rich, Zoltan. You can go back to Buda, buy a palace.'

'What would I do with a palace?'

'Anything you like.' He picks up one of the little bags of coin, weighs it in his hand, listens to the *chink*. 'That's one bag. Look at it. No bigger'n a bollock, and it's heavy as a cannonball. And we've hundreds of them. Zoltan, how do we shift all this?'

UP IN A bare and dusty bedchamber, Rafe is dreaming. He is walking up that hill again, to the little chapel. The black pool is opening before him. He wakes, flailing his arms. 'There is no floor!' he shouts. 'There is no floor!'

Ulf throws a cushion at his head. 'There's a floor, you're lying on it! Take a bit of water with it next time, Scribbler, eh?'

SAYS AVA, 'I want you to go back up there again and ask them about Viktor.'

Such a pretty day outside, Otto had been thinking. The first with true warmth in the air. He has been on the riverbank all morning, fishing (well – he has been avoiding his sister all morning, to be honest). He puts down his knife. Outside he can hear the hens fluffing themselves through their dust-baths. 'Ava—' he begins.

'I want you to go back up there again. They were drinking last night, drinking and singing, and speaking of him. I heard his name.'

At the other side of the table, their father has lifted his head.

'How,' Otto begins, 'how would you have heard his name?' He is picking threads in what she says, he knows, as an alternative to doing something about it. As Ava is so clearly about to demand that he does.

'I was on the path below the cannon—'

'Ava, I begged you to stay here. I don't want them knowing you exist!'

She waves his protest away. 'I was on the path below the cannon and I heard them. Now you must do something.'

'Ava, what am I to do? They are armed men! They are the Prince-Bishop's men—'

'They are not the Prince-Bishop's men,' his father says.

'Remonstrate with them! Shame them! Whatever they are here to do, *stop* them.'

'Ava—'

'They are not the Prince-Bishop's men,' his father repeats.

'Otto,' Ava is saying, 'if Viktor Lopov is here, it is for the same reason *we* are here.' Her eyes flash. Ava looks like their mother, her features are strong and dark and exciting. Before their exile here, when Ava was younger, her eyes danced. The way she has of pursing her lips that made her look as if she were always on the point of jumping into the conversation, now it smacks of judgement. Judgement of her brother, usually. She says, 'We have to help him. We have to try, at least.'

She is four years Otto's senior. There is probably no woman on earth, thinks Otto, of whom a man stands so much in awe as he does his older sister.

'Ignore me then, you idiots,' his father says. 'Like I would care.'

'Tata, forgive me. Forgive us.' (Ava turns away, with a *tchoh* of anger.) 'What is it you said? Why would these not be the Prince-Bishop's men?'

'Why? Why? Do they look like them? Do they act like them? Do they sound like them?'

'But whose else would they be?'

'Maybe,' his father says, 'you should go up there and find out.'

The moment he sets foot in the courtyard, Otto knows his father is right. There are those patchwork uniforms; more, there is the friendliness of these men to each other; and then their low-voiced speech, the alien rhythm of it, the way it stops as soon as they see him, to be replaced with something both louder and more familiar. Even the way those there with the horses are investigating how the horses have come through the night. *But if they have Viktor*, he asks himself, *who else can they be?*

They have seen him. Otto chooses the youngest as being the least alarming; also, surely, any being who (God above) looks so much like a seraph could not possibly do you harm. '*Guten tag*,' Otto begins. 'Might I speak with your captain?'

The seraph looks troubled. 'I think he sleeps.'

'Oh, I will—' He is about to say *I will come back*, then he remembers Ava. 'I will wait. I am happy to wait.'

An early morning rain has begun to fall. He was right about the seraph. 'You should not wait out here, *mein Herr*. Please, follow me.'

He does. He finds himself being led upstairs, to the great room on the first floor. His heartbeat becomes audible, but apparently only to him; he tells himself he is only a very little way away from the outside world, that this is nothing, that he has been this far inside the castle before and lived to tell the tale. The boy pulls out a chair for him, then seeing how its seat is broken, selects another. 'I will find the captain,' the boy declares, and Otto is left alone. Every so often there are noises overhead – other sleepers, waking, rising, shouting greetings. He hears footsteps descending the stone stairs, and a young man enters the room, a trim black dog at his heels. The young man nods to Otto, says, 'Ah, rain,' as if this were conversation, and exits the room, the dog trotting after him.

Not the captain, Otto thinks. He finds his heart has eased back a little. He starts to rehearse his first line. *Captain*, he will begin. *Captain, of your mercy, sir. Captain, one of those you brought with you—*

Outside the sun appears. One of the horses gives a sort of horsey shout, then it does so again, even more loudly. Otto is peering through the window, to see which animal it might be, when he hears a voice behind him. It says, 'You were waiting to speak with me?'

He turns about. Close to, the man is even taller than he had looked before. A long, lean face, not without humour, Otto assesses, hopefully. The recent white chop of a scar through one eyebrow. He had come up behind Otto as silently as a cat. 'Fiskardo,' the man says, holding out a hand. 'I am the captain here.'

'Otto Franka,' Otto replies. 'I am the – the caretaker.'

'Is that so?' the man says. 'We were not expecting you.' He has a peculiarly unreadable gaze with much going on beneath it. Otto finds he is thinking of the Elbe, as it had been, running along under its winter skin of ice. He starts speaking, in a rush – *you have prisoners, I think, it is possible one of them is known to me, Viktor Lopov, would it be permitted, of your mercy, might I see him?* The rush of words dries to a trickle, then dries completely.

'Viktor Lopov,' the captain says, 'believed this place to be deserted.'

'Yes,' says Otto. 'It was.'

'Yet here you are,' this man Fiskardo says. 'The caretaker.' Is Otto imagining it, or is the man leaving a space for him to fill?

He takes a breath. He feels, rather than sees, that more of these strangers have now come into the room. 'I am not exactly the caretaker,' Otto begins.

'No?'

'No.' The blood is pounding in his ears. 'But then I think you do not exactly work for the Prince-Bishop, either.'

The laughter starts behind him, uncertain at first, then it swells, and then the captain raises a hand and it dies away.

'How if,' Fiskardo says, 'you tell me your story, and if I like it, I will tell you ours, and you will see Herr Lopov. Fair enough?'

Very well.

'My father,' Otto begins (he is marshalling his facts with care), 'is a foundryman. A specialist in the casting of iron and bronze. Perhaps you know something of the casting of metals, Captain?'

'I do not,' comes the reply.

'People think,' Otto continues, 'that casting is a matter of mere heat and force, but it is not. It requires much skill, the most delicate judgement, and great exactitude. The greater the item to be cast, the more precision it requires. The item my father was to cast was a cannon, an enormous piece, to be used against the Turk, so we were told.'

He looks up, takes a breath. *Ah, Vainglory*, he thinks. *She must languish yet somewhere in Prague, unfinished and forgotten. Just as we languish here.*

Still that watchful gaze.

'I think now the whole purpose of the piece was the taxes the Prince-Bishop could demand, to pay for it. There was something awry with the commission from the start. And Viktor Lopov, Captain, he is – he is a great chaser after detail.'

At last, his audience reacts. 'Hah,' says the captain. 'Ain't he just.'

Otto is encouraged. 'He had uncovered these – these anomalies in the record-keeping. Entries that made no sense to him. For example, there was the copper, to smelt the bronze – it was sourced through Yosha Silbergeld, in Amsterdam, but payment to him was recorded against another name entirely. And there were other examples—'

He stops. The captain has lifted his hand. 'Say that again. Payment to who?'

'To Yosha Silbergeld. In Amsterdam. A merchant.'

Something peculiarly intent in that listening face.

'Captain, do you know the name?'

'I think I've heard of it. Go on, Herr Franka.'

Otto lines up his thoughts anew. 'The debt to him was set against another name entirely, a man who did not seem to exist. Then when the first shipment of copper came down to us, while the *Guid Marie* yet rode at anchor—'

The hand is raised again. 'The *Guid Marie?*'

'Yes, Captain. The ship Mynheer Silbergeld used to bring the ore to us, down the Elbe. He has an interest in her, a partnership—'

'She carried the copper to you? Down the Elbe, to Prague?'

'Oh, no, no, no. This was summer, Captain, and her draught, and the shallowness of the river – she carried it to Dresden – below us, but not so far as Prague. We used barges after that.'

'But below us. Past Hoffstein. She could sail down past us here.'

'She must have done, Captain,' replies Otto, bemused.

Much thought, much activity, beneath that steady gaze.

'Captain, I would dearly love to speak with Viktor Lopov.'

'Herr Franka,' says the captain, getting to his feet, 'I will bring you to Viktor Lopov, I promise you, but first I have something to show you. Will you come with me?'

This is exactly what he had been dreading. In fact, did he not have this captain, this Fiskardo, behind him on the spiral stairs, now is when Otto Franka would turn and run.

Down they go.

'Straight ahead, Herr Franka,' Fiskardo says. 'Follow your nose.'

Into the archive. Through the archive, into a second room. He sees the door.

'Did you know of this?'

'I did not.' Otto has to swallow, to wet his mouth. 'I doubt anyone did.'

'It does indeed seem to be something of a mystery. Or so we thought. Keep going.'

Through the door. Oh, dear God, more stairs, and even further down. He has to stop.

'Are you unwell? Is it the air?'

'It is the everything,' says Otto, indistinctly.

'This place disagreed with Viktor Lopov too. I am not given to fancies, Herr Franka,' says Fiskardo, 'but Hoffstein has a reputation, yes?'

He nods his head. 'Yes. The reputation of the Prince-Bishop's dungeons in Prague was bad enough, but to be sent here was worse.'

'So anything below would be unlikely to be disturbed?'

Again, all he can do is nod.

'Just a little further, Herr Franka. Down to the bottom of the stairs.'

He takes the last stairs with his eyes tight shut. He feels the coldness of the air of the cavern on his face. 'Captain, whatever you wish to show me—'

He feels Fiskardo's hands upon his shoulders. 'Trust me, Herr Franka. Keep going. To your right.'

To the right? He opens his eyes. He can make out that pair of men with the white-blond hair, stood to either side of a low door.

'Good day, comrades,' Fiskardo says. 'The door, if you will.' He turns to Otto. 'Now, Herr Franka. Whatever else the Prince-Bishop may have been up to, I can promise you, he had one very good reason for discouraging folk from coming down here.'

The men with the white-blond hair are smiling. They are opening the door.

Oh—

Oh, my God—

*

'Viktor!'

Viktor Lopov lies with his face to the wall. When the Frankas first came to Hoffstein Ava too took to her bed like this, lay there unspeaking for days. Then one morning there she was, up, dressed, demanding help in rounding up the scrawny feral chickens. But Viktor is not Ava.

'Viktor, it is Otto. Otto Franka. Will you let me see your face? Will you turn around?'

'Otto?' The narrow shoulders twitch. Viktor Lopov turns, slowly, away from the wall. The face, same as ever, the great eyes – haunted, bloodshot, moist. 'Otto? What are you doing here?'

'This is where he sent us,' Otto begins. 'We are all here. Me, Ava, my father – here in exile.'

'He sent me here too.' Lopov has twisted himself about. 'I thought I had escaped, but here I am.' He closes his eyes. 'I worked for him all my life, and yet he sent me here. He sent me here to die.'

Fiskardo is waiting for him on the stairs. 'How does the patient?' he asks.

'I think his spirit is oppressed,' says Otto. 'I think being in the castle is oppressing him. I think perhaps if we might move him to our house…'

'We can do that,' Fiskardo says. 'And then there is something you can do for me.'

CHAPTER 3

Weights and Measures

'No sweet without sweat.'

John Ray, *A Collection of English Proverbs*

ONE *PFUND* IS sixteen *unzes*. Twenty-two *pfunds* is a *stein*. Or, by Rafe's reckoning, about the same weight as Dart.

'You sure you got that right, Scribbler?'

No, he is far from sure. Rafe's sleep has been much broken into; his thinking feels like it has silt in it. But the scouts have been tasked with getting the gold out of that cellar and down to the riverbank, and that, by God, they are going to do. As means to which, behind Rafe in the courtyard is what may look like a scaffold, with that rope and beam, but is in fact a dog-weighing machine. There is a platform for Dart to stand on; another, smaller, where they plan to put the gold. It is a fine spring day, a little breeze, a little sun.

They lure Dart up onto the platform with a chunk of sausage, then they pile bags of coin on the smaller board, one by one. The board descends to the ground. By Rafe's estimate, they have therefore—

They have at least fifty Darts to carry downhill to the river, simply to move the coin.

They try to lift the golden galleon. It takes four of them, staggering, and they can hardly get it to the door.

They make a sort of sled. They place the galleon upon it. Now Ulrik and Elias can drag it to the bottom of the stairway. Elias peers upward, up the stairs. 'So now what?' he asks. 'Where do we go from here?'

Ava Franka, in her garden, chickens scratching round her feet. The small breeze – Hoffstein always catches a breeze – plays with her skirts, and makes the primroses bob their bonneted faces, and usually, this is where she finds her peace. But not today.

'You will go *where*?'

'Amsterdam. Sister, I am as amazed as you. But it seems our captain –'

Our captain, she notes. *Ours!*

'– our captain has a connection to Yosha Silbergeld, and to the *Guid Marie*, and the *Guid Marie* is what our captain needs. I even have a script. I am to say that the captain knew their dock-rat… I will have an escort,' he adds, as if to reassure her. 'He is sending me with those two they call the Gemini. I am not going on my own.'

He must be able to see the fury gathering in her face; Ava can most certainly feel it. 'Sister, what am I to do? Refuse him? You don't refuse him. Trust me on that.'

'But you are not a soldier! You are not one of his men!'

He tries again. 'This is our means to escape, don't you see? Do you want to die here?'

'Do I get no say in this? What am I, chicken soup?' And she picks up one of the hens and shakes the bird at him. 'There is wood to chop, there is water to fetch uphill, I am tending to Viktor – how do I take care of all of that, and him, and manage Tata, while you are gone?' She pulls away from him. 'You and your captain, you make this nonsense plan, you can unmake it. Right now. And I am going to tell him that *myself*.'

A world of men up here, she thinks. *A world of men, and each one more stupid than the last.*

'CAPTAIN!'

She sees him turn about. Yes, her brother is right, you would not mistake him for any other. Only there is some idiot in her way. The whole courtyard to stand in, this one decides to stop dead, right in front of her. She pushes past. '*Captain*, you would send my brother –' She can feel now what her eyes must be doing. When she used to lose her temper like this as a girl, her father teased her by calling her his little Medusa, saying her eyes blazing in temper could turn you to stone. She sees the captain almost in a blur. And who *is* this ignoramus in her way? '– You would send my brother to Amsterdam. It cannot be. You must send some other.'

'There is no other,' he replies, calmly. His voice is not at all the boorish thing she had expected. That, and its calmness, only maddens her the more. 'Yosha Silbergeld knows your brother's name. He will trust your brother. Your brother is who it must be.'

This – this block, he is *still* in her way, he and his moustaches, you would think she was Medusa, you would think the man had turned to stone for real!

'Then who cuts firewood for me, while my brother is away? Who will bring up water for me, from the pump, for my father, for Viktor Lopov? How am I to manage all this on my own?'

She can tell from the way he draws in his breath that she has annoyed him. None of them have time for anything but how they are to move their precious gold. But instead of addressing her again, he looks right over her head. He calls, 'KAI!'

Oh, this must be the one her brother called the Seraph. She sees now what Otto meant – or she would see, if this fool in front of her would finally *move*.

'Kai,' says the captain, 'introduce yourself.'

The Seraph bows from the waist, brings his heels together. '*Gnädige Frau*. My name is Karl-Christian von Lindeborg. How may I serve you?'

'Madame Ava, this is my ensign,' the captain is saying. 'How would it be if I make him yours, while your brother is away? He can haul water for you, he can make sure your woodpile is replenished, and any such other task. How would that be?'

She feels a little of the heat go out of her. 'He would be our servant?'

'If you like. He is well trained, and fully house-broken.' Now he is smiling. The smile, too, differs from what she had expected; it is engaging, it invites you to smile back.

That would make it too easy for him. 'Very well,' she says, stiffly. 'Very well, then, Captain, I accept.'

He puts out his hand, as if she were a man like him, striking a deal, and she shakes it, despite the way he has desecrated it with tattoos. Then she puts up her nose and turns on her heel. Can you believe it, the one with the moustaches is still in her way!

ANOTHER SMILING MORNING. On the green slope down to the river, there are now spring flowers in profusion. And in Ava's imagination, as there is every morning, somewhere between here and Amsterdam, the tiny dot that is her brother and the two blond dots that are his escort are inching forward, day by day. How long will such a journey take, if nothing goes awry? Three weeks? More? It is April already; that will see them into May. She glances up at the sky, which strikes her as being as open and as welcoming this morning as an embrace.

Oh, what fancies! And when, in this world, did nothing ever go awry?

A smart rat-tat-tat upon her door. Here is her servant.

'Here in the garden, Kai!'

She hears him battle through the house to her, lugging a barrel of water. Her father, in his chair beside her, where he can look out on the river, turns his head. 'Is it Kai?'

'Yes, Tata.'

Kai appears. In his usual formal fashion, he bids them both good day. 'But where is Herr Lopov?'

'He has taken himself off to the tower again. One of his walks.' She disapproves; in Ava's view, if Viktor is well enough to walk about, he is well enough to be doing something more useful. She nods her head in the direction of the castle. 'How goes it up there?'

Kai slumps his shoulders, winds his neck; a pantomime of long-suffering that reminds you what a child he still is. 'Not good,' he says. He digs into his pocket. To Ava's surprise, she sees that he is blushing. He brings from his pocket a tiny paper packet, obviously folded in a hurry, and by one with no skill whatsoever in the wrapping of gifts. Some attempt has been made to letter her name upon it. 'Madame Ava,' he begins, 'I bring you this from our lieutenant. He begs you to accept.'

Twenty-two *pfunds* is a *stein*. One hundred *stein* is a ton, or near enough. So a ton of gold now sits incongruously, in a heap, in Hoffstein's dusty courtyard. It is a sizable heap, but it seems ridiculously small compared to the effort of getting it up there, and the days and days that effort swallowed up. And there is still more to come. And they still have to get it down to the river. For when this boat gets here. If it ever does.

They try dragging a load on the sled, and the sled slips and overturns almost as soon as it leaves the courtyard, scattering ingots down the road. 'Don't do that again,' the captain warns them, mildly.

They try carrying the ingots downhill, and the bowls, and the chains, and the earbobs and other little bits as well. 'And now you can carry it back up again,' Zoltan tells them when he sees what they are at. 'You think we simply leave a pile of gold here on the riverbank, for all to see?'

They have to—

They have to find some way to get it down there, quick and easy. Lower it by rope?

They have no rope.

'We need a cart,' says Rafe.

But they have no cart, either.

'Oh, fuck me,' says Ulf. 'You know what we got? We got too much gold!'

It sits there, in the courtyard, obdurate; it glowers at them, down there in the cavern. It defies them. And whatever they come up with, it defeats them.

Says Ulf, 'Never thought I'd hear me say it, but I am beginning to hate this fucken stuff. And this fucken place, and all.' He rubs his eye; sleeplessness has given him a twitch. 'Is anyone else getting these fucken fearsome dreams?'

A GOOD DOG's work is never done.

Here sits Dart, or lies, rather, just outside the courtyard, where she can keep an eye on both the doings in the courtyard itself and on the road down the hill. She has her chin on her paws; her anxious eyebrows move perpetually. There is not one single member of her pack at present about whom she is not troubled. There is Rafe, her beloved, startling awake at night, or whimpering so in his sleep that she has to waken him herself. There are the scouts, who keep disappearing down into the cavern, a place that necessitates Dart negotiating two spiral staircases if she is to follow them (and of course she is to follow them). Spiral stairs confuse her, especially going down, then she remembers how that wall had moved – walls are not meant to move – and then in the cavern there is always bad temper, loud voices, cursing, and how is a dog to know if the curse is directed at her or no? Also, it is all too easy for her to be tripped over in the dark, and then at the far end of the darkness there is the well. It is obvious to Dart what is in the well. But Rafe – her alpha, her omega – he seems not to know this. He is down there for hours, every day.

Then there are the strays: Viktor Lopov, who she feels about as every dog everywhere feels about something that cannot be trusted to look after itself; who spends his days in mournful silence wandering about the round tower, as a moth veers round a flame. Or Kai, who keeps appearing and disappearing – one minute up with the rest of them, where he should be, the next (she lifts an eyebrow) down there, in and out that place where she is not allowed to follow him because she finds the chickens irresistible.

Even the courtyard is strange to her now. There are all those unfamiliar objects in it that gleam and glister in a way that might be dangerous or harmful – how is a dog to tell? And the other creatures in the courtyard, whose shape and movement registers as being so like hers, however much bigger – first of all, her favourite is not amongst them any more, which is a sadness, and then there is one amongst them whose investigating nose, under her belly, is big enough to lift Dart off her feet, and who seems to have taken a liking to doing so, what's more, such that occasionally he must be warned off with a bark. And there are the droppings, another task, as sometimes some inner sense of obligation tells her that the droppings must be rolled in. The round of duties is endless.

Dart puts her head back and yawns the high-pitched yawn of a dog ill-at-ease. Worst of all, where is their alpha? The alpha of alphas, what has happened to him?

The alpha of alphas is standing waist deep in the Elbe, although you'd never know it, so thick and strong is the new growth of rushes that he is almost invisible. He is streaked with mud and weed, his hair is in sodden rat-tails, he is naked but for his drawers, and altogether so aquatic in appearance that you might be forgiven for thinking that even if the Elbe still hides her Undines, today she certainly has a river-god. Neck deep in the water beside him, held almost captive in the mats of rush and root, is his *nix*, the river-god's own helpmeet, in the form of Luka, who is holding steady the latest of the posts with which they are mending Hoffstein's ramshackle jetty. What might be fluff, what might be insect-life, drifts through the air about them; in the background the old reeds rattle and hiss in the breeze. It is, if you are Jack, pleasingly reminiscent of boyhood. Even if the river then did smell and taste of the sea, and its bed was sand and gravel, rather than the goulash he feels now under his feet – mud, old timbers, rotting leaves, releasing their gasses up to the surface in mighty bubbling burps.

Up on the bank, keeping watch, is Thor.

'So how big is this boat?' Luka wants to know.

'Big enough,' says Jack. He gives the post a final belter with the stone that is his mallet, tries it; *good*. Obviously too much to hope for, that there might be an actual mallet lying about this place. 'So she ain't ever going to be able to come up to the bank. And we'll need to load her fast, Luka; we'll be out in the open when we do. Which is why we also need a jetty that ain't about to collapse.'

Thor, lying amongst the grasses on the riverbank, rolls his shoulders, settles his musket anew. Zoltan has told Thor he will pay him if Thor brings back a brace of good fat duck. Or even better, some fat goose, gorging itself in its springtime home.

'And how come you know of her?' Luka asks, as Jack lifts the next post off its floating barge of reed, swings it over his head.

'There's a Dutchman –' (more blows from the stone punctuate the conversation) '– name of Yosha Silbergeld.' He rubs with the edge of his thumb at his breastbone; the scar from the silver wolf is still there, beneath where the silver wolf itself swings on its cord. 'He's a share in the *Guid Marie*. I knew him when I was a lad, and I knew her captain too, a Scotsman. I was an unrighteous little bastard when I was a lad –'

A pause; he looks down. Luka is shaking with laughter.

'And I'm flattered as you so clearly disbelieve me, Luka, but I was. Yet they were both of 'em very good to me.' Two-handed, Jack brings the stone down on the post; the post goes down six inches into the riverbed. 'So –'

Another pause, to wipe the sweat from his face.

'So let's hope they remember me now, eh?'

'She ain't going to be too big, is she, Domini?' Luka asks.

'Too big how?'

Luka taps at the waterline on the posts they hammered into place just yesterday. 'The river's dropping, Domini. An inch since yesterday.'

A moment while his captain stares off into the sky. Then his captain says, 'I swear to God, Luka, I have never known a place as cursed awkward in *everything* as this.'

'No, Domini,' says Luka, with feeling, then adds, 'Viktor Lopov says as it is cursed for real.'

TO BE FAIR, it is the prettiest of springs, this spring of 1631, in that way the gods have of giving you something perfect, before all is changed forever. Today the air is soft as milk, and Leo

Franka says he wishes to feel it on his face. Like Viktor Lopov, he too wishes to take a walk.

'Tata, you cannot go out on your own,' Ava tells him. There are feathers sticking to her apron, goose-down all over her hands. Really, she does not have time for this! 'You know it is not safe for you. You will trip, or you will fall, and then where shall we be? And I cannot come with you.' She points to the goose lying with all the helplessness of a casualty on the table behind her. 'I must get this bird to the fire or it will spoil.'

'May I help Herr Franka?' asks Kai. He too is flecked with goose-fluff, and it is not the most martial of appearances, truly. 'I have been a walking stick before. Might I assist?'

Yes, he might. 'Where do you wish to go, Herr Franka?' Kai asks, once they are safely outside, and all the perils of the door, the doorstep, the path, safely behind them.

From the courtyard above, more noises of bad temper and complaint. Kai's cheeks have flushed; it is just as well Leo Franka does not speak Swedish.

'What are they up to, up there?' Leo asks.

'It is the gold,' says Kai. He waits, one arm about Leo's midriff, while Leo finds a place for one foot, then aims and stabs his stick as a guide for the other. 'My brothers-in-arms say it is because it does not wish to leave here, that it wrestles with us so.'

'Eh,' says Leo. 'Gold is the most obedient of metals. Trust me on that.' He moves the second foot into line with the first. 'I suffered an apoplexy,' he explains.

'Yes, sir. I thought it might be so.'

'When I was imprisoned.' Leo straightens his back. 'And that was the Prince-Bishop's doing, also.'

They move another yard or so downhill, as slowly as before. 'The road is very bad,' Kai comments. 'Where is it that you wish us to go, Herr Franka?'

'Down there,' says Leo. With great care he uses his stick to point toward the linden trees. 'The little temple.' He raises a finger to his lips. 'The Prince-Bishop's old laboratorium is inside, and in it, there is everything we need.'

Readying a goose for the fire is exactly the kind of task the busy housewife would usually pass on to her underling, but not today. First of all, her underling has been requisitioned by another, has he not, and then cooking anything at all in this kitchen requires the kind of ingenuity Ava is convinced is hers and hers alone. In her kitchen in Prague there would have been a proper spit hanging before the fire, a scullery maid to sit there turning and turning it in the sweltering heat; there would have been caraway and cinnamon and honey to roast it with; while here there is but one dented pan, and onions, and without her garden there would not even have been those.

But nonetheless, she strews chopped onion into the pan, and tucks the goose neatly in above them, and then she stands there, and sighs a sigh. An onion-scented finger plays with her earlobe, where hangs a golden earbob, a tiny hoop, hung with a miniature dragon. She thinks it is a comment on her temper. She will have to give them back, of course.

She will have to find their lieutenant and give them back.

Of course she will, there is no question!

But she thinks the lieutenant is perhaps not quite as great an idiot as she took him for at first.

She finds him up in the courtyard, himself standing moodily over that great and ever-growing heap of gold they have up there, shrouded under the Prince-Bishop's flag. Truly, you would never believe these men had stumbled on such a fortune, the way they frown and grumble. But when he sees it is Ava come to speak with him, then his expression changes at once. 'Madame,' he says, gravely, and sweeps her a bow, and comes up, dark eyes all a-welcome. It is a shock every time she sees him, how handsome he is. He would be good-looking as a woman, as a man, he is ridiculous. That flashing eye, the golden skin. If she isn't careful, she is going to blush.

To cover this, she already has the earbobs in her hand. 'Thank you,' she says, briskly, holding them out to him, 'but these, I cannot accept.'

His amazement is so – well, amazed, it must be genuine. So *young*, thinks Ava. And so unused to being turned down. 'But why not so?' he asks.

'Because there can be nothing between us,' says Ava, bluntly. 'But why not?'

She had not expected to be questioned. It catches her off-guard. 'Because – because you see me only as I am *here*,' she begins, 'and that is not how I am at all. This is not *who* I am. I am not – I am not this woman in need of earbobs.' Or perhaps it is that she does not wish to be that woman, she who once had earbobs of her own. And servants. And a kitchen with a spit. Oh, this is so much more complicated than she had thought it would be!

He is smiling at her. There is every conquest he has ever made in that smile, and she is damned if she will be one of those women, either. 'And I am old enough,' she tells him, 'to have met men like you before.'

Comprehension. How confident he is that he has got this right! 'You think you are too old for me?'

'No,' says Ava. She is brisk, she is heartless – yes, yes, yes, she has been called all these things before. 'No. It is that *you* are too *young* for me.' She takes a breath, puts her shoulders back. 'And so there can be nothing between us. And so I wish you good day.'

Oh, she thinks, *oh*, as she goes back to her kitchen. None of that feels like what she meant to say to him at all!

'Now,' Leo is saying to Kai, 'you see this?'

'Yes, Herr Franka.'

'This is a crucible. We put this here, in the centre of the fire. These are the bellows. Do you see?'

'Yes, Herr Franka,' Kai replies. He has taken off his jacket and his collar, rolled up his sleeves. Everything in this place is furred with dust.

'This will be our mould,' Leo says next. He holds it, one half in each hand. 'Now what you have to do, my lad, is go up to the courtyard and abstract a little of that gold. Two bags of the coin should do it. Are you game for that? Because the problem your brothers-in-arms have here is that they are trying to use brawn to solve a big problem, instead of brains to solve a very little one.'

THEY COME UP the hill, Jack and Luka, and the first thing they hear are the shouts of disagreement and dispute from above them in the courtyard, which sadly is no surprise, and the first thing they smell is—

The charcoal whiff of smoke. Which is.

There, set back behind the trees, the tempietto with its door wedged open, and smoke exiting its chimney in great untidy puffs, and the roar inside of fire, so loud in the small space that from the doorway Jack must shout to be heard, and inside – God a'mighty, is that Kai, leaping about in there, stripped to the waist and black as one of Satan's imps? And old man Franka, Otto's father, clumping forward, on his stick?

'Domini!' comes Kai's exultant yell. His teeth gleam in his face. 'Look what we have done!'

He sees the old man is holding something out to him – an orb. A small orb. The ball for a culverin perhaps. *The devil—*

The thing is veiled in a film of carbon, as if it wears a caul. It is warm to the touch. It is small enough to fit in one hand; it is heavy enough to need two hands to hold it. He rubs his thumb across it.

Gold.

'We melt it down!' Kai shouts to him, across the noise of the suck and draw of the fire. 'We melt it down here, we cast it into these cannonballs, do you see? And we dig a track, down the hill, in the road, where the rains have begun one for us already, and when the boat is here, we roll the gold downhill!'

He weighs the orb in his hand. 'Have you tried it yet?'

'Not yet, Domini. But it will work, we are sure!'

'Then I reckon that's what we do next, don't you?'

Oh, what a difference. What a transformation, now they have a plan. 'Although it hurts my heart,' says Rafe, as he and Ulf carry a basketful of broken gold downhill to the linden trees, 'it hurts my heart to see such artistry all melted down to nothing.' He gazes down at the contents of the basket – the flat gold mask, the bowls, the head and antlers of the golden stag, the golden binding of the book, a handful of the chains.

Says Ulf, 'You do know as you get a share of this, Scribbler, do you?'

He does?

'Sure you do. We all do. The captain gets the most, then the lieutenant, then Kai, then the Executioner, then Ziggy and the Gemini, then everyone. Viktor Lopov, and the Frankas, for being so handy, and you.'

'Me?'

'O'course you! Ain't you played your part and done your bit, just like to the rest of us?'

Good Lord. 'Do you –' Rafe begins, 'I would not wish to seem ungracious, but how much might such a share be?'

'Well,' says Ulf in the tone of one to whom dealings in the laws of loot are second nature, 'little as they are, one of them golden orbs is ten pound weight, ain't it? And I reckon there'd be three or four with your name on 'em, once we're done. So how much is London rates for gold?'

'Three pounds and ten shillings an ounce,' says Rafe, at once. 'When I was first affianced, I wished to commission a posy-ring for Belle, one of those with the secret verse inscribed inside. But I found I could not afford it.' It irks him still.

'How much is that, then?' Ulf asks. Mental arithmetic is unknown to the scouts. They can smell the weather, they can steer by star, they can tell a good haul with one pull on the nets – who needs more science in their life than that?

Sixteen times three pounds ten shillings. Times ten... times three...

'But that's fifteen hundred pounds!'

'There!' says Ulf, cheerily. 'Think you'll be able to buy your Belle a fair few posy-rings with that.'

BY THE TIME they have dug out a track down the hill, top to bottom, curving it carefully about those corners, digging a gradient on every straight, there is a basketful of those golden orbs ready to go. Ten *pfunds* of gold in each. Jack has men posted at every bend, every corner of the road, right down to the river. He says, 'We do *not* want any of these to go astray.'

They give the honour of sending the first on its way to Ava. She gasps at its weight, then releases it from her hand as if this were a game of boules. Down it goes, down it bounces, this tiny gleaming sun, spinning at the first bend then finding its way. Dart goes running after it, paws skittering on the stones. A shout from downhill: 'Here it comes!' Another: 'There it goes!' It seems to pause, rotating on the spot. A shout from Sten, 'Ow me little golden arse!' And laughter. And how long is it, Jack wonders, since he heard his men laugh?

Now to the second corner. Now along the straight again.

'Here it comes!'

'There it goes!'

'It's working, Domini!' says Kai. If the boy were only a little younger, he would be jumping up and down with excitement. And there is Ava, squeezing her father's hand. And there is Zoltan, studiously turned away from her.

Well, well.

'Here it comes!'

'And there it goes!'

The shouts are now from too far off to hear them clearly. He looks out, over the waving tops of the trees, full of leaf, tossing this way and that, like the sea.

More shouts from the bottom of the hill. He hears Dart, barking. He says, 'Roll another.'

Down by the jetty, Rafe waits with Viktor Lopov, and a few yards ahead of them, Ulf and Ulrik, both hunched over, arms a-dangle, peering up the road with furious intensity. As is Rafe himself. 'We have a game like this at home,' says Rafe to Viktor. 'I played it a little when I was up at Cambridge. There is a fellow with a bat, and another with a ball, and the rest of us to defy the batter and retrieve the ball, wherever it is hit. It is called cricket,' he concludes.

Ziggy, on the bend above, signals to them: here it comes! And here comes Dart in furious pursuit, as well. Can Viktor be lured into a reply? Can he be brought out from his melancholy? 'And of course,' says Rafe, 'one is put in mind at once of Atalanta and the golden apples of the Hesperides, not so?'

Ulf and Ulrik have caught the first of the golden orbs, are holding it up, exclaiming over it. Shouts of warning from uphill: here comes another!

'What do you think, Viktor? Did you imagine you would ever play a part in anything like this? Viktor?'

But now something does have Viktor's attention. He straightens up, he points out to the river. Something is in gliding motion there. A flash of white. An alien upright. Another. There is a boat, midstream, a three-master, under one single sail. Rafe rubs his eyes, the sun is in them. Shouts of warning from above: "Ere! Scribbler!' He ignores them. He sees men lined up along the gunwale, hallooing, waving, he sees two blond heads, stood together; he thinks perhaps he makes out Otto Franka, and without any doubt at all he can fill in the grotesque outline of that hideous figurehead. There are more shouts, already carrying the news uphill. 'My God,' Rafe hears himself exclaim, 'that's the *Guid Marie!*'

By the time Fiskardo comes in view, loping down the road, the *Guid Marie* has thrown her anchor out midstream. Her sail has fallen slack, and there is a ladder of rope – the same ladder of rope? Rafe wonders – hanging down her side. And a man climbing down it, a man with hair rough and brindled as that of some old dog, tied in a pigtail at his neck. He is followed, much more uncertainly, by what can only be Otto himself.

The man lands on their jetty. The sappy wood springs beneath his weight. He strides toward them, toward Rafe, who he clearly recognizes not at all. 'Now then!' he shouts. Gaining the bank he surveys them, rocks on the heels of his boots. 'Which of you villains is this son of a whore says he knew my dock-rat?'

Fiskardo steps forward, his grin as broad as Rafe has ever seen it. He has doffed his hat. 'Greetings, Captain,' Rafe hears Fiskardo say. Their audience, all save Rafe, look on, wholly bemused. Rafe is not bemused. No, Rafe is simply astonished. But nothing like as astonished, it would seem, as Mungo Sant.

Fiskardo holds out his hand. He says, mysteriously, 'Heard you was come home.'

For a moment, nothing. Then: 'I don't believe my eyes.' Sant takes a step forward, as a man might toward a mirage. 'I don't believe my bluidy eyes!' Then in a rush – of the man, forward, of the words, tumbling out: 'Oh, my lad, my lad!' He has his arms around their captain, in a bear-hug. "Tis you! 'Tis truly you!'

CHAPTER FOUR

Ways and Means

'... early in the morning, before the break of day, the sign was given by the discharging of thirty pieces of cannon, and Pappenheim, Mansfeld, Tilly and the Duke of Holstein did from their several quarters furiously set upon the city walls...'

Count Galeazzo Gualdo Priorato, *An History of the Late Warres*

I T's AN EXCELLENT place to take stock, a quarterdeck – up above the river, up above the toilers on the jetty, up above everything. Jack spreads his hands along the *Guid Marie's* rail, feeling the quiver of her constant gentle pull at anchor, the echo through her timbers of the river. They have warped her about; she has her prow headed for home. You might almost think she knew. He says, 'I have missed being on a boat.'

Says Mungo Sant, beside him, 'Seems to me you've nae done so bad without.'

Below, within the *Guid Marie*, and outside on the bank, the heavy sounds of loading: bumps, shouts of warning. Six tons of gold, cunningly hidden in the ballast. *Six tons of stolen gold*, thinks Jack. It is the strangest thing, to imagine a future with that buttress behind you.

'My lad, we've matters to discuss. Chief amongst 'em, our river is flowing away from us by the hour. I can make way in five foot of water, but no less than that, and she's a jade, the Elbe. You blow out your candle with her holding you fast; you wake and she has you on your beam ends, on the mud.'

'In other words, you want to be gone.'

'In other words, aye. This place,' says Sant, casting a darkling glance up the hill, 'there's something here is all awry. Yon wee fella of yours, with a face like a hare?'

'Viktor Lopov?'

'He's the look to me of a man about to cast himself over the side. Added to which,' says Sant, nodding downstream, 'Magdeburg.'

'We saw the camp,' says Jack.

'You'd see one ten times bigger now. Tilly at the front door, Pappenheim at the back.'

'And if you were flying the Prince-Bishop's colours?'

Sant rocks back and forth, considering. 'It would help,' he says.

'And if you had the Gemini with you, for the look of it?'

Ava's voice reaches them, strident as a trumpet. Down on the quayside, for only a second, Zoltan is motionless.

'Yon lassie's a scald,' comments Sant, then, 'Aye, mebbe.'

And now for my good deed of the day. 'And maybe,' says Jack, 'maybe if I let you take my lieutenant with you, as well?'

'Aye, that would help too.'

'We've not come this far, to be thwarted.'

'Nooo,' says Sant, 'I dare say you have not.' A sideways squint. Jack waits. Sant seems to be working himself up to something.

'Do you know how braw it is to see you again?'

'People keep telling me that.' He looks ahead, over the river, over the green of the land, all of it there for him, all of it waiting; all his force, all his will bent toward it. 'I'd no idea I was so popular.'

'Aye, well,' says Sant. 'Now it's said.'

Jack waits. Sant clears his throat, munches up and down a little, as on some feeling too delicate to expose to the light of day. 'And we'll need to set a rendezvous,' he says, sounding gruff. 'There's a wee village, maybe ten mile above Magdeburg. She's a church with a stone tower, and a good stone quay. Hohenwarthe. There.'

Says Jack. 'It's braw to see you too, Sant.'

Oh, the business of packing up one's life, how it defies all logic. Ava wishes to take her hens with her.

'Ava, I am quite certain,' Otto tells her (and really, he feels he can speak with some authority on this), 'I am quite certain Captain Sant is not about to permit your hens aboard the *Guid Marie*.'

'He will have to,' says Ava. 'I am not leaving them.'

'Ava –' He is baffled. 'Ava, we came here with almost nothing, and survived. When we get to Amsterdam I will buy you the fanciest fowl you could desire, I will buy you a whole flock—'

'No,' she says. 'You don't understand.' His sister, his imperious sister, she is almost in tears. 'They are mine, do you understand? They are *of me*. I would leave everything else behind, but I will not leave my poor hens behind to – to suffer here. I cannot – I cannot –' The *cannots* become fan-shapes in the air, fluttering from her waving hands. 'And – and –' her gaze moves past him, out to their bags and bundles, out there on the slope of the road, '– and where is Viktor Lopov going? And *why is he wearing no clothes?*'

*

It is odd how warm he feels. How warm and how very much, at last, at peace. He pads across the courtyard, bare toes over the stones, over the weeds, lantern in one hand, rock in the other. He hears the startled shouts behind him, but once he is inside the tower, he can hear them no more. Which is delightful, that silence. *They will be going to fetch the captain now*, he thinks. *They will be going to get Fiskardo.*

Viktor Lopov goes up to the first-floor chamber, crosses that too, down the stone stair to the archive. The air is cooler here. He takes no notice of the documents littered across the floor, having to be shaken, some of them, as he passes, from his feet. He takes a small breath, and goes through the second door, down the stairs to the cavern. He thinks of how it had been, all those days before, the continual passage of the gold up to the light, busy, busy, busy, they had been, like ants, but all is quiet now. Quiet and cold and dark.

He lifts his lantern. He turns left, pads toward the end of the cavern under the round tower, toward the well. This is where he was meant to be. This is where he was meant to die. Where God knows how many have perished before him.

There is no cover on the well. He never thought there would be. He swings his legs over, into that gelid darkness, and seats himself on its edge, bare stone beneath his arse-cheeks. He sets the lantern beside him, with its chain neatly coiled beside it; he positions the rock beside the chain, and he waits.

'Viktor?'

A sigh, in response. The small pale creature sat there at the far end of the cavern, in the lantern-light, shifts its position. Viktor's voice comes from it, hushed, as if this were a church. 'Captain, is that you?'

'It's me.' He comes closer. 'Viktor, that looks most perilous.'

'Are you alone?'

'I am. I thought that would be best.'

'Yes,' Viktor answers. 'You are – you are most aware, Captain. Of others. I have often noted it.'

Possibly, thinks Jack. 'Although you have managed to take me by complete surprise with this.' He goes a couple of steps closer, casually as he can. It would seem wrong to approach as if about to leap, to pull Viktor back from his precarious seat, but then again—

'This well,' Viktor begins. He swoops an arm over the void before him; Jack feels his heart give an answering lurch. 'It is dug through basalt. Do you know the properties of basalt, Captain?'

'I don't. Will you tell me?'

'You've no need to humour me, Captain,' says Viktor, in a sharper tone. 'I am not run mad. I want nothing of this place with me when we leave, that is all. Basalt,' he repeats. 'It has a natural power of filtration. It dissolves impurities, continually.'

'Viktor, you told me that the water in the well was bad.'

'Oh,' says Viktor, 'it is. It is.' He adjusts his position. 'I went to work for the Prince-Bishop when I was no older than Kai,' he says. 'I worked for him all my life. I set up his archive, where he might keep all his secrets hidden. Yet this is how he served me. I am not made of basalt, Captain. I cannot rid myself of him so easily.'

'Viktor, trust me,' Jack begins. 'I know what the Prince-Bishop is, as well as you. I have met those he imprisoned, I have met those he scarred and one he blinded, and I know what kind of men he employs to do his black work for him. I have crossed swords with them, as well.' *And I have hunted one of them for years, and I am hunting for him still.* 'But we will take from him that letter, and we will take from him his gold, and there is nothing will hurt him as much as that.' *And damn it, Viktor, we need to be gone.*

'It is not enough. For what he has done, it is not enough. Look there.' And Viktor directs the lantern upward, up into the interior of the tower. 'Do you see the door there, Captain?'

He sees that Lopov sees he does.

'Do you see there is no floor beneath? How the tower is hollow? That is where his victims were brought. When he was done with them, he had them brought here, from Prague, and thrown through that door, and down —'

He directs the beam of the lantern down again, into the well.

'— and there they were left to die,' Viktor says. He lifts the lantern, begins to lower it by its chain. 'And he had that door made, that secret door in his archive, so that he might come down here, and either view them as they died, or take a prospect of his gold. As it pleased him. None would know.'

The lantern is low enough now to cast a beam across the water, which is indeed clear as if filtered, until it deepens to a blue too dark to see beyond it. Viktor lifts the rock and throws it in. For a moment, nothing. The water closes over the rock, it sinks from sight. Then something, disturbed by its passage, lifts slowly to the surface. It rotates, as if to stare up at them. Now something more — fragile twigs, still bound one to another; fingers, perhaps, or toes. They lift, they sink. Story told.

Viktor is saying, 'There might be a score down there, or more. There must once have been hundreds.' He lets the lantern drop. 'Do you see, Captain? It is not enough.'

He comes up into the sunlight, with Viktor Lopov now more or less decently covered by Jack's own buff-coat. He calls his men together. We are, he says, going to take every scrap of paper out of that archive. Every paper, every folder, everything. Bring it up here. We are going to burn it. We will leave the Prince-Bishop *nothing*.

And that bloody crest of his, there on the wall, that bastard bloody eagle, we are going to carve a damn great TACK across

it. We are going to tell him thank you. We are going to let him
know that we were here.

And we are going to take a barrel of black powder from the
store on the *Guid Marie*, and we are going to mine the round
tower, and we are going to blow it to smithereens.

Then we can be gone.

And when his men go to Zoltan, and they ask him *Why*,
when they ask *What's going on*, all Zoltan will tell them is, *You
see his face? You see that face, you don't question, you don't quibble.
You get on and you do.*

BY MOONRISE THEY are under way. Viktor Lopov (clothed, qui-
escent) and the Frankas on the *Guid Marie*, with Zoltan and the
Gemini, for some convincing martial colour, and a crateful of
softly *bok-bok-bok*-ing hens. We will be with you until you are
safe past Magdeburg, Jack says to Sant. We will track you, we
will keep you in our sights.

Aye, says Sant. And we rendezvous at Hohenwarthe.

That we do.

And with any luck, we meet His Swedish Majesty, sweeping
south.

Which would be so perfect an alignment of folk and
circumstance, you would think the gods would grant it simply
out of a sense of what is right and proper.

They pass the high bluff, where they had watched
Pappenheim's army on its way to Magdeburg; so many men
that even now you can see the scars they left: the trees cut
down, the grass trod away, the broken earth. The river is once
again empty of craft, other than the *Guid Marie*. Through the
spyglass Jack watches Sant's first mate at her prow, dropping
his line into the water, over and over again. Next day they ride
through the clearing – they know it must be the same one from

the marks left by the tents and fires, but all abandoned now. He thinks of Hoffstein, of the bonfire in the courtyard, of the crack as the powder detonated under the tower, of seeing it slump. Wonders how and when the news of it might get to Prague. Pats M'sieu's neck, and tells him, 'You are good.'

Ziggy rides up beside him. Ziggy says, 'Domini, the horses are no longer used to being ridden hard as this. We risk them going lame. They need to rest.'

'They rest once that gold is past Magdeburg. We can all rest then, Ziggy. Not before.'

And feels his will, his force, again like an arrow, flying ever forward.

Magdeburg comes in sight, Magdeburg with her spires and islands, and her bridge, and the *Guid Marie* riding at anchor in front of her bridge, where the channel splits, and still under her single sail, because to look hurried here, to draw attention, would not be the thing to do. The woods they trotted through before, unhindered, now have a camp set up in front of them, a camp that might be almost the size of that at Stettin. *Pappenheim*, Jack thinks. *Those thousands upon thousands of men.* It is so early in the day even the sun is not fully up, just a marbling of pink and gold breaking through the clouds to the east. A bugle call, as the guard rotates; watching through the spyglass, hidden here, back within the trees, he sees the earliest risers come out of their tents, knuckling their backs.

Now there are figures on the bridge. 'Cross your fingers,' he whispers to Kai, 'hold your breath. Think her through.' Lifts the spyglass once again. There is Sant, on deck, there is the small figure of the marshal, on the bridge itself. Here comes Zoltan, wearing a jacket of mustard and blood, pointing back to the colours trailing off the *Guid Marie*'s stern.

An unexpected early morning salvo from behind the city. Everyone in view through the spyglass reacts. Then fast on its heels, another, firing through the echo of the first. The marshal seems distracted. *Come on*, Jack's thinking. *Come on. You don't need to inspect her. Look at her flag.*

One of those moments of perfect stillness; the exact point where dawn meets day. Now here is Otto, walking to the *Guid Marie*'s prow, joining the conversation.

He sees the marshal, on the bridge, turn about. A breeze lifts the Prince-Bishop's flag. The first breath of the new day.

Let. Her. Through.

Another double salvo. The marshal is no longer in sight. The breeze is strengthening. And there are men at the windlasses of the bridge, at either side.

The line of the bridge is no longer quite so perfectly true.

Sant's crew, in the rigging, lowering an extra sail. The line of the bridge now broken, unmistakably so. Kai gives a yelp: 'Domini, she is moving! The bridge is up, they are letting her through!'

There she goes. They can hear the windlasses now, hear them working, hear the creak of timber as the draw of the bridge is raised. The *Guid Marie* is half obscured, only the tops of her masts slowly moving forward; oh so slowly, so agonizingly slowly, the draw of the bridge at an angle, leaning down over her – *don't let her foul! Don't let her foul!* – then the wind carries her through, through the deep channel, out past the bridge, out and away. They watch her go, as the river turns toward them, as it curves away.

Another salvo. Then a fifth.

The *Guid Marie* passes beyond the curve, and she is gone. 'Bon voyage, Captain Sant,' says Jack, under his breath. 'We will see you in Hohenwarthe.'

There is a sort of stir now, before them in the camp. There are men standing outside the tents, watching, shielding their eyes against the sunrise.

And now one final deafening salvo from the cannon behind the town. Even here, on the far bank of the river, it has them putting their fingers in their ears. And then – nothing. A shout or two drifts over the Elbe toward them, but to be honest, might have only been the cries of startled birds.

And then one single, awful, piercing scream.

'Domini,' he hears Kai gasp. 'Domini, there is something happening in Magdeburg!'

CHAPTER FIVE

Magdeburg

'… no more terrible work and divine punishment has been seen since the destruction of Jerusalem. All our soldiers became rich.'

Gottfried Heinrich Graf zu Pappenheim

NONE OF IT should have happened as it did. The siege should never have lasted so long, nor become so bitter. There should never have been so many men – two entire armies, General Tilly's, General Pappenheim's, camped outside Magdeburg's walls; unpaid, unfed, fever rippling through them, fever and fury at being held there while it cut them down like corn. Gustavus Adolphus should have come sweeping down from the north, attacked some other target, drawn them off. Magdeburg's councillors should have sued for peace when the last of the sconces outside the city fell; in fact Rumour would have it that this very morning, the 20th of May, that was their plan, to send out a party to negotiate under a white flag. They were starving in the city too, they too had fever; everyone wanted peace; and Tilly wanted Magdeburg as a base for operations just as Gustavus Adolphus had Stettin. That was the plan. And the wind should never have been so frisky, so determined, the air so dry; and Dietrich von Falkenberg, commander of Magdeburg's defences, should never have been so intransigent, and it would have helped too had he not been so certain Gustavus Adolphus would arrive any minute, instead of being eighty miles away, and had Falkenberg not climbed to the top of the walls to ascertain what was going on out there, and had a sharpshooter's bullet not caught him full on. None of it should have happened, but it did.

There is that one, long, final deafening salvo from the artillery behind the town, and the cries of birds, and then that single marrow-chilling scream.

He lifts the spyglass. He hears Kai ask, 'What is happening? Why have the guns ceased? What is happening, Domini?'

He knows why. There is only one reason why you cease to fire upon a city under siege: because your own men would be under your guns.

Now, to the left, men at the base of Magdeburg's walls, as small from this distance as had been the few birds flying above the *Guid Marie*'s rigging. They go splashing through the shallows, there, then not there. A far-off rattle of shot. Now horsemen, following them. Also disappearing. And he hears Thor give the answer, Thor who needs no spyglass to have worked it out: 'They're in, Kai. The Emperor's men, they've breached that gate.'

Almost at once a thread of smoke, fine as the stroke from a single hair, lifting off from the city, drifting right.

They all know what happens now. A city stormed is a city sacked.

'Domini,' says Kai. 'Domini, my tutor. Dr Silvestris. His wife.'

The smoke has changed colour. The white of timber, of a roof going up in flames, he knows it, he remembers it so well.

'Domini, my tutor. Domini, we must help them, we must!'

He lowers the spyglass. 'Kai—' he begins.

But Kai gives him no chance to finish.

'Domini, *you said*, if you can see the thing to do, you have to do it!'

God a'mighty. Is he the more angered, or is he the more impressed? Already he feels that pull, that beggar-child he thinks of as his conscience, reaching out its hands. 'You're using my own words against me?'

'Yes, Domini! Yes, if I must!'

From across the river a shout, and then again, a scream. It has that same awful note to it as before; it might be an adult, screaming as mindlessly as a child in pain, or a child so terrified it's found an adult voice. Kai's face contorts. 'Then I will go!' he declares, and sets off, stomping down toward the riverbank, the camp.

Damnation! 'Kai! *Kai!*' and the boy turns back, face with that tight, white look of complete, insane determination. 'Kai, what the hell do you think you can do on your own?'

'I will take a boat!' the boy shouts back. 'I will take a boat, I will find them—'

'We don't need a boat, you idiot, we're in the Prince-Bishop's colours. We can walk in.' He turns to face them: his troop, his men, his company, his family, his *souls*. He says, 'I won't order any of you to do this. If you can't be a part of it, step back.'

Not one of them does. Not even the Scribbler, not one.

'Domini—' There is more noise reaching them now, from across the river; gunfire, opposition to it; more movement on the far bank.

'No, Kai, *wait*. We get this wrong it will be the end of every one of us.' Because this is life, ain't it: you make one plan, you make another. Apparently no amount of gold waiting for you makes any difference to that. *Think*, he tells himself. *We go in. How do we go in?* 'Ziggy, you have to take the horses. Take them on to Hohenwarthe.'

'No, Kapten, I come with you—'

'No, you don't. We go in on horseback, like officers, we'll stand out. We have to seem like foot-slogging troopers; like them,' and he points to the men already running from the camp to the bridge. 'Take Luka and Ansfrid, to help.' *Move the counters off the board.* 'And you take the Scribbler with you too.'

'He does not,' says Rafe. 'No, Captain, where you go, I go.'

'Scribbler, I am giving you an order.'

'Then I resign my post, Captain, and I will go into Magdeburg as a common man.' And as if to prove it, Endicott takes a step sideways, as if away from himself as soldier altogether. 'But into Magdeburg I will go, and whatever is done there, I will see it and write of it. That is my contract. That is what I am here to do. But –' and here the Scribbler picks up Dart and carries her to Luka, '– it would do me the greatest service, Luka, if you would take my dog with you. So that I know she is safe.'

IT'S A STAMPEDE. A stampede, but not out of the city – in. There are men pouring from the camp and down to the bank, onto the first bridge to the island, a bridge as tottery as ever was the jetty at Hoffstein, but will that stop them? There are even those braving the mudflats, hauling their booted legs across the creeks; one or two, the older, the weaker, halting, breathless with effort, and their fellows – stronger, or on horseback – simply pushing past, pushing them over. The horses toss their heads, roll their eyes, panicked by the press of men about them, and then inevitably,

as they reach the bridge, one horse goes over, disappears, surfaces again, starts paddling for the shore, but the officer riding
it, carapaced like a lobster, back and breastplate solid steel, he
must have sunk like a stone. Now the second bridge, past the
windlasses, over the draw, with it bouncing under their tread
the way housewives flap a sheet – Jack glances left and right;
yes, all still there, still with him. 'Watch yourselves,' he shouts.
'Watch your balance,' and there, just ahead of them, there's a
musketeer, dripping with cartridges like a crop of fruit, he goes
over the edge as well. No-one stops, no-one hesitates, the man's
place is taken at once by another, a halberdier. Jack shoves out
an elbow, and that one goes over as well – one less! – then to his
left Ulrik does the same. *Good lad!*

They are coming up to the city wall, up to its gate. For a
moment he thinks, *Good Christ, there is a woman hanging there,*
but it's a sculpted figure only, set above the gate, life-size, with
yellow painted hair, red lips, holding out a carved and painted
garland, and on the garland the words—

WER WIRD ES NEHMEN?
Who will take it?

Oh, sweetling, he wants to say, *don't ask, don't ask.* Beside
him, Endicott is gaping upward too, must have made the like
mistake. Magdeburg's Virgin, the city's proud symbol, she has
her answer now.

And now they are in. The first thing he sees are men in that
chequerboard of blue and white, running from house to house,
smashing in the windows, kicking in the doors. 'It's ours!' they
shout. 'Everything is ours!' *Jesus, this is going to get ugly. This is
going to be bad.* And now more, running in from the left – and
the smoke, where does the smoke come from? It comes to him
that the men running in from the left are in fact running from
it, as it rolls down the street after them – fast, Christ, fast like

an incoming tide, the wind behind it, pushing it on. The spires of the cathedral, like two arms raised to heaven, are already in smoke up to their elbows. They need to move. 'Kai!' he shouts. 'Kai! Which way?'

'The marketplace!' comes the answer. Kai, already half-obscured by smoke, coughing, bent in two, but summoning them on.

He tries to remember, in that prospect from the bank, how far would the marketplace be? He tries to fold what he remembers into the machine now running in his head, wheel upon wheel, the turn, turn, turn of it, where else men might be entering the city, the north, the west… A headcount: Ulf, Ulrik, Thor, Sten, Elias, even the Scribbler, all running with him. So far, so good.

'Watch out for each other!' he tells them. Then, 'Kai, lead us. Show the way!'

There's a tavern, easy prey, door already hanging off, men inside, looting the place, liquor running out the door. They run past an alleyway, which is as silent as if the plague had emptied it; then the next street holds a row of shops, and men there trying to lever their shutters off or open them with anything to hand. He sees a drummer standing on his drum, walloping the shutters with the butt-end of a musket, while up above a girl, a maid maybe, sticks her head out of a window, then slams it shut, and a man, hauling two children with him, runs unseen behind the drummer, bolting down the street and out of sight. Now a trooper running with an empty wheelbarrow, wooden wheel bumping. No-one who sees them takes any notice of them at all.

'Domini, this way! Here, here!'

What can only be the Rathaus, the town hall, up ahead, looming over every other building. Out into the market square – *and this*, he thinks, *this is where it starts*. Because there are men in the square already, hauling open the doors of the houses, yelling for coin, for silver, for food; what have you got, what have you got, silver, food, now, now, now, pulling the inhabitants out into the street, throwing them to the ground, going into the houses, still bellowing, *Meat, bread, silver, what have you got?*

Kai is running for a house on the corner of the square, a house with a painted gable. Its door is already open. Jack launches into a run, comes through the door, sword in hand. Kai is being swung about the room on the arm of a scarlet-behatted trooper, in fact it looks as if Kai has his teeth in the man's sleeve. Briefly he registers a staircase, he registers people on the staircase, a table in the centre of the room – macabre, a table laid with what appears to be a feast – and beyond the table a chimneybreast, and a man at the chimneybreast; he sees out the corner of his eye the swift upward movement of a musket being raised, ready to fire. He turns his hand and puts a foot of steel straight into the back of the scarlet-behatted trooper, that lovely narrow *slippery* blade of Solingen steel, straight in; with his victim thus gaffed, swings the man in front of him; the man's comrade at the chimneybreast fires; Thor, just behind Jack, fires as well, straight past Jack's ear and the man at the chimneybreast drops. Jack puts his foot on the back of the trooper, frees his sword. The hearing in his left ear, he realizes, is gone. Now Thor fires again (Jack hears it as if it is a hollow thump, something being dropped outside maybe), and one of those on the stairs falls backwards. Ulf runs toward the fallen man, pulling him to the floor, breaking the banister as he does so, and those on the stairs turn about, revealing two figures cowering beneath them. There is Sten, vaulting forward; there is Kai picking himself up off the floor. Now a man comes toward Jack, brandishing – no, *waving* – a pistol. Jack launches a kick at the pistol, hurls himself at the man, turns this one about as well, and Ulrik, swinging the cauldron from the fireplace on its chains, like a priest swinging a censer, hits the man with it on the side of the head. Down he goes. Now two more, and he ducks, goes for the first man's legs, brings this one down, punches him in the balls; as the man twists into that figure four there on the floor, Ulrik brings the cauldron swinging down onto him as well, and then again, and then again. Another shot – and that was Elias, and the sound of another body falling. Now Kai is on the stairs. Now Kai is bending over those two cowering figures. 'Dr Silvestris,' he cries, 'Dr Silvestris, it is me, it is Kai!'

Jack picks himself up. His hearing whines back into use. Where's the Scribbler?

At the door, open-mouthed and unmoving. 'Rafe, the door. *Rafe!*

The Scribbler springs back to life.

'Close it, block it, anything.'

Ulf and Elias drag the table to the door. The floor is covered in food – bread, sausage, biscuit, and what must once have been a rumtopf as the kitchen now smells eye-wateringly strongly of rum. He tries to straighten up, feels a sting at his hip. Looks down. Blood. Investigates inside his shirt. Good God, the bullet that went into Red Hat must have gone right through; bit Jack as it passed. 'You caught one, Domini,' Elias tells him.

'Nicked me. So did you.' There is blood on Elias's collar, and his shirt. Jack straightens up, properly this time. He looks over to Kai, and what must be Dr Silvestris, and what must be Frau Silvestris, he would guess, Dr Silvestris in spectacles with one lens starred, and his wife with her cap pulled awry. 'Dr Silvestris,' he begins, and tries for a bow, which all in all is a mistake. 'Dr Silvestris, my name is Jack Fiskardo. These are my men.' He points to Kai. 'This Galahad you know. We are here to help him rescue you.'

Dr Silvestris gets to his feet, fits one arm of his spectacles more securely round his ear. He's small and spare and you could carry him piggy-back, if you had to. Frau Silvestris, still sat upon the stairs, is the same, a tiny wrinkled face, downy-cheeked. He thinks, *This thing can be done.*

Dr Silvestris says, 'But there are more. There are more in our parlour upstairs.'

Scheisse.

There are ten more. Three are children. There is a babe at the breast. Two families, the Hannemanns and the Brandts; a maidservant, a manservant who might be a gardener, from his clothes. Frau Brandt is finely dressed and has a sort of rigour to her; Herr Hannemann – 'Johannes', he keeps telling them, 'Johannes', whose wife is cuddling their infant – is teetering on the verge of hysteria. 'These are our neighbours,' Dr Silvestris says. 'We thought if we all put together the food we had, if we put it out for the – for the soldiers, they would think better of us, they would leave us alone.' He has to raise his voice. Mere moments they have been within the house, but the noise outside is increasing all the time and has now entirely changed in character as well. What they are hearing now is not robbery but destruction, riot, capture; and without a doubt some of those shrieks are the last sounds those making them will ever utter.

And there is smoke. There is the horrified human chorus that runs ahead of fire; he knows it all too well.

'We have to move,' Jack says. 'You cannot stay here.'

The door downstairs is now bolted, but every few seconds it is tried, it is hammered, it is rocked.

'The nearest building made of stone. What is it, and how far?'

They look from one to the other. 'Now,' Jack tells them, '*now*. We have to move.'

Thor, at the parlour window, the shutter open by an inch, looking out onto the square – 'Domini, the fire is coming.'

I can hear it, he wants to say, because there it is, that voice fire finds with a wind behind it, when everything ahead of it not made of stone is fuel.

The manservant – the gardener – steps forward. 'The church,' he says. 'St Augustine's. It is three streets away. That is stone.'

Then that, good people, is where we're headed. 'What's your name?' he asks, and the gardener replies, 'Tomas.'

'Tomas, you are going to lead us there. Dr Silvestris, do you have a garden?' and the old man nods. 'Quickest way to it. Nearest window,' and the old man points into the room next door.

'My study,' he says.

'Then that's our way out.' But he sees Frau Silvestris knit her hands, Frau Hannemann clutch her baby all the closer.

'If you can't make the jump, we will lower you down. But we must move, good people. Now.'

They make a human rope, with Ulrik at the bottom, arms raised, ready to catch. There is a rain-pipe and a water-butt – that helps – and there is spare cloth in Frau Brandt's over-skirts, which she gives up with perfect grace, without demur. Of them all, Frau Brandt seems to be the one most equal to what is happening to them. The children scramble, dropped from hand to hand; Tomas takes it in one, as the scouts do them-selves. Johannes Hannemann stands at the window, gripping its mullion; he says, 'But if we were to talk to them, if we were to wait downstairs, I think it would be worth the trying, truly.'

The door downstairs is already being battered to pieces.

'Herr Hannemann, you jump, or I will throw you out. Up to you.'

Down they go, out through the garden, into the lane behind. To the left, a building at the end of the lane, built across the archway in, already with its roof aflame, shreds of burning thatch lifting off into the air; and that is no doubt how the rest of the lane will go up too, at the caprice of the wind. But Tomas turns to the right, waiting for them to come up. '*Go,*' Jack tells him, and Tomas starts to run, steady strides, like he was measuring something out.

There is a window above the archway, there is something standing at the window, kite-shaped, white with flame, but still moving purposefully, the grid of the window's leading stark black against it, diamond-paned. They can see it scream. It is opening the window – it is falling back. Little drops of fire from the thatched roofs above, already raining down upon them. 'Keep going! Go!' Frau Hannemann shielding her baby's face; Thor, just as carefully, shielding the cartridges on the bandolier beneath his coat. Endicott, at the back, is hobbling. 'My ankle,' he gasps.

'Scribbler, no-one died yet of a turned ankle. Go.'

Another street, but this one littered with furniture – burst mattresses, broken chairs; with household pots and pans; the houses turned inside out. And the fire is still chasing them. A trooper staggers toward them – drunk or mad, who can tell? – and grabs at the necklace at Frau Brandt's neck, as if the rest of them were invisible, and whirls her around. The maid gives out a scream, lifts a joint-stool from the ground, hits him with it; now he turns on her. Ulrik plucks the man away, throws him against the wall. He comes at them again. Jack springs the blade on his knife, slides it into the man's throat, keeps it there, so he dies without a sound, because now there are other figures coming toward them, three or four or five – 'Prisoners!' Jack yells, pointing at the Brandts, the Hannemanns, at all of them. Thor lines up beside him, musket at his shoulder, tracks the men as they approach. 'Our prisoners, for ransom! Fuck off – get your own!'

'Where'd you find 'em?' comes the yell.

'Marketplace. Plenty there – all the big houses!'

'*Danke, Freund!*'

He turns about. Another street full of smoke ahead of them, smoke and Christ alone knows what else. Tomas is saying, 'We need to be there. That turning, down there.' He says, 'Give Tomas a knife,' and Elias hands one over.

Shielding his eyes, Jack peers down into the smoke. He says, 'Anything that isn't screaming, kill it.'

Now they move as a pack; Dr Silvestris, Frau Silvestris, the women, the children at their centre. Brandt has his arm about Johannes Hannemann. Somewhere ahead of them, horsemen. Somewhere behind them, the sound of running feet. And to the right, a pool of burning spirit, dancing with blue flame, and a soldier, a sergeant maybe, plumes sizzling in his hat, lying in it, his chest likewise dancing with blue fire. Dead? Dead drunk? The maid has gathered the children to her skirts. Figures moving back and forth in the smoke, across their path, and now a terrible rhythmic wailing coming from somewhere ahead, and a man screaming a woman's name, 'Isolde! Isolde!' Figures advancing on them – Thor has dropped to one knee, is taking aim; the crack of shot, the figures retreat. Thor reloads at once. The figures begin to advance through the smoke anew. Beside him he hears Sten fill his lungs, and then the boy yells loud enough to echo from the walls, 'Pappenheim! Pappenheim! Lord Pappenheim! Make way, make way!' and the figures all draw back, and Tomas darts ahead, into the side street, and beckons to them to follow. 'Here! It's here!'

There is the church, in its scrubby graveyard. Tomas is at the doors, pulling them open. In they go. Jack runs for the altar, starts to clear it. 'Everything,' he tells them. 'Anything. Anything that could be loot, hurl it out of doors. This place has to look as if there's nothing left.'

Elias disappears toward the sacristy. Ulrik gives the font a shove. 'This too?'

'Does it have water in it?'

Ulrik nods.

'Then leave it. We might yet need the water to drink. And block the doors. Pile the benches against them.'

Tomas can carry a bench on his own. Even the maid lends a hand. Whereas the Hannemanns, the Brandts, Dr and Frau Silvestris, they have huddled under the pulpit. *And these*, Jack thinks, *these are the ones who used to be in charge.*

And then a yell – 'Domini!'

Huddled in a cupboard in the sacristy, hiding under the vestments, a man in the long dark robes of a churchman. He is thin, he is yellowed, he is unshaven, he has a savage cut across his scalp. He is on his knees. 'Is this your church?' Jack demands, and the man nods. He seems incapable of speech. 'Take him out there with the rest.'

But as they come out of the sacristy Tomas gets to his feet. 'Pastor! Pastor Theo!'

'Oh, Tomas, Tomas,' the man calls back. 'What is happening to us? What is happening?'

So that makes—

Twenty-two souls to get out of here. Christ All-bloody-mighty. He sees the same expression on Ulf's face as he feels on his own. 'Where's Thor?'

'Bell-tower, Domini.'

Indeed he is. On his knees, musket pointing out over the graveyard. 'How are we doing for shot?' Jack asks.

'Depends how long we're here.'

He watches with Thor, watches the smoke roil and open in the streets about them, watches it close and roil again. Sparks are blown through the air about their heads. He glances up – the bell-tower roof is tile, but supporting the tile are timbers. 'Keep an eye on that roof,' he says.

'Domini,' Thor answers, 'the whole world is on fire.'

Every so often some crouched shape darts across the churchyard, helps itself to some of what is strewn out there, and disappears. The smoke is thick below them, thick as fog. Thick enough to taste it. They won't be able to stay here long.

'Where,' Jack begins, 'where has it been quietest? Which direction?'

'That way, Domini,' says Thor, pointing.

Toward the river. That might make sense. Fewer houses, and those there are, smaller, meaner, less worthy of attention.

Footsteps coming up to join them, and here is Kai. He offers them his flask. 'Domini, downstairs, everyone is coughing.'

'I know,' he says. 'I know, we'll have to move soon.'

'Not quite yet, Domini,' says Thor. He is up on his knees, peering down into the smoke. Something down there?

Yes. Two men, dragging a girl between them along the ground; one by her hair; the other with his hand down inside her dress, under the stomacher. They are making for the graveyard. One throws her down. Thor leans forward over the parapet, shoots him through the head. The girl scrambles onto her hands and knees. The second man looks up, looking directly at them, as Thor reloads, and even if the man can't make them out, Jack can see him, him and the red scarf tied at his throat. Thor fires again, the man spins about, lands on his back. The girl pulls herself to her feet. Kai is leaning out across the parapet, is yelling at her, 'Here! Come here! Come to us! In the church!' but even if she hears him, even if she can make out where the voice is coming from, she isn't about to do it. She is gone, gone at once, a crouching run, back into the smoke.

Kai, calling after her, sounding broken, 'Oh, no, no, no, no, no.'

He turns the boy about, to face him. 'Kai,' he says, 'we cannot save them all.'

'I know, Domini, I know.' But he can see Kai doesn't know, not at all.

Time to go.

He makes his way down the tower, signals for Ulf to come over, Ulf and the Scribbler, both. He keeps his voice low. 'I'm going down to the river,' he says. 'I'm going to find us a boat. We're getting out of this. Till I come back, Ulf, you're in charge.'

'Yes, Kapten!'

'And me, sir?' Endicott asks.

'You'll be more use with me than you will be here.'

*

Out they go, clambering over the benches; easing themselves out through the door. The street ahead is maybe eight houses long, and nothing but fire on either side. They pull their jackets over their heads and run. But once past the houses the smoke begins to shred. There is a breeze coming from the river, even though you cannot see the sky. Everything the same filthy yellow-white. But he can hear the boats, moving on their moorings, and he thinks at first it is miraculous that there should be any boats left, and then begins to wonder if it is because so few survivors have made it this far, to make use of them. And Endicott is hobbling still.

'Did you turn that ankle, or do something more to it?'

'No idea,' comes the answer. But the Scribbler has that set look of one in pain.

'Don't try to make sense of it. There is no sense to this.'

Here is the river's edge, its surface covered in cinders and ash. One boat tied to its moorings, but full of water, sunk, and another, still afloat, but black and burned, right down to the waterline; but beyond that, one there, still afloat, still with her sail bound to her mast, a pair of oars lying across her seats, and that is going to have to do. He gives Endicott his pistol and is wading out into the filthy water when he hears Endicott gasp. There is something floating out there, blackened, human-size. Jack reaches it. He turns it over. Endicott cries out, 'Oh, Christ! Is it a woman? Oh, good Christ!'

It was a woman. It was once the sculpted wooden Virgin, from Magdeburg's gate. Jack looks down toward the bridge, shielding his eyes from the fire-drops, but the smoke is so thick down there, you can't even see the bridge any more. But you can hear what is happening up there. You can hear the screams, the cries, the pleas for mercy; the impacts with the water.

He looks down at the sculpted Virgin. The flames have licked off her paint, and the glass in her eyes has melted, and gone running down her cheeks like tears.

He lets her float away. Get the boat, that's what matters. Get the boat.

He goes deeper into the filthy water, wading, then swimming, finds the rope through the layer of black, turns the boat about, hauls her behind him. Pulls her up onto the bank. 'Keep her here,' he tells Endicott. 'Use that pistol. Guard her with your life.'

He has no idea how to get back to the church unless he goes back up that street again, and since they came down it, the house at the end has collapsed in its entirety. Burning thatch, smoking timbers spread across the street, ruffling with flame. He can see right down into its cellar – also blackened and consumed. A gust of wind lifts the flames; he shields his face, he staggers past, and as he does so, that scarred left hand of his begins to sing and he is flooded with the absolute conviction that there is someone there, behind him. He spins about.

He does so just in time for the shot to miss him. It's so close a call that he sees the sparkling wadding flying ahead of the bullet, and the bullet itself, black as some enormous buzzing fly. He turns on one heel, sword already in his hand, and there is the other's blade, ready to meet his. The smoke is thick as on a battlefield. All he can see through it is this shape, circling him, first one way, then another. Then that blade again – another lunge, interrupted by a dragon-tongue of flame as the wind veers round them. Jack swings, waist-height, and something wallops him hard across the ribs. The butt-end of the pistol. *Oh, this one knows his stuff.* He sees a boot, in the small space of air above the ground, stamps on it, goes in with his elbow, hears the fleshy crump of connection, swops his sword – that old trick – from left hand to right and as the shape falls back one way, he goes in the other and meets it. *Got him.* The shape staggers away, lopsided. The flames rear away from them, the smoke comes in.

Where is he?

He's beginning to get the measure of his adversary now –
fast, strong, not so tall as Jack is himself, less reach of arm and
leg. A heavier blade than Jack's own. Jack has to put both hands
on his own sword to turn the next blow; sends his own blade
skirling up the other, steps forward into the noise of the scrape
of steel, blades raised in a spire, punches the man in the gut. A
grunt; his adversary falls back, into the smoke.

Falls back, yes, but not giving up. Still there. Christ, he's
determined. *Who is this? Who the fuck is this I'm fighting?*

Here he comes again. First left – a feint – then right, a blow
Jack has to turn aside to evade. They are both of them wheezing.
Their blades move the smoke like milk through water. Now the
wind shifts again and for a second Jack sees opening before him
like a maw that open cellar. They have fought themselves into
the hot litter of the collapsed house. Now they circle each other
again: two men, in the middle of two banks of roaring flame.
He thinks, *I'm going to have you come forward. I'm going to have
you move first.* There, now the man does, closing in, but now he
has armed himself with one of those flaming timbers from the
ground as well, is whirling it one way at Jack's head while he
comes in with his sword from the other. Jack twists away, parries
the sword, turns, but the timber catches him on the back of his
sodden leather coat, sends him staggering. He hears the timber
whirl again, ducks, comes up, into a vortex of clear air, and there
the man is, the lard-white chops, the tiny, lizard-like teeth bared
in a snarl and the eyes, unaltered, in just the same way, above it.
And the silver wolf, on the front of the man's coat. The memory
opens: Hoffstein. The yard behind Fat Magda's. Face to face, a
dress rehearsal, before they had come for him in earnest.

'Carlo,' Jack hears himself say, and in that split-second of
shock, the wind roars back in, hurling before it a barrage of
fire-drops, and he is down. Here comes the flaming timber
once again, aimed at his head. He rolls. Here comes the sword.
He raises his own, to hold it off, rolls again, gets up onto one

knee, and the timber catches him across the back of the neck, scattering sparks and cinders and he is down once more. This is savage. This is not about to cease. He twists his head around, and Carlo Fantom is standing over him, standing on one of the collapsed roof beams, as it lies, calcined, charcoaled against the edge of the cellar, so Jack kicks at it, kicks it away, as one would the boom of a boat, and the entire mass of timbers goes down into the cellar and Carlo with it. Not a sound comes from him. Just Carlo's face, staring up, sword still raised above his head, and then this gout of flame, like the last breath the house has in it. Like one of the mouths of hell.

Jack pushes himself up. He touches his forehead, finds it is bleeding; touches his neck and the sting tells him his neck is blistered. And something has happened to his foot. Back he goes, limping, back up the street, back to the church. Thor spots him yards away; they have the door open before he gets there. 'Move,' he tells them. One of the children, one of the Brandts' little girls, sees him and starts to sob. 'Move. All of you. Out. Down to the water. The Scribbler has a boat.'

They move. Out of the church, down the street, shielding their faces. Ulf is beside him. 'Domini,' he says. He's staring. 'Domini, what the fuck—'

'Do I look that bad?'

'Worse. Jesus. There's devils in hell don't look as bad as you.'

Past the ruined house. He peers into the smoking cellar, close as he can get, but if there is anything moving down there, he can't see it. *Leave it*, he tells himself. *This matters more.* Down to the water's edge, the little girl still crying, Frau Brandt trying to comfort her. There is the Scribbler, clambering to his feet, and he still has the boat, only it is so obviously too small for all of them that Jack cannot think how he imagined this would work, that this would ever work.

They put the children into it, with the women, then one man at a time. Even with him wading on one side, and Ulrik the other, there is still no more than an inch between river and gunwale. He hardly dare lay a fingertip to it; the smallest ripple will come over the side. Frau Silvestris, leaning against Kai, has closed her eyes. They push the boat forward, Sten at the rudder, Thor with his musket trained on the bank. Elias, at the mast, lowers her sail, but there is nothing to fill it. The fire is sucking all the air into itself. The boat is being pulled back to the bank. 'We must lighten it,' Brandt is saying. 'Johannes, we must get out too.'

They hold the boat steady as the two men climb out, splash round to the stern, make ready to push her forward. Pastor Theo, on his knees, hands clasped, is praying. The crying little girl has folded her hands too, Frau Hannemann as well, but she prays with a rosary draped round her knuckles as she whispers the words. Now he sees the Scribbler, head to his hands, also praying, and Ulrik doing the same. Every god there is in this war, almost every tongue, and a boatful of bowed heads, a boatful of murmured prayer. 'Try again,' Jack says. He, Hannemann and Brandt put their shoulders to the stern. Ulf rattles out the oars.

Something must be listening. The sail curves, flattens, curves again. Out they go, through the smoke, across the Elbe.

CHAPTER SIX

Be Ready

'Great fortune bringeth with it great misfortune.'

Giovanni Toriano, *Select Italian Proverbs... Newly Made*

WHERE TO START?
Here, perhaps, on that good stone quay at Hohenwarthe, looking back over the fields and water-meadows, all the way back to Magdeburg – or where Magdeburg used to be. Or perhaps from the top of the tower of Hohenwarthe's church, which is where Zoltan had to stand, before he could believe what he was seeing. Because from there you can see the few buildings yet rising from the great flat plain of ash and rubble, where the city stood. An entire city, and you

can count what is left. In some places, you can see where it is
still alight, where the smoke still rises. You can for sure smell
the smoke in Hohenwarthe, all the way through the village, and
where laundry has been left forgotten on the hedges, you can see
where it has caught the smuts of what was Magdeburg; smuts of
a particular greasy tenacity. You cannot see the sun. You cannot
see the sky. Above you all is that yellow-white, like tallow.

Jack sits on Hohenwarthe's good stone quay, in the shadow
of the *Guid Marie*, and watches the boats from Hohenwarthe
go back and forth across the Elbe, collecting corpses from the
water. The bodies tend to mass and lock together, and most of
the boats are small, no bigger than the one he and Endicott had
stolen, so there is difficulty in hauling the bodies aboard. Those
out there on the river have adopted a technique something like
herding, and simply shepherd the largest rafts to the far bank,
or urge them, encourage them, send them, floating, on their
way. You cannot row through them, there are so many. You
cannot sail through them, that's for damn sure.

'We are losing our time,' says Sant.

'Well then, Captain, we are losing it. God himself could not
do more right now than wait.'

They came here in their stolen boat, sail up, wading,
swimming, urging her along. Tomas rowing one side and Ulf
the other. As they pushed off, the heat was so great that the
ropes began to smoulder. When Hohenwarthe came into view,
through the smoke, the villagers were all along the quayside,
watching what was happening across their river in soundless
disbelief.

At first, in Hohenwarthe, they had waited for more survivors
to come, rowing or paddling or drifting across, as they had
themselves. One boat arrived with everyone in it asphyxiated,
one with its sail on fire. But by midday on Tuesday the whole
city of Magdeburg was ablaze; and after midday no more boats
came. They watched the flames consume her, and the sky above

them turn black, turn day to night; and then they watched the smoke by day, and the glow by night; and then on Friday General Tilly recalled his troops to camp.

What they are hearing is that twenty thousand died in Magdeburg. Tilly's troops will be pulling corpses from the ruins and throwing them into the river for days – her defenders, her citizens, her men, her women, her children; Protestant, Catholic; and many of her attackers too – caught when the fire changed direction; suffocated in the smoke; dying weighted down with plunder; dying drunk, insensible. Maybe two hundred buildings have survived the fire; mostly those of stone, like the cathedral, still raising its arms to heaven. There will be no base for Old Father Tilly. Magdeburg is gone.

The fire that destroyed her was an accident. 'They are saying,' says Zoltan, also lowering himself down to sit, 'that the fires were set only to flush out sharpshooters from the attics. Or that some infantryman was careless with his match. Or that the citizens of Magdeburg had brimstone and powder in their cellars, stored away.'

'All a mistake, in other words.'

'Yes. All a mistake.'

Further up the quay, Ava is in conversation with Frau Brandt. Jack thinks how similar the two women look: their stiffened movements, the determination in their faces. They see him watching, and they turn away.

Zoltan is staring down at where the ashy waters circle in the shadow of the quay, watching how they marble, how they streak and pool.

'Did you speak with Ava?' Jack asks.

'I wanted to.' Zoltan rubs a hand against his forehead. 'God knows I wanted to. I think she wished me to, as well. But every time I made to do so, the words died in my mouth. She and I spent three days on that boat, staring at each other in silence. And how can I speak to her now?'

No, because right now there is not a woman in Germany does not wish every man in Germany all the ill she can.

Zoltan is saying, 'They broke into the cathedral, did you hear? Tilly's troops. They even took the women sheltering in there.' He gets to his feet. 'They are calling it the Magdeburg Marriage. They are saying how Tilly and Pappenheim and their soldiers, this was how they married the Virgin of Magdeburg.'

Frau Silvestris wants to give them money, and cannot understand why they won't take it. She and her neighbours all have coins and bits and bobs of jewellery sewn into their clothes; and it distresses Frau Silvestris so much to be refused, and she asks so continually, that in the end Jack accepts, and gives the money to Tomas, and to Anka, the maid.

They will go back, they say. All of them, that he and his men rescued from such danger, and with such difficulty, all they want to do is go back. 'We have lost all we had,' says Pastor Theo, attempting to explain. 'But if we lose our home as well, then truly, we will have lost everything.'

Dr Silvestris cannot stop coughing. 'Domini,' says Kai, 'if they could but go back on the boat, back to Amsterdam. I will take care of them after that, but if they could but be found room—'

'I'll speak to Sant,' Jack says.

The Scribbler sits in the Antelope, in Hohenwarthe's only tavern, which now has people living in its garden, sleeping on its stairs. He sits with his foot up on a stool and his ankle so swollen that he cannot even wear a sock. Dart lies under his chair; she makes one swish of her tail when Jack comes up, but that's all.

Jack looks at the ankle and he says, 'You're not riding far like that.'

'No,' says Rafe, 'I know. I think I am going home.'

'I think you are.'

'Yes, sir.' Blenching as he does it, their Scribbler shifts the foot into a better position. 'A friend of mine,' he says, 'he warned me I might come to this place. He made me promise, if I did, I would go no further.' A sigh. 'When I was first in Germany, all I heard of was the army of the dead. Once I even dreamed of them. I think we need no army of the dead. But if there is, who could be surprised by it?' Another sigh. 'We are at the end of something here, aren't we? Magdeburg has changed the war.'

Christ, I do so hope.

'Captain, will you go on to Amsterdam?' Rafe has shuffled forward in his seat. 'Because if so, Captain, I must tell you something. Luka says you were in Amsterdam before, is that so? When you were younger – very young?' He leans over. 'Captain, I have wanted to speak to you of this for days. I think we have a friend in common. I think I know who you are.'

Out on the quay, the Brandts' little daughter and her even smaller sister are playing a game. They have bunched their skirts up, and are hopping from one square paver on the quayside to the next. They stop when they see him, watch him with great seriousness as he passes by, then get on with the game as if nothing had happened at all.

Sant is waiting for him. Sant says there is a problem.

'And what is that?'

'We have inches underneath our keel. Inches, that is all. It's one on, one off. If the Englishman is coming with us, someone must make way.'

'Zoltan,' says Jack. 'He comes with me.'

'Aye, and his place gets taken by the doctor and his wife.'

'For Christ's sake, Sant, they can't weigh more than a grasshopper apiece!'

But Sant knits his arms. 'Mah boot, mah rules.'

Kazimir says he and Konstantin will go.

'Noo ye don't. We need you. I'm moving six tons of gold, I want a guard upon it.'

Says Viktor Lopov, 'I will make way. Herr Endicott shall have my place. Captain, I will come with you.'

M'sieu welcomes him back like a long-lost lover. M'sieu goes capering round and round the field behind the Antelope, scattering the other horses before him. Ziggy tells him his horse is a menace.

'I know he is. It's why I love him. For God's sake, Ziggy, let's get out of here. I think I was never so happy to find myself back on a horse in my life.'

'Where are we headed, Domini?'

Now that's a question. 'We need to get this blasted letter back to De la Tour, and we need to find our fellows and we need to tell 'em that they're rich, and *then* we need to get to Amsterdam.'

So does anyone know where their army might now be?

No-one does.

'Are we discoverers or are we not?'

Yes, Domini!

'Right then. Let's go discover 'em.'

EAST. EAST INTO Brandenburg. He watches his men's heads come up with every mile, he watches Ulf and Ulrik and the rest start to shake themselves free of Magdeburg, he watches them look about; he listens to them making plans. *And why should I not too?* he thinks. *Why not say after that, enough?* Enough of marching, enough of scouring out the byways, enough of laying your head on a different bit of cold ground every night; enough. 'You know what I want?' he begins, to Zoltan, jogging along on Reena beside him. 'I want – I want to eat more pastry. You never get pastry, out in the field. And I want to wake in places that have names.'

'I want to wake in Ava's arms,' says Zoltan, mournfully.

'Only because she's the one who got away.'

'That is not so,' says Zoltan, with dignity. 'You are a stranger to love. You would not know.'

They ride on a little way in silence, the lovely noise of their troop behind them.

'You're telling me that Cupid scored a hit?'

'There is an arrow for every man,' Zoltan declares. 'Even for you.'

They ride on a little more. Behind them, one of the scouts begins singing 'Ein feste Burg'. Others join in. Turning about, he sees to his astonishment that one of those singing is Lopov. *Let Magdeburg rest in peace*, he thinks, *and to hell with Hoffstein.* 'Zoltan, you do still have that blasted bloody letter?'

'It would almost be worth saying no,' says Zoltan, bringing it out from his shirt, 'just to see your face.'

'Read it to me. Let's find out what all of this was for.'

Zoltan folds back the seal, holds the letter in one hand, steering Reena with the other. His forehead starts to crease. 'Jacques, this makes no sense.'

'Why? What's it say?'

'It says only what we know already. It sets out the agreement with the French. What they will do, what His Majesty will do – why would this matter?'

He holds out his hand. 'Let me see.'

Their path is wooded, pine and oak and birch, and thicker in leaf than the lindens were in Hoffstein. Light comes through in little broken pieces, and he lets them dance across the paper, over the lines of script that mean nothing and then over the occasional figure, which does, and then there is one short line of numbers, under the great slanting loops of the signature, and that must be—

'Zoltan,' he says. 'Look there. Look when it was written. Is that the date?'

Zoltan peers down at the letter as Jack holds it out, then lifts his head and leans back in his saddle. 'That,' he says, 'that is a long, long time before November last. That is before we even disembarked.'

'Ain't it just?'

Behind them, the singing has ceased. Instead the sound of a horse being spurred up the path toward them. 'Domini?'

It's Ulf. 'What's up?'

'Domini, Thor says he thinks that we are being followed.'

They're being followed by something, that's for sure. And enough of a something to raise sufficient dust from the road to hide itself in. All the same, they can make out that what follows them is on horseback too, and that it's moving fast, and nothing about it suggests it is theirs.

'Can anyone see a flag?'

No-one can, not even Thor.

'Do they not have one?' suggests Ansfrid, sounding worried.

Men riding without a flag. That does not sound good.

There's a high heathland ahead of them, might give them a better line of sight.

They spur the horses up, up; through the trees. It's a small enough advantage, but once they work a way out from the trees, they can look down on their followers on the road below, for long enough to make some estimate of numbers. 'Domini, there must be fifty men down there.'

Can anyone make out their colours?

No, they cannot. Too much dust.

Down through the woods they go, the horses picking a way. There are low runs of walls, ancient with moss; shapes within the trees that might once have been buildings. Zoltan asks, low-voiced, 'Do you like the feel of this as little as me?'

'Even less.'

They find a road. They find a ploughman, working his way in patient lines back and forth, back and forth across the field beside it. It's his horse who sees them first, or rather M'sieu, who sees the horse and shouts at it, causing it to stop dead halfway up its furrow. The ploughman waits, stock still, as Jack dismounts, crosses the field toward him, leaping from line to line. *Frieden*, he calls out. Peace. There is a child, he sees now, watching from the margin of the field, boy or girl he can't make out, watching as he comes up to its father.

The ploughman removes his hat. Peace to you too, he answers, warily.

'We are looking for our comrades,' Jack tells him.

The man narrows his eyes. 'And which would they be?'

'Blue and gold,' Jack replies, and the man turns about, pointing out across his field, up to another rise, more sandy heath, another crest of trees.

'Potsdam,' he says. 'Your brothers are at Potsdam.'

'How far?'

The man scratches his head. 'Three days,' he says. He squints at M'sieu. 'Maybe two for you.'

He leaves the ploughman staring at the golden florin in his palm.

A little rain begins to fall. Up that next rise. They are almost at the top when Luka calls out, 'Kapten!' and there on the road behind them, there are their followers once more. Still at a gallop. Still coming on. The ploughman has halted again.

And the rain has quelled the dust. 'Thor,' he says, 'take the spyglass, tell me who those sons of bitches are.'

The horsemen halt. One rides across the field, to the ploughman, and there is a conversation. The horseman seems satisfied, turns about. Then he turns back, lifts a pistol from before his saddle and shoots the ploughman where he stands. The child jumps to its feet. The horse – big, white, patient, steady – goes lumbering across the field dragging the plough behind it. The horseman dismounts, ignores the child, goes instead to the body of the ploughman as it lies there, across the furrows, opens the man's hand, where the coin had been, and lifting his head stares straight across the field, straight to the top of the wooded rise.

'Domini,' Thor begins, 'they are—'

'In the Prince-Bishop's colours. I can see.'

'And that one,' says Thor, lowering the spyglass, 'he has a burned face.'

Now he knows.

They are two days from Potsdam, two days from safety. These men cannot pursue them much further. Whatever they intend to do, they have to do it soon.

The country round them has changed again, grown watery. Standing pools, and mills, and mist, and every so often a steeple rising out of the mist marks another village. One big river, islands all across it, everywhere, and trees, trees, trees. The wriggle of roots, the horses picking their way, leaving a track through the moss as clear as across velvet. And good God, how the river winds about. Pushing ever eastward they cross it once, and then again, and then again, island to island; sometimes over a gravelly ford, sometimes the horses must high-step through the water. Slow, slow progress. *But more of them than us, so slower for them than us.*

A world of green. *God a'mighty*, Jack finds himself wondering, *these last twelve months, how many miles have there been? How many rivers? How many roads?*

Ahead of him, Ulf comes to a halt. 'Domini!' A hiss.

Way ahead, splashing across, four figures on horseback. As they watch, one turns about, halloos. Four more. Their pursuer must have split his force.

Split it into hunting parties.

They wait until the birds come back to the trees, then go forward once again.

Oh, for a road. Oh, for a chance to run.

And now, just as Ziggy had warned him, Kai's horse goes lame, and it's that part-way decides him, and part-way he had already resolved upon it. 'You take Kai,' he tells Zoltan, 'take Kai, and the letter, and you run like you had a hedge of pike behind you. You run, and we lead them astray.'

'We meet in Potsdam?'

'We meet in Potsdam. Go, brother, now.'

They turn Kai's horse loose. They watch as Zoltan and Reena, with Kai hanging on behind, disappear up the bank. Then the rest of them turn back to the river once again.

The sun goes down. They keep on, island to island, ford to ford, working upriver, breaking branches, being sure they leave a trail. They hear the sound of horses, but well behind them now. Ulf whispers, 'Domini, is that them?'

'That's them. Too many to be anything else.'

'So we've got ahead of 'em?'

'Yes, we have.'

On they go. Every so often they stop to listen. He imagines their pursuers doing the same. Go forward, stop and wait. Go forward, stop and wait. The trees along the bank grow tight and close, the river to their right is broader, the water makes more noise. It's so dark you have to use your ears to see. Then the moon rises, lighting the water, the darker trees on either bank, and the sky, which is maybe one shade less dark than both. And then an opening-up, within the trees, and lo and behold, below M'sieu's hooves, he hears not grass but stony track. A track going down to the riverbank. And opposite, on the far bank, the trees open again.

Ulf whispers, 'What's that noise, Domini?'

A soft metallic clinking, which seems to be happening in tandem with the sound of water bumping up against the underside of something made of wood. He lets his eyes follow the sound, and his eyes find a chain, reaching out across the river at head height, and then another, and at this end, at the bank, a flat-bottomed ferry. A chain ferry. And opposite, on the far bank, that gap within the trees. *That's our road.*

There it sits, open as a book. There they are, on the opposite bank. There are their pursuers, maybe half a mile behind. And there is the river too, deep, and in absolute darkness. He thinks maybe he heard a riddle like this once.

He steers M'sieu down the bank, dismounts. The ferry works by human sweat: you haul yourself along. He lifts a hand to the chains – well used, but equally, well worn. They'll squeak, they'll grind, they'll rattle. The minute the chains start to move, those pursuing them will hear it. He puts a foot to the ferry itself, rocks it up and down. Good. Solid. But nothing like big enough to take all of them at once, and once is the only chance they are going to have.

He takes a prospect up and down the river, listens to it rush and run. You can understand why a ferry was needed here. But once they are across, if they pull down the chain, break it, nothing else is getting across this way tonight. And the nearest ford miles downriver, behind them. They'll be ahead by hours before their pursuers can find a way across.

Worth it. More than worth it.

Back up the bank. 'That's our way home,' he tells them. 'And we will have to be quick about it. So who's feeling hearty?'

Up go the hands: Ulrik, Ulf, Ansfrid, Sten.

'And who ain't about to swim?'

Viktor Lopov, predictably.

'Right then. The rest of you, boots off, coats off, into the water. And keep your heads down.'

They lead the horses onto the ferry, then wade in themselves. Waist deep. Chest deep. Ulf and Ulrik take up position to one

side, Ansfrid and Sten the other, hands to the chains. He hears
Ulf whisper, '*Go!*' and the ferry moves out from the bank by
a yard. An admonishing word from Ziggy, as Ansfrid's horse
begins to lose its nerve.

'*Go!*' The chains protesting.

'*Go!*' For those in the water, the trick is to keep a hold of your
horse with one hand, and hang onto the ferry with the other.
Jack feels his feet leave the bed of the river, sees M'sieu lift his
head and start to paddle. '*Go!*' The half-dozen horses on the
ferry start to whicker, to stagger a little, keeping their balance.
He thinks they have about fifty yards to go. Beside him in the
water Thor hisses, 'Domini – behind us!'

Four horsemen, on the bank. One rides his horse down into
the water, takes a shot, and a cloud chooses just that moment
to shift across the moon. The bullet stings the water, but their
pursuers have pistols, not muskets, and it's dark, and all they
can aim at is the noise of the chains.

'*Go!*' Those on the ferry are hauling now, hand over hand.
He hears the noise of more horsemen crashing down through
the trees, the sound of a horse losing its footing altogether,
rolling down the bank. Shouts. Curses, maybe. Their pursuers
are searching for wherever it is the chains turn on the bank. But
the ferry is halfway across, more than halfway, the water not so
deep. M'sieu at times has his hooves on the riverbed, you can
tell, the way he rises up out of the water, shakes his head. Luka,
hanging on at the front of the ferry, has remounted already, is
making for the bank. '*Go, go go!*'

It's like shepherding that boat away from Magdeburg. He
finds himself thinking *in the dark places, in the fire and flame.*

Where you cross over.

The first grenade arcs over them, just as the moon slides out
behind the clouds, fizzing as it flies. Lands on the corner of
the ferry, wooden plug facing him, the round clay body rolling,
rolling, then—

They hold about five ounces of black powder, do grenades. The fuse is meant to be slower-burning, but even so, they have an evil reputation – they go off in your hand, or not at all, and if they fall in water, obviously they do nothing. All the same, five ounces of black powder is enough to separate you from a limb, and enough of them, raining down, will overturn a ferry, snap its chains, blow those on it, man or horse, into the river. Send the chains whipping down into the water, carrying Ulf with them. Send fragments of hard-fired shrapnel into your face. Light up trees and bank, so you can see those standing there hurling more and more; have your horse scream in fury as the grenades burst over him; deafen you, as you grapple your way toward him, rip your arm open. Send you under water. Illuminate, through the water, in a firework-starburst over your head, the body of one of your men floating past, too disfigured to make out who but wraiths of blood attending him like water-sprites, wrapping him as in a shroud; burst over you again as you fight your way one-armed to the surface, and then again, and again, and again; as the wreckage of the ferry looms up before you – the hanging chains, the splintered timber – as the river carries you *bang* straight into it; then drags you around it, and away.

SUNRISE.

Much disturbance at the site of the old chain-ferry across the Havel this morning – or at least what was the ferry, before last night. The banks trampled bare; the remains of the ferry on its side, the chains sunk to the riverbed. No more crossing over here. The odd unexploded grenade bobs harmlessly against the bank, soaked through; and in one place a soldier's boot, and in another a jacket, watermarked with blood. The body of a horse, the mound of its belly. And a row of human corpses, laid one beside the other on the bank, decently covered, to hide the mangling they have suffered. And men on the far bank calling to each other, scanning the river, searching, searching, searching.

Far downstream, a horse, pushing at something lying in the shallows. Pushing with his nose, like a dog. Giving vent to a noise of deep annoyance from the back of his throat. The creature before him still doesn't move. But then it doesn't nose, to M'sieu, quite like something dead, either.

So M'sieu does what he does when the world makes no sense to him: he stands over the thing that is vexing him, and shouts. Head up, ears back, loud as he can. Velvet rippled back to bare his teeth. When there is no response, he shouts again, even louder; rearing up, sending the echoes knocking up and down the river, bank to bank, that stallion scream that echoes half a mile or more.

And that is how they find him.

CHAPTER SEVEN

The Traveller's Tale

'A friend is in prosperity a pleasure, in adversity a solace, in grief a comfort, in joy a merry companion and at all times a second selfe.'

Nicholas Ling and John Bodenham, *Wits Common-wealth*

To the hand of Sig. Tino Ravello, at the sign of the Fleur du Lys, Rue Serpente, Paris

My friend, the fact that I know not what to write here should tell you all you need to know. There is no news. There is nothing. I have asked, high and low, I have sent word out north, south, east, west. Our friends have vanished. All I can tell you is that they must have been passing close by Magdeburg, when that unhappy city fell. Then, in that conflagration, that destruction, they were gone.

I think we must endure the likelihood that we may never know.

I remain your most willing servant, in all things,

Achille de la Tour

STRANGE, HOW YOU can always tell an Englishman. Something in the stance, perhaps, their way of viewing the world, and the fact that they always have an animal with them (in this case a silky-coated dog), and how they always seem to be leaking their stuffing. Especially this one, with his straggling and uneven beard, and much-stained clothing – *Guter Gott*, that jacket of his has taken a beating, hasn't it? What is he doing, waiting here upon the quay? What is the paper that he has there in his hand, at which he stares with such intensity?

Oh, and what is his business now? The landlord of Hamburg's Green Boar watches the young man approach his door – watches not askance, necessarily, but certainly with the expression of one who has heard enough travellers' tales, all of 'em ending in a plea for charity, to last an honest taverner a lifetime.

Here he comes, the silky-coated dog nosing at his heels. Herr Maier is a tender-hearted man; even after the many hardships of the last more than several years he is still tender-hearted; refusing pleas for food, for assistance, does not come easily to him. As an aid in doing so, he clamps his teeth more forcefully about his pipe.

'Do you remember me, sir?'

Now that's a surprise. An Englishman who speaks a language other than his own.

'Do you remember me? I remember you. Herr Maier, is it not?'

Herr Maier's pipe drops from his mouth altogether.

'Rafe Endicott,' the young man says. 'Rafe Endicott from London. I was here a year ago. I came to write about the war. Do you remember me?'

'Good God in his sweet heaven! I do, Herr Endicott, I do!' Herr Maier comes forward, pumps the young man's hand. 'And here you are again!' *What a – what a resurrection*, Herr Maier thinks; although perhaps, seeing the young man's wan, drained face, his red-rimmed eyes, not a happy one. 'What brings you back here, *mein Herr?*'

'Passage,' says Herr Endicott. 'Passage to London. I am waiting for the lighter to return, to take me to the boat out there.' He points, out beyond the harbour-wall. 'I came here –' (it is as if he has to focus his thoughts) '– I came here up the Elbe. But the ship that brought me this far, she will go on to Amsterdam. I have no need to go to Amsterdam. I need only to be home.'

He looks, now Herr Maier sees him, quite exhausted, as well as most miserably sorrowful. 'A taste of beer, sir, while you wait?'

'No. No, thank you. But if you would, an answer to a question.' The Englishman places his pack upon the floor, then spreads the coranto in his hand out on the nearest table. 'Is this the latest, do you know? Is it trustworthy?'

Herr Maier peers over to see. The dog pokes its nose over the table's edge, as if it needs to know this too. 'Why yes,' Herr Maier replies. 'Yes indeed. That is from Johann Carolus, in Strasbourg. It is most terrible, is it not?' He sees how the young man's face is working. 'The fall of Magdeburg. We must beg God's mercy. We must pray for those lost.'

'No, this,' the young man says. He is pointing to a sentence, no more, midway down the digest of news. Herr Maier looks, he reads. A company of Swedish adventurers, fleeing that sad city, most troublesome thieves and bandits all, pursued and destroyed by one Croat, Carlo Fantom, an officer in the household of the Prince-Bishop of Prague.

Why, this is of no consequence at all!

STRANGE, HOW YOU can always tell a traveller, coming home. It's not only the worn and wrinkled clothes (stained, in the case of this particular traveller, by the tar of the ropes upon which he slept, and with fans of sea-salt dried upon them, too). It's not the size of the pack he hoiks upon his shoulder, nor his sad need for a barber – no, it's that faraway look, as if he can hardly believe any of the buildings he sees around him are real. Here he stands in Leadenhall. Perhaps he arrived on the coach from Tilbury. Been gone long enough to have forgotten how to negotiate a path through London's jostling crowds, that's for sure. Look how he lets the dog trotting along ahead of him find the quickest way through. There he goes, up Leadenhall to Cornhill, Cornhill to Cheapside, and then he turns up Foster Lane, because that is where the offices of the Goldsmiths' Company are to be found. His business there takes longer than it should – there are difficulties first of all in even having the doorman admit such a tatterdemalion, but Rafe takes from his battered pack the thing that makes it so extraordinarily heavy, and when a clerk approaches, states that there are three more, just like this, held against his name in the Wisselbank in Amsterdam, which institution he is certain the clerk has heard of, yes? And this one he wishes to deposit here.

Eventually, with pack far lighter than it was, Rafe re-emerges into the London day. Now he glances up, getting his bearings from the mighty gnomon of St Paul's. Now he turns down toward Watling Street. Now he quickens his steps. The dog runs on, as if she knows the way – but perhaps, thinks Rafe, by some miracle of doggy nosing there is yet some year-old trace of him upon the air, upon the ground. They come nearer to St Paul's, and nearer yet, and he sees the first of the booksellers' stalls on the pavement there ahead of him – but no, it is not a stall. It is stock, crates of books and papers, all spread about in confusion, all across the road. It is chairs, and tables, and other household stuff – and surely he knows those pots and pans, surely he has seen that jug before, however sadly orphaned and unloved they now appear, out here in the open air. And the woman sat there on that packing case, with her apron over her face – why, surely that is Mrs Butter—

Mrs Butter, sat in the street outside the Butters' yard, weeping, and there, the gate opens, and there is Mr Butter, directing his two boys, who are hauling another chest of books out into the street. Mr Butter, shoulders slumped, disappears back into the yard. Mrs Butter stares blankly after her husband.

But who is this young woman, standing so straight, so slender, with her hand on Mrs Butter's shoulder? This young woman, who stares at him, and then cries out in wonder, 'Oh, Rafe! Oh, Rafe!' Belle – his Belle, in the middle of the street, with a rag tied over her hair, and a great smudge of dust upon her forehead, and a sack over her dress, like a drayman's overalls. 'Oh, Rafe!' The lift of joy, of disbelief in her voice is enough to have Dart twirling on her back legs, as Rafe has not seen his dog do in weeks. 'Oh, Rafe!' Belle's hands are to his face; Rafe, without even knowing he has done it, has dropped his pack and has his arms about her. 'Rafe, you are home, you are home! You have come back to us!'

He sees Mrs Butter rising to her feet. 'Yes,' he says, 'yes, I am home, I am home at last – but Belle, heart's delight, what is all this?'

'Oh!' Mrs Butter's voice is a shriek. 'Oh, Mr Endicott! Oh, my dear good Lord!'

Rafe, to his amazement, finds he now has both Belle and her mother in his arms. 'What has happened here?'

'It was Mr Bourne,' says Belle. 'While Mother and I were out of town, he had Father speculate on a new venture—'

'Oh, Mr Endicott, my poor husband!' wails Mrs Butter.

'And Dadda signed the lease of the shop over to him as surety, and then there was a fire,' says Belle.

'A *fire?*'

'Father left a candle on the stairs,' says Belle, and makes a face. 'So Father could not trade, and Mr Bourne, he says as Father cannot pay the rent, he must quit the shop—'

'And to think,' says Mrs Butter. She grips Rafe with one hand, she lifts the other, shakes it at the heavens. 'To think, that – that heartless *grinder*, Mr Endicott, dared imagine our Belle might be his! Oh, we have seen his real feathers now. Never, Mr Endicott! Never!'

'No indeed,' says Rafe. He still has his arm about Mrs Butter's waist. Now he gives that waist a squeeze. 'We shall see about this, Mrs Butter,' he says. 'I cannot have you – I cannot have my family treated so.' Then he looks down at Belle, and he kisses her, in full view of her mother, indeed in full view of the whole damned world, and lo, that world does not end. He feels as mighty as the Colossus of Rhodes. No man can stand against him, least of all, as Mrs Butter puts it, that *grinder*.

'Now where,' says Rafe, 'is Mr Bourne?'

'He is with Father,' says Belle, promptly. Her eyes shine up at him. 'He is in the shop.'

Indeed he is. Rafe enters the shop with Belle on his arm, and Mrs Butter calling out behind him, 'Nate! Nate, look who it is! Look who is here, it is Rafe Endicott!'

Mr Butter turns about. Rafe thinks he has never before appreciated how truly small Mr Butter is, without the bustle, without the hurry, without the snap. While Nicholas Bourne, by contrast, seems to have swelled like some great slow-moving human spider, fattening on its prey. Dart, he is delighted to note, on first sight of Mr Bourne, disappears behind Rafe's legs with her ears back and teeth silently bared.

Nicholas Bourne is the first to speak. 'Why, *Endicott*,' he says, and the displeasure in his tone falls upon Rafe's ears like nectar. 'You're returned to us, are you?'

'I am,' says Rafe, dismissing Mr Bourne and turning to his one-time employer. He sees now the damage of the fire, a sort of porthole charred through the wall, and the stains of smoke upon the ceiling of the shop and through the door, it looks as if the stairs are gone entirely. Mr Butter's sons (sooty-handed, but slack-jawed as ever) stand at what was the door through, and Rafe can only imagine the damage above, if the stairs were chimney to it; the stock gone up in smoke. 'Mr Butter,' says Rafe, 'I cannot tell you how it hurts my heart, sir, to see you in this plight.'

''Tis very good of you to say so, Endicott, 'tis very good.' Mr Butter is wet-eyed. He sniffs. Mrs Butter goes to him. 'Oh now, Natty,' she says.

'But it is only the littlest matter,' says Mr Butter, bravely. 'A bit of business to be sorted, that is all.' A glance at Nicholas Bourne, a sideways glance, as if Mr Butter – Mr Butter of all people, Mr Butter who bounced through life with as little care for those he bounced on as a ball of cork – must nigh-on ask for permission now before he speaks.

Rafe puts his shoulders back. He faces Mr Bourne. A rush of moments pass through his head, from the loss of the unfinger onwards. He thinks how almost any one of them is a hundred, a thousand times more difficult and dangerous than this. He thinks how the Bournes of this world are no more than nutshells, as on the floor of the Globe, to be trod beneath the feet.

He thinks how Mr Bourne can go to hell.

'Mr Butter,' he begins. 'I understand the business is a debt, from you to Mr Bourne. Occasioned by the fire. Is that so, sir?'

'Why yes—' Mr Butter begins. He glances at his wife. He looks, to Rafe, like some small animal poking its nose warily out from its burrow.

'Nothing *little* about it,' says Nicholas Bourne. 'There is the matter of the quarter's rent, plus the damage to the property, and the stock, in which I have an interest.'

'Put a figure on it, Mr Bourne,' says Rafe.

Bourne blinks at him. 'A figure?'

'Yes. Your debt, sir. To quit Mr Butter of it, here, today. The total.'

'The total?' For all the calculations kicked into instant life in Mr Bourne's eyes, the rest of the man looks dumbstruck. *I was wrong*, thinks Rafe, *to call this man a field of mud. He is infinitely less than that. He is nothing but bubble. He is nothing but air.*

'The total, yes.' He turns to Mr Butter again. 'It will be my honour, Mr Butter, if you will let me settle this matter for you.'

A squeak from Mrs Butter. Rafe feels Belle seem to fold into him. 'Do you have a figure, Mr Bourne?'

'You made your fortune out in Germany, have you?' says Mr Bourne, nastily.

'Yes,' Rafe replies. 'I have.'

The calculations in Mr Bourne's eyes accelerate, ease back, accelerate again. 'Two hundred,' he says, and then, 'and fifty.' He says it with the confidence of a man who knows such a sum will be wholly beyond Rafe's reach. 'Two hundred and fifty. But there will be interest.'

'No, there will not be, Mr Bourne, because the amount will be settled in full, today. You and I will go to the Goldsmiths' Company, and I will pay you from my deposit there, and you will give me a receipt, sir, and transfer the lease of this shop to me, and that will be the end of the matter. Because as Freemen of the Stationers' Company we are, as I am sure you recall, sworn and bound to deal fairly and honestly with each other. Is that not so?' He takes Belle's hand, he lifts it to his lips. 'And I cannot have my father-in-law treated in any wise other than that.'

The stars are out in the sky over Watling Street, and Rafe stands in the yard of the newly christened enterprise of Endicott & Butter (Books and Fine Bindings), looking up at them and pondering what they have seen, and he has seen, and all (insofar as any man can guess it) that is to come. Well, carpenters and plasterers, he supposes, painters and wainscotters. Cabinet-makers. Oh, yes – and a wedding.

Behind him, in the kitchen, Mrs Butter is humming to herself as she reinstates her kitchen. Belle was assisting her, but now she is not. The kitchen door is open, and Belle stands in the Butters' yard with her husband-to-be, gazing up at the stars. She leans her head upon his shoulder.

'I love you, Belle,' says Rafe.

'I know it,' comes the reply. He feels her squeeze his hand.

Behind them, Mrs Butter tiddley-tums her way along the shelves of her kitchen dresser.

'I cannot tell you how I dreamed of this, and how in the worst of times, the very worst, it was my dreams of you that got me through.'

Belle holds the hand with the unfinger. 'All I prayed for was to have you back,' she says. 'Mr Watts and Mr Vanderhoof, they let me read some of your letters, I asked so many times. But they would not let me read what you wrote of Magdeburg. Cornelius said Mr Watts wept over that letter, and then he burned it. He said such horrors ought not to be set down.' She lifts the hand to her mouth, she puts a kiss into its palm, she folds his three-and-one-half fingers over it. 'Rafe, I think you must have seen terrible things.'

All he can do at first is nod. But then he finds his voice. 'I did, Belle, yes. We all did. But there was great comradeship also, and times of great wonder, and times when I think I did not quit myself too badly, all in all. Even if it has ended in such sorrow.' He turns his face against her hair. 'We lost our captain, Belle. He was Cornelius's friend, then he was mine, and we have lost him. And tomorrow –' (and again he has to find his voice) '– tomorrow, I must go to Cornelius, and I must give this great sad news to him as well.'

CHAPTER EIGHT

All Together

'Greater is the injury that proceeds from great iniquity.'

Thomas Hobbes, *A Briefe of the Art of Rhetorique*

SOMETHING HELD HIS head; the rest of his body like a river, flowing downhill. A susurrus of voices, like the sea. And lights. Lights as big and bright as pumpkins.

And dark. And lights again. The river flowing backwards, the first ripple of panic. The first wave breaks across his face. *I'm on my own*, he thinks. *They've left me on my own*. It comes to him that he is unmoored. His sail has fallen over him. A single voice, just one. It says, 'Stay with us. Stay with us, Jacques.'

*

And lights. And dark again.

He's drowning. As soon as one wave has done with him another starts. *God... God...*

What's doing this to me?

And instantly, *Fight it.*

There's a wolf, has his leg between its jaws, is trying to tear it from his body.

There's a bird, pecking through his skull, its beak in his brains.

He can't breathe. It hurts too much to breathe. The wolf has given up, lies beside him, panting, he can hear it. Then it starts again.

And dark. *God, make it stop.*

'Stay with us, Jacques. Stay with us. Hold my hand.'

Something pushed against his mouth. Flowing like oil over his tongue. A taste under the taste. He tries to twist his head away, spluttering. A voice, a different voice. It says, 'Jacques, please. Take it down. Stay with us. Please.' If this was all happening somewhere else, some other time, he'd say it was Ilya.

Make it stop make it stop make it stop

Lights again, but not for him. Things moving. Somewhere not so far away, a rough untutored sobbing.

He thinks he can hear hoofbeats, galloping through his head.

Floating.

Everywhere, nothing but light. Radiance without end. Floating in it, weightless.

Where am I?

Flowing forward. *Where am I going?*

Moving faster. *Am I afraid?*

A great space, and a burst into the space, and there they are, all of them, Ulf, Elias, Sten, somehow multiplied, endless as a dream. *Ah*, he thinks, *we're all together*. He gives a sigh, filling his sails, and the movement forward slowly dies away. Ziggy bounces up to him. He hears Viktor Lopov, at his head, ask, Is he coming with us? And Ziggy answers, No. Not this time. Not yet. And lifts from his head a hand as cold as rain.

Lights. The lights are back. He's cold now, trembling. Going to snap, like glass. A thread of glass, pulled out too fine. The pulses of his heart, caught in the space above him. Every other beat, a sound that's half a moan and half a sigh.

He moves his head; the sound stops.

There is a shape squatting beside him, a blacker blackness.

'Hey.'

Hey.

'You back with us? You coming back?'

Maybe. He can't get his eyes to open properly. Why is that? Nor can he lift his voice above a whisper.

Try it again. *Why is it so dark?*

'It's night-time, Domini. That's why it's so dark.'

One arm, itching. The other hand finds it, scratches it.

'Hey. Leave that alone.'

The hand lifted away, the arm held up into lantern-light, to show him. His own arm, unmistakably. Line of dry brown skin wrapped around it, like the cast-off from a snake.

'It's healing. Leave it alone.'

Can't move my leg.

'That's because it's splinted up.'

I broke my leg?

'Your leg, your ribs, your head. Every bloody thing, near enough.' The shape heaves itself up. 'Sleep now.'

Secretly, he picks at the snake-skin. There is a scar under there. It feels like bark.

He wants to sit up. Can't do it, can't get purchase.

Arms about him, lifting him up. He lolls against them.

'Is that good, Kapten? Is that better?'

He squints upward. A pudge of a face; freckles, like lichen, across the nose and cheeks. 'Who are you?'

'I'm Jens, Kapten.' More shapes moving there, in the background. He has the sense that they were keeping watch. 'Jens, and Per, and Magnus and Alaric. Do you remember us, Kapten? Do you remember?'

When he pushes with his elbows, his head comes away from the mattress like a rock.

'Domini, you've got to lie still.'

He squints at the voice. 'Ilya?'

'That's me.' The figure settles itself beside him.

'You found us?'

'We're discoverers, of course we found you.'

'Rosa –' he begins.

'Yes, she's here. She and our little girl.'

He pushes himself up again. 'You have a daughter?'

'Yes, we do.'

He squints upward. 'And you've grown a beard.'

'So have you.'

He touches his face. So he has.

'Where is this?'

'Potsdam, Domini. You're in hospital. The Krankenhaus.'

'We made it?'

'Yes. Yes, you made it.'

We made it. He closes his eyes.

*

Rosa finds her husband outside the Krankenhaus, leaning his forehead against its wall. 'Ilya,' she begins, gently as she can, 'Ilya, someone has to tell him.'

'I know. I know we do. But I don't know how.'

'Get Zoltan,' Rosa says. 'You and Zoltan together. You do it.'

'Ilya? That you?'

'That's me.'

'Who's with you?'

'Me,' says Zoltan's voice, and Zoltan's shape comes forward.

'Where's my horse? Where's M'sieu?'

'He's here. In better shape than you. We are all here, Jacques.'

They sit him up. A circle of figures round him. No, wait, this is all? And then a sudden panic, some half-remembered thing… his heart is thudding. The fragments of memory, drawing together.

'Who didn't make it?'

A long silence. 'Easier if you look and see who did.'

He looks, he sees. He looks again, but it isn't going to change. No Ulf. No Elias. No Sten. No Viktor Lopov. No—

No Ziggy.

He hears Zoltan's voice. Zoltan is asking something.

'Where do we go now, Jacques? What do you want us to do?'

CHAPTER NINE

Ça Va?

'In time comes she whom God sends.'

John Ray, *A Collection of English Proverbs*

WHEN TIMES ARE hard, the road to Laon, through St-Étienne-des-Champs, stays country-quiet. The only folk who use it are the villagers themselves, going out to their fields in the morning, chattering like the sparrows in the hedge; then at sunset, wearied by the day's work into monosyllables, making their way home. The bells of the church ring for vespers, the villagers of St-Étienne (some of them) lift themselves from their hard-earned ease with a silent groan and go put their souls right with their creator; the day draws to its end; night settles; the village sleeps. So it has always been, so it always is.

But when times are good, as now, at summer's end and coming up to harvest-time, when the market in Laon is thriving, then the farmers and drovers and shepherds make their way back through St-Étienne-des-Champs with their pockets heavy with profit and disposed, before the precious francs are swallowed by this debt or that plan or that promise, to indulge themselves with a small reward. The journey by foot from Laon to St-Étienne takes about six hours, so those setting off at dawn from Laon itself (that inexplicable great plug, rising out the flat of Picardy) reach the village as the clock comes round to noon, by which time the notion of a little self-reward begins to look a lot like a jug of cider at the Écu de France, brought up from his cellar by Robert, the landlord, and accompanied, maybe, by a slice of *flamiche* baked by his sister Mirelle, who uses eggs from her own hens and turns out a tart almost as tasty as did her grandmother. How the girl has never married is a mystery. There she stands: not pretty but not plain, capable, dependable, courteous, deferential; possessing all the qualities in a woman that St-Étienne most admires – and single. The girls Mirelle grew up with have children at their skirts by now, some have two or three. Is Mirelle to be left an old maid? Surely not. Particularly not when it must be evident to everyone that brother Robert has his sights set on matrimony of his own with the Marin girl; and two hens in the one henhouse? You know what they say about that.

Cou-Cou Marin (she was christened Claudette, but no-one bothers with that) is Old Marin's favoured child, and Old Marin is the owner of the biggest farm in the village. So it is understood in St-Étienne that any man asking for Cou-Cou's hand will need to show that he can keep her in the manner her father would expect, which means wine, not cider, on the table for high days and holidays, and no stinting Cou-Cou on any of the little things that make her happy, such as sugared cherries, and necklaces of marbled glass, and new gloves. Although it must be acknowledged that having set his sights on her, Robert is making as good a case for himself as he can to be considered her suitor. The pressed-earth floors of the Écu de France have been laid with flagstones; her ancient barn patched up and re-roofed; passing trade has been courted so skilfully that it has doubled, and first Sunday of every month Old Marin gets a barrel of cider of his own, stencilled with the warning: *XXXXX*. He's a man on a mission is Robert, a man with a plan, and everything that can be put to its service, is. Even the old horse that the Écu so unaccountably came to possess, from the stranger who so inconsiderately chose to die there – when it died itself (despite the tears of his sister, who had made of the animal almost a pet) Robert paid for the Écu's chimney to be swept and relined with the sale of its carcass. No-one would have dared touch the creature when it was alive, it being an article of holy writ that anyone or anything from outside the village, let alone anything from even further afield than Laon (almost unimaginable!), had the potential to bring unheard-of trouble in its wake; but surely at this remove, making a little money from the stranger's horse was safe enough. And if a thing can do good for others, either in this life or out of it, then so it should, *n'est-ce pas?* Everything in St-Étienne is commodified, sooner or later: apples, horses, daughters, sisters... this is not to judge, it is simply how it is. Which brings us back to where we began: what is to be done with Mirelle? What can be made of her? Has Mirelle ever pondered this herself? No-one has any idea. Serve, and step back, that has been Mirelle's life, for years. Serve, and step back. Perhaps she'll do the same with Cou-Cou. Perhaps Robert will be able to manage with two hens in the one henhouse, after all. 'Oh,' says Cou-Cou, laughing off the notion of a rival (the very idea!). 'It makes no difference to me!'

Cou-Cou Marin has a laugh so delicately rippling it can only be the result of practice (so thinks her putative sister-in-law). But for all the daintiness of her person and the preciseness of her needs, there is something clumsy about Cou-Cou. She elbows aside. She barges through. She's the kind who will tell you, on meeting, that you look *so* much better than when she saw you before. Time spent with Cou-Cou is painful – as if the girl's tiny feet can nonetheless raise a bruise akin to being trodden on by a cart-horse.

Obviously Mirelle does not share these opinions with her brother; in fact Mirelle shares these opinions with no-one. They are aired only when she finds herself alone in St-Étienne's graveyard, where it has been her habit to go since girlhood, to make a daily salutation to her parents (even though they have never been much more to her than names), and to talk with her grandmother, who was everything: bringing her up to date on all the latest doings in the village, asking her advice: 'Madame Bertin wants to sell me one of her beehives. Should I take it?' 'The cat has kittened – three little ones. May they be as good mousers as she!' And confiding her secrets. Thus, Mirelle's grandmother is the only one to know that in fact it was not one stranger from outside who came to St-Étienne, but two: the man who died here, and caused such consternation in St-Étienne's heart; and three years later, the second man, who arrived here at the end of so long a search for his friend, to find only his grave and the board clumsily lettered

UN ÉTRANGER
INCONNU

Not unknown to Mirelle, however. According to the second man, the searcher, the stranger had a name; she's never forgotten it, so strong in the mouth was its flavour of the world beyond the village: Jean Fiskardo. According to the searcher, the stranger had a family too.

It became Mirelle's habit, after visiting with her grandmother, to walk round to the far side of the church to the grave of the stranger, she being the only one who knew anything about the man; to free his grave of bindweed and clear a little space for the daisies that scampered across it to see the sun. She came to think of the stranger's family as being a daughter like her, on her own in the world (when she was young herself, the notion of this anonymous little girl could almost make Mirelle weep), one who, as she grew, might face the same dilemmas and annoyances as did Mirelle: neighbours who commented behind their hands on her unmarried state; a prospective sister-in-law telling her how to liven up her dress with ribbon or teaching her a more becoming way to tie her shawl; and a brother, sitting up late at night, endlessly, endlessly, planning a future in which Mirelle seemed to have no place at all.

It's good to be outside this morning. The air is clear, the sun just pinking the sky; night is still there under the hedgerows; in the churchyard it lingers under its trees. Mirelle stands, hands folded, head bowed, at her grandmother's grave. 'Here we are again, Grand-mère, in St-Étienne-Always-the-Same.' She describes the setting-up of the beehive; she relays the unheard-of price achieved by Old Marin for one of his bulls. She does not let herself contemplate her own future, or lack of it, she does not wail to the spirit of her grandmother, 'And me, Grand-mère, what is to become of me?' She does not voice her loneliness, her sense of life slipping past her; no, instead she crosses herself, murmurs her usual farewell ('Au nom du Père et du Fils et du Saint-Esprit. *À bientôt, Grand-mère. À demain!*') and walks around the church through the dew-wet grass to see how the stranger's grave finds itself today.

She sees the horse first, because it is so enormous you can't miss it, and against the shadows of the trees looks as if it has been collaged on top of them. She sees its head turn toward her, the movement of the tasselled reins; but even as she steps back, with a gasp at its size, at its scarlet saddle, at the fringed harness, she is also aware of the man kneeling at the stranger's grave, down on one knee, and the boy beside him, supporting him as he kneels. The horse gives a whicker when it sees her, takes a step in her direction – *thud* as its hoof hits the ground – and the man tells it 'Stay…', as if it were a dog; then he too sees Mirelle. With the boy's help, he pushes himself up. At the same moment she becomes aware of the others, more men, more horses, standing within the trees, some nearer, some further. *His* men, she knows it, at once. He is staring at her. The Bertins had a sheepdog born with pale blue eyes, which was one of the only two times in her life she had seen eyes like this stranger's, that light, seemingly impenetrable colour that is almost no colour at all. The other had been when as a child she had waited upon the man who had died here, the stranger who now lies in that grave. She had been almost the last to speak with him. Almost the last. *He had family*: this is it. Not a daughter, not a girl like her, a son. A man. This man.

He moves toward her, limping somewhat. The others move forward with him. She has a sense of small creatures fleeing through the grass of the churchyard as this – this – *horde* begins to move: some walking their mounts, some riding. She has seen soldiers before, in Laon, but not like these. In Laon they wore tabards, they looked cheery and predictable. They might have been members of a guild, rather than an army. These – these are armoured, back- and breastplate, and you cannot miss their weaponry: the protrusion of swords, the swing of muskets, the pistol hilts, the criss-cross of bandoliers. They could overrun her village. They could snap their fingers, do it as easy as that.

The man is in front of her. She must look up; even that small thing seems to rob her of breath. 'Mam'selle,' he says. He has scars on his face, new enough to be glossy, on his forehead and under his eye. He must see how she is staring, try as she might to do something – anything – else. She lifts a hand (it shakes

– it shakes so badly that it flaps), and points behind him to the
grave. 'It's you,' she says. 'Your father. It's you.'

He tilts his head. 'You're from the village, mam'selle?'

She manages a nod. 'There,' she says (the hand points again,
but wildly, trying to intimate *there*, beyond the church, the
village, *there*). She thinks – she only thinks, it is the maddest
thing to hope – that somewhere within that quarry of a face
there might lurk some understanding of her fright. 'At the inn.'

'The Écu de France?' he asks next.

She nods again, up and down, like a puppet, like her head is
on a string.

'Then,' he says, 'then you must be Mirelle.'

She is astonished beyond speech. He takes her hand by the
fingertips in his. In that moment she thinks of her hand as a
butterfly against a window, being scooped up. 'My name is
Jacques Fiskardo.'

Here is the field-path from St-Étienne's church to St-Étienne
itself; here is the procession (there is no other word for it) of
men, of horses, making its way along. Here is St-Étienne's one
street, its early morning quiet burst asunder by their noise: the
drum of hooves, the rattle of those straps of cartridge. Here is
Madame Bertin's house, which is the first in the village; here
is Madame Bertin herself opening her bedroom window to see
what's making all this racket; here is the squeal from Madame
Bertin as the horsemen go past her window. Here is Mirelle, at
the head of the procession, wincing at the sound. Here, beside
her, the limping man with his giant of a horse. Here, more
of the villagers, hauling open their front doors. Here are the
thoughts in Mirelle's head: one, that she has never been the
focus of so much attention in her life; two, that she understands
now how Cou-Cou lives, at the centre of so many eyeballs; and
three, that these men court such attention as consciously as ever
Cou-Cou did: they with their headfuls of hair, like Samson,

their crazy combinations of beard and moustache. The boy, walking along in front of them like a page, is the only one who looks the way people commonly do. And here, finally, is the inn, and her brother Robert standing in its doorway. It isn't often Robert gives evidence of his sister mattering to him, but he does so now: Robert is standing at the door with his old arquebus levelled to his shoulder.

'No, no,' she calls out, at once. 'Robert, *ça va, ça va*! These gentlemen mean no harm.' The man with the scarred face is behind her – oh how strongly she feels him there.

He whispers, 'Your husband?' and she whispers back, out the corner of her mouth, 'No, my brother.'

He goes forward, holding out his hand. The boy steps back, out of the way. 'Monsieur Robert,' the man says, 'your sister is right. Forgive us how we look. We have travelled a long road, but we mean you no harm at all.'

The hand is not taken, although the muzzle of the arquebus is now put up. 'What d'you want?' Robert demands.

The man, Fiskardo, digs in his pocket. This time the hand, when it opens, is filled with gold. She sees how her brother's eyes widen at the sight of it. 'Right now, Monsieur,' Fiskardo says, '*food* would be a very fine thing indeed.'

It is the work of the entire village to feed them. Every egg from under Mirelle's hens, all those from Madame Bertin too; then they need more ale, more cider, then they need more bread (tangy and suede-coloured; Mirelle is ashamed of it, she's sure these men are used to the sweet white stuff, but they empty every basket, even scoop out the crumbs). And while breakfast for the men is found or bargained for, their horses must be taken care of too; which means more stabling than the Écu can provide, so some must be tethered in the street, then they also need feeding, although thank God the one thing St-Étienne has plenty of at harvest-time is fodder.

The gold swills round the village: Mirelle to Madame Bertin's, her brother to Georges Artaud for the hay now piled out there beneath each horse's nose; then to the Salles' youngest, to fetch water for the horses too; from Madame Bertin to Catherine Thibault for cheese; and then up to the Marins' for a ham, or two, or three, or however many Old Marin can spare, and then of course the gold brings Cou-Cou Marin down to the Écu in its wake. Cou-Cou appears in the dress with the yellow striped sleeves she wore in church at Easter, in fact she's dressed herself up as for a festival, and announces her arrival with her usual musical *Oh-oh-oh-oh* of laughter – although this time, Mirelle notes, laughter modulated to sound suitably amazed at the company now sat about the Écu, inside, outside, smoking their pipes. 'Oh, Robert!' Cou-Cou cries, as if she is scared by them, as if she dare step in no further, despite the fact that those small bright eyes of hers are busy assessing each of these men as comprehensively as if she were entering them into an inventory.

Robert, mighty daring, puts an arm about her, where she stands there on the path to his front door, and Cou-Cou settles herself against him in the same way as Minou, the cat, might settle herself on a cushion. 'We shan't let 'em worry you,' he promises. Mirelle, watching through the kitchen window, feels how her mouth has set itself in a line, wipes her hands on her apron, and goes out the back door to the yard. She's standing there, eyes closed, the sun on her face, telling herself, *I must be more charitable, I must find more in my heart for Cou-Cou*, when she hears Fiskardo's voice, behind her, in the stable, talking to his horse. She takes herself a little closer. There he is, but standing with his face hid against his horse's shoulder, and his hand on its neck. He has a ring on his hand, a gold ring, massy, with a blue stone.

I am intruding, she thinks, but before she can retreat, the horse espies her, shakes its head and gives a snort, and the man

comes back, out of his thoughts, and he looks round. Seeing
her, he says, 'The snort means hello. It means he remembers
you.' He is favouring that leg again. When he smiles, the scar
under his eye wrinkles up as well.

She comes forward. Mirelle has an habitual gesture, when
she is nervous, of running her fingers round her face, under the
shading of her cap, as if clearing her face of invisible strands of
hair. She makes that gesture now. 'Hello,' she says. She isn't
sure which of them she says it to, the horse or the man. She
says, 'I never saw a horse so tall.'

'I know,' he says. 'Everyone is scared of him, on sight.'

She comes forward a little further. 'They shouldn't be,' she
says. Then just to show how much (unlike Cou-Cou) she is not
afraid herself, she puts out her hand, and knuckles the horse
down its nose. The horse moves its head to sniff her palm, then
jerks its head, cuffing her hand out of the way. 'He's looking
for this,' Fiskardo says. Takes from his pocket a screw of paper.
A moment while he seems to ask permission (Mirelle feels her
cheeks flare; she drops her gaze but doesn't move away) and he
has her hand in his, is scattering a pinch of seeds from the screw
of paper over her palm.

Now her hand sits in his again, his fingers under hers. She feels
the warmth of it; how warm, how dry. And again, how scarred.
He places her hand under his horse's nose, and the horse inhales
deeply, then proceeds to clean her palm of the little seeds as
thoroughly as a mother scrubbing her infant's face: she feels its
lips (so soft!), its tongue, which is diligent and muscular. She dares
a glance upward. 'I thought, all my life, that you would be a girl.'

'A girl?' he repeats.

'The stranger,' she tells him. 'Who came here. Looking for
your father. He said your father had a family. I imagined a girl.
Like me.'

'Balthasar,' he says. The way he says the name, you can tell
the man is someone he misses.

Balthasar, she thinks. After all those years, a name. 'Did he find you? Did he take care of you?'

'Yes, he did.'

'I'm glad,' she says.

Cou-Cou's laugh floats right over the roof from the garden. The horse puts its ears back. 'Who *is* that?' he asks.

'Cou-Cou. Cou-Cou Marin.'

'Cuckoo,' he says. 'Well named,' and when she laughs, and tries not to, hiding it behind her hand, his eyes light up as well. He shifts his weight, and momentarily his mouth sets itself, as against a pain. It's as if now he knows her well enough to let her see it. One of those uneven male mouths, like a length of unironed ribbon. Now he stoops and kneads at the leg. 'Were you in a battle?' she asks, and he replies, 'Oh, so many,' and of a sudden he looks so tired. She thinks that she has never seen a man so tired. She says, 'Why don't you come inside? You can sit.'

He follows her, settles himself in the window-seat, on the old flat cushion that Grand-mère had stitched. Stretches out the leg along the seat. His men are sat about out there just as before, only some are at work now on their saddles or their harness and two with ridiculous bright blond hair are picking over each other's heads. One, out front, the handsome one, dark as a Spaniard, who looks as if he also has some measure of command, is talking with Robert. She sees him glance over at the window, where Fiskardo is (eyes closed, head back against the wall), and speak to Robert again, although the conversation must be part in words, part in dumb-show, and part with the boy translating. Cou-Cou, meanwhile, is gazing up at the man as if she has never seen anything so wonderful, for all she has her hand on Robert's arm, and Robert has that look he gets upon his face when someone is talking money. For the first time she sees how they might work together, Cou-Cou and Robert, how they might make a pair.

She looks back at Fiskardo. Minou has jumped on his lap, is circling round, then sitting down, and though his eyes are closed, she sees Fiskardo's hand come up around the cat's head, rubbing behind her ears. She thinks, *They are going to stay.*

Robert comes in from outside, Cou-Cou on his arm, as if she now gives the orders here as well. Mirelle sees them both register that here she is, in the same room as this man, on her own, and she sees it register as a completely different thing for both of them: her brother looks wary; Cou-Cou looks taken aback. Says Robert, 'Better start making up beds.'

She makes up the beds, then they pool their stores of bean and sausage, she and Madame Bertin (more gold changing hands), and Madame Bertin sacrifices a pot of her own confit, and between them, they cook up two vats of cassoulet, and bake more bread, and there is more cider too. The boy (the young boy, whose manners are so lovely) conveys to her in broken French their gratitude, and how impressed they are with her cooking. Mirelle goes round and round the room, with ladle and pot, filling and refilling the men's plates, listening to them talk. Can't understand hardly a word they say, but the way they talk, she likes it, at times it sounds like lapping water, like this is what happens to speech that has come from so far away: as if it starts to gather about itself the sounds of the journey to get here. And then they draw lots for who shares a bed/who gets a floor; all save for Fiskardo, who it is understood gets a bed of his own. He gets the bed below Mirelle's, in fact, where she sleeps in the attic. She thought he would. She gave that bed the pillow with the most feathers.

Madame Bertin kisses her and goes home, pocket heavy; Old Marin sends his wagon for Cou-Cou. *Bon nuit, bon nuit! Dormez-bien! Dieu te garde!* The Écu has rarely been so full. Mirelle lies in bed thinking of all those souls asleep beneath her. It makes her feel as if her bed is floating. Also, she did take some of that *XXXXX* cider tonight.

The noise from downstairs wakes her; at any rate there she
is with eyes open, in the warm summer dark, looking at the
slanted square of moonlight on the attic floor, and there's the
noise again. It's footsteps. Someone pacing up and down in the
corridor below, slowly, someone with a limp.

Holding up her nightdress she picks her way down the stair
from the attic in the dark, feeling for the edge of the steps with
her toes. There, the one big step at the bottom. She unlatches
the attic door.

There he is, at the end of the corridor, resting, arms up
on the windowsill. His head is lowered, like his thoughts are
heavy. He has a sheet round him, sort of round him, but even
so, Mirelle is looking at more naked man than she has ever
seen before – his shoulder, the edge of his hip, a dint at the
top of his backside, where it goes into his spine, one great long
thigh. There are more scars. She feels herself blushing. Even
under her nightdress, she is blushing. He turns about, starts his
lopsided walk back along the corridor, and sees her.

And walks forward. She sees the fur across his chest, darker
than on his head, grows down his belly like a path. 'Forgive me,'
he whispers, when he is close enough. 'I woke you.'

She is still on the step. She is the same height as him. She
whispers back, 'Why are you wakeful? Is it your leg?' and he
replies, 'It comes and goes.'

She should not be doing this. She should not. She knows
that she should not. She says, 'Let me help you,' and steps
down. She puts her arms, in her nightgown, round him, and
fits her shoulder under his. They walk. The door to his room
is ahead.

He stops. He says, 'I have been thinking of my father. I
came here to make my peace with him, but I never thought
before, how it would have been for him. I never lost before,
Mirelle,' and as he says it, she hears his voice narrow, and she
sees the *pomme* rise in his throat. 'I never lost such that others

had to pay.' He is still not moving. He says, 'I think that never heals. I think it never will.' Then he says, brokenly, 'I loved my father.'

Either he puts his head against hers or she draws it there, she is never sure which. At any rate, her arms are now about his neck. Then his round her. His arms are warm as his hand, she feels that; and she lifts her face up to look at him, to ask, with the look, *What is happening, what are we doing?* but instead the lifting of her face becomes a kiss, against that mouth, that unironed ribbon, then it becomes another. She thinks, *I must be drunk.*

His mouth is as warm as his arms. Mirelle has been kissed before, paid a little court to, in her time, but it always felt like something you did because it was expected of you. She kept herself back; the men who courted her could tell; they moved on to other girls more welcoming, more interested. Now, she opens her own mouth under his, she wants to, how silly to keep it closed. Her mouth is interested. Her body is interested. Her breasts are interested. She is again all a-blush.

He lifts her off her feet. His fingers are in her hair. For the first time in her life, something punches through her: *lust,* that's what it is, she knows it at once. She has to part her legs; something is in the way, under the sheet.

Oh—

It's as if he is waiting for direction. Mirelle watches herself remove one arm from round his neck and point to his door.

Now: enough to keep her thinking, wondering, examining the inside of her head for months. To have her pause, midway through whatever she is doing, duck her head, hide her face and smile. He lays her on the bed. He does that, that happens. The next thing she remembers is that they are skin to skin, legs stretched out together, nightdress wedged beneath her. Her breasts are aching. It feels as if her nipples are shouting *Me, me!* He kisses her breasts. This is a thing that has never happened to them before. Then he touches her between her legs where she has her own fur, and she seems to liquefy beneath him. She draws her legs up, she knows what will happen next, at the same moment she is thinking that this has never happened before, that she is virgin, that this shouldn't be happening now, this is sin, and then an evil, evil imp in her thinking tells her, *You're going to know what this is before Cou-Cou does*, and at that she rolls all her thoughts up into a ball and throws them away. She thinks how the bed must not make a noise, so she braces herself, then she feels his hand under her bottom, lifting her up, and her whole body seems to open, as her mouth had done. This extraordinary moment, where she can feel more of herself than she has ever done before, all the places inside. A clang of pain, but like a bell, it dies away. Another; then it too is gone. Oh, his face. Oh, the feel of that hand beneath her. Oh, to be joined like this, how incredible it is, but at the same time, isn't this why we were made? Oh, some little fire. Oh, his face. Oh, she wants to be like this forever.

In a way, they are. There is a timeless time after, when they lie together on their side, this creature they have made, she with her legs one hooked over his hip, one buried under the hollow of his waist. Her thighs feel silky, wetly silky. She says, 'I am glad you are not a girl.'

A huff of amusement. 'I am very glad you are.' He has his fingers in her hair. Again, this has never happened before, to have a man see her like this, hair loosened, hair uncapped, not since she was a child.

He wears a little silver pendant. She never noticed it before. But when he sees it has caught her eye, he puts his hand over it. 'A memento,' he says, and she understands not to ask of what. Instead she turns his face toward hers. Her fingertips hide the scar under his eye. She aches a little, but differently to before. 'We are both better now.'

He lowers his head into her hair. She dare not close her own eyes, or at least, not for more than a moment. She pulls her nightgown from behind her. There is a bloodstain on it. She thinks, *I will take it away with me and he will never know.* 'I have to go back,' she whispers. 'I must go to my bed.' Because she will need to look out for herself now.

The morning comes, and she makes sure she is up before anyone else; up, dressed, hair bound away, her nightgown washed and hanging on the line, hiding amongst cloths and napkins. His men arrive downstairs in ones and twos, and then they must be fed again, and then there must be some kind of reckoning-up for the bill, which seems likely to take some considerable time, and she doesn't want to be about for that, the preparations for them leaving, so she takes a stool and goes down to the beehive and talks to the bees, just as Madame Bertin said she should. She feels light-headed. No, she feels light-bodied too, as if when she walks, her steps aren't quite making it down to the ground.

That's where he finds her, sitting at the bottom of the garden, talking to the bees. How different he looks, by day. Much older, more serious, as if his thoughts are already leading him away. Better rested, though. She stands up.

He is holding out a handful of coins. She looks at it, raises her brows. 'This is from all of us,' he says. 'This is to settle the bill.'

'But that's too much.'

'No,' he says, 'this is what we owe, I promise you.'

'Then you should pay Robert.'

'But you did all the work.' He puts the mound of coins down on the stool. 'Up to you,' he says.

She wants – what does she want? She wants there to be more than this. She asks, 'Where do you go now?' and he answers, 'Amsterdam.'

Amsterdam. So far away. 'Is that home?'

He shakes his head. 'Nowhere is home.'

'Then you can choose your own.'

He looks down at his boots then at her, so directly at her, it is almost as if they are nose to nose again. He says, 'I lost my men. It was my fault, my doing, but they died, not me, and I have to put that right. Do you understand?'

She doesn't, not at first. Then she does.

He says, 'I want you to have this.'

He is taking the ring from his finger, the gold ring, heavy, with the blue stone. She tries to stop him, to push it away. She says, 'I need nothing from you.'

'But I need something from you. I need you to take this. Mirelle, please.'

He knows, she thinks. *He knows. There must have been blood on the sheet as well. He knows.* An uncharacteristic flash of anger – why, Mirelle demands, in her head, why must it be only we who bleed? Why must it be only our secrets, on display?

She's watching his face, his throat, his hands, trying to memorize them, to fix them in her head. The words fly into her mouth. 'I will make you an exchange. A trade.' She reaches up, takes off her cap, undoes the ribbon binding her hair. It is a very pretty ribbon, not from a pedlar's tray but from the *mercier* in Laon; it is the prettiest she has ever owned but she bought it gritting her teeth and feeling forced into doing such a thing by Cou-Cou; now it's going to have a better home. 'You take this,' she says. Her hair tumbles down, over her shoulders. 'When you bring it back to me. I will give you back the ring. *Ça va?*'

He takes the ribbon from her, and now she concentrates on memorizing his touch too. He goes to put the ribbon in his pocket, but there is something else in there must be taken out first. A letter, by the look of it – old, creased, tired, thick paper, folded round a heavy seal. 'Good God,' he says. 'I'd almost forgotten that we had this.'

'But I know that,' she says. 'I know that seal. I have seen that before. Your father, when he was here, he had a letter with him, with a seal on it like that. Just like that. A beehive with ribbons. Just the same.'

CHAPTER TEN

Gefroren

'There were full 15,000 of the Enemies slain upon the place of battle, or in the chase... the Enemies whole leaguer near unto Leipzig was taken, full standing... this was as complete a victory as could possibly be gotten.'

William Watts, *The Swedish Intelligencer*

Mrs Rafe Endicott, here on the doorstep of her house in Coleman Street, behind the Guildhall ('To think,' Mrs Butter says, 'I have a daughter with a house behind the Guildhall!'), dressed for the changing season in a gown of delicate sarsenette, in a shade known as 'Maiden's Blush', and with a smile of pure content upon her face. Where might she be off to? Perhaps to stroll over to Wood Street, to bid Mr Watts good day, or to wander down to her father's old bookshop by St Paul's – although really and truly, that is her husband's bookshop now, ain't it? Perhaps she plans a stroll to the Stationers' Company in Ave Maria Lane, to collect her husband from one of his frequent meetings there (Rafe has become a most diligent man of business since his marriage, with plans to open further Endicotts in Cambridge and Oxford, both). Or perhaps a longer walk is desired. Perhaps beyond St Paul's, to Newgate Market, although Belle generally hates to go there, it is so noisy with all the poor animals, so if something is needed from Newgate Market, she tends to send the maid. ('To think,' says Mrs Butter, 'I have a daughter with a maid!') Perhaps the other way, then, to Leadenhall, which she finds much more pleasant, especially the sellers of herbs to make the house smell sweet when Rafe comes home, and of slips and seedlings of new plants from the Continent. The house in Coleman Street has brick footings and a window in every room (says Mrs Butter, 'To think!'), and it has a garden, which has become Belle's pride and joy.

This morning, however, she will go to none of these places, do none of these things. This morning, Mrs Rafe Endicott is to meet her husband at the bureau of his friend Cornelius Vanderhoof in Green Dragon Court, and then they will dine (Belle hopes not at the Mitre, as they do go there so very often!), and then they will wend their way to this afternoon's performance at the Phoenix Theatre in Drury Lane. They are going to see *The Wedding*. Rafe and Belle take it in turns to choose which plays they see; *The Wedding* was Belle's choice. Firstly, all the characters in it are young and full of hope, just like her and Rafe, and secondly there is nothing whatsoever in *The Wedding* (unlike almost every other play, or book, or broadsheet published in London this summer) about the war in Germany or, especially, what befell all those poor people in Magdeburg.

Belle feels an outrage at what was done to Magdeburg that is deeply personal, what with Rafe having been there, and with Rafe still getting that stab in his ankle when he first sets his foot to the floor in the morning that makes his dear good-natured face go tight as a fist. Belle's own imaginings of what was done in Magdeburg, especially to so many of the women there (no-one goes into detail about this, but that is only because everybody *knows*) are a big part of the reason why she has so taken against going to Newgate Market. A heartbroken howl from inside the house interrupts her thoughts. 'Oh now you be good,' says Belle, tapping on the window, where Dart's nose has appeared. Dart has become quite the child of their household, although surely with she and Rafe being so diligent in this respect, it cannot be long before real babies appear?

Of course, after Magdeburg, all the kings and princes everywhere were sending soldiers to fight against the Emperor; not just the French, but the army of Brandenburg, and that of John-George of Saxony, and even their own King Charles. Which is all fine and good, but in Belle's opinion, would it not have been better if the men of Brandenburg and of Saxony and the King had joined the fight before? While the people of Magdeburg were still alive? ('Now, Belle,' Mrs Butter tells her, ''tis all very well Rafe speaking out about such matters, him having travelled the world as he has done, but you don't want your neighbours thinking of you as getting biggity, do you, my girl?')

Here is Green Dragon Court. Belle dismisses her mother from her thoughts and enters the court with a swirl of silk sarsenette, lustrous enough, as it swirls, to have a helter-skelter of reflections pass over it of all the windows of all the little enterprises with a home here. Her hope is that she will prevail upon Cornelius to join her and Rafe for supper, once the play at the Phoenix is done. Belle, despite her mother's suspicions that she is becoming 'biggity', is quite wonderfully happy as a newly-wed, and likes to share her happiness, as unconsciously as the sun does its warmth. It has always struck her as a great shame that Cornelius should live so modestly and on his own, and she has seen too how deeply it has grieved him, the death of this captain who had been his friend, and who (as it turns out) had been the one to keep Belle's precious husband safe through all his time in Germany as well. She likes Cornelius to dine with them so she can see he is eating as he ought, and present him with her and Rafe as an example of what else he might have a mind to, in due course.

And there is her husband, at the window to the Vanderhoof bureau, hand over his eyes, peering in. He sees her.

'Belle, now here's a thing!' he calls.

'What is, my hubby?' asks Belle, presenting her face for a kiss.

'Why, it is Cornelius. He is not here. He has left word that he is called back to Amsterdam!'

AND HERE IS a place with a name. This is the Wisselbank in Amsterdam, beside the old Town Hall. One way or another, every bit of business done in Europe leaves a fingerprint here. It comes in through the door as bullion – coin, ingots, even (recently) rough-minted orbs, brought up under armed guard from the docks; it goes out again in feather-light notes of exchange. The French crown pays the Swedish army through the Wisselbank, indeed you can hardly engage in any transaction of any size without it. More than a few rough-minted human types have come through the doors of the Wisselbank recently as well; stood there glaring suspiciously about them, as that noble young soul Cornelius Vanderhoof – or Cornelius Silbergeld, as he is known in Amsterdam – explains the extent of their good fortune to them, witnesses as they sign or more likely make their mark upon one of those same notes of exchange, takes them (dazed) to a tavern to toast that same good fortune, and listens as they describe futures hardly conceivable before. Duty done, Cornelius returns at the end of the day to another place with a name, the house of Yosha Silbergeld on the Prinsengracht in Amsterdam, a house built to a scale that would leave both Mrs Butter and her daughter speechless: a patrician front six storeys high; topped by a gable of white stone, as if the house were wearing a wig. It is a little strange perhaps that these rough-minted martial types should so linger round it, finding themselves beds in the inns and hostelries close by; it is odd how reluctant, even with their new-found good fortune, they seem to be to leave Amsterdam. But then men move back and forth between the world of the army and that of the civilian in most informal fashion all the time. Perhaps these are simply making a pause.

And the house of Yosha Silbergeld has had plenty of other visitors to keep it occupied, as the year has moved through summer and into autumn. There are the Frankas, for a start, who have settled themselves in Haarlem, which of all the cities in the Dutch Republic is still the easiest in which to be a Catholic, and plan to begin a business there. Otto wishes to speak over their ideas with Yosha, while Leo Franka wishes to say hello to young Kai, see how the boy does, while Ava – oh well, says Ava, I suppose if you are both going, I will come too. *Particularly* as the idea for the business was originally mine.

She strides into the great black-and-white tiled hall of Yosha Silbergeld's house, takes in the mighty window that lights it, takes in the polished sheen on the oaken staircase, reaching forever up, up, up, and she says not 'How handsome!' or 'How noble!' No. Ava looks about her and she says, 'How *clean!*' and Zoot Vanderhoof, housekeeper to Yosha and (privately, quietly) mother to Cornelius, takes to her at once. The two of them decamp to Zoot's private parlour, to sit on chairs with padded seats at a table covered with a Turkey carpet, and sip gin; which Zoot serves with a drop or two of healthful cinchona cordial from the New World, or Jesuit bark, as it is also known, and that other lovely exotic, sugar, to taste. 'And this,' says Ava, raising her glass and enunciating her way around her new Dutch vocabulary with care, 'is exactly what I mean.' She blinks as the bitterness of the quinine makes itself felt behind her nose. 'Our proposed endeavour. You have so many plants and simples here that are unknown elsewhere.' She sips again. It is indeed a most novel flavour, cinchona, although it, and the aromatics of the gin, and that touch of sweetness – the combination is certainly pleasing.

'It would be no bad thing,' says Zoot, with consideration, 'if more men would devote themselves to gardening. Instead of what they do.'

'You speak of our captain, I think,' says Ava, and when Zoot gives a small sad nod of confirmation, 'I wondered if we might see him, while we were here.'

'No-one sees him,' says Zoot, regretfully. 'When Captain Sant first told us our lost boy was found, I tell you, Madame Ava, we were all of us beyond delight. But what has come back to us – this is not our boy. This is a changeling. Mynheer Silbergeld—' (as always, Zoot is most carefully formal when speaking of Cornelius's father) '—Mynheer Silbergeld says he is a golem.'

'A golem?'

'It is a creature that acts as if it is alive. But inside it is dead.' She shakes her head. 'He hardly eats, he hardly speaks – or only to Lieutenant Zoltan, and even then, barely a sentence.'

'Oh,' says Ava, ingenuously. 'I hadn't thought of that. Is the lieutenant here too?'

Those not invited to Zoot's private parlour, or not engaged in consultation with Yosha himself, tend to congregate in the house's kitchen. Rosa is to be found here, with her daughter, Rosetta, who is at the stage where she seizes everything within reach, and throws herself rigid against her mother if it is denied her. Just for once, however, it is not Rosetta who is the centre of attention with the cook and the maids, but her mother and the news Rosa brings: a mighty battle, outside Leipzig, in which the combined armies of His Swedish Majesty (huzzah!) have wholly routed those of Old Father Tilly and General Pappenheim, after which the Swedish lion, all a-roar, is set to sweep on into the very heartland of the Empire itself. Says the cook (now dancing Rosetta on her lap), 'And will your husband go back to war now, Mevrouw Rosa? Will we lose this little one?'

But Rosa shakes her head. 'I think none of them know what they will do now. With the captain as he is, we are all in limbo.'

She retrieves her daughter from the cook, and carries her upstairs. Out in the garden, she spies Kai sitting with Leo Franka, heads together, and as she walks out into the light September air upon the Prinsengracht, and heads back to the lodgings she shares with Ilya, she spies at a discreet distance up the street Madame Ava, standing with Lieutenant Zoltan. The two women exchange shorthand acknowledgement, without breaking step (the one), or interrupting her conversation (the other). A liking has grown up between Rosa and Ava. Their paths might never have crossed before, with the world as it was, but now that those paths have met, they find they have much in common, not least their belief in taking what they have and making the best of it they can. Rosa, in fact, wonders if she might not also set up a business, just as Ava plans to do. Haarlem, she has heard, is famous for its bleaching grounds and its linen, and there cannot be that much difference between laundering the stuff and the finishing of it, can there?

If only any of the captain's men could be brought to think of moving forward too!

'We have leased a house,' says Ava to Zoltan. She finds it helps keep her pulse steady, in talking with him, to be laying out her plans. 'It has some land. My thought is to begin a business, bringing on plants and bulbs. Especially the novelties. Gardens are so all the fashion now, in France, in England – we will grow and we will sell.' She glances up. Oh, the softness of his regard! 'It seems – it seems as benign a way to make a living as could be found, and that – that matters to me, now.' The words *since Magdeburg* sit there in the air, unsaid.

'Madame Ava—' Zoltan begins.

She knows that tone. 'Lieutenant, there must be ten years, *more*, between you and I. The thing would be absurd.'

Now he is offended. 'I was about to say only how *bene* you look.'

Oh. This of course being what men say when they mean you are cutting a finer figure than they remember, or have plumper cheeks – but then she does look well, she knows she does. Gone are her old skirt and bodice, with their gardening stains. Ava is in tobacco-coloured velvet, crisp with pintucked poplin at neck and cuffs; her hair is dressed; there is even a touch of rouge upon her cheeks. What a lot of fuss, simply to visit Amsterdam!

'Then I thank you,' she replies. 'Also, I am glad you are alive. And I am also – I am most sorry, for everything I hear of the captain. Truly.'

'He has given up his commission,' says Kai. He sits with Leo Franka on the smooth-worn marble bench in Yosha's garden, facing the canal that runs along its rear. Autumn leaves float across it, flecks of amber, flecks of gold. 'He has sent notice to General Åke Tott. He made me write it, from his dictation. He made me write he was not fit to lead.' Kai's voice has at last begun to break. It swoops up and down as if it is learning to fly. 'And the letter – the letter from Hoffstein? He has given that to Mynheer Silbergeld. It is as if he is ending everything.'

'Kai,' Leo begins, 'his heart is bruised. His spirit, likewise. But in time, he will heal –'Although having caught sight of the captain, thin as a corpse, haunted of eye, Leo is tempted to cross his fingers as he says it.

'Others of us were hurt as well, you know,' Kai declares, angrily. 'Ansfrid broke his shoulder. Luka's knee was twisted all out of joint.'

He glares at the ground.

'He is sending me home,' he says next. 'When Dr and Frau Silvestris return to Stockholm I am to go with them. I am to take the gold that should have been Ulf's and Elias's, and Sten's, and I am to give it to their families. I am to light candles for them. And for Ziggy and Viktor. And when I asked what should I do after, should I return here to him, he ordered me, *No*. He said I must make my own life now.'

Because he thinks he is why his men are dead, thinks Leo, remembering how he had felt, when he thought he had imperilled his own children – ah, God, that pit of dread. That fall, that dreadful well. That's where their captain is.

'He says he failed us. How did he fail?'

Because he never thought he could, Leo answers, in his head. But out loud he says, 'You are his family. All of you. This is grief, it is a mourning.'

'*We* are in mourning,' Kai replies, with heat. 'All of us. But now we are mourning him as well.'

HE CAN'T SLEEP, that's the worst of it. He closes his eyes and the images are there in front of him at once; the worst things he has ever seen, things worse than any he has ever seen. Memories that were never his: the instant of his mother's death; the tumble of his father's body into the grave. Bloodied children. Broken animals. Everything that was ever precious to him, all being destroyed, and somehow it is always he, he, who is the agent of destruction. Things impossible to speak of, impossible to describe. Thoughts that slide over each other, spitting and hissing like serpents, coiling in and out, writhing and biting.

At night he walks, and walks, and walks. It's not as well regulated a city as it might appear during the day, is Amsterdam. If he hears the sound of a fight, he makes toward it. He comes home scraped, contused, knuckles swollen; goes up to the room in the attic where he slept as a boy, lies there in silence while his body screams at him. Waits for it to get dark and the snakes to start slithering again.

Yosha Silbergeld, a man who has seen his share of good and of bad, summons his prodigal to him; to his first-floor chamber, with its darkly polished floor, the light streaming in through the window, and Yosha, in his burgermeister's chair, wheeling himself out from behind his desk. He holds the mysterious letter in his hand.

'What would you have me do with this?'

'Keep it,' comes the reply. 'It might prove useful.'

'And why would you not keep it yourself?'

No answer.

Yosha gives himself a push. He rolls across the floor and up to Jack, right up to his toes. 'Do you remember when you first stood in this room?' he asks. 'You were thirteen. Do you remember what you asked me? You asked me what had happened to my legs.'

At last, a little life in that hard, scarred face. 'I was an insolent little bastard, wasn't I?'

'Yes, you were. But I answered you. I told you, how they were burned in a fire.'

'In Russia. I remember. And, you said, a long, long time ago.'

'So it was.' Yosha squints upward. He has managed his usual trick, of keeping the light behind him. 'Turn aside,' he says. 'You think I can't see what you're up to? Turn aside from this.'

'Yosha—'

'No. You listen. I know what you are planning. I once had those same thoughts in my head. Turn aside. Revenge is a demon. It will eat you alive.'

'Yosha, I—' For a moment it seems to Yosha that there might be tears rising in those pale eyes.

'Think what you have. You are a wealthy man now, Jack Fiskardo. You can make any life you please. Turn aside.'

'I cannot. This is different. He killed my men, Yosha, and he killed them because of me. It was my fault, but it was my men who suffered. It's not as it was with you. He has to pay.'

'So you wait for these men who love you still, you wait for them to give up on you, and then you sneak away, is that it? Sneak away to your revenge.'

No answer.

'On your own. To Prague. To get yourself killed. That's it, isn't it? That's the plan. Kill him, and put an end to yourself as well.'

Yes, Yosha, that's it. That's it exactly.

And then to everyone's amazement, the army of that distasteful old drunkard John-George of Saxony takes Prague.

PART IV

November 1631

CHAPTER ONE

Pilgrims

'... I am in blood
Stepp'd in so far that, should I wade no more,
Returning were as tedious as go o'er.'

William Shakespeare, *The Tragedie of Macbeth*

AND SO I write this, in the hope that if we are murdered in our sleep, as seems entirely likely, this will be found and our fates will be known.

There are seven of us. Henry Kempwick, the leader of our merry troupe. Alembert, our leading man. Martin, who has been with us since Sheppey, poor stage-struck little rabbit. Lucy, who gives our audience a song. Blanche, our wardrobe mistress, who gives nothing to nobody. Saul, who has crawled under the wagon in which I sit and scribble this, the useless drunken sot, and I. I am our dramatist. We are the—

They're still awake out there, those two, beside the fire, I'm sure of it. One of them, I think, just moved.

Forgive me, I have run ahead, fatal for any story, most fatal on the stage. Upon the boards your story must proceed in good consecutive order, much like a marching army, else your audience is lost. I know this, I know it, so elementary a mistake, it is a measure, I think, of my nerves.

Very well then, set the scene. The seven of us, the road to Prague, an afternoon so late in this year of 1631 that it is almost dead and gone, a pepper of frost in the air; and then those two.

We must have watched them for an hour or more, as the road unrolled behind us, sometimes there and sometimes not, but always when we saw them again, closer than before. Then we came up to the crossroads, and there they were, their horses reined in and blowing like dragons.

At first sight of them, Lucy and Blanche jumped into the wagon and hid. It might have been wiser had we all done the same. We've seen our share of ruffians and ne'er-do-wells, some rowdy few in our audience most nights, but never two with OUTLAW writ so clear across them as these.

As they saw us, one of them raised a hand in greeting, called out, '*Guten tag!*'

'Good day to you too, my fine fellow,' Henry called back. Henry prides himself on his manners and reasons that a civil word never goes amiss, even if that civil word should be utterly incomprehensible to those he addresses. It is up to them, says he, to learn the language of Master Shakespeare; it is up to us, says he, to show the way. We have traversed the length of Germany on our travels; we have all done our best to gain some little understanding of its tongue, but not one word more of Deutsch does our gallant leader speak than he did when we embarked.

'Hah!' said the man. 'Engländer! Hello!' He seemed delighted. His companion, wrapped in a cloak, and with his hat pulled down over his face, had yet to say a word.

'Why yes,' said Henry, much surprised (as were we all). 'We are indeed.'

'Where you going, Inglish?' asked the man. He was a handsome fellow – lustrous moustaches, and lace at his cuffs, although everything else about him – jacket, boots, horse – bore the signs of much travel and long wear.

His companion merely stretched in his saddle and knuckled his back. Now where are you headed? I wondered, and where might you be from, come to that? – when the man pushed back his hat and let me see his face, and I decided that I had no wish to know.

Hair waxed and plaited off his face. A rough beard. The line of a scar across his forehead and below one eye, and good God, the eyes revealed—

Cold. Dead. Cold as ice. Well, thought I, if I ever find myself attempting to outstare a shark, I will be able to tell it I have met one of its relatives.

His horse, though. That horse is something. Biggest animal I've ever seen. Legs as long as organ-pipes, a coat like watered silk, ears curved up like the horns of the Devil, and a cicatrice on its chest as thick as my thumb.

I was not the only one to be impressed. Martin had hopped down from his seat beside Saul and come running up, curious and incautious as ever. 'I like your horse,' he said, edging toward it. 'That's a fine animal, that.'

The man swung his head around, stared down at him. Martin flushed brick-red. The man smiled. Well, thought I, if I am ever smiled at by a shark...

''Tis, ain't he,' the man said, and gave the animal a pat.

His friend held out his hand. 'Kaiser,' he announced.

'Henry,' Henry replied, shaking the hand, and transferring his reins most carefully from right to left to do so. We are none of us what you might call natural horsemen, certainly not when compared to centaurs such as these. 'Henry Kempwick, my good sir, late of the famed Red Bull Theatre in Clerkenwell, in the fine city of London. This,' Henry continued, pointing to me, 'is Andrew Frye, our dramatist. The driver of our wagon there is Saul. The boy Martin you have met.'

'Pray don't feel,' came Alembert's voice behind us, 'that you are by any means required to introduce *me*.'

'Ah, yes,' said Henry, 'and this is—'

'Oh my dear fellow, no,' said Alembert, riding up to join us, 'I count for nothing, till I am on the stage, I'm well aware of that.' He leaned forward, flipped a cuff, extended his hand. 'I am Alembert.'

'Alembert, yes,' said Henry. 'Our leading man.'

'Nonsense, nonsense,' said Alembert. 'I play my part, that's all.' He turned his horse to face the shark. 'And you are? Don't believe I caught the name.'

'Jagiello,' the shark replied.

Jagiello. The name, I believe, is Polish. Beyond that, I have no idea.

'Charmed, I'm certain of it,' said Alembert.

'And your ladies?' Kaiser enquired, in well-judged tone.

'Oh, in the wagon? Lucy and Blanche,' said Alembert, with a lordly wave of his hand. 'Took fright, I dare say. Women!'

'Ladies have to be careful,' commented Kaiser, generously.

'Exactly so,' Henry put in. 'We are the Pilgrim Players.'

There was the usual silence. I, for one, have long since given up expecting our name to be recognized, but never Henry, God forbid.

'We're on our way to Prague,' Martin announced, piping up again.

'Now there is coincidence,' said Kaiser. 'This is our destination too.'

Coincidence my eye, as Blanche would put it. Milestones set ten Imperial leagues apart had been announcing PRAHA XL, or PRAHA XXX, as it is now, for the last day and a half.

'We're going to play for His Grace the Prince-Bishop of Prague,' announced our infant prodigy.

We are not going to play for His Grace the Prince-Bishop, though I regret that Henry, in a moment's excess on our last night in Erlangen, carried away by the season perhaps – that time of year when we all start believing there is better to come (fools that we be, as Blanche would say) – announced to the boy and several dozen others that we were. We know who *will*, of course we do, we have followed them all across Deutschland as a – as a rowboat might bounce along in the wake of some mighty galleon; but it will not be us. We will play anywhere we can hang a row of lanterns, set up a stage (assuming, after tonight, that any of us are still alive to do it). At Henry's insistence we had given Erlangen his favourite, the Scottish play, which may be marvellously brief but there are the witches, there is the walking wood, there is Henry's Scottish *accent*, above all… I think half our audience had left us by its end. So when the curtain fell (literally, I regret to say, Saul's usual shoddy workmanship), I was not surprised that Henry should feel he must announce our next engagement as being in so lordly a venue, rather than to more of the human turnips we faced there.

'Well, well,' said Kaiser, kindly as before. 'That is a great thing for a little fellow.' At which Martin, beaming with delight, announced, 'Why! We should all travel together!' He looked to Henry, he looked to me, he seemed surprised that none of us should say at once *why, excellent idea!* 'Don't you think?' he added, uncertainly.

Ah, the innocence of youth, how many lives has it destroyed? (Good grief, I really am beginning to sound like Blanche.) Let me, as it were, costume our reservations for you: Kaiser, along with the splendid moustaches and the handsome smile, had a sword at his hip, a bandolier of those wooden powder cases across his chest and a musket across his shoulders. Jagiello, meanwhile, had all of the above, a pistol either side his saddle (pistols which, were I any judge of such things, I would have thought rather fine) and a knife a-dangle at his belt. All this time, I had been aware of Alembert eyeing the pair of them up and down; I can imagine all too well the complaints next time Blanche robes him up to tread the boards – how, how is he supposed to play the hero, armed only with a pasteboard shield and a sword made from a poker?

Assuming that we have a next time, obviously.

Henry cleared his throat. On stage, this can still silence the house; out here, it only seemed to point up the complete desertion of the countryside by all save us, and these two. And while I'm sure there's many a man in Germany chooses to go about as an ambulant arsenal for no other reason than a quiet life, with these two, aloft on their horses, I rather doubted it.

'Ah, now,' Henry began, 'I don't think that would suit.' It is one thing to pass the time of day with creatures such as these, but throw your lot in with them? God above.

'Why not?' demanded Martin, pouting out his lower lip. I don't know what it is happens to children when you put them on the boards, they lose all sense of their proper place at once.

'Because we travel rather slow. We would delay these gentlemen—'

'Oh, we have no hurry,' Kaiser said.

'No,' said Jagiello. 'We've time to kill.' And did that sharkish smile of his again.

If this were a joke, I must say I found it in very poor taste. But we are, as Henry constantly reminds us, English gentlemen (and women); if some dubious remark is passed in our presence, even if it is hurled at us as we strive upon the stage, we are to ignore it. We are to carry on as if nothing had happened.

And now, we are going to get ourselves killed.

'So I don't think it would suit,' Henry concluded manfully. 'Not at all.'

'Sirs,' Kaiser began. He shot a pained glance at his companion. 'We have travelled a long road. We tire of our own company. To travel with you – it would be an honour.'

Strangely, I almost found myself believing him. War creates a great hunger for anything that is *not* war (this was Henry's chief argument in proposing our expedition in the first place – well, that and his difference of opinion with our paymasters, the family Holland). When Lucy sings a ballad that in London would fail to raise a tear in the eye of a child, here it has grown men weeping on each other's shoulders, and when, in Regensburg, we gave them *The Winter's Tale* with Henry, as Hermione, rising from her plinth, to embrace Martin (Perdita – flaxen plaits and virgin white), when Leontes (Alembert – not his best performance, not at all) realizes his daughter is not lost, but found, we positively had to stop the play, until our audience ceased bawling.

I am not a coward, at least I do not think I am, but one does hear such tales. At Regensburg there was a man whose friends brought him backstage afterwards to thank us. He too, they said, had a daughter, and had lost her in the worst of ways. A gang of soldiers took her, and whether it was the violence they did to her, or the shame she felt of it, the girl had died. And the only thing that made this man's story different from I have no doubt a thousand others, is that he had sought out the men responsible, found them, and laid his complaint against them with their officer. Do you know what the officer said? That had his daughter not been such a niggard with her virtue, the heartbroken father might have had her with him still. The poor man, who could hardly speak for his tears, told us that when he saw Martin on the stage, it had reminded him of her, the one that he had lost, and when Perdita and Leontes embraced, it made him think that there would be another meeting for him and his dear child, not in this world, but the next, for on this earth there is no justice left.

'Ah,' said Henry to Kaiser. 'Ah, well now. In that case – that is a noble sentiment, good sir, nobly expressed.'

Myself, I think his vanity was touched. Myself, I think that it was meant to be.

'In that case,' Henry concluded, 'gentlemen, we would be pleased. There is safety in numbers, after all.'

'So they say,' said Jagiello, turning his monster horse about. 'If you travel slow, we'll take the lead.'

I pride myself I have an instinct where Blanche is concerned, the moments when for all her fierceness, she'll appreciate a reassuring word. I let my horse drop back, past Alembert, past Saul (in his usually glassy-eyed slump – it is a mystery to me how the man always contrives to find drink somewhere, how does he do it? How does he pay for it? Certainly not from what we give him), and as the rear-end of the wagon came abreast, gently called her name. Immediately the corner of the canvas was pulled back. 'Have you gone *mad*?' she hissed. 'What are you thinking of, letting them ride with us?'

'Blanche,' I began, 'I cannot see that we had any choice. Nor do I think that they intend us any harm.' I was thinking no such thing, but for Blanche I would swear black was white, up down, and any matter else. 'Besides, technically *we* are joining *them*.'

'You are insane,' she said. 'You are an idiot! They are *freebooters*, *land pirates*, *mercenaries*!' She glanced over her shoulder; I saw Lucy, cowering behind her, guitar clasped to her breast. Blanche lowered her voice. 'Andrew, they will kill us! They will lure us off the road, they'll strip us and rob us and leave us for dead, and that's if we're *lucky*. You wait until it's dark, you mark my words.' And at that the flap of canvas was yanked down, and would not open again, no matter how many times I whispered her name.

I rode back up to Alembert. Dusk was creeping in across the road ahead. As I came up to him, Alembert leaned across. I saw he kept his eyes on Kaiser. *Remember*, I told myself, in encouraging tone, *Alembert is your friend, your true friend, he takes your words and into them he breathes the breath of life* – here it comes, I thought, a plan. I waited to hear it: *I don't care for the cut of these at all, no matter what the old man says. If they try anything, I'll take that rogue with the black hair.*

'I say,' said Alembert. 'D'you think I should try a moustache?'

I must say, they accomplished it superbly, I could not have written it better myself.

Scene: the road to Prague. The sound of water – a river, falling over rocks. Night draws in [the lights are dimmed]. A clearing to the left, ringed round with ghostly birch. [You could accomplish all that on a backdrop.] The audience waits. The party of travellers approach. [How would one simulate the sound of horses? A pair of tankards on a tabletop, perhaps.]

Horseman 1 (Kaiser, offstage, but as if reining his horse to a halt, dismounting): She has picked up a stone. (We imagine his horse lifts its hoof.)

Horseman 2 (Jagiello, also offstage): Then let's call a halt. Let her rest up overnight.

Horseman 1 (as if noticing the clearing for the first time): Here, you think?

Horseman 2: Why not? Good a place as any other. (He holds up his hand. The party of travellers [more tankards on the tabletop] comes to a halt.)

Horseman 2, loudly: Time to make camp. The clearing over there. (Enter, stage left. And we follow. Like lambs to the slaughter.)

We are rarely at our best, come close of day. The excitement of performance fades and leaves us fractious, like tired children, yet there are still costumes to restitch, scenery to repaint, props to repair. There are post-mortems to endure – who spoilt whose entrance? Who blocked who? Roles from whole months, whole seasons back, are summoned forth as witnesses. There is, above all, the tedious business of feeding ourselves, and this, of course, is all compounded by the fact that it will be dark, it will be cold, it will very likely be raining, and before we can do anything, we must make a fire, which thankless task, invariably, falls to Alembert and me. Lucy says she cannot do it, this battling with tinderbox and sticks, it makes her fingers too rough to play, Blanche that she will not – at least, did any of us have the nerve to ask her, I think we all know her response – and Henry, though he would help, sure, is afflicted with a swelling of the knuckles of his hands. Henry is getting old. (So are we all, Blanche would say.)

And that, of course, would be without our two new travelling companions, lurking, watching, big as bears.

Having taken an unconscionable time to tie up, unload, rub down and generally make comfortable their horses (while Henry, Alembert, Martin, Saul and I – still no sign of Lucy and Blanche – went back and forth from the wagon, unloading tent and blankets), they folded their arms, and for a good five minutes watched in apparent amazement as Alembert and I, kneeling on the ground and our heads bent hopefully over a handful of dry moss, amused ourselves with one of us blowing, and the other striking sparks. Our progress from smouldering moss to little twigs to something that Prometheus might recognize is generally attended with far more failures than successes; the whole progress has been known to take an hour. It was not, thank God, raining, though it was bitter cold, and by now so dark I could not even see where our handful of moss lay on the ground. I merely struck sparks in the direction of Alembert's nose.

'I think they try to make a fire,' we heard Kaiser comment, wonderingly.

'Oh,' answered Jagiello. 'Is that it?'

They both plunged off into the trees. We heard them crashing round us, then Kaiser reappeared, hid from the waist up behind a double armful of thick-stalked bracken. He walked into the centre of the clearing, opened his arms and let the heap fall on the ground. Jagiello, reappearing behind him, let fall upon the heap an equal armful of timber. 'I cannot wait,' said Alembert, under his breath, sitting back, mopping his brow, 'to see how they intend lighting *that*.'

Kaiser took a step back. He plucked one of the wooden cartridges from the bandolier across his chest, pulled out its stopper with his teeth, and shook its contents across the pile, like seasoning. Jagiello pulled the pistol from his belt, loaded it, primed it, took aim and fired. The pile went up like a beacon. Martin clapped his hands. 'That's how to do it!' he exclaimed.

'Well now,' said Henry, coming closer, rubbing his hands together over the warmth. 'That is a blaze! Andrew, the pot!'

Our cooking pot has been with us through thick and thin; thick and thin too, what usually emerges from it. Blanche is our cook, and it is not a role that she is happy with. We assure each other that so long as we are certain she has got the contents boiling before she doles them out, all will be well; nonetheless we are all frequently afflicted with loose bowels – all save Saul, that is, who must have the stomach of a jackal, and has even been known to finish up our leavings. Henry says Blanche needs encouragement, providing this with many lip-smacking, squint-eyed compliments as he attempts to swallow the last spoonfuls down ('No, no, my dear, I could not eat another bite'); Alembert has been heard to wonder why we do not simply ask her to poison us outright, and so be done with it. The truth of it is, none of us would dare suggest that we might make a better cook than she; the task fell to her, and she despises it, yet will not give it up. Much about Blanche presents this same conundrum. She seems to hate her life with us, yet it is unthinkable that she would follow any other; her own bad temper (I maintain) makes her miserable, yet should I try to lure her into any other mood, all I get is all that same temper shot at *me*.

The canvas flap of the wagon lifted, and there was the lady herself, Lucy peeking out behind her. They must have seen the fire.

She let herself down from the wagon, shook out her skirts, as women do, taking the measure of things, then stalked across the clearing as if toward the finest *pension* in France. I remember this same straight-backed walk of hers, exactly, from when I first clapped eyes on her in Southwark, stalking across the yard of the Tabard, the pilgrims' inn – as proud and as disdainful as a queen, looking to neither left nor right, while the frank stares of the multitude muddled in her wake.

She went straight to the cooking pot, lifted its heavy lid. The usual unsavoury odour welled up from within. Blanche smiled, apparently well satisfied, and went next to our box of foodstuffs. What, I wondered, might be added to her witch's brew tonight? Bitter aloes? Toadstools? Mud?

Onions, it would appear. She sat herself upon the ground, began to slice them into her lap.

Lucy, meanwhile, stood hesitating at the wagon's end. Lucy is a pretty creature, plump of cheek and bright of eye, and her hesitations generally provoke one of us to come to her aid, generally Alembert, it being generally understood between us that there is a general understanding (much to Blanche's loud-voiced scorn) between them. Like calls to like; contempt brings only contempt in its turn, the root of most of Blanche and Alembert's fallings out, which are many; those fair of face (Lucy, our leading man) draw together, it would seem.

But not tonight. As Lucy scanned anxiously across our camp, Kaiser was there to help her down. 'Oh, my!' said Lucy, faintly, seeing his extended hand. 'Well, I suppose –' and down she stepped, all a-blush.

Alembert (thank God, back turned) was warming himself at the fire, discussing with Henry whether his final soliloquy as Leontes 'had, you know, quite enough weight. I thought perhaps if I were to deliver it in armour, and were crowned, and maybe with attendants...'

'Oh, quite, quite,' I heard Henry saying. 'Speak to Andrew.'

Jagiello had approached our cooking pot. Removed the lid, and sniffed. Martin sidled up to him; God forbid a stranger, knowing no better, should offer criticism of our cook. 'It's not as bad as it smells,' Martin informed him, earnestly.

'It couldn't be,' came the reply. He crossed to where he had tethered his horse – the creature gave a snort, as if to welcome him – I saw him opening his pack; when he returned he carried two squat bottles by the neck in one hand; and in the other, a pair of pheasants. 'Here,' he said, dumping this booty upon the slumped, if not slumbering, Saul. 'See what you can do with that.'

Our cooking pot lies pushed off to one corner of the clearing; in moving it, I contrived to tip the thing over – in the morning I foresee a patch of bare, of poisoned earth. Those two lie out there beside the fire; Saul is under the wagon, Lucy and Blanche, with Martin between them, cocooned at the other end of it; I (hunched in a blanket) sit here on one of our hampers. The lantern by which I write is growing dim, its candle burning low; I would have more light did I remove the candle from its prison, but we all have a great horror of naked flame. This wagon is our ark, our world, and so much of it composed of pasteboard, gauzy tulle, glue, paint, a fire would wipe us out. Henry and Alembert are just the other side of us, roofed under canvas. Sometimes I hear Henry coughing. He *is* old, he is certainly too old to sleep outside, yet will he let us tell him so?

I never saw such quantities of stars. I feel like the lone sentry, left upon the walls.

I have a cramp. I must move.

There, I heard it again. They are most definitely still awake. I heard their voices, a deep murmur, impossible to catch the words, I'm not sure that they're even speaking (now) in English.

There is an owl. There are things moving, in the woods. There is another world out there. I do not think that we belong in it.

A strange pair. Kaiser one almost warms to – affable, voluble, full of questions: How long had we been in Germany? Where had we travelled? What had we seen? Perhaps it was nothing, how he had helped our Lucy down; Alembert had not marked it, that's for sure. Martin had sat as close to our new companions as he could, as we ate, fascinated by them, spellbound. Fascinated by that damn great horse as well, he sidled close to it; the creature raised its head and took a lazy snap at him. 'Come away from there,' Jagiello commanded; Martin obeyed at once.

Otherwise, Jagiello has hardly said a word. As Kaiser talked, he only leaned forward, now and then, to tend the fire. He has another scar on his forearm, I saw that. Oh, there's something dark about that man, yes, very dark.

He's talking. Jagiello. Out there. His voice has a *basso* rumble, puts the hairs up on your neck; now *there* would be a good voice for an auditorium that would horripilate an audience most satisfactorily, even Alembert at his finest would be hard put to match it. What a thought, those two, Jagiello, Kaiser, costumed, motley, burnt cork, rouged, disguised, *acting*.

My candle is a ruined *Schloss*, in miniature, poised above a lake of molten wax. The wick is bending over, the flame it dips, it dips again, I think this time it's going out; God, what will I do, if I should hear them stir, approach?

—⟨∞⟩—

ONE GREAT ADVANTAGE of Rotwelsch – it sounds so blood-thirsty, even the most determined eavesdropper is deterred. 'Is he still awake in there, d'you think?' Jack asks.

'Who, Herr Andrew?' Zoltan casts a glance over his shoulder. 'So it appears. Too scared to blow out his candle, probably.'

'It offends me,' says Jack, 'that we should be so misjudged.' He lets himself roll onto his back. 'So,' he begins, 'you are over Madame Ava I see.'

'By no means!' comes the affronted reply. 'I practise gallantry, is all. If I cannot woo Ava one way, I will win her the other.'

Jack tries not to let the laugh escape, but he is unsuccessful.

Zoltan's tone grows sharp. 'If you say she is too old for me, we shall be comrades no longer.'

'She is too smart for you, I know that.'

A sigh. 'Yes. So I must mend my ways. I must content myself with gallantry, for its own sake. Besides –' (another sigh) '– a man may lie to himself, he may lie to his enemies. He cannot lie to his cock.'

A moment's pause, then Jack lifts himself up onto one elbow. 'You don't mean it.'

'With Ava,' comes the reply, 'I would be as a phoenix. A phoenix made of *iron*. But with any other women – soft as the dove. She is all I desire, Jacques. I knew it as soon as I saw her.' A pause. 'You understand not one word of this, I know. We all know it. Your heart is proof, as well as the rest of you.'

Right.

He has slept, these last few weeks, with his hand through the grip of his sword, as if he were intent on slaughter even in his sleep. The ribbon woven through the guard is fraying now; so small and fragile no-one seems even to have noticed it is there.

SCRITCH, SCRITCH...

...They did not kill us as we slept (writes Andrew Frye). I must admit, this morning, over-reading what I wrote last night, I am put to the blush. In the daylight, all is changed – and a day so fresh and clear that far beyond us, on the horizon, I swear I can make out the white-topped bulk of mountains. Kaiser, when I woke, was already up, he and Alembert were standing by the fire, rubbing their hands over its remains. In fact every gesture Kaiser made, Alembert aped it – the hand to the face, stroking the fine moustaches (the one), skidding off the naked upper lip (the other), the contrapunto stance, with hands on hips. Alembert's voice appears to have dropped a good half octave too.

It is often in this portion of day I find my Muse most willing to come to me. Into the trees I went, chose one, stood watering its roots, encouraged by the sound of the tumbling river behind me, and running dialogue, as on a scroll, back and forth within my head. I buttoned up – and walked straight into Jagiello coming back up from the water's edge, riding his horse, leading Kaiser's, and with ours following behind him in a line, obedient as ducklings. They looked unusually shiny, suspiciously as if someone had rubbed them down. He gave me a nod as he passed, but that was all. A strange fellow, taciturn, without a doubt, but I would not like to misjudge him, scarred and forbidding though he be. Besides, it was evident even last night, it is Kaiser who is in command, and he appears to have a liking for us – a most civilized man, if I am any judge. I'd like to know his story, but I doubt I'll have the chance to get it from him. Prague is a day away at most.

I'll put this by but keep it close, I think. I never know when and what amongst my scribbled thoughts will come in useful. I am forever urging Henry that we might try adding *Much Ado* to our repertoire – well, now I have my forest, and a model, perhaps, for Don John too. Of course *Much Ado* has two great parts for women in it, so I would have to don a gown, but then I've not much of a beard, I can speak high, I have done such parts before. I also have, so Blanche informed me once, a woman's arse. It cut me to the quick.

Blanche would make a lovely Beatrice. Certainly a better actress than a cook.

Henry would not hear of it, of course. A woman on the stage? A shame. If she were Beatrice, I might play Benedick.

I am of course in love with Blanche. I never used to be; indeed it is a mystery to me how my fascination – even, I confess it, my fear of her – changed like the chameleon and became this ache, this fire. Yes, the *how* is a mystery, but I can tell you to the minute *when*: it was in Regensburg, after the father had left us, poor man. We were all much affected by his speech (Lucy, indeed, was in tears), and I turned to Blanche and said, 'That was so sad a story,' at which she, turning on me, replied, 'Was it? Evil was done, the evil-doers went unpunished. It happens everywhere, a hundred times a day. It was a *pointless* story.' And as a parting shot, 'No doubt you will put it into one of your speeches.'

I tell you, there is a rage in that woman as deep as the sea, and ever since Regensburg, I think I know why it is there. I don't know who he was, the London scoundrel who did her wrong; all I know is that it has become my fate to suffer with her. It is – oh, if this is love, it is torment akin to hers. It is *agony*.

I must add here unexpected news, received but moments past from Alembert. Kaiser, he reports, believes we might find lodgings in the same place he and Jagiello intend putting up, and, indeed, this season of the year, nowhere else. Prague being over-swelled with folk – its newcome Saxon overlords, those visiting the city for the Christmas markets, and then all those for the Prince-Bishop's great Twelfth Night feast, and without lodgings previously reserved, we risk finding none. But at the sign of the Black Swan (says Alembert), Kaiser assures him we will be welcome.

I am by no means as cheered as Alembert at this. I had thought one more day and we were done with our new companions. I must admit some of the sparkle of the morning came from this thought; now it has gone off. I am not at all sure what Blanche will make of it, either, though Henry, I am assured, thinks it a fine idea, most generous.

I think I will keep this to hand a while longer; I anticipate I may yet need to unpack my thoughts in words.

Oh. We are off...

POETIC LICENCE.

Andrew Frye of the Pilgrim Players does not of course commit all this to paper in one single go. In fact he will still be scratching away at it that very night. *Prague*, he will write then, *is a weary blur...* for now, however, he takes his place at the front of the Players' wagon, on his horse, and when Prague comes into sight at noon, he gasps at it, as do all of its visitors, as he takes in quite how completely it is two places at once – the shining castle on its hill, with the palaces of the nobility ranged all about it (that of His Grace the Prince-Bishop amongst them); and opposite, divided from it by the river, the Old Town – lower, darker, a place of smoke and shadows, pierced by alien spires. In between it and the Pilgrims, seemingly half the population of the world. There is, to begin, the Saxon camp, on either side the road, and on the road itself carts and wagons like the Pilgrim Players' own, plus herders, drovers, folk of every caste and die, some walking, some riding, some (the littlest) on piggy-back, and all moving slowly down the road together to the city gates, above which flies the flag, striped green and white, of Saxony. 'Christ,' Alembert demands, riding up beside him. 'This sea of folk! I'd no idea!'

'Our audience,' Andrew answers. He feels, of a sudden, buoyant. Why should Prague, this great city, not be good to them?

'Not *our* audience,' says Alembert, darkly. 'Look there. Damnation!'

Ahead of them at the gates, unmissable in their silver and scarlet, the wagons of Duke Leopold's company of players. *Well, of course*, thinks Andrew. Within a moment, he is utterly cast down. Duke Leopold's men, *ahead of us here even as they have been ahead of us right across this country.*

The scarlet and silver wagons are so large, they seem to swagger as they roll. 'I do think,' Alembert continues, bitterly, 'the gods might have let us have a moment more to relish our arrival.'

'Don't tell Henry,' Andrew says, lowering his voice.

Neither of them notices the boy sat watching from the bank beside the road, hands clasped about his knees. They do not mark his spiked hair nor his pointed fingernails, nor do they see him stand of a sudden, and head off at a run toward the distant woods.

PRAGUE, ANDREW BEGINS. On the bed behind him Alembert is already a-snore, while on a mattress on the floor Martin sleeps in the sort of flattened-out exhaustion only ever achieved by the young. Outside in the courtyard the Black Swan itself, beating the air with its wooden wings, squeaks a little on the chains that hold it captive. Hanging modestly beneath the board, the sign, announcing

STEFAN SAFRAN

(Then another line, but all blacked out, and followed by)

KARTOUNKA

The blacked-out line used to read *A BRATA*. And brother.
Stefan Safran, *Kartounka*, has had a bad year.

Prague.

Scritch, scritch, goes Andrew's quill.

...Prague. My notebook must forgive me; there will be no
elegant description of Prague. Prague is a weary blur. It took
us all day to gain the city gates, and even then there was a
moment when I feared we would be turned away. There I sat
with licences and passes stamped and sealed and all to hand,
but we all know bureaucracy – the incomprehension, real or
feigned, the necessity for bribes here and douceurs there, all
very real indeed. And this was such an interrogation as I had
never seen before, the guards beneath their flag of green and
white demanding what is this and what is that of every soul, and
being in that unpleasing wanton mood to boot, when sudden
power makes men capricious. But lo, just as we gained the gate,
a gang of wandering Gypsies descended upon it and proceeded
to make such a nuisance of themselves, what with mobbing the
guards and clambering aboard the waiting traffic, that when it
came to us, the sentry merely stuck his head in the back of the
wagon, squinted at us, squinted a moment longer at Kaiser and
Jagiello, and decided that he'd done his duty.

Prague itself is but the noise our wheels made on its streets,
it is torches guttering in the dark, it is shrouded passers-by,
an incalculable number of inns, and the most extraordinarily
rich, ripe odour of roasting hops. Turn your nose one way, there
it is, turn it the other, there it is again. It is drifting through
the window now. Henry has remarked that it reminds him of
his boyhood, spent in the hopfields of Kent; so strong is it, so
all-pervasive, I would not be surprised to find that river *made* of
beer. Saul has cheered up considerably.

The streets became so narrow that I feared our wagon
would stick in them, the last (the turning in here), we were

positively brushing the sides. We turned under an arch, it being by then so dark the only thing that told me we had, the sudden echo of our wheels, and followed our guides, or rather the slick rumps of their horses (the air was wet, it had begun to sleet) into a courtyard.

Now, how to describe this place? Or, indeed, our arrival here? I will do my best.

The home of our host, Stefan Safran, might be some segment of a castle, shucked off and plummeted to earth. It has a staircase rising to a door studded with nails, and the building itself is two turrets, circular, like donjons, rising up above on either side. We rolled into the yard, and to a stop. At the top of the stairs, there fluttered a torch. Kaiser dismounted, climbed toward it; we heard the tinkling of a bell.

At the top of the left-hand tower, a candle appeared at a window. The candle descended (we watched it circle down, narrow window to narrow window); the door was opened. A figure stood there, a figure in a nightshirt voluminous as a sail.

'Hallo, Stefan,' we heard Kaiser say. 'A long, long time.'

There was what I can only call an explosion of words, like the blast of a rocket, but in syllables of speech. Is this the language of the Czechs? God help us all, if so. 'Mother of God!' the figure said, but now, thank heaven, in Deutsch. Holding the torch, he – no, I should call him Stefan now, for he has proved a most accommodating host – came down the stairs. His flat feet slapped across the stones like fish. Revealed in the torchlight, his nightshirt sailed across a belly the size of a barrel, and his calves, in the nippy chill, looked each of them solid and un-nipped as salted hams. He went straight to Jagiello. 'Get down from there,' Stefan commanded, and Jagiello did, so slipping from his horse's back to stand there, motionless, arms at his sides, while Stefan played the light of the torch across his face. 'You owe me a brother,' he growled.

'And I can never pay you,' came the reply.

Stefan gave a grunt. 'You look tired,' he said.

'I am.'

Stefan raised his torch one more time. Another scrutiny. 'You don't look dead to me,' he said.

At which point Martin, so I think it was, sneezed.

Now Stefan turned to us. What spectacle we presented I have no idea – wet, cold, lost, utterly mystified. 'What is this?' he boomed. 'What are these?'

'Ah, now these,' said Kaiser, 'these are the Pilgrim Players. From London.'

'Londin?' Stefan repeated, as if the effort of stretching his mind that far might fell him. '*Londin?*'

'They have been travelling with us,' said Kaiser. 'They are going to play for the Prince-Bishop.' And then he winked. Stefan shot him a look of absolute disbelief. There is another thing will no doubt keep me from my slumbers, weary as I am (my writing arm is aching now, as well), why?

Yet here we be. Yet here we are. Alembert and I room together, Martin in the truckle bed at our feet, Lucy and Blanche the next room along; Henry has a room all of his own; even Saul has a bed in the stables, with the horses, ours and theirs. There was a little girl too, Danushka, I think is her name, half-asleep as we trooped into her kitchen, the poor child, but who served us a soup of marigold yellow, smooth as velvet, quite delicious. Some sort of oil upon its surface. Was it pumpkin? I wonder now. Oh, my brains are sagging, my eyes burning, I have wore them out. Prague and the Black Swan and their secrets – and this brother, what was all that? – they will have to wait until tomorrow.

TWO FLOORS BELOW where Andrew turns from his window and throws himself upon his bed, Stefan Safran bends to a cupboard in his kitchen and emerges with a stoneware flask and three squat, heavy-footed glasses. Straightens up, and sees on the table behind him there is now a small sagging pile of little canvas bags, all of them carefully tied and sealed. Stefan puts the flask down on the table, and picks one up. Weighs it in his hand.

'There are more with your name on them in Amsterdam,' says Jack.

'Thank you,' says Stefan, with dignity. 'I would sooner still have my brother.'

'So would we.'

The glasses are filled. '*Na zdraví*,' Stefan says. 'No, *Prost*, that's what you say in Deutsch, Zoltan, yes?'

Zoltan raises a finger. 'Kaiser,' he says, reprovingly.

Stefan rolls his eyes. 'Kaiser, then. *Zdraví a bohatství*. Health and wealth.' He lifts his own glass, tilts it to the unseen. 'To Sigismund,' he says.

'To Ziggy.'

'To Ziggy.'

Stefan pulls out a chair and sits, fixes his guests with his glare. 'What the *hell* are you doing here?'

'Not a question your brother would have bothered asking,' Jack tells him.

'Listen, Kapitán,' says Stefan. 'God knows I want the man dead as much as anyone, but it's not possible. The Prince-Bishop's palace is a fortress, especially at this time of the year. You think you would be the first to try?'

'John-George of Saxony opened the gates for us,' says Jack. 'And our friends out there are going to do the rest.'

'Them?' Stefan gapes at him. 'Those innocents? How are they going to help?'

'They are going to get us up the hill,' says Jack, sitting back. 'They are going to play for the Prince-Bishop. Hadn't you heard?'

Stefan looks at them in disbelief. 'But it is Duke Leopold's men who play for the Prince-Bishop,' he begins. 'Always.'

Jack lifts his glass; tilts it. 'Not this year,' he says. 'Not this Twelfth Night. *Na zdraví!*'

CHAPTER TWO

Sir Subplot

'We must talk in secret...'

William Shakespeare, *Romeo and Juliet*

ANDREW FRYE, WAKING.

Andrew Frye, waiting for his thoughts to shake themselves free of this dream of being churned like cheese, the paddle coming round over and over again with a thump... thump... thump like the tread of a giant. It persists. Andrew's hearing, also waking, informs him that the thump comes from across the courtyard, and that it comes in chorus with the sharper din of carpentry, and with Henry's voice, directing operations. He takes himself to the window. There is their stage, in embryo: a wooden platform, two uprights, a pole between them. Hanging from the pole, a canvas, and in paint upon the canvas to the left, the badge of Capulet, and to the right, the arms of Montague, and Saul, stood on a three-legged stool, even now twitching this backdrop into place.

Andrew dresses, speedily as he can. He clatters down the stairs while yet tucking in his shirt. 'Henry,' he begins, bursting out into the day, a day so brightly blue, so freshly cold that *whew!* at your first breath it finds the nerve in every tooth and sets them jumping. 'Henry, if you will – a word.'

'Aha!' Henry comes down off the stage, and throws an arm about his playwright's shoulders. 'What do you think? *Romeo and Juliet.* What say you?'

Again that same relentless thump... thump... thump... coming from behind wooden gates on the far side of the courtyard. Together with the thumping, Andrew hears the squeaking of wheels, then as if refined by the coldness of the air, the drifting scents of linseed oil and turpentine. *Kartounka, carton,* paper... what lies beyond those gates is a printing press.

'It was Alembert first put the notion in my head,' Henry informs him. 'But now I think it a most excellent idea. Tragedy of sweet simplicity. Couldn't be bettered.'

Thump... Thump...

'But Henry,' Andrew begins. '*Romeo and Juliet* has three crowd scenes before we are even beyond Act Two. There is – God help us all – a chorus. There's musicians, there's attendants, there's a riot, Henry, there's citizens of Verona, there's a – what's the phrase? – a fair assembly, servants, masquers – we have a company of *seven*.'

'Oh, you will find a way,' says Henry. He is beaming. 'Look to the plot. It is a trick all of you writers, how you let one story wrap around another. You must strip off those wrappings, Andrew. All secondary business, that must go.'

Andrew is aghast. 'But Henry,' he begins again. 'This secondary business, as you call it – these are the very harmonics to the tale! The moment where plot and subplot embrace, where branch and ivy cling most closely...' Is this not the very essence of the writer's craft? Is this not, in fact, what he is here to do?

Henry flaps a dismissive hand. 'What emerges,' he declares, 'that is what we need. Pure, clear, untrammelled.' The hand on Andrew's shoulder delivers an encouraging pat. 'You go to it. You will find a way. And speak to Alembert. He has some thoughts that may be useful. Useful, and dare I suggest –' and here a snicket of laughter (nothing puts Henry in better spirits than a new production) '– *germane*.'

'It is the death scenes,' says Alembert. So eager is he to share his thoughts with Andrew that he does so still abed, knees up beneath the blankets, hands clasped about them.

'The death scenes?' Andrew repeats.

'Exactly so. The death scenes. Juliet, d'you see? Has two of 'em. Perfect heart-wringers, the pair, any actor would give his teeth for. First the sleeping draught, and then the hussy stabs herself. Whereas Romeo takes poison. Poison, I ask you. Is that a hero's death? And dies the first of them. It's she wakes up, has centre stage. No, no, the thing won't do. Won't do at all.'

'You would prefer, perhaps,' Andrew suggests, 'if I should rearrange matters so it is Juliet dies first?' Part of him refuses to believe such irony can be lost, even on Alembert, but apparently that part of him is wrong. Alembert is beaming.

'Precisely! And only the once, mark you. Only the once.'

'If I should have her banished, then,' Andrew suggests, 'after the duel, for brawling. Would that suit?'

It is at last borne in upon Alembert that this may not be meant entirely seriously. He gets to his feet, his blanket wrapped like Caesar's toga round him. 'I think it could be done,' he says, magnificently. 'I think it would improve the piece immensely. And after all –' (and here Caesar pauses at the door) '– it is called Romeo *and Juliet*, y'know. Not Juliet *and Romeo*, not at all.'

Andrew sits at Stefan Safran's kitchen table, in the good light from its window. There is a quire of a paper, newly breached, before him, and the Pilgrim Players' copy of the Master's works in Folio upon his lap. Its binding gapes. Its pages hang. It represents exactly how Andrew feels. No, never was there story of more woe. To add to his misery, the thumping from outside now has a counterpart in the pounding taking place in Andrew's head. He has reread all five acts of the play, twenty-five scenes plus prologue. He has stared at its pages till dots jump over them like fleas, and his Muse has taken one look at the task ahead of him, and fled.

In the room above, he hears Blanche, fossicking for costumes in the hampers. She is singing to herself. Her voice is lower than Lucy's, and gentler than when she speaks. Oh, the distraction of it; she might be searching through his brains.

Thinks Andrew: I detest Romeo and Juliet, God-damn their eyes, beyond anything else our Master ever wrote. Detestable milksops, the pair of them. Do they know true suffering? The misery of *I would, but she would not*, of living, thus tortured, day after day? The heart that is ate out, and ever grows anew? No. They kill themselves, rather. Coitus and quietus is their lot. What have they to complain of? *Nothing*.

In the corner of the kitchen, Danushka, hearing his sigh, lifts her head from the plucking of the chicken in her lap. There is very little of romance or excitement in Danushka's life, and even less now her uncle Sigismund is gone, but she is of an age to be keenly alert to such in the lives of others. She sees the unhappiness in Blanche, now she sees the same in Andrew; she puts them together as simply as that.

At this moment, at the table, Andrew is having one of those conversations with himself. Be calm, he tells himself, sternly.

This is your craft; you know how to do this. This needs not one iota more of skill than Procrustes, lopping his guests to fit his bed. Craft can come later, for now, blunt butchery. Begin by cutting all those there merely to raise a titter in the crowd. A line through all comedy gravediggers, gatekeepers, yokels and the like. Which means no Sampson, Peter, Gregory, Abraham; and farewell musicians, officer, old man; Friar John, adieu!

Which leaves—

Which still leaves FOURTEEN parts for FIVE actors—

Andrew feels his thoughts slide into the dreaded whirligig. He jumps to his feet and is gone.

Poor gentleman, thinks Danushka. Also, the poor lady, Blanche, who was so kind to her. Seeing Danushka at her door, staring in amazement at the quantity of clothing in the hampers, the lady had beckoned Danushka in and explained: *Kostüme, wir sind Schauspieler, Aktoren, jah? You understand?* Actors? How exciting! And then, after Danushka had helped the lady hang up and inspect the costumes, and shaken out the wigs, and had explored Blanche's workbasket, and been greeted by her own reflection in the Pilgrim Players' mirror (polished steel, a yard high), Blanche had offered Danushka a Christmas gift of a Kreutzer piece, and not a worthless copper one, either, but silver. It's clear to Danushka, something should be done to apprise these two folk of their feelings for each other. Rip, rip, rip go her fingers over the chicken. Its head flops, beak half open; its limp little legs are akimbo. Danushka regards it sadly. Something should be done.

And then a thought like a comet: perhaps she, Danushka, might do it!

Outside, as well as backdrop, the stage has now acquired a row of lanterns at its front. Kaiser is nailing the last of the hooks for them into place, and Lucy is there too, running arpeggios up and down on her guitar, with Martin trilling along beside her.

Every so often she glances up at Kaiser; when she looks down, she is dimpling. Lucy is unused to attention – in her relationship with Alembert, it is always he who must be centre-stage; to be taken notice of (and so gallantly!) leaves her both excited and confused. 'Ah, Andrew!' Henry calls out, seeing his playwright. 'How goes it? You see how well we progress here. I see no reason why we should not have a performance ready by the end of the week.'

The end of the week? Andrew is appalled. He clears his throat. 'Henry, this is a drama with much *matter* in it. It is somewhat intractable. It may take a little time.'

'You have excised the minor characters?' Henry asks. 'All those there merely to raise a smile upon the vulgar cheek? Our Master never would have put them in had he had free rein, Andrew, his hand was forced by his paymasters.' A sigh. It is obvious Henry has the Holland family in mind. 'The drama is a cruel mistress, forever spurning the true suitor for he with the deepest pockets, no matter how coarse his tastes—'

'Yes, yes,' Andrew tells him, tetchily, 'Dogberry and Fart and all, they're gone.'

Martin, at the edge of the stage, sits up. 'How will His Grace the Prince-Bishop know to come here to watch us play?' Martin is endlessly persistent in this enquiry; seeding all their consciences with guilt.

'Peace, shrimp,' Alembert tells him, but now it would appear Henry has a better answer.

'Our good friend Herr Safran,' Henry begins, as the man himself appears at the door of his print-shop, wiping his hands on a rag. 'Our kindly host. Zoltan tells me that Herr Safran will print handbills for us. We will take them all around the city, and thus His Grace will learn of us, and after that, why our renown –' (a glance at Alembert) '– our renown must do the rest! Oh, and Andrew? I meant to say, we will need a text for the handbills, of course. I know, I know –' (the hand descends to Andrew's shoulder once again) '– one would think it was enough to write the drama, but these days, no, one must announce! So could you? When next you have a moment?'

Andrew looks at the hand upon his shoulder, and removes it. 'Henry,' he announces, 'I am going to take a walk.'

IT IS MIDNIGHT. The presses of Stefan Safran's print-shop have fallen silent, their thumping heartbeat stilled. The windows of his house are dark.

All save one. Up there, one candle flickers. *Scritch, scritch, scritch.*

I think (writes Andrew, in his notebook) *that I begin to see how this thing might be done.*

...Let me set it down: blundering out the yard of the Black Swan, I must have had as much muddle in my route as in my thoughts, for mere streets from its arch I was as lost as in a labyrinth. I was aware, as one is ever, of those shining buildings on the hill, but all about me was confusion. Prague is – Prague is—

Prague is two places, but the Old Town, it is *dark*. Dirt stains the streets and soot the walls. The brightest colours seem to lose their lustre. The streets are narrow as ravines, as bad as any London alleyway; in some you cannot even see the sky; and the crowd is all about you, swilling, milling, pushing you on. Only when a body of guards in Saxon uniform clanked past, a prisoner in manacles gibbering between them, only then did the crowd react, with a hissing and a drawing back.

Then you come up to the river and there is light and space at once. Before me was a bridge so wide one might have run four carriages across it. My feet rang out on stone, not squelched in dirt. A carriage did pass me, at that moment, heading to the shining castle stood there in the wintry sunshine on the hill.

Then one coming in direction from it. Not another soul on foot but me.

Since none appeared to tell me I might not, on foot I crossed the bridge. It is a mighty river runs through Prague, a great slow stately toiler, and it has been cold enough, I saw, for there to be pans of ice along its banks already. At the far end of the bridge, outside a little shop of knick-knacks for the traveller (I spied the shopkeeper, in bright embroidered headscarf, inside), a part of the Old Town lingered yet: a one-legged man on crutches, who held out his bandaged hand and cawed at me.

A note here: the language of the Bohemians is an impossibility. One sees it written up, but surely it must have been created for a joke. The letters have hats, they have tails and eyes; what any of it means a mystery. So as the beggar shuffled forward, poking out one crutch as if it were a hazel-rod with which he would divine my being, I made haste to say the one phrase in German we all have off pat: 'Forgive me, good soul. I am a stranger here, and have none of your language.'

He: Engleesh?

I (vastly surprised): Why, yes.

He: I haf Engleesh. Lee-sen. (Strikes a pose): *GEEF* off your charity, alms for ein soldaten. *GEEF* off your charity—

I (anxious to stop the din): Why, so you do!

What a sight he made. All three and a half of his limbs bandaged like a leper's, even the fingers, bandaged individually, and an eye-patch wholly obscuring the top right-hand quadrant of his face. Yet he had his *GEEF off your charity* in five languages, pat. And then of course I had to hear his tale. He'd enlisted as a boy in Styria, he said, in his local regiment, fought his way all over Germany in the first years of the war, up as far as a town on the Polish border. There a sudden attack by the Swedish (here, he spat) all but wiped out his regiment. In fact, he said, modestly, it was he saved the boys he served with, led them to safety. He enlisted again and found himself at D'sow Bridge (I have no idea how this would be spelt, I put it down as it sounded); but at D'sow, disaster. He mimed a cannon (very good! His entire body became its barrel, as it fired and rolled back); 'Aaargh! Aaargh!' he cried, scythed a hand across his knee, then clapped it to the eye-patch. He lifted its edge, pointed up beneath; did I wish to see? I demurred. So now, he said, he begged here, outside this little shop with its trays of maps and pennants and souvenirs, and (so I gathered) had become something of a landmark himself. 'I famoos,' he said, balancing carefully on his crutches and the remaining leg, before freeing a hand and striking himself on the chest. 'I famoos man.'

'Famous?' queried I, and he drew in his head, looked left and right, then told me his secret. He touched his one remaining eye with a bandaged finger, dropped his voice. 'I watch for the Dead Man.'

'The Dead Man?' I repeated, and he cackled, laid the finger alongside his nose. He was a sharp-featured fellow, and for all the sorry plight of his physical self, watched me in that unmistakable manner of one who trafficks in sharp practice too.

Suddenly pulling me close, he asked, 'You vant to see it?'

'Want to see what?' I was pulling away from him with some determination at this point – the fellow was feculant as a farmyard. (I say, that's good. I must use that again.)

'The hole,' he said. 'Two pennies, I show you. The hole where the war was born.'

Good Lord. It had never struck me till that moment that this was indeed the place where it all began. Protestant Bohemia (as it was!), and the Emperor's men hurled from the castle walls, thirteen long years ago – and then the army of the Emperor, vengeful, unstoppable, marching in. Frederick the Winter King, monarch for one season only; our own poor sad Elizabeth, his Winter Queen. Could any soul, then, have seen that it would grow to this – a war that has covered half the world?

My guide led me up the hill. Halfway, the castle loomed down over us, much like it frowned at such impertinence. A gate appeared, with turrets, and portcullis, and a lazy sentry at last wandered into view – striped breeches, green and white, twin to the guards upon the city gate, and levelled (as it were experimentally) his musket at us. My guide called out a cheery greeting; the weapon was lowered.

'I famoos man,' my guide repeated, reassuringly. 'You look there.' He pointed through the gate, where some part of the height of the castle wall was visible. 'There. Oop. Vun, doo, tree.'

And I looked oop, or up, rather. There – a corner window, high within the thickness of the walls. I had expected grandeur; this was inconsequential as could be; although its very smallness made the thought of the mob forcing the Emperor's men through it all the more horrible. One could put oneself in that window, imagine the catching of clothes in the frame, the desperate scrabbling of hands, the final scream, the drop.

And it happened as it always does. I felt it rising in me like a single note; swelling, growing stronger, more insistent by the second. Catholic. Protestant. Bohemia. Austria.

Two households both alike in dignity.

Habsburg. Wittelsbach. It could be any city, that's the genius of it. It's like the man could see into the future.

From ancient grudge—

Montague. Capulet.

It could be this.

Hah! By God! Every bell in Prague is tolling! It must be the New Year!

THUMP.

Thump.

Thump.

Also the satisfyingly wet kiss of the pad that inks the type; and the constant background chink-a-chink as the trays of lead type are sorted through; various small wooden taps and knocks as the type is set in the frame for the next job, and the under-the-breath whistling of the lad amongst Stefan's three apprentices absorbed in this essential task. Then the noisier goings-about the print-shop of the other two, one re-inking the pad, one presenting the paper, getting it onto the bed of the press; followed by the sound of the bed rolled under the platen, and that thump as the long handle lowering the platen is pulled around by Stefan himself. Back rolls the bed. Off comes the protective blanket, and there is your printed text – in this case, the precious handbills, which now, drying, decorate the print-shop in their dozens. Andrew has forgotten what a pleasing place a print-shop can be. Sadly he has also forgotten that it is the abode of that printer's nightmare, Titivillus, demon of the misprint, of all the ills, in fact, that so upset the orderly plans of men. For now, however, Andrew's spirits are high as can be. He is thinking only how beautifully black the ink, how good that paper-smell. And how magical it is: the Muse sits down beside you, puts her arm about your shoulder, begins her whispering song into your ear, and the blessing of her presence casts its magic over everything. Outside Henry strides across the stage like a man half his age; Saul is *sober*, Alembert rehearses his lines without comment or complaint; Lucy trills away like the nightingale. And Andrew has advanced upon his rewriting with a speed that would do credit to Gustavus Adolphus himself. 'Excellent!' he says to Stefan, as another handbill comes off the press, and then, feeling bold, 'Vin-ye-kay-itsy!' The language of the Bohemians is still a mystery to them all, but by dint of pointing and repeating, in interrogative tone, '*Wünderbar? Wünderbar?*' he has at least mastered the phonetics, in Czech, for that. Vin-ye-kay-itsy – very good! Emboldened, he tries something more. 'We take,' he says, in German, 'all over Prague! You make us famous!' Ah, that word. 'We give to man on bridge!' Andrew continues. There in the print-shop he does a little mime, hopping about on one leg with a hand over his right eye.

'Man on bridge,' Stefan informs him, patiently, 'is spy. Spy for Prince-Bishop.'

Andrew ceases to hop. '*Wirklich?* Truly?'

Stefan nods his head. '*Wirklich.*' And continues, in English, 'He vatch for Dead Man.'

And that is another phrase Andrew has heard before. 'Now who,' Andrew asks, 'is the Dead Man?'

Stefan heaves a sigh. 'Many year ago,' he begins, 'is Roma.'

Roma? Ah! A Gypsy! Like those at the gates!

'Is tell fortune. Is tell fortune the Prince-Bishop. Is say the Dead Man kommt, and send the Bishop down to hell. Is say at great feast. Three King Day. Epiff,' says Stefan.

'Epiff?'

Mentally, Stefan rolls his eyes. These godless English! 'Twelve Night,' he says.

'Twelfth Night?' asks Andrew. 'As in next week, Twelfth Night?'

'*Ja wohl.* And the Prince-Bishop much fear. So every year all strangers search, and many guard, and no man near him is to carry sword or pistol.' Stefan wonders if he might elaborate: the Prince-Bishop's fury; the years the young Roma then spent imprisoned beneath the Prince-Bishop's castle; the tireless petitioning of the young man's brother for his release, even after that persistence had cost the brother an ear. He decides against it. The English (all save the one woman, with her quick way of looking about) strike him as remarkably stupid; and the way they speak of the Prince-Bishop downright witless. The Roma are more godless souls, of course, the outcasts of the world, but try asking them what manner of man the Prince-Bishop might be.

'Well!' Andrew is saying. 'What a tale! What strange, dark superstitions stalk this city!' As always at these moments he feels himself akin to some glittering insect, feelers out, sensing the vibrations in the air. A story! 'Our friend upon the bridge,' Andrew begins, 'an old soldier. He had a tale to tell of his own.'

Stefan thrusts a basket of rustling handbills at him. A man less intent, at this moment, than Andrew might feel his absence was being encouraged. 'These,' Stefan says, 'is dry.'

So out Andrew goes, out into yet more bright cold sun. On stage, in flaxen curls new-dyed a Tuscan brown, Martin as Juliet paddles hands with Alembert as Romeo, while a pleasing crowd of the Black Swan's neighbours not only watch, but when Martin is done, applaud. The Pilgrim Players have become an object of much curiosity within the neighbourhood, and an audience is an audience wherever. Martin, speech complete, drops a curtsey; Alembert gives them a bow. And here comes Blanche. Ah, how Andrew's heart lifts to see her!

'I have been stitching sequins to Lucy's bodice till my eyes cross,' she announces as she comes up. She points to the handbills. 'Are those ready to go? Henry is all of a fret to get them out across the city without delay.'

'Oh,' says Andrew, at once. 'I will come with you!'

'Oh, no need, no need,' comes the reply. 'I have an escort already.' The smile grows wicked. 'Do you see? There by the gate.'

Andrew looks. He sees. *Jagiello!*

Jagiello. Andrew is a-seethe. Jagiello, that great – that *ink-blot* of a man. That shark, that brooding *crocodile*, he and his smile and his way of moving about so you never know he is behind you till he is; Jagiello, who even now escorts his Blanche about this city; Jagiello, who had turned that beaked profile of his down to Blanche as they walked out of the gate, and said something to her that made her sparkle with amusement; Jagiello, damn him, who – who—

There is a knock upon his door. Andrew has stewed up here by himself all afternoon, he is not of a humour for company. 'Bugger *off*,' he shouts, but when the door opens, there is the lady herself. Returned unharmed, and sparkling still. 'Andrew,' she says. 'Do I have a tale for you!'

───❧❦❧───

AND NOW PRAGUE lies in darkness, awaiting the many chimes of midnight, one of the first of the year, by the still-newish calendar of Pope Gregory. And here sits Andrew, at his window. *Scritch, scratch, scritch.*

So this, he writes, *is the tale Blanche had to tell.*

… Out they went, out into the city, my lady and her escort (damn him), and being Blanche, says she to him, right out (as I could have told the man she would), was he escorting her because he thinks her incapable to handing out a handbill? And he says no – and this is Jagiello speaking, *Jagiello*, Don John to the life – he says no, but he fears for the city if she and her scorn are let loose upon it unsupervised, and so he would come with her, if she will do him that honour.

It was at this point that I realized my Blanche, as she told me this, did blush. 'Oh, forgive me, Andrew,' she said, hand spread out across her collarbone to hide her colour, 'but you must admit, that man – he does have a certain *force* to him.'

Damn him!

'I am quite certain,' said I, 'Jagiello would have gone with you only because Kaiser told him to.' At which my lady, with a laugh, said, 'You think *Kaiser* is the one in charge?' And shook her head. 'Oh, *Andrew*.'

Anyway, says she, out they go, my Blanche and her strange escort, into the city, and what with her spirit and her pretty, pliant way of bending at the waist, and his – well, *presence* – none they gave our handbills to refused, or threw the bill away, and then Jagiello says he has a great curiosity to see the ways up the hill, to the castle, or at least, close as they can get. So soon enough they find themselves upon the bridge, beside the little shop, and on the bridge there is this mighty crowd of folk, all cheering and waving flags, and trundling down the hill toward them, pulled by God knows how many oxen and escorted by as many men-at-arms, there is an enormous bronze cannon.

'It was immense, Andrew,' says she. 'It must have been twenty feet long if it was a yard. I asked where was it being taken – *Wo, wohin*, you know, as best I could – and it seems it is being sent as a gift from the Prince-Bishop to John-George of Saxony. Andrew, I tell you, this thing – I saw down inside its maw, and truly, you could have lost two hogshead barrels in there, side by side. And the name they have for it, Andrew, you will never guess – *Vainglory* – that's what the thing is called. Vainglory!

'But,' she said, 'what I truly came to tell you happened after. The cannon trundled past us on its way, and the crowd, all cheering, fell in behind the men-at-arms, and set off after, all a-waving of their green and white flags, until Jagiello and I were the only souls left upon the bridge – and there, on the opposite side of the road, there was your one-legged friend Herr Geef Off! And he stares, and then he points, and then he shrieks – he positively *shrieks*, Andrew – "YOU! GOD A-MIGHTY, YOU!"

'And then,' says my lady, 'your Herr Geef Off undoes some string or other at his waist, the missing half of his leg appears beneath him and the rogue takes himself off as fast as his two legs will carry him.'

I never heard her laugh so merry as she did describing it to me.

'And the most extraordinary thing, Andrew,' says Blanche, 'is that other than myself and Jagiello, there was no-one else on that bridge at all. So, Sir Subplot,' says she, eyes again all a-sparkle, 'what are we to make of that?'

I know what I make of it. No good at all, is what I make. A force, had he? Escort my lady, would he? And Herr Geef Off knows him, does he? 'And where is our Jagiello now?' says I, thinking, *I will have it out with this fellow here and now, tonight*, but Blanche replies, 'Oh, he is gone again.'

Gone?

'Yes,' said she. 'He saw me to the gates here, then he said as there was something he had forgot, and back into the city he went. That was the last I saw of him.'

Very well then, Andrew writes (*scritch, scritch*). He looks out from his window, over the darkened streets. Is he the last awake in Prague tonight? *Herr Geef Off knows something of this man, I am quite certain, and so shall I! I am determined, I am resolute! I will find him out!*

You will not escape me, Herr Jagiello! Tomorrow it is!

Also, it has begun to snow.

Andrew is not quite the last awake. In the top-floor window of the shop upon the bridge, another lamp burns late. The one-eyed (but not, as it turns out, one-legged) man watches the lamp as he has been doing this last hour and more, and finally concludes he must be safe. Nothing is moving up there in his lodgings. Viki must have lit the lamp for him and took herself to bed.

Well then, he will wake her. This is too good not to share.

He tiptoes lopsidedly up to the back door (no-one will ever know, he thinks, the pins and needles you must live with, with your leg tied up under your coat day in, day out), twists his key in the lock, makes his way upstairs. 'Well now, my little pumpkin,' he begins, as he walks into their room. 'You'll not believe what happened to me today—'

He stops. Viki, still dressed, still in her workaday headscarf, sits there upon a chair placed in the centre of the room, her face seeming to supplicate him for forgiveness. Behind her stands a man in a mighty studded leather coat, the real soldierly business, whose hair gleams like a candle-flame. And another – younger, skinny as a weasel, hair in these strange points, sat on their bed itself.

And a third. Who comes forward, smiling that same great smile of his that the one-eyed man remembers so well.

'*Guten Abend*, Matz,' says Jack. '*Fancy* seeing you!'

CHAPTER THREE

A Turn of Events

Scapino   Cap. Zerbino

'Titivillus: Here I come, with me legs underneath me!'

Thomas Hyngham, *Mankind*

'I KNOW YOU,' Matz says, sourly. 'Just you remember that. I know you.'

He too now sits on a chair in the centre of the room, although in his case with his wrists tied to the posts of its back. Beside him, in her chair, Viki is doing her best not to snuffle. Hell-fire...

'You think so, do you, Matz?' Jack is asking. 'I tell you, I was so much more reasonable a creature when we last met. These days I scarce know what I am. Now,' he says, crossing the room, 'introductions. This gentlemen here, his name is Kazimir. He is skilled at – well, everything another soul might baulk at, if you

understand me. The imp sat on your bed –' (he turns to Viki)
'– forgive him, Madame – his name is Emilian. He is skilled at
climbing. Up walls, drainpipes, over rooftops… you get the idea.'

He crouches down before Matz exactly as if (thinks Matz)
he were the one in need of help here. Those same God-damn
pale eyes, whatever he's done to the rest of himself. Fucken
unforgettable. *I remember every God-damned thing about you*,
thinks Matz. *The way you prowled about. The way you was always
in charge.* He glares at Jack. *What the fuck are you now?*

'One of two things can happen here,' Jack continues. 'You
can do as I ask, in which case I will pay you such an amount
that you and Madame Viki here – all your troubles will be over.
Or, you can refuse, in which case all your troubles will be over
in the other way.' He stands, places a hand on Viki's chair. Viki
gives a sob. 'Do you understand me?' he asks, looking at Matz.
'Madame Viki does. She understands. Don't you, Madame?'

'What are you up to?' Matz demands, with some sense that
saying *yes* at once is not the way to go. 'Who are you with? The
Saxons, is it?' He wriggles his wrists against the ropes. He'd
been so proud to own these chairs. Proper chairs, pads to the
seats, proper backs to 'em. *Hah.*

But this, it seems, is not a question with an easy answer. 'You
know, Matz,' says Jack, considering, 'at this stage of things I'd
have to say I'm working only for me. For me and –' and he
indicates the bruiser, Kazimir, standing there motionless, and
then the wriggler on the bed, '– for my men.'

'So how much are you going to pay me?' Matz asks next,
because this, of course, is what truly matters.

Instead of answering, Jack bends down and whispers
something in Viki's ear. There's a moment's silence, in which
Matz watches Viki's eyeballs go round as a sheep's. She makes
a sound like a gulp gone backwards. 'How much?' he demands.

Viki leans her head toward him. The snuffles and sobbing –
all have ceased, like magic. She names the sum. Matz stares at

her, then up at Jack. 'You are – you are—' His mouth, his entire
throat has gone dry. 'How can you?' he demands. 'How can you
have that much?'

'Oh, believe me, there could be a hundred such as you, Matz.
I could pay each and every one.'

Matz licks his lips. 'So what is it I'm meant to do?' he asks.

'You're going to help Emilian make sure our friends the
Pilgrim Players get to play for the Prince-Bishop,' says Jack.

Of all the requests that might have been made of Matz in
these circumstances, this would not even have made it onto the
list. 'An' how am I supposed to do that?'

'You're going to find Emilian some little window, or some
unlocked door,' Jack tells him. (At mention of his name the
weasley little wriggler hops off the bed.) 'Some small way in
amongst those buildings on the hill you know so well. That's
all. Then you will spend a couple of days here, in the care of
this gentleman,' says Jack, indicating Kazimir, 'and another who
looks just like him, who is even now waiting to escort you and
Emilian upon your little errand. I regret, we will have to keep you
tied up, because sad to say, Matz, I wouldn't trust you as far as I
could spit, but then it will all be over. You may open your shop
anew, you may get on with your lives, you may do anything you
wish, secure in the knowledge that you will never see me again.'

And now Viki is leaning toward him once more. 'And,' she
says, 'the gentleman is going to be paying *me*.'

WINTER SEIZES THE city overnight. Winter cleans it, numbs its
stink, freezes and most thankfully hides the muck underfoot
beneath a first soft coat of white. Little icicles hang sparkling from
the roofs; and every one of the few souls up and about so early in the
day is rosy-cheeked, where old Jack Frost has pinched 'em. Even
Andrew, lurking here in the Black Swan's yard, beating his arms

against his sides, hopping up and down before his toes benumb. Momentarily, his attention is taken by the smoke rising from the buildings on the hill, straight up against the blue sky, like a string. He is just beginning to wonder what might be beneath it, when—

'You're up betimes, Mr Frye,' comes the greeting, behind him.

Damn him, thinks Andrew, *how does he creep about like that?* 'Why yes,' he says. He squints. His interlocutor has the sun behind him. *Yes, the soft-footed rogue, of course he has!*

He squares himself. 'I thought of walking to the bridge,' he begins. 'You know it?'

'Prague has only the one,' comes the reply. Is it Andrew's imagination, or does the fellow have the gall to sound amused?

'Yes,' Andrew continues (fiercely determined). 'I made an acquaintance there. The beggar-man. It seems he thinks he knows you too.'

Nothing changes in that face. Not a flicker. 'Old soldiers always know each other. Ain't that what they say?'

From the top of the stairs, the sound of the bell. Alembert, already costumed, stands there. 'Andrew, Andrew!' he calls. 'To arms! The lists await us!'

'I think you're wanted,' says Jack, stepping away in the direction of the stables. 'Mam'selle Blanche –' (*Mam'selle* Blanche? thinks Andrew, in a fury. He has his own name for her.) '– tells me you will rehearse a swordfight today. I look forward to it.'

… *THE DUEL*, writes Andrew. *Good God, I have, I am—*

I know not what I am. One single day, and the whole world is upside down!

To begin at the beginning.

… the duel in *Romeo and Juliet*. When we have played it at the Red Lion, we have had much sport with this scene. Indeed,

last time we played it, as Benvolio and Mercutio enter, I had
Benvolio declaim, 'I pray thee, good Mercutio, let's retire / The
day is hot, the Capulets abroad,' only I had him say *Skinners*
for Capulets, d'you see, and it quite brought down the house.
Ah, happy days. And Alembert adores to strut across the stage
with sword in hand, it is his favourite bit of business, not a
doubt. Here, though, the day was very far from hot and we
had no Benvolio nor no Mercutio, neither; stripped to its bones
the scene has me as Tybalt, and Alembert as Romeo. I offer
insults, he replies, we go to it, I am stabbed, Henry enters as
the Prince, banishment is pronounced. The fight itself, our
rehearsal – well, it is nothing: left right, left right, clack-clack
of pasteboard sword on pasteboard sword, than back again right
left, right left; I shriek, I fall. I look up. Jagiello is there at the
front of the stage, he and Kaiser both.

'What the devil,' says he, 'what was that?'

'The swordfight,' says I, getting to my feet. I was as frosty as
the air. Was I about to explain my business to this fellow? I was
not.

'Romeo and Tybalt, d'you see?' says Alembert, behind me.
'They duel.'

'That?' says Jagiello. 'That was a swordfight? That was a duel?'

Next thing I know, both he and Kaiser have climbed
atop our stage. Kaiser takes up a position behind Alembert.
'Gentlemen, please,' I hear Henry declare, in indulgent tone,
and then, 'Gentlemen! Please!' for Kaiser has thrown away
our Romeo's cardboard sword, and Alembert, with arms
outstretched and Kaiser's own hands over his, now flourishes
Kaiser's rapier in my face. I pull my head back; of course I do,
and that voice rumbles behind me: 'Let's give them a fight,
Andrew.' Jagiello is there. Jagiello has my arms outstretched,
my hands in his. Jagiello places his sword in my grasp. 'Turn
your hand so,' says he, *sotto*, in my very ear, and there we are,
Alembert and I, Kaiser and Jagiello, each one of us held tight

to the one of 'em. And they – we – start to circle. 'Oh, I say!' I hear Alembert gasp.

It is – it is—

I think I hardly have the words. There was the feel of this man's body pressed to mine, its tension, its steel strength, its *force*, as Blanche would have it. Oh, by God, it is another thing entirely, compared to mine. There was the feel of his sword in my hand, the hilt in my palm (this little tickling ribbon tied about it), and held correctly, held aright, I tell you, these blades have no weight at all. They support themselves, they feel alive, like they strain at the traces, like they yearn. And a swordfight – it is not a left-right, right-left thing, it is not a back and forth, it is a whirlwind. It is a typhoon. 'Which of us triumphs?' Kaiser asks, and Jagiello, behind me, replies, 'I think that would be you,' at which Kaiser behind Alembert's head gives a mighty laugh. 'Now, Romeo,' he declares, 'this is a chance neither of us is ever like to have again. Are you with me?'

'I am! I am indeed!' Alembert cries out, and then to me, 'Have at you!'

I am side-on – we are side-on, I should say. They make their lunge toward us. CRASH! 'Gentlemen!' I hear Henry wail. CRASH again! We turn – my free arm is raised, yanked upward, I block (somehow) Kaiser's next blow, I force his sword-arm away, I arc my own blade in beneath. Alembert screams. (I am aware, dimly, that Stefan's prentices have come running from the print-shop, indeed our noise seems to be drawing folk from all over.) We part. Applause! Cries of excitement, applause! We crouch, both pairs of us, like great cats about to pounce, one upon the other, circling, circling – by now we are off the stage. How did that happen? I have no memory. Kaiser (and Alembert) comes dancing in. Another CRASH. I see both Lucy and Blanche in the crowd, I remember that. A sort of up down up, a-this-a-way, a-that, Alembert and I jerked back and forth like puppets – by God, that was close!

I hear Alembert give a *hah!* of triumph; I remember all those
rewritten speeches, all those complaints; my heart pounds; my
skin warms; my temper rises; I shall give him a fight! Tybalt
will not go down easy, not this time! CRASH! We push up to
it, blades above our heads, Alembert's face in mine – 'Stamp
on his foot!' comes the hiss in my ear – I do – Alembert gives a
wail, staggering sideways – 'Oh, foul!' Kaiser declares; 'Nicely
done!' comes the voice in my ear, but also from our gathering
crowd yet more applause, more and more, and cries of *Sanguine!*
as well. Now Stefan is there, Danushka too; heavens, there
is Saul, there is Martin, all yelling encouragement or – or
something. Now we dance our enemy back across the ground
CRASH CRASH CRASH – more applause! I look across our
crowd – my God, our noise must have drawn in every bully-boy
for streets around! There, a fellow with ears like the handles
on a loving cup, and a face like dried leather, hat in hand,
whooping; there a pair of lads with jackets so studded and
metalled they all but strike sparks from each other as they lean
in, yelling *Sanguine!* again. By now I know not who I am most
angered by, Alembert/Romeo, or the man who has me in his
grasp. He lifts my sword-hand, ready to stab, and rage pours
through me like strong drink. We twist left, they right, we
push them back; I see Kaiser and my puppet-master exchange
a glance; he bends me sideways, Kaiser's blade goes past my
gut – my God, my shirt is cut to ribbons! – we fall back. I am
done. Tybalt is slain. I am lying under Jagiello, on the snowy
ground, sword-arm thrown out beyond my head, and he, on
hands and knees above me, is laughing into my face. I feel his
breath. I see the merriment in his eyes, the lethal merriment,
you might call it. Everyone is laughing, but not I. I scramble
free, I stagger up. I am a-sweat, I am untucked, I know not
what I am. I see my lady, come toward me, eyes a-sparkle, and
she looks at me and in that look there is – there is amazement.
There is admiration. There is awe!

'Andrew!' she says.

At which moment, marching into our yard, there comes this square of men, like a Roman tortoise, shoulder to shoulder and halberds lifted to the skies, and all decked out in that unlovely combination of mustard and blood so favoured by His Grace the Prince-Bishop. Every soul in our yard rooted to the spot, upon the instant. Good God, we think, what have we done? What ordinance offended? And then from within that square of men, another elbows its way free. He brandishes one of our handbills. 'Eeeez this,' he begins, 'the Peeelgrims?' He has a look to him of intense annoyance before he has said a word. Also, it must be said, compared to his escort, he is quite a little fellow, even with the length of his brocade robe and the height of his fine tall brocade hat, which he now removes and begins brushing, like contact with something – his escort? Our yard? – had soiled it. 'The Peeelgrims,' he repeats. 'Players. Yis?'

It was Henry first came back to life. 'Why yes,' our Henry says, going forward, sweeping a bow. 'Yes, that is we.' Meanwhile, the brocaded one looks about our yard, and if anything, his annoyance seems to increase.

'You kom mit me,' he says, to Henry.

'Why certainly, certainly,' Henry replies. He looks over at the rest of us, panic in his face. 'But if I may ask, who do I address?'

'Magister Ieronymus,' the brocaded one informs us. A twirling motion of the hat, a sort of shorthand bow. A testy tapping of the foot. 'You players, yis? You kom mit me to Prinz-Bischof.'

'My dear sir!' says Henry, going backwards and forwards like a thing made of clockwork. 'Of course, of course, the greatest honour. But if I may ask – why?'

'Because I am steward for Prinz-Bischof,' Magister Ieronymus informs him, 'and because there is fucking *fire* –' (he really was most annoyed) '– and all clothes and stuff for Duke Leopold men is burned up, so there is you, and now you play for Prinz-Bischof.'

Imagine here, if you will, a sort of collective gasp from us all.

'And you play for Twelfth Night feast,' Magister Ieronymus finishes. 'And so you come now.'

'AND OFF WE go again,' says Blanche. Once again the open hampers, once again the sorting, folding, packing. 'And this time we leave our little helper Danushka. For which I am very sorry.'

From her side of the hamper Danushka gives Blanche a wan little smile.

'Just as I began to learn something of the language here too,' Blanche continues. 'Is that not so? *Jmenuji se Danushka. Jmenuji se Blanche.*'

Danushka's wan little smile grows more sure of itself. 'Moy nim ist Danushka,' she says.

'I too,' says Lucy, beside them, also sorting, folding, stowing away. 'I don't wish to go up there amongst all that great company. I shall be all a-frit, I know it, and my fingers will tangle. And Alembert will mock me. He will say they should replace me with a monkey.' She gives a sigh.

'And it will be back to Saul as our only help lugging the hampers about, I suppose,' says Blanche. 'No more Kaiser and Jagiello.'

'Oh, no,' says Lucy. 'No, they are coming with us. Stagehands,' and turns her own face away from Blanche's sharp eyes as she says it. 'But we will miss our little helper Danushka, very much.' Little Danushka, who has been so invaluable in stitching and mending and in the sewing-on of buttons; little Danushka who likes nothing more than to sit and go through the costumes with them.

Little Danushka of the mournful face, who has just secreted in the pretty bodice with its sequins a love note. Little Danushka, who can hardly believe she had the cunning to do such a thing. Of course she has hardly any English, but she wrote it out the best she could, and no-one fusses about spelling anyway. *Meine Liebe, yor King ist erwait du...* The bodice with the sequins is, she knows, Blanche's favourite, so of course she put the note in there. And she is certain that Cupid has given her enterprise his blessing and will see to it that she succeeds, because what else has he got to do? There, she thinks, as she watches the bodice folded and stowed away. The lady Blanche will find it, she will think it is from the gentleman, Andrew – all Danushka has to do is wait.

Oh, she does feel so grown-up!

CHAPTER FOUR

The Dead Men

'*First Witch*
When shall we three meet again
In thunder, lightning, or in rain?

Second Witch
When the hurlyburly's done,
When the battle's lost and won.'

William Shakespeare, *The Tragedie of Macbeth*

'A MOST NOBLE, CULTIVATED gentleman,' says Henry. 'Most noble. I am sure everything they say of him is true.'

He stands before his players, rocking on his toes. Were they less painful, in this bone-cracking cold, he would be rubbing his hands together with glee. Ah, if those vulgar philistines, the Hollands, could but see him now! Especially that upstart Aaron. He to give Henry direction! On the very stage of the Red Bull itself! But look at Henry Kempwick now. Triumph, triumph, all his dreams come true! 'Do you know, he did me the honour of conducting some of his business before me. The Prince-Bishop. With me in the room, I mean. Such informality! Such condescension!' Full of benign content he surveys them, his company, his children. In this moment, Henry feels a little like a noble patron himself.

They sit (or the players sit; Henry is standing) in the building in which they will perform, a building something like one of those enclosed courts for *jeu de paume*, so popular these days. It must be temporary, put up especially for the Twelfth Night feast, as it entirely blocks the front of the Prince-Bishop's palace (Henry cannot even think those words without a warmth coming over him almost akin to the pleasure of love), but it is marvellously well done. On the outside it is gaily painted: contesting panels of green and white, mustard and deep red, like the tent for a champion at an old-fashioned joust; inside it has a stage (properly sprung, and with wings, what is more), at the edge of which, right this moment, the Pilgrims sit, swinging their legs. Behind Henry there are rows and rows of benches, where the audience will seat themselves, on cushions. And at the centre of the front row, there is a great high-backed, velvet-padded throne. *That*, thinks Henry, *is where the Prince-Bishop will be.* He should pinch himself!

'And what does the man look like, Henry?' asks Blanche.

Into Henry's head there swims the image of the Prince-Bishop, who was (let's be frank) not at all the cultured aesthete of Henry's imagining; the cultured, *appreciative* aesthete with whom he had seen himself discussing all the mysteries of

Melpomene, the tragic Muse. Still, one must not judge upon appearances. A thespian knows that; none better!

'Oh, most venerable. Most – uh – august. You will see.'

The space echoes. Thin, wintry light shafts down through the windows (which sit as high as if they were a clerestory), and brings with it still a ghost of the scent of smoke, of the conflagration that had robbed Duke Leopold's men of the chance to perform here – *but*, thinks Henry, *what man can stand against the force of destiny?* Already he sees himself announced to some fine company at home: 'Henry Kempwick *Esquire*. His patron is the Prince-Bishop of Prague.' Perhaps even (good God! But why not?), perhaps even, like his beloved Shakespeare, at the royal court?

'But what did he actually *say* to you, Henry?' Alembert wants to know.

'Well,' Henry begins. 'He did not as such *say* anything. But as you know, the language of the Bohemians is an impossibility. And His Grace was at first in his private chamber, while I attended without – but then he came through, talking with this other gentleman.'

A gentleman most sadly burned about the face. Henry had done his best not to stare. 'Magister Ieronymus announced me, and then His Grace gave me his most gracious salutation. Most gracious. I bowed. I sensed the noble inclination of his head. Some men,' he concludes, 'some men can make the smallest gesture speak of everything.'

He sees Alembert and Andrew exchange glances, but again it is Blanche who speaks. 'And that was it?' she asks. 'No welcome, no enquiry as to what we were going to play? No comment, in fact, at all?'

'I am sure,' Henry replies, with some heat, 'those who find themselves selected to play for the Prince-Bishop are also *trusted* to present entertainment fitted to the occasion.'

'Of course you are right, Henry,' says Blanche. 'Words would have been superfluous, I'm sure.'

'Quite.' Does he imagine it, or does Andrew hide a smile? 'And he had this other business, don't you know.'

Martin pipes up. 'What was his other business, Henry?'

'Oh, some great thing about that mighty cannon, so Magister Ieronymus told me. As we walked through the Prince-Bishop's hall of mirrors, don't you know. Which is a wondrous room, I have to say – a hundred Henrys followed me, from one end to the other. But this, my friends –' (and now he does rub his hands together. How his knuckles crack!) '– this is hardly our concern. No, our concern should all be how we can make the most of this our marvellous opportunity. Don't you agree?'

'So what is it,' Alembert asks, 'that we are to play?'

'Why, *Romeo and Juliet*,' Andrew answers. 'Surely! We have the thing ready to go.'

'Oh, no, no, no,' says Henry. 'A simple romance? Such a trifle might entertain the Black Swan and its neighbours, but here, Andrew, here – dear me, what a mis-step that would be. No, here we shall have grandeur, here we shall have resonance!' He cups a hand to his ear as the echo dies away. Such an acoustic! 'Here, for these tragic times, we shall give them the greatest tragedy of blood the Master ever wrote! Here we shall give them *Ma* – here we shall give them the Scottish play! No, no –' (as uproar breaks loose all about him) '– I am resolute! We know the piece, this is the place and that shall be our play!' And he, Henry Kempwick, raises a finger, and with a mighty *harrumph!* clears his throat, and begins. 'Is this a dagger that I see before me? The handle t'ward my hand? Come let me clutch thee—'

'Damnation, Henry!' roars Alembert, on his feet. 'Macbeth is my part! You play Macduff!'

ON THE EASTERN EDGE of the noble palaces on Prague's remarkable hill, and seemingly almost forgotten by most of those who live upon it, there is a tiny crooked lane of tiny crooked houses. Houses so small they might have been intended for children to play in, no more – one room deep and with doors so low and windows so miniature even Martin must bend his neck to look out of them. It is here that Magister Ieronymus lodges the Pilgrim Players, along with the now so-sadly unemployed members of Duke Leopold's company, who with sour looks and angry whisperings make no secret of their dissatisfaction with this arrangement. For all the brocade robe and hat, it is Blanche's contention that Magister Ieronymus is pretty low down the list of the Prince-Bishop's servants, and has thrown them all together back here behind the palace because it is the only place available to him; anywhere else his writ runs not at all.

'But ain't we the centrepiece?' Lucy asks.

They sit at the window of the little house that is temporarily their own, in the best light it affords them. Blanche is putting the finishing touches to a pair of orange plaits for Lady Macbeth, who Blanche has decided as a Scotswoman must have been a redhead. She intends pinning them in two Celtic knots about Martin's ears, where, aside from anything else, they should do a splendid job of distinguishing Martin as Lady Macbeth from Martin as Lady Macduff, not to mention Martin as all three of the weird sisters, whom Andrew has rolled into one. She turns the wig around on her fist. 'Are we?' she asks. 'Don't it strike you, how nothing here is quite as it should be?'

Lucy frowns at her, perplexed. Lucy is threading ribbons of Saxon green and white through the lugs of the drum on which she is to rattle out the approach of Macduff's army. She strikes it with her fingers, *Tatatataa!* 'Not me,' she says.

Ah well. Perhaps it is only Blanche who feels this way. But even so – the Players are banned from the palace proper, but straying around its lower corridors, Blanche had been shocked at their shabbiness. Patched-up plaster, ragged curtains, the bubblings of damp, and in one corner what can only, from its size, have been a human turd. And this persistent sense of – of simply not getting the full story. 'Don't you feel it?' she had asked Andrew, only that morning, as he had scribbled his way through his rewrites.

Andrew had looked up. 'Hmm?' he said. He'd had that faraway look she knew so well, of one frantically composing in his head.

'Don't you have the sense that we are not seeing something here?'

'Hmm?' Andrew said again. A long slow blink, coming back to the here and now. 'Not seeing what?'

Ah, no matter. She gets to her feet. 'Are you ready?' she asks. 'Henry will be fretting!'

Outside, another dusting of snow. It adds a further gruesome touch to the blackened costumes, half-consumed by fire, of Duke Leopold's company, thrown out into the lane. But there at the end of the lane, a lad wearing the grubbiest mustard-and-scarlet doublet, making half-hearted passes back and forth with a broom. Does this mean the wreckage of the fire is at last to be cleared away? 'Good day to you,' Blanche calls in passing. He lifts his head. Poor lad – one eye half the size of the other. But he calls back, '*Heute Nacht, jah?*' Tonight, yes?

'*Ja wohl,*' Blanche replies.

'*Toi toi toi,*' the lad calls after them. Good luck!

Beyond the lane, what a frenzy of folk! The front of the palace is being festooned with bunting – yet more green and white – being hooked and nailed up into place from a forest of teetering scaffolding, obstructing her and Lucy's path. How could anyone keep track of who is who and what is what amongst so many? It's a relief to get into their theatre. Blanche hands Martin his wig, then slips in beside Andrew. 'How goes it?' she asks. On stage, Alembert declaims, and behind him, eyes closed, Lady Macbeth practises her sleepwalk. Saul lurks, as Banquo's ghost.

'Do you know,' says Andrew, in a whisper, 'I am amazed to hear myself say it, but we might in fact acquit ourselves with honour here tonight.'

'There's not a one of them,' Alembert declares, on stage, 'but in his house I keep a servant fee'd.'

'Very good, Alembert, very good!' Henry calls up to him. 'But if we might skip ahead, and rehearse Lady Macbeth's sad end, and Birnam Wood to Dunsinane, one final time? Saul, are you ready? "The Queen, my Lord, is dead." Do you have it?' A glance up at the darkening windows. 'And I fear me we are running short of time. We have but a scantling hour before our audience is due.'

'But the duel, Henry!' says Alembert. 'Macbeth and Macduff, remember, you promised. The duel! I would not waste such good tutoring for anything.'

'Yes, certainly, certainly. Although I would remind you, Alembert, of the Prince-Bishop's strictures on actual weaponry. We must not alarm our noble patron with our seeming violence.'

'Ah, the *duel*,' Blanche repeats, beside Andrew, low-voiced. No-one is near them, not by yards. Andrew, with one hand, mimes a miniature thrust and parry. Blanche covers her mouth with her hand. Her shoulders shake. It is the smallest thing, a single shared moment of silliness, but it feels to Andrew as if it has opened up some little door between them.

'You laughed at me then too,' he whispers, sadly.

'It was not mockery, I promise you. Only I had never thought to see you so impassioned, that was all.'

'You think of me as not passionate?' Of a sudden, Andrew's mouth has dried with nerves; he has to wait before he can speak again, but he senses Blanche waiting with him; he senses the moment he has longed for is as nigh as it is ever like to be. 'Oh, Blanche,' he begins. 'If you only knew. I put so many words into so many people's mouths, yet when it comes to you, I am completely tongue-tied.' His eyes hold hers.

Wonder of wonders, hers let themselves be held. He hears her say his name – 'Andrew' – low-voiced as before, but softer. Everything else – Henry, Alembert, Lucy in her sequinned bodice, lifting her drumsticks – is merely noises off. It is as if his and Blanche's two seats, side by side, have become the only place there is in the whole world.

Tatatataataaataaaa! The acoustic is marvellous, indeed. Lucy raises her arms to try it again, and a slip of folded paper flies from her cuff, twirls through the air, and lands at Alembert's feet. He picks it up. He unfolds it. Reads.

'What is this?' he asks.

Somewhere backstage, Titivillus weeps with laughter.

THERE ARE NO curtains on any stage known to the Pilgrim Players; there will not be for centuries to come, so if you wish to watch your audience arrive, you must apply an eye to a hole in the backdrop and squint. Which is what Blanche is doing now, at Henry's pleading, as Henry himself has other matters on his hands: to wit that two members of his company are in furious disagreement, with him and Andrew as a sort of living barrier between them.

'And what matter,' Lucy is declaring, 'what matter if the good gentleman did pay me court? If Herr Kaiser paid attention where others do not, what of it? If others do not, they have *only themselves to blame.*' A stamp of her foot.

'Now Lucy,' Henry begins, 'that is not helpful—'

'Hah!' Alembert exclaims. 'So you admit it! You – you Jezebel! You *jade!*' He rushes forward, but not with so much force that Andrew cannot hold him back.

'I admit nothing. I am innocent as snow. But I will not be accused like this! Blanche,' Lucy implores, 'you know I have done nothing shameful.'

'Of course you have not,' Blanche begins, turning her head. But only briefly. To her amazement, she sees Duke Leopold's company, in its entirety, seating themselves on the benches at the back of the hall. What are they doing here?

'Don't you appeal to her!' she hears Alembert declaring, as he struggles with Andrew. 'She is as unnatural as you. You, you lickerish *viper*, and she frigid as a polar bear!'

Andrew drops his arms. 'And with that,' he says, 'you are on your own.'

'Henry!' Alembert wails. He seems to realize he has gone too far. 'Henry, Macbeth is betrayed! He is traduced!' He has taken the crown from his head, thrown it to the floor. Now he steps forward. The crown crunches underfoot.

There are no lights backstage. If repairs cannot be conducted in the auditorium (and now they cannot be, for the auditorium is full), the nearest place is outside, where flaming torches have been placed to light the way in, and where Blanche now stands, attempting to bend Alembert's crown back into shape. It is bitter cold; she intends giving this no more than another minute of her time. *Be damned to Alembert*, she thinks. *I should make this fit tight enough to scalp him.* But then she remembers Andrew, and surprises herself with a smile. What a strange moment that had been, as they sat together. Strange, but not – not unpleasant, not at all. Might there be another?

The torches flare and flicker. Above her head, the bunting stirs in the chilly darkness. She glances up. So much of it, good Lord! And what is that other sound she hears, under her feet? Someone moving something about in a cellar, perhaps?

The small sound is eclipsed. Inside, a great blare of trumpets announces the arrival of the Prince-Bishop of Prague.

Blanche's way back in is out of sight, all a-ways around behind the theatre's canvas walls. What a fragile skin, she thinks, dividing the two worlds. In one, golden torchlight, carpets, cushions; bright-coloured silks, rich jewellery; the well-fed guests, complacent, waiting for the evening's entertainment to begin; while hidden away out here, heaps of frozen mud, ends of rope, broken benches, all furred with white. Now wooden steps. Now she is once again backstage, with the hazy light of the auditorium ahead. She hears Magister Ieronymus, upon the stage, introducing the players, the performance, and leading the audience in a first round of applause for what, unless Blanche's ears deceive her, has just been announced as *The Tragedy of Macbeef*. She sees Martin waiting for his cue. Lucy is peering through the backdrop. Blanche tiptoes up beside her, does the same.

There is a figure occupying that mighty velvet throne, with Magister Ieronymus sat smiling at its feet. It is wizened. It is sere. It is of the age when all a man's weight drops down, so that the sharp, peaked face – eyebrowless, almost sexless – sits atop a body that widens like a pear. The nose is like a rodent's. The eyes are a curious red-brown. *Bletted*, Blanche finds herself thinking. Gone beyond ripe to rot to something else altogether. 'That's *him*?' she whispers. '*That* is the Prince-Bishop?'

Lucy's only reply is a sniff. She strikes her guitar; a disunited chord designed to evoke whistling winds across some Scottish heath. From behind them, Henry's voice, pianissimo, but enraged: '*Where* is *Saul*?' and then Andrew's, in calming, eventoned reply: 'I have it, Henry, never fear.' Their thunder-sheet is shaken. Martin takes the stage.

Andrew has shifted upstream the speech of 'Double, double, toil and trouble' as a suitably dramatic beginning. Into the cauldron, from Martin's hands, go toad and snake and eye of newt. But the audience shift in their seats. They appear baffled. Blanche hears the low hum of whispered queries, the equally mystified replies.

'Hah!' comes the shout from the back of the auditorium. Duke Leopold's company, without a doubt. '*Englische kochen!*'

Enter Alembert as Macbeef, and Andrew as Banquo.

Riotous laughter from the benches at the back.

The witch makes her prophecy. Now we are in Inverness, in Macbeef's castle, or would be, if Saul were here to change the backdrop, but Saul's mysterious disappearance continues. Instead Lucy and Blanche must do it. More riotous laughter and that particular male roar as they struggle with its weight. Also, it must be obvious to all that Lucy is in tears. Safe backstage again, out of sight, Blanche reaches for her hand. 'What is it?' she whispers. 'What did Alembert say to you?'

'He said I was a pig,' says Lucy, collapsing against her. 'He said I was a fat-fingered sow!'

Andrew makes his entrance as Duncan. Alembert and Martin, the latter now bewigged as Lady Macbeth, do him to death. Henry returns as Macduff, and brings the audience tidings of Macbeef's elevation. The audience roars anew. The Prince-Bishop is rocking in his seat; he leans down, pats Magister Ieronymus on the head, Magister Ieronymus closes his eyes like a cat. Ah, these English! What ridiculous comedians!

Now Banquo must be slain, but there is no-one to do the slaying, First Murderer also being Saul's part, so Andrew, holding his side as if mortally wounded, staggers across the stage from one side to the other. Now the banquet. Andrew, draped in floss, reappears as Banquo's ghost, and receives the loudest laugh yet. Backstage it is as if time has stopped, or rather to the remaining Pilgrims it is as if they find themselves falling from one maelstrom to the next, and within the maelstrom, there is no bottom, no release. Alembert slaughters Macduff's family, and goes to his final meeting with the witches, or witch, rather, and Henry seizes Andrew by the arm. '*Where is Saul?*' His face is wet with sweat, his eyes are moist with desperation.

'Henry, I have no idea—'

'Find him! Find him! He is our Seyton, he is our Siward! Andrew, please, for the love of God.'

Behind Henry, Andrew sees Blanche. Her eyes meet his. It seems to Andrew that there are but two sensible sane adults left in all the world, and he is one, and Blanche the other. 'Very well,' he says. 'Very well, Henry, I will find him. Never fear.'

Saul. Off he goes, Sir Andrew to the rescue. Down the lane he strides. *Saul. By God*, Andrew promises himself, *if he is at the bottle, I will, I will*— 'SAUL!' He throws open the door to their lodgings. 'Where the devil are you? Are you in here?'

He stops. For a moment he cannot work out what it is he's seeing. The low voices, the two seated figures, sat here in the almost darkness; one candle, lighting their mirror, and in it the reflection of two skulls. One figure stands, the unearthly whiteness of the skull rising up the height of the mirror, then disappearing as the figure turns. 'Hello, Andrew,' it says. Hitches the strap of its sword across its shoulder. 'This is a surprise. What brings you back here?'

Jagiello. The beard is gone; the whole face has been painted white, with inky pits round those pale eyes. Andrew takes a step back, but the second death's head, Kaiser, has already closed the door. 'Oh, good God,' Andrew hears himself saying. 'She was right, wasn't she? She was right. It is you, is in charge.'

'What, Blanche, do you mean?' Jagiello asks. He comes closer. 'Now that,' he continues, 'is an interesting woman. Very clever. I thought we might have to do something about her.'

'You wouldn't −' Andrew begins (his throat has closed, he finds he has to swallow), '− you won't hurt them, will you?'

'What, your Pilgrims? Not a hair of their heads, I promise you.' He steps closer yet; Andrew, in falling back, finds Kaiser right behind him. 'We look after our friends,' Jagiello, or the man Andrew has known as Jagiello, is saying now. 'And you have been our friends, whether you knew it or not. We could never have got here without you.'

'No,' says Andrew, swallowing again. 'Good.'

'It is a shame that you won't see this,' Jagiello says next. 'It will be something, Andrew. We've learned a lot from you.'

'Oh,' says Andrew. 'Well. I am glad.'

'And we are very sorry,' Jagiello continues, 'that we have used you in such a fashion. That we lied to you, and treated you like dupes. Which you are not, by the way. Not even Alembert.'

'Oh, well,' says Andrew. 'He is a bit, you know.'

And Jagiello smiles, that great sharkish smile of his. 'And I am most sorry of all,' he says, 'for this.'

And swings his fist.

Let us return to the theatre, for there is one final act to come. We are just in time for Lady Macbeth's demise, but who will announce it? Saul was to do it, but now it seems they have lost not only Saul but Andrew too. Henry, at his wits' end, seizes Blanche by the shoulders. 'You must do it!' he tells her. He shoves the doctor's gown at her. 'You must go on!'

On stage, Macbeth cries how he will hang out his banners and defy them all. In the wings is Lucy, with her tearful face. Blanche dons the gown, sets her shoulders, Martin wails the wail of Lady Macbeth's bereaved maidservants, and Blanche strides out onto the stage thirty years before the next woman in English theatre will do the same. She glares at Alembert. She thinks of Lucy, and how Lucy weeps. She thinks of how she too was once left weeping, wretched, humiliated, desperate. Blanche lifts her chin and announces, 'The Queen, my Lord, is much improved.'

'Much improved?' says Alembert, blank.

'Yes, my Lord,' says Blanche. 'Sat up abed and is requesting breakfast.'

'Breakfast?' Alembert repeats.

Frühstück! some genius in the audience declares, and the first piece of bread is thrown onto the stage. It catches Macbeth on the nose.

They struggle on. The gales of laughter now are such that they can hardly hear themselves. In the front row the Prince-Bishop is positively rocking with delight, leading the audience along. There is the type of merriment that carries actors with it, and then there is this other sort, that glories in their misery. Now Henry takes the stage, with Martin gamely waving Birnam Wood over his head. More items thrown upon the stage – apple cores, nuts. There is the mighty duel of words, there is 'Macduff was from his mother's womb untimely ript', there is 'Lay on, Macduff'. Lucy, drum in her lap, raises her sticks ready to indicate with its *Tatatataaa* the martial activity taking place out of sight. She brings them down.

The thunder of a kettledrum explodes behind the stage: *BOOM-BADDA-BOOM. BOOM-BADDA-BOOM.* Lucy, with a cry of shock, throws her drum from her as if it were possessed, but the *BADDA-BOOM* continues. It grows louder still. It grows an accompaniment: the stamping, or perhaps the marching on the spot, of booted feet – of many feet. The stage is shaking. The audience at last is silenced. What is this?

Out of the wings they come, all with their faces whited-up like death's heads, pistol in one hand, sword in the other. The audience, for a moment taken aback, breaks into startled applause. Some of the more enthusiastic get to their feet. 'Bravo!' they cry. 'Bravo!'

The men on stage level the pistols at their audience, and fire. These weapons are real as can be. The volley is above the audience's heads, but of course the effect is the same as if it had been aimed at their hearts: blind panic. As one, they jump from their seats and rush for the doors, only to find the doors they came in by are blocked. There is no way out of the theatre but through the door back up into the palace. The men on stage have jumped down from it, bearing Henry with them. Henry has a topsy-turvy glimpse, for but a moment, of the Prince-Bishop's bodyguard bearing the Prince-Bishop overhead (did he imagine that? Surely he must have done), through the door to the palace and up the stairs, then on hands and knees, scarce knowing what is what, he finds himself carried forward by the shrieking crowd, forced up the stairs by the press of folk. Later, when the hurlyburly truly is done, Henry will learn that some of those of Duke Leopold's company had thought to run at the barricaded doors with benches – trust actors to find a prop – and that the doors had splintered, given way. With half the audience now streaming out across the courtyard into the night, his Pilgrims started calling out for him, but find only each other: Martin, Alembert, Lucy, Blanche, all four staggering outside to be met by Saul, in the wagon, fighting folk off with his whip and yelling at them to get aboard. Blanche begins screaming, 'Where is Andrew? Where is Andrew?'

Saul points down. Andrew is lying across the bottom of the wagon, completely insensible, and with a bruise coming up on his jaw like a bubo.

Meantime, where is Henry?

Carried along by the throng is where, knocked nearly senseless, pleading for help, when he feels himself lifted up once again and this time set on his feet. He is facing one of the death's heads. Only when it speaks does he realize this is Jagiello. 'Where are they, Henry?' Jagiello asks. 'Those rooms of the Prince-Bishop. Where are they?'

Henry can only point. 'And I did think,' Henry will say, later, 'whether I would or no. I did ponder that. But then I remembered how the Prince-Bishop laughed at us, and so I pointed.'

They pass along the corridor at the top of the stairs. 'He held me by my scruff!' Henry exclaims. 'My feet were dangling!' They hear the shrieking of Magister Ieronymus. Ahead of them, a door is closing. They pass from the corridor into the Hall of Mirrors. The flames of a hundred, hundred candles greet them, reflected back on either side. Jagiello comes to a stop. There is a long, long pause. Jagiello, dragging Henry with him, strides first one way, then the other, watching his reflection, seeing how it works, this strange effect, how one part of what each mirror catches lingers for a moment even as it passes into the next, then to Henry's amazement he says, 'I will be damned,' gives an almighty laugh, and they are off again, through the final door and into the enfilade of the Prince-Bishop's own chambers. One of the guard comes running at them. Jagiello produces a second pistol, fires, and the man folds and drops.

They go forward again, but more cautiously now. The tumult from the courtyard reaches them through the windows, but Henry, gawping upward at his captor, sees it register not at all. Another guard. Henry is thrown up against a wall, the man is dispatched. A third, but this one chooses the better part of valour and runs away. They are at the door of the room where Henry was presented, he remembers it well. They hear Ieronymus struggling inside. For the first time Henry hears the Prince-Bishop's voice. It is pettish, unexpectedly high, tight with panic, poisonous with rage. 'A curse on you,' the Prince-Bishop is saying, 'be *still*.'

Jagiello pulls open the door. Ieronymus runs out, and down the enfilade. The Prince-Bishop takes one look at Jagiello and runs behind a table. Jagiello throws it over. The Prince-Bishop hurls himself to the floor. 'Mercy,' he shrieks, 'mercy!'

Jagiello stands over him. He says, 'Does your God still know your name?'

'I was watching from the doorway,' Henry says. 'The Prince-Bishop is squirming, *squirming* I tell you, on the floor. Jagiello says, "Can you guess who I am? You know who I am. Say my name."'

The Prince-Bishop answers something, but his voice is so attenuated with terror, Henry cannot hear it. But Jagiello can. 'That's right,' he says. 'I am the Dead Man. I am the man foretold. I never knew it either, but we both know it now.'

The Prince-Bishop is silent. 'Tell me,' Jagiello asks him, 'did you truly think you could live as you have lived, do what you have done, and this day would never come?'

Now the Prince-Bishop is moaning, 'I have gold, I have gold.'

Says Jagiello, 'No, you don't. All you have left is your life. And I am going to take that too.' Then he lifts the Prince-Bishop up onto one knee, holding him there, even as the man shrieks and thrashes. 'Look away, Henry,' Jagiello says, and Henry does, but there is a mirror in the Prince-Bishop's chamber, and Henry is looking directly into it as Jagiello holds his sword over the kneeling figure and says, 'You have deserved this. You have had this coming to you for years and years and years. Do you know what it is, to open a window for a man?' He lifts his sword. He says, 'I am going to open one in you.'

And then—

Never once at this moment in his account will Henry manage to get the words out. Instead, when he comes to describe it, he mimes what he saw happening: the arm up, the open mouth. It must be hard to scream with your gullet full of steel, but the Prince-Bishop manages it. It is a sound that engraves itself in Henry's memory as if put there with a diamond-headed drill.

Jagiello stands over the body for some little while, long enough for the pool of blood spreading from it to enclose it completely. Then he sheaths his sword, goes to Henry, lifts him to his feet. 'Time to make our exit,' he says.

'Oh yes,' Henry replies, faintly, 'but how?'

'In the traditional manner, for Prague,' Jagiello tells him.

He turns about, with Henry grappled to him, and runs at the nearest window. Out through it they go. They fall, they fall, they fall… a mighty wallop, and Henry finds he is rolling like a boy down a meadow, rolling down a pile of straw and kitchen stuff and any and everything soft that could be found, just as the Emperor's men had survived their plunge all those years ago, 'and whether it was there by accident or by design,' says Henry, later, 'I neither know nor care.'

He sits up. To his amazement he finds he is alive and unbroken. He looks about for Jagiello, but the man is gone. Instead he sees Martin and Alembert, who run to him, seize him by the arms, and pull him with them to the wagon. It is Blanche, looking up, who sees how the bunting strung all ways across the front of the palace is starting to burn. But it is burning in a most peculiar manner. It is fizzing. And there is an odour of sulphur and saltpetre, and all of a sudden Blanche works out what she's looking at, and screams, 'Oh, my God, it's *fuse!*'

Saul points the horses' heads downhill, and down they go, folk streaming down the hill on either side of them, everyone from the fine ladies and gentlemen to the lowest kitchen scullion. At one point they see Magister Ieronymus, running as fast as his legs will carry him. And Blanche, looking back, sees the bunting form a giant death's head across the front of the palace, two staring eyes, the grinning mouth, and as she watches, one of the eyes opens and closes in a wink. Bursts of flame shoot from the mouth, then more from the windows of the cellars, and the Prince-Bishop's palace disappears before her eyes, in this immensity of red and gold, of purple and black. Edges of sparkling flame fall through the air, coming down to rest like ribbons. The noise is like a tidal wave, consuming all around it. But the Pilgrims are down the hill. They are on the bridge. They are galloping through the streets of the Old Town with this conflagration lighting the sky behind them, with people coming out of their houses to see, but Saul doesn't stop till they are through the city gates and out into the countryside beyond. Only then does Saul rein their horses in, with that blush in the sky behind them like another dawn. Andrew, propped against Blanche's arm, at last opens his eyes, looks up at her, smiles, says, 'My darling, let us go home,' then passes out again.

*

Scritch, scritch.

... A postscript. So there we were, the red of the Prince-Bishop's palace, yet alight but far off one way, and the true sunrise the other. We Pilgrims get down from our wagon, and watch them awhile, until we realize some of us are hungry, and some of us are cold, and some of us nursing our hurts, and there is nothing in sight for miles around, nothing but snow and a frayed dark line of trees. 'Good God,' says Henry. 'My children, my Pilgrims – what are we to do?'

'If I were you,' says Saul – I swear, I never knew the man so sober or so sensible – 'I would look to your take from the night.'

So we do. We lug our strongbox out from the bottom of the wagon, and we open it, and it is stuffed, it is *choked* with gold. As much as we might make in a year.

'An' I hope you realize,' says Saul, 'as I could'a kept all this for myself. Only I know what trouble awaits those who don't follow his orders.'

Whose orders? we ask.

'Why,' says Saul, 'him. Fiskardo. Or your friend Jagiello, as he would have it. The Dead Man. Didn't you know?'

We gawp at him. Says Alembert, 'You mean you did?'

'Of course I did,' says Saul. 'Knew it soon as I saw him. You think there's another horse like that in all of Germany? You think there's another *man*? No, I knew it right from Erlangen. Where it was you said as we would play for the Prince-Bishop, if you remember, and he first spoke with me, and made me part of his plan.'

'But, Saul,' says Henry, 'you said nothing. Not a word.'

'Of course I did not,' says Saul. 'First, he asked me not to, and he is not a man whose wishes you'd ignore, not without you're very tired of life indeed, and second, he paid me not to.' He digs in his pocket. 'This here's my portion,' says he. 'Your good health!'

So there you have it (Andrew writes). He who we all discounted knew everything, all along; we were the actors, but it was others in disguise, and our hero, for want of any better word, cannot have a name for he is dead. And now we, we Pilgrims – we are heading home.

Henry tells me I should write this up, make a drama of it of my own. He tells me his plan for his share of our takings is to use it to come to an accommodation with the Hollands; enter into equal partnership with them at the Red Bull. He says this tale of our adventures might be our first production.

I cannot agree. Put this on the stage, *no-one* would believe it.

CHAPTER FIVE

Vainglory

'... there appear two actions in the Play, the first naturally ending with the fourth Act, the second forced from it in the fifth...'

John Dryden, *Of Dramatick Poesie, An Essay*

ALL ACROSS EUROPE, the printing presses greet the year of our Lord of 1632 with their thumping heartbeat. News, good people, news!

The Lion of the North, that Alexander of our days, begins the year with FRANKFURT, MAINZ AND HEIDELBERG all held in his fist.

The Swedish despoiler moves against Bavaria and all of southern Germany. Woe, woe! SHALL ALL THE LAND OF GERMANY BE LAID WASTE, and made into a desert?

A great and extraordinary eruption of THE VOLCANO OF VESUVIUS, with fire and smoke as the mountain writhed in torment, and a cloud like an umbrella pine, so high it could be seen from Rome, black and evil, stained and livid… Woe to us, woe, for God has turned his face from us!

That notorious harlot, Bess Holland, is retired; her bawdy-house of sin, HOLLAND'S LEAGUER, IS CLOSED by order of King Charles, who sends his soldiers to besiege the place, but the women there empty their chamber-pots upon them and pelt them with such filth, even the cloths stained with their monthly issue, that they force the soldiers to withdraw beyond the moated gardens…

The TERRIBLE DEATH OF THE PRINCE-BISHOP OF PRAGUE, in all his pomp and pride, his household scattered, his house destroyed by fire…

IN HERTZBERG, IN common with so much else, the news arrives on horseback. It receives a deal more attention than would once have been the case, when Hertzberg fancied itself a centre of the world; when the war was young, when Hertzberg was both mustering place and winter quarters for army after army; but since then the war has moved on, as they do, as they must, and Hertzberg finds itself as hungry for news from outside as any other place. And where better for the news to launch itself in Hertzberg than from Fat Magda's, where so many folk gather to drink and sup and chew the latest from the outside world into gobbets too?

'Morning, little sis,' says Jo-Jo, dismounting (it must be said) with something of a swagger, since it still seems a fine thing to him to arrive here at Fat Magda's on a horse rather than his long-suffering feet, and if you were the heft and build of Jo-Jo,

you would think the same. Even if his steed is only Eberhardt
Rauchmann's old dray, and the true reason for his arrival here
no more than Fat Magda's weekly delivery of Rauchmann's
doppelbock beer.

'Morning,' says Ilse, at the door, in her usual slow way,
although she does look very well this morning, even to her
brother's eyes, she with her hair all curled about her cheeks and
drawn up into that tight glossy bun at the back, as *à la mode* as
any on the streets of Paris. As a finishing touch, Ilse also sports
a glittering chatelaine of keys about her waist, a chatelaine she
wears as proudly as ever officer wore his sash.

'They still abed, are they?' asks Jo-Jo, following her into the
kitchen and pausing to inhale deeply of its mingled odours of
salt-raised bread and roasted pork. He tilts his head upward,
to where Fat Magda and Paola must lie in the Land of Nod.
You'd not say they was getting old (you wouldn't dare), but
they are easing up on themselves. Eberhardt Rauchmann,
Jo-Jo's employer, is the same. In fact, now Eberhardt has the
duties of a burgermeister to keep him busy, he's talking of
having Jo-Jo take over more than just deliveries. There – yet
more news for today!

'I'm letting 'un sleep in,' says Ilse, and then with one of her
craftier smiles continues, 'Means I'm in charge, that do.'

'Ain't you just,' says Jo-Jo, proudly. Then he digs into his
pocket. 'When they wake,' he says, 'you'll want to show 'em this.'

'What is it?' Ilse asks. 'What's it say?'

'That's the Strasbourg news, that is,' says Jo-Jo, laying the
coranto on the table. 'An' it says plenty. You remember the Roma?'

'Ye-e-es,' says Ilse, but wary now. The Roma share a part in
memories she avoids revisiting at all, if she can.

'You remember how they kept saying how the Prince-Bishop
of Prague 'ud get his?'

'Ye-e-es,' says Ilse, again.

'Well,' says Jo-Jo, 'they was right.'

*

And on a fine frosty morning in London, Clayton Proctor, landlord of the Mitre, looks over at the table where young Mr Vanderhoof, and his friend that most reputable man of business Mr Rafe Endicott, and even that pious gentleman the Reverend William Watts, have just called for their third bottle at eleven of the clock, and the floor about their table all littered with copies of the latest corantos from abroad, and wonders what news it can possibly be, to have such quiet, well-mannered gentlemen in such rambunctious spirits so very early in the day.

And on a handsome street in Stockholm, an elderly lady leans from an upper window, and calls down to the aristocratic young gentleman approaching her door, 'Master Kai! Karl-Christian! Have you heard the news?'

And in the dining room of the Cardinal's Hat, Tabby looks out over the terrace, and the man asleep out there, on the couch she had set up for him, with its fine view of the road down into Annecy, and, turning to her daughter, puts the latest copy of the *Gazette de France* into her daughter's now ten-year-old hand and says, 'Take that out to him, little sparrow.'

And her daughter replies, 'To Signor Ravello? The gentleman who always seems sad?'

And her mother answers, 'That's right, little one. See if it don't put a smile on his face.'

THIS IS WHAT gold can do. It means you can purchase everything you and your men might need for a winter sojourn in the mountains: boots of Russian elk-hide, bearskin cloaks; rusk and cheese and air-dried beef and ham; oats for your horses; schnapps for those nights about the fire. It means you can scout out the mountain valleys as only a discoverer can do, until just above the treeline you find a fissure in the rocks, and if you twist yourself through it one way, and then the other, inside there's a cave, and another beyond that. It means you can store in it all your provisions; stack it with logs, from which to make all the Swedish torches you might need, to light and warm your cave with; and then you and your men, you make your way back to it fast as your horses can carry you. Fifty miles before the mountains come in sight, another twenty before you can truly say you are amongst them, and it's a gamble, yes, but your guess is anyone pursuing you – if any are pursuing you – will reckon on you hightailing it straight back to Germany. And once you are surrounded by snow unmarked by anyone or anything, then you're satisfied. Nothing big enough to be a threat to you can follow you up here, not from the army of Saxony, nor anyone sporting the Prince-Bishop's colours of shit and blood, assuming any of them would care. Assuming there's any of them *left*.

They spend the first evening sat outside their new home, round their fire, howling to the wolves on some nearby peak; one pack of wild beasts singing to another. In the morning they walk out into a fog too dense even to see the trees below.

They carpet the cave with pine needles. They hunt – snow-hares, deer, wild goats. Thor and his fellows find another, smaller hollow within the rocks, block the entrance with more pine, heat rocks on the fire and sit in there naked, while snow-melt drips down upon them and fills the hollow with steam. 'Domini, we stay here,' say Luka. 'We have everything we need!'

'Eh, not quite. But we'll give it another month or so. There's still those small fortunes with your names on 'em in Amsterdam, remember?'

And then one morning, maybe a week after they'd reached the mountains, Per is out on the scout for deer, and hears from somewhere below him the bellow of an ox. He circles down, and hears more. There is a road beneath him, far beneath, so far that his finger, tracing the line of it, blocks it from sight entirely. He settles his bearskin cloak around and beneath him, lies on it, on his belly, with his feet lifted up behind him, out the snow (one of the *Kapten*'s tricks), and waits.

He sees it first as a moving cloud of animal steam, steam like in their sauna. Faint shapes beneath it, brown and dun. Smaller shapes round them, quicker-moving. Men, he thinks, men on foot, and oxen. Horsemen too. And then this great, greenish log, out of scale with everything about it.

'Fuck me,' says Per, under his breath. 'That's Vainglory.'

None of them believe him, but Per is adamant. He draws a map out for them in the snow: here is where I was, here is the road, here are they, this was the cannon.

'*Zehr gut*,' says Jack. 'Then show us.'

So Per leads them to what had been his vantage point and shows them the tracks left down there on the road – the tracks of wheels, the shuffled lines left by the men, the horses, the lumbering oxen; and they follow Vainglory's spoor another mile or so, under the ridge of the mountain, eyebrows gathering hoar-frost from their breath, and there below them again, exactly as Per said, the men, the oxen, the cannon. Well now.

'Now that,' says Jack, 'is not the way to Saxony.'

They wait, their breath making a little fog of its own. They watch the cannon's lumbering progress, yard by painful yard. What are the men down there trying to do, pull a cannon over a mountain? Why?

'Thor,' Jack says, 'you and that little eye of yours. Scout up ahead, see if you can see what they might be making for.'

Thor heads off. They wait again. They watch the cannon. What is it doing here? What the hell?

Thor returns. 'There's a stone bridge, Domini. The road turns across it. That must be where they're headed. But why?'

'I have no idea. But I think we should find out, don't you?' He looks down – through the trees, over the aprons of rock, down to the small shapes of men and animals and that great cylinder of the cannon, its almost imperceptible, inexorable progress forward. 'And I think time for that thing to come to the end of its travels too.'

The bridge. A single arch, pinched between the sides of the ravine; and the ravine itself – narrow but deep, like so many in this land-scape; and the river tumbling around down there at the bottom.

So, Jack thinks. *Viktor, here is your gun, here is Vainglory. What would you have us do?*

Nothing but boundless silence. Maybe that means Viktor is resting easy.

Sixteen oxen to drag its weight this far, twenty men on foot, three on horseback, urging them on. And it's another day of fog, thick fog, the breath of some sleeping giant, wafting up on either side of the bridge, breaking over it like cresting waves. The noise of the river is swaddled. The trees drip, the oxen strain and groan, the men curse, the horses skitter.

You should be listening to what those horses are trying to tell you, thinks Jack, aloft on M'sieu, back amongst the trees. He strips the gloves from his hands, raises them to his mouth, and whistles that soft warbling note – we're ready.

From the far side of the bridge, Zoltan's whistle in reply.

This will be so easy it is almost indecent.

Luka – bootless, feet and legs lagged like a peasant's, blanket tied about his shoulders, hat tied down round his head – Luka, who is such a bantam no-one could see a threat in him if they tried – shuffles along the bridge and stops, apparently open-mouthed at the sight of Vainglory and her escort. Possibly even a tad weak in the head (these mountain folk!), so stark is his amazement. The troopers pass him by as if he were invisible. The oxen pass, in pairs. As the last pair pass, Luka darts forward, pulls at the pin on the nearest wheel of the gun carriage. Will it shift? Will it give?

Yes, it will. The pin vanishes with Luka, back into the fog. There, you see? Smallest part, greatest weakness, always.

The oxen continue pulling. The wheels grind. The unpinned wheel, at each rotation, moves along its axle, nearer and nearer to disaster.

And now one of the horsemen notices something amiss. The one wheel on the carriage leaning out more than it should, the timbers of the axle protesting at the torque; the fact that the chains holding Vainglory in place are straining to one side. He gives a yell.

The yell that comes back is that of men under attack. The trees on the far side of the bridge conceal Ilya, Magnus, Ulrik, Per. They have a new trick: they have discovered you can both take cover behind a snowdrift and fire through it; then they race down between the trees to finish the job.

The horsemen gallop halfway across the bridge, stop, consider – one thinks better of it, turns his horse and runs. Thor takes care of him. A shot from Ansfrid on the near side of the bridge takes the next; the third, finding himself under fire from both sides of the bridge at once, throws himself from the saddle, flat to the ground. One pistol shot comes back at them, over the parapet of the bridge, and is returned tenfold. No more foggy blur of human movement after that. No, what moves is Vainglory. There's a crack, sharp as a shot, and the unpinned wheel starts to collapse on itself, the wood splintering, the iron rim springing free. Everything about this gun happens with mind-benumbing slowness: it slides from its carriage pulling timber and chain behind it; it rolls toward the parapet of the bridge, twisting, almost bouncing, under its own momentum – will the parapet be enough to hold it? No, it will not. The parapet sunders, stone falling from it, then more stone, then almost its entire length; going down into the fog as one, and Vainglory follows; hits the side of the ravine and rings like a cathedral bell, hits again, tolls again, a final third massive chord from its great bronze throat and then the double splash of parapet and gun into the river. Which folds over it, and it is gone.

Now this, thinks Zoltan, *this would be a subject for a painter.* This clearing in amongst the trees, the trees themselves, how they thin out toward the bridge, the sense beyond of space, of air, and in the foreground the white of snow and the single trail of red. And there his man sits, against the trunk of a tree, hunched forward, arms across his stomach. A couple of yards away, the Gemini, trying to look as if this is nothing to do with them.

Zoltan approaches, wary. Dying men are not predictable. Some depart in silence, some in tears, some want to take you with them.

The man lifts his head. One hand reaches out in entreaty. Zoltan comes closer. '*Peccavi,*' the man whispers, '*Peccavi.*' He stretches the one hand further out, and groans. *Peccavi.* I have sinned. What this one wants, it seems, is to make confession. Zoltan comes closer by another step, crouches down, into the stink of human shit. The man is holding his bowels in his lap.

Holding his nose, Zoltan peers in under the hat, into the face that is emptying itself of life even as he watches. There is something there... Good God. Under the dirt, under the blood—

'Signor del Ponte!' he exclaims.

*

It is not quite communion with the dead, but it has something of that in it. He closes his eyes and lets the faces come. He knows they are not there, but perhaps wherever they are, they close their eyes and see him too, and honour on either side is satisfied. *Now*, he thinks, *now, shall we leave each other in peace?*

'Domini?'

Ulrik lumbering up to him, through the snow. 'What is it?' Jack calls down.

'Domini, something down here you need to see.'

So he slides from M'sieu's back and follows Ulrik down through the grove of trees, and there, sat against one of the pines – dragged himself there, judging by the mess in the snow before him – is the corpse of a man, bloodied and with that stillness to it that is unmistakable.

Zoltan is waiting beside it. Zoltan steps forward, removes the man's hat.

I'll be damned. Jack crouches down on his hunkers. That polished smile, fixed in a rictus; those busy eyes, empty and in this temperature already starting to cloud. 'A shame,' he says, standing up. 'I'd love to have heard what this one had to say.'

'*Jah,*' says Zoltan, '*jah,* you would. Jacques, it was a ruse, this notion of the cannon going to Saxony. It was to be lost, here in the mountains, and the Prince-Bishop was to claim recompense for it from John-George. There was to be an ambush.' He points to where the road disappears over the bridge. 'Somewhere out there is a place with a hermit's shrine, and a tree with two trunks, and the ambush was to be there. You want to know who is to lead the ambush, steal the cannon, take it to the Emperor in Vienna? You want to know who Del Ponte was to meet?'

'Go on,' he says, although he already knows. By the twist in his gut, he knows.

'Carlo Fantom. Charles the Ghost. Out there, a place with a hermit's shrine and a tree with two trunks, that's where he'll be. This next full moon. Waiting. Jacques, he is there for the taking. He is in your lap.'

CHAPTER SIX

The Pigboy...

'The Mountains of the Giants, in Bohemia... are famous for three things: for their Signification and Prognosticks of all Tempests; for the rarity of Plants, Stones and Gems there growing; and for a spectre called Rübezahl, which is said to walk about the Mountains in the form of a Huntsman.'

Robert Morden, *Geographie Rectified*

HIS NAME WAS Pyotri; he was ten years old. He didn't count for much. Pigboys rarely do.

Pyotri's father and his grandfather had kept pigs, but now they and Pyotri's mother were dead, Pyotri lived with his brother, who had gone up in the world. Pyotri's brother had married Lenka, who owned a cow, two chestnut trees and a bit of pasture, and his brother regarded pig-keeping as beneath him, so the family pigs had become Pyotri's.

Pyotri liked his pigs. He admired their phlegmatic and philosophical characters, and their many useful qualities. They cleared the ground of dockweed, to grow beans on; and in the woods beyond the village, where he drove them in the summer months, their sharp-edged trotters kept the paths clear, and come the end of the summer they sometimes rewarded his care of them by turning up truffles for him to carry home in his handkerchief. In the winter a dozen or so would be slaughtered, and provide the only meat the villagers saw for months: smoke-cured hams, chitterlings, joints of salted pork to be soaked and roasted at Christmas, boiled brawn solid enough to butter like bread. The pigs were Mangalitzas, big and tough and covered in coarse wool, like they'd been rolled in glue and horsehair. Good eating; very lardy. More like wild boars than domestic swine. Get between a nursing mother and her piglets and she'd go for you without hesitation. Get between a sow and her suitor and he'd kill you, slice you behind the knee with his tusks and, when you fell, clamp you in his jaws and shake you like a terrier with a rat. It took skill to handle them, to lead them from one place to the other without mishap. The villagers were more than happy to leave Pyotri to it.

The fiercest of all was Boris, the prize boar. Boris was the height of a calf, and had tusks that rose on either side of his snout six inches into the air. His testicles dangled outside his woolly coat to his heels. His eyes were small and mean and missed nothing, glinting in their tangle of hair, and the calves of Pyotri's legs were a lattice of near-misses with Boris's jaws. But Pyotri reasoned any boar who could father as many piglets a season as Boris deserved to have his worst points overlooked. He was proud of Boris. Boris was one of the two most interesting things about him.

The other interesting thing about Pyotri was that he wanted to marry beneath him. He wanted to marry his sister-in-law's serving girl, Tink.

Tink's mother had also married beneath her. Tink's mother was the most beautiful creature ever born in the village, and it was a source of amazement that she had survived into adulthood at all; something that had arrived so unexpectedly could, it was felt, vanish just as easily, on a whim – and she could have married anyone. She chose to marry the blacksmith. He was a good blacksmith, when he was sober, but he was also capable of laying out any man pestering his wife, and it was thought this had perhaps been Tink's mother's reasoning, that she married him just to gain a little peace. After her death (it wasn't known for certain she had died, but all the evidence pointed that way), the blacksmith had been drunk almost continually, one night setting fire to himself and his forge and his cottage, all three. Tink wasn't living with him by that time, fortunately, otherwise he'd have immolated her too. The villagers had taken her away.

Tink's real name was Christina, but the villagers called her Tink because she had one leg shorter than the other and had to wear a built-up wooden clog upon it, with an iron sole. The iron sole ground against any pebbles it hit as she walked, hence Tink.

Pyotri thought Tink the loveliest thing on earth. She had eyes the colour of violets and hair the same softness and darkness as mink. Her skin was baby-clean, and scattered with freckles over the shoulders and bridge of her nose. In Pyotri's dreams these freckles tasted of cinnamon and nutmeg, and could be licked off, on the tongue. He described the dreams in detail to Boris, as he drove the pigs through the woods and knocked down acorns for them to munch. He would never have dreamed of discussing such things with another human being, nor in any other location but the wood, with its dark shadows and the whispering spaces between the trees. It had no roof or walls, but one could be more private there than anywhere else Pyotri knew.

The house where Pyotri lived, or rather where he was more or less tolerated, was strongly but simply built. The ceilings of the downstairs rooms were no more than the whitewashed undersides of the floors of the rooms above. Sound carried; one room opened from another; privacy was almost unknown. For this reason, in summer Pyotri slept, more often than not, in the hayloft above the pigs. In the summer the smell, if you were unused to it, could have felled a grown man, but Pyotri was used to it, indeed he scarcely noticed it any more and found his sister-in-law's sniffing commentary on his summer odour most uncalled-for. She'd have a deal less rose-water to strew across her linens without the money the pigs brought in, he thought. And it was common for the boys of the village who worked with the stock to sleep with their charges. Josuf slept above the few bony horses and mules in his father's stables, Henrick out in the fields with his father and the goats, and poor Marcus was required many a night to sleep rolled up on a mat surrounded by his mother's hens, a circumstance the other boys in the village considered girlish, and a poor reflection on Marcus's character, and for which in general bullying and insults he paid a fairly heavy price.

Pyotri's sister-in-law, Lenka, had sharp elbows, narrow pinching fingers and a nose whose end (as her husband could attest) was as permanently cold and wet as a dog's. But she was a competent cook, she could write her own name, and she sewed the prettiest linens in the village. Amongst the women of the village she was highly respected, amongst the men somewhat feared, but she'd come with her dowry and Tink, and Pyotri's brother, Egan, was widely regarded as having got himself something of a catch. Pyotri would lie on his back in the hayloft, while the pigs went about their piggy business beneath him in the dark, and he would dream of a day when Tink would be his, and they would have a house and piglets of their own, perhaps, and his own name would be uttered with the same respect his brother now enjoyed. The day when he'd give orders to his own pigboy, instead of taking them. Like all the villagers, his dreams were practical, cyclical and, one might say, local. There was good reason for this. The world beyond the village was a place of horror and chaos, had been this way as long as any of them could remember, and had been this way as long as any of them could remember because of the war.

The war had begun before Pyotri was born, and if anybody could remember who had started it, they were long dead now. All Pyotri knew was that way to the east there were awful things called the infidel, and way to the west there were equally awful things called heretics, and in between was the world he lived in, guarded over lovingly by the Emperor. (Pyotri knew there was an emperor, they prayed for his continued good health every Sunday in church, though if you'd asked him to describe what an emperor was he'd have been at a loss. Something, he assumed, rather like *Pán* Siegel, who was the richest man in the village, and perhaps a bit like God.)

News of the war reached the village with the pedlars in the spring, or rumours from other villages, or from the summer fair at Malenikov, the nearest town, the largest place Pyotri knew or could imagine, where Boris's progeny were taken to be sold. There one might hear of another town, taken and left smouldering, or villages like their own obliterated; of great men performing acts of monumental madness, of the treachery of the enemy and the mighty goodness of the Emperor. Sometimes the stories were old, though told as if they were new, sometimes they were new, and told as if they were fables, centuries old. No-one knew what to believe. So long as the war stayed where it was, and didn't come near them, that was all. And if it did – well, if it did, there was nothing to do but pray for Rübezahl, the Lord of the Mountains, to come out from under the mountain and put the world to rights again.

The Lord of the Mountains brought down the winter weather. He hunted all across the mountains on a horse that could fly, and his hunting party were the souls of the dead. He could shape-shift into any form he liked – an old bearded man, a great grey wolf. To those who lived in the mountains he was kindly, giving them sourdough-and-mushroom soup (Pyotri knew that when mist rose from the river, it meant the Lord of the Mountains was cooking), but if he asked for your help and didn't get it, his wrath could split the world in two.

Pyotri pondered nervously on the Lord of the Mountains sometimes, as he drove the pigs through the woods, tapping their backsides with his stick if they stopped to rootle too long in the piles of fallen leaves. It was foolish, he knew, to arrive on the outskirts of the village sweating with anxiety and in full view of Josuf or Marcus or Henrick, but he couldn't help it. It was just being in the wood that did it. It put strange notions into your head, as if the twisted black branches could grow through your thoughts; and strange and terrifying things could happen there.

His grandfather, for example, on the hunt for a fox for Marcus's granny, which had been worrying the hens when they were hers, had once gone so far into the wood he'd been on the very last and furthest path anyone knew of, and had seen lights through the trees, and creeping closer, watched under the light of flaring torches as an entire army passed by. He'd said there'd been so many it had took all night for them to pass, only a few miles from where his wife and son and village slept, oblivious. Then Josuf's father, when he was young, had been out hunting one sharp cold winter's morn, and found lying in the middle of the path that led over the ridge the corpses of two men, still locked fast in combat. The first had his sword thrust through the other's breast; the second had his sunk to the hilt in the other's belly; and so they had died, and so the freezing air on the ridge had found them, and so it had preserved them, frozen solid.

Then when Pyotri was a baby, a young man had come running into the village out of the tanglewood, stark-bollock-naked and mad as they come, babbling in an accent none of them knew that there had been a massacre. He'd run miles, judging by the state of his feet, so God alone knew where the massacre had been. They'd sent out men to the neighbouring villages, dreading that one would come back saying some place full of souls they knew had been razed to the ground, but in all the other villages life was going on as normal; though quite a lot of folk came back to see the babbling young man, wrapped in a blanket and sat in Mauritz Siegel's kitchen, alternately weeping and shrieking. In the end they sent him off to Malenikov in a cart. Best not to keep that sort of thing around too long. Didn't want to attract the wrong sort of people's notice. That was it, do you see, that was how you survived. Kept your head down, stayed close to home, kept your dreams small and practical and the tanglewood out of your imagination; prayed once a week for the preservation of the Emperor, and privately, under your breath, for the continued benefaction of the Lord of the Mountains.

And there was the fate of Tink's mother, of course, but that was still seen as too raw and recent to be the subject of the tales told around the fire of a winter's evening. Anyway, Tink might have heard them, and her feelings been hurt, or worse, her memories awakened. Because Tink was so very quiet, the villagers assumed that she remembered nothing, or very little, of what had happened to her mother. Only Pyotri knew that she remembered almost everything, and what she didn't remember she had nightmares about, things that fell on her out of the dark and left her weeping and wretched and Pyotri wringing his hands with grief. He and Tink told each other everything. Nor did anyone but they know that when in the winter months Pyotri slept indoors, he would wait until the house was quiet and creep into the cupboard in the attic where he slept, silently remove the loose board at the back, and like a homing salmon work his way down between the panelled walls of the house until he came to the framework enclosing Tink's bed, built into the wall of the kitchen beside the stove. And Tink would remove one of the squares of panelling above her head, and the two of them would spend the night together, Tink safe from her nightmares, and with her nightdress tucked round her, like a bag from which only her hands and head protruded, and Pyotri burning with love and afloat or afire or aglow with bliss.

And all the time the war went round and round them, like a hungry sea.

NOW WINTER WAS upon the villagers again. Pyotri led his charges out for one last rootle through the undergrowth, one last snuff of the frosty scents of the tanglewood; and Boris the boar took it into his head to go wandering. He had never done such a thing before, and heaven alone knew why he should have chosen to do so when he did, with the skies lower every day as they grew heavier and heavier with snow. Some porcine intuition, perhaps. A sense that some winter not too far away it might be his carcass hung up by the corners like the crucified Christ's, to drip its blood into a barrel. Anyway, off he went, and Pyotri stayed out till his fingers were blue, hunting and whistling for him, and when he came home was beaten for his negligence and for staying out so long. That night when he shared Tink's bed it was with a smarting sense of fury at the injustice of the world. 'I'm going to find him,' he vowed, 'if I have to search right through the wood to do it!' This was the greatest vow the children of the village had.

'You can't,' Tink said, calmly. 'He's gone.' She was an expert at loss. 'How would you find him again?'

'He'll find me,' Pyotri had declared in a furious whisper. 'He's my pig. I won't be beat for losing him.'

So early next morning, while the sky was still more dark than light, Pyotri pulled on all four of his pairs of knitted socks, his winter boots, his three shirts, his two jackets, his knitted cap, and a felt blanket for a cloak, and filling his pockets with food, he set off. The cold was not a thing to trifle with, but neither, where his pigs were concerned, was Pyotri.

He set off at a march, straight for the heart of the tanglewood, where the paths ended and any fugitive, porcine or otherwise, would imagine they must be safe. He walked till the sun began to make the frost drip off the branches, then he sat and made his breakfast: bread, bratwurst and cheese. Then he set off again. It was hard-going, but he let himself think only of Boris pushing and barging his way through here before him, making small oinky noises of relish at all the new sights and sounds and smells. It began to snow, but only very lightly, a dusting of frost crystallizing out of the air. Pyotri halted at the ruin that had been the blacksmith's house, with its chimney pointing like a blackened finger up toward the sky. He had never been this far before, and few, so far as he knew, had been further. Near here, where there was no more need for them, all the paths ended, all at once. Here he sat and ate his nuncheon – more bratwurst, somewhat moulded from its passage in his pocket, and another hunk of cheese. And here he also found his first clue. A fresh scar on the blackened stone, where something had stopped to strop the side of its head. Pyotri ran his fingers along the grooves. He had seen the same marks left around the wooden walls of the sty. He remembered how nosy the boar had been, always pushing and barging at things to see what they were made of. Boris.

Pyotri took a sooty timber from the ruin and continued walking. Every so often he would whack with the timber against the snowy side of a tree. Every so often he would stoop and examine the ground: little pointy tracks in the frozen ground (astonishingly delicate, considering the size of their maker), the small rootled holes where an eager snout had caught the scent of beetle or mouse. A fallen branch turfed out of the place where it had lain for years. 'You old pig,' Pyotri said to himself. 'You old bugger. I'll get you now.' The light snow ceased to fall. Cold seized the wood and squeezed it, as if it were squeezing out the air. It hurt to breathe. Pyotri buried his nose and mouth in the felt of the blanket and kept on. In the village he imagined first the ruts in the road would freeze and the water standing in them. Then the ice on the rainwater tubs would begin to support a soft fleece of hoar-frost. Henrick and his father would exchange glances and start driving the goats downhill. His brother would be splitting logs. Tink would be sent to stuff up any cracks or chinks round the windows, and people would stand outside each other's houses, blowing on their hands and stamping their feet and watching the big clouds in the sky and saying to each other, aye, here it comes, this is the start of it, we're in for a bad'un. Cats would creep in from under the floors of the houses, and declare their intention of living indoors from now on, thank you, with the present of a rat, and the dogs would lie in their kennels, one eye open, and their muzzles laid drooling on their paws. And he imagined also, any minute, a scream of piggy rage from the bushes and Boris charging out of them. He took a firmer grasp of his stick.

A definite path had been ploughed through the undergrowth. The hard ground held the impression of four sharp pig feet. The trunks of the trees bore the shredded marks of collisions with the boar's tusks. Every so often, Pyotri would stop and pick a strand or two of pig bristle from bramble or twig.

He walked on, very warily, another few yards. He stopped.

In the ground before him, dusted with snow, there was a bare black depression, where something heavy had landed on its side. In the ground around the depression, the earth was torn up as by a tiny plough, going round and round. And the earth in the hollow was thick and wet. And the snow around the earth was stained.

Pyotri knelt down and touched the snow. He was too late. The pig would never charge at him again, never raise his snout to the frosty air as he heard Pyotri approach the sty in the morning, never again mount a sow. Pyotri knew exactly what had happened here: something had killed his pig.

Pyotri surveyed the trees all round him with new respect; he crouched over the dent in the ground, and pondered. Boris had been a prodigy, a miracle of size and aggression. What, in the wood, was big enough firstly to dispatch him, then spirit the body away without a trace? Wolves? No, wolves would have feasted on the body then and there. A bear? Could there be a bear in the wood?

Pyotri stood up, wiping his hands. His face set, the way it did when he was scolded. Not even a bear was going to take his pig and escape the consequences.

Circling out from the spot, he began again, cutting in ever-wider circles around his own track. There must be something left – either a path where the body had been dragged away, or the head, or the trotters, or something. He pulled the remains of the cheese from his pocket, mashed it up with the end of the sausage, and as he walked, he ate. The brambles pulled at his cloak, and the cold stung his fingers, the trees raised their roots from the ground to trip him, but still he pushed and shoved and forced his way onwards. He stopped only when his legs began to ache so much his knees felt as if they could bend as easily backwards as forwards. And only then did he notice something else had been taking place around him, while he pushed ever further on. It was getting dark. Pyotri had no desire to come back to the village having poked an eye out on a branch, with the remains of pig or pig-killer or without.

It also meant he could no longer see his markers on the trees.

The wind was growing stronger. In the few places where it could stab through his clothes it hurt.

Pyotri turned and began to follow his own footsteps back. But the ground was a snarl of frosted bracken, and what he thought was his own trail might have been anything or nothing. After a while he stopped again and looked about him, and realized that he recognized nothing and that in a very little while more it would be too dark to see his feet. He looked up at the sky. No moon, no stars, all hidden by the clouds.

Pyotri tried to think. Generally he avoided hard thought – it always made his head feel as if his woollen cap had shrunk – but he understood now that he had done something staggeringly foolish, and that unless he thought extremely hard, and right this minute, a bad situation was going to become a great deal worse. He could feel the dead fronds of bracken crisping up underfoot. He was ravenous again. He felt in his pockets. His pockets were empty. 'Ow, fuck it,' he said. Even as he stood there the cold began to seep under his skin, and the dark sky above the trees began to toss and billow in the wind like a stormy sea, and Pyotri realized he was going to have to do something no-one he knew had ever attempted before. He was going to have to spend the night in the tanglewood. And what he needed now was shelter from the wind, and the freezing drop in the air and anything else that the darkness might bring.

Ahead of him there was a tree. An old tree. A hollow tree, its insides blasted out by lightning.

On tiptoe, Pyotri stuck his head into the hollow. He smelt owl – that combination of dander and old meat – and long-dead wood, and leaf mould, all collected inside. With some difficulty, much incommoded by his clothes, he scaled the trunk and lowered himself in. It was like lowering himself down inside the panelling, on his way to Tink. He collected some of the dead stuff together round him and, tucking his knees up to his ears, pulled his blanket over his head.

In the village they lit torches and left them along the paths, in case the boy should by some miracle be able to see them. The same wind blew them out. Pyotri's sister-in-law wept. She should never have been so strict with the boy, never. Her husband came in, stamping his feet. He wouldn't look at her as he stood over the fire, saying only that they'd search again in the morning, there was nothing more they could do tonight.

Tink lay awake in her box-bed beside the stove, listening to the wind as it roared, then stilled, then rushed back in again, as if it thought to take the houses by surprise. The clouds above ripped open, one by one, along their swollen bellies, and it began to snow in earnest, driven by the wind. By midnight, there was a blizzard blowing.

The worst fears Pyotri had ever entertained, even in the darkest parts of the tanglewood, were exceeded within minutes of the storm hitting. The tree creaked and moved as if it were the hollow mast of a ship, and the wind whirled about its few remaining skinny branches and tore at them. The noise of it was like some beast of prey, roaring away outside and trying to claw its way in. Pyotri raised his own voice in holy terror at the tumult raging all about him. He tried to tuck himself into a ball like a baby, arms over his head. He was sure that any minute he and the tree would be flung into space. The wind bellowed back at him, and tore at the tree again. He was too scared to remember the words to any of his prayers. He could hear something whistling through the air like shot. 'Holy Father,' he tried, and the wind hit the tree with such a whack he lost the words in a cry of terror. He tried to brace himself and the tree shuddered as if it were cracking open. *I'm going to die*, he thought. *I'm ten years old and I'm going to be dead.*

Snow is a warm blanket. Tiny plants and animals live happily beneath it, all winter long. The noise of the storm was deafening, but they slept through it all.

IN THE MORNING the villagers tried again, but were defeated. 'Drifts in there could bury a horse and cart,' Henrick's father said, coming back, wet through from boots to armpits.

Marcus, Josuf and Henrick followed him and the other villagers in miserable silence. 'That's it then,' Marcus said at last. He had a tender heart – maybe it was all the hours spent watching over things as daft as poultry. 'Poor Pyotri.'

Josuf nudged him. 'Look,' he said, pointing up at the windows of the house. 'There's Tink.' But when she saw them watching her, she turned away.

PYOTRI WAKES with his head pressed against his chest as if a sack of sand were holding it there. With his legs sunk into the leaf mould as into a quicksand. In a panic, still with the blanket over his head, he tries with his blind fingers to find the hole he had come in by. Reaching above his head, he punches two holes through the weight of snow that had settled on the blanket, pulling and pressing it back until, squinting up, he can make out the dazzling blueness of the sky and the brightness of the sun. Hauling and scraping, he gets himself upright, and sticks his head out of the top of the trunk. Then he wakes, truly, to a world transformed.

Every tree is buried to its branches. Every twig carries six inches of snow. What had been a wild wet dark tangle of bracken and timber and thorn is gone, buried under a blanket of snow whiter than the whitest linen Lenka ever sewed. Any movement, every tiny bird alighting, blows a breath of snow into the air as fine as a dust of diamonds, against a sky so blindingly blue it's like its paint is still wet. He hauls himself out of the tree, and rolls to its base in a drift as soft as feathers, as deep as a bed. He is alive, and alive in a wonderland, a magical kingdom. He can hardly believe his eyes. Where is the chaos of the night before? The woods open themselves to him in vistas of black on white, each with its path of snow, and the trees arch over them as if displaying themselves for choice. It doesn't matter where he goes; each way is as wondrous as the next. He wanders a few steps one way, then comes back and tries another. He begins to shout, then to laugh, because it is so beautiful there is nothing else to do. He feels like the first wanderer in a new world. He would not have been surprised to see his footsteps disappear behind him.

He is surprised to see the horse.

At first he thinks his eyes are playing tricks on him. The horse is a deep and dappled grey, and wears a saddle – an immense, high saddle – of crimson and gold. Its reins are two more solid stripes of crimson; it has golden tassels hanging over its eyes. It is a horse from a dream. And it's huge. It looks, with the saddle, ten feet high.

Its great dark eyes watch him from under the tassels. It's a gaze that in its contempt would have done Boris proud.

'Wo-ow-ow-ow-w,' Pyotri says, losing his breath in the single word, drawn instantly as any boy his age to anything large and potentially dangerous. He takes a few steps toward it.

The horse tosses its head about a little, but that's all. Plainly, it would take more than Pyotri to make it consider flight. It pulls a length of yellowed vine from the snow-shrouded mass of a bush, and chews it up, like a noodle, mouthful by mouthful.

'Whose are you then, eh?' Pyotri asks, coming closer. 'What're you doing here?' He likes horses. Anybody would like this horse.

The firm snow squeaks and sighs beneath his tread.

The horse, apparently noticing Pyotri properly for the first time, pauses in its meal and regards him straight on. It begins to make the most curious noise in its throat. In fact, if Pyotri hadn't known better, he'd say it was growling at him. He stops. He measures the distance from his hand to the crimson of the reins. He has a picture in his head of himself leading the horse into the village. 'No,' he'd say, 'I couldn't find Boris. But I found this.' And he'd put Tink onto it, and lead her round and round...

The horse moves its head, so from being front on, it is now watching him with one eye only. Pyotri extends his hand. He reaches a little further. An inch more. His fingertips touch the reins.

The horse swings its head, like a mallet. It catches Pyotri square on the side of his face, and so hard he thinks his face must have been knocked clean off, but somehow he can still see the snowy ground coming up to meet him, and the spreading darkness as it does.

He comes to with the coldness of the snow being forced up the back of his shirt. He tastes blood in his mouth and his right ear feels as if it is on fire. His eyes water with pain, and the water freezes on his cheeks. Branches jerk over his head, in a tracery against the sky. He is being dragged on his back through the snow, by something that has his feet clamped together under one arm. The horse is being led along beside him. What is this? What is dragging him? Where is it taking him? *Oh, God*, Pyotri thinks, *it's a monster. Don't let it turn round.* And closes his eyes, and the water runs down his cheeks a little more copiously than before.

Whatever holds him is dragging him uphill, he can feel that. Bars of light and dark fall across his eyelids as they pass under the trees. Then a place of thick uninterrupted darkness, and the feel of the snow beneath him is gone. He hears the monster urging the horse onward, and then with a sudden jerk, Pyotri's passage ceases. His heels hit the ground. He smells woodsmoke, and horse shit. He hears the rumble of voices. He has a sense of figures moving round him, also of being now not outside, but within.

The voices move away. As stealthily as he can, Pyotri opens his eyes. A dim curved space arches over his head, its limits undefined.

He sees the smoulder of a fire. He smells the juices of cooked meat, and his stomach gives a groan. He sees the shapes of men, of men who seem as tall as giants, stood back from him, consulting with each other. His eyes accustom themselves and the darkness drops back, as if it were being cleaned away, layer by layer, to reveal—

The glimmering curve of a pair of tusks. The brownish end of a snout. Boris!

No, Boris's head. Sat there, upon a shelf of rock, like a trophy, and driblets of sticky liquid running off the shelf beneath it.

Pyotri springs to his feet. He points, with an arm that shakes with indignation. He shouts, 'THAT'S MY PIG!'

CHAPTER SEVEN

... And the Warlord

'The life of man is a winter's day...'

John Ray, *A Collection of English Proverbs*

GENERATIONS BEFORE (pursued by the terrible heretics), Pyotri's ancestors had come over the mountains from Saxony. They had been miners and farmers and in a small way hunters, as they were now, and very few of them were tall, neither the work nor the diet favouring the making of long bone. You did best close to the earth, and thick-set, so the winter winds couldn't get you.

'THAT'S MY PIG!' Pyotri shouts. He hurls himself at Boris, or at Boris's remains, throws an arm about the pig's severed head. 'Boris!' he wails, gathering it to him. 'Boris!'

The giants are nonplussed. 'MY PIG!' Pyotri yells again, but as an accusation this time. 'YOU KILLED MY PIG!' There are more tears on his cheeks, but this time of rage.

Now they understand. One giant steps forward. His face is scarred, as if some iron-clawed bird has walked across it, but he hunkers down to make himself a little less giant-like, and points, first at Boris, then at Pyotri. *Yours?*

'Yes, MINE,' Pyotri says. 'Boris!'

The man points at Pyotri. 'Boris?' he asks.

Everyone knows how stupid giants are. Pyotri points at the remains of his boar (how sad and sorry Boris looks! His eyes all sunk, his snout dried up, and all that meat and muscle behind him, all that gone!). 'Boris,' he says. He points at himself. 'Pyotri.'

'Ah,' says the giant. '*Verstanden.*'

Verstanden. There are hard-grained nubs of German scattered throughout the dialect Pyotri and his neighbours speak; *verstanden* is amongst them. *Verstanden* – got it; understood.

'I was looking for him,' Pyotri says. The tears have dried, now he is all furious accusation. 'I searched all through the wood.' He waits for the man to register the monumentality of this.

'You,' the man says. He's talking as if he thinks Pyotri must be the simpleton. 'You live in mountain? You home nearby?'

'Of course I do,' Pyotri says. 'Right near.' He touches his face, his swollen cheek. 'And,' he adds, remembering, '*and*, your horse *hit* me.'

The scarred giant murmurs to the others, and there is a nodding of heads. And as they growl and murmur together, in Pyotri's own head the smallest seed of thought puts out a shoot. Pyotri takes off his cap, to give the thought space to spread its leaves about. Above him the ceiling of the cave curves away into a darkness. He says, 'Is this your cave?'

The scarred giant replies, 'Is now.'

I am under the mountain.

The scarred giant picks up a stick from the fire, and goes to stand by the wall. When you get used to it there is plenty enough light to see by, and look at that! The giants have been painting on their cave! Above Pyotri's head there they go, skinny little figures capering after deer and horned and humpback oxen, and even pigs, like Boris. Pyotri is amazed. But now the giant turns him round, so that they face each other.

'Pyotri,' the giant begins. 'You help us. We look –' (as he talks, he does a dumb show, scanning all about him with a hand above his eyes) '– for this.'

He taps the wall and then begins to scratch upon it with the stick from the fire. He draws a little dwelling, then puts a cross on top of it. A church? Pyotri wonders. The giant draws a tree – a cloud with a leg (they're not much good at drawing, these giants, thinks Pyotri; see, for example, how they've shown themselves hunting with spears and bows and arrows!), then adds beneath the cloud a second leg, so now the tree has two trunks.

The other giants wait in silence. They are still as statues. Thinks Pyotri: *This is a trick, to test me. To see if I will help or not.*

So he taps the little dwelling. 'Hermit shrine!'

The giant points – left, right, back, forward: which way? He hands the stick to Pyotri. So Pyotri draws upon the wall a line, like string, for the road. He puts a knot upon the string, taps it, says its name – 'Našemísto' – taps at himself again.

'You place?' the giant asks.

Pyotri nods. He continues the line of the road, up, up – he adds in the jagged points of the ridge, so the giant can see Pyotri knows that yes, you have to go right up, then over – then brings the line past the tree to the shrine.

'How far this?' the giant asks, tapping journey's end.

How far? And now, of course, Pyotri knows full well that he is only being asked to prove he tells the truth. His questioner must know how long it would take to get up to the shrine; none would know better. His sister-in-law employs the same tactic. So he walks his fingers along the road, to where the jagged points begin. For his audience's benefit, he mimes cold – *brrrr!* He mimes sleep, hands together, at his cheek. Then his fingers walk on, and there they are – the tree with two trunks, the hermit's shrine.

'Very good,' comments the giant. He stands there, hand to his chin, considering. The other giants make their low rumble, offering suggestions, when Pyotri's stomach joins in, so loudly that the men stop talking and stare at him, and one of them laughs.

He with the scarred face points to the fire, and to the pot sat in its smoulder of ash. 'Hungry?' he asks.

Ravenous.

The giants sit Pyotri down and put a wooden bowl into his hands. Lenka would never be satisfied with such a soup as this – it should have onions, it should have barley; a spoonful of sour cream never goes amiss; and of course it has no mushrooms nor sourdough – but it is soup, all the same, and has a fatty, meaty unctuousness Pyotri tells himself won't be thanks to Boris, but which no doubt is. He eats, tipping the bowl to his mouth, being careful to favour the untender side of his jaw. It is warm in the cave; as warm as in a house. The air is unmoving, and smells of wet rock and wet earth and he sits on pine needles, thick as fur. As he eats, he watches. He sees how there is another cave beyond this, where the horses are – he hears them move, and one of them occasionally gives out a resonant, imperious whicker, as if for no better reason than to hear it echo. He sees how the giants differ – some are younger, some are older, some seem to him almost as old as Egan. One is twice the width of the rest; two look the same; one has moustaches but keeps his chin clean; one has a beard right down his chest, in a plait, and ears that stick out through his hair. They have drawn on their clothes as well. Leaping flames; death's heads; serpents. There is one half the size of the rest, who catches Pyotri's eye, points to Pyotri's swollen cheek, mimes the way the horse had swung its head, then raises his hands as if to ask, *What can you do?* And they have swords. Pyotri has had a lifetime's acquaintance with wood-choppers and axes and scythes, but not with swords. No man in Našemísto wears a sword. No man in Našemísto has any use for them.

The man with the scarred face is standing over him. 'Done?' the man asks.

Pyotri nods.

'On your feet. I take you home.'

OH, THE BRIGHTNESS outside, it is dazzling. Oh, the cleanness of the air, the smells of pine and snow. Oh, the size of the horse, and the height of it, as for one breathtaking moment the man sits Pyotri up on its saddle on his own, before swinging himself into place behind him. 'Našemísto?' the man asks, and Pyotri points, and the man turns the horse's head and off it trots, with the snow mounding up about its knees like foam. The sun on Pyotri's face is warm as if he were sitting in front of a fire. He closes his eyes and the world glides past in yellow light. Unconsciously, under his breath, he starts to hum.

'What's the song?' the man asks.

So Pyotri sings a little louder: 'Sleep, child, sleep, your father tends the sheep...' It's meant to be a lullaby, but Pyotri and the other children of the village sing it with martial force, beating out the time. The man listens, then he says, 'I know a song too.' Above his head, the man starts to sing: 'A mighty fortress is our God, a shi-ield never fai-ai-ai-ling.' The horse swivels its ears and gives a whinny. 'He knows it too,' the man says. He sings on: 'Our helper he-ee ami-id the flood, of danger all prevai-ai-ai-ling.'

Pyotri has a good ear for a song. He starts to la-la the tune, and then the man goes back to the beginning and they sing it again. All the way down through the trees, the warlord and the pigboy, and the horse high-stepping through the snow, singing 'Ein feste Burg'. And then—

The snow is not so deep now; in fact you can see a path, and right across it, there's a chasm. 'We have to go round, here,' Pyotri says. 'It's the old road, it got broke.'

The man stands up in his stirrups. He looks up, to the right, where the chasm snags its way uphill. You can hear the water that broke through the mountain, tumbling away at the bottom. 'Round how far?' the man asks, and Pyotri points back up to where the trees thin out.

The man dismounts. He goes down to the edge of the chasm, and looks into it, and then across it, then comes back. 'Fuck that,' he says. Up he gets. Turns the horse's head, and they go back up the path a little way. Turns the horse about again, to look downhill, facing the chasm. The horse seems to know something is expected of it; Pyotri can feel how it is tensing, readying itself. 'You can't—' he begins, but then the man bends down over him, an arm about Pyotri to hold him tight; he shouts '*Yar! Yar!*' to the horse, and the horse surges forward beneath them. The world, the path, the trees come at Pyotri in a series of bounces, each bigger than the last. The edge of the chasm comes nearer. You could hear the water, if it weren't for the thud of the horse's hooves. 'We can't!' Pyotri shrieks, then 'Noo-o-o-o!' as they take off. For a moment he thinks he sees the edge of the chasm behind him, the little plants clinging to the rock, the thick green water below, the froth and foam, and then there is nothing ahead but air and sun and the blue of the sky. 'WE'RE FLYING!' Pyotri shrieks, 'WE'RE FLYING!' but even as he says it, they land, in a fountain of snow, the horse skidding, legs braced, the man fighting the force of the landing that wants to put all three of them in the snow at once, but no, the horse comes upright, snorting, shaking its head, and the man too, Pyotri clamped against him. Pyotri's heart is up between his ears. His face is like it's frozen. He can't end his smile, no matter how much it hurts his swollen cheek.

The man dismounts, pats the horse's neck. 'Good boy,' he says, and then to Pyotri, 'There. That was something, eh?'

The man walks his horse the rest of the way. Down from the mountain, out from amongst the spruce and pine, through the trees of the tanglewood, all the way to the ruin of the black-smith's house. 'What was this?' the man asks.

'Blacksmith,' Pyotri answers. 'It burned down.' It's not the whole story but it's close enough.

The man turns about and looks behind them, all the way back the way that they have come, right up to the far-off ridge, under which his cave is hidden. He says, 'Pyotri, listen. You can help us again. If more men come here, men like us –' (and he taps the hilt of his sword) '– I want to know. Put two green branches here, yes?' And he shows, with his boot, where to put them in the snow outside the ruin. 'Put them in the shape of a cross. We'll see them. We'll be watching.'

'Yes, my lord,' Pyotri says.

'And we're your secret, *verstanden*? You keep us to yourself.'

'Yes, my lord.'

The man gives him a look, quirking his face so the scars change shape, but says nothing.

On they go. Over the top of the trees, the tower of Našemísto's church pushes forward to greet them, and when the breeze comes to finds them it brings with it the sounds of the village: hallooed greetings, the bark of a dog, even the squeal of Pyotri's pigs, rootling in their sty. They go another few yards, and the last of the bushes and bracken and the bare-branched trees around the village come to an end; and the man says, 'You know the way from here?'

'Yes, my lord,' Pyotri says again. There in the garden of his brother's house is a small figure, sweeping the snow from the path. Up down, she goes, as she sweeps her broom in arcs across the path. Pyotri feels how his eyes yearn toward her. The man lifts him down, then, mounted up again himself, sees where Pyotri had been looking. 'Who's the nymph?' he asks.

'That's Tink,' Pyotri says. A ripple flows through his heart. 'I'm going to marry her.'

The man watches for a moment, then he says, 'What's up with her leg? She break it?'

'Her father did it,' Pyotri says.

The man stares down at him. 'Her *father*?'

'He did it to spoil her, in case more soldiers came. After they took her mother. He did it on the anvil in his forge. He was drunk,' Pyotri adds.

The man watches Tink a moment more. 'Christ All-bloody-mighty,' he says. 'What a world we're making of it.' He reaches down toward Pyotri. He is holding out a silver coin. 'That's for your pig,' he says. Then he turns his horse about, twisting this way and that through the trees, and is gone.

Pyotri's homecoming. There is first of all Tink's embrace, then Lenka's screech through the window, and once inside, her hysterics. His brother's hug, which lifts Pyotri from the floor, and for appearances' sake, concludes with a wallop across Pyotri's breeches. The other villagers hear the noise and come to the door. There are cries and exclamations, far too much pinching of Pyotri's cheeks, much praising the goodness of God for preserving him. And at the end of the day, a village supper that ends with pancakes and jam and plum brandy. At long last, after everyone has left, when the house is at last quiet again, Pyotri loosens the board in the cupboard and swims his way down to Tink, in her bed in the kitchen.

Tink weeps against him, just a little. 'Never go away again,' she tells him. 'Promise. I don't have no prayers left.'

'Tink, listen,' Pyotri whispers. 'It wasn't prayers brought me back. Look!' And he shows her the coin in his fist. 'It was the Lord of the Mountains. He's up there. He's true.' But then he grows serious. 'An' we mustn't tell anyone. No-one at all!'

CHAPTER EIGHT

The Lord of the Mountains

'I know that grass was made for the Horse to eat, and that the Horse was made for man to ride, so do I discover that the strong was made to protect the weak.'

William Stevens, *A Sermon Preached at the Temple Church*

WHEN THE GIANTS who made these mountains were at work on them and the clay still wet, one of them must have caught his toe as he strode over that ridge, and left a mark, a flattening of the terrain, in the slope above the cave. It makes a splendid vantage point. You get up there and, by Christ, you'd think you could see back to Prague itself. The mountains fold away from you, one after the other, white as the clouds above; valleys like theirs spooned out between them; tiny tracks laid over their heights, and acre after acre of frozen trees standing below, unmoving as a forest of stalagmites, sparkling like quartz. A crystal forest. Ah, now, who was it said that?

They laugh at him, the number of times they find him up there. There's a place where a man can stand with a spyglass as in the crow's nest on a ship. 'What you looking for, Domini?' Thor calls up to him. 'This fucker, Charles the Ghost?'

'Maybe,' he answers. 'Maybe. I'm well aware I should have you up here instead.'

'We'll find him for you, Domini. He's not going to get away.'

Looking down on those frozen trees, he's keeping half an eye out for the Roma as well.

The moon is a thumbnail-crescent in a sky that dazzles with stars. Pierced with them, like there was some mighty candlelit room up there. You turn your face up to them, squinting from under your frozen eyebrows, with the frost of your own breath weighing down your beard, and you could almost believe there was something hiding behind that night sky, something more than all of this. And then you go back to the cave, and lie down to sleep on your bed of pine, and sleep, and dream not at all.

In the morning there is low cloud caught against the mountains, blotting out the way over the ridge. The trees drip. We've time, he tells his men. It'll clear, we've time.

Also, their larder is bare.

Out they go, he, Thor and Magnus, to see what more they can find on this mountain to hunt, and the trail of a roebuck leads them all the way back to the bridge where Vainglory fell. The river already runs so much more sluggishly than it did before; the pools to either side the flow are solid with ice, and there, by God, the cannon lies, tilted up, its mouth mere inches below the surface of the water.

'That is a lot of bronze,' says Magnus, sadly. 'To think of it, left there for all eternity.'

True. Can't deny it, the lad is right. But once that river is ice – what then?

They check on the pit where they threw the bodies. The wolf-pack has been scratching over it, but the ground is too hard-froze even for them. The roebuck thinks to tiptoe past while they are engaged in examining the scrapes and diggings of the pack, but it thinks wrong. Back they go, with its body flopped behind Thor's saddle, and as they come up to the cave Thor spots something below them, peels off to the side, gets up in his stirrups to be sure, then calls back, 'Domini? I think there is a cross been left for us down there.'

Down through the trees, letting M'sieu find the way, and there they are, outside the blacksmith's ruin, Pyotri and three more, just like him. 'Good morning!' Pyotri calls. The other three gawp, fish-faced, open-mouthed. 'Good morning, my lord!'

'These are all the ones you ain't told of us, Pyotri, would that be right?'

'That's right,' says Pyotri, beaming. He holds up a sack. 'We have brought you a present!'

Onions, as big as your fist. 'Very kind of you,' says Jack. All four now all a-smile. Pyotri introduces him – this is Henrick, he keeps goats; this is Josuf, his father has the stables; this is Marcus. 'Hens,' Pyotri whispers, low-voiced, as if this were a childhood ailment.

And the little nymph? When he was ten, he had been in love as well.

'Tink can't walk this far.'

Tiny children, lagged like you would lag wine bottles in a cart, every limb wrapped and double-wrapped, hats tied down over their ears. He watches them go, they with much turning about and arms lofted to wave, smiling and shuffling along.

These mountain-folk, he thinks, shaking his head. There is an instinct to warn them – wolves, dips in the snow, horses that swing their heads too fast to see – but he holds it back.

Two days later the cross is there again, and the four have become eight, one so tiny it arrives strapped to an older sibling's shoulders, and in the sack there is—

'What's this?'

'Plum jam, my lord!'

Then it's poppy cake. Then cheese flavoured with caraway. Cabbages and a hand of carrots – soft to the point of being bendable, but carrots all the same. 'Pyotri, we're still your secret, are we? You ain't told anyone else of us? You and your friends?'

They seem shocked. 'No, my lord!'

Very strange.

The moon is half-full. The snow has grown a crust. The way over the ridge lies open above them; nothing between them and it and the stars.

PYOTRI'S BROTHER, EGAN, returns from Malenikov, full of news. A bushel of wheat half again as much as it was; peppercorns not to be had for love nor money; the Swedish lion rampaging toward them across Bavaria, and Lenka will not believe what he has heard took place in Prague.

Lenka says she has been robbed of a pot of plum jam; and Henrick's mother is missing a cheese, and everyone is saying it is imps and goblins.

'Lenka, love,' says Egan, putting his arm about her, 'if all we have to worry about is imps and goblins, we have little enough to complain of, trust me on that.'

THEY COME OUT of the wood, and truly, anyone can see what they are, with their mismatched clothes and their dented armour and their boots with the seams agape, and they themselves a-twitch at every sound. Their swords are slung crooked, the barrels of their pistols dull with tarnish, and no-one anywhere else in the world would spend more time on these than was needed to give them a kick up the arse, *but*—

– They do have those pistols. They do have those swords, and they have that lurking, hulking manner of men all too disposed to violence. There's an unpredictable boozy sway when they stand; they snarl when they speak; and they say they have a diktat from the Emperor, that the people of Našemísto are to give them billets in their houses, and hand over whatever they ask, or the Emperor will send his army down upon them, and will utterly rout the place and raze it to the ground. 'We were at Magdeburg,' these men say, 'and we will see you served the same as they!'

The villagers are divided. Some say the war was bound to find them one day, and that what they should do now is exactly what these men ask, and they will be on their way all the sooner. Those of this opinion (who tend to be older, and wealthier, and friends of Mauritz Siegel) point out that while these men may be ragged, there are all too many of them, and none of them well mannered. We should do nothing to provoke them, these folk say. There's a corporal with them, who gives his name as Tobias, and who might once have been a proper soldier – Josuf's father says the man spoke civilly enough as they took over his stables and warned him, do as his comrades asked. 'There is no ruling them,' Tobias said, sadly.

Their sergeant (at least, he says he is a sergeant) takes Egan to one side. His hand is twisted in Egan's sleeve like he would throttle it, and his face is uncomfortably close to Egan's own, and it is not a face you would welcome being close to. The man's nose has been squashed flat as a frog. Listen, he says. I am Salvatore, and that would be Hauptmann Salvatore to you. You hear of what was done in Prague?

I did, says Egan.

You think on it, Hauptmann Salvatore tells him. Now you bring us the best you have. You bring us everything we ask for, and maybe we'll let you be.

Hauptmann Salvatore and his men have scarce set foot in Prague. They have been brought together the way you sweep dirt into a pile. But the death of the Prince-Bishop is so notorious an event, every blowhard between here and Leipzig is claiming they were part of it. Also, Salvatore and his men should be getting a deal more than will now be the case from their miserable winter in these God-forsaken mountains, and the untimely death of the Prince-Bishop is the whole reason why. To grab what you can by laying claim to the deed – surely it's no more than compensation?

Hauptmann Salvatore now holds Egan's sleeve between finger and thumb. Now where is it? he asks. All you peasants always have gold hid away somewheres, ain't that so? Where's Siegel keeping his?

All we have is all you see, Egan tells him.

Hauptmann Salvatore gives a snarl of disgust and lets him go.

Going up to her bed that night, Dora Siegel, Mauritz Siegel's daughter, finds two of Salvatore's men waiting for her in her room. Dora shouts and screams, and the household comes running before the men can do her too much damage, but they meant to, not a doubt. They'd blocked her bedroom door with the chest that holds her dower. Herr Siegel moves his daughter, scratched and trembling, to the house of his neighbour Herr Egan, where in the middle of the night Pyotri finds himself evicted from the attic, and sent downstairs to a mattress on the kitchen floor. When the house is at long last quiet once again, he moves over to the box-bed, and to Tink, and lies there all night, eyes burning with tiredness, keeping her safe.

The soldiers deal with the high spirits they couldn't get rid of on Dora by breaking into the field where Henrick's father overwinters his goats, and chasing them hither and yon, even the nannies in kid, even though Henrick is there and begs them to stop. Henrick's father hears his son's cries for help and arrives armed with his old fowling piece, upon which the soldiers overpower him, and stab him through the heart.

Hauptmann Salvatore calls the villagers together. 'We're getting altogether too much trouble from you people,' he says. 'First blood's been spilt, now there'll be more. You bring us all you have, your gold, your silver, everything, or we'll take one of you for every night we're here.'

It's Alaric has the last watch of the day, up there with the spyglass, up above the cave. He comes in, serious as ever, saying, 'Domini, I think those wankers in the village, they're setting up a gallows.'

At first light, while Henrick's mother still weeps over her husband's body, while her husband's blood is still a soft red mush at the edge of the paddock, Pyotri knots the blanket once more under his chin, hefts the wood-axe over his shoulders, and sets off through the tanglewood. When he gets to the ruined forge, he chops branches off the trees until he has enough to make a cross in the snow the width of the ruin itself. Then he sits and waits.

HE COMES DOWN on foot this time, saving M'sieu for that trek over the ridge. The moon is a wink off full, no more.

'There's soldiers,' the boy announces, as he comes up. 'Soldiers in our village.'

'We know,' Jack says. 'We spied them. They ain't the ones we're waiting for. The ones we're waiting for will be over that ridge, at the hermit's shrine, a day from now.' *And so will we,* he thinks.

'But these are here *now*,' says the boy. He sounds mystified that this must be pointed out. 'They say they were at Magdeburg. They say it was them killed the Prince-Bishop in Prague.'

Do they indeed?

'They say we must have gold. They say we're hiding it. They killed Henrick's father. Everyone is all a-feared.' He takes a breath. 'You have to help us.'

'Pyotri,' he begins. 'We're leaving. We have to leave. I came to say goodbye.'

The boy stares at him in disbelief. 'But you can't,' he says. 'We need you. If you don't stop them, they are going to kill us. One every night, for as long as they're here.' And in a rush of childish fury, the boy stamps his foot. 'We *helped* you. So now you have to help *us*.'

He trudges his way back up the mountain, and it's hard-going on foot. By the time he gets within sight of the cave his leg is cursing him. He has to stop to ease it. *God-damn*, he thinks, *will it be like this forever?* You get to fifty in this life you're beating the odds; he's more than halfway there already.

Outside the cave the horses wait in a line, Ansfrid and Magnus loading them, one by one. Zoltan comes forward. Low-voiced, he asks, 'Jacques, do we stay or go?'

He pushes past. He has no answer.

Here is Thor, coming down from that vantage point above the cave. 'Domini, there are more snow-clouds on the way. If we are going over that ridge, we need to do it now.'

I do not need telling, he thinks.

'Domini,' Thor calls after him, 'even you cannot be in two places at once.'

He hears M'sieu, doing that shout of his. 'He's got his yard out,' Luka says, stomping past, and yes, his horse has, glistening red, swinging beneath his belly. 'I ain't going near 'im.'

He goes to M'sieu, pulls his horse's head down against his shirt, feels that hot huff of air, the anger in it, the endless striving against everything. 'What is it?' he asks. 'Is there a mare down there?' Stands gazing down, with M'sieu at his shoulder, chuntering away. Put up the spyglass and you can see it plain, the one street, the lanes a-branching off it; what must be the headsman's house, the only one that is three storeys high; and closest to, this end of that one street, a gallows, that upended *L*.

He can feel those snakes in his head again, slithering and hissing. Ah, God-damn… one little village, what difference will that make?

Ja, tell yourself that. And then M'sieu puts up his nose, rolls back his lips and sends a scream down the mountain that has every four-footed thing down there scampering for cover, every bird sent skywards; and in the silence that follows, out of nowhere, he knows. His sigh is so immense, it even has his horse turn its head.

'Yeah, you're right,' he says. 'Zehr gut. Fuck 'em.'

ALMOST SUNRISE ON the day that is to end with the first full moon of February. Blue shadows cross Našemísto's single street. Its gardens are stiff with frost; there is rime on every window, inside and out.

There is a trail of footsteps down the lane at the side of the Siegels' house, as if someone had been making an early morning inspection of its barn. There are two more, into the garden of Pyotri's house, and some odd new scuffs up its back wall; and was that the end of a dangling rope, being pulled swiftly in through the attic window? A cockerel crows; from somewhere – in the village? Maybe in the woods just beyond? – it is answered by a horse with too much to say for itself, always. Also, this is a horse with a sense that it is shortly to be called upon, as all the finest horses have.

Dora Siegel wakes to find a man again kneeling by her bed, with his hand across her mouth. He has the brightest, whitest hair, stuck out all around his head. Now he lifts a finger to his lips – *shhhhh*.

Dora feels herself go rigid with terror, down to each individual toe. There is a second man, also with bright white hair, leaning out of the attic window, looking down into the street. He makes a signal, then withdraws his head. The man beside her bed bids her *shhhh* once more, then both men bow to her, go out the attic door, and she hears them going down the stairs. Quiet as cats. Hardly a creak.

Dora Siegel waits until her breath comes back, then she too tiptoes downstairs, to the bedroom where Herr Egan and Frau Lenka sleep. She scratches on the door. 'Herr Egan?' she calls. 'Herr Egan, forgive me, but there's men in your house. Only – only I think these are different to the ones before.'

And down in the box-bed in the kitchen, Pyotri wakes to a voice softly humming 'Ein feste Burg' outside the shuttered kitchen window.

He comes barrelling out the kitchen door, hopping from one foot to the other as he puts his shoes on, hurling himself forward, wrapping his arms around Jack's legs. 'I knew you'd help us! I knew you would!'

'Steady there, Pyotri,' says Jack. 'We ain't done it yet.' Takes the boy by the shoulder and guides him to the corner of the house. Points down the snowy street. 'You see that son of a bitch stood at the corner?'

There is a lazy guard outside the Siegels' house, lounged against its wall, packing his pipe.

'We need him gone,' says Jack. 'Think you can shift him?'

Oh, indeed.

No creature in Nature can saunter like a ten-year-old boy. Jack watches as Pyotri wanders down the street, past the guard, as innocent-looking a dawdle as you could ask for. Then Pyotri wanders back. He stops.

'What do you want, you little fucker?' the guard snarls at him. 'You'll get the flat of my hand.'

Pyotri takes a mighty breath. At the top of his lungs he bellows, 'SHIT ON THE EMPEROR AND SHIT ON YOU!'

There is the guard's roar of fury, then the man comes pounding after him. Pyotri charges back the way he came, skidding round the corner; Jack puts out an arm, yanks him out of sight. When they peer back around the corner again together, the guard is face down, unmoving. After a second or two, they see the body being pulled silently and stealthily out of sight. Then Jens's freckled face comes into view. Jens lifts a hand – all clear.

'One down,' says the Lord of the Mountains. 'Come with me.'

Over the wall into the next-door garden, with a helping hand as the boy scrambles over it after him. This is the place with three floors to it. 'Pán Siegel's house,' the boy whispers. The shutters of the parlour window are open, and there are two men sat at breakfast there, one either end of the dining table, in a pair of high-backed chairs. The mess made of the parlour is exactly as Jack would have expected from such human dreck as these – an arc of wine splashed up the wall, a target scrawled upon it, food thrown at the target, and outside in the garden broken dishes, broken bottles, sitting in the snow. But something else about these two. Jack has a pair who work together, does he not, and there's an instinct whispering to him that these might be the same.

He crouches down. In a whisper, to Pyotri, 'Would those two in there be the two as took Henrick's father from him?'

'That's them,' and Pyotri's small face goes cold and tight and hard.

Jack straightens himself up, flattens himself to the wall of the house. Inside, one of the men begins thumping his fist on the table. At an angle, Jack sees a maid enter the room, carrying a tray; her eyes pink with mortification.

'Do you know her?' he asks.

Pyotri darts a glance over the windowsill. 'Hannah,' comes the reply. 'Pán Siegel's maid.'

'Once she's back in her kitchen, you go in and you keep her there. Close the door through. Off you go.'

Pyotri, scampering out of sight.

Jack crouches down below the sill, searching with his hand under the snow by his boot. One pebble. Two. Three for luck. Throws the first up at the window. Hears one of the men inside move his chair. Second pebble. Both heavy chairs pushed back. Third. Both men come to the window; he hears them there, right there, above his head. No-one at a ground-floor window ever thinks of looking *down*.

Snarls of annoyance. Back the two men go. He hears them settle in their seats, then he stands up outside the window himself. Sees the men turn, sees their surprise. Lifts his arms.

There is, of course, now no guard outside the Siegels' house.

The Gemini rise up, one behind one chair, one behind the other.

Let us begin.

Each man is now watching a mirror-image of what he also finds happening to him: first, an arm under the jaw, in case they feel like being noisy, and—

'Hello,' says Kazimir to his.

'Goodbye,' says Konstantin. Then the knife into the throat; then use the knife in the throat to press the larynx down into the windpipe, and wait. It takes a little time, of course, but Jack has never known anyone manage more than a few bubbles of blood as a result, and they go limp long before they're dead. He watches from outside; when it's done he gives the Gemini a round of silent applause (both of them bow), then makes his way round to the kitchen himself.

*

Pyotri's previous dealings with Hannah had been restricted to her complaining of him fidgeting in church, but this time when she hears his voice she turns about, drops to her knees and pulls him to her. 'Oh, Pyotri,' she wails. 'Oh, Pyotri! What will become of us all?'

'Slečno Hannah, the Lord of the Mountains has come down to help us, and he says we are to close that door and stay put.'

'What?' says Hannah. At which moment the Lord of the Mountains himself walks in from the garden. 'Good day to ye, ma'am,' he says, dipping his head. 'God's love, but it is cold out there.'

Hannah has retreated across the kitchen and armed herself with the pestle. 'Good lady,' says Jack, 'I promise you, we are on your side. Are any of those others billeted on you awake?'

Hannah manages to shake her head.

'Excellent. Now I must borrow this boy –' (he takes the pestle from her hand, before it drops to the floor) '– and it would do me the greatest service if you would wait here till he comes back. Oh, and don't go into the parlour no more. Pyotri – after you.'

Out they go again. 'Not much more of this, Pyotri, I promise you,' says Jack. He takes the purse from his pocket. 'You take this, use what's inside, and make a trail. Start in the street, go all the way down the lane. Do it like you were sowing beans. One long row, down to the barn.'

Pyotri gives the bag a bounce in his hand, hears the chink of what it holds, and opens it, just as Jack knew he would. Little lights flit across the boy's astonished face. 'But that's *gold*!'

'So it is. And once you're done, you go back in there, you and Madame Hannah, and I want you to start up the loudest racket that you can. I'll be across the field, and I want to be able to hear you from there. You yell out *Herr Siegel, Herr Siegel! The men have found your gold!*'

'What are you going to be doing across the field?' Pyotri asks, in a whisper.

'Wait and see,' says Jack.

In Pyotri's hand the coins have a strange feel – so small and yet so heavy, like they are somehow more than real. He strews a small selection in the street, then down the lane, makes a grand circle of them at the barn door, and throws the rest on the bare earth inside. He goes back to Hannah. She hasn't moved.

'We got to make a noise,' he tells her.

To show her, he starts by beating on the mantelpiece with a wooden spoon, then on the cooking pots, then Hannah, getting the idea, upends the mortar and begins walloping it with the pestle. 'Herr Siegel, Herr Siegel!' Pyotri shouts. 'The soldiers have your gold! They found it where you hid it! They found it in the barn!' They hear Mauritz Siegel's bemused shout above them, then the first of the soldiers arriving in the street. Pyotri goes to the door. 'Gold!' he yells. 'Gold! In the barn! They found the gold!' For good measure he adds, 'Everyone's gold! They found all of it!' The villagers, most knowing full well that they have no gold in the first place, put their heads out their windows, but this is in fact exactly as Jack wants it – divide the village into layers, is what he's thinking: the villagers all safe abed above, the soldiers below, in the lane. And here they come, pulling on boots, tucking in shirts; not one of 'em ready, not one of 'em armed. Fighting over the coin like pigeons over corn. Banging and knocking against each other, they barge their way down the lane. They hesitate at the door of the barn, as if for the first time it has occurred to them, *isn't this just too good to be true?* but they don't have time to do so for long: Thor, up on the roof of Siegel's house, has a perfect view of the door of the barn, and the men gathered outside it.

The whip-crack of shot. So fierce is the scrabble for the coins that it takes another, and another after that; it takes one of those elbowing his fellows out the way to slump against the side of the barn before any of them understand what is happening here, and then they all catch on at once: this is the barrel, they are the fish. And now, down the lane, here comes Ilya and those bruisers Ulrik and Magnus, in that same drill they used advancing down the streets of Stettin: fire, reload, go forward, fire, reload—

The men in the lane drop back as if in disbelief. But there is open ground at the end of the lane, and woods beyond. They take to their heels and run.

Oh no you don't.

They come out from under the trees, the Gemini holding the ends of the line, he and Zoltan at its centre. True enough, his discoverers ain't cavalry men, but nor are those they're charging, and just in case any of them might think to make a fight of it, his discoverers have whited out their faces and made wings of pine-branch and birch-bark to sit behind their saddles once again. Ah, what music – *thrum, thrum, thrum!* The men running across the field stagger to a halt, eyes round with horror, mouths agape, as this apocalypse thunders out from the trees toward them. He fires once, he sees the puffs of smoke all the way along the line, he fires again, then he unsheathes his sword and lets M'sieu go to it, the point to the arrowhead; and the thing with an attack such as this, you have to make it fast, you have to give your enemy no time to think at all, you have to make it one fucken thing after another, because once they are operating on instinct, they are yours. And there they go, just as you want them to, staggering back across the field, into the lane, but now Ilya has the lane blocked, don't he, so into the barn they go. *Perfekt!*

He brings M'sieu to a prancing halt outside, dismounts, strides in sweeping off his hat to display the scars across his face. 'Who's in charge here?' Jack demands. 'And which of you misbegot apes, which of you sacks of skin, which of you walking fucken corpses can guess who *we* are?'

*

Salvatore – never an early riser. Wakes with a snort, hears his men cheering some discovery – about time, but then he's never known the gallows fail – and then the very minute he was about to stroll outside, ready to go claim the lion's share, it all goes arsewards. Shots. Shrieks and cries. Horsemen – *horsemen?* – at the gallop in the lane, and only at the last minute was he able throw himself over that garden wall and hide himself in here, the kitchen of that bastard Egan's house. He waits, crouched, catching his breath. Oh, this has gone to hell, all to hell, they should be rich by now, rich and on their way out of this shit-hole village; instead what are these – these – these *raveners* who have fallen upon them?

Still in an ungainly crouch, knees akimbo, he creeps to the window, peers through. Not one of his men left out there, not one; the fucken witless blockheads. And now the villagers have come out of their houses, are joining the men in the lane – he hears that bastard Egan and his skewer of a wife out there for a start. How is he meant to get out of here now? And what's that noise he hears within the walls – is it rats? It might be rats. Is he not alone in here? Where is that damned noise coming from?

The noise Salvatore hears is Tink. Tink, who had just finished strapping on her iron boot when she heard the shots outside, and had scrambled through the panel in the ceiling of her bed, hauling herself through it, boot and all. Tink, who is now pulling herself up, up, up, within the walls, reaching from lath to lath, scraping her hands, scraping her elbows; Tink making the journey in reverse that Pyotri has made so many times down to her. *Up*, she thinks, *up*, away from the noise in the street, away from the memories of horses and pistol shots, and her mother's screams. And her father, coming to, where the soldiers had thrown him. Her father's drunken sobbing. Her leg held to his anvil—

She hears something beneath her. She looks down. In the narrow space below she sees a man's face, peering up, peering through the hole where the panel should be. He sees her, and his face twists with rage. Tink knows what that face means. She wedges the iron boot against the timbers like a mountaineer would wedge a pick. Up!

Here is the attic. The boot is so heavy, and it was never designed for this, and she's sweating now, sweating but triumphant. Here is the panel in the cupboard in the attic. She kicks at it, then kicks again, reaches forward—

An arm, a hand, grabbing at her. He's here! The man is here!

This one, Salvatore thinks, *this one, the cripple*. She matters to them, he's noted that, for all that she's so marred. This one, this is how he's getting out of here. Thought she could escape by going higher, did she? Two can play at that.

Christ how she wriggles, how she squirms! Maybe he'll keep her. Maybe he'll have her. But for now, though, he needs to get them both out that window, get them both onto that roof—

She's biting his hand. Salvatore whips the hand away, slaps Tink across the face. 'You little *bitch*,' he snarls. 'Keep still!'

THERE'S NOT MUCH dignity a man can muster, hiding in a barn, but this one does his best. 'Tobias,' this one says, standing up. He clears his throat. 'I am the corporal here.' He dusts off his sleeves, seeming as he does so to slap himself back into some sort of shape as well.

'And where's your fucken Hauptmann?' says Jack.

Tobias's eyes are braver than he is, keep darting toward Jack, then running away. 'Kapitän, if I knew, I would tell you,' the man says, sadly, and again his eyes do that flick and scurry.

'Do I know you?'

'No, Kapitän. But you are one of the only two men I have ever seen who wear a silver wolf.' And Tobias points to the pendant, where it hangs against Jack's coat.

He hears Zoltan coming into the barn behind him, he hears the murmur of the villagers, tiptoeing up to its door. 'That so?' he says. He keeps his voice steady, but his heart has quickened at once, the way women say the child does in the womb. 'And who's the other?'

'Carlo Fantom,' the corporal answers. 'The man who sent us out here.'

'You,' Jack says, 'you were to be the ambush? Over the ridge, at the hermit's shrine? You?'

The corporal looks at his boots. 'We were. We were, but all to naught. We never saw hide nor hair of the mighty cannon, and then we heard the news from Prague, and after that, Kapitän Carlo was gone in any case.'

'Gone? Why so?'

'Because that was his father. The Prince-Bishop.'

Out the corner of his eye, Jack sees Zoltan come to a dead stop. It feels as if the same has happened inside his own head as well – everything stilled. Like when the wind falls away. Like when some great tumult ceases. 'Say that again.'

'The Prince-Bishop of Prague. Carlo Fantom's father.'

And then from outside the sudden shouts, a woman's wail. 'On the roof, on the roof! He has Tink!'

Against the whiteness of the sky, the silhouette of a man, and the child held to him. They're on the tilt of the roof, the man unsteady, finding footholds in the thatch. He has a knife at the child's throat. 'Now you let me be,' he shouts down. 'You let me be, I let her go.' The child with that iron on her leg, built up like a patten, nothing else to her, the wee scrap, but the hugeness of her eyes, huge with fright. 'TINK!' Pyotri is yelling. 'TINK!' The corporal, Tobias, comes out from the barn too, calls up, 'Hauptmann! Hauptmann Salvatore! For the love of God, let the child go!'

'You let me have a horse!' Salvatore calls down. Edging sideways, wobbling as he goes. No, thatch can't be any too easy to keep your balance on. Now Salvatore sits. The child gives out a cry – did the knife prick her? A sharp-featured woman running back and forth under the eaves, wringing her hands, and Pyotri's heartbroken cry, 'TINK! TINK!'

'You gimme that horse!' the man yells, using the knife for a moment to point at M'sieu. 'You bring it there.' He points again, to the spot where the roof dips lowest. 'You do it now!'

'*Sehr gut, sehr gut!*' He goes to M'sieu's head, tells him, *Play along.* There on the Siegels' roof, flat to it, like a lizard, there lies Thor. Salvatore has his back to him. But if Salvatore falls, the child will fall as well.

He leads M'sieu forward. 'You stop there!' Salvatore orders. 'You step away!'

'Very good,' he says. 'I'm stepping back, do you see? I'm stepping back. Nothing in my hands.' Salvatore comes down the roof another foot or so, bracing his feet. The child, Tink, gazing down at him, the blank, expressionless gaze of one who knows already she is lost.

'Look to your soul, Salvatore,' Jack calls up. But seated on the Siegels' roof, Salvatore is still below Thor's line of sight. 'Now this is a big horse,' Jack begins. 'You sure you're of a size enough to ride him?'

'You shut the fuck up and step the fuck away,' comes the reply.

'A'cause,' Jack continues, 'you look like you might not even reach his stirrups to me.'

Salvatore swings the child from him. 'I'm plenty big enough for any god-damned animal you brung with you,' he roars, standing up, full height, and Thor takes the shot.

And this is another thing that gold can do. It means that when you hear of this odd-sounding novelty, a musket with a rifled barrel, you can purchase one of those as well, and present it to your sharpshooter with the comment, 'See what you can do with this.'

Mind you, you never know, with those soft lead bullets, what the effect will be. Salvatore's head goes half one way and half the other, clean as if you'd cleaved it. He pitches forward. Tink falls from his grasp. Salvatore falls from the roof altogether, still curled, knees to his chest, and Tink slides down the thatch, grabbing at it as she goes, finds something within it to hold onto, and hangs there, at the edge of the roof.

'She'll fall!' the woman screams. 'She'll fall!' A rush for ladders, blankets, but the iron boot is swinging like a pendulum, like an anchor, it is dragging the child off the roof even as they watch. He hauls himself onto M'sieu, swings the horse around, gets him close as he can to the wall, pulls on the reins, gets him in tight, pulls again. M'sieu is chuntering with annoyance, uncomprehending – what does his rider want him to do, climb up the wall?

Yes, he does. 'That's it,' Jack tells him. 'Up the wall. Get your hooves on it.' Pulls on the reins again. M'sieu rears up. Tink is right above them. 'Tink!' he calls. M'sieu's hooves hit the wall, rear legs paddling to stay in place, great wings a-sway. A swinging arc of faces left and right of him as he stands up in his stirrups. 'Tink, let go! I'll catch you!'

She's staring down at him, right into his eyes. He is a creature from her nightmares, no mistaking terror as naked as that. 'Tink!' he calls. There is maybe five foot of air between them. 'Tink, I know you're scared. It's no excuse for being stupid. Let go!' His leg has started cursing him, and even louder than before.

And then Pyotri's voice. 'Tink! It's the Lord of the Mountains! He's come to help us! Let go!'

Does she let go? Or does the weight of the boot finally pull her down? Whichever it is, there is a cry, she drops, and he has her in his arms. A bump back into the saddle. A bump as M'sieu brings them back down to earth, and he hands Tink down to the sharp-nosed, tearful woman, dismounts himself, his damned leg nothing like as steady as it should be.

The little maid stands rigid, exactly where the woman puts her, eyes tight shut. She is commendably direct. 'Is it over?' she asks.

'Yes, Tink,' he hears Pyotri answer. The boy has taken her hands in his. 'All over and done.'

ONLY OF COURSE it's not, because these things never are, not as tidily as that. They have to deal with those bodies first of all, in the field and in the lane, and what's left of Salvatore, because you can't leave a spoor like that, no matter how unloved these corpses were. He has the survivors load the bodies onto a wagon, then take the wagon up through the trees, high as they can get, until they find the ravine, and into it the corpses go.

Listen to me, he tells Tobias, once the last body has been flung over the edge. The war is that-a-way. Go, and keep going. If any of you come next or nigh this place again, it'll be the last thing you ever do. I find I'm feeling oddly merciful today. You're not going to get another chance like this.

In point of fact he's feeling oddly fragile. As if this familiar world had just revealed itself as something entirely new, which has to be negotiated for the very first time, and with care. Almost as if—

Almost as if there is some design to it, after all.

And one more thing to do, as the full moon rises. They stand out under her, and they sing out the names, toasting each one: Ziggy, go to God. Ulf, go to God. Sten, go to God. Elias, go to God. And Viktor Lopov, go to God.

Pyotri has sidled up to Luka. Who were they? he asks.

They were our brothers, Luka whispers. And we lost them. But we will see them again.

'Domini,' says Thor, beside Jack, 'we missed him. Your ghost. He got away.'

There's not one chance in hell Thor will understand this, but even so. 'This time,' says Jack, 'this time, I think the one who got away was me.'

It'll be a midnight ride out of here, across the snow, under that moon. They ready the horses, with the expected audience, and it would be pleasing to think the villagers are there to wish them on their way, but it's more likely they are there to be sure they do indeed leave; because what is today's hero, tomorrow? He sees Pyotri, stood with the sharp-featured woman, and a man who keeps a solid hold of the boy's shoulder, but Pyotri breaks free, all the same, comes up to M'sieu. 'Where do you go now?' he asks.

'That way,' Jack says. 'Over the mountains.'

'What's over the mountains?'

'Don't know. We find out when we get there.' And then – and he means it almost as a joke, but not entirely so – 'You could come with us, if you like.'

But the boy shakes his head. 'I have to stay here,' he says. 'I have to marry Tink.'

'Because no-one else would?'

'She wouldn't have no-one else,' Pyotri answers. 'It has to be me.'

When it is cold as this, the skin of his scars tingles when he smiles. 'You're a man who knows his own mind, Pyotri.'

'Yes, my lord,' Pyotri answers.

'Then I wish you long life,' he says. 'Long life, and a happy one.' He turns M'sieu about.

But now the boy is calling, 'No, wait, wait!' so he turns M'sieu about again, in a circle, reins him in.

'What is it?' he calls, as Pyotri comes running up.

'You ain't the Lord of the Mountains, are you?' the boy asks.

'I doubt it.'

'So who are you?'

'What do you mean, who am I?'

'Your name,' the boy says. 'What's your name?'

'What do you want my name for?' He can feel the scars tingling.

'So we can tell your story,' Pyotri says. 'So you are not forgot.'

Well now. Never thought of that. 'My name,' he says, considering. 'Very well then. My name is Jack Fiskardo. And once, a long, *long* time ago, I was a boy like you.'

WHERE DO THEY GO?

Back to the bridge. Back to Vainglory. They make camp, then he and Zoltan go into Malenikov with a tale of being prospectors; saying how they've heard there's chunks of rock crystal can be prised out the mountains hereabouts, and how they want to try their luck. And are laughed at as idiots, of course they are, but nonetheless they're sold chain and rope and pickaxes, and one shopkeeper even warns them, if they are going into the mountains, to watch themselves. 'There's Gypsies use those tracks this time of year,' the man says, 'and if that weren't bad enough, there's a band of freebooters, it's said did that business in Prague. They're meant to be up there in the mountains too.'

That so?

'That's so.' And the man darts a darkling glance over his shoulder before he speaks again. 'Folk are calling them the Dead Men.'

They use the pickaxes to hack down into the frozen river, cutting steps for themselves and a slope for Vainglory. Out from the ice she comes, with it packed solid down inside her still, but once they have a big enough space cleared round her, they wrap her first with rope and then with chain, and warp the chains round the rocks at the river's edge and start pulling her free, free of the silt and weed on the riverbed, where a little water runs even now, and tilt her over onto that slope of ice, with the chains grinding and his men shouting in time as they pull and pull and pull, and just as they have her laid out on the ice, riding on the glassy surface of the frozen river, they hear wheels upon the bridge, and looking up he sees a man with red hair, and a cap with a tassel, and there is Rufus, smiling down at him, and shouting through his hands, '*Sastipe*, Kapitán! What do you have there?'

The Roma set up camp beside the river. They will take Vainglory, they say, and send word they have her to the metal-workers, the Kalderash, and the Kalderash will come, and into the Kalderash fires and smelting pots Vainglory will go. From ingots she came, to ingots she will return. There's a lesson for you. She will become knives and cooking pots and horse harness and pestles and mortars and bells. She will travel on to Rus, and into Wallachia, and into Serbia. 'But you, my friend,' Rufus asks, as he and Jack sit together, watching the icicles all a-drip along the riverbank, listening to the rustlings in the trees, 'What will you do now?'

'That's a good question, and I must admit I have no answer. What does the Dead Man do now?'

'Now?' says Rufus. He scratches with his pipe-stem at his remaining ear. 'Now, he has to learn to live.'

At the entrance to their tent, the three old women sit and watch. They see the scouts, all of a busyness: adjusting saddles, stirrups, girth, strapping their packs into place behind their saddles. 'So that's that then,' Pernilla says. She taps out her pipe, rests her hands upon her knees. 'What's next?'

Kizzy has that dreamy look to her. Her arm is round her boy, Benedicte, and now he puts his mouth against his mother's ear, and there is the dry-grass whisper of his voice.

Zoltan strolls past, leading Reena. 'What happens to our handsome lieutenant, for a start?' Pernilla asks. 'I'll miss him.'

'Oh, I think our Lady Ava might take a little pity on him, when she and he meet again,' says Kizzy. 'He is trying so very hard.'

Now Roxandra leans forward. 'And our Lady Soap-Bubble, and her little girl?'

'Our Lady Soap-Bubble will do very well indeed. You needn't worry about her. She's another three daughters to come, for a start.' More whispering from Benedicte. 'And it is going to be a fine and handy thing for all,' his mother adds, 'to have friends in such a peaceable place as Haarlem, we can tell you that. There's a storm headed for England, a great one.'

Pernilla tuts her tongue. What an untidy place the future is, for sure. 'Then what about the Pilgrims? What's going to happen there?'

'Lucy can do much better than Alembert, and will,' Kizzy announces. 'And Andrew and Blanche – they've found each other now. I think they will not let each other go.'

'That's good,' says Pernilla. Her gaze wanders across to where Jack and Rufus have got to their feet, are doing that strange gadjo thing of shaking hands. 'Yet our brave captain,' she comments. 'Always on his own.'

'Eh,' says Kizzy. Her eyes may be closed, but she's smiling. 'We'll see about that. Although he does have a bit of business of his own to sort out first.'

CHAPTER NINE

His Eminence

"Tis no strange thing, that a Foreigner should make his fortune out of his Country...'

Letters of the Cardinal-Duke de Richelieu

THE PALAIS CARDINAL. It will sit – no, no (thinks its creator), so splendid a building does not sit, it *resides* – in the Rue Saint-Honoré, behind the Palais du Louvre. It will be perfectly situated – apart, not *a part*. This little jest never fails to make him smile. In order to create it, historic mansions by the score have been reduced to rubble, and their remains used to level the ground over which Jean Le Nôtre is now laying out the design for an immense central courtyard; with lines of chalk marking paths and parterres, and pipework erupting from the mud to show where fountains will play; he is already wearying the Cardinal for decisions over planters and arbours and the views of His Eminence on the use of box, which as everyone agrees, produces *parterres en broderie* of marvellous crispness and elaboration, but unfortunately also smells of cats.

From around this central courtyard, in this new augmented
plan, there will radiate four more. The wings of the palace will
surround them, the gold mount about the stones. Its rooms will
be galleried, columned, high-ceilinged, those within the rooms
will view the world outside through acres of flawless, blown-
plate window glass. There will be a chapel, and a ballroom.
There will be a theatre – in fact there may be two. Ah, such
fancies, such possibilities, such delight. The Cardinal smiles
again – *What is this fascination we have, we men of the church*,
he thinks, *with building?* There was Wolsey (poor Wolsey!)
with his dreams at Hampton Court; today there is Barberini,
redesigning his palazzo in Rome. And once this, the Palais-
Cardinal, is finished, it will be fit to rank with either of them,
and into it he will move his paintings, his tapestries, his massy
plate; his vase of rock crystal, his tortoiseshell cabinets, his
clocks, his books; his tables inlaid with jade and amethyst,
with mother-of-pearl. For now, though, it sits in miniature
on the largest table in the Cardinal's private office – not his
grand salon, through which the petitioners and flatterers and
fawners come and go; not the bureau nor even the petit bureau;
but here, his cabinet, here beside his bedchamber, here in his
most private and particular space, this panelled room with its
comfortable chair and old-fashioned, unmatched firedogs and
its little closet with the narrow window over the courtyard
below; and every evening when the day's work is done, His
Eminence takes a restorative glass of the cognac of Charente, of
the type he grew up with, and stands here, like this, candlestick
in hand, and lets the candlelight play over the model of his
palace, and his imagination wander at will through its rooms,
uninterrupted by headache, immune to the agonizing bristling
of his nerves. Perhaps he will enlarge this wing, or raise that
pediment. Perhaps another fountain here in this westernmost
corner of the central courtyard, where it will sparkle as if
spraying rubies in the setting sun. He loves his creation (*que*

Dieu pardonne!) almost as much as he would have loved an infant heir. And like an infant, it will be un-shadowed. It will be without ghosts. He lifts the candle higher, as if in salutation to that same *Dieu* who has granted him so much and saved him from such perils – and then he sees it. There, propped against what will be the south-facing façade of the principal courtyard, a letter. Attached to it by a ribbon, a seal.

He takes it up. He is aware his hand is shaking so badly that he must lay the candlestick aside. He examines the name upon the letter – his – and then the seal. Ah, the Fates, the Fates that whisper to a man that he is safe at last, even as they open up a chasm beneath his feet!

He feels some shape, some sort of moulding on the seal's reverse. In his shaking hand, he turns it over.

There, impressed in the wax: the outline of a wolf. To the Cardinal it appears the creature might be dancing in triumph.

Some small sound at the far end of the room. He looks up. The door to the closet overlooking that courtyard is open, and a man stands there, outlined against the dark. In his hand, the gleam of steel, the cocked flint, the barrel's awful empty eye.

The Cardinal gives a gasp. Before the gasp becomes a shout for aid, his visitor speaks.

'Your brains will paint that door before any of your attendants are through it. And you have need of your brains, Monsieur, do you not? You listen to them. And right now they are telling you, you should listen to me.'

His visitor steps forward. He is tall, he is scruffily unshaven (a detail that impresses; *this is a man*, thinks the Cardinal, *with one thing to do*), he wears a soldier's buff-leather coat, a soldier's sword. He has three dark scars across his face, above and under the left eye. He indicates the letter, still in the Cardinal's hand. 'It is a copy,' he says. 'But of course, I am sure you realize that.' He tilts his head and his eyes catch the candlelight. Oh, they are like *ice*. 'A copy, but a good one, don't you think? We used china clay on the original, to make a matrix for the seal, and took this impression from that. As you see, it worked. It would convince −' (he lifts the unencumbered hand) '− anybody. It would even convince a king.'

Richelieu places the letter carefully upon the table − due deference to the work that went into its creation, and to that eye of the pistol barrel, now six feet from his heart. 'Would you tell me who you are?' he asks.

'You know who I am,' comes the reply. 'You made me.' A moment's pause: the nascence of a thought. 'You were *my* matrix, if you like.' Now his visitor indicates the closet behind him. 'Was it in there? Was that the window where you stood, to watch Concini die? I'm sure you watched, Monsieur. You would want to see the thing was done aright. And then my father looked up, and − well. From that, here we are. From that, everything. Not so?'

Ah. *From this point on,* thinks the Cardinal, *if I were but an animal, a brute beast, I would know all hope is gone. But I am not, so—*

'I do know who you are,' he begins. 'I know who you are, and I know what you have done. In Hoffstein *and* in Prague.'

A tip of the head in acknowledgement. 'I figured you might work that out. They have a sense of humour, the Fates, don't you think, Monsieur? That we should end up on the same side? Me fighting for the Swedish, and you paying the bill? This invasion would have stalled months ago without France's gold. Now where are we? Almost down to Munich. The Habsburg eagle is being clawed to bits. It was a masterstroke, Monsieur.' As he speaks, his visitor is moving step by step around the table, between the Cardinal and the door. 'And it would be such a shame if King Louis were to discover you had set up this brilliant alliance quite so far ahead of ever consulting him. Especially now you and he are such firm friends. Sit, please, Monsieur, I beg of you. Be comfortable.'

The Cardinal sits. He takes the letter into his lap. It is, he supposes, after all, his. From outside the sound of a gentle night-time rain. Paris, tomorrow, will be sparkling, her trees abundant with leaf, her gardens heavy with flowers. The Cardinal says, 'You are not here to kill me, I think.'

'Oh, don't be fooled, Monsieur. I find I have a capacity for vengeance that astounds me. But no, I am not here to kill you. Not this time.' An easy smile. 'Do you know, Monsieur, the first thing you do, as a soldier, when you find yourself shifted, as it were, to some new position?'

'I do not,' the Cardinal replies.

'You put an earthwork about it. You look to its defence. And that is what you are going to be, Monsieur. An earthwork, for me and my men. First, you will call off the Prince-Bishop's attack dog –'

'That,' says the Cardinal, 'might be easier said than done.'

'Nonetheless, you will do it. You will leave him to me. Second, you will tell everyone that I and my men are no more. You will say you have it on authority that we went sky-high with the Prince-Bishop's palace. Do you understand?'

'I think you underestimate your notoriety,' says the Cardinal. 'There are already stories –'

'Stories are nothing. They are mist. They help obscure the picture, that is all. My men, such as are still with us, are going to live long and happy lives, Monsieur, now they are dead. And so long as they do, you do. If we can agree on this, I see no reason why our paths should ever cross again.' His visitor shifts the pistol, as if to improve his grip. 'So. Do we agree?'

The Cardinal raises a hand – like a child, he thinks, like a boy in school. 'I suppose it would be too much to enquire after the safe-keeping of the original?'

'Not at all,' comes the reply. 'Very safely kept, Monsieur. Very safe indeed. You may trust me on that.'

Oh, such a moment. Oh, how he longs to refuse. How he

longs to shout *NO!* into the barrel of that pistol with all the force his lungs can manage. Instead he says, 'I never met your father. I understand he was a Poitou man. Like me.'

'If you had, you would have found him a realist. Don't play for time, Monsieur,' his visitor warns. 'Yours has all run out. I have nothing to lose here.' That free hand moves again, over the entire width of the pasteboard palace. 'You have all this.'

Very well, then. *Our whole life,* thinks the Cardinal, *is but one negotiation, one master, after another.* He leans back. Briefly, he closes his eyes. Such concessions, he has found, irk less if one makes them with the world shut out. 'We agree.'

For the first time, a smile. The pistol stays where it has always been, but the free hand reaches for the cognac. *Do we drink together now?* wonders the Cardinal.

No, we do not. 'And now, Monsieur, we need a small diversion. You must choose. Your curtains or your palace. Which is it to be?'

At first he doesn't understand. Then he sees how his visitor has raised the decanter – a favourite, blue glass, with criss-cross moulding to its belly (ah well, such things come, such things go) – and is waiting for a decision. 'My curtains,' says the Cardinal, rising out of his seat, to step safely out of the way. 'Only wait, one moment, wait. Tell me – after this, where do you go? Back into the army? Will I be paying you still?'

'Well now, that might be difficult,' his visitor says. 'Seeing as I am a dead man. In any case, Monsieur, your concern is not where I go now. *Your* concern is all whether I come back.'

The arm is raised. The Cardinal shields his face. He hears the bottle smash, the sound of candlestick following it; he feels the warmth of flame. He looks for his visitor, he sees the man's back, turned, as the man moves away into the closet, behind the flames already leaping across the floor. Now at last the Cardinal can shout, 'Fire! FIRE!' The first of his attendants is already there, rushing in from the petit bureau. 'Fire!' the Cardinal tells them. 'Save the model! Save my palace!' In they run. The fire leaps, as if from a sudden draught, as if a window has been breached, but as his attendants pull down the curtains, stamping on the flames, the Cardinal sees that the window behind the curtains is untouched. The draught came from elsewhere. And his visitor is gone.

CHAPTER TEN

Ça Va

'It is not good for man to be alone.'

Genesis 2:18

PITY THE POOR innkeeper, whose work is never done. On fine summer days such as these it seems he barely has a chance to lay his head upon his pillow before the sun is bidding him get up again, and this morning Robert doesn't even get the chance to take the nightcap from his head, so persistent is the hammering upon his door. In his nightgown, he pulls the door open and stands there, peering out, a hand shielding his eyes. He sees the horse, he sees the man.

Mirelle's roses nod about the door. 'Oh, for Christ's sake,' says Robert, turning, stomping back indoors.

'And it's a delight to see you too,' the man comments, following him in.

Robert goes to the shelf at the back of the room, returns with two glasses in one hand, a jug in the other. 'You'll take one? Get the dust out your throat?'

'You're a good man, Robert,' says his guest, seating himself.

'And where's the rest of them?' Robert asks, once he too has taken a seat. 'They about to pitch up here, likewise?'

'Just me this time.' The man lifts his glass, holding it by the foot. 'Your health.'

'And yours.' The roses peer in at them. Outside now there is village noise. A cockerel. A door slamming shut. A greeting in the street – *Salut! Salut, ça va?*

Robert leans forward, scrutinizing. 'You've a different look to you.'

'I have?'

'You look less mad,' Robert announces, bluntly. 'Less like you're trying to work out how best you might put an end to whoever you're talking to.'

'Is that how I truly seemed, to you?' His guest sounds shocked.

'To everyone,' says Robert. 'Not her, though.' He takes another pull at his cider. 'Never knew if I should thank'ee kindly for being so generous in settling up, or challenge you to a duel.'

'Which d'you fancy?' comes the response. From outside: *Mon Dieu! Regarde ce cheval!* His guest shifts his sword, to prop more comfortably behind him. 'Is she here?'

'Upstairs,' Robert informs him, with a sigh. 'I know you know the way. Or shall I give her a shout?'

The man gets to his feet. 'No, let me,' he says, smiling. 'I'll surprise her.'

Robert, alone at the table, drains his glass. Sunlight is chiselling itself a way across the floor; outside it sounds as if the horse has drawn a crowd. '*Ouias*,' Robert comments, to himself. 'And she's got a surprise for you, and all.'

*

The stairs have been painted. As he goes up them, his palm brushes limewashed wood. It makes this narrow tunnel through the house a different space; you're thinking when you reach the top there will be light and air. There's a rope been hung along the wall as well, as an aid to going up and down. He touches it, thinks of those roses and their scent outside, about the door. He thinks, *She's been laying down the law.*

Here's the attic corridor, and it has been limewashed too, and more, the paint on the doors tinted a gritty blue-green, and on the windowsill the dried petals of what must be last year's roses, sat in a little bowl. He'd never thought before of women marking a territory, but he does so now, pondering it as something new, and then immediately he hears her voice, in conversation, to his right. 'And there's the sky,' she's saying, 'and there's a cloud, and there's a tree – do you see?'

He opens the door.

She's standing at the window, in silhouette against the summer brightness. She's in her nightdress and her feet are bare, with a shawl hanging in a drape below her shoulders, and her hair in a great bunch at the back of her neck, disordered from her pillow. He thinks he can see the softness of sleep upon her still, feel it in the gentle un-hurry with which she turns to face him, bare feet marking out a three-step on the floor, because she has to keep her balance, because there is a child, an infant, held against her, cradled in her arm. The two of them regard him, each as untroubled by his presence as the other, and he'll think later it was this that told him, this was when he knew, not any semblance that the baby might have to him, but the fact that there is this same calm gaze from both of them, that this is hers, and if hers, then it is his as well.

'Oh,' she says. She sounds surprised, but only a little, as if he had done no more than return earlier than expected from some local errand. But then with a small unguarded gesture, her free hand goes to her face, the fingertips running round it, one side then the other, as if clearing it of those invisible strands of hair, as if she were wearing her cap, rather than bareheaded, uncombed, fresh from her sheets. He thinks his own arms lift toward her, unsteady, opening in amazement. He thinks there is some word, or sound, or something, in his throat.

She adjusts the child's weight slightly; sits it up. 'Oh,' she says. She's smiling now, very possibly at him. 'And there's Papa.'

Acknowledgements

This must be the favourite part to write of any book for any author, not least because it marks journey's end, but also because this is where you get to thank the many, many folk who have contributed to that journey, and without whom it would never have been completed.

Specific thanks therefore: to R. Guy Erwin and Rob Flynn, for guidance on all things Lutheran; to Kit Maxwell for sharing with me his experience of Latvian black butter and its surprising effects; to Jenny McKinley, Barbara Schwepcke, Lucy Saunders, Lee and Maxwell and Kate, Guy and Lucy Kirk, for periodically pulling me out of the word-mines; and to Lydia and Rich Rumsey for blowing away every remaining cobweb and reminding me what good places woods and trees and forests can be. To the crew of the *Götheborg* of Sweden, for mooring outside my front window just as I set about imagining the *Guid Marie* sailing up the Elbe to Hoffstein; and to Lucian Staiano-Daniels for his thesis, 'The War People: The Daily Life of Common Soldiers, 1618–1654', which was a particularly happy and useful find, especially for the authentic sound of seventeenth-century soldierly slang. Thanks too, as ever, to the British Library; to the Rijksmuseum in Amsterdam, the Art Institute of Chicago, the Metropolitan Museum of Art in New York and all those many other museums generous enough to place their images on open access, to the delight and heartfelt appreciation not only of us writers of historical fiction but also, now, I hope, this writer's readers.

Heartfelt thanks to my agent, Chelsey Fox, and to Charlotte Howard, of Fox and Howard, and to the wonderful team at Allen & Unwin: Joe Mills for such a handsome cover design, Ed Pickford for the equally handsome pages and Jeff Edwards for creating our map. More of the same to Tamsin Shelton, copy-editor extraordinaire, and to Rachel Wright, who proofread those same pages with such acuity. And for guiding *The Dead Men* out into the world, Dave Woodhouse, Kate Straker and Sophie Walker; and to my ever-patient, ever-supportive editor, Kate Ballard. You people are the best. This is also my first opportunity to thank Peter Noble, who has recorded the audiobook versions of Jack's adventures. It was an extraordinary moment to hear my hero's voice – no narrator could have done it better.

And finally to my family, and to my partner, Mark Polizzotti, who lost me for weeks if not months at a time to Jack Fiskardo and his Dead Men: this journey needed you above all, and you were there every step of the way.

What lies in store for our hero?
Read on for an exclusive early extract from Book Three
in the Fiskardo's War series, *The Wanton Road*.

PROLOGUE

London, February 1620

Crossbones

'... these single women were forbidden the rites of the Church, so long as they continued that sinful life... therefore there was a plot of ground, called the single woman's churchyard, appointed for them, far from the parish church.'

John Stow, *Survey of London*

EVEN DEAD, YOU don't want to end up here.

Ask any man what this place is, he'll tell you it's the burying ground for St Saviour's, ain't it? And if he's a native of Southwark, look at you askance for not knowing that in the first place. The burying ground for St Saviour's, he'll say, in a manner that leaves unspoken (but not unheard) the *What's it to you?* because they are a tribe within a tribe, the people of Southwark, as those at the bottom of any such great place as London tend to be, and suspicious of strangers, as well as being most perversely proud.

Not that this is the proper burying ground, you understand. It's not that round St Saviour's itself, where you might already lie in company with old John Gower the King's poet, and that mad lad Will Kemp, with that iron-fist money-machine Pip Henslowe, even with Shakespeare's little brother Eddie, and thus be altogether as respectable as, in Southwark, you are ever like to be. No, this – this acre of wasteland, humpy and unmown, dotted with those lozenges of naked earth (don't look too close at them, don't go too near 'em, either) – this is St Saviour's other burying place. This is where they bring the outcasts, the nameless, the friendless, the penniless. Those who lived in sin, died in misery, and are buried here in shame. That's what a man will tell you.

But ask any woman you might find hereabouts – in the yard of the George, maybe, just up the road, warming her hands this February morning on a cup of London porter, mulled with gin – and she'll tell you something different. She'll give this place a name, for a start. She'll call it Crossbones.

Why is it called that?

Because so it always has been, that's why.

But who is buried there?

The women.

What women?

(It might take a moment for her to answer. Who are you, after all? But give her time.)

The women of the Southwark stews. Them, and their little'uns what never grew up, and their babbies what died of being born, or what never got out of their poor dead mothers in the first place. Hundreds of them. Hundreds of hundreds. All buried there.

And she'll look at you, out her black-rimmed eyes that might be young, that might be old, that might be any age at all, and sip from her cup with her wrinkled red lips, and she'll dare you. Judge me not. This is my ground, not yours. Crossbones.

Old Bess Holland (and don't you ever let her hear you call her that), but Old Bess Holland, all the same, she could walk it here from her place, Holland's Leaguer, so she could, but will she? Will she the fuck. You don't work hard as Bess has done these almost-twenty-years to walk through Southwark's streets, you don't get rich as Bess has done these almost-twenty-years to go dragging your petticoats in its mud, not no longer, and you don't get as feared and as reviled as Old Bess counts herself to be to chance yourself to the outside world and those plague-rat bastard Skinners for no good reason neither.

So when Bess Holland leaves Holland's Leaguer, when she has its literal drawbridge lowered over its actual moat, when she processes through its gardens (noted for the arts of flirtation and arousal practised within their shady groves, although admittedly, not when the weather is as bitter raw as this), to begin with there's the getting of her ready, which can take two hours or more; then there's the fanfare (Bess keeps a trumpeter on her staff – she does, truly) to warn all her girls to tumble out of bed, run to the stairs, and when Bess appears at her bedroom door, start with the cheering and applause. Abigail, Bess Holland's maid, is never sure how much of this is genuine, and how much is no more'n a joke to which everybody knows the words, but cheering and applause, nonetheless. Then there's the processing outside, past old Spikenard, Bess's doorman, still as hefty as in his days trailing a pike, and out to Bess's carriage, waiting there within the garden gate. Then there's the bowing and the handing of her up into her carriage by that handsome young buck Miguel Domingo (coachman, waterman, bodyguard, all rolled into one) and only then does the journey proper begin; and only then can Abi let out her breath.

Don't huff so, you creature, Bess Holland says. All these years, ain't I taught you no better manners than that?

All these years. Bess set up Holland's Leaguer the same year Old Queen Lizzie died and King James of Scotland came down to the English throne. 'Elizabeth was King, now James is Queen' was the joke in Southwark, har-har-har, when the rumours first began to run about (and how Bess rubbed her hands when they did!), but James is old now himself, a widower, and drinking hard, and ailing, and beset by all the troubles of this damned new war in Germany, and his proper heir, young Henry, he died years ago, and the remaining son, Charles – God save us, the ninny, what poor watery shot was it engendered him? The

Hollands – Bess, her brothers Cosmo and Greville, their sons Jenkin and Titus – are all of them readying themselves for times that may be nothing like as free and easy as those they've known. There's been many a recent family council at Greville's house in leafy Rotherhithe, plotting how to move on from London's taverns and its brothels and theatres into – well, whatever takes London's fancy next. Expand their business on the other side the North Sea, too, maybe, see if they can't claim a bigger share in trading with the Dutch. Don't they have the name for that already? All of which is most exciting, entertaining stuff to listen to, at Greville's chamber's inner door, while minding Titus's youngster, little Aaron, who ain't even in breeches yet but already you can't take your eye off him for a minute; and all of which is (in Abi's opinion) a far safer and warmer way to spend a Sunday than a goose-chase such as this – trundling all-a-ways along Bankside and past the Bear Garden and Winchester Palace and the evil old Clink and then bossing and fighting a way through the traffic coming off London Bridge – Lord! It's like being tossed about at sea! – and then right down the High Street and right past the George and then oh, thank the saints, we're safe arrived. Surreptitiously, under her cloak, Abigail draws a cross upon her bony bosom. Above them Miguel Domingo gets down from the coachman's seat, and the carriage rises slightly on its straps. Abigail lets down the slide. Miguel's face appears (oooh, it still gives Abi such a start, to see an African as close to her as that!), and the door to the carriage is swept open.

'Out my way, you kipper,' says Bess, as she stands up. A nose-tingling waft of Hungary water, creamy with neroli oil, fills the small space of the carriage. Now the susurration of silks: silk chambray for the winter petticoats, silk brocatelle for the gown (textured like a pelt, and in that oh-so-fashionable colour known as goose-turd green), silk velvet for the cloak and hood. Chinchilla for the muff. Sheeny kid, the gloves and boots. Lace, lace, everywhere.

And pieces to pad out the hair, and belladonna for the eyes, a wash of dew-and-white-ceruse for the face, mouseskin for the eyebrows, and a patch to hide the scar that horrid chancre left upon Bess's forehead, long ago. It's such a playful disease, the pox. God knows what goes on underneath the silks these days – what ulcers, what yellowings, what wastings-away – but the Bess Holland that Bess Holland presents to the outside world is so richly, lushly fine she could walk unchallenged into Whitehall Palace.

Abi, in her wool fustian, the humble colour of ink, gets down behind Bess and starts whining at once. 'Oh, milady, 'tis so cold! Oh, that wind! 'Tis Arctic!'

Bess, striding away, ignores her.

'Oh, milady, must we do this? Must we?' Abi gathers her cloak about her. It's a good thick cloak, it was Bess's own once, but Abi's shivers come not from the icy air, nor the chill of the ground, but from the sense of being so exposed out here, at the mercy of every passing thing, be it a keening disembodied spirit wafting about in that colourless sky or an all-too-embodied Ingram Skinner, or Ezra, or Asa, or one of their boys. God knows, Miguel is a handy man to have about, but it is such a wasteland, this. A place where nothing but bad could befall you. No proper paths through it at all, and sticks and markers here, there, everywhere: the flutter of a tattered ribbon, the glint of some gew-gaw set into the earth. A pair of women's shoes, laid neatly side by side, all faded by the weather. Ghost shoes. A wee cross of sticks, and a child's bonnet tied to it. Every place you set your foot, you're walking on the dead. Although the cold at least keeps down the lurking background sewage-stink of putrefaction.

She's falling behind. Bess, ahead of her, turns and says, 'What, you'd give Dainty Jane your word and break it, would you?'

Well, no. Even if the woman do be dead. Especially now she do be dead, truth be told. Dainty Jane had a way to her, a look.

Sweet-faced as she was (and she was! Oh, she was!), no-one crossed Dainty Jane. If she could lay her hand on you and melt a cramp, fade a toothache, take your hand in hers and read it like a book, what might she also do with them same hands of hers if you should sour her piss? Dainty Jane was a moon-girl, a Roma. No-one wants to get the wrong side of one of them.

'I promised her. First Valentine's after her passing, just as she asked of me. I'll be there, I said. I'll be at your graveside, girl. And soon as she heard me give my word, she closed her eyes and was gone. Never saw so quiet a death. You have them flowers?'

Abi has, a great bunch of 'em, under her cloak. But it's February, so the flowers are all waxed silk, hand-brushed with colour – peonies and roses and irises and lilies, paper stems and leaves, all tied with a stiff-wired silver ribbon. She can't believe the cost of 'em. And all to moulder away out here.

'Now where's that place we put her?' Bess asks, looking about.

'There,' says Abi. Abi never forgets a thing. She's a walking almanac, is Abi. Bess's life is as much Abi's as it is Bess's own.

Where Abi points is Crossbones' only landmark: its yew tree. Or at least, what was its yew tree. No churchyard is complete without a yew, but this being Crossbones, and unconsecrated ground, its yew was chopped down lifetimes ago to make good English longbows. The tree's roots, however, seemed to draw unnatural sustenance from this dreadful ground, so the tree grew anew – wispy and crabbed and hollow and curved over its stump. Just to look at it gives Abi the shivers again. It's like the tree's grown carnivore, feasting on all that rotting flesh below. But that was where Dainty Jane wished to be laid, so that is where she—

'The devil in hell is that?' Bess demands.

There's something lying at the centre of the yew, within the jagged hollow of the stump. All wrapped up, like a pasty, cloth tucked in at either end.

'Oh, I don't like it!' says Abi, at once. 'I'm not looking!'

'Abigail Skinner, how did your family ever produce such a shivering mouse as you?'

Bess goes forward on her own. She bends over, hips a-creak, backbone protesting.

There is some point within the bend when she knows exactly what that carefully wrapped parcel will contain, just from the size of it, the shape. 'It's a babby,' says Bess. There's every modulation in her tone – pragmatism (such things be), pity (that such things be), anger (that such things be) and then Bess's own habitual way of drawing a cover, at once, over anything you might call feeling, weakness, hurt. Her hand reaches the little bundle. Abi behind her is wailing, 'Is it perished? For sure it's perished of the cold!'

'No,' says Bess. 'No, Christ, it's warm as a new-laid egg.' She straightens up, holding the bundle in the crook of one arm, lifts the cloth laid over what she thinks to be its head. Peers down.

The bud of a mouth, bright pink and pouting. Such well-marked brows, too, for such a baby-thing. The tiny miracle of every single extravagant eyelash, swept over the plump cheeks, and then the eyes open and gaze straight up at her. That deep, deep blue, like a starless heaven.

Under the cloth, the child is naked. Kicking feet, soft fat arms reaching up. Nipped at the navel, tied off, but no time yet for it to scab. No piddler. Little cleft.

'She's bonny!' says Bess. She cups the infant's head. There's some few faint curls of hair, slick to the scalp. Darkish. Reddish. Dark amber, polished cherrywood. She holds the baby toward Abi, for her to see. 'Look at that!'

'Oh!' says Abi, in the high ecstatic voice of the childless, the manless, the loveless. She's a hand laid flat to her heart. 'Oh, the weeny worm! Oh, the duckling! Bless!'

The baby kicks and wriggles. Abi offers it a fingertip. Which is grappled onto at once, and brought to the pouting mouth.

'Oh, she's hungry!' Abi exclaims, delightedly. 'Oh, are you hungered, pipkin? We must find you some peck! We need to find her some milk, milady! Yes, ducky, we must, we will!'

'Abi,' says Bess, 'when did we bury Dainty Jane?' Something's prompted her to start counting backwards. She'll never be sure what, but it may have been the colour of that hair. Dainty Jane had hair dark as garnets. 'When was it we brought her here? When did we lay her to rest?'

'It was May-time,' comes the answer, in a coo down to the baby, 'May-time, wriggler! Nice and warm! May-time, milady. Sure of it. All them bushes in the garden was in bloom.' She looks up. 'Why?'

January, December, November... all through this last foul winter, back and back. October, September, August, July, June...

'Abi,' says Bess. She chooses her tone with care; the last thing she wants to deal with is Abi in a fit of hysterics. 'It was nine months ago we brought Jane here. It was nine months to the day.'